Southern Women

Lois Battle
Southern Women

St. Martin's Press/New York

Design by Manuela Paul

Library of Congress Cataloging in Publication Data

Battle, Lois.
  Southern women.

  I. Title.
PS3552.A8325S6 1984   813'.54   83-22999
ISBN 0-312-74747-0

10 9 8 7 6 5 4 3 2 1

Acknowledgments

In Savannah: To Gene Jones, whose love of the city took me there; Bill and Mary EuDaly, who welcomed me; Rosemary Daniell, who encouraged me and gave me the pleasure of her company; W.W. Law, who shared a history that is yet to be written; and Shirley Carson, whose keen mind and true heart were a constant inspiration.

In New York: to Jane Rotrosen Berkey, for her continued confidence and guidance; Thomas L. Dunne and Pamela Dorman, for their enthusiasm and patience; Petya Fluhr, for everything.

Southern Women

Chapter I

The square belonged to the city of Savannah, but Eunnonia Grace Hampton had lived beside it for so long that she had come to think of it as her own property. She walked along the path as quickly as she could. At eighty-three she still had a well-turned ankle, and since her legs were her only remaining vanity, she refused to go out in "old lady shoes," by which she meant anything less than a three-inch heel. She held herself erect—carriage was so important for a tiny woman with a deep chest—and her head bobbed slightly as she took in the beds of crimson, pink, and white azaleas and the monument to General Pulaski. Her favorite bench, the one beneath the grandest live oak, was unoccupied. She didn't mind the tourists as long as they stumbled around and gawked, but it was quite another thing if they proposed to take up her space. She settled down, slipped her feet out of her shoes, and breathed a sigh of relief. A few moments of contemplation would, she was sure, restore her spirits.

It had been a trying day, with one thing and another. She'd made her morning phone calls, gone to a meeting of the Lifelong Learning Association, and then stopped by the old grocery store on Broughton Street to see how the restoration was progressing. She'd bought that property five years ago and was just now about to lease it to a restaurateur from Atlanta. As she'd picked her way through the sawdust and paint cans, she'd noticed that the workmen, disregarding her explicit instructions, had taken down the wooden ceiling fans. Drawing the foreman aside, she had fixed him with a withering look and told him to stop everything until he'd heard from his boss, Mr. Dozier. Then she'd hurried over to the Pink House for her weekly luncheon date with her friends Joan and Lethia. After calming herself with a glass of sherry and commenting on the weather and Joan's new dress, she'd excused herself to go to the telephone.

"Mr. Dozier? I'm so glad I got you in," she'd said in her sweetest voice. "I guess I was just so scatterbrained at our last meetin' that I forgot to mention that those pretty ol' wooden fans will have to stay up." She held the phone away from her ear while he buzzed an objection. "I know I've spent a mint on air conditioning, but the fans will have to go back up. And they'll have to be functional as well as decorative. Do have your boys replace them this afternoon, won't you? An' give m' very fondest regards to Mrs. Dozier." Mission accomplished, she'd rejoined Joan and Lethia, finished her bowl of she-crab soup, and started off to the meeting of the Building Review Board in a lighthearted mood.

But George Naughton, her sometime escort but chief adversary on the Board, had made her peevish again by trying to push through a motion for new construction. He'd made a flowery speech about not being buried in the past, but she knew he was only trying to push the deal because he was a silent partner in a construction firm that employed a slew of Vietnamese workers at non-union wages.

"Why don't we table this motion till everyone's here an' we can have a further discussion? Motion to table?" She'd smiled around the table, fixing on Julia Elkins. Julia would be the swing vote, but she was so wishy-washy there was no telling what she'd do.

"Well, Eunnonia . . ." George had drawled. Even before she'd turned to see his wattle shaking and his mottled cheeks suffused with blood, she'd known he was angry, because everyone with whom she had more than a nodding acquaintance always called her Nonnie. "Well, Eunnonia, we have just enough members to vote, so . . ."

She'd looked at Julia again, and when Julia had stared back with all the comprehension of a sheep who wasn't sure which pasture she was being driven into, she'd started to gather up her things.

"But we don't, George," Nonnie had said as she got up, "because I have to leave. I have a very important meeting with my lawyer."

"Goin' to rewrite your will again?" he'd inquired tartly.

"Lord, I should've left ten minutes ago. I'd love to stay, but"— she'd turned at the door and blessed them all with her smile—"I guess we'll just have to table the motion."

It was too bad about George, she thought as she pressed her toes into the grass to see if it had been properly watered. Fifty years ago he'd been a real gentleman, mindful of his responsibilities toward others in the community. Now he was just one of those mean old men who, gripped by the knowledge of impending death, resented everyone and everything that would survive them. He cared only about blood pressure and profits. That was the trouble with people. They couldn't make the transitions that life demanded. Most never stopped being children, and fewer still were able to cope with old age.

Her husband Lonnie, bless his heart, had been just the opposite. Whereas George acted horsey and high-handed, desperately trying to hold on to his power, Lonnie hadn't wanted to hold on to anything but his golf clubs, his bourbon, and his TV set. Why, in 1961, when word got around that the Freedom Riders were coming through Savannah, he'd wanted to give up the house. Just wanted to throw in the towel and shuffle off to some retirement village in Florida. She had to put her foot down then, telling him that if he was going to run away to ride in a little cart with a parcel of dodderers who couldn't figure out what to do with themselves, why he would find his clubs on the back veranda and no hard feelings. He had brought her to this city as a bride. She'd lived through gossip to acceptance, hard times to prosperity. She'd birthed and buried her own here. It didn't matter that the children and grandchildren were now scattered from Boston to Arizona. Savannah was her home and she wasn't about to leave until they carried her out.

The Freedom Riders had used the Union Bus Station rest room and cafeteria and passed through the city without incident. And Lonnie, grudgingly, had lived to play another ten years of golf on a local course. Those retirement years had been hard for her. Lonnie's growing lethargy had, in a perverse way, made her feel more energetic, as though she was in a three-legged race with someone with a hurt foot. Since she'd talked him into staying, she tried to slow her pace to his, but the aimlessness of their days fairly drove her crazy. She fussed over the breakfast menu, then found herself watching the clock until lunchtime. After lunch she would take a nap. When she opened the newspaper, she automatically turned to the obituaries. Nothing was too small to unhinge her. She would nag Bernice about a stain on the tablecloth, or remind Lonnie that it was time for *As the World Turns*, then criticize him for watching it. Knowing she was being cantankerous and not being able to control it, she tried to absent herself from the house mentally if not physically. She took to sitting in the wing-backed chair in the front parlor for hours at a time, gazing out onto the square while visions of bygone times floated into her mind's eye. There was that holiday they'd spent on Jekyll Island when the children were small: a glorious summer even though all four of the children had simultaneously come down with measles. And that day she'd had her hair bobbed, knowing she'd made a horrible mistake the instant the barber's shears had whacked into her waist-length curls but bragging that she loved the freedom of it when her mother-in-law had criticized her. Or that humid summer night when she was only fifteen and her cousin Andrew had kissed her and asked her to run away with him.

As the memories tugged at her, threatening to pull her down, she would get up and rummage through the house for proof of her past. Where was that cascade of glorious hair wrapped in tissue paper? What had become of the hand-painted "I Love You Mother" valentine from Vivian? Or Wade's diploma from the University of Virginia? She had torn the carriage house upside down trying to find the sepia-toned photograph of their rowboat with a dashingly handsome Lonnie, shirt sleeves rolled up to expose powerful biceps, resting on the oars. And when she couldn't find it, she had sat amidst scattered photo albums numb with regret. It was a sad thing when one's only reliable source of pleasure was in memories of the past.

With a tremendous act of the will she began to find activities that would take her away from the house. Lunch dates, hairdresser's appointments, committee meetings—any self-imposed obligation, no matter how trivial, that would force her to live in the present. Lonnie teased her about her gadding, but she could sense his relief when she set his breakfast tray in front of him and kissed him goodbye. "Giving each other space" was what the young people called it, though she suspected that they meant a good deal more than forcing yourself to go to a book discussion group. She tried to revitalize their social life. They were still the gracious fixtures of the old community and people loved to get an invitation to the house on Monterey Square. Apart from the beauty of the house itself, the food and liquor were always first rate, and Nonnie, pert and gossipy, was always the perfect hostess. Sometimes, warmed by drink and company, Lonnie would come round, teasing her in that gruff way that showed them to be fellow veterans of many ancient campaigns. But when the guests had gone, their relations cooled imperceptibly. After more than fifty years of marriage she'd refused to follow his lead and had made him buckle under to her demand to remain in Savannah. He couldn't quite forgive her for it.

Most evenings, as soon as Johnny Carson had finished his opening monologue, she would put aside her book to go upstairs and braid her hair. By the time she had finished her toilet and gotten into bed, she would hear Lonnie in the bathroom. He would empty his bladder and brush his teeth. Occasionally, in a departure from routine, he would shower. Then he would slip into bed beside her. She would turn off the bedside lamp and move into the curl of his arm, feeling their bodies brush against each other like dry autumn leaves. Sometimes, after he'd dropped off to sleep and rolled away from her, she would wonder where all the moisture of the past years had gone. Then, focusing on the chinaberry tree that brushed the bedroom window, she would go over the next day's activities until she too dropped off.

Then, one afternoon in early January, when the air was so unpleasantly chill that it made you think of lung infections, she came home to find him on the library floor. He had had a stroke. The children unanimously recommended that she put him into a rest home. The ease with which they all sought to abandon him made her feel lonely for the first time in her life. They reminded her that she was getting on in years herself and might not be equal to the burden, and when she said that she'd helped with births and deaths at home, they looked at her as though she was hopelessly old-fashioned. So she didn't even bother to tell them that she intended to see it through. But from that bleak January afternoon to the Fourth of July weekend, when, to the pop and frizzle of firecrackers, Lonnie drew his last breath of humid air, she was at his side.

With Bernice's help, she bathed and fed him, translated his slurred speech to friends and relatives, sat by him when he was restless, and made sure that the medicines on the bedside table were always camouflaged with flowers.

For a month after his death she went out only rarely, dressed in the black suit with the wide lapels that she'd bought when their only son Wade's body had been sent home from Germany in 1945. Then, with an alacrity that made people question her mental balance, she called in the painters, rearranged the furniture and gave up her widow's weeds for the high-necked silk dresses she was fond of. She still refused invitations from sympathetic friends, but was seen trotting around town at odd hours, pausing in front of decaying buildings and taking notes. She changed her affiliation from Christ Church Episcopal, where she and Lonnie had been married, and turned up at the second floor of the wooden house where the Unitarian Fellowship held their meetings. Less than a week after that scandalous defection, she phoned her three daughters and announced that she was going to invest all the money Lonnie had left her in real estate. Since Lucille and her husband Jake were the only ones still living in the area, they drove straight over from Hilton Head.

Lucille was in such a state that she neglected to put on her eyelashes. She'd been on the phone all day, she said, calling sisters, cousins and uncles; and the consensus was that Nonnie was making a horrible mistake. Lonnie's estate, though not massive, was surely large enough to see her through a very comfortable old age if conservatively invested. But if she was foolish and pigheaded (she knew the word Lucille really wanted to use was "senile") enough to start speculating in real estate she would only disappoint herself.

And maybe burden you, Nonnie thought as she nodded and refilled the iced-tea glasses. After listening politely, and long enough for Lucille to exhaust her arguments, she got to her feet. "It was real good of you to come, sugar. But y' see, I've already made up my mind." Jake shrugged and said something about just trying to help, but Lucille was so outraged at Nonnie's willfulness that she stormed out of the house.

It was a failure of the family's collective imagination that they couldn't see what a shrewd businesswoman she would turn out to be. If there was one thing she understood, it was property. Why, hadn't she known every inch of her daddy's five acres and guessed that he'd sold it at a loss? And even before Lonnie had married her and forced the Hampton clan to accept her, hadn't she known about the frantic trading in land that had brought the Hamptons to wealth and prominence over a period of two hundred years? And though it wasn't public knowledge, hadn't she advised Lonnie in every successful deal he'd ever made? She had always regretted not being able to put her abilities to full use before, but there *was* some advantage in being a dowager.

She cultivated her reputation as being a bit of a character, because when people thought of you as a character they told stories about you but they didn't spend much time examining your motives. She perfected her habit of toying with her handkerchief and seeming to drift off during business meetings, only to become sharp-eyed at the conclusion of a deal. Within five years she'd managed to double her capital, and the doubting relatives had actually come to believe that they'd all encouraged her venture. And buying the neglected houses, restoring them, and selling them at a profit gave her the sort of compulsive secret joy she hadn't felt in years.

The bells at St. John's tolled the hour. Five o'clock. Time to see to supper. Force of habit almost made her rise from the bench, though there were no children, grandchildren, or friends expected for the evening meal. Only Bernice would be there, sitting in front of Lonnie's color TV waiting for her to arrive. Bernice had a family of her own to go home to, yet she stayed after the work was done, knowing how hard it was for Nonnie to walk into an empty house. "I must be gettin' senile," she muttered to herself, settling back onto the bench. The pouches under her eyes constricted as she examined the azalea bushes again. The flowering this year had been particularly fine, great bursts of color that shone in the sun and scattered blossoms on the ground like confetti. There were a couple of tourists now, getting down from a horse-drawn carriage and "oohing" and "ahing" over them. And there was Foster Jenkins sauntering home from his law office, his suit as rumpled as if it had been a summer day. He waved a greeting, and her hand fluttered in response.

She slipped her feet back into her high heels and took a deep breath. The air had a sulfurous, slightly rotten smell from the wood-pulp factories upriver. Just last week some young man had called her attention to the "stench" and pushed a pamphlet about air pollution into her hand. Yet she didn't mind the odor at all. Whenever she came back from a trip it fairly welcomed her, for it was the smell of commerce in her city.

As she approached the house, she paused as she always did, her eyes slowly going up and down its three stories, appraising its needs. The shutters needed painting, the drain spouts in the form of open-mouthed dolphins were sadly chipped, but the arch and fanlighted opening above the front door welcomed her with its simple beauty, and her hands caressed the graceful ironwork railings as she mounted the stairs. As soon as she was in the hallway, she balanced herself against the umbrella stand and took off her shoes. The mail was waiting for her on the silver tray. She took a quick look at the envelopes: an announcement of a meeting, two bills, four requests for charitable contributions, and a note on Lethia's lavender stationery, which would either be thanking her for dinner last week or inviting her to dinner next week. She had been hoping for a letter from Cordy, her favorite granddaughter. None of the others took the trouble to write. The telephone seemed to have robbed people of the ability to compose a letter, just as stereos and televisions had taken away their ability to entertain themselves. Still, any mail was better than none. She would open it after supper, a substitute for the conversation she'd always relished over her coffee cup.

Bernice's carpet slippers slopped down the passageway. The heat from the stove gave a waxy sheen to her high forehead and broad nose, and her smile was wide enough to expose her gold back tooth.

"Miz Hampton, have I got some news for you!" She wiped her hands on her apron and almost clapped them. "A phone call from guess who."

"George Naughton, I'll bet. He was actin' so horsey at the meeting he prob'ly wants to take me out to dinner to cajole himself back into my favor."

"No, ma'am. It was Cordy. Yes, it surely was. She's comin' home on a surprise visit. Called from—oh, I forget, where—someplace in Tennessee. She's gonna be here late tonight. All the way from Chicago an' bringin' lil' Jeanette with her. Isn't that somethin'? An' here we didn't expect her till summer vacation."

"Well, isn't that a surprise." The deepest vertical line in Nonnie's forehead creased and her hand went up, nervously touching her chignon.

"Could be she's finished writin' her new book already, an' she's comin' home fer a rest. Now you remind me to bring back that copy of *Tempes'us Love*. I sure do hope she's finished this next, 'cause I can't wait to find out whether that Lord Buckingham is ever gonna do right by that Roxanne girl. I made up the two back bedrooms 'cause I figured Jeanette is old enough to want a room of her own."

"We'll see when they get here, Bernice. So she's driving back alone? Without Lupton?"

"That's what it sounded like."

"Well, this is going to be a treat, isn't it?"

Bernice focused her eyes on the front door and smoothed her apron. "As it happened"—her voice dropped slightly—"Miz Lucille called too. 'Bout twenty minutes after Cordy. But she didn't say anythin' 'bout Cordy coming, so's I didn't either. I figured maybe Cordy wanted to surprise her, so . . ." The sentence trailed off.

Their eyes met in quick and intimate recognition. After thirty years of working for the Hamptons, Bernice's mind could move through the maze of family names, tastes, peccadillos, and relationships faster than an advanced computer could do a printout: Lonnie's brother John had cirrhosis, though everyone ignored his drinking and called it gout; Vivian's husband had died owing Nonnie fifteen thousand dollars for some miniature golf course he'd bought in Arizona; Cousin Curtis was a little funny about the ladies, though everyone said he only went around with his male friends because he hadn't met the right girl yet; and despite what granddaughter Stephanie said, no baby that weighed nine pounds, fourteen ounces had come into this world before its time. And Cordy could no more get along with her mother Lucille than Lucille was able to get along with Nonnie. If Cordy was coming back home unexpectedly, without Lupton, why then . . . Bernice's nostrils flared slightly, as though marriage trouble could be sniffed in the sultry air.

"Yes, she must be going to surprise Lucille and Jake," Nonnie smiled. "Thank you for waiting, Bernice. You can go on home now if you want."

"I ran to the store and got some more groceries, an' I made some pies, but I haven't finished washin' up yet."

"Don't fuss with it. You go on home. I'm sure everything's going to be just fine."

When Bernice had put on her hat and changed into her street shoes, Nonnie went upstairs, took down her hair, and put on her wrapper. Coming back to the kitchen, she started her supper but found she was too worked up to sit. Between mouthfuls, she moved around lining up the canisters, opening her mail, and fixing herself a pot of coffee. Lonnie always used to say that only a horse could eat standing up, but as the oldest girl in a family of ten she'd grown up serving others, and anybody could see that if you had to be leaping up and down it only made sense to stay on your feet. Once, when they were courting and Lonnie had brought her to the house for dinner, she'd made the mistake of getting up from her seat when the maid had been slow to bring in the roast. Her mother-in-law Ettie had fixed her with a gelid stare, and Nonnie had blushed at her faux pas. She'd exposed the fact that she was the daughter of a mill manager as surely as if she'd turned up in a calico dress. From then on, whenever she was in Ettie's presence, she'd made a point of gluing herself to her chair and affecting the slightly bored expression that marked the faces of most of the Hampton clan. But she had never

given up cooking, for Lonnie had praised her for it, and during the
Depression the simple recipes she'd learned from her mother had
come in mighty handy.

Bernice had turned out two fine pecan pies, and a check of the
refrigerator showed enough food for a dinner party; yet, in her restlessness, she began to open cupboards and assemble ingredients.
Cordy had a passion for buttermilk crullers, she recalled. In fact,
when Cordy was twelve and her baby fat was struggling to re-
distribute itself into curves, Nonnie had forbidden her to eat them.
But ever since she was fourteen, Cordy'd had a dangerously fine
figure. Though much taller than Nonnie, she'd inherited her lines.
She was deep-chested and slim in the hips—top-heavy, as Lucille
called it.

She reached for the recipe book, flattened its spine, and ran her
finger along the stained page. Couldn't trust herself to know it by
heart anymore. Why, just last week she'd made biscuits and left out
the baking powder, and what a sorry mess that was. Her hands,
which had just a touch of arthritis, gave her some trouble as she
kneaded the dough, but cooking was a fine thing. You never had to
act coy when people praised you for your cooking. It gave you something to show for your troubles, busied the hands while it freed the
mind. What they called therapy nowadays. She covered the dough
and set it to rise, then wandered into the library to pour herself a tot
of bourbon. After turning out the lights, she felt her way to the
wing-backed chair by the window. The streetlamps had come on,
but the square looked deserted. Ah, dear little Cordy. Her head
bobbed in sad recognition, for she knew her intuition was right.
Cordy must be leaving Lupton. And it must be Lupton's fault.
Why, the first time she'd set eyes on him she'd known he was the
sort of young cock who thought the sun rose to hear him crow. But
everyone else had been blinded by his charm.

At nineteen Lupton was already a man's man as well as a
ladies', and Lonnie and Jake were so impressed by his prowess on
the football field that they sat around swapping sports stories with
him instead of looking at his character. He'd easily seduced Lucille
with that combination of flattery and exaggerated politeness that set
Nonnie's teeth on edge. You'd best go through a few more of life's
battles before you pull that "Hail conquering hero" routine with me!
she'd thought as she'd watched him swagger. Handsome he was.
Smart too, if that calculation of the effect he was having on others
that showed in his eyes could be taken for intelligence. But he just

wasn't man enough to win the hand of her favorite granddaughter. Given a few more years of experience, Cordy would have come to realize that. But the girl was too infatuated to think any further ahead than the next time she'd be in his white Corvette. Yes, the automobile had surely changed the nature of courtship.

Knowing that the objection of elders was the strongest aphrodisiac for young love—and this romance needed an aphrodisiac like a hog needed a morning coat—Nonnie had moved cautiously at first. She'd praised young Clay Claxton, Cordy's previous beau: "He's a fine stamp of a young man an' even if he is goin' off to Yale, you can be sure he'll be back." "He's got blackheads," Cordy had flounced. Next she'd suggested that perhaps Cordy would like to go up North to college. Cordy said she wasn't so old-fashioned as to quit school just because she was getting married; she planned to go to Georgia Tech along with Lupton. Then, shamelessly, Nonnie had dangled the prospect of a European vacation. "Debs stopped doing that European thing fifty years ago" was the only response to her bribe.

As a last resort, she'd tried to talk to Lucille. She knew in advance that it was a risky proposition. She and her daughter had never seen eye to eye. In fact, if she hadn't remembered the labor pains she might have believed that she'd found Lucille under a rosebush. Even when Lucille was a bitty thing there'd been no real closeness between them, though Nonnie had been hard put to find an acceptable reason to complain, for Lucille had been the prettiest and most docile of all her children. She had done her homework without coaxing, she had never mussed her clothes, indeed, she seemed to have had an almost perverse willingness to conform to the expectations of others. Perhaps, Nonnie thought, it had been a perversity of her own that made her long for the outbursts of defiance and self-assertiveness that most other parents would find disagreeable. Lonnie had called Lucille his "candy girl"; and Nonnie, with secret shame, had agreed: Lucille was sweet as a cherry cordial and just as sticky. Naturally the two women had been at odds about Cordy ever since the child had drawn breath. What Nonnie saw as high-spirited, Lucille put down as rebellious; what she perceived as intelligent, Lucille said was sassy and too smart for her own good. So Nonnie had approached the subject of Cordy's engagement with uncharacteristic trepidation.

She had waited until a Sunday evening after supper, when the rest of the family had left the house. Lucille sat in the library, legs curled under her, absorbed in the pages of *Today's Bride*. Perhaps,

Nonnie had started slowly, Cordy was still too young to make an intelligent choice of a mate. Lucille, without bothering to look up, had pointed out that Nonnie had married at seventeen and had permitted her to marry at eighteen. "Times have changed," Nonnie had shrugged, unable to admit that at the time of Lucille's marriage she had been so grief-stricken about the news that Wade had been killed in Germany that she hadn't really cared what happened to anything or anybody. "People live longer now, though. Why my mama died when she was just forty-nine, but I was readin' the other day that life expectancy for women is now up to . . ." She struggled to recall the exact figure.

"We're preparing for a wedding, Mother, not going into death charts," Lucille had drawled, still keeping her eyes on the page.

"But she's got her whole life ahead of her, an' right now she's starry-eyed about Lupton 'cause he's a football hero. This lil' fling she's havin' is gonna wear itself out and I just wouldn't want her to marry because . . ." She took a deep breath and plunged into it: "Have you ever talked to her about what you do not to have a baby?"

Lucille's head came up slowly, her eyebrows arched and mouth open in that dazed but slightly hostile expression affected by models in fashion magazines. "Since when did you become an advocate of sex education, Mother? I don't recall your ever talking about birth control to Vivian or Constance or me."

"It just wasn't *done* in those days," she'd said, flustered, then, bowing her head apologetically: "I didn't know too much about it m'self."

A piercingly accusatory look flitted across Lucille's face before she smiled and held up the magazine. "I'm helping Cordy to choose her patterns. She thinks she likes this Danish Modern." She tapped the glossy page. "But I'm in favor of this Bordeaux Lace. It has a lovely traditional style."

Nonnie had left the room. Trying to force Lucille to confront her own motives would be like lifting up a pretty stone to find the worms, larvae, and dank earth underneath. Though she didn't want to believe it herself, she knew that Lucille was jealous of Cordy's blooming sensuality and wanted the girl off her hands.

Accepting defeat, but none too graciously, she'd dragged the old hope chest from the carriage house and filled it with crockery and linen. She'd taken her beige lace out of mothballs and had the skirt shortened. And since Lucille had made such a point of saying that no expense was to be spared for the wedding, she'd added another forty names to the guest list.

After a time, she too had been caught up in the preparations and found herself looking forward to the event. Standing on the veranda with the throngs of well-wishers, throwing rice and calling out congratulations as Lupton and Cordy set out for Atlanta, she'd been more optimistic than resigned. She had greeted the birth of Jeanette, her eighth great-granchild, with pride, even though it did mean that Cordy dropped out of college. She'd been pleased when Lupton got the football contract with the Chicago Bears. Even when he'd had that terrible accident that had cut short his professional career she'd felt that they could weather it. If the marriage had held for seven years, there was no reason, given the strength of Cordy's character, that it wouldn't continue to hold.

But then she began to notice a subtle change in Cordy's letters. At first the hints of discontent—brutal winters, homesickness, troubles with Lupton's sports-equipment store—were offset by the occasional piece of good news: Cordy had written a romance novel, or a "bodice ripper" as she called it, which had been accepted for publication. Then the letters had taken on a humorous, self-deprecating tone, excluding any mention of Lupton. Nonnie had written back asking some intimate questions, which stopped the correspondence altogether. She was patient for a month, then curiosity and concern drove her to make a long-distance call. Within minutes of Cordy's bright hello there had been a silence that had made Nonnie think the phone had gone dead. Then she'd heard the sharp intake of breath that comes before tears, and Cordy had wept that she was profoundly depressed. She suspected, without any real evidence, that Lupton was being unfaithful to her. Nonnie had advised toleration: Men had their little foibles; Lupton might be nursing sorrows of which Cordy could know but little; coddling could build a man up faster than a good tonic. Divorce, she pointed out, was a very serious matter, especially when a child was involved. Of course, if Lupton continued to treat her badly . . .

Nonnie's head jerked up. She'd started to doze off. And here Cordy and Jeanette were speeding toward a homecoming and she hadn't finished making the crullers! She picked up her empty glass and reached to turn on the lamp. It was dark outside now. She could barely make out the figure—no, it was figures: a couple entwined in an embrace—on her favorite bench. "Why it can't be but fifty degrees," she tutted, pressing her forehead to the glass to get a better look. "An' there they are canoodling. Green as salad. Neither one of them with the sense to put a sweater on."

Still, she reminded herself as she shuffled to the kitchen, the real wisdom of age was the ability to feel, through muffled memory, the compelling passions of youth. And yes, loving in the park amidst the azaleas, it was possible not to notice the chill in the air.

She was glad that Cordy would be home in time to see the azaleas. Cordy had always taken pleasure from the blooming. And present pleasures were so important, especially for a girl who couldn't tell what sort of a future she would have to face.

Chapter II

Like most of the actions of her life, Cordy's decision to walk out on Lupton came from emotion rather than thought. Now, quite literally, she didn't know where she was.

The gas station attendant rested his arms on the hood and leaned into the window. "Sure don' see how y' coulda made the wrong turn back there at the junction. Signs is marked real clear. You've gone 'bout fifty miles outta yer way."

She wanted to sob at her stupidity, but she tilted her head and smiled up at him. "Guess I just wasn't paying attention." Better to sound dumb than desperate. "If you'd be kind enough to put some gas in while we go to the ladies' room . . ."

"I'll not only check her out, I'll fill 'er up," he grinned.

"That'd be real nice of you." She smiled again, ignoring the double entendre. "It's good to know that the service is still more polite here than it is up North."

She reached into the back seat and stroked Jeanette's arm. "Wake up, honey. Let's go to the bathroom."

Jeanette wiggled around in the pile of winter clothes she'd shed during the journey, her eyes wide. "Where . . .?"

"It's O.K., honey. We're not home yet. Let's just get out and go to the ladies' room while the man fills up the gas."

The smell of hamburger grease and the thrump of disco music

assaulted her as she led Jeanette through the formica tables and vending machines toward the washroom.

"This place is all yucky." Jeanette wrinkled her nose and looked at the crumpled candy wrappers and dirt on the bathroom floor.

"We're not here to do a review for *Holiday* magazine. Just go."

"What?"

"Just go. Put some toilet paper down on the seat first."

Cordy blinked into the washroom mirror, her hands clasping the edges of the sink. Her thick blond hair, yanked back from her forehead and held with one of Jeanette's plastic barrettes, needed a touch-up. Her heavy-lidded brown eyes, framed with thick lashes and icon-like brows (Nonnie mentioned a distant uncle who'd injected some Greek blood into the family's otherwise Anglo-Irish stock), were swollen from tears and fatigue. The phosphorescent light made her skin look blotchy. Hard to believe she'd been called the prettiest girl in her senior class.

"Oh, I look like a turtle," she whispered, fumbling in her bag for some makeup.

Jeanette was dancing from foot to foot, spelling out the graffiti on the grubby tiles. "'Debbie loves Lance for-ev-er.'"

"Wash your hands."

"I just did wash them. Didn't you see me? You must be preoccupied."

"Preoccupied."

"Hey, look, Mama. They have one of those wind machines to dry your hands. I love these." She punched the button and waved her hands back and forth, eyes still focused on the scribbles. "'Toni gives good head.' Hey, Mama, what does it mean to—"

"Damn, I've smudged this mascara. Run on into the stall and get me some toilet paper, honey."

"It smells bad."

"I know it smells bad. Just do what I tell you."

When had obscenities started to appear on women's bathroom walls? She didn't remember seeing them in her childhood. Had she simply failed to notice, or was it because her own mother Lucille had been careful never to expose her to crummy roadside washrooms? Lucille would never have walked out on Daddy, thrown her belongings into the back of a car, and dragged her halfway across the country.

She patted Jeanette's head as she took the toilet paper, wiped the smudge from beneath her eye, and reached for her hairbrush.

"'For a good time call—'"

"I told you to stop reading that trash."

"You told me I should try to read, 'member? You told me to spell out everything I see."

"Not trash," she said impatiently, whipping the brush through her own hair then stroking it through Jeanette's.

"How do I know if it's trash before I read it?"

"For pity sakes, let's go." She shoved the brush back into her purse, took the child's hand, and hurried her through the swinging doors.

"Can I have some potato chips?"

"No. No more junk food. There'll be plenty of food at Nonnie's."

"But I'm hungry now."

A woman with straggly hair and a baby on her lap sat hunched over a cup of coffee. Her eyes shot up to Cordy in a quick appeal for sympathy. "God, kids," she said loudly. "Ain't travelin' alone with a kid 'bout the most miserable punishment on earth."

Cordy nodded noncommittally and pushed open the door. The attendant was squatting near the left rear tire.

"Think y' got a lil' puncture here that could use some repair.

"I'm only going another hundred miles. It'd be okay till then, wouldn't it?"

"It's low," he shrugged, getting to his feet and wiping his hands on his backside. "Woman travelin' alone . . . Y' wouldn't want no trouble. You could check into that motel 'cross the way an' I'd repair it for y'. No charge, course."

"But will it be all right till I get to Savannah?"

"I get into Savannah m'self some weekends."

"How much do I owe you?" she asked quickly.

"That'll be twenty-four fifty for the gas an' oil."

She counted out the money. Jeanette was twirling around in circles singing, "I love it here, Mama. It's so warm." Cordy stuffed the wad of bills back into her wallet. She'd cleaned out the savings account of two thousand dollars. How long would they be able to get by on that?

"You want to get into the back seat and nap again, Jeanette?"

"No. I want to ride up front and play the radio."

"I figured you would," she sighed. "Buckle up the seat belt and let's go."

The attendant pocketed the cash and turned away before she

could ask him to repeat the directions back to the main highway. She pulled away from the pumps and gunned out onto the road, her ears tuned to the idiosyncratic knocks and thumps of the car as they never had been before. Jeanette pushed the radio button and the last bars of a hymn blasted out. Cordy's mouth curled into a smile of recognition. She knew she was back home when a choir or a preacher was the first thing you got on the radio.

"Woman," the preacher's voice exhorted, "cleave unto your husband. The Bible tells us that a house divided cannot stand. The Bible also tells us that woman was created to be sub-servient unto her husband. Why do we see this strife and discord around us today? Why are lil' children turnin' into joo-ven-ile delinquents? I'll tell you why. Because the hand that should be rockin' the cradle is poundin' a typewriter so that it can buy worldly goods. That's why! Worse yet, that hand is all too ready to pick up a beer bottle or flick on a TV. An' the woman who stands against the will of her husband is bringin' down the rafters of her own home, callin' disaster an' the disrespect of her own blood upon her head. Woman—"

"Shut that thing off," she commanded.

"You said I could play the radio."

"Just shut it off. If I don't concentrate on the road I'm gonna get us lost again."

Jeanette wiped her fingers across the dashboard, eyeing her.

"Shut it off or I'll pull over and you can get into the back seat. I mean it."

Jeanette punched the button fiercely, rolled her sweater up, and pulled away toward the door as far as the seat belt would allow. Her lips were drawn together as though they'd been cobbled with basting thread. "Daddy doesn't get lost when he drives."

"Sorry, Mama's tired," she said after a pause. She had almost blurted out a reprimand, and that would have been unfair. Jeanette had accepted the "Mama and Daddy aren't getting along so we're taking a little vacation" story with equanimity, but it was difficult to guess how upset she might be. The domestic upheavals of the last year had turned Jeanette into a miniature diplomat, and she'd developed a capacity to mask her feelings that was far beyond her seven years. Though she would still race through the house to see if Lupton was there, she never asked where he was if he didn't come home. She would automatically go to her room when she sensed Cordy's anger, or comfort her with a hug when she saw her misery.

Cordy reached over and pulled her closer, stroking her head

until her body relaxed against her. She slowed the car, rolled the window down, and peered through the darkness at the sign that showed the entrance to the main road. As she accelerated onto the highway, strands of hair blew into her face. She swept them back, took a deep breath, and started to croon, "Southern nights, let me tell you 'bout those Southern nights." It was so good to be back home. The heavy, fragrant air engulfed her, stirring memories of strolling through the downtown squares, watching the ships come up the river, sitting on Nonnie's veranda sipping iced tea on those timeless, indolent afternoons. If only Lupton had seen how important it was for both of them to come back home.

"If only . . . I should have . . . Why didn't I see . . ." The turning points of her marriage whizzed past her like the markers on an unfamiliar road. She struggled yet again to give some chronology to her decline from ardent fan to unwilling critic to hysterical wife. Apart from the postnatal depression she'd suffered after Jeanette was born, they'd never faced any real emotional problems until the accident that put an end to Lupton's career in pro ball. But even before that there had been cracks and fissures in the relationship—hints that were so minor it was easy for her to ignore them. The way Lupton would stride ahead when they were walking, leaving her and Jeanette to bring up the rear. Or the way he never seemed to listen to what she was saying unless it concerned some practical aspect of their daily lives. She'd dismissed the public swagger—Lupton was a man of action, not a college professor—and she could still flirt and cajole him if she really needed to get his attention. But it was harder to dismiss the deeper character faults that had initially gone unnoticed in the glare of their blinding sexual attraction.

Even before she became the victim of Lupton's lies, she was the audience for his exaggerations. She would sit at parties, momentarily released from the show of having a good time, and listen to his stories. The thirty-yard run became the sixty-yard run; the newspaper article that had mentioned him became a feature; the celebrity he'd just met was transformed into a buddy. And she would smile, fiddle with her drink, and cast her eyes to the floor in an attitude that passed for shy pride. She never had the nerve to tell him that his bragging embarrassed her. And if he guessed her feelings, he never acknowledged them. She was his wife after all. He assumed her complicity. She would never be disloyal enough to expose him, even to himself.

Lucille had always stressed the importance of sweetness and

docility. Confrontation, any open expression of opinion, was not desirable in a woman. A woman went *around* a man, not *to* him. "If a man sees you can take care of yourself, he's not gonna have any cause to wanta take care of you," Lucille had said, and being taken care of was the mark of a woman's success. In that regard she had been successful, at least during the early years of the marriage. Lupton was openhanded with his money. She had the finest clothes, an expensive house in the suburbs of Chicago, an allowance for the health club and gourmet cooking classes. And if Lupton's generosity verged on being spendthrift, if he insisted on a Jacuzzi as well as a sauna and bought a new car every year, she had no cause for complaint. He was the one who was bringing home the paycheck after all.

Another thing that bothered her was the difference in their sense of humor. Lupton laughed at off-color jokes and situation comedies, whereas she was amused by human behavior and the play of words. Lupton invariably laughed when someone was hurt, but this she knew was part of his code of toughness. A woman shouldn't be critical of a man just because they didn't laugh at the same things. And if he loved female attention it was because he was a glamorous figure, always in the limelight. Noticing other women did not mean he was neglectful toward her. He always commented on her grooming and showed her off when they were in public. So, she reasoned, as long as she was first in his heart it was really better to be with a man who genuinely loved the opposite sex. Their marriage was better than most. His braggadocio, his inability to handle money, his need to be admired by women, and the lack of harmony in their humor, surely none of these was sufficient reason for complaint. Their continuing need for each other in bed made it possible to overlook the flaws in their relationship.

She'd heard her mother say that withholding of favors was a wife's chief leverage, but she'd never been able to follow that advice. Her own desires were too strong to be manipulated. And Lupton was a tender as well as energetic lover, suspending their shared knowledge that she was always available to him and continuing to court her in endearing, silly ways. And if she felt a little foolish in the Fredericks of Hollywood nighties he bought for her, she knew that they gave him pleasure, and giving him pleasure was reward enough.

And so they might have bounced along, buffeted by the hundred and one annoyances that make up any marriage but steadied by their shared past, their material comforts, and the sacred rites and power of sexual love. If only . . . If only Lupton hadn't injured his knee in the first game of the third season.

Even before the cast was taken off his leg and the team of doctors had pronounced their verdict she knew that Lupton's football career was over. Yet as she stood by his hospital bed she felt closer to him than she had ever been. His jaw was clenched in the stoic denial of pain that had always elicited her admiration. He disengaged his hand when she tried to hold it and stared at the ceiling. She knew he was too depressed to take in her words of comfort and encouragement, but later, when he recovered, she was sure they'd not only be able to cope with but overcome this painful turn of events. They both knew that a career in football couldn't last forever, and in a strange way she even looked forward to the challenge. Now she would prove that she was a real wife, capable of loyalty and endurance, and not just an attractive appendage.

Throughout his recovery, Lupton remained sullen and uncommunicative. His clenched jaw never relaxed. She could hear him grinding his teeth in his sleep. He moped around the house and refused to see his teammates. His depression lifted when the possibility of a job as a sportscaster on a local TV station presented itself, but months later, when the offer failed to materialize, she was almost as disappointed as he. Any effort to discuss their future was met with hostile silence. Then one afternoon he'd come home to announce that he might take his insurance money and invest it in a sporting-goods store that one of his buddies wanted to sell. She'd asked him to think it over. There was no real need to stay in the Chicago suburbs now, and if Lupton was going into business she was sure they'd be better off in Savannah, familiar territory where they had friends and relatives.

She thought she'd convinced him of the wisdom of moving when he suddenly announced that he'd already signed the contract to buy the store. In some misguided effort to show that he was still master of his fate, Lupton had ignored her counsel and her feelings. It was as though he were stalking away again, leaving her to bring up the rear, asserting that the decisions that affected their lives were his, not theirs. Beneath his gruff apology and her own anger and grudging acceptance, she knew that they'd come to a terrible fork in the road.

After the first year, the business was barely limping along. Lupton told her that she would have to fire the gardener and the cleaning woman. She insisted on seeing their bankbooks and was horrified to discover how little money they had. Though she continued to play cheerleader to Lupton's struggle for an improvement in their fortunes, she secretly began to worry about her own ability to earn a living. On Monday mornings, after he'd gone off to the store, she would retrieve the want ads from the trashcan. With Jeanette starting in the first grade, there was no reason why she couldn't augment the family income with a part-time job. But she discovered that even a part-time job was not easy to come by if you had no college degree or prior experience. Thinking that her looks would at least get her something as a receptionist or a hostess, she tried businesses and restaurants, but it seemed that no one wanted to hire a woman with a small child. The afternoon of her tenth rejection, as she'd stopped off in the mall to do grocery shopping, she'd seen a HELP WANTED sign in the window of Koegh's Bookstore. Impulsively, she'd gone in and had been hired without even having to fill out an application.

"Until we're on our feet again," she'd convinced Lupton, having already paved the way by telling him how bored she was at home. She did want to escape from the house. The neighbors had sniffed out financial trouble and wandered by on the least excuse, leaving magazine recipes for various "budget surprises" as though they were calling cards. Sometimes she was tempted to confide in one of them, but she feared that their continued interest could only be purchased with a full confession, and she didn't want to be the object of gossip. Besides, there was nothing interesting about being broke.

"A clerk in a bookstore, honey?" Lucille had cried when she'd called to give her the news. "Even if you have to work, surely you can do better than that. I know Lupton's folks can't help you out, but if things are that bad, maybe—"

"It's okay, Mama, honest it is," she'd cut in, hearing Lucille's tone change from solicitude to embarrassment. "I like working at Koegh's. My boss has a crush on me, so I don't do much mor'n read all afternoon." It was one of the few times she'd been honest with her mother. Her boss, Joe Koegh Junior, was a nervous but amiable man with a mouthful of tombstone teeth. Koegh Senior rarely bothered to check up on him as long as he stayed out of his way. Joe Junior had more trouble staying out of Cordy's way. He was always coming up behind her when she was in the back room doing inventory or bumping into her in the narrow space behind the cash register. At first she thought he must have an uncorrectable case of nearsightedness, but even when he gave up his glasses for contact lenses (a change that made him look as though he had a permanent case of pink eye) his sense of spatial relations didn't improve. It dawned on her that his fumblings were the expression of desire. Since she knew he would never become aggressive enough to proposition her, she started treating him with the indulgence she'd show to a pet. She still turned up within ten minutes of her scheduled time and worked efficiently in the mornings. But in the afternoons, free from the pressure to find busywork, she would sit on the stool behind the cash register, her back warmed by the sun on the plate-glass window, and read for long stretches. The books, even the silly ones, transported her to other times and places, eased the boredom and the persistently nagging feeling that nothing in her life would ever change.

"I think I could write one of those romance novels," she'd announced to Lupton one night when he'd teased her about always having her nose in a book.

"Don't see how you can read one let alone write one," he'd shrugged. But evenings when she was alone, dishes done, Jeanette tucked into bed, she'd set the Underwood (a graduation gift from Nonnie) on the kitchen table and pound away. She told a story of lust and adventure in which a heroine of humble origins was forced to yield up her virtue but found riches and happiness in the arms of a moody, handsome nobleman. Nonnie, who was the only other person who knew about the enterprise, suggested that the writer of a romance should have three names—"So's the reader knows she's either married or comes from a family she's proud of." So Cordy typed *Tempestuous Love* by Cordelia Simpkins Tyre on the front sheet, wrapped the fat stack of paper, and sent it off to Chrystallis Books. Four months later, when she'd given up hope of even getting a rejection, she came home to find a letter of acceptance in the mailbox.

"They're going to pay me fifteen hundred dollars," she cried, waving a smudged Xerox contract in front of Lupton's face. "And better than that, they want me to write another!"

Lupton didn't read the book, but he took her out to dinner. Joe Koegh Junior bought her a bottle of champagne and promised to make a display on the rack as soon as the novel was published. Nonnie called and said she'd already told everyone in Savannah that her granddaughter was a writer. Buoyed up by her good fortune, Cordy went to the library, checked out another stack of history books, and started on a sequel. Reading the history books made her conscious of all the gaps in her knowledge. At one time, before she'd become interested in boys, she'd been an eager student. Lupton had majored in business administration at Georgia Tech, and for some reason that was still obscure to her—since he had no interest or discipline—he'd chosen history as his minor. After she'd become pregnant and dropped out of school she would read his textbooks and write his papers for him. The disappointment she'd felt when he'd pulled a C in a class she'd particularly enjoyed was softened by a note from the professor: "After your impressive paper on the Court of Charles II, I'd expect more from you in the final." Lupton had said he didn't care about a bunch of guys who went around looking like hippies, but she'd kept the professor's note. At a time when her life was little more than Pampers and pureed carrots, it was good to know that someone felt she was capable of thought.

Between the job at Koegh's, the care of the house, and the obligation to earn another fifteen hundred dollars, her days became very busy. Lupton was away a good deal, but more often that not she was grateful for his absence. At first she didn't even question his excuses of car trouble, problems at the store, or an obligation to spend the evening with a divorced buddy. Then, even before she had any evidence, it began to dawn on her that he was seeing another woman. The idea threw her into an almost schizophrenic frenzy. On the one hand she wished that he would give up his implausible stories and be honest with her. Even if the truth caused her pain, it would at least put an end to the gut wrenching suspicions. At other times she only wanted him to conduct his double life more shrewdly, to keep her in ignorance and preserve the illusion that he was committed to the marriage. Neither choice was ideal, but each in a compromised way held some hope of respect and harmony.

But Lupton did not choose to be honest. Nor did he choose to protect her.

He began to leave evidence where she was bound to find it. There was lipstick in the glove compartment of his car, a phone bill with a toll number that had been called four times during the week she'd filled in for the night cashier. For some reason she couldn't understand he seemed to want her to know. Yet when she confronted him, hating the prosecutorial tone of her voice, he made up stories that were so puerile that she'd actually started to laugh. He said the lipstick in the glove compartment must belong to the salesgirl at the store. The girl's car was in the shop and he'd probably given her a lift home. The phone calls were to a buddy she'd never met. The guy was having a drinking problem, and he was trying to give him some moral support. But she knew Lupton hated telephone conversations, and the only moral support she'd ever seen him give to a buddy was a quick slap on the ass. He kept his eyes on the floor. When she said she'd called the number twice and both times a woman had answered, he'd dropped his head and cracked his knuckles.

Without thinking what she would do if he took her up on it, she offered him a divorce. He looked into her eyes then, his big face blank yet contorted, as though he'd just witnessed an accident and couldn't figure out who to call for help. She tried to give him another opportunity to tell the truth. They'd been married young, she said, it was almost inevitable that boredom, vanity, or curiosity would lead one of them to stray. She had been tempted herself. (The only instance she could fix upon was an intense foreign-looking student with black hair and sad eyes who worked at Koegh's on the weekends.) Lupton said angrily that he had nothing to confess. If she didn't realize that he was working his butt off because she and Jeanette were the most important things in his life then she must have started to believe the plots of the melodramatic books she wrote.

Her desire to believe him was stronger than either evidence or intuition. She allowed as to how she was feeling pressured. Perhaps the house, the job at Koegh's, and writing the book were too much for her. Christmas was coming, and since they couldn't afford a trip back to Savannah, she would quit work and make it a real holiday for them at home. They would spend more time with each other, explore all the changes they'd observed in each other but hadn't quite caught up with.

There was a month of calm. She made special recipes. He called her pet names. Though her eyes crossed with boredom, she watched TV shows he liked. He sometimes scrubbed her back when she took a bath. They stayed in bed on Sunday mornings. They talked elaborate plans for the vacation they would take once business picked up. On Christmas Eve, after he'd carried Jeanette into bed, they snuggled on the couch correcting each other's versions of how they'd met and who'd proposed to whom. Sitting there in the firelight sipping brandy, it all seemed too pat, as though they'd studied a *How to Make the Relationship Work* manual and were going at it with a vengeance. "If it weren't for this see-through nightdress I'd swear we could be on a Norman Rockwell Christmas calendar," she'd laughed.

"I don't know who Norman Rockwell is, but you look like the *Penthouse* centerfold to me," he'd answered.

On cue, they'd gone into the bedroom. Executing turns, changing positions like seasoned acrobats, she still felt an unfamiliar distance, so that her mind seemed to leave her body and float about them watching. She couldn't interrupt their lovemaking to tell him that she felt somehow phony, but after he'd dropped off to sleep she'd crept into the bathroom and taken a Valium. The next morning, watching him play with Jeanette under the Christmas tree, she decided that the distance she'd felt the night before was a passing thing. And even if it weren't, she could live with it.

Except for an astronomical bill for roof repairs that sent Lupton into a funk for days, January passed uneventfully. But in late February, as Lupton approached his thirtieth birthday, it was as though she'd drawn a GO BACK TO GO card in a Monopoly game. Nothing she did seemed capable of pleasing him. He came home after midnight two nights in a row. The weekend after that he said he was going to Chicago for a stag night with old teammates and didn't come home at all. Monday morning, when she'd gone through her Valium supply and was about to call the police, he'd phoned from the store. After a gush of invective she didn't know she was capable of, she hung up on him. Four days passed. Her rage dissipated into concern for his safety. Ignoring her resolution to force him into making the next move, she called the store. A salesgirl, presumably she of the magenta lipstick and the faulty carburetor, took the message. Lupton phoned back around five o'clock.

She spoke to him calmly at first, but within minutes she'd lost control and forgotten the speech she'd prepared. He held on through her tears, shushing her with "Now baby's" and "You know how much I love you's." She was on the verge of asking him to come home when he added, "And let's just forget about the whole thing." Then she roared with reflexive rage, as though her fingers had been mashed in a door. Even as she yelled she knew that she was doing the wrong thing: her tears might evoke his guilt, her sobs could elicit avowals of his love, but Lupton simply would not put up with her anger. But she couldn't stop herself. She kept on screaming even after she heard the click at the other end of the line.

Jeanette was playing in the family room with a school friend. Cordy'd crept past them, her fist stuffed into her mouth, rushed upstairs, and locked the bathroom door. Sitting on the edge of the tub with wads of tissue in her hands, she'd howled and sobbed until she'd exhausted herself. Numbly staring at the tiles until the colors seemed to merge, she choked back a hysterical laugh. "Sarah Bernhardt of the washroom, that's what you are," she said aloud. As far back as she could remember her emotional catharses had always had the backdrop of toilets and tubs. She flushed the soppy tissues down the toilet and washed her face.

In all likelihood Lupton didn't really care for this other woman, or women (she hoped it was plural). He had suffered some terrible blows over the past few years. The woman wouldn't necessarily have to be prettier, just as long as she was *different* and saw him in the way in which he wanted to be seen. He might stray, but he *did* love her. The weight of their shared experience and his concern for Jeanette would bring him back. If she could face the fact that she was suffering from wounded vanity as much as moral outrage and get him to *talk* to her about what was really going on, she'd be able to get them back on the track. Besides, she didn't have any money. Her only alternative, should she walk out, was to go to Nonnie's.

Nostalgia for their shared past and an overwhelming fear of being alone fused into the need to make it up with him. She went back downstairs, called him again, apologized for screaming, and asked in her sweetest voice if they might not have dinner together and talk.

"If only . . ." If only she had been able to present him with a clear set of demands. If only she had been able to overcome his resistance to any sort of conversation about his feelings. If only . . . Instead, she'd gone to bed with him.

She arranged for Jeanette to spend the night with a neighbor and spent an hour in an elaborate grooming session. Lupton arrived promptly at eight. He stood in the hallway and helped her on with her coat, saying that he'd made reservations at the Lamplighter. She suppressed an impulse to tell him that it was too expensive (only a wife nagged about money and it was tactically better to start off with the illusion of courtship).

The first hour was so full of physical awareness glossed over with small talk that, had it not been for her anecdotes about Jeanette, they might have been on a date. He opened doors and pulled out her chair for her. He asked what she'd like to drink, though he knew she always had bourbon and water. Barely touching her own food, she watched him cut into his veal piccante, another gesture toward her taste, since he was usually a meat and potatoes man. She avoided asking him any but the most mundane questions and answered his in a soothing, controlled voice.

As he leaned toward her, his hands blond-brown in the candlelight, she asked for another drink. She was feeling very mellow now, humming along to the faint strains of piano that drifted in from the bar. She took an after-dinner liqueur. He played with her fingertips. They even seemed to be laughing together, not at any particular joke but as an expression of good will. Lupton finished his drink, moved quickly to her side, took her by the fleshy part of her arm, and guided her to the exit.

He peeled out of the parking lot, one hand on the steering wheel, and swerved down a series of side streets. They'd stopped talking now. As he pulled up to a stop sign, a neon light slashed a diagonal line across his crotch, leaving his face and torso in darkness. She took off her glove and slowly reached across, stroking his leg just above the knee where the bunch of muscle started. He gave the slightest recognition—a stiffening of the neck muscles, a slow exhalation of breath as though his chest had been tight—and stepped on the accelerator. She clutched the seat with her free hand and bit her lip. Only wives nagged about drinking and speeding.

Relieved that they'd made it safely home, she opened the car door and slid away from him as soon as he pulled into the drive. The night was moonless and the air had a bitter chill. She waited at the front door stomping her feet in the slushy snow, feeling her armpits sweaty underneath the fur coat he'd bought her the first winter they were in Chicago. How could she ever forget the first time he'd made love to her; that never-to-be-repeated combination of fear and ecstasy, alarm and intoxication. And that desire, persistent and enduring, was still here after all these years. Lupton might make jokes about positions and performance, but she knew they were real lovers, not just actors in a sex manual. Their deep mutual need was like a long rope, and each was tied to an end of it. It might go slack with apathy, lose its tautness because of jealousies and squabbles, but it still bound them. A real tug would pull them together again.

He waited until she was well into the hallway, then closed the front door noiselessly behind him. They were hard against each other, hands and mouths everywhere, pulling at the bulky clothes with the same urgent, almost combative energy that marked their best couplings.

They rarely touched after they'd made love; but now she let her hands play over his chest and face, tracing familiar moles, touching the scar beneath his chin, which he'd gotten not on the playing field but by falling out of a tree when he was ten.

"Want some orange juice?" she whispered. Lupton was always thirsty afterwards, and she particularly enjoyed serving him, fancying herself as a sensitive geisha.

"Hmm? No. I'm fine."

There was a preoccupation beneath his sleepy drawl. She rolled out of bed and stretched in an exaggerated way, throwing her head back and lifting her hair through outstretched fingers. She knew he liked to watch her when she was in this languid, exhibitionistic mood, so she held the pose until she realized that he wasn't looking at her. He was staring at the wall, his lips drawn back over tightly clenched teeth.

"Then I'm gonna get myself some water, 'cause I'm parched. Sure you don't want some, Lupton? Is anything the matter?"

The absolute stillness of his body told her that something definitely was. Shivering, she wrapped her arms around her breasts and sat back down on the bed. "I know we haven't talked. An' I know I said I wanted to talk. But I don't mind if we wait until morning. Even with the Valium, I haven't been sleeping much. Guess that's natural. I miss you in bed."

"I thought you came."

"Oh, Lupton, that's not what I meant." His misunderstanding annoyed her. She reached out to touch him again and stopped. He might think that her touch was a request for more sex. "I meant that I miss sleeping with you, waking up with you, being held by you. Even though you do always hog the covers."

"You gonna get that water now?"

"In a minute. Lordy, what's the matter with you?"

He was getting out of bed, feeling around on the floor.

"I said what's the matter with you?"

"I'm looking for my shorts."

"Your shorts?"

He flicked on the bedside light. She shielded her eyes and watched. He found his shorts under the bed, turned his back, and put them on. Maybe he was going to show his willingness to change old patterns by getting her something to drink. But he stood very still and, without turning around, said, "I don't know how to tell you this, Cordy. But you're the one who's always saying we should be honest, so I guess I'd better come out with it. It's about Susan."

He said the name casually, as though she should know who he was talking about.

"Susan?" she repeated flatly.

"She knows I'm seein' you tonight, an' she might call here."

She had never imagined that he would make such a confession, and certainly not in this nonchalant way.

"You just won't answer the phone then, will you?" Her voice sounded as though it was being played back on a tape recorder, offering advice about how someone might avoid a bill collector.

"I sorta have to. You see—"

"No, I don't see. You tell me what I should see." She was gripping the sides of the bed now, afraid that if she didn't hold on to something she would be propelled across the room. "I don't see why you picked this time, this time when we're, when we're . . . to tell me about . . ." She couldn't say the woman's name.

"I didn't have it in mind to come back here, Cordy. I meant to tell you first, honest I did. It's just that— Christ, you know. That part's always been good with us and we'd had a few drinks and"—he turned now, looking at her dumbly—"and hell, you wanted it as much as I did."

"What the hell are you sayin' to me?" Her throat was so tight she felt she was being strangled, then her voice rose in a screeching crescendo. "What the hell are you sayin' to me!"

"I'm trying to talk, if you'll just shut up a minute," he yelled back. "You want honesty. I'm givin' it to you. I got involved with this girl—with Susan—it didn't mean anything. It's just that . . ." He stopped and looked around as though he'd forgotten the next line of an important speech and was hoping an invisible prompter would whisper a hint. "I want to do the right thing. I sure didn't mean for any of this to happen. You gotta know that, Cordy. I didn't want any of this mess." He opened his arms and lifted his palms up in a helpless, conciliatory gesture. When he spoke again, his voice was so low that it was almost inaudible: ". . . and Susan thinks she's pregnant."

Her head jerked forward, mouth open, eyes squinting, asking him to repeat what she thought she'd heard but couldn't have. He dropped his arms and looked at the carpet, then took a step toward her. She staggered up and moved about the room, reeling with disbelief. The right thing. What could the right thing possibly be now? Holding on to the bureau for support, she saw the jewelry box where she kept her birth control pills. She hadn't wanted to stay on the pill, but Lupton had insisted that they couldn't afford to take any chances. She squeezed her eyes shut. She couldn't think. She didn't want to think.

A silence so long and deep that it threatened to swallow her up and obliterate consciousness followed. He was beside her, stroking her naked shoulders and muttering something about the right thing again. She whirled around, striking him in the face with her fist. "You son of a bitch," she howled. "You rotten, selfish son of a bitch." He jerked his arms up in a quick, coordinated defense, grabbed her wrists, and pushed her backwards onto the bed. "God-damn it, woman! Get control of yourself."

"Get control of *myself*! How dare you tell me to get control of myself. I'm the one who's kept this rotten marriage together. I'm the one, you selfish bastard. You've never had control over anything. Not your brain, certainly not your cock. All you ever had control over was a pair of running legs and now you don't even have control over them!" He let go of her and stepped back, his right arm flying into the air, ready to strike. She covered her mouth with her hands and stared up at him, the triumph of scoring a direct hit mingled with the anguish of having wounded him. His eyes filled with tears and his arm froze. "Lupton"—she reached toward him—"Lupton, I'm sorry, I—"

Whack, a stunning blow across her face. She recoiled in shock. Lupton pulled his clothes on while she wept. She did not see him leave the room but felt an incredible calm as she heard the front door slam. Then she screamed his name, ran down the hallway, and flung the door open. A blast of freezing, damp air knocked her back. His car disappeared down the deserted street.

She had stood stark naked at the door and watched as it started to rain. That much she could remember clearly. What she'd done after that was still a jumble. Somewhere during the next few hours she'd tried to call Nonnie, then, realizing the time, she'd hung up. She'd thrown Lupton's clothes out of the closet and ripped up the cashmere sweater she'd saved to buy him last Christmas. She'd packed up her typewriter and taken the manuscript she was working on out of the refrigerator (her editor Maggie Brocksen had told her to store it there "in case the house burns down"). She'd put ice on her jaw. She'd woken up on the couch to the screams of a Bela Lugosi movie. And she must've left the TV on, because she could remem-ber stuffing clothes into plastic bags (she couldn't find the key to the basement where the luggage was stored) when *Good Morning, Chicago*

came on. The guests were discussing incest and how women should
dress for the corporate world. She'd called Jeanette's school to say
she would be picking her up early. By noon she'd cleaned out the
savings account and had the car lubed and oiled. She'd done the
dishes. And as she looked around the kitchen she'd seen a six-page
letter to Lupton that she'd left on the table. She wasn't sure when
she had written it or what she'd said. She ripped it into tiny pieces
and threw them into the trash.

She flicked the headlights onto high beam and tried to
straighten her back without disturbing Jeanette, who had burrowed
into her side and was making soft, wheezing sounds as she slept. Her
jaw still ached. Her eyes felt gritty. She slowed the car as she approached a sign. Hilton Head turnoff to the right. She stayed left.
She had her bearings now. The fact that she was within twenty
minutes of her parents house and had no intention of calling them
caused her a spasm of guilt, but she barely felt she had the strength
to get to Nonnie's, where she knew she would be comforted. The
notion of facing Lucille was out of the question.

She pushed the accelerator to the floor. Soon she would see the
deep, curving river for which the city had been named, the ships,
the cupola of City Hall, the ribbon of lights along River Street. She
would cross the Gene Talmadge Bridge, follow the silent, rhythmic
one-way streets past one square and then another, be sheltered by
the overarching oaks decked with Spanish moss, see the house with
the lights shining from the high parlor windows, and be welcomed
into the arms of the one person in the world whose love for her was
steadfast and immutable.

Chapter III

At a distance of three feet, bathed in the diffused light of the crystal lamps she'd brought home from Italy, Lucille Hampton Simpkins was still lovely. The emollients, creams, sun and wind shields she called into daily service had preserved much of the elasticity of her fine-pored skin. Her hair was not so luxuriant as it had been, but the fall she'd bought recently gave it a pleasing fullness. She watched her diet carefully, and though her ribs did not show as they would in a young girl, she was sure that none of the clichés about ripe fruit would ever apply to her. Yet as she leaned into the mirror stroking Eterna 27 into her throat, the creases running from the sides of her nose to the corners of her mouth became visible, and the hazel eyes had a tired, worried look. Of course she couldn't expect to look her best now. It had been an evening of unbearable tension, and all the creams in the world were no armor against anxiety.

She wiped her fingertips on the pastel-colored tissue and pulled the fall from her head. Jake was whistling "Stardust" in the bathroom. Whistling! As though nothing had happened. As though their entire anniversary party hadn't been ruined.

Just a few hours before, dancing with Jake on the Premins' patio, she'd caught a glimpse of herself in the sliding glass doors and the image had given her a sense of relaxed well-being. Then Ellen Hamilton had cut in, looped her arms through theirs, and cried,

"You two look as though you've just come back from your honeymoon. What is it, thirty-two years? Ah'd never believe a couple could look so happy after such a long time." There was a hint of self-satisfaction beneath Ellen's effusive congratulations that had immediately put her on the alert; so that a few moments later when Ellen said she'd been in Savannah that morning and had run into Cordy at the Oglethorpe Mall, Lucille had said, "Oh, yes," as a statement instead of a question. But before she could reach behind Ellen and give Jake's arm a warning pinch, he'd flustered: "But Cordy's in Chicago." The humiliation of it: Ellen's smirking, Jake's making it worse by trying to cover, saying they expected to see Cordy tomorrow. And then, when they'd started to dance again, Ellen's running around greeting everyone with loud hellos then dropping her voice to spread the news: Lucille's daughter was back in town and Lucille didn't even know about it. Cordy had done it again.

"Jake, if you have to whistle, please switch to another tune. You're about to drive me crazy," she cried.

"I thought you liked that song."

"Not enough to hear it forty times over."

He walked past her, touching her shoulder in a gesture both familiar and dismissive, as though he were patting his own belly. Why did he persist in wearing only his pajama bottoms when his stomach protruded over the elastic band like that?

"You gonna be much longer, darlin'?" He sat on the edge of the bed before easing himself into a supine position. "I see you've got your wig off, so's you must be ready for bed."

"It's not a wig. It's a fall."

"Just teasin'. You gonna be much longer?"

She could see in the mirror that his eyes were already at half-mast. He was ready for sleep, not lovemaking, not even conversation. She set the jar down hard on the marble-topped dressing table.

"What's the matter, Luce?"

"What do you mean, what's the matter? You know very well what's the matter."

"Now ease up, Luce. I told you I wanted to drive in to Nonnie's an' find out what's goin' on."

"It's after midnight. Too late to drive to Savannah."

"Then let's call 'em."

"I don't want to call. I want them to call me. The idea that she'd come back without telling us! And having to stay at that party with everyone talking about it. I swear, I could have crawled under the rug."

"Ah, hell, honey, it doesn't matter what Ellen and those other hens think."

"It matters to me. It's *my* anniversary," she cried.

"I know it is. So come on over and give your ol' man a kiss. Show off that pretty nightdress I got for you."

"This is typical of Cordy," she went on. "Just typical. It's like the time she was arrested for speeding with all those drunk kids an' she gave Nonnie's address to the police."

"Luce, Luce," he said tiredly, throwing his arm over his face. "That was fifteen years ago. Besides, everybody's been through stuff like that with their kids."

"Jake Junior never gave us any trouble."

"We probably just never found him out. An' how about when Ellen's boy was arrested for runnin' cocaine up the Florida coast?"

"That's what I mean. This was a chance for Ellen to get back at me. She was real happy to let me know I have problems I don't even know about."

"Cordy'll call tomorrow. I know she will. She prob'ly didn't want to come tonight 'cause she knew it was our anniversary and didn't want to interfere with our party." He was tempted to tease her about how cranky she got whenever social plans were disrupted, but the way she was slamming those jars onto her dressing table let him know that she was in no mood for teasing. If he tried to sympathize, admitted that he too was upset that Cordy hadn't let them know she was coming, that would only prolong the conversation. Why was it that women always wanted to talk at bedtime? Must be one of those things, like credit cards and sudden mood changes, that a man just had to accept about marriage.

He moved his arm from shielding his eyes and watched her. The way she was patting the cream into her face reminded him of a cat washing itself. His impatience gave way to tenderness. He felt an aching need to have her beside him, to press his mouth against her cool cheek. He even liked the slightly oily, perfumed taste of the face cream. He'd had sentimental thoughts about their anniversary all week. It was more than pride in the fact that they'd survived while so many of their friends had suffered acrimonious and costly divorces. He loved her. He loved the little pad of flesh beneath her chin, though she saw it as an indication that she needed a face-lift.

He loved the sense of delicacy she brought to everything she did. He loved the stylish home she'd created. Other people might see her as capricious and demanding, but if it hadn't been for her influence he might have spent his life in aimless adventures and found himself rootless and alone.

"Now, Luce," he said firmly—a pleading tone never worked when she was like this—"Cordy did send a card, didn't she?"

"I don't want a damned card. I want to know what's going on. I want to be treated with some respect. I want—"

"Now hush up. You know Cordy's always been unpredictable. It's part of her charm." He turned on his side and patted the space next to him. "Come on over here an' show me that pretty gown I bought you."

"Nothin' bothers you, Jake. I swear the house could burn down about our ears an' you'd just want to roast marshmallows."

"That's 'cause I know when to use up energy and when to save it. Now goddamn it, come over here an' calm down. C'mon, lil' girl. It's our anniversary. Admit you're acting foolish."

She shrugged. "All right. I admit it." To submit was to display her reasonableness and get insurance that he would have to listen when she brought it up again. She turned out the lights, untied her peignoir, and got into bed beside him.

"I might take you sailing tomorrow," he whispered, playing with the tangle of ribbons at the front of her nightdress.

"I remember the first day you took me sailing," she murmured. "I'd never seen a man so hairy."

"You'd never seen a man."

"Like a big brown bear." She pulled away. "How do you know I'd never seen a man?"

"'Cause you were the youngest daughter of a fine family, an' your mama had eyes like a hawk."

"I'd seen my brother Wade."

"First time I saw you I knew you'd be the mother of my children."

"Polar bear now," she said softly, touching the hair on his chest.

"No, honey. Not that cold. When I get that cold you'll bury me."

Slowly, slowly. Nowadays it always took such a long time for his affection to change into active desire. His hands were on her breasts. He always started with her breasts. Then he'd nuzzle into her neck and bite her earlobes. His right hand would slide between her thighs, gathering up the nightdress. She knew the pattern. He'd settled on it decades ago. She closed her eyes, remembering the young bartender Dulcie Premin had hired for the party. He'd had long, sun-bleached hair tied in a ponytail, an unconventional but not unappealing contrast to his starched shirt and bow tie. Their hands had touched when he'd given her the champagne, and he'd said she must've been a child bride if this party was to celebrate her thirty-second anniversary. She'd dimpled her cheeks and said that she had been, her eyes still on his hands. Those hands were on her now. He was looming over her. His long hair brushed the side of her face. His mouth tasted of sea water and ozone. The bristles of his beard were scratching her neck and his legs were hot against hers, forcing them apart. He—

Jake pulled away, his hand still on her thigh. The phone was ringing. "That'll be Cordy."

"Don't answer it."

"Don't be foolish. Course I'm gonna answer it."

He leaned across her, his weight on her stomach. She kept her eyes squeezed shut and pulled the front of her nightdress together.

"Hello. Yes, darlin', this is Daddy."

She could hear Cordy's voice, muffled but high-pitched, saying something about having called earlier. Jake cupped the receiver and started to whisper what she'd already heard. She shook her head and wiggled out from under him. "Your mother's asleep, honey. Yeah, we had a party over to the Premins', remember them? Just let me press the hold button an' wait till I get into the other room." He put the receiver down and got out of bed.

"Sure you don't wanna talk to her?"

"Not now." When he'd felt his way out of the room she had an impulse to pick up the phone and listen but decided against it. Nonnie was sure to be on the line too, and she had no intention of being in on a three-way conversation. Typical of Cordy to go to Nonnie's first! That was because Cordy knew Nonnie would take her in, coddle her, and never ask any questions. There'd been none of that kid-glove approach when she was a child. Nonnie had been strict. She had always expected her children to live up to her own well-defined standards of conduct, but once Nonnie became a grandmother she'd taken on all the cliché indulgence of the role. She was always bobbing about, blind to misbehavior, handing out sweets and advice. Half the trouble with Cordy was that Nonnie had always favored the girl and made no attempt to hide it. Now Cordy and Nonnie were joined in another conspiracy, disrupting her life, ruining her anniversary, and making her look foolish in front of her friends. And Jake would feed into it as usual.

"Luce? Luce?" he whispered with insistent sibilance as he crept back into bed. He kissed her shoulder. She drew her legs up and fluttered her hand, feigning a disturbed sleep. "I'm sorry, Luce. I only answered it 'cause you said you wanted to know what was going on." She pulled the sheet up around her chin and turned on her side. "All right," he said, almost to himself. "All right. She'll be over first thing tomorrow to talk to us."

As the misty light of dawn sifted through the center panel of the draperies, Lucille woke up gasping, her nightdress stuck to the prickly sweat that had broken out all over her body. No matter what time she went to sleep lately, she always woke at dawn. She'd made the mistake of mentioning these waking sweats to Nonnie. "It's what they call the biological time clock, sugar, an' yours is winding down" was the only comfort she'd gotten.

She pulled the clammy gown from her thighs and lay perfectly still, palms pressing into her hip bones, fingertips resting on the soft mound of her belly. The concave smoothness she'd been able to keep even after the children were born was gone forever; even flat on her back there was that little bulge of flesh there now. "Oh, I was such a kid," she muttered softly to herself. "Such a kid."

Now, when it was too late, now she realized all the circumstances that had conspired against her in her seventeenth year, when she had accepted Jake's proposal. Her beloved brother Wade had been killed. She couldn't really believe it. She stillkept the last letter she'd written to him in her diary and felt that if she only dropped it into the mailbox it would reach him somewhere in Europe. Her sister Constance had married and moved way to Boston, and Vivian was studying singing and working for the Army in Atlanta. Lonnie was a manager in the shipbuilding factories and rarely came home, and Nonnie seemed so preoccupied that she didn't even notice when Lucille came in late from serving punch at the Savannah U.S.O. club. Even when she did come home on time, it was taken for granted. She was expectd to be the obedient daughter.

Nothing she did brought more than a matter-of-fact acceptance. The smile she got when she presented a perfect report card was nothing like the flush that came to Nonnie's face when Constance told a funny story or Vivian squeaked through some silly aria. Why, she hadn't even been given a proper coming-out party. And then Jake came on the scene: handsome, mature, protective, the hero who'd known her brother and understood her loss. She'd said yes the instant he'd proposed, when she might have had . . . well, anybody. Anybody at all.

Yet the first hints of dissatisfaction that had now metastasized into a constant regret had not started until she was in her mid-thirties. Jake, fifteen years her senior, was already making noises about retirement. Her friends seemed to be placidly accepting the role of middle-aged custodians, calling their children "the young people" and gossipping about their romances. Her son Jake Junior's chin was sprouting tufts of downy hair, and Cordy, her eyes red from chlorine or possibly even marijuana, walked around in a bikini, jerking her body to a rock beat and singing, "I want you-o-o, I want you so bad it's drivin' me mad." And that summer Lucille had realized that though she was at the height of her beauty, no one would ever again think of her as being young.

She started taking Italian lessons. She took up the piano again, but gave it up when she realized how rusty she'd become. She wanted desperately to *do* something, but the activities in church or political groups that interested Nonnie only promised another stone in her premature internment. In her need to stop time, she tried to create an order that couldn't be disturbed, and from inside herself, she began to watch and listen. She became acutely aware of even minor social slights, keeping a tally of each rejection, a balance sheet of the minor triumphs of each successful dinner party, each envious glance. Her self-awareness became an invisible deformity that prevented her from enjoying herself even when she appeared most abandoned. It was too late to change anything, that she knew with sinking certainty. If only she could shrink the world to things she could control—her home, her appearance—but even that struggle frustrated her daily.

Jake muttered something in his sleep and rolled onto his back. He was sucking the air into his mouth as though he was giving artificial respiration. She slid her hand between her legs, imagining the deck of the ship that had taken them to Europe. It smelled of tar and oil and salt spray. Strong male scents. And the band had been playing some ballad from the 1940s that had been popular when she was a girl. But now she hummed lovingly to herself, "I want you-o-o, I want you so bad it's drivin' me mad."

Chapter IV

There was no need to push, Cordy told herself. She'd reach her parents' house on time even if she dawdled. The greenery along the roadside was still sparkling from last night's shower, and even the faded signs for fireworks and home-grown vegetables looked new. It was so good to have escaped the final slush of the Midwestern winter that she was able to dismiss the upcoming interview from her mind and kid herself that she was just out for a drive. Then the first billboard for Hilton Head loomed in front of her.

It showed an elegant couple sipping cocktails by a marina and promised "A Lifestyle Where the Sun Always Shines." It was followed by another showing a golf course, and yet another depicting ocean-front restaurants and scenes of boating, shopping, and sunbathing: all the ordered and acceptable indulgences of the upper middle class.

She crossed the bridge, taking in the expanse of clear, shining water and marveling that the tight little island still looked so lovely. Its marshes had once been battlegrounds for Spanish and English colonists, hiding places for pirates and bands of Indians. Now it was a hiding place of another sort, where the worst insecurity was a fluctuation in the Dow Jones average, and the fiercest battle was a pro golf tournament. She reached for the antacid pills she kept on the dashboard.

The man-made bumps in the turnoff to Spanish Wells slowed her to twenty-five miles an hour. Through the lush foliage on either side of the road she glimpsed a few older houses, out of place now in the more elaborate design of leisure living. A couple of cows and a horse, picturesque additions to the bucolic scene, lazed in a paddock. She slowed down to look at them, then crept on for another half a mile, unconsciously putting off the reunion. And finally she saw "Casa Felicidad" burned into the wooden post that marked the circular driveway. The house, placed well back from the road, was sprawling California Modern with enough ersatz Spanish influence to make it seem out of place in the South. The first time Nonnie had seen it she'd shaken her head and muttered, "Architecture's gettin' so damned homogenized you don't know if you're in Santa Fe or Boston. Pretty soon they'll put a parkin' lot over the marshes and fly a Confederate flag over McDonald's."

Cordy switched off the ignition and checked her face in the rearview mirror. She'd had a crying jag last night when Nonnie had forced all the details of the breakup out of her, but twenty-five minutes in front of the bathroom mirror had camouflaged most of the ravages. She tucked in her blouse, walked to the front door, and rang the bell. Lucille and Jake had bought the house after she'd married, and as she stood on the tiled stoop waiting for someone to come, she felt like a stranger peddling the *Watchtower* magazine on a Sunday morning: "Hello. Could I have a few minutes of your time? I've come to tell you about the apocalypse." She rang again, then opened the door. "Mama, Daddy? It's me, Cordy."

Lucille moved across the expanse of beige carpet dressed in a pair of wide-legged hostess pajamas. Her hair was a shade lighter than Cordy remembered it, and her face was artfully highlighted with blushers and turquoise eye shadow. "Darlin'." She opened her arms wide before she reached the landing, then leaned forward to offer her cheek. "Darlin', what a surprise. Why didn't you tell us you were back in town?"

"I didn't know I was coming, Mama. It was a quick decision an'—"

"Where's my baby? Daddy said you were going to bring Jeanette."

"I was, but she was so tired I let her sleep in. Nonnie said you're invited over to Sunday dinner if you don't have other plans."

"But you got in night before last, didn't you?"

"Yes." Cordy stopped, ensnared.

"You must've forgotten how fast word travels in this neck of the woods." Lucille smiled brightly. "Ellen Hamilton told me she ran into you over to the Oglethorpe Mall."

"Ah, yes. I'd forgotten. I was there buying some shorts for Jeanette." She disengaged herself from the embrace. Lucille was still smiling, but there was the hint of accusation in her eyes. "You look wonderful, Mama."

"And so do you, darlin'. Plump as a little partridge."

"Where's Daddy?"

"He's run over to the store. We didn't expect company, and we've got into the habit of eating out, so the pantry's almost bare."

"That's all right. I'm not hungry."

"You gotta be hungry, darlin'. I'm fixing us some eggs Benedict, and Daddy's only allowed to have 'em once a month 'cause of his cholesterol. Now don't just stand here, come on through! I know the house is changed since you visited last."

"Yes, it has, hasn't it." Without even looking around she knew there would be a shift in the furniture, an addition of some painting or lamp, because Lucille's bouts of dissatisfaction usually found their outlet in a passion for redecorating.

"Let's see, the sofa . . ." She took a stab, knowing in advance that she'd be wrong. "Wasn't the sofa over near the windows?"

"No. Sofa's in the same place. Guess again." When she remained mute, Lucille swept her arm around the room and extended a bejeweled index finger. "It's the coffee table and the drapes. The drapes used to be beige and now they're white, and I replaced that ol' coffee table with this chrome and glass one. It has a much cleaner line, don't you think?"

"Yes, it is. I mean, it does."

"Don't just stand there, honey. Come on through." Lucille led the way down the steps and through the living room, gesturing as she went. "Course the sofa is reupholstered, but I think I'll have to get rid of it. I about drove your daddy crazy on that last trip to Europe. He said I'd brought back more stuff than William Randolph Hearst dragged over to furnish St. Simeon's and it would just be simpler if we moved to Italy. Now this credenza . . ."

Cordy couldn't quite believe that Lucille was going to give her the grand tour instead of asking what was going on. But Lucille always showed people through the house, pointing out this or that possession. She claimed that it was a fine conversation opener and put people at their ease, but Cordy felt the real reason was to establish territoriality. "I've simply *got* to tell you the story behind how I got this lil' ol' table," Lucille would say, touching the guest lightly on the arm, only the mouth smiling if the guest was a woman, but the eyes promising a mischievous secret if it was a man. Some of the visitors actually seemed to take an interest in the china and the furniture, but most just seemed to be intimidated, as though they knew they could never bring such choice and order into their own untidy lives.

"An' I've had another window cut in the wall here. Seemed a shame not to take advantage of the view of the water when we have people over to supper." Lucille swept into the dining room. The table was set with enough glass and silver for a full course meal. "I'll just take away this place setting," she sighed. "I thought Jeanette would be coming too."

Cordy stood near the window and looked out at the dock. The antacid pills hadn't helped. She felt an oily, burning sensation in her chest. "It's lovely, Mama. The window was a fine idea."

"Let me get you a glass of orange juice. Or would you prefer some coffee?"

"Neither. Oh, juice will be fine."

Lucille indicated that she should take a place at the table. Cordy took her jacket off and draped it across the back of a chair. The same claustrophobia that made her want to giggle during long church services was beginning to seize her. She picked up a knife, then replaced it, lining it up in perfect symmetry with the other silverware, and folded her hands in her lap. Lucille had called her "Slew Foot" when she was a child, and the nickname seemed to be a self-fulfilling prophecy. She always felt graceless when she was in her mother's house. Lucille hated spills. Or rips. Even random movements seemed to disconcert her. And breakage was a cue for real anger. Rules of order were not so strictly enforced for her brother Jake Jr. He had tracked in dirt, left dishes in the sink, tossed his smelly socks into the corners of closets, but his behavior was accepted as a natural male boisterousness. Cordy, on the other hand, was reminded that she was a little lady. A little Southern lady. She was encouraged to be vivacious, because a certain amount of vivacity was charming, but warned that her exuberance must never be allowed to slip the bounds of control. When as a child she had heard her mother referred to as sophisticated, she had thought the word must mean the opposite of clumsy. Now she understood that sophisticated meant that one's reach never exceeded one's grasp of either an object or a situation.

"Here, let me hang up that jacket." Lucille's eyes flashed a quick rebuke as she placed the orange juice on the table. "And then let's have some girl talk before your daddy gets back. You aren't having any troubles with Lupton, are you? I expected to have both of you back for a visit, but not till the summer."

"The business hasn't been going very well," she began slowly.

"Still havin' trouble? That's too bad, sugar. Course, the way the economy's going . . . But you have been able to help out a little with pin money from that book, right?"

Pin money. That's all it was. How could she possibly hope to live on it? How could she begin to explain the chaos of her life?

"Why I was proud as a peacock when I got that book," Lucille went on, stirring a few drops of saccharine into her coffee. "I never expected that I had such a talented daughter! Now this one you're working on, do you think you'll get more money for it?"

"I'm getting a bit more, but not much."

"But I always hear all those wonderful things about girls making millions on these romance books."

"Ah yes, well, Mama . . ." The claustrophobic feeling was getting worse, as though there were dials on all of her senses and they'd been turned to the halfway mark. She didn't seem to be able to hear or smell anything properly. A nervous laugh escaped her as she fiddled with the top button of her blouse.

> "There was a young girl in distress,
> Whose nerves were all in a mess,
> He said, "Yield up yer virtue,
> An' I'll jest barely hurt you,'
> So she wiggled right out of her dress!"

"What's that?"

"It's just a silly limerick Maggie told me."

"Maggie?"

"Maggie Brocksen. She's my editor."

"You mean she publishes the books, but she makes fun of them?"

"She works at Chrystallis. I don't think she likes the job much, but she's divorced, so she's sorta stuck there."

Lucille's spoon was going round and round in the coffee cup, though she'd always stressed that it was unladylike to stir more than once.

"She's a real hoot," Cordy went on quickly. "I mean romance books are silly, aren't they? It's the same old thing: girl meets rich man, loses rich man, and gets rich man."

"Doesn't sound too bad to me."

"But no one's life is like that, is it?"

"What about Lady Di's," Lucille said archly.

"I don't know anyone who lives in a castle. Besides I've always imagined that Prince Charles had spindly legs."

To Cordy's surprise, Lucille tossed her head back and gave a throaty laugh. "That's not what I imagined."

"What I really love about writing is that it gives me an excuse to read. When I read history books I try to imagine what life was really like back then. Driving onto the island today, I was thinking about it. Not the dates of battles and the coronations and that *crap*"—she used the word on purpose, knowing it would rankle—"but trying to imagine things as they really were. What do you s'pose it was like for women in plantation days, being laced into corsets when it was a hundred and three degrees? No wonder they got the vapors. Anyhow"—she paused, conscious that her hands were gesticulating wildly—"I do love to read history. I think I might have made a good teacher."

"But Cordy, you never got along with your teachers. You surely didn't feature yourself as one, that I remember with clarity."

"I still don't." She shrugged. "I'd just like to know that I could really do something. Anything."

"You're a wife and mother. Surely that's enough to keep you occupied. That's a full-time job if you do it right."

"I know it is, but . . ." She couldn't bring herself to confess that somehow she'd failed at that too. "I guess I am hungry. Eggs Benedict, you say? When's Daddy coming back?"

"I told you he'll be here directly. He's sure gonna be upset when he finds out you didn't bring Jeanette. He does dote on that lil' girl, you know. I think he featured himself having a slew of grandchildren, and so far Jeanette's the only one."

"Then you'd better tell my brother to hurry up and get married."

"Jake Junior's not even finished his internship yet. It would be a mistake for him to rush into any sort of commitment. I'm sure he's got lotsa friendly dental assistants to keep him company. But you don't want to leave much more time between Jeanette and the next one. Believe me, I can understand the loneliness of being an only child."

"You weren't an only child, Mama."

"Might as well have been. Constance and Vivian and Wade were all but grown when I came along. I remember . . ."

Cordy rested her elbows on the table and leaned forward. Over the years she'd cultivated the ability to appear attentive, while actually tuning out what her mother was saying, especially when Lucille rehashed the supposed deprivations of her childhood. Looking without really listening helped to sharpen her observation of her mother's moods. This was one of a vague, almost misty dissatisfaction. Familiar enough, but still unfathomable. Lucille possessed all the things she said she prized: an adoring husband, genteel respectability, material comfort, the admiration (and sometimes the envy, which she seemed to enjoy even more than admiration) of her friends. Yet there was always this note of unhappiness that hinted that her inner life was as barren as an unfurnished room.

". . . course, I knew that Vivian's singing would never come to much. Vivian had a sweet voice, but not of operatic quality. Nonnie thought Vivian was going all the way to the Met, but Nonnie has no understanding of music. Closest she ever came to music appreciation was going on about how her silly ol' cousin Andrew played a fiddle. She just believed Vivian was the talented one, and Constance was the smartest. And Wade, well, both Nonnie and Lonnie thought Wade had the power to make the sun come up. And I—"

"You were the prettiest."

"Pretty is something you're born with. It's not something you have to work at."

"Now that's not what you've taught me, Mama. You're always saying how important it is for a woman to look after her looks. And you're an example of that."

She toyed with the silverware again, aware that she was pandering to Lucille's vanity in order to keep the conversation away from herself. She heard the front door open and jumped up, grateful for the reprieve. "Daddy!"

She was struck by how much Jake had aged since her last visit. His mutton-chop whiskers, a compensation for his inability to grow hair on his head, had been salt and pepper the last time she'd seen him. Now they were snowy white. His carriage had changed too.

She could sense the effort that went into holding his large bearish body erect, the strain of keeping his shoulders squared. But the expression in his eyes was the same: generous and pleasantly self-satisfied, ready to forgive the faults of others more easily than he would forgive himself. How could such a man manage to live with Lucille's perfectionism?

"Daddy! It's good to see you. You look wonderful."

"Hello, darlin'. You're looking mighty good yourself."

He put the bag of groceries on the table and put his arms around her. "We were real happy when we heard you'd come home for a visit. Where's my granddaughter?"

"She was sleepy, so Cordy left her at Nonnie's," Lucille said, linking her arms through theirs. "Guess we're gonna have to drive over to Nonnie's to see her."

"No, Mama. I said I'd bring her over. She remembers going on your boat last summer, Daddy, and she's rarin' to go again."

"How long you planning to stay?" Jake asked, easing himself into a chair.

"I don't rightly know," she stalled. "A few weeks anyway. The winter up there is brutal."

"You didn't mind taking Jeanette out of school?"

"There was only another couple of weeks to go and she's doing fine in school. I didn't think it would hurt her any."

Lucille took the groceries into the kitchen, pausing to switch the wall dial that piped music through the house.

"Damn it Luce, not that Musak again. Makes me feel like I'm living in a shoppin' mall."

"It's relaxing," she called. "Don't you find it relaxing, Cordy?"

"About as relaxing as being in a traffic jam," Cordy muttered, then raising her voice, "Tell you the truth, Mama, I'm not crazy about it."

"But everybody has it in their homes." Lucille thrust her head around the door again. "How long did you say you were fixin' to stay, honey? A few weeks?"

"Uh-huh."

"Well, we're real glad to have you back, but you mustn't stay away too long." Lucille wagged her finger. "No sensible woman leaves a handsome husband alone for too long."

"Indeed she doesn't." Jake laughed. "How is that son-in-law of mine doing anyhow?"

"Fine. Just fine." Cordy dropped her head but raised it almost immediately, feeling his eyes on her. His look was curious and concerned, a plea for intimacy. She lifted her shoulders then let them drop, mirroring the helpless gesture with her eyes. He nodded a promise: they'd steal some time for a real talk.

The meal was so much like every other she'd had with her parents that it seemed like a movie she'd seen too many times. Lucille at mealtimes elevated daintiness to the level of ritual. She centered the flower arrangement and fussed with the serving dishes. She chided Jake about eating too fast. Jake winked and said the food was so good that his taste buds had overtaken his manners. Lucille talked about calories and slapped his hand playfully when he took a second helping. He smiled like a naughty ten-year-old, then called her little girl and reached over to butter her toast.

Cordy had never been able to explain to Lupton why these family meals made her so uncomfortable. Lupton, whose father had deserted his mother when he was a boy, loved to have dinner with his in-laws. He thought Lucille and Jake were the perfect model of a loving couple, and Cordy could never articulate the reasons for her embarrassment. Now, spooning into her fruit salad, she put her finger on what it was that unnerved her. Lucille and Jake reminded her of Jeanette and one of her schoolmates playing house. They obeyed the same unspoken rules, the same effortless trading off of authority: parent/child, child/parent. The roles were given, as immutable and clearly defined as the performance of a Noh play. And the remarkable thing was that they seemed to enjoy playing it.

She pushed her bowl aside, carefully leaving two strawberries ("Neither wasteful nor unladylike"), and thought about her grandparents. Nonnie and Lonnie had never gone through this charade of togetherness. In fact they'd routinely voiced their exasperation with the opposite sex. "Men!" Nonnie would sputter, "Lord preserve me from men." Men were stubborn, impractical, welded to wrongheadedness out of pride, helpless in day-to-day problems. And Lonnie had railed against women: Women were talkative, given to outbursts of emotion that no reasonable man could understand, they were frivolous and demanding. Yet there was no real malice in their outbursts. After letting off steam they would shrug and look at each other tenderly, as though any attempt to alter the situation would be foolish. They had a depth of toleration, not just for each other, but for each other's sexual differences. Whereas she and Lupton seemed to stare at each other across a great gulf, almost as if they belonged to different species. They were united only by sexual need rather than any broader enjoyment of each other's sex.

"You're not eating enough, Cordy. Here, have some more salad."

"You just got through telling her she should watch her weight," Jake reminded Lucille.

"Fruit salad isn't fattening. Here." Lucille ladled another helping into Cordy's bowl.

"I really don't want any more."

"You're home now, honey. You've gotta do as you're told. Jake, please don't light up that cigar. You promised me that you were gonna cut down."

"I didn't buy it. I ran into Jacques Haur at the store, an' he gave it to me."

"Have I told you about Jacques Haur, Cordy? He bought that fancy two-storied place at the end of the road. I swear the traffic's been so heavy since he moved in I think we're gonna have to put up a stoplight. He's always givin' these big parties. Don't think he does anythin' else but party."

"He doesn't," Jake agreed, lighting up. "He told me that's why he took an early retirement."

"Must have a heap of money."

"An' my guess is it's not all from legitimate sources," Jake laughed.

"Wouldn't surprise me. He's been through three wives already. He's in with a pretty wild crowd from what Ellen Hamilton tells."

"That woman's like an X-rated version of the six o'clock news, Luce. By the time Ellen gets through embroidering her stories, a fund-raiser for crippled children is turned into an orgy. She's the one got your mother all riled up 'bout your being back in town without tellin' us, Cordy."

"I did leave sort of on impulse," Cordy explained. "I'm sorry I didn't let you know.

"No matter. Anyhow, Luce, when I ran into Jacques at the store—an' I must admit he was lookin' the worse for wear—he said he was gonna shower and shave and then drop by for a drink."

"He said he was coming by, an' you're just now gettin' around to tellin me," Lucille cried.

"Your mother's been dying to get an invitation to one of those wild parties."

"That's not true, Jake. I'm sure we wouldn't fit in at any of those parties. But if Jacques is comin' to my house . . ." She was already on her feet, gathering up plates. "I do wish I hadn't given that girl the weekend off."

"I'll help you," Cordy offered.

"No. You come on down to the pier. I wanta show you the boat," Jake insisted.

"Yes, you two run along. Anything to get that cigar out of the house."

Jake waited on the patio while Cordy took off her sandals. They started down the grassy incline toward the dock. Neither of them spoke. Cordy was pleased to be out of the house, barefoot, with the warmth of the sun on her head. They reached the pier and stood side by side looking out at the water. Jake often said the chief attraction of the outdoors was that it seemed to discourage conversation, and Cordy, grateful for the silence, leaned on the railing and listened to the waves slap against the moorings. Jake pushed his palm against the center of his chest and belched. "'Scuse me. Your mother's right. I shouldn'ta had that second helping of eggs. Been trying to keep the ol' blood pressure down and keep the weight down too. But I'll never have the discipline your mother has."

"You're not so vain as Mama."

"Don't have to be. I'm a man." His eyes narrowed, squinting against the glare of the water. The muscles of his face were drawn down introspectively. "Ah, the water's so pretty. I swear I could just sit here and watch the sun come up and go down. I used to kid m'self that once I retired I'd read all the books I put aside when I was a young man. All through college I wanted to read something more than my engineering books but I never had the time. Then I worked my butt off at my first job, then the war came along, and after that . . ." He shrugged, passing his hand over his scalp and looking down into the water. "But now I find I don't have the will to read. Caesar's *Gallic Wars* has been opened to the same page on my nightstand for weeks. I just want to sit and soak up all this beauty that's around me. Other people, I don't know, they just seem to ignore all this, think of it as a sorta backdrop." He sighed. "I think your mother's plotting the next trip to Europe, and we've only been home four months."

"You always like to travel, Daddy."

"Used to. It's different now. People in foreign countries used to treat us with respect. Now they don't even like us. In France during the war you could go up to anybody an' be treated friendly, get a civil word. Now you don't feel safe 'less you're sitting in a bar at some Hilton Hotel. Luce don't mind the Hiltons, but I'm damned if I wanta lounge around some bar an' not know if I'm in Berlin or Houston. Still, she's got her mind set on goin' back. She's just so . . . *restless*." He was still in love with her enough to make it sound like a virtue.

Cordy nodded. She knew what it was like to subjugate your own tastes out of affection. And she knew the defeat you felt when your denial led to further compromises instead of harmony. She admired her father's flexibility, but her admiration was not without annoyance.

"An' even when we do traipse around the world, it just doesn't seem to make Luce happy. When we were in Italy, she was jittery as a filly at the starting gate. I swear . . ." He talked on, clucking at examples of Lucille's dissatisfactions, until Cordy realized that she'd misinterpreted the look they'd exchanged at the table. He didn't want to find out about her; he wanted to unburden himself. "An' I've told her I'm not Croesus. We live right up to the penny, and living beyond our means has always bothered me. We can't go back to Italy and have her get a face-lift too."

"I didn't know she wanted to get a face-lift," she said without surprise.

"Isn't that the craziest thing you ever heard tell? Everybody thinks Luce is at least ten years younger than she is. She gets a face-lift an' I'm gonna have people thinkin' she's my daughter. But she's so damned anxious about it. An' I don't think it'll make her happy, Cordy. I guess I don't have any idea anymore what will make her happy. Maybe you could talk to her."

"Oh, Daddy," she interrupted with a laugh, "I don't know what I'd say to Mama. I don't know what's bothering her. Sometimes I think certain people were born unhappy. It's just a given, like the color of their eyes or a disposition toward indigestion."

"Hell, I don't know." He leaned forward and started to splinter the wood with his thumbnail. "Guess you've got troubles of your own."

Take the plunge. Confess. Ask for help. "Yes," she began slowly. "I came home 'cause Lupton and I are having problems."

He turned. His gaze did not waver, not even to the slightest flickering of his eyelids. Paterfamilias: The more he was shaken, the more stolid he became. "When did this start?"

"I've been trying to figure that out. I don't know. I'm so confused now I think maybe all the seeds were there from the beginning."

"How . . .?" She could feel him groping for words.

"How bad is it? Pretty damned bad. I may . . ." If she said the word it would mean she'd really left Lupton; it would drive her further toward the decision she wasn't capable of making. "I may get a divorce."

"Good God, Cordy. There's never been a divorce in the family," he said hoarsely.

"What difference does that make? I'm talking about me, not the entire clan," she bristled. "I'm not rushing into anything. That's why I'm here. I wanted time to think. And I don't want to tell Mama anything yet. Damn it." She turned her back to him and tossed her head. "Damn it. I've always hated all these convolutions in the family."

"What do you mean?"

"All this intrigue. All the plotting and crossed alliances. Whenever I come home I feel like I'm part of a conspiracy in the court of Louis the Fourteenth. Mama has secrets from Aunt Vivian, Vivian knows but she won't tell Constance. Like when Uncle John went into that detoxification program an' everybody pretended like it was a vacation, or when—" She broke off; the list was endless. "And now I'm doing it too. I don't mean to hold out on Mama, but I just can't bring myself to tell her about my troubles with Lupton. She'll think it's all my fault."

"No she won't. It would upset her no end, but if he hasn't been treating you right . . . Hell, I'm gonna get on that phone and have a good talk to him."

"Please don't, Daddy. That would only make it worse."

"Hell's fire, if I'm giving him a hand I have a right to know 'bout how the business is going. An if he's treating you bad I've got a right to set him straight. You're my daughter an'—"

She turned slowly, lifted her hands from the railing, and hugged herself. "You loaned Lupton money?"

"He's 'bout twenty thousand dollars into me." He shifted his weight uncomfortably. "I thought he would've told you."

"That's what I've been saying, Daddy," she sputtered. "Everyone is always doing things behind everyone else's back. And, no, I didn't know."

"Your mama doesn't know either," he said. "An' maybe I

shouldn't've told you. Lupton prob'ly wanted to spare you, an' we did sort of agree to it man to man. But if he's in that much trouble, I guess you don't have a whole hell of a lot of cash now."

"I'm fine," she said quickly. "I took some money out of savings." It was bad enough to think about being broke, but not nearly as bad as it would be if she took money from her father. If she asked him not to tell Lucille she'd be doing the very thing she was criticizing everyone else for doing. If, on the other hand, they told Lucille, it would expose the depth of her marital problems. It would be like having an allowance again, opening her up to an unmanageable amount of interference and criticism. It was bad enough that she might be out of her job as wife, but if she came out of the divorce a pauper, Lucille would count her stupid as well.

"Now, honey, you'll let me know if you need anything, won't you? I want you to stay close to me. I want to know what's happening." He reached over and took her hand. She laced her fingers through his, wanting to put her head against his chest. "Course, if Lupton's having business problems . . ." He opened his free hand to a host of excuses and possibilities. "There's nothin' can upset a man more'n feeling he can't take care of his own."

"It isn't just problems with business, Daddy. I'm tough enough to survive that," she said, knowing she'd never really be tested, but willing herself equal to the challenge.

"What the hell else has gone wrong?"

She paused, wondering how much to divulge. It was ridiculous to feel that she was betraying Lupton, but it was hard to put aside the years when they'd joked about their parents' foibles, criticized their habits, and formed a united front against them. Besides, if they did get back together again, there were things she wouldn't want anyone else to know.

"Maybe you should make the effort to talk to your mother, Cordy. There are things that women can tell each other—"

"No, Daddy, it's not *that*. If we'd had trouble with sex I probably would have noticed the other troubles sooner." The innocence of his remark won her trust. His characteristic concern for anyone else's privacy was something she cherished about him. "Though in a way . . . yes, it definitely is about sex."

"You can come and talk to me any time you want." He let go of her hand and shifted his attention to the boat, indicating it with a nod of his head. "You say Jeanette wants to go out on the boat again? I'd sure enjoy that. You see there where the rigging . . ."

The moment was not to be. He was too embarrassed by the possibilities of her confession, too unsure of the boundaries of fatherly affection. He hated emotional scenes. He prided himself on gentlemanly reserve. Even with the family his occasional outbursts of temper came equipped with apologies. Noticing that she was chewing the inside of her lower lip, he left off his description of the boat. "And Jeanette," he asked, fixing on a subject of mutual concern, "has she been all right? You haven't let on that you and Lupton are having troubles have you?"

"Nope. I've been real cowardly about that too."

"That's not cowardly, Cordy. Children should be protected."

"But they can't be, Daddy, can they? She's a very smart little girl. She knows what's going on even if she doesn't understand all of it. Oh, please." She had hoped for comfort and advice, but seeing how miserable all these questions had made him, she felt inclined to dispense rather than receive concern. "Please don't worry. We'll be all right." And then with forced brightness: "Did you say you'd had the *Lady Luce* painted? I thought you were just gonna have her scraped."

"That was such a hell of a job that I decided to go the whole hog."

She started toward the boat, manufacturing more questions. Lucille called from the patio.

"Guess your mother wants us." He grinned. "Maybe I'll drive on into Savannah one night this week and take you to dinner. Just the two of us . . ." his voice trailed off.

Lucille was standing, one hand to her hair, the other stretched forward beckoning them, in a pose that might have been copied from an operetta. She looked back over her shoulder as a tall man with ear-length sandy hair walked onto the patio. He was dressed in white pants and a white shirt, opened to expose his chest. A jeweled leather belt with a sunburst design was clasped around a middle that had thickened slightly. Catching sight of Cordy, he stood absolutely still, watching her so intently that she rounded her shoulders as she walked toward the house. Coming closer, she could see the hollows beneath his eyes and in his cheeks, the slack sensuality of his lower lip. He was deeply tanned, but even standing in the sunlight he reminded her of darkened rooms. I could use him in a book someday, she thought. What was the modern counterpart of the world-weary buccaneer? Record producer? Disco owner? Did he run guns with Cuban refugees?

"Jacques dropped by to have a drink with us." Lucille's voice, which had been almost strident during the meal, was now hushed to a confidential whisper.

"Good to see you Jacques." Jake offered his hand. "This is our daughter Cordy."

She started to offer her hand.

"Cordy"—Lucille laughed—"is that somethin' they taught you up North? When did you get into the habit of shaking hands?"

"I don't rightly know." She clasped her hands together and made an idiot face. "It's an ancient ritual, you know. Meant to show that you aren't holding any weapons."

"Women don't normally carry weapons." Lucille settled herself on the chaise.

"No. They conceal them," Jacques said, a smile lurking at the edges of his mouth.

Cordy opened her hands and turned them upward. "Neither carrying nor concealed."

Jacques made a mocking bow and stayed forward, staring at her bare feet. "The pleasure is mine, Miss Simpkins."

"It's not Miss Simpkins. It's Mrs. Tyre. Or Cordy."

"Actually it's Cordelia," Lucille sighed. "Such an old-fashioned name, but my mother picked it. Perhaps you've heard of Cordy's husband, Lupton Tyre. He used to play pro ball with the Chicago Bears and now he owns a chain of sporting goods stores in the Chicago area."

Cordy slipped into her sandals, keeping her eyes on the ground. Why did Lucille insist on giving information nobody wanted and then exaggerating it?

"How about a drink?" Jake said.

"I'd like a drink," Cordy answered quickly. "In fact, I'll fix them."

"Would you, darlin'? The bar's in the living room now, right next to the stereo."

"You need a map to find your way around this house," Jake laughed. "Lucille's always changing things around. Why I came home one night, didn't bother to turn on the lights, threw myself down where my armchair used to be and damned near broke my back."

"Don't exaggerate, darlin'."

"I did sprain my back, Luce. You remember that."

"Cordy, tell your daddy not to exaggerate. He didn't have a sprained back at all, Jacques."

Jacques looked as though this single example of a domestic joke had already brought him to the brink of a yawn. Not, Cordy imagined, that his face was capable of much emotion.

"What shall I fix? Bloody Marys or would y'all like something stronger?"

"Bourbon, scotch—whatever." Jacques turned to watch her as she went to the door.

"Make that two scotches," Jake said.

"An' just a white wine for me. I do get so languid in the afternoons," Lucille stretched seductively. "Anything more than wine jest puts me into the mood of a siesta. When I was in Mexico . . ."

Cordy went straight through the hallways toward one of the bathrooms. It didn't seem likely that Lucille would change the location of the bathrooms; but she had, Cordy discovered as she opened the door, installed new mirrors with strings of lights around them so that the place looked like a movie star's dressing room. Damn her mother! Everything Lucille did annoyed her. Lying about Lupton's business and then scolding Daddy for telling the truth. And that Jacques. He probably thought his reptilian stare was sexy. King Cobra looking to transfix bunnies.

She grabbed a brush and started whipping it through her hair, then took the Jungle Gardenia from the cluster of perfume bottles. Typical that Lucille's favorite perfume had something to do with the jungle; Lucille was a sort of domestic guerrilla. She was touching the stopper to her earlobes when she stopped. She'd come inside to have a moment's respite, and here she was checking her complexion and dolling herself up just because there was a man on the patio. And not even a man she wanted to impress. How many years of relentless "a girl's nothing if she's not pretty" had made her respond so thoughtlessly? She replaced the stopper and wandered into the living room, trying to get her bearings. Of course the place made her nervous. It would make anyone nervous. It had all the individual warmth of a furniture display room. It was a wonder Lucille didn't put little notices up: "You break it, you've bought it." That was how Lucille felt about girls' hymens, after all.

She slopped the drinks into the glasses and went to the kitchen to add the ice. Lucille's laughter, now in the upper registers of delight, floated in through the window. Balancing the tray—"Genuine lacquer, from Kyoto, not Taiwan," Lucille would be sure to point out—she walked slowly to the patio, eavesdropping on the conversation.

"I get up to Virginia a couple of times a year," Jacques was saying, as though the trip were a major accomplishment. So they were still into travel talk. Since Jacques didn't look like a sportsman, they'd zip through boating and golf to arrive, breathless but secure, at property values. "Matter of fact, I'll be going up there in a couple of weeks. Two of my mares are getting ready to foal and I want to be there." And I bet you'll hand out cigars, Cordy thought.

"Thank you, Cordy." Jake accepted his drink. "We were talking about horses. Jacques here has some. Cordy loves horses. When she was 'bout thirteen she was a mighty fine horsewoman."

"Yes"—Lucille touched her curls—"she was. I do wonder why girls that age are so fond of horses. I guess it's—"

"Sublimation," Jacques offered, raising his glass.

"Sublimation?" Cordy arched her brows and smiled, challenging his rudeness with her eyes. "Sublimation for what?"

"I think that's pretty obvious."

"It isn't to me. Sometimes, as I think Freud said, a cigar is just a cigar."

"I think Groucho Marx said that, sugar," Jake laughed.

"Even at thirteen I didn't confuse riding a horse with anything else. I enjoyed it because I love beautiful animals. There's a sense of simultaneous freedom and control when you ride well."

"Just as I was sayin'," Jacques said laconically.

"You don't have to make such a fuss about it, Cordy. After all, you don't even ride anymore," Lucille reminded her.

"If you like horses so much, do you bet on 'em?" Jacques wanted to know.

"I don't need to gamble on horses. I guess life has enough gambles built into it."

"Well, I've got a real beauty now, an' I'm gonna start racing her next year, an' when I do I'm gonna let you folks know about it 'cause I'm sure she's gonna be a winner. Nothin' as fast as a Southern horse or a Southern woman."

"I'll drink to that," Jake said.

"I do s'pose you mean that as a compliment, Jacques," Lucille laughed.

"Oh, I do. I do indeed." He touched his glass to Cordy's and leaned back in his chair. A smile that bordered on smugness curled on one side of his mouth.

"Tell me," Jake said. "Y'all havin' much problem with erosion on your part of the shoreline?"

Just as Cordy had anticipated, the talk now turned to property values. She examined her toes and held her tongue for another twenty minutes, but at the first possible break in conversation she put her glass down and got to her feet.

"Won't you have another?" Lucille asked.

"No. I really should be getting back."

"Cordy is stayin' in Savannah with my mother," Lucille volunteered. "She just came in last night an' she has so many old friends to look up, she wanted to be in the city."

"I 'spect I'll see you again." Jacques now made a point of offering his hand. "I do quite a bit of entertaining, an' a pretty woman is always a welcome addition to a party."

"I think I might have just another splash of wine, Jake darlin'." Lucille held out her glass. "Will you do the honors? Jacques, you will join us in another, won't you?"

"Surely. Let me just escort Miss Simpkins to her car."

Cordy leaned down to kiss Lucille's cheek then walked over to give Jake a hug.

"Now call us when you get back to Nonnie's so's we'll know you arrived safely," he ordered.

"Daddy, it's only forty-five minutes away. You know I drove all the way from Chicago." Then, catching his look of concern: "All right, I'll give you a call."

She walked through the house and out into the drive. Jacques was right behind her. She turned on the ignition as soon as she got into the car, but he leaned into the window.

"I meant what I said. What's your grandmother's number? I'll give you a call next time I'm having a party."

"Thank you, but I don't think I'll have much time. I'm writing a book you see and—"

"What's it called?"

"I don't have a title yet."

"Your father said you'd written something else. *Tempestuous Love*, wasn't it?"

"Yes," she admitted, feeling foolish.

"You ladies do have active fantasy lives. *Tempestuous Love*. But there's no other kind worth having, is there?"

"Excuse me. I really do have to be going."

"Remember my offer."

"I'm a married woman, Mr. Haur." And you're an arrogant son of a bitch to be coming on with me at my parents' house.

"And your husband's in Chicago, isn't he?"

"Goodbye."

He whacked the fender as she pulled away. Through the rear-view mirror she could see him watching her with that same air of superiority. She wished she'd been able to maintain a similar coolness instead of getting flustered, but she was no longer used to men acting as though she were available. At least his visit had helped her to get through the initial homecoming; it made escape that much easier, and for that she was almost willing to forgive him his rudeness.

Nonnie was sitting on the floor of the library playing jacks with Jeanette when she came into the house.

"Mama!"

"How did it go, Cordy?"

"Ask me no questions an' I'll tell you no lies. *They* didn't. Ask any questions, that is."

"Hey, Mama, how come you didn't wake me up," Jeanette whined.

"Don't be stringing out your voice like you're a homeless cat," Nonnie smiled and patted Jeanette's bottom. "Run on out to the kitchen an' get your mother an iced tea."

Jeanette moved reluctantly to the door, frowning at the unfairness of being excluded from important secrets until Cordy acknowledged her good behavior with smile.

"He called," Nonnie whispered. "'Bout ten minutes after you'd left. Thank god for small blessings, the baby was still asleep."

"Did you tell him I was here?"

"Didn't want to, but I felt I had to," she confessed. "He was 'bout crazy with worry for you. Course, I would've given him a piece of my mind in a heartbeat, but I just held my peace. You know I don't like to meddle. I just told him you'd call him back this afternoon, if'n he could stay in his own home that long. And I told Jeanette I'm gonna take her for a ride in one of the horse-drawn carriages, so's you can call him just as soon as we leave."

"If it's too much trouble . . ."

"No trouble at all. You need privacy. Besides"—her eyes narrowed critically—"I've always wanted to hear what those guides are tellin' those tourists."

*   *   *

Lupton picked up on the first ring. "Oh . . . Cordy." She could hear the relief as he drew out her name.

"Yes. Nonnie said you'd called."

"Are y'all safe?"

"Of course we're safe."

"You've never driven that distance alone before."

"I know." She wanted to spit at his concern. "Now I have."

"Well, what the hell do you mean runnin' out like that?" he demanded. He had always maintained that the best defense was a good offense, on and off the field. "You like to drive me crazy."

"Since it took you two days to call, you couldn't have been too concerned. Maybe you just didn't notice we were gone."

"I had to get things straightened out here first. And I have, Cordy. I've straightened things out."

Straightening things out, she knew, was something Lupton was good at. Like doing the right thing, stonewalling it, and hanging tough. She held her breath, feeling some small measure of retribution as she imagined him squirming at the other end of the line. Not that she could have spoken. Her rage almost strangled her.

"Susan . . ." he began. Again she held the silence, refusing to give him so much as a grunt of recognition. "Susan's all right. She's not pregnant."

She wanted to ask if it had been a false alarm or if something had beed done to terminate. For the briefest moment there was a flicker of concern for this unknown woman, but it was quickly obliterated by her own misery. The sweat broke out on her hands. She tried to swallow to ease the pain in her throat, but couldn't. Did bitterness dry up saliva as it dried up compassion?

"I'd appreciate it if you would call again tonight," she said finally. "Jeanette will feel better if she talks to you. Just tell her hello and say that you love her."

"I do. Goddamn it!" The declarative gush, its sincerity genuine but irrelevant. "I love you. You gotta know how much I love you, Cordy."

"Spare me, Lupton." She sounded bored, almost mocking. She thought she might sink to the floor.

"When can I expect you back?" Gruff, too bright, toughing out his growing panic.

She looked around the hallway. Her mind slipped its gears as she recalled a paper she'd done for a history class: "Sanctuary: Inviolable Asylum in the Middle Ages." "I don't think you can." She mouthed it so softly that it might not have been heard. But that didn't matter, because she was already putting the telephone back on the hook.

Chapter V

"I'm telling you, Cordy, you've got to think of this divorce as a positive experience."

Maggie Brocksen tipped back her chair, hunched her shoulder to keep the phone near her ear, then lunged forward to take another cigarette. The gold lighter, an unimaginative gift from an unimaginative former lover, was out of fluid. She tossed it aside, rummaged in her desk for some matches, and scanned the jackets of the new releases that were tacked to the pegboard above her head. The romance line, all cavaliers and cleavage, was to her right. The contemporary offerings (*Female Independence: Mystique or Mistake?*; *How to Firm Your Thighs in Ten Days*; and *Solitude Can Be Sexy*) were to her left. A ripple of smoke drifted into her eyes. Squinting, she checked the photo of the fifteen-year-old model on *Exercises to Save Your Face* and automatically arched her brows and opened her eyes wide in the "shock" expression recommended in the first chapter.

"A positive experience . . ." Cordy's voice drawled with an upward inflection, mocking and questioning. "In the first place, I didn't say I was getting a divorce."

"Does that mean you've heard from Lupton again? Cheez, Cordy, I don't see how you could even go out with someone called Lupton. I was introduced to this guy called Archibald, and I knew it would be a mistake to go out with him. A name like that can scar a man for life. Can you imagine yourself saying 'I want you, Archibald'?"

"As a matter of fact, he has been calling regularly. But I asked him to. Jeanette misses him so much, and I don't want her to think that she's being rejected."

"Has he sent you any money?"

"A little."

"That's what I figured. Wise up. It's been over a month now, hasn't it?"

"A few months doesn't mean . . . I just need some more time."

"Look, I'm not minimizing the pain of making a real break. I've been through it myself. But *tempus fugit* and all that. The faster you can get on your own feet, the faster you're going to recover. Why don't you take this chance and come to New York? Just see how you like it."

"I've never been alone before."

"You make it sound as though a judge just read you a life sentence in solitary. I'm only offering you a two-month sublet. I'm going to be working for an old friend, you know, and that's iffy. I might be back even before the two months are up. California scares me."

"I didn't think anything could scare you, Maggie."

"Are you kiddin'? Crossing the Hudson gives me the shakes. And I already know what California's going to be like: If you're over forty or don't surf they put you in relocation camps. They don't like sharp people, they like pretty people. But I've gotta take the chance because the salary's so much better. And speaking of business, did you get your new jacket yet?"

"I got it yesterday."

"I know. I know. Don't tell me. Roxanne's hair should be red instead of blond, but you don't expect a schlock outfit like Chrystallis to have artists who actually read the books, do you? All things considered, this is an improvement over your first one. At least Captain what's-his-face has muscles instead of a case of elephantitis. And I'm sorry I had to cut the chapter where Roxanne gets pregnant, but you know the rules with romances: no kids; no old folks; rags to riches; and a handsome, brutal, but deeply misunderstood hero."

"I think I can get that last part right."

Maggie snorted and coughed. "Couldn't we all, sister, couldn't we all? Listen, I've leaned on that creep in accounting, so I think you'll get the rest of your advance in a coupla weeks. Why the hell don't you use it to come up here and scout around? You're on what?—your third book now—and you're still makin' lunch money. You're never going to get outta the rut unless you find a good agent and another publisher, and you can't do that long distance."

"I do appreciate the offer, Maggie. Really I do. But with Jeanette to take care of and—"

"You said she was going to spend the summer with your relatives, didn't you? Hell, the number of relatives you've got down there you could probably cast the *Forsyte Saga* at a Sunday dinner. I'll bet your grandmother wouldn't mind taking care of Jeanette. I don't think you realize what I'm offering you. A sublease on a good New York apartment is harder to find than a fundamentalist with a sense of humor. You know, I have a friend who's been itching to get a divorce for the past year and a half, but neither she nor her husband can find another place to live, so now they're in therapy together. You'd better make up your mind real fast."

A short, soft chuckle came through the receiver. "Why does everything have to be so fast with you Yankees?"

"I'm not a Yankee, Cordy. I'm from Rahway, New Jersey, and my ancestors didn't hit Ellis Island until after the Civil War. I know that a Georgia education doesn't do more than teach you to cross the street when the light turns green, so just listen to me for a minute. I think you've got some talent. You need a lot of work, but some of the things in your books—the historical descriptions, for example— are first rate. Not that anyone here's gonna notice; they're into heavy breathing and happy endings. Point is, you could go somewhere. But not if you're always so broke you're cranking out the next one. And once I'm gone you won't even have an editor who'll see you get paid on time. So think about it."

Maggie stubbed out her cigarette and glanced over her shoulder. The Sierra Club poster she'd appropriated from her son's room when he'd gone off to college was taped next to the narrow strip of glass that passed for a window. The glass was smoked, denying any hint of climate or time of day. "God, I hate this place," she muttered, scrounging in her purse to find her watch. "I can't believe it, it's almost five o'clock. I've gotta get my hair streaked and I'm supposed to meet this sci-fi creep for drinks at six-thirty. I know he can't write and I won't be surprised if he can't talk either. He's invented some sort of futuristic language that's absolutely unintelligible. He thinks it's creative. I think he must've gone to one of those colleges where they let the kids drop acid and tell'm that sentence structure blocks spontaneity. I can see it now: I'll be on my fourth martini and this space cadet will be slurping goat's milk and lecturing me about environmental impact. Have to rush. Let me know if you want to take my apartment, because once word gets out that I'm going away there'll be squatters on the stoop, and the Puerto Rican super will start giving out numbers." She made the little clicking sound that signaled the end of her conversations. "All the dollars, cookie. Bye."

Cordy heard the drone at the other end of the line before she could get out her farewell. Shutting her eyes, she leaned against the hall mirror. Conversations with Maggie left her breathless, even though Maggie did most of the talking. Maggie's husky, abrasive voice was always demanding something in a hurry. Could she get the rest of the manuscript in by the end of the month? Could she send the revisions back special delivery? And now, would she leave Savannah and come to New York for two months while Maggie tried out a new job in Los Angeles.

She felt queasy, as though she'd swallowed the question whole and couldn't digest it. Placing the receiver in the cradle, she started to move away, automatically averting her eyes from the mirror. Mirrors were not her friends these days. She used them only as a tool to check herself, the way she might look at a plant—quickly and objectively—to see if it needed pruning. Still, she couldn't resist a sidelong glance as she moved toward the front door. The image that flashed by her was that of a compelling rather than beautiful face marked with the strain of showing a confidence she no longer felt. And if she began to care for herself again, made a face to meet the faces, could she fool anybody? Or would the slash of mouth with the full lower lip be a giveaway that she was too easily led by emotion? Surely any sharp eye could detect that she was a woman approaching thirty, anxious about money and sex, soon to assume the dubious label of divorcee. And Maggie had advised her to think positively. What half-baked psychology magazine had she lifted that from?

She sighed and continued toward the front door. Late afternoon sun came through the leaded glass, dappling the hardwood floor and the edge of the umbrella stand with gold. There was no sound except the faint drone that came from the living room, where, she knew, Bernice would be standing, dustcloth in hand, transfixed by the television. The aroma of pumpkin bread bloomed through the house. Bernice always made it on Wednesdays—a heavy concoction that seemed to use up all its goodness creating that sweet, homey smell. "To Grandmother's house we go," she and Jake Junior had chanted, bouncing on the back seat of the Oldsmobile as they were driven to Nonnie and Lonnie's for those endless Sunday afternoon dinners. And it was still here, solid and familiar, secure on a bedrock of the past when the whole world seemed to be trembling on an earthquake fault.

"Sounds so cozy it could make you catatonic," she heard Maggie's voice heckle. "You going to take up needlepoint and celibacy, and get the vapors when you hear about Lupton's second marriage?"

She took up the imaginary conversation with a confident rebuke: "I'll stay here, take care of Jeanette, and keep writing until I get on my feet."

"Given the piddling amount of money you make, that at least sounds like a challenge. Why don't you do what you should've done ten years ago: Get out and do something for yourself. Learn what you should've been learning when you were taking ballet lessons and memorizing football scores."

"But New York is like a fortress, an ant hill."

"Don't mix metaphors."

"It's mobs of wise-mouth, cynical people who don't care about each other, it's crime and garbage and no manners—"

"No worse than seventeenth-century London, I'll bet. Pick up your skirts and sail through the sewage like your heroines always do. Seek love and adventure. Make a buck."

"But it scares me, Maggie. My body goes rigid with fear when I think about it. No that's a lie. Roxanne's body would go rigid with fear. Mine just feels waterlogged. Fear bloats me; it makes me soggy."

"God, you wishy-washy types bore me! Stop forcing me into the role of the tough physiotherapist who just knows sweet little Annie can kick away those crutches and walk again if only she believes in herself."

"But you don't understand . . ." She'd almost said it aloud. But even in hypothetical conversation she couldn't find a rejoinder to Maggie's wisecracks, because behind the imagined taunts was the force of indisputable truth. Like it or not, she would have to take charge of her life or else go under. She would have to make some money. Ultimately, she would have to move out and find a place of her own. When she thought of living alone she imagined a small room with minimal furniture. The faucet would drip, the refrigerator would never hold more than a jar of instant coffee and half a dozen eggs. The telephone would not ring.

"'I'll think about it tomorrow.' Honest I will." She searched her memory for the line that preceded that famous procrastination, but couldn't find it.

Opening the front door, she looked out on the square. The azaleas had all but died out now, only here and there a bush showed a hint of color. A young man lazed on a bench reading. A family of tourists stood near the monument to General Pulaski—the father staring up absently, the mother quoting from a guidebook, the child picking her nose as she watched a gangly black boy dribbling a basketball. A predictable, muted, and lazy scene. It soothed her now, just as it had filled her with raging boredom when she was a teenager.

A bright blue sports car careened around the corner, barely slowed at the stop sign and zoomed off. It was just like the car Lupton drove now. No matter how broke he was, Lupton always had a new car. The first one had been the white Corvette, on loan from his brother who'd been shipped off to Vietnam. She could still feel the vinyl upholstery sticking to her naked back, still see the glow of the radio light. Then they'd had the Ford. Jake's wedding gift. They'd roared off to Atlanta in that, and six months later Lupton had stripped the gears. She'd thought it was funny until she realized they'd have to pay for the repairs themselves. She'd taken the Ford then, and Lupton had bought a new Pinto. After that . . . This was the problem, damn it. So many things—cars, the smell of liniment, a Willie Nelson song—triggered her memory, and now, after a month at Nonnie's, the unhappy memories had started to fade while the pleasant ones lingered, bloomed with colors, scents, and forgotten scraps of conversation.

She could almost see him on the football field, his head and shoulders thrown back, his hips moving with that relaxed swivel that could go into a quick, violent jerk as he pivoted around the safety man and raced across the goal line, or—more painfully recalled— changed his rhythm in bed. Lupton, fifteen pounds heavier now, his cropped hair longer, styled to camouflage his prominent ears, his thick neck adorned by a gold chair he would once have labeled "effeminate." But still smiling that "nothin's gonna stop me" smile. The athlete turned dandy, the playing fields of the past replaced by the bedrooms of the present. The pleasant recollections took her on a winding road that brought her back to the same point. She could not forgive him. Even if Jeanette did miss him. Even if she didn't know how to support herself. Even if she couldn't bear to consider the prospect of living alone.

She closed the door and started down the hallway, damned if she was going to let any more obsessive memories ruin what was left of an already disrupted afternoon.

"That you, Cordy?" Bernice called over the drone of a detergent commercial.

"Yes. I was just taking the air."

"Y'all finished typing yet?" Whether out of humor or a veiled critical judgment, Bernice always referred to Cordy's work as typing.

"I'm not through, but you can go on home if you like. I'll clean up the kitchen," she called over her shoulder.

Nonnie had told her she could use Lonnie's study, but since she'd started writing on a kitchen table she had a superstitious need to work near cabinets and appliances. And she mustn't be too far from the refrigerator. Snacks momentarily eased frustration even if they were followed with instant remorse.

A stack of clean paper, a few typed pages and a bottle of correction fluid were scattered beside a half-eaten chicken leg and a glass of iced tea. She pulled up her chair and stared at the page in the typewriter.

> *He pulled the lavish satin gown trimmed with ermine from her creamy shoulders and gripped her roughly. His lips were on hers, bruising her tender mouth. To her horror, she felt herself respond to his fiery embrace. She tore his pillaging hands from the soft mound of her bosom. "You are a captain in the King's guard," she sobbed. "While I . . ."*
>
> *"Be silent, wench. I'll take my pleasure with you, struggle as you might."*

Could she have written that? Ripping the page from the machine, she crunched it into a ball and threw it onto the floor. Being a hack was one thing. She needed the money after all. But this was enough to make her retch. What parts had Maggie said were good? Ah yes, the historical parts. Another legacy of Lupton's. She finished the rest of the chicken leg and wiped her fingers on her jeans. Maggie's advice was "Don't get it right, get it written." She rolled a clean sheet of paper into the typewriter, decided to abandon Lord

Buckingham's seduction, and hammered away at a description of the Black Death.

"Hello darlin'." Nonnie was standing next to her. "Didn't mean to startle you. Bernice is gone, I guess."

"She left about"—she checked the clock—"about an hour ago."

"Figured as much when I didn't hear the TV goin'. Lord, she's worse'n your granddaddy. I wanted to throw that set out, but I figured she'd quit on me if I did. Where's m' baby?"

"She's gone to a Brownie meeting, then she's gonna stay the night with that little friend of hers."

"The one whose teeth are comin' in every which way?"

Cordy nodded as she started to pick up the wads of paper from the floor.

"Don't be stoppin' for me, darlin'. I'm just gonna fix myself some iced tea and read the paper in the other room."

"I'm grateful for the interruption. I've just gotten to the part where my heroine comes down with the plague."

"Oh, dear, does poor Roxanne have to go through that too? That girl does get herself into a heap o' trouble," Nonnie laughed.

"Don't worry, she comes through it all unscathed."

"I figured she would."

"Just gets a little ol' pockmark on her cheek, which she covers up with a beauty patch when she goes to court."

"Would she get a pockmark from the plague?"

"No, she wouldn't. But I'm working fast. This is all formula stuff, you can't really describe anything unpleasant. Pox, plague, who cares," Cordy said tiredly. "As long as she gets married in the end." She put the plastic cover on the typewriter. "It's been one of those days. My mind was already wandering, and then I got a call from Maggie Brocksen. That completely derailed me."

"The woman with the raspy voice?"

"That's her. She wants me to come to New York and take her apartment for a couple of months while she tries out a new job in California."

Nonnie sat down, undid her top button, pulled the collar of her dress away from her neck, and appraised her. Cordy's T-shirt, her worn jeans, her fine head of hair yanked back from her unmadeup face, made Nonnie feel the sort of impatient disgust she felt when she looked at neglected property. It was as though the girl no longer realized that she had a face and body to care for.

"Well, that's an interesting proposition, isn't it?" she said. "Why

don't you run on in an' get us something from Lonnie's liquor cabinet and we'll talk about it."

"There's nothing to talk about. I mean, I can't go."

"Don't say 'can't,' Cordy. I've told you not to say 'can't,'" she
scolded. Cordy opened her mouth to speak, but took in a breath
instead. Sometimes Nonnie's homilies, no matter how well in-
tentioned, were wearing.

"Sounds to me like the sorta chance you've been waiting for."

"I haven't been waiting for any chance."

"Then you should've been. Gracious, girl, you can't be lollin'
around here for the rest of your days. It's all right for me; I'm too
old to be uprooted, but if I were a young woman . . . Ever since I
heard "Rhapsody in Blue" I've wanted to go to New York."

"George Gershwin's been dead for a long time, Nonnie. I don't
think New York is a glamorous place anymore."

"I expect that's just foolish publicity. You know how people
who've never been here think we're still runnin' around with sheets
over our heads with a hole cut out so we can sip our mint juleps.
Only way to see what a place is like is to go there yourself. I remember Sophie Meldrim went up to New York. Started a—what do you
call it—boutique. She surely did. Attracted a fine clientele and made
a heap of money. That Maggie'd introduce you to some people,
wouldn't she?"

"I'm sure she'd do what she can, but—"

"How much is the rent?"

"Four hundred and fifty. She says it's a bargain."

"Can't be too bad at that price."

"I wouldn't be so sure. Besides—"

"You might meet some nice young man." Nonnie raised her
hand to prevent interruption. "All right. All right. The way things
are these days . . . Oh, did I tell you that Eunice Clauson's Sam is
wanting to get a divorce? Yes, ma'am, a divorce! After forty years of
marriage. An' worse than that, because I never held any brief for
Sam Clauson, he doesn't want to share his retirement money with
her. Isn't that shameful? Don't go talkin' it around, because she
hasn't told a soul yet. She's just beside herself. It's surely not the
way it used to be. Nowadays when I get an invitation to a wedding I
feel foolish putting money into a present, because, bingo, in six
months the one you didn't even know may end up with it. Like that
silver tea tray I sent to Julia Stalker's niece? Julia told me that
what's-his-name—Fred? Randolph?—anyway that sad-looking boy

she married, he took it when they split up. It like to break m' heart. If I'd thought . . ."

Cordy hitched up her jeans and carried the typewriter over to the counter. She didn't feel like listening to anyone else's marital problems, and once Nonnie got into a discussion about the division of property you could count on a twenty-minute digression before she picked up the original topic. And the way Nonnie had brightened at the mere mention of New York, as though the trip would be as easy as running to the drugstore to pick up a pair of panty hose. In her own way Nonnie was more relentless than Maggie Brocksen. "I'll go and get us that drink," Cordy interrupted.

Kneeling in front of the liquor cabinet, she paused, staring at the carpet. The early evening breeze made the loose glass in one of the windows tremble, but didn't stir the heavy damask drapes. She could feel all of the possessions that crowded the room, the Empire sofa with its hairy pawed feet, the eighteenth-century prints done by an English naturalist, the Hepplewhite chairs carved with sheaves of wheat, the velvet footstool, the needlepoint covers, the statue on the mantelpiece of Diana cavorting with hunting dogs. These things had been accumulated over a lifetime—over several lifetimes. They'd been lovingly cared for, handed down from one generation to the next. How many times had she and Lupton bought and sold and given away their belongings? Nonnie insisted that if they did divorce, Cordy was to go back to Chicago and reclaim everything. But she wanted none of it, except perhaps the old hope chest. No other object was so individually hers that it hadn't been tainted by having shared it with Lupton.

She turned the key in the cabinet and gingerly took out the bourbon decanter. She'd been clumsy last week and broken a crystal glass. Even though Nonnie had assured her that it didn't matter, she'd winced with embarrassment because she knew it could not be replaced. In her own house, she'd never minded clutter, but being in someone else's territory, even someone as easygoing as her grandmother, required constant care and accommodation. She was always trailing around after Jeanette, quickly picking up any mess. If Nonnie went to bed early and she stayed up, she moved around furtively, afraid to make a noise. When she went out, there was a self-imposed obligation to call and say when she'd be back. And there were times like tonight when she really wanted to be alone, if only to mope. Nonnie didn't cotton to moping. And Nonnie's opinions, like her presence, always demanded some response.

How wonderfully relaxing it would be to eat and sleep when she wanted to instead of fitting into another person's habits and rhythms. What a joy to act without interference, to move freely without prior design, to close the door on the world when she wanted or open it to a friend or lover. The possibility of a lover seemed remote. Not that she'd made any attempt to meet anyone. Except for the obligatory visits to Hilton Head, she had hardly gone out of the house. The thought of grooming herself for a public viewing filled her with lethargy. But word of her presence had circulated; this was Savannah after all. If she didn't start going out soon the gossip would be that she'd had a nervous breakdown.

Nonnie's cronies came by the house regularly; and though Cordy always excused herself "to write" and went up to Jeanette's room, she could hear their questioning voices and Nonnie's brisk interruptions before she even reached the top of the stairs. It was only a week before that her cousin Cissy came to call. Cissy was five years Cordy's senior, and Cordy could remember tolerating her at family gatherings when she was still too innocent to be aware of social toleration. Cissy hadn't changed at all. She still affected ruffled dresses, sibilant speech, and gushed with expressions like "dashing," "stunning," and "cute as a bug's ear," though, to demonstrate her modernity she added phrases such as "with it," "fun time," and "too much." The furthest move Cissy had made toward independence had put her in the refurbished carriage house behind her father's house on Gaston Street. Cissy could barely mask her delight at seeing Cordy join the ranks of "us girls." She telephoned periodically to invite Cordy to parties that promised to be "swinging, but not in a tewky way, y' know."

"What would I do about Jeanette if I went to New York?" Cordy demanded as she reached the kitchen door. Her voice sounded almost hostile. Nonnie drew her lawn handkerchief from her sleeve and fanned her face. The faint fragrance of violet eau de cologne surrounded her like a mist.

"Why, Lucille an' Jake are right over to Hilton Head, aren't they? And Jeanette could go down to Jacksonville and spend some time with Lupton's clan. But Lordy, I'd advise against that—not that you asked me. She'd come back with no manners and T-shirts with nonsense printed on 'em stuck to her little chest. Course, I could straighten her out. But I think it best that I take care of her. I took care of you when you were a child, didn't I?"

"That was different," Cordy objected, pouring them both a shot of bourbon. "That was because Daddy was still in the Army an' they had to move around. And then later, when he got the job with—"

"Don't you trust me?"

"It's not a question of trust, Nonnie. At your age—"

"Don't start up with me, Cordy. I'm not a monument yet."

"I meant that it would be a burden."

"How could my own great-grandchild be a burden? You do come up with the silliest ideas. Besides, Bernice is here all day, even when I'm not home. And nobody is better with children than Bernice. She's raised her own up fine and, let me tell you, against incredible odds. Only reason her son Malcolm got arrested in Miami is 'cause the police are so evil down there. And as for as her daughter runnin' off leaving her child with Bernice, why that could happen to anybody."

"It's about Jeanette," she said impatiently.

"Oh, Jeanette," Nonnie shrugged. "Jeanette is all puffed up with her this and her that. Brownies, swimmin' lessons. You know she told me the other day that she'd like to be a girl astronaut. No. Jeanette is a very independent little miss. Just like you used to be."

Cordy dropped the ice cubes into the glasses and carried them to the sink, her teeth biting into her lower lip. "Perhaps it's not so much that she'd miss me, but that I'd miss her."

"Sure you would, sugar. That's natural. Hey, just a splash of water for me. I don't mean to say anything to hurt your feelings, but you haven't been all that good for Jeanette lately. She knows what's goin' on even if she doesn't understand it. Doesn't help for her to see you moping around. And it surely doesn't hurt the child to be with lotsa different relatives; that way she'll get to know all kinds of craziness instead of just one kind. This—what's it called—nuclear family is something they dreamed up during Lucille's time and it looks to me like it's already goin' out of fashion." She took a long swallow, then blotted her lips with her handkerchief. "You've got to think of yourself, otherwise you'll end up being worthless to everyone else. That's what I've always told you, Cordy."

Even as she said it she knew it wasn't the exact truth. She'd always stressed the importance of serving others, and she'd cautioned toleration when she'd first heard that Lupton was acting up; but, she forgave herself, only a fool honored consistency.

"I am trying to think of myself. For the first time in years I'm really trying. And that's why I get so frightened. Because even though I'm almost thirty I don't have any idea what I should do next. I'm worried about making money, and . . ."

Nonnie sipped her drink. She knew Cordy wanted to go even if the girl didn't know it herself yet. She would just let her exhaust herself with all of her objections, then she would nudge her toward a decision and step in to plot the practical side. Still, it was difficult to know how to advise a young woman these days. So much had changed. She'd tried to take it all in, to balance herself between the dinosaur attitudes of a George Naughton and the slow letting go she'd witnessed in Lonnie, but it wasn't easy. In her heart she was afraid for Cordy. Even a girl who laid no individual claims to liberation could no longer expect the traditional rights of her sex. A place like New York had never been famed for manners or kindliness. How would an inexperienced and trusting girl like Cordy make her way in such a place?

Oh, she had seen them. Girls rushing out of offices, wearing their salaries, clasping magazines and self-help books to their breasts, opening doors for themselves instead of letting men do it for them. They were going to have career and marriage both—which was about as sensible as trying to ride two horses at the same time. They seemed to have been raised by parents who were too confused about their own values to guide them in any particular direction. They had been led to think that they had independence but hadn't been taught any of the harsh lessons of self-reliance. Their mothers and fathers expected them to marry but thought it old-fashioned to make sure that their prospective husbands had enough money and sense of social obligation to honor the contract.

And they wanted so much, these bright young things, yearning for freedom but unable to earn enough money to make their expectation of choice a reality. They craved both autonomy and tenderness, but wanted even more than that. They entertained hopes of equality and friendship with men they expected to be consummate lovers. Surely that was a misguided dream. In all her years she'd never witnessed equality or friendship where sex was involved. And they just didn't seem to realize that men had desires that were not connected to consequence. The old myths of female fragility, the games of romance and manners—and most intelligent women of her generation had recognized them as such—had been tossed aside. Without them, what leverage did a girl have in an unequal struggle?

Perhaps their demands for sexual expression did make them happier in bed. But common sense told her it couldn't have changed all that much. Every new generation thought it had invented sex. Why, there had been a few years, after the birth of her first baby, when she'd lost her shyness and before she'd been worn down by too many pregnancies, when she and Lonnie had done things for which she'd only recently learned the names. Of course, you didn't talk about it in those days. But even the secrecy had a protective sweetness. Nowadays you only had to turn on the TV to hear someone fussin' about their open marriage or their orgasms. And it didn't matter to her if the whole country thought such jabbering was acceptable. It was tacky. More than tacky: it was dangerous. If a woman gave openly and did not exact some tribute for her vulnerability, why, men who only understood a market economy would hold her cheap. She would end up alone, without support for herself or her children.

"Nonnie?" Cordy touched her hand. Apart from taking conversations down meandering paths, Nonnie had an increasing tendency to drift off.

"Yes, darlin'."

"What were you thinking?"

"I was wonderin'"—Nonnie tilted her head to one side, a youthful gesture of coquetry that had taken on the color of thoughtful self-absorption—"wonderin' how my life might have been if they'd had better birth control when I was young."

"Oh, Nonnie"—Cordy laughed—"I've known you since the day I was born and you still surprise me. Do you think you'd have been a wild-eyed woman runnin' around the county with a pack of lovers trailin' after you?"

"Can't rightly say. Anyhow, I was listening to you. Heard every word you said." She held up a finger to illustrate the first point. "You're worried about the money. You know I can fix that, an' you must let me. That little piddlin' sum you're getting from Lupton isn't enough to get you from here to Macon in style, and I'm not gonna live long enough to spend what I'm makin' now. It's just a game I enjoy playing, y' know. I love to see the houses all fixed up and I love it when I go to the bank an' they all act respectful 'stead of treating me like an ol' pest. You're gonna get some of the money when I go, so why not use it now? Next"—she tapped her middle finger—"you went on about Jeanette again. I already told you what I think 'bout that. After that"—her hand was now circling—"you started up this long weepy thing as to how you're scared. You should be scared, Cordy. Only natural to start a new enterprise with a case of the willies. But to cut it to the bone, what I think you didn't mention is that you're afraid of leaving because of Lupton. You're still confused about wantin' him back, aren't you?"

"That's got nothing to do with it," Cordy said impatiently. "Nothin' at all."

Nonnie smoothed her handkerchief, pretending to be interested in the fraying lace around the edge. She'd gone too far with that remark. Couldn't expect Cordy to see the truth while she was still nursing her wounds. It would take some time for her to realize that she'd outgrown Lupton. Even if he hadn't acted like a jackass, sooner or later Cordy would have had to own up to that fact. But he'd been brutal and damaged the girl's trust and wounded her pride. Cordy was aching more from hurt pride than from true love now, but she didn't realize it. It was hard to admit that anger and jealousy could be just as galvanizing as love.

"Ah, the fumes of Bacchus." Nonnie sighed. "I do believe I'm beginning to think more clearly now. An' I always get hungry when I have to think. What did Bernice leave us for supper, the last of that okra gumbo?"

While Cordy heated the food and set the table, Nonnie jabbered about suitcases and reservations. She sounded so excited that Cordy wanted to suggest that *she* go to New York. As soon as the meal was over, Cordy had the same queasy feeling in her stomach that had plagued her that afternoon. As she got up to load the plates into the dishwasher, she surreptitiously popped some of the antacid pills she kept on the windowsill into her mouth.

"I suppose I could go," she muttered, staring out into the garden.

"You can and you must. Being alone up there, you might could get some good writing done. You just think of it as a business trip an' do your best to hook up with one of those folks—"

"Agents."

"Yes, agents. An' think about branching out an' doing something you're proud of 'stead of these little quickie things. Write about something you know about."

"Ah, but I do. I'm up to my eyeballs in the past; I wallow in romantic illusion."

"Now talk sense, girl. Do somethin' better. An' for more money."

Cordy turned away from her inspection of the avocado pits Jeanette had skewered in glasses along the windowsill. A quick, mischievous smile brightened her face. "What'd you have in mind, Non-nie? A family saga?"

"That'd be racy enough if you told the truth, wouldn't it? An' everybody could understand it."

"Sure, I could have one uncle who gambles and makes lying his favorite pastime—"

"An' another who's kept a fancy woman so long she's not fancy anymore." Nonnie laughed.

"An' a cousin who's a homosexual."

"Now, Cordy, I'm still not sure 'bout Curtis."

"I am."

"An' another cousin who goes around convincin' people that there can be a Virgin birth, even though she's not a Catholic. Oh, yes, darlin'. We've got 'em all."

They were both laughing wildly now. Nonnie dabbed a tear from her eye and pressed her hand to her breast. "Course, you'd have to do it in good taste."

"Fictitious names?"

"Yep, an' change the hair color." She breathed heavily, calming herself. "Ah, wouldn't it be a sweet revenge. I wouldn't mind if you exposed the whole pack of 'em. Course, your mama would be even more upset with you than she is now."

"Do you think I should call and talk to her about the trip?"

"That's up to you." Nonnie pursed her lips and wagged her head slowly. She could imagine Lucille regurgitating all the objections that she'd just succeeded in helping Cordy to overcome. "I always think it's best to make up m' own mind, then let others prattle on after the fact."

"I suppose you're right." Their eyes met in a flicker of recognition. "But I want to think about it some more."

"You turn it over in your mind. But don't lose your nerve. Seems to me that's the thing the whole country's missing these days: nerve. Don't let it happen to you. Oh, I do wish you'd have known your granddaddy when he was young. Lonnie was 'bout the nerviest young man I'd ever set eyes on."

She was suddenly quiet. Cordy stood beside her watching her drift into another reverie, then squeezed her shoulder and started to leave the room.

"An' don't be calling Lupton either." Nonnie turned her head sharply as Cordy reached the door. "I'll tell Lupton all he needs to know after the fact. Remember, he broke the bond, now you break the bondage." Cordy nodded and moved into the hallway, only to be stopped again by Nonnie's voice. "An' darlin', do your ol' grandmother a sweetness an' wash your hair and set it before you go to bed. You're looking real pitiful, an' I'm not going to let you leave here till you've started to do something to make yourself a treat again."

"I know I need a touch-up, but I don't have any dye or conditioner."

"You don't hav' ta get it from a mail-order catalogue. Run on over to the drugstore an' buy some. Go on, now. Don't put it off."

Chapter VI

The insistent blare of a horn caused Cordy to slam on the brake. She looked around. A lumpy-looking couple were pushing a shopping cart out of the grocery store; a boy who was big enough to know better was battering a gum machine; but no cars were moving. She started to back out again. Again the insistent blast of a horn. A car door slammed, and she heard a wild screech: "Cordelia Simpkins! Cordy, hey, *Cordy!*"

A woman was running toward her, arms waving crazily. She was scarecrow skinny, in tight magenta pants. Her small breasts bounced under a cheap Indian blouse embroidered with mirrors and her close-cropped hair under the fluorescent lights of the parking lot was the brilliant orange of a child's building block. She almost collided with the couple pushing the cart, bent down to retrieve a plastic thong, then broke into another uncoordinated run and arrived, panting, next to Cordy's car.

"Cordy. My god, Cordy Simpkins. I just knew it was you. Don't sit there with your tongue hangin' out, it's me. It's Alidia."

"Alidia! Of course. Alidia. I had no idea—"

"I know. I know."

The couple had stopped to stare. Alidia's back was toward them, but she seemed to sense their disapproval. She turned to stare back defiantly, then swiveled her head to smile at Cordy. "I know how different I look. But you! I recognized you all the way across the lot. Oh, am I glad to see you." Her face broke into an expression of pure joy.

"I didn't know you were back in Savannah."

"I didn't know *you* were back in Savannah. Y' couldn't have been here very long, could y'?" she asked; and without pausing for an answer: "I woulda heard if you'd been here long. You know this town. You sneeze one morning, next day word's out that you're dying of pneumonia, day after that your enemies have you buried. How long you been back? How long? Come have a drink with me."

"I've been back a couple of months but I've been hiding out."

"Come on, let's go have a drink."

"How's about we just have a cup of coffee. I'm not dressed an'—"

"Still playin' the belle? Doesn't matter if you're dressed up. You look fine, Cordy. Let's go have a drink. Please. I'll buy. I just stopped by this ratty place to pick up my check. I was a cashier at K Mart till last week. Thank god, they fired me. Oh, it's great to see you. C'mon! Don't say no. I know I look tacky, but we'll just go over to Shuckers an' have us some raw oysters and a coupla drinks."

"I just came out to get some—"

"Cordy!" She put her hands on her hips and feigned exaspera-tion. "You have got to come and have a drink with me. Follow my car, that way you won't have to bring me back here." She leaned in, grabbed Cordy's face with both hands, and kissed her on the mouth. Before Cordy could raise another objection, Alidia had raced away. Moments later she pulled up behind her, honked again and roared out of the parking lot. Cordy waved and fell in behind the beat-up white Chevy. No use trying to resist. Alidia had an incredible talent for rousing others to action, for making them feel that her whims promised the best time they'd ever had. Even in high school Alidia was the brightest, wildest, and—yes, even then—the most miserable girl Cordy had ever known.

She was always getting into trouble. She came to school with a flask of whiskey in her purse, and was suspended. She drove the car her daddy had given her as a bribe to better conduct into a tree. She hitchhiked to Atlanta. She read more books than anyone, yet she failed the most elementary classes. She actually bragged that she'd lost her virginity. And there was another side to Alidia: She had depressions that left her limp as a rag doll, as though her energy was supplied by electric current and someone had pulled the plug. She listened to Chopin as well as the Doors. Though she refused to go to church, she talked about death and resurrection, saying that she knew absolutely that the body felt all the stages of decay before the soul was freed. One of the worst arguments Cordy had ever had with her mother was when Lucille forbade her to bring Alidia to the house. Cordy had responded with a violent defense that was partly prompted by guilt, for she had often heard the girls at school say that Alidia was trashy but had been too cowardly to defend her. Goaded by her sense of betrayal, she'd declared that she would continue to be Alidia's friend even if it meant sneaking around to see her. But her threat never materialized, because Alidia had run away shortly afterwards. She was brought back by the police, then shipped off to a boarding school. Word had it that she was pregnant, but Cordy had never countenanced that story. A lone postcard from Virginia—"I am serving my sentence on Devils' Island, but like Papillon, I shall escape"—was the last she'd heard from Alidia.

Throughout a decade of rumors—Alidia had been kicked out of Sarah Lawrence; Alidia was in Europe; someone had seen her hawking flowers on a street in Key West; she was living with a black man—Cordy had held to her own fantasies: Alidia was living in New York or Paris, she was painting or writing songs, collecting unique breeds of cats and lovers. But here she was in Savannah, working as a checkout girl. Judging from her appearance, Alidia's life had gone wrong in a far more bizarre way than her own had.

Stopping at a red light, she lost sight of the Chevy. She saw a pay phone and considered calling home, but sped on toward the bluff. As the car bumped down the steep cobblestone ramp to River Street, she saw the moonlit expanse of water and she thought of Nonnie. This spot, she had often been told, was the scene of her grandparents' secret rendezvouz, where Lonnie, "bless his soul and manly courage," had, in spite of the objections of his Better Family and most of Savannah Society, proposed to Nonnie, the daughter of a mere foreman in one of the Hampton mills. Lonnie had not, however, gone down on his knee, "because we were both of a Progressive frame of mind and sealed our troth with a kiss." Now the street, which had been the old cotton exchange, had been "restored;" into a collection of specialty shops, restaurants, and bars.

Alidia's car was parked in front of Shuckers, facing the river. Cordy pulled in beside it, brushed her hair, and crossed the street. There were more customers than she would have expected for a weeknight when the weather was still cool. She walked purposefully past the bar, ignoring the row of male backsides and focusing on the raw hands of the black man who was shucking the oysters.

"Cordy, over here."

Alidia was at a corner table toward the rear. She jumped up, her face lurid above the single candle, and pulled Cordy into an embrace. Cordy smiled into the frantic green eyes.

"Hey, I didn't think you were coming. Look"—Alidia reached out and grabbed the arm of the waitress—"this is my dearest friend from high school. I'll have a cognac. Oh, yes, and a dozen raw oysters, lotsa horseradish. What'll you have, Cordy? Bourbon? Scotch?"

"A glass of wine."

"Too tame. Bring her a Courvoisier. Here, sit. Next to me." She brought the chairs closer together and pulled her mouth into a clown's grimace of sorrow. "So you're back. You must've lost your way in life if you've wandered into this damned swamp again. Where you staying?"

"I'm with Nonnie just now."

"God, is she still alive? What a tough ol' lady. But you and Lupton are still married aren't you?"

"Separated."

"Should I say sorry?"

"I don't know."

"Honest enough. You always did have that annoying trait of honesty. You were a bit chicken here and there, but basically honest."

"I try," Cordy said, trying not to sound offended.

"I can't believe I'm seeing you," Alidia blinked and shook her head. "You are here, aren't you? I know I've blown the entire front panel of my brain, but you are here. So what else? Tell. Tell."

"I have a daughter. Would you like to see her picture?"

"Hey, she's pretty." She held the photo Cordy had fished from her purse up to the candle. "Course, with you and Lupton as parents she'd have to be. Hey, tell me about Lupton. Boy, was he a hunk. Not too much upstairs, but then we didn't care about that in those days, did we? I'm not real sure I care about it now. Hey, here're our drinks." She raised her glass. "'Live fast, die young, and have a good-lookin' corpse.'" She downed the cognac in quick, determined gulps. "Who else have you seen since you've been back?"

"No one. I told you I was hiding out."

"That's prob'ly wise. You wouldn't believe . . ."

Cordy's eyes had adjusted to the darkness now, and she

watched Alidia's face, saw the acne scars beneath the thick makeup. Years ago, when Alidia's complexion had erupted with pustules and liverish blobs, Cordy had felt no more than a shiver of gratitude that she had not been so cursed. Now, seeing the map-of-the-moon pits and craters that disfigured a potentially beautiful face, she felt a stab of pity.

". . . an' the weird thing is that everyone's just like they used to be only more so. Prissy Greer, she's married. I think her name'd fit her husband better'n her, but they do have three kids. She owns an antique shop over on Bull Street. When her parents died she solaced herself by cleaning out the ol' homestead and turning it into a business. And Michele-Jane Receed, 'member her?" Cordy shook her head. "Sure you do. Soulful an' anemic but with a positive lust for power. She was the first one to get married, 'member? To a guy from the Citadel. Had a gap between her front teeth. Class president."

"Oh, yes."

"She's the most interesting of the bunch. She's the regional director of M.I.A.s."

"What?"

"Missing in Actions. Her husband got shot down over Laos. She flew over to Vietnam and she's been on TV an' all. Bet she'll run for the legislature in a coupla years. Young widow, grieving and praying, perfect package for a campaign here 'bouts, don't you think?"

"What about Pamela? Last I was in town I heard—"

"What could happen to Pamela? When you're that rich, only thing that can happen to you is boredom. Forget about all of them," she insisted, as though she hadn't brought up the subject. "Tell me about you."

"I don't hardly know where to begin." She stalled, disarmed by Alidia's bitchiness. But Alidia's eyes, which always had a look of shock about them, were now warmly inquisitive. And it didn't matter that Alidia had said some insulting things, or that the laugh that punctuated her conversation was almost a bark. Alidia's feelings ran deep. In matters of importance she could be trusted. Cordy checked her impulse to beg for secrecy. You couldn't negotiate trust. As she started to talk Alidia grew hushed and attentive. A plate of oysters was put in front of her and she ate greedily as a slum child, sucking the oysters into her mouth, letting the juice run between her fingers, her eyes interrogating but going moist and sympathetic as a dog's.

She interrupted only briefly: to ask a question, to order another drink, to mutter, "Men!" or "Goddamn Lupton's eyes," or clap her hands when Cordy said she'd written a book.

"And so I'm toying with the idea of going to New York," Cordy concluded.

"You must, Cordy. You absolutely must. If I could earn a living without having to report to some S.O.B. and punch a time clock, I'd fight tooth and nail to hold on to it."

"It's funny. I always thought you'd be the one to write."

"So did I, years ago. I just don't have the concentration. I always see things in a flash, and the illumination goes when I try to put it on paper. Still keep a diary though, just like I did when we were kids. Say, won't you have another drink?"

"I guess I might have one more. And you? Tell me about you."

Alidia was in stasis now. She looked worse than tired. She looked abused, burnt out. Cordy noticed the sallow yellow of a bruise on her arm, the deep hollows in her throat.

"Aw, you know me. On the edge. Always on the edge. Tallulah's style on Norma Rae's budget."

"Did you ever get to Paris? I remember you had that poster of Notre Dame in your bedroom."

"Yeah, I got there too," she sighed.

"Did you ever marry?"

"Sure. Yes. Naturally. Got a Cuisinart and tried to find salvation. Wouldn't stick. Married a lawyer. Can you imagine me with a lawyer? Met him when he bailed a friend of mine outta jail. Guess he was into redemption too. And I tried real hard for a coupla years. I really did try, Cordy." Her voice was pleading. She started to reach for Cordy's hand, remembered that her fingers were sticky, dipped them into a glass of water and flicked the drops into the air. "One night"—the little barking laugh again—"one night we'd started out to this dinner party. And we were already late and we'd got about twenty minutes from the house and James had forgotten his little printed name cards. He carried his little cards with him everywhere. He turned the car around to go back for 'em and when he stopped at a red light I just got out."

"Got out?"

"Uh-huh. Outta the car and outta the marriage. I never went back. Tried to go back once because—" A dead stop. A look of bewilderment. Another barking laugh. "What was I saying? Yes. Left James. Another great circle. Ended back in Savannah. With six months in Baton Rouge working as a go-go dancer. And believe me, honey, with my tits that was an act of courage."

"Oh, that must've been something," Cordy said, trying to hide her disapproval."

"I had to do it. I just couldn't find any other job. We were none of us brought up to earn our own living, were we? But I saved some money an' took this class to be a checkout gal. Thought that sounded steady enough, but fact is it only depressed me more. You ever watched those women in K Mart? It's like *The Night of the Living Dead*." She raked her fingers through the convict haircut, taking in the two young men who were sitting down at the next table. "Damn, I hate it here. Oh, how I hate it. You could walk down Bull Street and if it weren't for the cars you'd think you were back in the nineteenth century."

"I kinda missed it."

"And everybody knowing everybody's business. That's all there is to do around here. Drink and talk about other people. Hell, if they didn't have TV's they'd never know there was a world beyond the Talmadge Bridge. And when they find out, they don't care. It's a curse for a woman with an I.Q. over eighty to grow up here, Cordy. Eighteen's the high point. After that it's quicksand. And y'r supposed to giggle girlishly as you get sucked down."

Cordy put her hand up to her mouth. Each little pinprick of Alidia's venom was forcing ripples of laughter from her throat.

"'Member that poem by what's-his-name?" Alidia's speech was slurred, but she pitched her voice louder, whipping herself into the performance level of a nightclub comedian. "You know, 'Farewell to Savannah.' 'I leave you, Savannah, a curse that is far/The worst of all curses: to remain as you are.' It'll never change. And I'm not just talking 'bout all the charming architecture. People don't like to *think* around here. You question something and they say you're fussin' at them. And the hypocrisy! Everywhere you look, landmarks. But no landmark to the whorehouse, no landmark to the slave cabins."

"There weren't too many slave cabins in downtown Savannah," Cordy murmured, hoping the softness of her voice would give Alidia the hint that she was talking too loudly. There was no point in asking her why she'd chosen to come back. That would be like asking an alcoholic why he liked the smell of scotch, like asking an outnumbered general why he continued to fight. "I've lived up North, Alidia, and I can tell you, the South hasn't cornered the market on hypocrisy."

"You probably want to know why I came back, don't you?" Alidia asked. She cupped her hands beneath her chin, dimpled her cheeks, and affected a thick drawl. "Ah jest had to come home, sugar. Ah' heard that homesick song whistlin' through the pines. I wanted to wiggle m' toes in that ol' Georgia clay. An' I thought, Jesus an' germs, manners an' meanness, carbohydrates an' calamine lotion! How can I resist? Aw, fuck it, Cordy. I'm really hangin' around 'cause I've got no place to go. And if I hang around long enough an' my daddy's new wife hasn't spent all of his loot, I expect he or one of my other relatives will pay me to get out of town. My family's always been most obliging about clothes and travel expenses. I slit my wrists once, and they ran right out and bought me a whole closetful of long-sleeved dresses."

Was she being funny or had she really tried to commit suicide? Cordy looked around, wondering if Alidia's remarks had caused offense. Apparently the thrump of the jukebox prevented her from being overheard by anyone except the young men at the next table. The one with corn-colored hair and the aqua shirt had tipped back in his chair laughing. The other ducked his head and curled his hands around his beer mug but smiled shyly when Cordy caught his eye.

"I think I'd best give Nonnie a call. I don't want her to worry."

"Sure, sure." Alidia waved her hand. "Phones are near the bathrooms, right near the video games. Want another drink."

"I don't think so."

The phone rang five times before it was picked up, and she knew Nonnie was lying when she said she hadn't been woken up. Cordy apologized and said she'd be home soon, but Nonnie encouraged her to stay and "enjoy the company of the other young folks."

She wouldn't say that if she knew what the young folks were up to, Cordy thought as she hung up. She leaned against the wall of the booth wondering what to do next. She was far too restless to want to go home, but the increasingly noisy mood of the bar and Alidia's agitated drunkenness were making her uncomfortable. More than anything, she wanted to be alone in a place of her own.

There was a tap on the door of the booth.

"Sorry," she muttered, trying to ease past.

"Miss Simpkins, where did you park your horse?" Jacques Haur was blocking her way, smiling indulgently, as though he'd caught her in some misdemeanor.

"Oh, Mr. . . . . ?" She pretended to have forgotten his name. Alidia was right about one thing: It was impossible to go out in this town without bumping into someone you didn't want to see.

"Jacques. I'm sure you remember our meeting at your parents' house."

"Yes, of course. And how are you?"

"Ah'm just fine. Didn't know you were still in town or I would've followed up on that invitation to party."

"I don't go to parties."

"You just come to bars, is that it?"

"I ran into an old friend."

"How's about sitting down and having a drink with a new friend."

"I'm sorry, but I really can't. Nice to see you."

Again she tried to move past him, but he wouldn't step aside.

"I don't like to take no for an answer, Miss Simpkins."

Lord, he didn't only look like some character she'd put into one of her books, he'd appropriated the dialogue as well. Next he'd be calling her "proud beauty" or saying that he loved it when she got angry. She couldn't imagine that there were still women around who responded to such a tired macho act; and as she said, "It's kind of you to point out a part of your character which is already obvious to me, but the answer is no," she couldn't help herself from laughing at him. His expression became vengeful, all out of proportion to her rejection. As she noticed his dilated pupils she understood the reason for his intensity and wondered if he'd still be welcome in her parents' home if Lucille realized he was a doper.

A girl in a see-through blouse pushed between them and closed the door of the booth. Cordy stepped past him. "If you'll excuse me, Mr. Haur," she said as demurely as if she'd been serving tea at a fund-raiser at the Telfair Academy. God, he made her flesh crawl.

It was no surprise to see that the men at the next table had moved and were sitting on either side of Alidia. Also no surprise to see another round of drinks on the table.

"It was kind of you to order me another, but I really must go."

"Sit down," Alidia said. "Carl here has bought you a drink. And this here is Johnnie." She placed her hand on the shoulder of the blond man in the aqua shirt. He couldn't have been more than twenty-two or -three, with a wide jaw and a nose that had been reset by a not very accomplished surgeon. "Carl and Johnnie are soldier boys from Fort Stewart."

"How do you do." Abandoning her resolve, she slid back into her chair. Alidia and Johnnie were busy sizing each other up. She turned to Carl. He was as big as a pro-ball fullback, hunching his shoulders forward and wrapping his huge hands around his beer mug. He nodded hello with that shyness she'd observed in very large men. "Are you from around here?"

"No, ma'am. I'm from Iowa. Been down here for almost two years, so I guess I'm startin' to talk like it."

"You don't sound very happy about being here. Didn't you know where you were going to be sent?"

"No, ma'am. They promised me I could go to Germany when I signed up, but then they sent me to Georgia." His eyes were innocently bewildered, as though he was still trying to sort out the bureaucratic mishap that had changed his life. "I got through college on the R.O.T.C., and I'm servin' my hitch."

"What did you major in?" Yes, she remembered from the old days, you just kept asking questions. You couldn't go wrong with polite questions.

"Don't say animal husbandry, Carl," Johnnie warned him. "Otherwise these ladies will know you're a sexual weirdo."

"Agriculture," he said, keeping his eyes on the table. "I'd like to have a farm. My parents were farmers. But an individual can't hardly afford to have a farm nowadays."

"You betchum, Red Rider," Alidia put in. "You ain't gonna see a farm less you go to business school and become an executive for General Foods."

"That's what I keep tellin' him," Johnnie said. "But ol' Carl here is one of those gung-ho guys who doesn't wise up till it's too late. He oughtta stay in the Army an' get special training in nukes. That's where the future lies."

"So the future lies in nukes." Alidia barked a laugh, looking sick. "Are you interested in the future, Johnnie?"

"Not me. I play it as it lays." He pulled his lips into a thin, hard smile.

"Are you from around here Johnnie?" Cordy inquired quickly.

"Damned straight. I'm from Jasper. An' it's just as well Alidia is from round here, 'cause if anyone else said all the stuff she'd been sayin' I'd have to take 'em on."

"She was only kidding," Cordy said.

"Like hell I was."

"If you don't like it, why don't ya get out?" Johnnie turned to her. "Nobody drafted you to come back here, did they? You can do what y' wanna do with yer life, y' know."

"Do you really believe that?" she smiled sardonically.

"I sure do. You want somethin', you go after it."

"What about Carl here? Weren't you just telling him not to go after a farm?"

"That's different. That's not realistic. You should only go after what you know you can get."

"I see," Alidia said archly. "Limit your horizons to what you know you can accomplish and shrink your dreams to fit your reality so that they aren't dreams at all. Now *that*'s a philosophy."

"What are you talkin' about?" Johnnie asked belligerently.

He's just smart enough to know she's putting him down, but not smart enough to figure out how or why, Cordy thought. She sipped her drink. Carl drew circles on the table. Alidia and Johnnie stared each other down. "I admire your limited horizons," Alidia said after a pause. There was no irony in her tone. She was the confused soul admiring the caveman; whatever antagonism she felt toward Johnnie seemed to fuel her attraction. Cordy had the uneasy intuition that much as Alidia spoiled for a fight she always anticipated defeat. She studied the bruise on Alidia's arm, then turned quickly to Carl. Crop rotation? Hog bellies? How could she best fill the gap in conversation. "I hear the modern-day Army is very different from what it was like when my father served. Do you find that to be true, Carl?"

"It's sure a lot different from what I expected. It's more like a regular job, and that's the last thing I wanted."

"Carl's a dumb-assed patriot," Johnnie slurred.

"Most times I have nine-to-five hours, so I have a lotta free time." Carl rested his arm on the back of her chair. "Some guys like that, but I think . . ." He talked on, grateful for her attention, losing some of his shyness. His arm slid down, tentatively resting on her shoulder. She moved slightly. Alidia sucked in her cheeks and winked at her, then turned back to Johnnie. Alidia was very drunk now. Her eyelids were at half-mast as Johnnie moved his face into the hollow of her neck. Cordy wanted to get up, but some feeling of responsibility kept her in her seat. Perhaps she should wait and offer to drive Alidia home.

"How 'bout another round?" Carl asked.

"I'm sorry, but I really can't. I have to be getting home. Alidia?" she said firmly, signaling an opportunity to leave.

"Naw. I don't want another drink. I've been listen'n to Sergeant Johnnie's philosophy. I think I should go after what I know I can get. An' right now, I wanna get outta here."

Carl peeled some notes from a roll of bills and threw them on the table. Johnnie got up and offered Alidia his hand with a gallant flourish. "How'd you ladies like to come over to our place?" he said.

"No, really," Cordy smiled. "I do have to get home." But Johnnie was already steering Alidia toward the door.

"I *do* have to get home," she said again.

Carl nodded. Either he was relieved or else he'd become accustomed to rejection. "I understand. Just let me walk you to your car."

Cordy wrapped her arms around herself as they stepped onto the street. The wind was up and there was a decided chill in the air. Alidia and Johnnie were nowhere to be seen, but as she and Carl approached her car, Cordy caught sight of them, locked together in the front seat of the white Chevy. "This is my car," Cordy whispered.

As Cordy opened the door to her own car, Alidia called out to her, "Come on Cordy. Please come with us."

"I can't. Sorry."

"Will y' call me tomorra? I really wanna talk to you some more."

"Sure. I'll call you."

"Promise?"

"Listen, Carl . . ." Johnnie disengaged himself and leaned out the window grinning. His teeth were large and bright in the moonlight.

"Yeah, yeah," Carl said. "I guess you should drive Alidia home."

"That's what I was thinkin'."

There was some shifting about in the front seat of the Chevy. Cordy tilted her head back, ignoring the giggles, and looked at the sky. The moon was watery and pale and the stars seemed to have disappeared. "Where are those damned keys?" she heard Alidia laugh. "No, Johnnie, they're not *there!* Hey, here. I just knew they were here somewhere. Now jiggle the ignition switch." The motor grumbled. "Remember, Cordy, you promised," she called out.

Cordy heard Johnnie say something about getting the damned muffler fixed and then they were gone.

"Well." She turned to Carl.

"You be all right gettin' home alone? I could follow you in my car."

"No. I'll be fine. Good night."

He reached to touch her hair, then stopped. When she made no attempt to move, his arms were around her, his grip too tight, clumsy with need. Oh, dear, she thought, he's so young and innocent and lonely. And the way he held the lower part of his body away from her, afraid that she would fell his erection. The powerful effect she was having on him filled her with tender disinterest.

"Could I have your phone number?" His voice was choked, his arms still wrapped too tightly around her.

"I have a little daughter," she said, catching her breath. What she really wanted to say was, You're the first man other than my husband that I've kissed in almost ten years.

He was nuzzling into her neck, still squeezing the breath out of her. "It's O.K. about your lil' girl. I'm crazy about kids."

"And"—she freed herself, her hand touching his chin—"and I'm going to be leaving town."

He released her, throwing his head back so that she could only see his thick neck and the outline of his jaw. "Sure is a watery old moon," he said at last.

She turned away, not wanting to compound his embarrassment by looking at him, and reached for the door. "Thank you for walking me to my car, Carl."

"See you around."

He loped away without looking back.

She was shivering as she drove home through the deserted streets and knew it wasn't because of the chill air. Sweet, clumsy Carl. Not that she really wanted him. She had nothing whatever in common with him. Unless she counted the great common denominators of fleeting lust and abiding loneliness.

The light had been left on in the hallway. She turned it off and felt her way up the staircase, stumbling on the top step. Sucking the air in between clenched teeth to stop herself from cursing, she rubbed her wounded toe on the carpet and stood absolutely still. She thought she could hear a noise in Nonnie's room. It reminded her of those nights years ago when she'd crept—face hot, mouth bruised, the front of her cashmere sweater stretched out of shape—into her parents' house and prayed that they were asleep. But Nonnie had the good grace not to appear, so she moved along the hallway, pausing at Jeanette's door before remembering that Jeanette was spending the night with a friend. Seersucker pajamas, hot chocolate, stuffed animals. She was sorry Jeanette wasn't here. Just now she wanted to hold her, to feel the protection of being the protector.

She crept into her own room, stripped off her clothes, and crawled into the big double bed with the goose-down pillows. The coolness of the sheets turned her nipples hard. She cupped her hands over her breasts, imagining Johnnie and Alidia thrashing about. The delicious shock of new flesh. If Johnnie of the bashed-in nose and hard mouth had come on with her, would she have been so quick to refuse? Johnnie would force his desire on a woman, help her to blot out her own responsibility. Just now that had great appeal.

"A swamp," Alidia had called it. And "eighteen was the high point." Perhaps it had been. At eighteen she'd been protected by all the rules she wanted to break. But more than that, it had been a time when desire was a great yearning forward, when clumsy movements had been made lovely by the force of their energy, when loneliness, technique, and mutual use were not even imagined. When there was no separation between sex and love. Was that all an illusion? She imagined Lupton beside her and hated him so profoundly it made her heart race.

She had told Carl that she was leaving town and that seemed to be justification enough for doing so.

Chapter VII

The sight of the New York skyline had made Cordy's stomach churn like a washing machine, and for one awful moment, as she stood in the swirl of passengers watching the
embraces of those who were being met and being shoved aside by
the loners who were making a quick getaway, she thought she might
be sick. Then she spotted the tall woman with close-cropped silver
hair and wraparound sunglasses. The woman held her ground as the
tide of people surged around her, her mouth pulling on a cigarette
the way a baby would suck on a bottle. It had to be Maggie
Brocksen. Cordy lifted her hand. Maggie stubbed out her cigarette
and moved toward her, her smile as big as the split in a watermelon.

"So kid, you made it. Thought you might get cold feet. Here,
the baggage pickup is this way." She pushed back into the crowd.
Cordy lunged after her, wanting to hold on to her shirt just as she'd
clutched her mother's dress when she'd been dragged through department stores during the Christmas rush.

"Come on out and take a good deep breath of filth," Maggie
grinned, hoisting one of Cordy's bags from the rotary pickup. Cordy
grabbed the other bag and followed her to the exit. Standing on the
curb, enveloped in clouds of exhaust from a tourist bus, she wondered why she'd let Nonnie talk her into wearing a white suit. Maggie had already stepped out into the traffic, her arm raised. "O.K.,

sister, here we go." She motioned Cordy into a taxi. The driver, a squat, dark-haired man, grumbled to himself as he threw the bags into the trunk. "Eighty-ninth between Central Park and Columbus," Maggie ordered. She ran her hands through her hair and sat back, giving Cordy a quick appraisal. "You're much prettier than I thought you'd be. Too bad they don't put your picture on the jacket."

"I just can't believe I'm here," Cordy gulped. "Jeanette had a toothache last night, and I got all guilty about leavin' her. Nonnie just about had to push me onto the plane."

"She sounds terrific."

"She is."

"Just as well you came in at La Guardia. I hear on the news that there was a bomb scare at Kennedy. Apparently . . ."

Cordy nodded with polite but divided attention. The driver was waving out the window, and it seemed he was using the hood of the taxi to butt his way into the line of traffic. "I just can't believe I'm here," she said again.

"Yeah, when I moved to Manhattan I felt the same way. Sometimes just getting across the Hudson from New Jersey is tougher than coming from Bombay."

"Yes. I suppose New York is still the symbol of"—she was jolted forward as the driver swerved into another lane, and had to brace herself on the plastic partition that separated them—"of aspiration."

"Sure. Sure. Everyone here is talented. Even the muggers are talented, so watch your purse."

"I'm sure I'll be all right." She smiled without much conviction. "It was real kind of you to come meet me."

"Dixie ain't the only place where people are hospitable. Besides, I'm all packed and ready to leave tomorrow. I've even had my hearts and flowers farewell with Marvin."

"Marvin?"

"Didn't I tell you about him? He's the space cadet who wrote *Glok to Earth*. The sci-fi kid. He's very cute in a weird way. After some of the slickos I've dated, I was kinda taken in by the messy hair and the baggy pants. And I figured a fling with a twenty-five-year-old vegetarian would prepare me for the West Coast. And for once in my life I made a graceful exit instead of sticking around to sing 'September Song.'"

Cordy gripped the seat. The shock absorbers in the car were

completely gone. The driver, darting from one lane to the other, gesticulating and cursing, seemed to think he was in a bumper ride at an amusement park. Maggie raised her voice over the Greek folk music that was coming out of the cassette he'd shoved into the tape deck, and described the infighting that had led to her break with Chrystallis. They made halting progress through the toll booths and finally swerved onto F.D.R. Drive. Around them was a depressing mix of gaunt high rises, doorways smeared with graffiti, and vacant lots strewn with iron pipes and broken bottles. But straight ahead was the reality of a million postcard fantasies. The sun was setting, and the famous skyline grew doubly distinct as it took on the shadows of evening. The silhouettes of the massive buildings were tinged with a rosy glow. A million lights were beginning to flicker on. Cordy felt a rush of adrenaline.

Maggie had pulled back the plastic shield and was telling the driver that her son was backpacking through the Greek isles. Cordy listened with half an ear as they whisked through a park, larger than anything she'd thought could be preserved in the city. They started down a broad avenue, the park on one side and large old buildings on the other, then turned onto a side street.

"Yeah, ease up. Middle of the block on the left."

Cordy checked the meter and reached into her purse, but Maggie was already thrusting bills toward the driver and reaching for the door handle. Cordy wondered if Maggie ever made a move that wasn't quick and decisive.

"I didn't expect the street to have trees." She looked around. "And such pretty buildings."

"Sure, we got trees," Maggie said as she started up the stoop. "'Bout one for every hundred dogs to cock their leg on." She unlocked a heavy oak door with glass panels and pushed the suitcase in. Cordy pulled the other bag into a narrow, poorly lit hallway. The heights of the walls were covered with a tasteful but worn paper in umbers and browns. Her eyes flashed over the names on the bank of mailboxes to her right. To her left was a radiator and an antique hallstand that needed dusting. A bike was padlocked onto the banister.

"Don't mind the hallway," Maggie called over her shoulder as she mounted the stairs. "It's a sort of no-man's-land. The superintendent has a limited command of English. He understands 'tip,' but he doesn't understand 'clean.'" She rounded the first landing, dropped the suitcase in front of a high dark door decorated with a Peace decal, and turned the locks. Cordy stepped forward, but Maggie stopped her with a quick "Wait a minute," then reached in and flipped the combination on a padlock. "Don't mean to scare you. This won't stop the bastards, but it'll slow 'em down."

Since she'd been so accurate in guessing Maggie's appearance, she was surprised when she stepped into the apartment. She'd expected something coldly chic with minimal furniture in primary colors; but Maggie's private side was distinctly homey: Laura Ashley wallpaper, overstuffed furniture in peach and beige, window boxes, and bookcases that almost reached to the top of the high ceilings. Beneath Maggie's low-cut blouse and tailored jeans she was probably wearing white cotton panties.

"I figured you could work in here," Maggie called from the other room.

A typewriter was set on an artist's worktable, and the famous picture of a dour Queen Victoria loomed above the brass bed. "Don't you just love her?" Maggie grinned. "I put her in here to give that sweet touch of the forbidden to the gymnastics. Now take off those high heels, and how about a drink?"

"I knew I was too gussied up," she laughed as she slipped out of the shoes and removed her suit jacket. "This outfit is Nonnie's idea of traveling in style. At least I didn't let her talk me into wearing gloves."

"I know what you mean. My mother thinks you're not really dressed unless you're wearing a panty girdle. And she'd always check to make sure we didn't have safety pins in our underwear. 'In case you're in an accident.' Anyway, you're here. White suit, underwear without safety pins, and ready to tackle the world."

"Thanks again."

"Cut it out, will you. Now let's take care of business first." Maggie walked around the apartment opening cupboards and pointing out where things were. Cordy trailed after her, sure that she wouldn't be able to retain most of what she was being told.

"I don't know if you've ever had one of these," Maggie said, flipping the knobs on the telephone answering machine. "This one's great. When someone calls you can hear your own recorded message, then their voice, so you don't have to pick up if you don't want to talk to them." Cordy nodded, hoping the steady stream of information was at an end. Maggie poured her a glass of wine, told her to sit down, and shoved a list of names toward her.

"These are the agents I think you should see. The name at the top, Abigail Pinkston Silverstein, is your best bet, and I've already talked to her about you. Don't go into her office looking like little girl lost. Give her a concrete proposal for the next book. Maybe that fictionalization of the life of Fanny Kemble that you were telling me about."

"I don't now if I could tackle that."

"It's a good idea. At least you got me interested when you told me about it. Type up a proposal and a sample chapter. Think it through so you can really talk to her about it. Now, if Abigail doesn't work out . . ."

Cordy scribbled notes next to the list of names and phone numbers.

"And as far as your social life goes"—Maggie cocked her head and winked—"check out the laundromat. I'll bet more couples meet at the laundromat than they do with computer dating. Just think how much you can learn about a guy by watching him do a wash. You can see if he lives alone, check out his taste in sheets and underwear, see what he reads while the dryer's going. And museums. If you meet come guy at a museum you can chat about Modigliani or Braque. Much classier than a singles bar or an ad in the *Village Voice*."

"I was just planning to work and find an agent."

"Sure. That's your first priority. You're going to have to work your butt off if you're going to support yourself by writing. I don't know how reliable Lupton is, but a hell of a lot of men run out on alimony and child support. Anyway, you'll go bananas just sitting around the apartment. I'll bet Lupton is going out."

"Since he was while he was living with me, I guess that's a safe bet," Cordy said, with a too bright smile.

"Hey, that can be a real karate chop to the ego." Maggie winced. "You start thinking you're unattractive, then it's an easy slide into hermitsville. Fact is, men always remarry faster than women. Charles started dating the only divorcée on our block right after we split up, and damn me if he didn't marry her six months after our divorce. After fifteen years of marriage I was replaced in six months. Course, with Charles it was more interviewing for a job opening than grand passion. He was just too busy with his business to shop around. If they still had mail-order brides I expect he would have sent away for one."

She spoke matter-of-factly, as though divorce was something everyone went through sooner or later, like having trouble with wisdom teeth or discovering the first gray hair. Cordy took another sip of her wine and stared out the window. "Oh, the streetlights have come on. The trees look so pretty with the light filtering through them like that."

"Yeah," Maggie said, "the neighborhood's getting gentrified. All the low-life crooks are being replaced by the upwardly mobile crooks. We've got more maids and gold nameplates around here than you can shake a lease at. Hey, Cordy, you're looking kinda drug out. Would you like to take a shower and freshen up?"

"I wouldn't mind." Maggie's rapid-fire comments and suggestions were making her feel slow and dull-headed.

"After you wash up, I'll take you upstairs and introduce you to Cliff. He's offered to fix dinner for us. He's as gay as New Year's Eve, but you'll like him."

Maggie gave Cordy a towel, poured herself another drink and settled into a cross-legged position on the floor. This time tomorrow she'd be in Beverly Hills. Despite the pep talk she'd just given, she was starting to get the jitters about leaving.

She had a new address book, but the only name in it was Murray Eisen's, or "Grind" Eisenberg as he'd been called twenty years ago when they'd met at New York University. "Grind" didn't have a sexual connotation; it tagged the fanatic dedication with which Murray applied himself to his projects at the film school, a dedication that helped to ease the pain of his constant rejections by the opposite sex. Maggie had been one of the unattainable girls. She'd managed to talk herself out of a pass and into a friendship that had lasted for two decades. And now she was going to Hollywood to be Murray's assistant. Life was strange.

The last time Murray had been in New York, she'd met him at Sardi's to discuss his job offer. He'd brought along a freckle-faced ingenue who looked as though she'd just graduated from the cast of *Annie*. It was embarrassing to watch him with the girl. His style—the lunge, the stroke, the compliment followed by conversation that completely excluded her—wasn't much of an improvement over the courtship dance he'd done in college. Beneath his dapper, trim body Maggie could still see an overweight, frustrated kid from Brooklyn. The girl saw a big-name television producer. She sat perfectly still as Murray rubbed his hand back and forth over her shoulder as though he were sandpapering a piece of wood. Her eyes met Maggie's with a "what else can I do?" look, and she rattled off a list of her credits, obviously trying to impress her with the fact that she was a "serious" actress.

Maggie had been tempted to take her to the ladies' room and warn her that sleeping with Murray would diminish rather than increase her chances of getting a part in his new series. Murray didn't mix business with pleasure, and success hadn't made any real change in his feelings about himself. The first flush of conquest was invariably followed by suspicions about the new girlfriend's judgment. But she decided against giving any advice. Freckles seemed to know what she was about, and Murray was even more generous when he was getting out of an affair than he was when he was getting into one. She excused herself and went to the ladies', glad that she'd resisted the proposition Murray had made five years ago when he was going through his second divorce. Good sense, and the suspicion that he might be a lousy lover, had triumphed over inebriated curiosity, and they'd remained buddies.

Now Murray was going through divorce number three. He was offering Maggie thirty-five thousand a year as a starting salary, so she knew the job would entail more than reading sit-com scripts. Murray was getting paranoid. He needed a friend at his side. She'd be confidante as well as secretary. She'd chaperone his kids and lie to the people he didn't want to see. She'd play Rosalind Russell, wise-cracking and efficient, helping him through the sixty-hour work week his compulsive nature and gigantic alimony payments had sentenced him to. She'd be the "good wife" at the office, while Mrs. Eisen number four lounged poolside. It was going to be tough. But the alternative—plowing through romances, sci-fi, and self-help books to the tune of eighteen thousand a year—was even less desirable.

When she had gotten back to the dining room, Murray's hand was under the table. The glow of anticipation on his face didn't quite dispel his harried look.

"I'll need to hold on to my New York apartment until I decide if I can take living on the Coast," she said.

"O.K., Maggie." He thrust his free hand toward her. "We'll throw in another grand. But I need you to start July first. Deal?"

"Deal."

As the food was brought to the table, Freckles started an anguished account of a summer production of *Titus Andronicus*. Maggie ate her scampi and mentally paid off her debts. Murray asked her to come with them to the Rainbow Room, but she begged off, caught the bus to her health club, and took a long steam bath.

She rolled onto her stomach and took a sip of her gin and tonic. She just wouldn't let herself be lonely in California. She'd work too hard to be lonely. She reached for the phone. She had already said goodbye to her friends, but if she called them again, tossed off a casual, anticlimactic farewell, it might calm her nerves. She dialed Thom's number first. He was her standby, her escort for social events she wouldn't dream of going to without a date. He was Peter Pan, charming but infinitely narcissistic, great for parties, though of course she wouldn't dream of calling him if she was sick or depressed. The Orlons were singing "Don't Hang Up" in the background of his recorded message and he was singing along with them. His voice broke off abruptly: "So don't hang up. I don't want to waste my time trying to figure out who's called. Talk after the beep."

She dialed Penny's number. Penny was bound to be home, curled up with herbal tea and Jane Austen. Though ten years Maggie's junior, Penny's style, like her taste in books, belonged to the nineteenth century. She was the sort of friend you invited over to finish up a pot of soup and watch serials from the BBC. Like as not, she was the one who brought flowers when you were suffering from the flu. "Hello, this is Penny. *Please* don't hang up," her tape pleaded. "I've been getting crank calls lately and they're very unnerving. I promise I'll get back to you if you leave your name and number. Thank you." Maggie left a brief message and thought of calling Maxine.

Unlike Penny, Maxine was as trendy as next month's *Cosmopolitan*. She'd left Lubbock, Texas, eight years before to find Mr. Right or a high-paying job, whichever came first; and neither her financial instability as a free-lance publicist nor "the failure of interpersonal relationships" (by which she meant her series of one-night stands) seemed to dim her essential optimism. Her conversations rarely got deeper than a jaded "girl talk," but her go-get-'em attitude was sometimes enough to boost you out of a mild depression. But it was Saturday night. Maxine had an almost pathological fear of being at home on the weekends. No point in trying to reach her.

Thom, Penny, and Maxine. What an unlikely trio. Yet each, in his or her own way, had come to her aid, entertained her, or made her feel less alone.

It didn't matter that Thom talked nonsense or sometimes stood her up, or that Penny occasionally turned childish about going home after midnight and slept on her couch. It didn't matter that Maxine had a habit of borrowing the odd twenty dollars and forgetting to pay it back. Friendships meant accepting each other's limitations. If you lived alone friendships were not just sweet, they were damned necessary. Otherwise you started talking back to the reporter on the eleven o'clock news, got hypochondriacal about hangnails, and found yourself reading statistics about suicide when the holidays rolled around. She wondered how Cordy would cope.

Propping herself up on one elbow, she looked at the books on the bottom shelf. Someday, when she had more time, she really had to get around to reading the classics. She'd bought the matched set of burgundy-colored volumes from a door-to-door salesman the week her son Robbie had started nursery school. Charles had been so critical of the purchase that she'd made a point of bringing them with her when they'd divided the contents of their eight-room house. Marvin had read the classics. Despite his futuristic language and his passion for extraterrestrial beings, he'd had a good education. He just didn't think that the classics had much to do with modern existence. Modern existence, nuclear disarmament, and the direction of his life were Marvin's favorite topics. But there was a caring young man beneath his crazed-scientist pose, just as there was an attractive young body beneath his baggy clothes.

Last night, after they'd made love, he'd noticed she was preoccupied and told her to wake him if she couldn't sleep. She'd lied and said she was fine. There were bed manners just as surely as there were table manners; and you didn't unburden yourself to a lover who was seventeen years your junior any more than you ate peas with a knife. Still, she was sorry she'd stopped herself from telling him how fond she was of him when they'd said goodbye this morning. Her days of bedding down with young men, even strange young men like Marvin, couldn't last forever. She wasn't a Russian peasant living on the steppes, eating yogurt, and looking forward to octogenarian sex. Despite grooming and a "youthful attitude," the span of her love life—of any woman's love life—was much shorter than a man's. In another ten years, when Murray could start on a fashionable second family, she'd be past the stage where she could have an affair with a young man without risking ridicule.

Not that she particularly wanted younger men—the few romantic fantasies she allowed herself always concerned a man of her own age—but men of her own age were hard to find. They were either married, recently divorced ("finding" themselves or going out with younger women), or "untouchables" (homosexuals, or men who'd never lived with a woman or guys who wore white socks and thought *The Texas Chainsaw Massacre* was the apex of cinematic art). If only she could imagine a time when she could stop caring about that Main Connection. But her desires were as strong as ever. And her resolve never again to let a man dominate her life had only increased her desire to really share it.

"You look solemn as an orphan at a family picnic, Maggie."

Maggie turned the corners of her mouth up. She had momentarily forgotten Cordy's presence. Now, looking at her standing there, her head thrown back as though the weight of her hair was pulling it downward, her skin still dewy from the shower, she was impressed by her beauty. It was a shame Cordy's confidence was at such an ebb that she had no idea of how pretty or capable she was. "Hurry up and throw something on, Venus. Cliff doesn't serve dinner, he stages it, so we shouldn't keep him waiting."

The meal restored Cordy's good spirits by reminding her what a social being she could be. During the last year she seemed to have forgotten how much she could enjoy a dinner party. Cliff's apartment was everything she'd imagined an artist's should be, with sketches of costumes he'd designed and autographs all over the crimson walls and books, fans, and feathers scattered around the room. He and Maggie talked like Gatling guns; and warmed by the wine and the excellent risotto alla Milanese, she'd sat on the floor stroking Cliff's cat Gielgud and sometimes joining in the conversation. But once she was bedded down on Maggie's couch, thoughts of Jeanette and Lupton returned. Not that it would have been easy to sleep. There was an unending cacophony coming through the windows— shouts of partygoers, blasting transistor radios, cars with broken mufflers, and drivers who seemed to think it was good sport to lean on the horn.

She'd almost drifted off when the phone rang in the bedroom. Maggie cursed and tripped over something as she got up to answer it. A few moments later she appeared at the door, a shadowy figure in cotton T-shirt and underpants.

"Cordy?"

"It's all right. I wasn't asleep."

"I don't know how you could've been. God it's been noisy

tonight. Real midsummer madness. There's a bar about a block and a half away and I think the bouncer brings all the drunk and disorderlies to our stoop. Mind if I have a cigarette?" She settled herself onto the carpet near the couch. "That was just my friend Penny calling to say goodbye again. We could close the windows and turn on the air conditioning if you like."

"No. I love the fresh air. My grandmother thinks it's dangerous for your health to sleep in a room without the window open. Lupton used to think I was crazy."

"Charles and I used to argue about the thermostat." Her face was briefly illuminated by the flare of the match. "He kept telling me we could keep the heating bills down if I'd wear two sweaters in the house. When things really got rocky between us he bought an electric blanket with dual controls. That was about as far as he ever got toward acknowledging my autonomy."

"How long have you lived alone?"

"'Bout four years. Ever since the last divorce." Because of the lateness of the hour and the darkness of the room, Maggie's voice had gone from trumpet to alto sax.

"Weren't you scared at all?" Cordy asked, conscious that her own voice sounded as thin as a penny whistle.

"I was frightened to live alone after the *first* divorce. I guess that's why I hooked up with Charles. It took me a long time to realize that I was still living alone, emotionally at any rate. So it was easier to live alone after Charles. See, Charles and I didn't have a real crisis. It was more like the slow separation of a cell.

"The worst part of the divorce was dividing the property. God how I hated to give up that house. I felt as though I didn't have anything to show for fifteen years except that damned house. But then I thought, Hey, am I gonna mow this quarter acre myself? Am I gonna make Robbie's room a shrine because he's gone off to college? Or clean the den even though Charles has moved out? I actually did for about three months." She coughed and chuckled. "Then I realized I just couldn't stay there even if I wanted to. I kept getting those I-know-how-things-are looks from neighbors who didn't have a clue about how things were. You know, I'd go to a barbecue and people treated me as though divorce might be a communicable disease. The suburbs are a definite no-no for a single woman."

"Don't you ever miss Charles?"

"Oh, I still want to call and tell him it's time for his annual checkup. And certain things he liked—Dave Brubeck or Cantonese food—remind me. But I can't say I really miss him. I guess I married him because he was a sort of insurance policy against passion. I'd gone through all of that violent emotional stuff with my first husband. I didn't want to suffer it again. Oh, no," she continued after a pause, her voice now so low that it was almost inaudible. "I remember it too vividly. The grand passion that makes you desert your own good sense, the jealous rages that make you lose your self-respect. No thanks."

She drew on her cigarette and shook her head. "Let me tell you: I rode on the back of a motorcycle from New Jersey to Nova Scotia because my first husband liked the outdoors. I went without makeup for two years because he thought makeup was an affectation. I sat in the rain, pregnant mind you, with a plastic bag over my head because he wanted to take pictures of a storm. And I got sick to my stomach every time he looked at another woman, even though I'd gone along, at least in theory, with his ideas of an open marriage. He didn't force me to do any of this, mind you. I chose to do it. And I still don't know why. Because I hate the outdoors, I know my face looks like shit without makeup, and I'd rather have the plague than think of myself as a suspicious woman. Whoever said green was the color of jealousy got it all wrong. Jealousy is all purple and yellow and brown, like a nasty bruise. So . . . when we split up and I was left with Robbie, someone like Charles looked very good to me. Charles worried about house payments instead of his Harley Davidson. He accepted Robbie. He had an integrity about how he dealt with people. He also had good legs." She stubbed out the cigarette and swung around grabbing Cordy's toe. "Hey, you! Did you get me talking about all this, or did I just start jawing all by myself?"

"I s'pose I started asking you questions. You're so strong and independent, I just wondered how you got that way."

"Necessity over character, Magnolia. I wasn't brought up to earn my own living either."

The "Magnolia" tag rankled, but Cordy decided to let it go by. "I didn't necessarily say that I think independence is a primary virtue in a woman."

"Independence is a virtue in anybody. What's more womanly?"

"Compassion, perhaps."

"Ah, dear," she let go of Cordy's toe and turned around to face her. "I don't mean to sound thick-skinned about what you're going through. I know you haven't been separated from Lupton long enough to have a handle on anything. And I've noticed that you always talk about him in the present tense, as though he might be eavesdropping in the next room."

"Of course I talk about him in the present tense. He isn't dead, y' know."

"Neither is Charles. But he's out of my life. If and when you get this divorce, Cordy, you're going to have to find some way to absolve yourself. Divorce doesn't always mean that love has failed; maybe it just means you're determined not to live without it."

"I know you're tryin' to be helpful, but I just can't stand all those pat little things you say about divorce. Divorce is a failure of love no matter how you slice it. An' I think about Jeanette. What's it gonna be like for her to grow up without a daddy, without any brothers or sisters? I know it wasn't my fault, but—"

"But you keep going back over it to see how you could've prevented it. Typical. Take all the crap, and then when you finally break free hit yourself over the head. It's like G. B. Shaw said: 'Women are called womanly only when they regard themselves as existing solely for the use of men.' Compassion is fine, Cordy. But independence is what you need to learn now. Not that pragmatism has ever made many inroads in your neck of the woods."

"Ease up, Maggie. The only thing you know about my neck of the woods you learned at a four-day book conference in Atlanta."

"I know this much"—Maggie's eyes glinted in the dark—"once, when we were first talking on the phone, you told me about your town."

"What's Savannah got to do with it?" Cordy asked impatiently.

"You said that when Sherman made his march through Georgia in the Civil War and burnt Atlanta and all, that the only reason the city of Savannah was saved was because the people had enough sense to know they couldn't resist. So they went on out and surrendered. Lived to fight another day and saved all those fine old houses your grandma's buying up. You've got to surrender to this change in your life."

Cordy was silent, then laughed with a tired helplessness. "You sure your granddaddy wasn't a preacher, Maggie? You're a natural at inspirational messages."

"I never knew him. He carted vegetables around Elizabeth,

New Jersey. But"—she laughed—"word has it that he was a bit of a bully. I guess I've inherited that."

A garbage truck was driving slowly up the street, grinding its jaws on the waste that people were throwing out of their lives.

"Ah, god, it's after two and I've got to be out of here by seven. Sweet dreams, magnolia blossom."

"I thought you were too smart for clichés." Cordy yawned without bothering to cover her mouth.

"All stereotypes are based on some reality; that's what makes prejudice so easy," Maggie laughed. "See you in the morning."

Cordy locked her arms behind her head and lay very still. The blessing of a summer breeze drifted through the open windows, making the shadows of the trees undulate on the walls. Tomorrow she would be alone. Tomorrow she would get back to writing. She was already toying with the next chapter:

> *Driven by an unquenchable desire for the menacing but magnetic Lord Buckingham, Roxanne gathered her meager belongings and set out upon the road for the great city of London. She had faith that when they met again, his lust would ripen into true love.*

How would Roxanne get the finery with which to bedazzle Lord B. when she met him at court? Perhaps she would be forced, just once, to succumb to a wealthy predator. Maggie said it was O.K. for the heroine to sleep with someone other than the hero as long as she was *forced* to do it.

Cordy smiled, remembering a girl in high school who'd bedded just about every available male in Chatham County but absolved herself with a lisping "Ah just don't know how it happened. He was so *insistent* an' ah guess ah'd had too many glasses of punch." These expurgated confessions half amused and half annoyed Cordy. She understood why the girl had to manufacture excuses to maintain an illusion of "niceness," but the hypocrisy irked her. Just as the excuses about car trouble she had given Lucille made her feel dirtier than anything she'd actually done in the back seat. All sorts of boys attracted her, and it wouldn't have taken too much insistence or too many glasses of punch for her to say yes. But Lupton was the one who had welded her will with her desire. He was the "true love" that everyone believed in but couldn't discover.

The street was quiet now, a predawn dampness heavy in the

air. Somewhere a police siren howled. Someone out there in that teeming mass was in trouble. Probably several hundred people were in trouble. They were also dancing, fighting, copulating on satin sheets and splintery floors, eating caviar or day-old bread, or trying to find a comfortable position in which to sleep. Cordy wished she could move back in time and be a girl again, untouched by fatigue or experience.

Chapter VIII

"Alone at last." Cordy closed the door and leaned against it, conscious of being the solitary witness to her own drama. "Alone at last!"—usually the gasp of passion when lovers reached their trysting place—but here she was quite literally alone.

Over Maggie's objections, she'd gotten up with the alarm and fixed breakfast while Maggie showered. Then she'd gone to the street with her and waited for the limo to arrive. Maggie was still shouting instructions when it pulled away from the curb.

Cordy looked around the room. The pleasures of privacy stretched before her like a beautiful landscape where she would be free to walk at her own pace. She could work when she wanted to, sleep when she wanted to, read whenever she liked. She could leave her underwear soaking in the sink and watch late-night movies. She could think without interruption; sift and examine all the assumptions, attitudes, and decisions that had brought her to this point in her life. Glorious, wonderful freedom.

She did the breakfast dishes—god forbid she should rush the typewriter and scare it—and unpacked her clothes, all the while giving herself a lecture: Freedom demanded structure; self-imposed structure required character. If she didn't follow up on all the tasks she set herself she would face the unique disappointment of letting herself, not others, down. She would create a regimen: early rising, protein for breakfast, a one-hour lunch break, exercise. "Sounds like you've enrolled yourself in a one-woman summer camp," she said as she changed the typewriter ribbon and set the manuscript next to a pile of clean paper.

> *Roxanne stood shocked, open-mouthed as the carriage passed by her. She saw a woman resplendent in mauve silk with ecru lace frothy at her décolletage. There was a man sitting beside this haughty beauty, and as Roxanne caught a glimpse of his profile beneath his plumed hat her heart leapt into her mouth. It was Lord Buckingham.*

Now to get Roxanne a job. Serving girl in a grog shop? Hawking oranges at the theater? Anything part-time would do until the lecherous but (thank heaven!) impotent Lord Perdiere (who was, after all, a French spy) supplied her with enough pounds sterling to compete with her rival's finery. Then Roxanne would be in Lord Perdiere's power until she came under the protection of Lord Buckingham. Women in romantic novels were either in a man's power or under his protection. But Roxanne would have no problems once she'd dressed herself up. Her face was her fortune. Peaches-and-cream complexion she had, and breasts like melons. *High melons.* No, strike that.

Cordy put her elbow on the desk and rested her chin in her hand. Had she ever known a woman who was satisfied with the shape or size of her breasts? Her mind flashed on Alidia bouncing to a disco beat somewhere in Baton Rouge. Not likely that Alidia would be taken under anyone's protection, or that she'd be able to put up with it if she were. She could imagine Alidia peeling off her pasties and dragging on her jeans, squandering her salary on a taxi that would take her unmolested to a room with paper-thin walls and phony wood paneling. Had Alidia's acne scars showed under the strobe lights? Would any of the customers look at her face anyway? And just how had she felt jiggling her childlike breasts in front of all those men? Of course, Roxanne would have a certain advantage when she unlaced her bodice, since Lord B. hadn't spent his youth poring over air-brushed centerfolds. And what about Roxanne's teeth? There were no orthodontists in Restoration England. In those days whole populations had blandly accepted gaps, overbites and snaggle-toothed smiles. But best ignore that piece of information. . . . *her heart leapt into her mouth.* . . . At least she should make a mess on the blank page.

By one o'clock Roxanne was flashing her perfect smile at Lord

Perdiere, and Cordy's stomach was rumbling. She combed her hair with her nails and grabbed her purse. As she reached the front door she saw that she'd forgotten to lock it. How would she ever survive if she was so busy daydreaming about her new freedom that she neglected to take the most rudimentary precautions for her own protection? She stepped into the hallway, tried various keys, and finally succeeded in turning all the locks.

At the delicatessen on the corner, she waited patiently until the customers who'd come in before her were served. But just as she opened her mouth to give her order, another woman pushed in front of her.

"'Scuse me," Cordy said gently. "I believe I was next."

"Yeah, she was next," the tough-looking counterman agreed. "So whadda y' want, blondie?"

"I'd like—"

"The hell she was. I've been here for ten minutes. I just walked over to look at the pastries 'cause you were busy. I'll have a pastrami on rye, hold the mustard, a half pound of potato salad, two sour pickles—"

"Cool it, lady. Blondie was next."

The woman folded her arms across her chest and set her feet apart. "You gonna give me my order or aren't you?" she demanded.

"I said this one was next."

Torn between politeness and assertion—she didn't want to start an argument, she just wanted a tuna-fish sandwich—Cordy hoped she could shame the woman with a show of good manners. "It's all right. I'll wait if she's in such a hurry."

"No, it ain't all right," the counterman told her. "It ain't all right with me. Now, what do you want, blondie?"

"I'd like—"

"Are you gonna take my order or am I gonna talk to your boss?" the woman asked belligerently.

"Talk to whoever you damn please, lady. I'm doin' this one's order first."

"No. Please." Cordy was backing off.

The counterman set down his knife and leaned across the counter. "Uh-uh. You're first. It's the principle of the thing, know what I mean?" His face grew wistful. "People gotta respect taking turns, otherwise the whole damn thing falls apart. Anarchy! Y' wanna know why democracy has lasted in England all these years?" Cordy shook her head. She wasn't prepared for this contretemps. "It's because citizens respect each other's place in line, that's why. I was over in London when they were havin' their subway strike," he continued, ignoring the customers who had just come in and were looking around, trying to discover their order in line. "You woulda been amazed at how those people behave. Lining up, or queuing up, they call it, one behind the other, peaceful like. Civilized! Here you don't have no civilization. You got a bunch of animals"—he glared at the woman—"screamin', anarchist animals. Blondie, whadda you want? 'Cause it's your turn, and this one with the mouth here, she can wait till hell freezes over because . . ."

But Cordy had already backed out the door.

Heat waves were rising from the pavement as she walked toward the greenery of the park. As she stopped to buy a hot dog from a street vendor, a group of Puerto Rican boys, standing in a semicircle bouncing mock-macho on the balls of their feet and yelling over the blare of a transistor radio, hooted at her. Embarrassed, she could think of nothing to do but to smile. The one in purple shorts, who'd caught her eye, spun back to his companions, hooked his thumbs into his armpits, and started to crow.

She moved on quickly, past an old man sitting on a bench, his hands crossed over a cane, talking to himself. The temperature was in the high eighties but he was wearing a topcoat. A guy with long, stringy hair and a blissfully stoned look almost pedaled his unicycle into her but swerved at the last minute.

As she went farther into the park she saw a couple in bathing suits entwined on an Army blanket. Since they seemed oblivious of the fact that they were in public, it seemed only good manners to be oblivious of them. The playground up ahead looked to be the safest place to sit. She took a bench under the dusty trees and ate her hot dog watching the children splash in the wading pool, fling sand at one another, and hang from the jungle gyms like spider monkeys. She watched the black nursemaids sweltering in white uniforms, saw the mothers clustered in groups of two or three, flipping through magazines or sharing snatches of desultory conversation because their real attention was always on the children. She licked the mustard from her fingers, stuffed the paper napkin into her pocket, and was about to leave when she saw a boy about two and a half crawl up the ladder to the slide and start down head first. She jumped and ran. He was down the slide lickety-split, miraculously landing on his backside and sending up a fearful wail.

"I saw him but I couldn't get here fast enough," she gasped to the young woman who'd rushed over and was picking him up.

"Jason, haven't I told you! *Sit* down when you come on the slide. Oh, god, he's got an egg on his head already. Both his parents are psychologists, so they'll probably want to sue the school."

"He's not yours?"

"Naw. The one in the red bathing suit is mine." She waved in the direction of the sandpile. "I help out at the school so I can get his tuition free. But I'm taking care of seven of 'em here today. Christ, I can't watch them all."

"No," Cordy nodded, reaching out to stroke the boy's back. "I think he's all right."

"Sure. He's made of rubber, aren't you, Jason? Hey, Debbie, I told you not to do that," she yelled, racing away to another accident on the jungle gym.

Cordy looked after her, then walked slowly back to the street. A few short years ago she'd been like these women sitting on the benches. She'd had the daily responsibility and routine. Lupton had been good about helping out during the off-season, and of course he'd written the checks year round. And there had been a certain poignant sweetness to those years. She'd felt a pride watching Jeanette's sturdy, pot-bellied body crawling to the top of the ladders or shedding her water wings, for Jeanette was as physically fearless as her father. And sometimes when Jeanette hurt herself and ran to her for comfort, or fell asleep on her breast, they'd breathed the same breath of drowsy contentment, as though they were still part of the same body. It wasn't until her first week back in Savannah, when she, Nonnie, and Jeanette had gone to a pancake house for Mother's Day, that she became aware of how many women were alone with their children. And it wasn't until Lupton had neglected to send a check that he'd promised that the full impact of her situation had hit her. She didn't want to have to go out to work and leave Jeanette in the care of others. She quickened her step, keys in hand, as she walked back to the apartment.

"Miss Silverstein, please."

"This is she."

"My name is Cordelia Simpkins Tyre. I think Maggie Brocksen may have spoken to you about me."

"Who's that?"

"Maggie Brocksen. She was my editor at Chrystallis. That is, she's not there anymore but . . ." Her heart was racing. She knew she sounded feeble-minded. "I'm Cordelia Simpkins Tyre," she started again.

"Oh, yes. I remember now. Maggie did send me one of your books. But I'm really backed up now. If you'll call again in two or three weeks I could possibly see you then."

"I'll do that. Thank you. I'll call back."

Mustn't interpret a simple postponement as outright rejection, she cautioned herself, reaching for the phone and checking the next number on her list.

Candidate number two was away on vacation.

"Third time's a charm, and if it's not it's all I can take for one day." She dialed a third time and counted herself lucky when she got through two girls at the switchboard and received a promise to return the call "before the end of the month." She made notations in her blank appointment book, fixed herself a pitcher of iced tea, and went back to Roxanne's dazzling smile.

By six o'clock the front door of the building was being slammed with frequency as neighbors came in from work. She folded her arms across the typewriter, hearing her neck crack as she moved it from side to side. "Oh, for god's sake, Roxanne, just get laid and get it over with." She felt clammy and disheveled. She put a "chicken tetrazzini, single serving" into the electric oven and showered. Later, turning on the TV for background noise, she lay on the floor reading *History of the British Theatre*, which she'd been lucky enough to find on Maggie's shelf. She made notes about the books she'd need to pick up from the library and did exercises to flatten her stomach. Around ten o'clock she turned off a panel discussion of the political situation in Zimbabwe, took another shower, and crawled into bed. The steady thrump of bass notes reverberated from the downstairs apartment. Above her, footsteps moved back and forth, caged-animal style. Judging from the heaviness of the tread it was a man. Strangers above, below, and on either side. Strangers all.

She woke to a strain of music so faint that at first she thought she might be dreaming it. Without turning on the lights, she groped her way into the living room and pulled aside the curtains. The street was deserted, the trees under the arc lights had the black and yellowish hues of an impressionist painting. A man was sitting on the stoop of the building across the street plucking a guitar. An old woman in a baggy shift lurched by, pulled forward by a bulldog straining against the leash. The woman's hair was a white bird's-nest, crinkly as a Brillo pad. It took all of her strength to rein the dog in and direct it toward the curb. "Come on now, Kenneth. Come on, baby. Make for Mommy." The guitar player watched as the dog lifted its leg against the hubcap of a silver Mercedes. When the woman, chortling with satisfaction, lurched on, he started playing again. It was a halting rendition of "Greensleeves."

> *Alas, my love, you do me wrong*
> *To cast me off discourteously . . .*

Cordy felt so lonely she thought she might cry.

By the end of a week her regimen had fallen apart. She woke only when it was too hot to sleep and went to bed in the early hours when all street activity had stopped. Except for her trips to the library and the supermarket, where, she thought, the checker looked pityingly at her stack of single-serving entrees, she might have been invisible. Certainly she had never been around so many people without any acknowledgment of her own presence. She missed Jeanette horribly. Whatever dreams of freedom and adventure she might have entertained gave way to feelings of isolation. From the window she became the secret observer, acutely aware of the patterns of the strangers around her.

Every morning at eleven she saw the nursery school worker she'd met in the park. The woman walked by holding a long rope. Several children clutched it, trailing behind her like a disconnected centipede. At three in the afternoon a black boy with the lean, high-hipped body of a Watusi met his redheaded girlfriend by the ginkgo tree across the street. He draped his arms above her head, holding on to the trunk of the tree as though he wanted to imprison her there. Sometimes they kissed, but mostly they talked in desperate hushed tones. Romeo and Juliet with racial problems. The man with the thick glasses and the Brooks Brothers suit who lived two doors down at 56 usually came home shortly after the lovers parted. He must have hated his conservative uniform, because he pulled at his tie and started to take his jacket off before he even went into his building. He'd emerge ten minutes later in T-shirt and shorts, hook the elastic band around his head to secure his glasses, stretch his withered shanks with limbering-up exercises, and jog off toward the park. The old lady with the dog continued to chant incantations that helped Kenneth relieve his bladder at the witching hour. The guitar player was having trouble with the fingering on "Black Is the Color of My True Love's Hair." Since he always chose songs in a minor key and refused to give the old lady so much as a grunt of recognition, Cordy assumed he was a melancholic type. But the strangest midnight wanderer was the middle-aged woman who lived directly opposite. It took Cordy several days to realize that the businesswoman who tucked her briefcase under her arm like a swagger stick and marched off each morning at ten was the furtive creature who, like a comic-book criminal, checked to see if the street was deserted at one A.M., then scurried around depositing her garbage in other people's trashcans.

And there were her immediate neighbors. The girl upstairs who never combed her hair and wore denim skirts and owlish glasses. Did she work in a place with an all-female staff or was she one of those Eastern girls'-school types who clung to dowdy clothes as a badge of their class? Despite her serious mien, she was scatterbrained, because she rarely got to the front door without dashing back upstairs to retrieve something she'd left behind. Cordy had never seen the man who lived directly overhead. He was troubled (witness the pacing), but it couldn't have been about the frequency of his sex life. She'd heard many different female voices at his door; and unless his hobby was moving furniture after midnight, the steady thrumps suggested more than the usual amount of activity. The disco addict downstairs was a striking black woman with a Nefertiti profile. She was either in the fashion business or had found her own version of Lord Perdiere, because every time Cordy saw her she was in a different outfit: tailored suits, jogging ensembles, dashikis, and flowing silk pajamas that would have made Lucille envious.

Cordy sat by the window now sipping her morning coffee and watching the jogger from 56 sprint into his building carrying the Sunday *Times*. Maybe she'd get dressed and go to the newsstand herself. She should at least be able to make it to the newsstand. There was a whole fascinating world out there: bistros and ballet, opera and four-star restaurants. And she'd promised Nonnie she would visit the Frick Museum, the World Trade Center, and see the Rockettes. But she wasn't up to tackling it alone. She'd work some more, then reward herself with a telephone call to Savannah, an hour of listening to one of Maggie's musical comedy records, or more watching out the window. Next week, when Roxanne and Lord B. were reunited and she was further along on her outline for the Fanny Kemble book, she would take an afternoon off, see a play, or maybe a movie, though the prospect of sitting alone in the dark gorging popcorn didn't really appeal.

Still, she must get out, even if it seemed a chore. She got up and stretched. Her body felt lumpish and disconnected. Sometimes when she scrubbed herself with the loofah or woke with her arms wrapped around herself, she went through Alice in Wonderland metamorphoses redolent of her adolescent dreams. She seemed to swell, grow so large that she could imagine her body pressing against the walls. At other times, eyes closed, she felt she was shrinking, becoming almost infinitesimal. She had the power of flight and could rise out of the room, up, up, and away, magically hovering above the city. From that height it was just dots of light, a giant insect swarm. The worker bees toiled during the day and crawled through common dugouts of subways and streets. They burrowed through hallways and finally became encapsulated in their separate cells. The distant hum of traffic became a sound they made when they rubbed their legs together to communicate.

She dropped her coffee cup into a sink already full of dishes. The phone rang but she ignored it. She had recorded a message giving Maggie's California address, and callers invariably hung up without talking. But this time, as her message came to an end, a familiar voice commanded, "Cordy if you're there pick up the phone. It's me, Maggie." She rushed over and fumbled with the switches, flicking "record," "rewind," and hearing an electronic squeal before she managed to find the "off" button.

"Yes. Sorry. It's me. I'm here."

"Glad I got you in, Cordy. How y' been?"

"Just fine. How are you?"

"I'm great. Still haven't found an apartment, so I'm staying out at Murray's place in Malibu. It's only slightly smaller than Versailles and all rooms face the ocean. I want to be downwardly mobile and become a beach bum. Really, the beach is fantastic. Reason I called, I left my old address book. My shrink would probably say that I've subconsciously decided to sever all ties with my past. Anyhow, it's a kinda battered red leather and it's in the upper left hand drawer of the desk."

"I'll put it in the mail right away."

"Thanks. So what have you been up to?"

"Working. Just working."

"Well, get your ass in gear and look around."

"I'm going to. Next week."

"Promises, promises! Do me another favor will you? Run up to Cliff's and tell him to give me a call at Murray's office tomorrow. I think there might be an opening on Murray's new show."

"O.K. I will. And thanks for calling."

"All the dollars, Magnolia. Bye."

An excuse was as good as an invitation. Cordy showered, dressed, and mounted the stairs to Cliff's apartment.

"I'm coming, I'm coming," he called. Moments later the peephole in the door was lifted.

"It's Cordy, Maggie's friend."

"Sure, sure, I remember. I wasn't that drunk when we met."

Snap, click, the locks were thrown back, and Cliff opened the door. His thinning hair was standing up in spikes and his Adam's apple wobbled up and down as he smiled. "I was going to come down and say hello later in the day."

"If I'm disturbing you . . ." She looked at his worn dungarees and bare feet, thinking that she might have woken him.

"Hey, I'm always disturbed." He gestured toward the living room. The cat carrier was out and several suitcases spilled their contents on the carpet. "I just got back from the Westbury Music Festival last night. God, it's hot today, isn't it? Come on into the kitchen. I'm cooking, but it's still cooler in there. Would you like a joint or a Bloody Mary?"

"It's a little early, isn't it?"

"Naw. Only the heavy users count the hours. My old man was strict about timing. He'd watch the clock for the cocktail hour as though it was the firing pistol for a race. Then he'd get jackhammered with a free conscience till they rolled him into bed at midnight."

"I guess I wouldn't mind a Bloody Mary."

"Good. Come on into the kitchen and help me cut up vegetables while we're talking. I always start cooking as soon as I hit the apartment." He nodded toward the pile of vegetables on the drainboard and the gourmet cookware hanging from the pegboards, cleared the *Times* from the table, and shooed Gielgud off the chair. "And after I've made this gazpacho I'm gonna take the phone off the hook and not leave the apartment for at least two days. How about you? Have you seen the Statue of Liberty yet?" She shook her head. "The United Nations?"

"No. I've just been . . . holed up," she admitted.

"Sometimes you have to do that."

"I was beginning to think I was the only one who burrowed in."

"Are you kidding? Half the population are secret shut-ins." He put a knife and a couple of bell peppers in front of her. "Two cups, diced. Listen, after the last two weeks I'm ready to find a padded cell. I've been working on this show for Gloria Duvall."

"I don't think I know her."

"Before your time. She was the other woman in just about every MGM musical made between 1940 and 1950. She'd tap her toes off, have one heavy seduction scene, and then the hero would walk off with Ginger Rogers or June Allyson. Poor Gloria. She ought to be home praying for a happy death, but every summer she gets out the twinkle shoes and she always asks for me. The money's good, but I have to put up with a cyclone of temper tantrums to get it. I try to tell her, 'Gloria darling, I'm Cliff the Costumer, not Merlin the Magician. I can't make you have a twenty-four-inch waist anymore.' But she just won't accept it. Oh, what a bitch." He shook the Tabasco sauce into the tomato juice with repressed rage. "Course, I don't blame her, because most of the audience hasn't come to see the show; they've come to see how Gloria's holding up. But let me tell you"—he handed her the drink—"after the fifth revival of *Kiss Me Kate* she's holding up a lot better than I am. I'm ready to donate my collection of waist cinchers to the Salvation Army and buy a roadside diner in Albuquerque."

"I don't think you'll have to do that. In fact, the reason I came up was to give you a message from Maggie. She says to call her 'cause there might be a job with that TV show she's working on."

"I'll give her a call, but I can't really take the idea of working in TV. Once a gypsy, always a gypsy. It's like a rotten love affair: You complain but you always come back."

"I hope I remember how to do this," she said as she sliced into the pepper. "I haven't cooked anything but TV dinners since I've been here."

"Bad sign. When I first lived alone I never cooked. Then I started giving parties so I could have the leftovers. When I got to the stage where I bothered to fix a decent meal for myself my shrink told me I only had to see her once a week. Yep, I can relate to vegetables." He selected an onion and fondled it. "And given the level of intelligence of some of my co-workers, that's a good thing. But if you're into TV dinners you should save the aluminum trays for Minnie Mouse."

"Minnie Mouse?"

"Yeah. She's this weirdo who lives across the street. She's got a seat on the New York Stock Exchange, but at night she sneaks out and puts her trash into other people's garbage cans."

"I've seen her," she laughed excitedly. "At first I couldn't put her together with the same woman I saw leaving in the morning."

"Maggie and I called her Minnie Mouse because she looks like a cartoon character when she does her sneaky trash dance. One night I came home and caught her red-handed. 'Excuse me, ma'am,' I said in my social worker voice. 'Why are you depositing your refuse in our garbage can?'"

"What did she do?"

"She looked right through me, handed me the plastic bag, and scampered back to her mouse hole. God, I miss Maggie." He sliced into the onion. "We used to sit there by her windows knocking back the gin and tonics and making up stories about the whole neighborhood. You get a real bird's-eye view from those windows. If Maggie doesn't come back from Tinseltown I'm going to trade apartments with her. Just sit there by those windows, watch myself go bald, and become the neighborhood yenta."

"I've been sitting there a lot. I like listening to the guy with the guitar."

"Oh, him. He's a real anti-social S.O.B. I'll be glad when the winter comes and he has to go inside to practice."

"And the old woman with the dog," she went on, pleased that she'd found a common ground for conversation.

"Mrs. Kelinsdorf."

"Is that her name? I do feel so sorry for her. She looks so poor an' lonely."

"You've let your sympathetic imagination run away with you there. She's just another nut case. She owns the first two buildings on the park, so she's not exactly worried about Social Security going bankrupt. She's an A.S.P.C.A. freak. Likes animals better than people. Believe me, she's more in love with Kenneth than she ever was with Mr. Kelinsdorf."

"That's a relief. That she isn't poor, I mean."

"Hell no. Who else do you want to know about? Have you met anyone else in the building yet?" Without waiting for a reply, Cliff chopped, sliced and chattered: The girl with the dowdy clothes was Carla Smalls, a graduate student at Columbia whose boyfriend had run off to New Mexico. The Casanova who walked the floors was Jerry Falkburg. He claimed to work at the commodities exchange, but he had so many girlfriends Cliff thought he might be in the white slave trade as well as bartering pork bellies and soy bean futures. "If he spots you at the mailboxes he'll be around to borrow a cup of scotch the next night." Two apartments were temporarily vacant ("Nobody who has a dime stays in New York for the dog days") but were normally occupied by a fledgling opera singer from Tennessee—"She *looks* as though she should play Brunhilda, but I don't think she has the range"—and a secretary at CBS.

"And what about Black Beauty—the glamorous one on the first floor?"

"That's Sylvia. She's in the rag trade. About ten years ago she ran away from home to become a model and during that Afro craze she worked a bit. Now she's a buyer from Teen Togs. Have you seen the limo outside when her boss comes to pick her up?"

"I don't think so."

"An old stud with silk suits and silver hair? Anyhow that affair's been going on for years. Yeah"—he waved a spatula—"it's all part of life in the Naked City."

"Shall I put in the peppers now?"

"Sure. Dump 'em in. And since you've been such a scout about helping fix the soup, why don't you come up around six o'clock and eat with me? There's a free concert in the park, so if you don't mind the thundering herd we could go to that."

"But you have to unpack. And you said you were going to hide out for a few days."

"I just said that to cover my bases in case I couldn't hustle up some company. If we don't go to the concert I'll just hang out till midnight and then get restless and wander over to the Golden Greek or some other rat hole."

"And?"

"And if I don't pick someone up I'll feel like a dog; and if I do pick someone up he'll probably *be* a dog. Come on up around six, won't you?" The invitation was offered lightly enough, but there was a hint of a plea. "What's the hesitation? Don't think I'm macho enough to protect you in the park?"

"No, no," she laughed. "I need to get out. I'll come up around six."

The drink had made her drowsy. She went back downstairs, shut the windows against the sweltering heat, and crawled into the unmade bed with her clothes on. She had a habit of falling asleep whenever she traveled, and now the drone of the air conditioner became the hum of a jet engine, lulling her into a dream that was distinctly though strangely erotic—a seaside picnic that turned into a bacchanal. Nonnie was there, a miracle of Biblical proportions as she fed a multitude with an inexhaustible supply of chicken taken from a single wicker basket. She'd brought a cake for Cordy, but as she turned it out of the pan it melted onto the sand, causing her great consternation. She pointed out a straggly palm tree and told Cordy to climb it because the tide was rising. But Cordy ran into the ocean instead. She mounted a dolphin. Riding him was an exquisite pleasure. His sides were a great slippery smoothness between her legs as she guided him through the waves. She could taste the salt spray in her open mouth. Her hair flew in the wind and slapped against her face and shoulders in wet, slippery tails. Diving to the bottom, she found herself in a tangle of bodies—arms, legs, cocks, and breasts everywhere, suffocating her. She struggled to free herself, but the mass of writhing flesh was heaved up onto the shore, squirming violently toward some unseen goal line.

Gasping mouthfuls of cotton-candy air, muttering gibberish, she surfaced into consciousness. After splashing cold water on her face, she tried to concentrate on Fanny Kemble's *Journal of a Residence on a Georgian Plantation*, but her mind was elsewhere. Lupton and Susan. Susan and Lupton: thrashing in athletic sexual ecstasy or, worse yet, lolling in post-coital intimacy, Lupton pushing back Susan's blond/auburn/black hair. (Susan's coloring changed according to the most recent advertisement or photograph of a beautiful girl Cordy had seen.) Annoyed, she threw the book aside, put on her prettiest cotton dress and went upstairs.

The jumble of suitcases was still on the living room floor, but Cliff had set the table and cleaned himself up. He offered her a joint ("to increase your appetite") as soon as she sat down.

"I don't need it," she said as she took it. "I haven't eaten all day."

"Fasting's an improvement over TV dinners. Here, break bread with me." Judging from his laughter and the redness of his eyes, he'd already had a joint before she'd arrived. He tore the loaf apart, popping a piece into his mouth and making short, affirmative grunts as he chewed. "I don't mind living alone. I don't mind sleeping alone. And I don't even mind the occasional return to the sexual habits of boyhood; but it's damned uncivilized to eat alone."

She noticed the cat's bowl placed close to Cliff's chair. "Didn't you ever live with anybody?"

"Sure. My beloved family, my college roommate, the U.S. Navy and once, in my callow youth, with an accountant from Des Moines. He left me with a broken heart and a five-hundred-dollar phone bill. It took me a while to get used to my own company again, but I've gotta admit, I'm too inflexible now to live with anyone else. Except Gielgud, here. He loves me. Strange though . . ." he turned thoughtful while ladling out the soup. "I never thought I'd be one of them."

She pulled on the joint, held her breath and sputtered, "One of who?"

"The people who eat alone. When I was a kid I used to envy them. There was this French restaurant somewhere in the East fifties. Le Coq d'Or. We went there every Friday night. See, my father knew the owners, and my father was the sort of man who needed to be recognized. Ah, I'll never forget those Fridays. Father wolfing down his frog legs, mother playing with her turban."

"Turban?" she asked, thinking it might be some exotic dish she'd never heard of.

"Turban. You know the thing you wind around your head. They weren't fashionable anymore, but then Mother was never too rigidly tied to the present. She was the sort of woman who continued to wear what was de riguer when she was twenty. Anyhow she'd get her escargot and after a couple of Stingers she'd start running her hands through what should've been her hair. After dinner my father would drag us into the kitchen to pay his respects to Maurice or Pierre or whatever the hell the chef's name was. Father booming out in that hail-fellow-well-met voice of his. Mother with her greasy turban. I used to shrivel with embarrassment." He swallowed the contents of the spoon that had been poised in front of his mouth and paused to appraise the soup, his Adam's Apple wobbling, his eyes dreamy. "So I always envied the people who ate alone. The out-of-town businessmen who brought their paperwork along, the widow who was such a regular she didn't have to open the menu. I used to think how lucky they were to eat without having to have someone watching them, talking at them, or embarrassing them. I sure didn't think I'd end up like them. Hey, what do you think—" he pulled himself back from the murky shores of reverie— "Does this gazpacho need more garlic?"

"Uh-uh. It's perfect."

"Coming from someone who's confessed to a steady diet of tin-foil dinners I'm not sure that's much of a compliment. Let's hurry up and finish, and we'll head for the park."

The bright corals and golds of the day were cooling into blues and greys when she and Cliff stepped outside. Cliff talked about his childhood, and Cordy, relieved of the obligation to tell about herself, listened with half an ear, more intent on watching the passing parade. She had never seen so many interesting and diverse examples of humanity. The overture of *La Boheme* had already started as they reached the Sheep Meadow. They picked their way through the squatters to a balding patch of grass. She looked into the faces around her. Cliff unfurled the blanket next to a group munching fried chicken out of a Kentucky Colonel bucket and swigging from a communal bottle of Gallo. The couple to their right were in a different league: They nibbled on foie gras sandwiches and dabbed their lips with linen napkins. The stage was too far away for them to see anything much, so she followed Cliff's example, took off her sandals, and stretched full-length on the blanket. A bearded member of the Gallo gang held the bottle toward her. She smiled, shook her head, crossed her arms behind it, and stared up at the sky. It was now a vivid, deep blue with nary a star in sight. Lying amidst these seemingly peaceful strangers, half listening to Mimi sing out her love, she felt she had captured some of the youthful anonymity she might have enjoyed had she not become Lupton Tyre's wife.

Cliff insisted that she hadn't seen New York until she'd ridden the subway, so after the concert they straggled out of the park and found the closest set of grimy steps leading underground. The vibrations of the train almost shook her guts out. She was appalled by the filth and graffiti and the noise pulled her mouth into a grimace, but she felt the childish excitement she might have on a rickety and possibly dangerous ride at the county fair.

"Hey, Cliff, I had a wonderful time," she sighed as they went up the front steps. "Did you see that Oriental guy sitting cross-legged in front of us at the concert? He had a flashlight and was reading the score. At one point—"

Cliff had stopped suddenly, tense and alert. His head pivoted back to her.

"What's the matter?" she asked.

"The front door. It's ajar. Didn't you notice?" He pushed it ever so gently and it swung open. Motioning for her to stay behind, he took a step into the hallway. She froze, scanning the street.

"Oh, shit," she heard him say with disgusted resignation. "Looks like Sylvia's apartment has been ripped off. Her door's open."

"Should I call for help?" she whispered.

He held up his hand in warning, pushed each of the apartment buzzers, and waited for a response. "Ain't nobody here but us chickens," he said finally. "Come on, let's see if they got your place."

They moved so stealthily up the stairs that they might have been the criminals. Glancing over her shoulder at Sylvia's open door, she broke out in gooseflesh. "Shouldn't we . . ." she said softly, but he'd moved ahead of her, flinging his hand back impatiently for her to give him her keys.

The rattle and click of the locks sounded unnaturally loud. Holding her breath, fumbling for the light switch, she stepped in after him. Everything was as she'd left it.

"Does Maggie have some scotch in her liquor cabinet?"

"I think so."

"O.K. Get it. I'll go up and check my place, and then we'll go back down to Sylvia's and call the cops."

He disappeared up the stairs. She locked up again and stood in the hallway, bottle in hand, trying to come up with a course of action that would either remove her from the scene or allow her to be more helpful. Just as she realized she had to go to the bathroom, Cliff racketed down the stairs. "A-O.K." He grinned foolishly. "A-O.K." She could imagine him at ten, mesmerized by the moon shot, planning a career as an astronaut. "Looks like they just hit on Sylvia's. And they must've left in a hurry 'cause they didn't bother to close either of the doors."

"Sloppy," she shrugged, wanting to sound callous.

Curiosity and a need to stay close to him forced her to follow him downstairs. She slowed as she neared the gaping door. Was it proper to walk into someone else's space, even if it had been burglarized?

"Is this 911?" Cliff was already talking into the white telephone. The room was off-white with carpeted risers and built-in furniture also in white. It might have been a waiting room. She moved to the bedroom, again white on white, feeling the sort of guilty curiosity she'd experienced when seeing her father step out of the shower. Drawers had been dumped onto the carpet. Wardrobes yanked open. A jewelry case upturned on the dressing table. The mirrors on the walls next to the bed doubled the image of chaos. A large high-contrast photograph of a nude Sylvia stared at the mess with veiled come-hither eyes. She turned to go, stepped on a pocket-size picture, and cracked the frame. A very proper Negro couple seated on the porch of a row house looked up from her toes. "Oh, Cliff I—"

"Looks like they got the TV. I remember when she had that color TV delivered. The stereo's still here. Worse luck. She always plays that damned thing too loud."

She reached for the photograph, but decided against a confession and picked up a stuffed Panda bear. Did Sylvia sleep with this when the silver-haired gentleman didn't turn up?

"Come on, let's have a drink," he called. "911 said the cops would be here right away. I don't suppose she'll mind if we use her glasses."

"I have to . . ." Throw up? Run away? ". . . use the bathroom."

"Right through that door. All the apartments have the same layout."

The bathroom was also white on white and mirrored. She kept her eyes on the carpet, damned her weak bladder—worse since she'd had Jeanette—and resisted a desire to open the cabinet. The final clue to anyone's private life was the bathroom cabinet. But she already knew there'd be a cache of sedatives next to the wrinkle cream. Nobody could live with their reflection in this snow-blinding cave without being tranquilized.

Cliff was wagging his head from side to side and muttering obscenities. The buzzer rang as they simultaneously downed the scotch. A cop with his belly bulging over his belt mopped his swarthy forehead with his arm, though both were equally sweaty.

"I'm Officer DelGeorgio," he said with infinite boredom, moving past them and flopping on the couch. "O.K. Y' wanna tell me about it?"

"We were coming home from a concert in the park," Cliff began.

"Names and addresses first," DelGeorgio said laconically. "You the guy who made the call, right?"

The younger, taller cop was moving about as though he might have been taking a leisurely walk in the woods. He stopped at the bedroom door, arms resting on the wall, one foot extended. The contours of his back strained against his blue shirt, which was stained with sweat, though his movements suggested that he wasn't easily perturbed.

"So then we went up to check Miss Tyre's apartment."

"Actually, it isn't my apartment," Cordy felt obliged to put in. "It's my friend Ms. Brocksen's. I'm just stayin' there."

"You from the South?" The good-looking one spoke for the first time, turning to her. His skin was fair and flushed, his dark hair, which curled over his ears, seemed rather too long for an officer of the law.

"Yes. I'm from Savannah."

"Pretty name, Savannah," he drawled. His eyes were half sharp, half dreamy, and decidedly blue. "Bet you don't have as many low-lifes down there, do you?"

"What are you tellin' me," DelGeorgio said defensively. "You know better'n that." And then, in the pseudo-serious tone of a television newsman: "Crime is a national problem."

"Yes," Cordy nodded politely. "I expect this sort of thing happens everywhere these days."

"Damn straight," Del Georgio growled. He was not a man to put up with disagreements.

"You're too charitable, DelGeorgio," his partner overrode him, his eyes sweeping the neckline of Cordy's dress. "This place is the biggest sewer. But I hope this lady won't go home and give us a bum rap."

"I don't think there's much we can do here." DelGeorgio got to his feet, hitching the belt beneath his paunch. "You guys can't even tell us what's missing. So why don't I just give you the complaint number an' you can have your friend call the station in the morning."

There was a noise at the front door.

"That might be her," Cliff started out. "I'd better warn her if it is."

DelGeorgio, disgusted that his getaway had been frustrated, grunted and sat back down. "He's a regular girl scout, ain't he?"

Cordy tried to take her eyes away from the bright blue ones that were returning her stare, but only succeeded in getting them as far as his badge.

"Name's Heandy." His smile was crooked, but broad enough to crease one cheek. "Sean Heandy."

Muttered explanation, pause, hiss, and expletives were heard in the hallway. Sylvia came through the door, somewhat unsteady on her feet. Cordy couldn't tell if she'd been drinking or was in a state of shock, but her face was impassive beneath the elaborate corn-row hairdo beaded with gold. "Son of a bitch," she said through clenched teeth. "Son of a bitch." She walked directly toward the bedroom in a straight line, ignoring all of them. Then, spinning back into the room, her gaze settled on Cordy. Cordy had a quick paranoid flash. Could Sylvia know she'd crunched the picture frame?

"This is Cordy Tyre," Cliff volunteered. "She's staying in Maggie's place."

"You wanna give us your name and birth date," DelGeorgio growled. No introductions outside of the line of duty on his time, by God.

"Sylvia. And I'd like a drink."

"Thought you might," Cliff slipped in sotto voce. "We brought some down from Maggie's."

"I think I'll go upstairs if you don't need me anymore," Cordy said. She was feeling very sad.

"Fine." DelGeorgio dismissed her with a beefy hand and turned back to Sylvia. "Now . . . what did you say your name was?"

Cliff walked her to the door, whispering as he went. "I'm really sorry about this. Really. We were having such a good time."

"Ain't it always the way," she shrugged. "Do you think she'll be all right?"

"Sylvia? She's tough as the nose cone on a missle. But if you get freaked, give me a call."

"No. I'll be fine. And thanks for dinner."

Unlocking her door again (how many hours in the life of the city dweller were spent in this futile defense?), she heard Sylvia shriek, "Whadda you mean you aren't going to dust for fingerprints? If I lived on fucking Park Avenue you'd be dusting for fingerprints!"

Cordy sat on the couch biting her cuticle. The street was quiet, luminously dim. She thought of the house in the Chicago suburbs. She knew less about some of the neighbors she'd lived next to for years there than she'd found out about Cliff and Sylvia in one night. But at least in the suburbs there was the illusion of protection. Feared as crime was—it came in fourth on the list of supermarket checkout conversations, following inflation, the weather, and children—no one she actually knew had ever been a victim. She'd felt safe in the suburbs. The sounds of lawn mowers, television sets, women summoning their children in drawn-out, plaintive syllables, Lupton bellowing that he was home, all had comforted her. She'd laughed along with Lupton at the women who took self-defense classes; even smiled when he'd said that the less desirable ones might enjoy an attack. Now she wondered what she would do if she woke to see a shadow climbing in the window or heard the door being jimmied. And Lucille's voice cautioning that she had more imagination than was good for her was not enough to stop her slide into scenes of more violence and mayhem: purses snatched, knives being thrust, little girls' bodies being held to the ground.

The knock at the door made her jump. She tiptoed toward it, calling out "Cliff" as she opened the peephole.

"No. Sean Heandy.

"I think this is yours," he said when she opened the door. He was standing one foot forward in that casual yet ready-for-the-lunge pose. For a split second he seemed to be offering himself. Then she noticed the bottle dangling from his hand.

"Oh, yes. Thank you." He held his ground for an uncomfortable pause. "Would you like to come in?"

"Just for a bit. My partner's waiting in the car."

"Oh."

Another pause.

"It's the end of our shift. DelGeorgio's nervous about getting home to his family and his food. You know how it is—when you're married your time isn't your own." Had he already guessed that she was alone, separated from her husband? "You seemed pretty cool downstairs, but I thought I'd come and check up on you." His eyes went from her face to circle the room, checking up on that too.

"That's real kind of you. I'm fine. Well, maybe a little shaky round the edges." She reached for the bottle. There was a slight reflexive motion of his hand—nobody moves on Heandy till he's ready for it—before he gave it to her. She offered him a drink, more out of politeness than in anticipation of his acceptance. He said he'd have a short one. His eyes never left her as she poured and handed him the glass.

"So what are you doing up in this neck of the woods?"

"I'm writing a book. And I'm up here looking for an agent." She was about to make herself sound less serious by mentioning that she wrote historical romances, but he just loosened his tie, spread his arms on the back of the couch, and said, "That's interesting. I've thought of writing a book myself. Hell, I guess everybody says that," he added with a grin. "That is, I've thought of writing a book once I get too old for the real action."

"I expect you see plenty of it." She moved to a chair and sat, pulling her skirt down.

"That's why I'm in the business. I'm going to school nights to get a degree in criminology. I'm gonna be a detective. Thought about being a lawyer, but it's too tame. I wanna figure out why things happen, not just pick up the pieces."

"I guess that's what I'm trying to do. Figure out why things happen instead of—" she broke off. It was hardly necessary to provide more information to a man who already seemed to know more than she'd like him to.

"Yeah. I know what you mean," he said evenly. "Hot in here, isn't it?"

She thought of her damp panties strung along the towel rack and hoped he wouldn't ask to use the bathroom. "I could turn on the air conditioner."

"Naw." He drained the glass and stood up. "I gotta go." He stretched with the slow movement that showed an acute awareness of his body. She could imagine him pressing weights in front of a mirror. "I thought since you were new in town I might show you around. Nothing safer than having a cop as a tour guide."

"That might be fun," she said coquettishly, though she knew that her eyes already betrayed an attraction that made her hesitation fraudulent.

"It will be fun," he determined. "How about next Saturday? I go to classes during the week."

"Saturday would be fine, I guess."

"Seven?"

"Fine."

"And don't be scared." He turned at the door, touching her chin with his index finger. "If the scums have hit on this building tonight they won't be back for a while. Besides, I'm not convinced that this wasn't a put-up job."

He turned and went down the stairs, obviously aware that he was leaving her with a remark so provocative that she'd have to think about it, if not about him, for several days.

Chapter IX

"I'm fancy free, and free for anything fan-cy," Cordy sang along with the Fred Astaire record, pasting her armpits with deodorant stick, slathering lotion on her just-shaved legs. She stepped into her beige lace pants. Lucille had been right about one thing: A girl couldn't feel really well dressed unless she started from the skin out. Besides, you never knew if . . . She straightened up, shaking her breasts into her brassiere. Self-deception was the worst dishonesty. Of course she knew: She was going to bed with Sean Heandy.

She took her birth control pills from the cabinet and popped one into her mouth, making a face at its bitterness. A few years ago, wanting another child but yielding to Lupton's decision to postpone it, she'd actually gagged when she took the pill, but she masked her feelings of anger and frustration by complaining about its danger to her health. Yet she'd kept on taking it even after the separation, rationalizing that hormonal change would add to her upheaval. Perhaps that had been another self-deception, but right now she didn't want to investigate it. She scooped some water into her mouth, swallowed, and turned her attention to trivial and more pleasant choices: blue or brown eye shadow, her own Chanel or Maggie's Cabochard?

She bent forward again slowly brushing her hair. It had been months since she'd spent so much time grooming herself. She'd moped about, wallowing in self-pity, letting her hair go stringy, and sometimes wearing the same clothes two days in a row. Now she patted, buffed, stroked, and polished herself. Was she the sort of woman whose ego was so dependent on male approval that she wouldn't even bother to clean her teeth unless she knew some man might smell her breath? "Yes," she muttered a quick benediction, giving herself a final check in the mirror. Her hair had frizzed slightly with the humidity, but fell around her shoulders in thick curls. Her eyes, wide and bright with anticipation, artfully shaded, were fringed with mascara; her lips were the same glossy red as her satin blouse. She'd pulled it off. She looked terrific. "Serves you right, Lupton." Dance-stepping into the living room, smiling at the slithery friction of her legs (it was really too hot to be comfortable in nylons, but men were always suckers for garter belts), she set the needle back to the middle of the record and settled down on the couch, as though she was the birthday girl waiting for her guests.

She read her horoscope in last month's *Vogue*, crossed and re-crossed her legs, and wondered if she was slim enough to look really good in the white suit. When the clock showed ten minutes past the hour, her fragile confidence threatened to shatter. Fred Astaire's breezy optimism evaporated, and she threw the magazine aside, listening to the click-slide-click of the needle, but rooted to the spot. What if Sean stood her up? She got up and flipped through the records. Something light and gay, in the old sense of the word, was required, but her hand paused on Billie Holiday's *Empty Bed Blues* album. There was nothing like giving way to an old-fashioned "I feel sorry for myself and I don't give a damn" blues. If he didn't come she'd go whole hog; for even self-pity demanded a certain style. She'd put on her robe, turn off the lights, plunk the bourbon bottle down on the coffee table, and listen to the whole damned record.

The buzzer sounded on the first chorus of "Mean to Me." She almost ran to hit the buzzer that would let him into the front door, but was composed by the time she heard his knock. She offered him a drink, but he declined, looking as uncomfortable in his suit as she felt in her nylons. "I'm double parked," he explained without bothering to apologize for being late. "Could you just get your keys? I've made reservations at the World Trade Center. The food's lousy, but I figured you'd like the view. I never go to places like that myself."

"You don't have to treat me like a tourist," she said, her relief at not being deserted making her voice sound overbright.

She was pleased and surprised that he had a big car. Maggie had said that few New Yorkers bothered to keep one in the city. She

stayed close to her door, acutely aware of the few feet of space between them, as Sean ran a red light, careened around other cars, and
pointed out buildings in a casual, husky voice. She gee-golly-goshed
her appreciation, amused at the way the concertgoers at Lincoln
Center rushed and shoved their way to their leisure, fascinated by
the panorama of lights, fountains, and banners. As they came to
Times Square she was appalled by the row upon row of porno mar-
quees and the grungy milling crowds that spilled over into the street.
But there was no denying the excitement of it all: this nighttime
subliminal beat, even more pulsatingly frantic than the city's
daytime rhythms, the neon lights, the masses of people, aggressively
fun-loving, motley, and elegant. How different it was from the near-
deserted tree-lined streets of home.

After he'd maneuvered the clots of midtown traffic, Sean turned
onto a darker potholed road near the Hudson River. His commen-
tary had wound down and he seemed lost in his own thoughts.
"What did you mean the other night when you said the burglary
might be a put-up job?" she asked.

"Oh, that," he answered laconically, shoving the dashboard
lighter in and reaching into his pocket for a pack of cigarettes. "For
one thing the locks weren't busted."

"But you didn't dust for fingerprints."

"Hell, y' know how many burglaries we do in one night? In one
week? You don't need fingerprints to see if a door's been forced.
That one hadn't been. If that guy you were with was as interested in
burglaries as he was in interior decorating he'd have noticed that. Do
you always run around with homosexuals?"

"He's an upstairs neighbor," she said quickly. "We were both
flustered. I mean, you don't walk into your building to find out that
it's been ripped off without being upset."

"O.K. First the lock. Second, you didn't see anyone leavin'
when you walked the half block to the building, and since no other
neighbors were home, we can assume that the burglar or burglars
didn't have to leave in a real big hurry. So, dummy"—he gave her a
sideways glance and a grin that took the edge off his words—"why
didn't they get that fur cape? Didn't you notice it hangin' in the
closet? A fur, a stereo—easiest things to unload, but they didn't take
'em. My guess is that they were after something else."

"But what?" She did feel dumb for not having noticed.

"Who knows. Drugs. Documents. Love letters. You'd appreciate that wouldn't you? Some guy pouring out his heart on a piece of

paper? They still do it, y' know. There's more crimes of passion here than there are in any Sicilian village. And your neighbor, the chick who looks like Diana Ross, she was onto it."

"Sylvia?"

"Yeah. You don't think all that screamin' she did was for Black Pride Week, do you? 'Cause she's an Oreo cookie if I ever saw one. But she's streetwise. She knew something was up. She'd probably given out several sets of keys and she wanted us to dust so she could try to nail the guy who'd ripped her off. You're a writer, aren't you? You should train yourself to be more observant."

"I don't write detective stories." She made a dismissive motion with her hand, wondering why she'd never bothered to take off her wedding ring. "Though since I've been alone, I have started noticing things more. I guess being alone makes you watch out for yourself."

"Only in the first stages. After that you get ingrown, like a toenail. And New York is the place for it: Ego City. Hey, look up ahead. See the twin towers? We're almost there." He started telling her what was wrong with the buildings at the same time he talked of them with pride. New Yorkers, she had noticed, were always quick to douse their praise with criticism and complaint, displaying a protective quick-wittedness that was opposed to the "If you cain't say somethin' nice, don't say anythin' at all" tradition in which she'd been raised.

The view from the restaurant windows was impressive, and she said so; the cuisine, as Sean had predicted, was nothing to rave about, so she made no comment. After his second scotch, Sean volunteered some information about himself. He'd been born in Boston, "closer to the Combat Zone than to Harvard Yard," and had run away to New York as soon as he'd graduated high school, because his mother had him marked for the priesthood. Sean, she saw, had enough trouble being confined in a suit, let alone a clerical collar. She lowered her eyes and swirled her shrimp in the hot sauce, imagining him as the perfect Hollywood priest. He would battle the corrupt cardinal, mortify his flesh, then succumb to it (just this once!) with a beautiful parishioner.

"And what about you?" he leaned forward, his eyes inviting confession.

"Oh, me." She smiled, imagining what her resume would sound like: height: five foot six; weight: usually ten pounds over what it should be; distinguishing marks: strawberry splotch on the left buttock; education: two years of college (though I'm vague on what happened between the Holy Roman Empire and the French Revolution); religion: agnostic (though I go to church on special occasions and "pray" in fits of despair); marital status: very confused; occupation: mother, former housewife, would-be writer; hobby: worrying about money. And I'd rather be in bed with you than be cross-examined just now. "Well, I . . ."

"Tell me about the book you're working on."

"I'm finishing up this piddlin' little romance now. It doesn't have a title, though I'll bet you dollars to doughnuts it'll be something about Surrender, Passion, or Ecstasy. But"—she gave a little shoulder and a little smile—"I'm working on a proposal for a book I'd really like to write. It's about Fanny Kemble."

"Who?"

"She was a famous English actress who later became a writer. Her life has all the elements of high romance, but the difference is that it really happened. When she was on tour in America, she met Pierce Butler and married him. Pierce had inherited plantations in Georgia, so he took Fanny and their children down to St. Simons Island. St. Simons is very near my home, so that's another reason I'm interested in her story. Anyhow, Fanny was violently opposed to slavery, which led to a good deal of strife between her and Pierce. She published a book called *Journal of a Residence on a Georgian Plantation*. Some historians think that it may have influenced the English not to come into the Civil War on the side of the Confederacy. Finally Pierce divorced her. It was a very messy and scandalous divorce, but since she destroyed many of her letters and diaries there's plenty of room for conjecture about their relationship."

He was nodding, but it was difficult to tell whether he was really interested, yet she kept on, too caught up in her own enthusiasm to care if his interest was genuine. For a split second she wanted to be back at the typewriter instead of sitting and watching him watching her, the ice melting in their glasses. "If I . . . if I can write it . . . if I can write it *well*, it'll be a departure from the formula stuff I've been doing. I want to concentrate on the reasons for the marriage and the divorce. You see, Fanny wasn't your typical Victorian lady panting after a rich husband. She'd made her own money, so there was no financial pressure to marry; and she was, as I've said, internationally famous, so it certainly wasn't for the prestige. I don't believe she was cut out for the married life at all, yet she chose it and then abandoned it. Not too many women left their husbands in the 1850s."

"There's sure enough women who'd do it now," he said flatly, leaning back in his chair.

This was one subject she had no desire to pursue. She pushed her plate aside and blotted her lips with the napkin.

"How was the shrimp?" he asked, reaching for a cigarette.

"Oh, fine. Just fine."

"So you're interested in crime."

She couldn't remember expressing interest in crime as such, but apparently he'd had enough information about Fanny Kemble's marriage and Cordy Tyre's aspirations. She nodded.

"I wish you luck with your book." He raised his hand, motioning for the check. "Now how about hitting a place where there's a little more action?"

"A place where cops hang out?"

"Hell, no. Most cops are hanging out in front of colored TV's in Long Island City. The joint I'm talking about is in Spanish Harlem. It's where the PRs who've made it take their girls. The band plays good salsa. Do you like PR music?"

She nodded again, though she had no idea what he was talking about. A club in Spanish Harlem promised more excitement than a restaurant full of Japanese and Arab businessmen.

He drove back uptown with the recklessness of his privileged status; and she, equally ready to show abandon, rolled down her window and let the breeze whip through her hair. He brought the car to a bouncing halt on a slum street near an open fire hydrant. A slew of near-naked kids dashed in and out of the spray of the hydrant, shrieking to each other in Spanish. She blinked at the neon signs: CUCHIFRITOS . . . DISCOMANIA . . . BODEGA. He guided her past a block of stores, one with garish religious statues and pop records, another with faded travel posters showing Anglos strolling the beaches of Puerto Rico, Jamaica, and Santo Domingo. She wondered why a tourist bureau would be open at eleven o'clock, but Sean said it was a front for a numbers racket.

Boxes of green bananas, oranges, pineapples, and coconuts were piled high in front of a grocery store, scenting the humid night with ripe-ready-to-decay smells that almost overcame the reek of garbage cans that overflowed into the gutters. Flies buzzed around a tray of sticky multicolored candy. Boys in T-shirts eyed young girls with brilliantly painted faces. Women with fat brown arms sat on stoops nursing babies and chattering like magpies. Chairs had been dragged onto the sidewalk, and the men crowding around the rickety card table that had been set up beneath the streetlamp hooted and slapped their money down.

Wild, repetitive drum beats throbbed from an upstairs window as they turned into a darkened street and Sean pushed the door marked SOCIAL CLUB. Maggie had said something about New York not being very different from eighteenth-century London, and as she sidestepped the garbage, followed Sean into the hallway, mounted the stairs, and looked down at her perspiring cleavage, she thought she might have stepped out of a Hogarth engraving: Country Lass Being Led to the Highwayman's Den.

The club's version of a maitre d' stood at the top of the stairs beneath a hand-lettered sign demanding a twenty-dollar cover charge. His black hair, plastered so flat that it might have been painted on, and his ruffled tuxedo shirt made him look like an agitated penguin. When Sean started to take out his wallet, the man smiled unctuously and waved them through the velvet curtains. The inner room was dark except for moving flecks of light from the mirrored ball above the dance floor and a pink spotlight on the tiny bandstand. The noise was deafening. The cheeks of the trumpet player distended to the size of tennis balls as he wailed high, insistent notes; the drummer thrashed about wildly, and the dancers were a mass of swirling skirts, tossing heads, and undulating buttocks.

"You wanna dance?" Sean asked as though it were a dare. "I'll get you a partner if you wanna dance."

She shook her head and felt her way to the seat at the ringside table. She could smell the waiter's hair oil as he inclined his face toward her to ask what the señorita would like to drink. Shrugging to Sean—it was impossible to be heard—she turned her attention back to the riotously exhibitionistic flash of legs, arms, and faces. A few sips of the piña colada that was put before her quelled the nervousness.

"That guy," Sean's breath was warm against her ear. She followed his eyes across the room to a man in a pale suit, white hat, and heavy gold jewelry. "He's the kingpin just now. He's got the coke trade sewed up from Avenue A to the Bronx." The man, who was sitting bolt upright like a wax judge, raised his glass to them before returning his gaze to the dancers.

"The chick in the purple—the one with the stems—she's his main squeeze." Cordy looked at the girl in the iridescent plum-colored dress. She was stomping flamenco style, flicking her petticoats high onto her dark thighs as her partner in the ass-constricting pants thrust his pelvis toward her. Sean sat back, one arm draped on her chair, his nostrils flared slightly, his eyes slit to the removed, totally absorbed gaze of the voyeur. The air conditioning was hitting her back, making her shiver, but as he took her hand, turning it over so that her palm was up, and covered it with his own, she felt flushed. It was the first time he had touched her, other than for the social nicety of taking off her jacket or guiding her along the street. She felt the excitement of danger at a safe distance, and rubbed her thighs together to feel that tingly friction again.

It seemed the musicians must finally take a break, but they kept on, mesmerized beyond fatigue, adding hoots and bird cries to the hypnotic rhythms. Sean was drinking slowly and steadily, his leg now jerking under the table, rubbing hers as he beat out the rhythm. She refused another drink, but scooped the foam that clung to the side of her glass onto her fingertip and sucked it. His eyes shifted to her and he leaned forward, staring into her face. Either the liquor had hit him and he was making a conscious effort to focus, or else he was about to say something important.

"You shouldn't write about the past. Only people who're scared or dreamy write about the past. 'Cause it's easier to try to understand what's already been than it is to try to figure out what's happening now and what to do next."

"I thought you said you were going to be a detective. Isn't . . ." The question was swallowed in the din.

"It's like my poor ol' grandfather getting a shine on and telling us about all the goddamn revolutions that didn't come off, or my mother bellyachin' about why she married my father in the first place," he went on emphatically. "The past is about defeat. Anything that's already happened to you, you might just as well forget because you don't learn from it. People don't learn. It's hopeless."

The tiny vertical line between her eyebrows creased as she leaned into him, straining to understand. Was he talking about a bad love affair, disillusionment with some religious ideal, or his work? The loss of faith was plain enough, but she wanted to know its source. He released her hand abruptly, as though she were incapable of taking the point, got to his feet, and stood behind her chair. "You wanna go? You can't hear yourself think in here."

The penguin man smiled a thousand smiles of farewell as Sean pressed a bill into his hand. The night heat assaulted her before she'd reached the street, and the receding beat of the music made her feel as though she'd left something behind. She would have liked to dance.

The street was quieter now. The fire hydrant still gushed, but the children and women were gone. As Sean opened the car door and she turned to get in, he pulled her to him. Looking over his shoulder, she saw the night hawks stumbling by—drunk, drugged, or dazed by the heat. He could have slid her to the pavement right there and nobody would have noticed or cared. Their cheeks brushed and his mouth moved onto hers, his tongue entering slowly, sliding over her partially closed teeth. Excitement struggled with apprehension and quickly overcame it. She closed her eyes, yielding to the pressure of chest, legs, and groin tight against her own, her mouth opening to receive the insistent probing of his tongue. Only when he released her did she feel the water from the hydrant sopping through the soles of her high-heeled sandals.

She slid into the seat and bent to take off a sandal, wondering if she should ward him off and arrange another date. "No self-respecting girl . . ." But that maxim was for other times, other places. He turned on the motor, then reached down, slipped the other sandal from her foot, and dangled it from his finger; then, with a smile of irresistibly audacious confidence, he let it drop to the floor. Slithering his hand up the length of her leg, he toyed with the clasp of her garter belt. She was grabbing him or he was clutching her, she couldn't tell which. All she knew was that she didn't want to think about anything, because he/she/they had already decided. "Hot in here, isn't it?" he said as he let go of her and reached for the steering wheel. She nodded, her eyes slits, her head lolling on the back of the seat. He took her hand, placed it between his legs, and pulled away from the curb. She knew that if he could negotiate the streets and she could get her legs to go up those stairs to Maggie's apartment, she was going to go to bed with him.

The phone rang three times before she bolted up in bed, realizing that she hadn't turned on the answering machine. Lunging for it, she felt a strange leg. Oh my God! A naked, hulking male body.

"Hello?"

"Mama, is that you?"

"Mmmm . . . yes."

"Doesn't sound like you."

"It's me darlin'," she whispered. "I was . . . still asleep."

"How come? Nonnie and I have already been to church an' had pancakes."

"Well, I . . ." She glanced back at the bed. He was beached, legs spread, arms extended (it was lucky he hadn't pushed her out of bed), the coil of his penis resting in the matted hair of his groin. "I was still asleep."

"Are you sick?"

"No, darlin'." She cleared her throat, but her voice still came out in a croak. "Hold on, Jeanette. I wanna take the phone in the other room."

"Why do you have to go in the other room?"

"Just hold on." Dazed and shocked, as though she'd actually been caught in the act, she pulled the crumpled sheet from the foot of the bed, struggling to drape it around her as she picked up the phone. Sean didn't move or open his eyes.

"I'm back, darlin'. How are you?" She was blinded by the glaring sunlight in the living room. She felt sticky and sore.

"I'm fine, Mama. We went to Nonnie's church. It's not like a real church." She could hear Nonnie's voice registering a correction in the background. "And we saw a movie about all kinds of things that grow an' then we held hands and sang a song."

"That sounds real nice."

"An' guess what! Nonnie bought me a hermit crab."

"Oh." She caught a glimpse of herself in the mirror above the bookcase. Her hair looked as though something could nest in it, there was a smudge of mascara beneath one eye, and her jaw was raw from the abrasion of his beard. "What does the hermit crab eat?" she asked, in the measured, inquiring tones of education majors or proud mothers on public transportation.

"He eats hermit-crab food." Jeanette disdained such an obvious question. "An' I'm calling him George after Mr. Naughton. You know that man Nonnie knows who has hairs in his ears?"

"That's nice." Sean's clothes were strewn on the couch and floor, as were most of her own. One of her high heels was on the coffee table, next to her beige lace pants and two empty glasses. A book of erotic poetry she'd seen on the shelf but never opened lay facedown on the windowsill. She tried to reconstruct the sequence. Yes, his hands had parted her here on the couch, and at his first shuddering gurgle she'd wondered if Maggie's peach upholstery would show the christening. They'd made it to the bed for the sec-

ond round. "And how's Nonnie?" Her eyes searched the pillows for
telltale stains.

"She's here an' she wants to talk to you."

"O.K., darlin'. You get back on so's I can tell you goodbye."
She worked up some saliva and swallowed, hoping to smooth the
roughness of her voice. "Hello, Nonnie?"

"Hey, there, it's me. How y' doin'? Jeanette was feeling kinda
lonely for your voice, so I told her we'd give you a call after breakfast. George took us to the pancake house. I swear, Jeanette's got
him wrapped round her little finger. How's the weather been up
there, darlin'?"

"Oh . . . hot. But I've got air conditioning."

"Yes, you told me before. Lord, did we have rain last night.
Real frog-strangling weather. Thunder got Jeanette all upset. Or
maybe she was just itching for an excuse to sleep with somebody.
Tell me whatch've been up to?"

"I'm fine. Just fine. I've been working real hard."

"But are you having a good time? Meeting some people?"

"Yes, I went out on a date last night," she said sotto voce, glancing toward the bedroom door.

"That's just wonderful, Cordy. What all did you do?"

"You know. The usual." If you only knew. "Dinner, then on to
a club with some music."

"I'm real pleased to hear that. What's the young man like?"

"He's . . ."—he's got a voice that sounds like wheels spinning
out over gravel, he drinks too much, he has a gold ring with a skull
on it, and that's just a minor clue to his slightly deranged personality, and he's terrific in the sack—". . . very nice."

"What does he do?"

"He works for the police department, but he's going to school
nights."

"Ah-huh."

"We went to this nightclub and listened to salsa." Cordy rushed
on, knowing that Nonnie would have already dismissed Sean as a
man "without prospects."

"What's salsa?"

"Latin-American music. Sort of a cross between a samba and
disco."

"Why, that's fine. I'm glad you're having a good time. Next
time he takes you out you get him to take you to Radio City Music
Hall. Hold on, Jeanette! This child is so persistent. I'm going to

hand her back the phone. I didn't see any harm in indulging her with a call, 'cause the rates are low on Sundays, but I'm gonna hang up now. I'll call you on Wednesday an' we'll have a real conversation. Take care, darlin'."

"Thanks for calling."

Cordy sat on the couch and waited for Jeanette to get back on.

"Mama, it's me again."

"Yes, Jeanette."

Sean came out of the bedroom, yawning and taking the sleep out of his eye with his index finger. He stared over at her, still dazed, before a slow grin of recognition curled one side of his mouth.

"I sure wish you were here, Mama."

"Why darlin'? Do you miss me?"

"No, I'm fine. It's just that"—Jeanette dropped her voice to a conspiratorial whisper—"Nonnie won't let me watch TV. She says TV makes you stupid."

"Well, you have to mind Nonnie, Jeanette." Sean stretched out on the couch, burrowing his face into her lap and making growling sounds. He grabbed her ankle, then slithered his hand up under the sheet. "I told you to do what Nonnie says."

"But what about the Muppets? I always watch the Muppets."

Sean's fingers were probing and tickling now. Ripples of pleasure were fanning out from between her legs, engulfing her belly and thighs. She shook her head for him to stop and tried to push his hand away.

"The Muppets?" she said, her voice caught between a moan and a laugh.

"I always watch the Muppets. Grandpa Jake and Grandma Lucille let me watch the Muppets."

He was pulling the sheet down from her breasts and she was struggling to hold on to it. She wrenched free, stifling giggles, and stood up, letting his head drop unceremoniously onto the couch. He lunged for the sheet and yanked it from her with one swift pull. She grabbed for it, but he held on, daring her to come after it.

"Jeanette, I don't want you to be givin' Nonnie any trouble, do you hear? She loves you very much an' she wouldn't be tellin' you anything that wasn't for your own good," she panted. "An' I'm glad to hear about your hermit crab." Sean stood up and held the sheet out like a bullfighter's cape, urging her to come for it. "I'll be callin' you on Wednesday night, darlin'. We can talk then. I've gotta hang up now. I love you."

"I love you too, Mama. Bye."

"Bye."

She dropped the receiver and ran toward him, grabbing for the sheet as he raised his arms, warding her off. "Oh, you creep," she laughed. "How could you do this to me?"

"You sure lay it on thick with the 'honeys' and the 'darlin's'."

"It was my daughter," she said, feeling embarrassed.

"I figured." He backed off and threw the sheet at her as though he'd lost interest in the game. She wrapped it around her and side-stepped him.

"Where do you think you're going, Cordy?"

"To the bathroom to brush my teeth."

"Come back here." He sprawled on the couch again and held out his hand.

"Sean, we're right by the windows!"

"And I could've sworn there was a bit of exhibitionism in you last night."

"Only in the bedroom. I'm an' ol'-fashioned girl."

"Then let's go into the bedroom." He rose and advanced toward her, backing her up to the door. "I'm kinda old-fashioned myself. I'm a morning man."

He grabbed her suddenly, pinning her arms behind her. The sheet fell to the floor. He caressed the fleshy part of her arms, then let his hands slide down, cupping her buttocks and pulling her tightly against him. His nose wrinkled as he sniffed the musk of last night's encounters.

"I could clean up," she whispered, her legs already trembling, anticipating exertions, and her gaze holding on his languid, slightly bloodshot eyes.

"Later," he groaned, already hard against her. "Later. If you're a good girl I'll take you out to brunch."

They stayed in bed until early afternoon, when Sean checked the clock and said they'd have to pass on the brunch.

As he showered, she hummed to herself and made a pot of coffee and scrambled some eggs. He was in a rush now. He came out of the bathroom toweling his hair, pulled on his pants, and only sat down for a few minutes, shoveling the eggs into his mouth. He gulped down the coffee but refused a second cup as he buttoned his shirt and said he appreciated the sort of woman who'd make breakfast instead of insisting on being taken out. "That's a great thing about women who've been married." He grinned. "They're house-broken."

"Housebroken?" She flashed an acid smile. "I think that applies to pets."

"Hey, touchy, touchy." He put up his hands in mock surrender and backed off. "I meant it as a thank you."

While he laced up his shoes, she busied herself by making toast she had no intention of eating. His remark had revived the annoyance she'd felt when he'd intruded on her phone conversation, and his rapid preparation for departure made her feel suddenly at a loss, as though she had something left to say but couldn't remember what. Should she walk him to the door, kiss him goodbye as though he were going off to work while she returned to the dishes? What a swift return to domesticity. She was scraping the last of the marmalade out of the jar with single-minded concentration when he came up behind her, wrapped his arms around her, and rubbed his jaw along her cheek.

"Ouch, that's still scruffy," she said, turning her neck at an awkward angle to look at him.

"You ought to keep an extra razor."

"I'll keep it in mind," she said casually, still intent on the marmalade. What did he think this was, the Hilton? On the other hand, it was good that he'd noticed she hadn't set up shop to entertain overnight guests. Last night, just at the point where there was no turning back, she'd wanted to let him know that she didn't make a habit of going to bed with men she barely knew. Now, leaning against him, chewing on the toast, she felt she liked him again. She waited for him to say something.

"What you going to do today? Write some more?"

"No, no. I'm going back to bed. Jealous?"

"No, baby. I've got work to do." Another quick squeeze as he released her, and then the words she wanted to hear: "Hey, I'll call you later."

When he was gone she reheated the coffee and took a cup into the bedroom where Queen Victoria glowered down in judgment. She threw off her robe, straightened the crumpled sheets, and rubbed moisturizer into the tender skin of her chin. She shook her head and chuckled. Just her luck to be woken with a call from home the morning after she'd taken the plunge. She hoped she hadn't sounded as shocked as she'd felt, otherwise Nonnie might have guessed. Broadminded as Nonnie was, she still thought of sex as the consummation of One Great Love. And Lucille, her head crammed full of notions of Togetherness and conformity from 1950s movies and magazines, Lucille wouldn't even be able to imagine the freedom of taking a lover just because you wanted him. But, she thought as she stretched out, surrendering to sweet morning-after lassitude, she didn't have to think about any of them now. She was in another city. No one knew what she was doing or cared. She was nobody's wife or daughter or mother. "Sean and I will have a hot, carefree affair that'll last the summer," she murmured. "I guess it *is* like riding a bicycle, you never forget how."

Chapter X

"George Naughton, I swear you take a perverse delight in thwarting my instructions," Nonnie complained as she opened the door to his Lincoln Continental and saw Jeanette sitting in the back seat licking an ice cream. "That child had a platterful of pancakes and syrup but forty minutes ago and now you've gone and bought her a cone."

"I just didn't want to sit here while you were inside, so we took a drive to the drugstore," George grumbled as he backed out of the parking lot of the Azalealand Nursing Home. "You know this place gives me the willies."

"I could throw the rest away," Jeanette volunteered.

"No. You can't be wastin' things. Now that you've got it you go on and finish it," Nonnie ordered.

Jeanette rolled her tongue around the rim of the soggy cone and kept silent, studying the folds in Mr. Naughton's neck. The creases of hard fat reminded her of a pink bulldog.

"So how's old Cora holding up?" George wanted to know.

"Looks about the same to me," Nonnie said. "I'm not real sure she even knew I was there."

"That's what I told you. Visiting Cora is just a waste of time. You only go out of your self-righteousness."

"I said I wasn't sure she knew *I* was there," Nonnie corrected.

"I didn't say she didn't notice the flowers I brought her 'cause I know she did."

"Well she sure wouldn't've noticed me," George said firmly enough to convince himself.

Nonnie pursed her lips and waved her palmetto fan in front of her face to circulate the blasts of icy air coming from the dashboard. If she fussed at George he'd just come up with more excuses for not visiting, so it was best to leave him to struggle with his conscience. Not that anyone could look on a visit to Azalealand as any sort of pleasure; it was one of those things that had to be done, then put out of your mind as quickly as possible. But it was hard to put it out of your mind. The sight of Cora Masters, her eyes the color of milk glass, her blue-veined, spotted hands never moving from her lap, always left Nonnie with a residue of sadness and impotence. But as long as Cora showed even a glimmer of recognition, she felt obliged to keep up her weekly visits. Some sixty years ago Cora had been one of the first ladies of the city to open her door to her and sponsor her into the ranks of the Right People. That was a debt of which she would always be mindful. She shook her head, her mind groping toward the murky but benevolent Providence that had, thus far, spared her the debilitation she'd just witnessed. Turning to George, she contented herself with an oblique reprimand: "There but for the grace—"

"Not me, Nonnie. When I get to that helpless stage I'll play the noble Roman."

The car went over a bump and the water from the can of flowers Jeanette was holding between her feet slopped onto her leg. She couldn't understand why Mr. Naughton wanted to play a Roman. She'd seen Romans on a TV show, and Mr. Naughton would look silly in a short skirt and a gold helmet.

"That's what everyone thinks, George, but something happens to people toward the last. Anybody's who's enjoyed living usually has to be pried loose from it. Me, I'm just gonna keel over 'neath a rose bush in m' back garden and you can leave me there for fertilizer."

"So you've got everything planned, have you? Think you're gonna be able to engineer that too."

"Don't see why I shouldn't try." She smiled at him now, tilting her head to one side. It was good of him to chauffeur her around like this. "I'll try not to take too long at the cemetery, George. Don't expect you'll want to stay and help us with the gardening?"

"I surely do not. I'll take a walk down by the river while you're about your business and pick you up in about forty-five minutes."

"That's right sweet of you." She reached into her purse for a handkerchief and waved it over her shoulder. "Here, Jeanette, lick your fingers clean an' wipe 'em on this. Be careful of Mr. Naughton's upholstery."

The car rolled past the open iron gates into Bonaventure Cemetery. Jeanette turned her head to see the statue atop one of the pillars—a woman with long hair with her arms wrapped around a cross. As Nonnie rolled down the window, Jeanette could feel the air hot against her face. There were no other cars or people in sight, but Mr. Naughton was driving ever so slowly because the dirt paths were narrow and winding every which way. There were huge oak trees trailing gray beards of moss; slabs, crosses, and statues sticking up from the ground; urns and pillars; six-pointed stars made of stone; and little ghostly houses without doors. She craned her neck, trying to catch a glimpse of a white angel statue. The car came to a stop. Mr. Naughton got out, held his hand to help Nonnie from the car, then opened the back door for her to get out. He wheezed as he lifted the basket of garden tools and the pail of flowers from the floor and put them beside a low iron fence. She tried to swing on the gate but it was rusted into the earth.

"All right, you two. I'll see you in a while." He lumbered back into his Continental and drove off.

Nonnie waved and set her straw hat on her head. "This is the Hampton plot," she explained, drawing on her gardening gloves and setting the rubber mat on the ground next to the biggest stone. "Do you want to stay with me, Jeanette?"

"No. I want to see that white angel." She pulled at her wet sock. "Can I take my shoes off?"

"Yes, you *may*. But don't go too far. The paths are all higgledy-piggledy and it's easy to get lost."

It was as quiet as quiet could be. Jeanette held her breath as she walked away. Soon even the sound of Nonnie's humming was lost in the still, heavy air. Spots of sunlight dazzled through the trees, and when the breeze blew from the marshes it had the clean, sweet smell of mud mixed with all the perfumey smells from the honeysuckle and the camellia bushes. She found the white angel and close by it the statue of a little girl wearing funny shoes that buttoned up the side. Looking around to make sure that she was completely alone, she crawled up and touched the girl's broken nose. The caw-caw of a bird made her jump. She twirled around three times to ward off any evil spirits, then ran toward the clumps of wild greenery closest to the marshes, standing absolutely still until another breeze came through the blanket of air and made the wet around her forehead feel cool.

Stepping over low iron fences, pausing to spell out the messages on the stones, she came to a patch that looked as though the ground had hiccoughed and sent the stones all crooked. Maybe she would get lost. Maybe she'd have to spend the whole night here with just birds to talk to. If she did she'd go back to the statue of the girl, and maybe if she brought her some berries or something the girl would come alive if the moon was full. She heard Nonnie call her name and ran as fast as she could in the direction of the summons.

"I saw a statue of a little girl," she panted as she reached Nonnie's side.

"That's Lil' Gracie."

"I know. I read her name. She died of ponu . . . I couldn't read it."

"Pneumonia."

". . . when she was only six years old."

"Don't worry 'bout that," Nonnie said without looking up. "It's most unusual for children to die these days. Course, when I was a girl we didn't have good medicines, and lots of children died."

"Any you knew?" Jeanette examined her dirty toes.

"Surely. Two of my own brothers died of diphtheria, an' another was carried off with polio. So any time you hear someone talk about the good old days, you'd better know they've gone soft in the head. It was a very sorrowful thing to have little children dying."

"How many brothers did you have?"

"I had"—Nonnie paused, tapping the dirt from the trowel against a stone—"five brothers and four sisters, counting the ones who died. One of them so small we could've buried him in a shoe box."

Jeanette pulled at her fingers and held them up, incredulous. "Nine. You had nine brothers and sisters?"

"That's right."

"What were their names?"

"There was Matthew, Mark, Luke, and John. There was Henrietta, Rosana Mae, Tabitha, and Hannah. And baby Benjamin. Benjie was my favorite. He was the last born, and Mama was so played out by then that Benjie was more like m' own baby than a little brother."

"That's so many kids," Jeanette whistled, squatting down. "There's only that many kids in my Brownie troop."

"Here, Jeanette, don't be acting like God took away the use of your limbs. Pull out some of these weeds."

"How can I tell which ones are weeds?"

"What are you, darlin', senseless or lazy? These are weeds." Nonnie yanked a handful of scraggy grass and held it up.

"My hands will get dirty."

"Then you'll wash them in the water from the watering can. Bless me, you'll try my patience yet." Nonnie looked at her sharply before she resumed her digging. Then she started to talk again in that soft singsong voice she used when she told bedtime stories. "Yes, Tabitha—or Tabby I used to call her, same as we called the cat, just to get her mad—Tabby was my closest. She had hair about your color. Prettiest hair, color of resin from a pine tree. We'd take turns braidin' each other's hair before we went to sleep at night. I'd tell her stories while she brushed my hair, an' when she stopped brushin' I'd stop tellin'. Oh, I could spin those stories out over a week or more just to keep her brushin' my hair."

"Did you get to sleep with her?"

"Not much choice about that, since we had but three rooms in the house," Nonnie chuckled, resting back on her haunches. "That place was so tiny you could hear each other's dreams."

"I wish I could sleep with somebody. Were you bossy to Tabby?"

"Naturally. I was her big sister."

"I wish I could be a big sister. I can't be a little sister anymore, can I?"

"Oh, we did have some fine times," Nonnie continued. "Tellin' stories and singin' to each other by the candlelight. An' my cousin Andrew! Now he was the one who could tell stories. I fell in love with Andrew because of his storytelling."

"I thought you were only in love with Grandpa Lonnie."

"No. Andrew was my first true love."

"Did he kiss you?" Jeanette wanted to giggle, but if she acted silly she might stop Nonnie's stream of talk. It was pouring out, slow and heavy like the syrup she'd drowned her pancakes in this morning.

"Yes he did." Nonnie smiled into the can of flowers and touched their faces. "He kissed me several times and scared the life out of me. He wanted me to run away with him."

"Where was he going?"

"He went off to fight in the Great War and he never came back. I don't mean he died. He just never came back. He didn't talk much 'cept when he was tellin' stories. I remember . . ."

Jeanette glanced over to the headstone nearest her: "Wade Andrew Hampton, 1920–1945. Lost his life in the service of his country." This was the man she wasn't supposed to talk about. He'd gone off to war too, but it couldn't have been the one Nonnie was talking about now.

". . . and Andrew had the most expressive eyes. You could look into Andrew's eyes and find out just about everything you ever needed to know about lovin'."

"But you married Lonnie instead."

"Never any question in my mind about marrying Lonnie. Only question was whether he would ask me. Probably the best moment of my life when he asked me to be his bride. Then I knew that all the things I'd ever hoped would be." She was breathing hard now, her eyes darting beneath the straw hat to appraise her handiwork. "Now"—she smiled contentedly—"we've made Lonnie's place all pretty and I suppose"—a deep, resigned sigh—"I suppose, I'd better do something to make Mother Hampton's grave look respectable."

"'Ettie Payne Hampton.'" Jeanette spelled out the name on the largest stone. "'Born in Savannah, 1871, died in the sixty-ninth year of her age, 1941. With hopeful eyes we look to thee, O Lord.'"

"Humph," Nonnie snorted. "That's what she wanted on the plaque, so that's what we put; but the only time Mother Hampton's eyes were hopeful was when she looked at her bankbook. Otherwise, she'd like to go cross-eyed looking down her nose at other people. Headed up every charitable organization in town, and the strain must've hurried her death, 'cause she didn't have a charitable bone in her body. That woman! May she rest in peace. Only way I could live without holdin' a grudge toward her was if I had an impaired memory. She made my life hell from the first day I met her. Course, Lonnie realized what was goin' on. He knew she'd keep him her baby boy for his en-tire adult life if'n we didn't strike out on our own. Yes, your great grandfather was a man of highly tuned sensibilities, Jeanette. I'm sorry you didn't know him, but never let anyone try to tell you that he wasn't just this side of perfect. 'And now abideth faith, hope, love, these three'"—she shaded her eyes and read from Lonnie's stone—"'but the greatest of these is love.'"

"Then it says, 'One Cor. thirteen,'" Jeanette piped up proudly.

"Cor. means Corinthians. I'd best start to read you the Bible, Jeanette, or your education will be sadly lacking. Just as long as you remember that it's just a book."

"I know it's a book." Not to be told that there was anything wrong with her education, Jeanette turned and started to spell out the stone next to Lonnie's. "'Eunnonia Grace Hampton, 1900—'" She spun back to look at Nonnie, her eyes round with a fearful question.

"Yes, darlin'. That's reserved for me. I used to think I'd want to go to my own family's place, but that was a long, long time ago. Besides, it's pretty here, isn't it? Smelling of the yellow jasmine, wind comin' off the marshes, two hundred years' worth of the best an' the worst company in this part of the world."

The breeze sent a tremor through the tops of the trees, dappling Nonnie's face with bright yellow and blue shadows. She sucked in her lips the way she did, so they weren't hardly any lips at all, and gazed around her, her eyes watering from the glare. "And you can hear the bees and the birds. The birds and the bees." She smiled again, making her lips reappear. "When I was a girl that's what we called talk about love and having babies and such."

"I know where babies come from. Mama showed me a book about how Daddy planted my seed. And my friend Janet in Chicago got to watch a TV show where you even saw the baby coming out. I wanted to watch it too, but Mama said—"

"Help me up, Jeanette an' set those flowers in the middle of Lonnie's stone." Nonnie shook her head and brushed off her skirt. She could feel her heart go phut-phut-phut as she took Jeanette's hand and struggled to her feet. "Now wash off your hands. I don't want you to be getting dirt on George's upholstery. I wonder if you'll have any stomach for dinner since he loaded you up with pancakes and ice cream and what all. Well, we'll see how you feel after you take your nap."

"Nonnie, I don't have to take a nap," Jeanette said disgustedly. She could hear Mr. Naughton's car coming toward them. "I stopped taking naps when I was four years old. I'm too old for naps."

"And I'm too old to be able to get through the day without them. You don't have to sleep. You can come into bed with a book for yourself, or just lie there and think about your navel, whichever you please."

"Can I watch TV?"

"There's nothing on TV on Sunday afternoons."

"There's football," Jeanette said mournfully. "I used to watch the football games with Daddy."

"Football's in the autumn," Nonnie said with a little snorting sound. Jeanette examined the scab on her elbow and slowly dipped her hands into the watering can. She knew the reason the air came through Nonnie's nose like that was because Nonnie didn't like to talk about her Daddy.

Mr. Naughton was getting out of the car and coming toward them. His trousers were wrinkled and his face had turned redder. "Godsakes woman," he mopped his forehead with his handkerchief. "It's about a hundred degrees out here. You won't get a chance to expire under that rose bush of yours; you'll die of heat prostration right now if we don't get into someplace that's air conditioned."

"Don't get yourself into an uproar, George. I'm packed and ready to go." She handed him the basket of gardening equipment and reached for Jeanette's hand. Jeanette smiled up at them. The way they talked to each other reminded her of how Cordy and Daddy used to be, except Mr. Naughton never slapped Nonnie on the behind or grabbed at her the way Daddy did with Mama.

"Now compliment me, George. Tell me if it doesn't look nice." Nonnie surveyed the weeded and decorated plots, creaking forward to pick up the watering can.

"Another exercise in self-righteousness, Nonnie. We could be sitting on your veranda sippin' a cool drink right now," George wheezed.

"You didn't think I'd impose on you to drive us all around without rewarding you with a glass did you? After Jeanette and I take our beauty rest you can come on back to the house. Just a cold supper. Lucille and Jake are drivin' over for dinner to pick up the baby."

"I was planning on having dinner at home," George said, not to be won over too quickly. "There's something on *60 Minutes* I want to watch."

"But I planned on your comin', George. I just forgot to ask you. Besides, Jake won't want to be sittin' there with a bunch of women."

"Trying to resist your orders is as hopeless as peeing against the wind," George chuckled.

"Lil' pitchers," Nonnie cautioned, her eyes moving to Jeanette's head. "C'mon, darlin'"—she raised her voice—"let's get organized. Into the car with you."

The windows were opened and though they were three stories up and faced the garden, the shutters were pulled to for privacy. The stripes of late afternoon sunlight glanced off the frames of the paintings and washed the pale yellow wallpaper of Nonnie's bedroom. The silence was as dense as an undisturbed pool of water. Jeanette, fresh from her bath and wearing only her underpants, hiked herself up onto the big bed and flopped around to make the canopy shake.

"If you don't stop that tituping around you'll have to go into your own room," Nonnie said in that way that showed she didn't really mean it. She walked around the room holding her cotton wrapper closed with one hand and touching things with the other. Her hand played over the silver brushes on the dressing table, switched on the ceiling fan, and arranged the rose satin coverlet at the foot of the bed. Satisfied, she eased herself down next to Jeanette.

"Want me to fan you, Nonnie?"

"That would be a blessing."

"But if I do . . ." Jeanette sat cross-legged, the fan poised above her head. "If I do, then you have to tell that same thing you told last night."

"That's just for the rainy weather. But I'll make a bargain with you. You lie down and close your eyes while you fan me and I'll tell it again."

"How come you always do a bargain when I try to do a bargain?"

"Because I'm a mean ol' grandmother," Nonnie laughed, stroking her head. "Did you get all the soap out of your hair?"

"I think so," Jeanette yawned in spite of herself.

"All right then, settle down an' I'll tell you the poem."

Jeanette propped the pillows beneath her head and wriggled down so that her feet could touch the coverlet. She would stroke the satin with her toes and close her eyes as she'd agreed to do, but she would not go to sleep. Instead, she would think her secret wish and count all the pictures in the room three times to make sure that the wish would come true.

Nonnie began in a soft, croaky voice:

> "I used to love those little rains
> That slip from out the sky
> Like the wraith of a storm that must move on
> But lingers in passing by."

The room went all pale and muzzy as Jeanette pretended to shut her eyes, and her arm felt heavy as she moved the fan back and forth. How she hated that boy in the playground! He'd showed her his football cards but he wouldn't believe her when she said her daddy used to be a football player. And when she'd told him that Lupton was in Chicago, he'd said she was from a "broken home." That made her so mad she didn't even want to look at his old cards anymore.

> "But now I hate those little rains
> All day I sit and cry
> When I hear their murmur on my roof
> 'Twas in rain that you said goodbye."

Jeanette's arm had dropped across her chest. Nonnie waited to make sure the child was breathing steadily, then took the fan from her and resettled herself onto her back, her breasts sloping to her sides, heavy and shapeless as bags of birdseed. Her own children and her children's children had collapsed against her like this. And before that, when her chest had been smooth and hard as a piece of pinewood, Tabby or Hannah, Mark or Luke, whichever came first into the lumpy iron bed. Oh, that creaky, nasty bed. And that stubborn little farm where she'd grown, its parched red earth suffering just to yield up turnips and corn. The cold, numb-fingered mornings with chores to be done. The lone cow Jessie, who'd died of the mastitis. The prayers and fights around the bumpy table. Mean enamel dishes that hit against your teeth as you slurped the last mouthful. And afternoons like this, the still, stifling oppression of Georgia heat. Sleepy, mean afternoons. The one scraggly tree in the yard, the clay around it beaten flat by bare feet seeking just that bit of helpless shade. Ignorance profound to dwell upon and be comforted by such memories, what with the ceiling fan cooling her now, this healthy child's sweet-smelling hair, and right outside the window her verdant, steamy garden.

"An' tell me what you did today, sweetheart," Lucille wanted to know when they were all seated at the dining-room table.

Jeanette moistened her lips and looked around. The dishes were shining in the candlelight, the roses in the center of the table reflected their petals in its high polish, and there were so many different things to eat it was almost like a party. Mr. Naughton was scraping a drop of cold peach soup from one of his chins. Grandpa Jake was smiling at her as he carved the ham, and Grandma Lucille, who was leaning forward encouraging her to speak, looked just like a peacock in her bright blue and green dress. She paused and turned to Nonnie. When they were preparing for the supper, spooning the relishes into the glass and silver bowls, Nonnie had told her that it wasn't polite for children to talk at the table. Jeanette had explained that she and Cordy always talked to each other while they were eating, but Nonnie had insisted that was different. But now Nonnie, her hair shining like a silver cloud in the glow of the candles, was nodding for her to go ahead.

"Went to the cemetery and read the graves," she said proudly.

Nonnie kept bobbing her head like one of those toy birds that keeps dipping until you stop it.

"You went to Bonaventure on a day like today?" Lucille cried, touching her hand to her neck. "Really, Nonnie! It can't be very entertaining for a little child to spend her day at the cemetery. What were you trying to accomplish? Heat stroke or depression?"

"That's what I told her," George said.

"I see nothin' wrong with going to the cemetery," Nonnie bristled. "Jeanette was interested in seeing where her relatives are resting. She had a fine time, didn't you, Jeanette?"

"She couldn't have had a fine time," Lucille insisted. "You are the only person I know who—"

"Bonaventure is a beautiful place. Why Mary Aiken visits the cemetery all the time. She goes to pour a libation on Conrad's grave. I've always thought that was both a loving and a civilized thing to do."

"It's morbid. That's what it is. Plain ol' morbid."

"This ham's delicious, Nonnie. And the potato salad . . ." As with any hint of unpleasantness, Jake seemed to be only superficially involved, but when he leaned forward to pass George Naughton the platter of ham, he nudged Lucille's thigh with his own. Her head stretched itself out of her already strained neck and she gave him a sidelong glance so chilly that he knew his touch had been misinterpreted. He had intended to show agreement and comfort, but she had taken it as a signal to stop criticizing her mother.

"Why thank you, Jake," Nonnie said with somewhat martyred dignity. "It's only a cold supper, but with the weather being so warm an' not even the gasp of a breeze—"

"Biscuits are hot." George helped himself to the plate Nonnie was offering. "That's all I care about."

Lucille folded her hands in her lap. Her lids drooped, so that she seemed to be admiring the roses, but Nonnie could tell that she had lowered the curtain on her thoughts and would probably pout for the rest of the meal. Does she ever go out of bounds except in sleep? Nonnie wondered, peeved at her daughter's passivity. She would have enjoyed a lively debate on the rightness or wrongness of exposing children to the realities of death. "Won't you take a biscuit, Lucille?"

"Too many calories, Mama." Lucille shook her head, then raised it to smile, apparently willing to join the conversation again. "I'd say that's the one fault of Southern cooking. Too many calories."

"If you're worried about calories how come you were raving on about how good the food was in Italy? How come you brought back that cookbook with all those spaghetti recipes?" Nonnie asked.

"Oh, pasta. I adore pasta. It's so"—she searched for the right word—"sensual."

Nonnie snorted and set down the plate of biscuits.

Jake laughed. "It's not the pasta that's sensual, it's lollin' around the beach and watching those young fishermen bring in the clams for the sauce that's sensual."

"I'd say Southern cookin' doesn't have *any* faults, leastways not when Nonnie's in the kitchen." George cut into his ham.

"Honesty compels me to confess that Bernice made the biscuits, George. But since you're enjoying that watermelon-rind relish so much an' that *is* something I can take credit for, remind me to give you a jar when you leave. And you take a jar home too, Lucille."

"Oh, Mother," Lucille said. "Isn't it possible ever to leave this house without being loaded up with a jar of this or a panful of that? You still cook as though the en-tire family lived at home. I expect that's just your Depression mentality actin' up again."

"Now, young lady," George said sententiously, sure of his ground if the conversation were to be divided along generational lines. "If y'all could remember the Great Depression you'd know it put scars on our minds that can never be eradicated. Why back in nineteen and twenty-nine, cotton was goin' for twenty cents a bale an' by thirty-one it had fallen down to eight. You'd see men walkin' the streets looking like they'd just been hit on the head with a two-by-four. Ships rusting in the harbor . . ."

"Why things were so bad even George here had to turn radical and support Mr. Roosevelt," Nonnie teased.

". . . banks closin', farms lying fallow, couldn't get credit anywhere," George ranted on, refusing to rise to Nonnie's bait. "Remember how ol' man Barnwell had to auction off his Packard?"

"I surely do," Nonnie joined in. "I remember the very night he came here to talk to Lonnie, trying to get a loan. An' that yellow-faced son of his trailing after him blubbering how he couldn't get over to Switzerland to see the mountains like he'd been promised. Course, Freddie Barnwell never did have a lick of sense. That weakness came from his mother's side of the family. Was Amanda Barnwell a McKelway or a Cook?"

"She was a McKelway. Don't you remember when Charles McKelway gave her away at the wedding?"

"Now let me think . . ."

Lucille pushed her plate aside and brought the napkin to her lips. Now that George and Nonnie were batting memories back and forth she didn't have to keep up the pretense of being involved. She touched her thigh where Jake had nudged her. The gesture had given her a mild shock, not because she was unaccustomed to his occasional squeezes under the table, but because it had reminded her of that first touch of forbidden flesh last night. She had thought it a mistake when Jacques Haur's knee had touched hers so she'd pretended not to notice. But when his eyes—full of challenge—had met her own, her suspicion, and perhaps her hope, had been confirmed. Then later still, when he'd walked her to the dock (Jake, thank God, had stayed in the house to watch the dancing), Jacques' hand had slithered to her shoulder and rested there as she'd chattered about the stars.

She'd been obliged to look at the stars every night since Jake, in one of his attempts at "lifelong learning," had bought a telescope and a stargazer's map. She'd repeated Jake's little joke of christening the constellation of the Three Sisters "Lucille, Constance, and Vivian." Jacques had cut her short by saying that he didn't need to learn about things, he only wanted to enjoy them. She'd stood, chastised and trembling, afraid to look at him, and turned her face to the darkened skies. The stars were beautiful. Luminous and lovely enough to bring an ache to her throat. How was it that she'd never been so moved by them before?

"Have you left us altogether, Lucille?" Nonnie wanted to know, pushing her plate aside and moving toward the sideboard.

"Luce is tired, aren't you, honey?" Jake said. "We slept in late this morning. Didn't even get up for church. But I still don't think we made up for last night. We went to a pretty wild shindig at Jacques Haur's place."

"Haur? Haur?" Nonnie pursed her lips, mentally shuffling through her vast list of acquaintances.

"I don't think you know him, Mother." Lucille smiled.

"He's a new neighbor of ours," Jake explained. "We'd heard tell he threw some pretty wild parties and Luce finally got herself invited to one. I tell you, I haven't been to a party like that since I left the Army; and if memory serves, I don't think Luce has ever been to such." Jeanette's presence prevented further elaboration. "It was still goin' strong when we left at two, which is way past my bedtime."

"There was a pit barbecue an' there were lots of young people there," Lucille said nonchalantly, sweeping her hair back from her face.

"Why don't you gentlemen go on into the library and make yourselves comfortable," Nonnie said as she opened the cedar box inlaid with tortoiseshell and offered it to George. She liked the custom of sending the men off after dinner so that she could take care of the more important business of putting the food away and giving herself a breather. If only she'd remember to stock the box more regularly. "I do hope these cigars are fresh."

George belched, covering his mouth with his hand, before accepting one. "I've sworn off smoking," he grunted. "But . . ." The pleasure of being back in Nonnie's good graces and the bourbon he'd had before supper encouraged him to abandon caution.

"Jeanette, darlin', help me carry these dishes to the kitchen."

George put his arm around Jake with the elaborate informality that men of importance use toward their inferiors. "Now, Jake, what's your opinion of this debate that's goin' on about raisin' the Talmadge Bridge," he asked as he led him from the room.

Nonnie watched George go with an indulgence that bordered on affection. She hoped she hadn't maneuvered Jake into a session of intolerable boredom, for George had a habit of never asking a question for which he didn't already have an answer. But, she forgave herself, Jake was a bighearted, charitable man. If he could put up with Lucille's foolishness he could surely put up with twenty minutes of George's rhetoric.

She did worry about George, though, especially since he'd had his bypass operation. His housekeeper, she'd learned from Bernice, only stayed with him out of economic necessity and periodically punished his cantankerousness by threatening to quit. What George really needed was a man servant, one of those snooty but devoted butlers she'd seen in English movies. Because George had a deep mistrust of women. He was always too ready to praise womens' natural superiority; and that was a sure sign that he didn't really know or like them. In the old days, the gossip—sprouted without a seed of evidence and nurtured by the growth elixir of wild speculation—had it that George was a great womanizer. She herself had been convinced that his frequent trips out of town "on business" had something to do with physical release, for she had occasionally received his lustful glance. But his escapades must have been of a purely biological nature. The only body George Naughton had ever really loved was the body politic. He had run for governor in the 1950s and she'd seen him almost swoon when he'd been applauded by the crowds. Perhaps because this passionate affair with mob adoration had ended in such a surprising defeat (he'd lost by a mere five thousand votes), George cherished and was haunted by the memory as much as any girl who'd been stranded at the church door.

"He's not such a bad ol' bullfrog," she muttered to herself as she picked up the soup tureen and started out of the room. Then, as though she had eyes in the back of her head: "No, Jeanette. Take one thing at a time an' use *both* hands."

Jeanette bit her lip with a fierce air of concentration, held the plate of ham at a respectful distance, and followed her out.

Lucille sat alone for some minutes before the muffled conversation from the library and the clatter of dishes from the kitchen intruded and forced her to rouse herself. She collected the crumb catcher from the sideboard and swept the table in long, slow strokes. Starting toward the kitchen to offer the assistance she knew would be refused, she paused in the shadowy passageway. Her hands trembled as she stopped to rearrange her hair in the mirror, and her face swam toward her, eyes questioning and accusing. She pulled the neck of the peacock blue dress away from her chest and sent a cooling breath onto her breasts. She'd started to wear her pink caftan tonight, but as she'd taken it from the closet, she'd remembered a game Ellen Hamilton had initiated at the last bridge party. "Of course it's just foolishness," Ellen had laughed, waving a copy of *Color Preference and Personality*. Yet after Lucille had selected her favorite, Ellen had smirked as she read, "'Pink is the color of tenderness, protection, and gentility. It is the choice of people who prefer the passion of red but haven't the courage to choose intensity.'"

She gripped the edges of the hall stand and shut her eyes. How many cold suppers on how many hot summer nights had she endured? How many recitations of past glories, stifled arguments, and comparisons of recipes had she submitted to? She had learned to suppress her emotion, grown to think that it was better that she didn't feel or know what she felt. Perhaps the core of Jacques' appeal was that he did what he wanted to do, and devil take the hindmost.

Of course he was a playboy. She was not so blind as to be ignorant on that score. She'd seen him eyeing the tight little backsides of the girls at the party last night, just as she'd surreptitiously watched as he'd hunched over the wicker table on his veranda indulging in some illicit ritual. Snorting cocaine, she'd presumed, though delicacy had prevented her from asking. Yet he had left the others and walked her to the dock. And she had seen those stars as perhaps she'd never seen them before. Jacques had made her feel alive. Thoughts of him had filled her all day long, giving everything a secret significance, making her feel that she had a real private life.

Why was she so stupidly timid? Almost every woman she knew had had an affair at one time or another. Some even said it helped their marriages. And her own daughter, without any visible emotional problems, was blithely walking away from her marriage, though she refused to discuss it with her. She could imagine what a high time Cordy was having in New York, so why shouldn't she seize this chance—perhaps her last chance—to experience the love affair she'd been waiting for all of her life? Her imagination reached out, grasping for some image vivid enough to support her yearning. The reality—a solicitation from the resident playboy—was not enough justification. But Jacques had sought her out with a purpose. Over all the younger women he had wanted her.

"Age cannot wither nor custom stale her infinite variety." Those words. She had had to ask the teacher what they meant when, as a girl, she'd been forced to read *Antony and Cleopatra*. Her teacher, a woman no longer young, at least by the standards of high school juniors, had stared out the window as though she, and not her pupils, counted the minutes until the bell released her from the imprisonment of the classroom. "Antony and Cleopatra were contemporaries," the teacher had explained. "That means that they were the same age. Cleopatra was possessed of physical charm, but she was more than a beauty. She was a woman of substance. Antony chose her because she was mature; a woman of profound appet—" The teacher had corrected herself: "Profound interests." Lucille had remembered that teacher because she'd committed suicide during the summer vacation. Everyone said it was because she was in poor health, but Lucille had always felt that those few short sentences about a play that had been written three hundred years ago had been the clue to the woman's self-destruction. Remembering the incident now, she felt a shiver of awe.

"Are you all right Lucille?" Nonnie's hand was on her wrist. Lucille turned to see her mother's face peering into her own with genuine though slightly annoyed solicitation.

"We'll have to be going soon, Mother. Jake told you we had a late night."

"But come on into the library before you fly away, honey. I want to talk to you about Cordy."

"She called us last week."

"I knew that girl could do wonderful things if she was just given a little push. She's gonna see an agent next week. She told me life's so hectic up there it's enough to make you tired by the middle of the day. Course, it's an adventure. I told her . . ." Nonnie released her wrist and started toward the library, sure that her voice was enough to oblige Lucille to follow.

Jeanette, who had been standing unnoticed in the kitchen door, came toward her and offered her hand with what seemed to be an intuition of Lucille's misery.

There was another half hour of conversation—George ranting on about local politics, Nonnie talking about Cordy as though she were nominating her for the Nobel Prize—before Lucille was able to catch Jake's eye and signal that she wanted to leave. When they had finally disengaged themselves from repeated embraces and injunctions to safe driving, they dropped old George off at his house, settled Jeanette into the back seat, and turned toward home.

Lucille was silent, lolling her head against the back of the seat, her eyes partially closed.

"You were awful quiet tonight, Luce. You feelin' all right?"

"Just tired," she smiled wanly. "I was limp to begin with, and listening to George always makes me feel like I've had two Valium.

Poor you, stuck with him in the library. What was he goin' on about? His influence in the state legislature?"

"No. He wanted to talk about Nonnie. Wants her to go to Europe with him, and he thought I'd put in a good word."

"Go to Europe with him?" she laughed.

"That's what he said. I told him I didn't have much influence with her."

"You have as much as anybody, 'cept maybe Cordy."

"Pull my shirt away from my back, will you, Luce," he bent forward, shoulders hunched to the wheel. "Lord, it's after midnight and it still feels like sittin' in a furnace. S'pose it will ever cool down?" And after a pause: "You think Nonnie would go with him? She's unpredictable if nothing else."

She stared out the window. After thirty-odd years of marriage they both asked questions for which neither one required or expected an answer.

"She's predictable enough to me," she said after a time.

"Hmmm." The half query, half acknowledgment eased him back into the conversation.

"Taking Jeanette to Bonaventure! It's bad enough that the child doesn't have her parents with her."

He jerked his head toward the back seat, and she nodded to assure him that Jeanette was sleeping. "And when we were all in the library," she went on, "Nonnie spelling out 'divorce' when George asked how Lupton and Cordy were doing. I swear! *We* don't know that they're going to get a divorce. Leastways Cordy hasn't seen fit to discuss it with me. And Nonnie blurting it out in front of George Naughton! It'll be all over town tomorrow, you can count on that."

"Ah, don't worry about that, darlin'," he said quickly, to relieve his own distress. "Nonnie's got ol' George so bamboozled that he won't dare gossip. You know what made me laugh? When she excused herself from spelling 'divorce' by saying that spelling in front of young'uns was an incentive for them to learn."

"Well, she always has the last word. You know that." He nodded sympathetically and she felt a sudden rush of tenderness toward him. "No, Jake, to me there's nothing as predictable as Mother."

"That's what families are like. It's not so bad." He reached over and squeezed her knee. "Maybe predictability is what makes us feel secure."

"No one's secure and no one's predictable," she flashed.

"Not entirely," he drawled. He was too tired to point out that she'd just contradicted herself. "But recognition, knowing each other"—he fumbled toward some distant but promising understanding of human relationships, for understanding of human relationships had occupied much of his thought since retirement—"knowing each other, even if it means accepting less desirable qualities"—and here he chuckled—"it binds us into a kind of unavoidable love. Or," he added humbly, "or at least an affectionate toleration." He loosened his grip but did not take his hand from her knee. Covered with the slippery stuff of her dress, it felt both soft and substantial. He could have spent an unmeasured amount of time in the contemplation of Lucille's knee.

His words caused her to look at him with the affectionate toleration he was talking about. She curled her arm around his neck and moved closer to him. He was, undeniably, a good man.

"I've planned out the whole week," she said with sudden energy. "I've invited Ellen's granddaughter to come stay the night tomorrow. Tuesday we'll go to that oyster roast at the Barneses' place. And Wednesday I'm gonna take Jeanette shopping. She's such a pretty little girl I hate to see her running around in jeans and tops, though Nonnie doesn't seem to mind."

She turned to look at the child sprawled on the back seat, her overnight bag clutched to her chest. She'd only been in her early forties when Jeanette was born and she'd hated the idea of being a grandmother, but now the child's presence restored her sense of proportion. It was shameful that she'd been thinking of no one but Jacques Haur. She vowed that she would never go the distance of a mile to his house.

"Lordy, will you look at those stars," Jake whistled, rolling down the window. "If you're not too tired when we get home we can take out my map 'cause I bet we can see Fomalhaut in the Southern Fish tonight if we use the telescope."

Lucille nodded and shut her eyes.

Chapter XI

Sean did not call on Sunday night. He did not call on Monday. By Tuesday afternoon, as Cordy sat at the typewriter and struggled to give Roxanne a final push into Lord B.'s crushing arms, her fingers would periodically freeze on the keys and her eyes would be drawn to the phone. It had now become a mute instrument of torture instead of an appliance.

She shook her head, rolled a page out of the machine, and read it:

The Lady Olivia's jet black hair glittered with jewels. Her self-indulgent lips, stained with cochineal, smiled at Lord Buckingham over the candelabra. Her bosom was thrust high, nestling invitingly in the delicate lace of her décolletage. The gold of her peau de soie gown cast shimmering lights into her seductive eyes, which were hard above the fluted edge of her ivory fan. Roxanne blushed to the roots of her hair and cast her eyes down at the lavishly set table. She knew that Lady Olivia was a wanton, a woman who gave herself without shame, caring nothing for the feelings which, Roxanne knew, lurked in Buckingham's tortured heart.

"Good for you, Lady O. Don't waste your time on the bastard," Cordy said as she took a swallow of her iced tea. It was too bad that she would have to punish Lady O. in the end, but those were the rules. The Rival had to be punished because she was not dependent on the Hero's Love. Historical, gothic, or contemporary (in which case Lady O. would be an executive in a model or advertising agency where Roxanne would be minimally employed until rescued by marriage), the Rival was always more interested in Sex than in True Love, and she was always tainted by those dastardly, unwomanly qualities of ambition and self-confidence. The Rival was never seduced and abandoned. She did not sob. She did not wait patiently for the Hero to discover his true feelings, nor did she leave home, family, or job to trail after him in hopes that he would make an honest woman out of her. She didn't need to be an honest woman. She already had her own money. "Poor isn't sexy," Maggie had instructed. "Aggressive isn't feminine. The Heroine has to get her money through a man. The man has to be handsome, older, *and* rich. That's the fantasy. That's what the readers want. Over and over again. Just change the costumes."

When Cordy had worked at Koegh's Bookstore and devoured three or four romances a week, she'd known this but had never taken the time to analyze it. She'd wanted to escape the dependency of her own life, and the happy resolutions the books provided were a comforting fantasy when she'd waited for Lupton to come home. Now she wished she could twist the ending and have Lord B. (who was, after all, better at swordplay than he was at figuring things out) succumb to Lady O.'s designs. Then Lady O. could have a playmate, Lord B. could have someone to direct his life, and Roxanne . . . What could happen to Roxanne? Cordy chomped on a piece of ice. She'd lost the thread of the plot. Here she was on the twentieth chapter and Roxanne was still battling for Lord B.'s affections. She looked at the telephone again, willing it to ring, then rolled another piece of paper into the typewriter.

Lord Buckingham skewered a hunk of venison on the tip of his knife and offered it to Roxanne. "You are pale, Lady. Your taste has deserted you."

"Let her be." Lady Olivia smiled. "We are not all fortunate enough to be possessed of strong appetites."

The phone bleated. Cordy sprang for it, knocking the glass of tea onto the completed page. It was Maggie's successor at Chrystallis. He asked if Maggie was having her mail forwarded or if he should still send it to the apartment. Mopping up the spill with the sleeve of her nightdress, Cordy suspected that he was really asking how Maggie was doing in California, and she gave him the address on the Coast. Almost as an afterthought, he introduced himself and said that he was expecting the Roxanne manuscript in another two weeks. Cordy assured him that she would have it ready by then, but as soon as she'd hung up she groaned. The thought of retyping one ruined page was too much for her. The temptation of an afternoon nap was so great that she knew she'd best get out of the apartment. A closer examination of the slipcover of the couch cushion had revealed a telltale stain. She would take it to the cleaners, then walk to the park. The walk might revive her enough to let her pound out another few pages before the six o'clock news.

The phone was ringing as she came up the stairs from her walk. She tore at the locks and ran to pick it up, already phrasing a surprised, lighthearted acceptance of Sean's apology.

"Goddamn it to hell. I am sorry," a tense female voice with a Western twang cursed. "I'm so screwed up, what with overwork and all, that I must've dialed Maggie's number out of habit."

The caller then introduced herself as Maggie's friend Maxine and by way of apology suggested that she and Cordy get together for lunch.

Cordy hung up in disgust and went back to lock the front door, which, in her eagerness, she'd left wide open.

After a supper of reheated pizza, she abandoned Roxanne and worked on the outline for the Kemble book. By midnight she had taken up her old position next to the windows. She turned off the lights and stretched herself out on the couch, her bare feet resting on the towel she'd wrapped around the uncovered cushion. The counterman at the dry cleaner's had stayed stoney-faced while she pointed out the spot on the slipcover, but she was sure she'd detected a secret sneer.

She cupped her hands over her breasts, blessing the whisper of a breeze that came through the open windows. The guitar player across the street had taken up his usual post and was fumbling through "Black Is the Color of My True Love's Hair," repeatedly breaking off toward the end of the song. It was a perfect accompaniment for her continuing postmortem on Saturday night.

She tried to think it through again. It must have been her fault. Because she was so unaccustomed to going out with men, she had been too conscious of herself to pick up any real clues about Sean. He had spotted her as needy. She had said yes too quickly; therefore he had thought of her as less desirable. But the physical attraction had been real enough. No man could fake that many encores. Per-

haps Sean was married. But if so, how had he managed to stay overnight? She almost banged her head against the wall when she
remembered Lupton's absences. It was the easiest thing in the world
for a married man to arrange for a weekend away from home.

But—she shifted about, unraveling, teasing, picking at her
thread of thought—intuition rejected the idea that Sean was married. He had probably considered her a one-night stand. That was
part of the trouble, for she had assumed that since they were sex-
ually compatible and she made no demands they would have a brief,
passionate fling. It might even be said that she had used him to drive
out thoughts of Lupton, thoughts which no longer sent her into crying jags but still had the compulsive, repetitive quality of a commercial jingle you couldn't stand but found yourself humming twenty
times a day.

Yes, she had used Sean. Used him to make her feel pretty, to
make her know that she was desirable. Why, then, did she feel used?
Because—she fixed on it with a vehemence—because he had lied.
He had sniffed out her unspoken plea for continuance and answered
it with a meaningless promise to call that had gotten him off the
hook. It wasn't fair.

She had a mind to call him up and tell him what she thought of
him. But even if she'd had his number, she knew that she wouldn't
call. A woman might call a man before she'd bedded down with
him, but afterwards the rules changed. The seeming equality of desire was lost once it had been acted upon. For what woman was
thick-skinned enough to risk rejection *after* the fact? Even though
she'd given herself willingly, more than willingly, she felt somehow
that she'd been conquered. She'd been had. And the damned cleaning bill for the damned slipcover was going to cost her twelve ninety-
five!

She jumped up from the couch, determined not to waste any
more time thinking about Sean. In the bathroom, she threw off her
clothes and stepped into the cooling spray of the shower, but as she
scrubbed herself with a loofah, a last insidious memory returned to
devil her. Just before Sean's empty promise, he'd said he was going
to work. Yes. Slam-bam, thank you, ma'am, but I have important
things to do in the world. Therapeutically relieved of sexual tensions, he had gone off to take care of his obligations, without a second thought for her. While she had allowed herself to be distracted
when she should have been finishing the Roxanne saga and working
on the proposal for the Kemble book. Her economic future de-

pended on that book, yet she hadn't given it a tenth of the attention she'd wasted on a hard-drinking Irishman with good pectorals.

Roughly blotting herself with the towel, she compounded her foul mood by blaming herself for it. She reached for the antacid pills. One day soon, if she didn't succeed in pulling herself into line, her anxiety would congeal into a nice big ulcer. And one day soon the money problems she'd stuffed like so much junk into a never-to-be opened mental closet would come tumbling out like the nasty, unmanageable mess they were. Tomorrow she must get up early and really work. Tomorrow she must call Abigail Pinkston Silverstein and do her best to get an appointment. She strode across the darkened living room and slammed the window shut. If that creep of a guitarist couldn't master the fingering on the tenth try then he'd damned well better practice inside, regardless of the heat.

Naked, lying on the bed, she watched the shadows on the ceiling and tried to ignore the thrump of Sylvia's stereo.

She completed the proposal for the Kemble book the next morning, but by midafternoon, when she returned to Roxanne, her concentration was gone. Sliding between nervousness and apathy, she cranked out another seven pages, pausing now and then to indulge in homesick fantasies. She longed to see Jeanette. She might be out at Tybee Island now helping her find shells. She might be lolling in Nonnie's garden listening to a funny story. As the temperature and the street noise peaked, she felt so enervated that she even fancied her mother's company. Lucille would be shopping or boating or sitting on the patio sipping a spritzer. Lucille's life was pleasant and secure, while she, Cordy, was sitting in a rented bedroom, her backside melting into the chair, trying to dream up a wardrobe for some imaginary characters from the eighteenth century. If only she were home in Georgia she wouldn't feel so irritable, so driven. She could slow down, drift half dazed through a sultry afternoon, but here, even in sweltering heat, the energy of the city vibrated, demanded that she *do* something. It wasn't "Y'all relax," it was "Youse guys keep movin'."

She got up, swung her arms around, and touched her toes. She had not had direct contact with another human being in four days, unless she counted the sour clerk at the dry cleaner's. Determined not to go through another stretch of solitary confinement, she picked up the phone. If she was lucky Cliff would be home and she would ask him out to dinner.

Cliff recommended a Szechuan restaurant on Broadway. The

Formica-topped tables, rubber plants with red ribbons around them, and tiny paper parasols in the tropical drinks didn't promise much; but the food was intriguing enough to make her postpone her diet yet again. Cliff tried to teach her to use chopsticks, but after she'd dropped the second piece of ginger chicken into the soy and scallion sauce she gave up and asked for a fork. Between mouthfuls of Moo Shu pork, Cliff told her about his current job at Yale Drama School, but she had trouble keeping her mind on the conversation. When she refused her fortune cookie he said, "You must be feeling down. How 'bout we go see a movie?"

They walked a few blocks and joined a line in front of a grimy little theater that was showing a double bill of Japanese films. The people who were waiting to buy tickets looked as tensely expectant as citizens of some Eastern European country who were lining up for a ration of rare consumer goods.

"Don't be ridiculous, Barry," the girl in front of them was saying to her date. "Truffaut was the first director to use the freeze frame in *The 400 Blows*. Everyone knows that!"

"You got your facts screwed up again, Rachel, and I'll prove it to you when we get back to my apartment."

"I'm not going back to your apartment."

"You have to. I have a copy of *Film History* there. Now when Bertolucci . . ."

Cliff brought his mouth close to Cordy's ear. "That's seduction New York style," he whispered. "Arguing about the cinema is foreplay."

Cordy nodded. They shuffled a few steps closer to the box office. She'd been looking at words all day and wasn't sure she was going to relish reading subtitles with an audience of superserious film buffs, so she didn't mind when the woman in the booth shoved a SOLD OUT sign into the window. There was general consternation in the line.

"I told you we should've left earlier," Rachel said. "This is the second time this year that I've missed seeing *Yojimbo*."

"We can go back to my apartment and I'll tell you all about it," Barry urged, steering her away.

Cliff turned to Cordy. "I don't have a single original thought on *Citizen Kane* and I'm not out to seduce you. Want to window-shop?"

He took her arm and they strolled a few blocks over to Columbus Avenue. The crowds were so thick that they sometimes had to walk single file around the outdoor cafes that spilled onto the sidewalks. "I remember when this used to be a neighborhood," Cliff said. "Right over there was the shoe repair store and next to it was a mom-and-pop grocery. Look at it now: a sushi bar and a store selling erotic postcards. The real necessities of life. When I look at them I start to sound like my father railing against the disappearance of the middle class." They lost each other momentarily in the tide of tourists, hustlers, middle-aged couples out for a night on the town, and street vendors. They window-shopped books, cowboy boots, antique clothes, and French pastries. They bought Italian ices and gave a dollar to a guy playing bagpipes who had a sign on the pavement saying he was trying to earn enough money to get back to Scotland.

"He probably owns a loft in SoHo and wouldn't leave unless they deported him," Cliff laughed as he took Cordy's hand and drew her away. As they crossed the corner near the Museum of Natural History, Cordy saw an old man standing under a tree talking loudly to himself. The crowd moved around him without even seeming to notice.

"I'd never seen people talkin' to themselves till I came here," Cordy said. "It always gives me the shivers."

"You mean people don't talk to themselves in Georgia?"

"Indoors, sure. But not out on the streets."

"I didn't even notice him."

She fell silent as they walked on. It wasn't that Cliff was insensitive, just that he'd had to become callous. It was an adaptive trait of city life, like wearing camouflage in a war zone. Moving through masses of people, you just couldn't let yourself notice and feel sympathy for every unfortunate. And so the tunnel vision became more narrowly focused: the young did not notice the old, the rich did not see the poor, and couples, their eyes so happily on each other and the future, how could couples see an individual muttering to himself? She had probably noticed the old man because she was feeling lonely and lost in the crowd. Just now she was a mouth, a pair of eyes, hands—like all the other hands and mouths and eyes around her.

"Don't get so shook up, Cordy," Cliff said when he noticed the expression on her face. "I was talking to the producer from New Haven the other day, and for all intents and purposes I might just as well have been talking to myself. That old guy under the tree is probably getting off on his own conversation. After all, there's no one to tell him he's crazy."

"Don't you be so mean. You know people only talk to themselves because they're alone. Or"—she smiled—"crazy. But maybe being alone makes people crazy."

"At least he got out of his apartment. You won't even venture out unless you're with someone."

"I work at home," she said stolidly, though she didn't quite believe that excuse.

"Wow, check out those clones." Cliff's head swerved to take in a couple of gay guys in punk makeup and matching silver jumpsuits. "Sometimes I wish no one had ever opened the closet door. But back to you. Maybe you'll stay lucky and all your escorts will come to the apartment to find you."

"What do you mean?"

"Stop acting so innocent. You don't think you're the only one who hangs out the windows and watches the neighbors, do you? I saw you going out with one of New York's Finest on Saturday night. I'm glad someone got something out of Sylvia's burglary."

"How is she?"

"If I were a gossip, what a tale I could tell. She's been screwed, blued, and tattooed. But we're talking about you. How was he? What's the matter? Cat got your tongue?"

"No," she answered slowly. "Truth is he said he'd call the next day and—"

"And of course you haven't heard from him. Hey, don't take that personally. That's standard operating procedure, the graceful way out."

"How can lying be graceful?" she snapped.

"You are a new kid on the block. You'd better get smarter at spotting the types. I could've told you that what's-his-name—"

"Sean."

"Sean's a city boy with city interests. He likes money, crime, politics. Not to say he doesn't like the ladies, but sex for him is probably on a par with the Boston Red Sox—you know, an enduring but seasonal passion."

"How did you get to be so smart?"

"Practice. I've been jilted about a hundred times. Of course, I've gotten my own back at least"—he rolled his eyes upwards, and the spike of his Adam's Apple wobbled as he counted—"at least three times."

"But I'm not promiscuous," Cordy protested.

"Hey, who's promiscuous? You just keep trying to find the

right one, and the numbers start adding up. Watch out." He guided
her a few steps from her path. "Dog shit."

"Thanks, I didn't notice."

"Head in the stars, that's your problem. Forget Sean. Go on to
the next one. Realistically, what's the alternative? Use it or lose it is
what they say. Just keep on trying. Think of sex as indoor sports.
Unless, of course, you've developed the Coyote Complex."

"What's that?"

"That's when you wake up in the morning, your paw is trapped
underneath some guy, and you'd rather bite it off than wake him
up."

"Oh, Cliff," Cordy laughed in spite of herself. "If my grandmother could hear you she'd wash your mouth out with soap. Indoor
sports indeed."

"Do they have soap in Georgia?"

"Don't get sassy," she said as they rounded the corner to their
block, "elseways I won't take you to the gay bars when you come
visit me in Savannah. An' you're wrong about one thing, Cliff. I am
going out alone. I'm going out tomorrow to meet this agent, so wish
me luck."

The interview with Abigail Pinkston Silverstein was so much
easier than she'd thought it was going to be that Cordy was still
dazed when she found herself back on the sidewalk at the corner of
Madison Avenue and 53rd Street. She backed up next to a store
window, stood between a vendor who was squeezing fresh orange
juice and a violinist who was frantically bowing the "Hungarian
Rhapsody," and tried to get her bearings. All of her fears—that she
would be clumsy and tongue-tied, that Abigail would treat her
rudely or, worse yet, be condescendingly polite but then reject
her—had been swept away in a fifteen-minute interview. Abigail
had been in a rush, though, Cordy suspected, being in a rush was as
much a part of Abigail's style as tailored suits and two packs a day.
Abigail had admitted to barely skimming *Tempestuous Love*—"I hate
romances; romances are to women what pornography is to men"—
but her brief perusal of the book, plus Maggie's recommendation
was enough to convince her that Cordy had some talent. And she
was genuinely interested in the Kemble proposal. She urged Cordy
to finish with Chrystallis as soon as possible—"They're not exactly
the creme de la creme of publishing, and now that Maggie's gone the
whole operation could fall apart"—and told her to get started on the

Kemble book. As she'd walked Cordy to the door and shook her hand, Abigail had gone so far as to say that she hoped to sell the Kemble project on the basis of the proposal and a few sample chapters.

Cordy's face, reflected in the shopwindow, had the faraway, slightly imbecilic, but altogether blissful smile of a viewer watching the last reel of a movie with a happy ending. She turned back to the street. It was a marvelous rainbow of colors. Skyscrapers were washed with sunlight. The crowds, which only an hour ago had reminded her of lemmings driven to devastation on concrete shores, now seemed to be boisterous guests at the world's biggest carnival. It was all here. It was all within her reach.

She plunged into the human current, not caring where it would carry her. Oncoming faces smiled. She had an impulse to grip friendly strangers by the arm and say, "Guess what just happened to me!" She bought herself a rose and tucked it into her lapel. She looked into store windows. She dodged traffic with balletic grace and helped a woman with a baby stroller cross the street. She met the eyes of fashionable, high-stepping women with smiling equanimity, acknowledging the sisterhood of the elite. Her affection encompassed sweaty tourists, shopgirls, ogling construction workers, newspaper vendors, children, and dogs. If she hadn't felt so ebulliently sexy, so very conscious of her bouncing rose-decked bosom and the flirtatious glances she shared with attractive men, she might have declared herself a candidate for sainthood, so all-embracing and radiant was her good will.

It wasn't until she'd reached Columbus Circle that she realized she'd worked up a sweat and that her high heels had worn a blister on her right instep. Stepping into the traffic, she raised her hand high, summoning a cab.

She leaned back in the seat, admiring the greenery of the park. She was even charmed by the angora dog and the family photos fixed to the dashboard.

The cabby eyed her in the rearview mirror and took his cigar out of his mouth. "Beautiful day, ain't it?"

"It surely is."

"An' you're beautiful too," he said gruffly, as though it was a statement of fact.

"Why thank you. I feel beautiful today."

"I can tell you do. Some kinds of beauty, y' know, they're only skin deep, but when the spirit animates the flesh, that's real beauty.

It's what y' call an aura. My youngest kid, this one here"—he jerked his thumb toward a snapshot of a young man with a mortarboard cocked on his head—"is a psychology major. He told me all 'bout auras. They do these experiments on 'em in Russia. Take pictures of people in the dark, an' if the people are, you know, feelin' good and powerful, this here red halo comes out in the photographs. That's the aura. But even in the sunlight, I can tell you've got an aura."

"That's one of the nicest things anyone has ever said to me, ah"—she checked his name on the cabbie's license—"Herb. Do you want to know why I feel so good?"

Lebowitz, Herb, much the roving philosopher, of course wanted to know. So for the next thirty blocks Cordy told him as much about herself as she'd ever told any stranger. When they pulled up to her building, Herb cut off the meter and told her to finish her story.

"Like I said, you've got an aura," he confirmed when she'd finished talking. "An' don't worry about that no-good husband of yours. If he don't know what he had he's a jerk who don't deserve no better'n he's gettin'. Good luck with your new book. If y' write as much as y' talk, it's gonna be a good long one."

She wanted to hug him. She shook hands and gave him a two-dollar tip instead.

As soon as she'd stripped down to her underwear, she started on the opening chapter of the Kemble book. Dedication was fine, but there was nothing like outside encouragement and the hope of a contract to revive flagging energy. She worked until after nightfall, then called home to get Nonnie's and Jeanette's congratulations and stories. Then she called Cliff, but his message machine said he'd gone to New Haven again.

Some of the steam went out of her when she realized she had no one with whom to celebrate. Up until now she'd felt her loneliness most acutely when things had gone wrong. Now she realized another, more poignant deprivation of not having someone with whom to share good news. But it wasn't just "someone" she wanted. She wanted Lupton. She wanted him to shower her with the kisses and congratulations she had given to him after a victory on the field. Perhaps, she thought as her fingers played with the dial of the phone, if she approached him in an entirely different way, asked only that he share her good fortune . . . She dialed the Chicago area code, then slowly put down the receiver. Determined not to let her "aura" fade, she called up and ordered some Chinese food, fixed a stiff drink, toasted herself and Fanny Kemble, and sat down to write a letter of thanks to Maggie. When the food came she took it and a copy of Kate Chopin's *The Awakening* into bed with her. Sitting in her underpants, reading and munching on egg rolls, she remembered the nights when Lupton had complained about her having her nose in a book or not fixing supper on time, and felt almost content.

During the next four days she was a prisoner working toward parole. She got up to the alarm, took breaks only to eat food that was delivered, revved herself up with a steady supply of coffee and tea, then doused the caffeine jitters with a heavy shot of bourbon when it was time to sleep.

On Tuesday night at seven-thirty, she tore the final page from the typewriter:

As the coachman whipped the horses onward across the darkening moors, Buckingham pushed tendrils of Roxanne's golden hair from her flushed face and caught her in his strong, sinewy arms. His mouth lingered in moist exploration of her lips. Now that she was going to be Lady Buckingham, mistress of his estates and, more importantly, mistress of his heart, Roxanne yielded as she had never yielded before to the fiery passions that fanned the flames of love.

Cordy got up from the chair, gave an audible whoop, and flung her arms into the air. "The End, Finis, Kaput, Finito, Goodbye Roxanne!" she cried. She stood breathless, as if she'd just finished a marathon. She wanted to dance, get wildly drunk, or make love. She called Nonnie, but there was no answer, so she poured herself the last of the bourbon and sat sipping it, grinning into space. Tonight, she told herself stoically, was destined to be an anticlimax, so she might as well finish up all the corrections. Tomorrow, after she'd delivered the manuscript, she would go to Bloomingdale's and buy herself a present.

She was dabbing Wite-Out over the typos on the final pages when the phone rang. She reached for it, thinking it might be Sean and juggling the possible pleasure of inviting him over against the even more transient satisfaction of telling him to go to hell. Scaling down her expectation to conform to reality—it was probably a wrong number or a magazine solicitation—she let it ring a few more times, then picked up.

"Cordy? This is Maxine, Maggie's friend. We talked about a week ago."

"Yes. How're you doin'?"

"I'm fine. How're you?"

"I'm feeling a little bit crazy. I just finished—"

"Forgive me, but I'm in a terrible rush," Maxine cut in. "Fact is, I'm between a rock and a hard place. I've taken this really fabulous summer place out in the Hamptons, and one of the girls who was supposed to take a share has backed out. I was wondering if you'd like to come out."

"That's very kind of you, Maxine," Cordy said, trying to determine if she was getting an invitation or a proposition.

"The shares are kind of stiff: a hundred and fifty dollars for the weekend. But the place is fabulous and you'd have your own room and everything. I mean, you have to invest in a classy place if you're going to meet the right people, and I just know you'd love the two other girls who are sharing."

"I don't think my budget—"

"You don't have to say yes right off. You can call and let me know tomorrow. I'll be driving out there on Friday afternoon, so if you decide to come, I could give you a lift."

"Thanks again," Cordy said graciously. "If you don't hear from me tomorrow—"

"Then we'll just have to get together for lunch sometime. But do try to come. You've got my number. It's a really swinging scene. Got to run. Bye."

By ten o'clock Cordy was lying on the couch. The typos had been corrected and the manuscript packed and ready for delivery the following day. Sylvia's stereo was pounding out some damned disco hit over and over again. Cordy couldn't really hear it distinctly. It was just the reverberation of the bass and the aggressive high-pitched wail of a proposition. Had she not been so pleasantly numbed by the three glasses of wine with which she'd washed down the hero sandwich she might have gone downstairs to complain. As it was, she cursed Sylvia's insensitivity, turned up the volume on the TV, and started to doze off.

There was a frantic banging. She jerked up as she heard her name being called and stumbled to the door, only remembering to ask, "Who is it?" as she slid back the locks.

"It's me. Cliff. Please open up."

His voice sounded hysterically urgent, and as she flung back the door she saw that he was white around the mouth and breathing hard. His hands were flapping at his sides.

"Cliff. You scared hell out of me," she croaked.

"I need you. Come downstairs."

"What?"

"I need you. Sylvia's tried to commit suicide. Come on," he ordered. "I can't explain now. Just come on."

She took a step forward. He thudded down the stairs, talking as he went.

"I got home about twenty minutes ago. Sylvia was taking care of Gielgud while I was away. I heard her stereo when I came in and figured the needle was stuck, but it didn't register. Then I called her and her phone was off the hook. So I came back down. I had her keys, but the door was locked from the inside, so . . ."

They were at Sylvia's open door. Part of the frame had splintered where Cliff had forced the chain.

"Is she . . . ?" Cordy couldn't bring herself to complete the question.

"I don't know."

He ran through the living room to the bedroom door, looked in, then turned and walked back slowly, his arms still flapping. He backed Cordy up as though he wanted her to leave, then placed trembling hands on her shoulders.

"Don't go in there. The ambulance should be here any minute. They told me not to touch anything. Just sit here until I take Gielgud up to your apartment, then I'll come back down."

Turning abruptly, he darted back into the bedroom. Cordy felt the bottom of her stomach drop as she heard him coaxing the cat to come to him. There was a hiss, a yowl, and a string of curses. A moment later, Cliff lurched back into the living room, a complacent Gielgud purring in his arms.

"Don't move. I'll be right back," he ordered as he ran out the door.

Cordy stood until she heard him going up the stairs, then, impelled by the universal compulsion to view the horrific, she moved to the bedroom door.

A crazy study in black and white seared itself into her brain. In the darkness of the bedroom the satin bedspread was luminous. Sylvia's body lay sprawled, limbs twisted as though she'd been dropped from a great height. Her white nightdress covered only her trunk, leaving her long black legs exposed. Her mouth was open, showing another slash of white. One arm was akimbo, the other drooped over the side of the bed. Her head was thrown back at an improbable angle, and though her eyes were closed she seemed to be looking at the high-contrast nude photo of herself. The eyes in the photograph stared back with heavy-lidded, seductive disinterest. Cordy turned her head away and closed her eyes, but the image remained, swimming like a negative in developing solution. White and black. Black and white. Working up some saliva, Cordy opened her eyes, swallowed, and focused on Sylvia's chest. She could hear Cliff behind her, talking to Emergency again in a too calm voice. As she heard him repeat the address, she thought she could detect some slight rise and fall, at least a tremor, in Sylvia's breast, but this too had the quality of hallucination.

Cliff was standing behind her and as if divining her thoughts said, "They said not to touch her, but I did feel her heart. I put my face close to her mouth. I think she's breathing. Christ, if only we could *do* something!" He grabbed Cordy's hand and squeezed it hard, as though he wanted to wring a directive out of her. She pulled away and moved to the bed. Her hand was slow and steady as she pulled the nightdress down over Sylvia's exposed thighs. Apart from this meaningless gesture to protect Sylvia's modesty, she couldn't think of anything to do.

"There's Elavil and Nembutal on the nighttable," Cliff whispered. "And half a bottle of Dubonnet. There was a note, but I took it. I have it here in my pocket. I figured if she pulled through . . ."

His voice begged Cordy's approval for his actions, but she wasn't able to speak. She looked at the nighttable and nodded, verifying the information he'd just given her, then watched the second hand move around the dial of the clock radio.

Some incalculable time later, men came to the door. They lifted Sylvia onto a stretcher as Cordy pressed herself against the living-room wall and tried not to get in the way. Cliff went with them to Roosevelt Hospital.

When she let herself into her apartment, Gielgud was sitting on the couch washing himself. She tried to take him onto her lap, but he was too aware of her tension to find her companionable and wiggled out of her arms. The cat's rejection made her feel as though she might cry. She poured him a saucer of milk, then rummaged through heretofore unsearched kitchen cabinets for Ovaltine or cocoa. If she took anything alcoholic it would push her over the brink. Finding a package of cocoa with round-faced, smiling children on it seemed to be a good omen. She put a saucepan of milk on the stove as though she were enacting some ritual to ensure Sylvia's survival.

If she didn't spill a drop of milk, or let it boil over, that too might be taken as a good omen. As she stirred the milk, the absence of sound from Sylvia's apartment was like a pain in her ears. She sat on the couch, hands wrapped around the mug, and waited. The fact that Sylvia, directly beneath her, had stuffed pills into her mouth, washed them down with Dubonnet, and lost consciousness, while she, lolling on the couch, had cursed the wailing disco, cut her adrift. Gielgud, mistaking her shocked immobility for calm, slithered up to her, rubbing his head against her leg.

"They pumped her stomach. It looks as though she's going to pull through," Cliff said.

They stood at the door staring at each other for a full minute before Cliff followed Cordy into the apartment. Without asking if he wanted it, she poured him a cup of cocoa. He took it, sat down, and pulled Gielgud into his lap.

"I should've seen it coming, but I didn't." He took a sip and stared at the carpet. "She didn't expect me back until tomorrow, so it was a serious attempt. And you know, all the way to the hospital all I could think of was what would have happened to Gielgud if I hadn't come home. That's pretty disgusting, isn't it?"

"Who knows what we think at a time like this," Cordy mumbled. "I was mad at her 'cause the music was too loud."

"I should've seen it coming. In all the years I've known her I've never seen her cry."

"Is there anyone we should notify? Any family?"

Cliff laughed helplessly. "It was a serious attempt," he said again. "If I hadn't come home . . . What did you ask about a family? Yeah. They're in Philadelphia. She asked me to call them about five years ago when I was doing a show in Philly. But she never went home for holidays or anything. I guess they didn't approve of her. She told me to tell them everything was going fine. Shit! I should've seen it coming."

"How could you?"

"I knew what was going on." He set the cup on the floor and rubbed his hands back and forth on his knees. "What an ass I am. I knew the burglary pushed her over the top." Cordy said nothing. She waited until his hands were still and he looked up to see her questioning expression. "The burglary," he went on impatiently. "She told me she thought it was a put-up job. She thought her boy-

friend had paid someone to do it 'cause a bunch of letters and photographs were missing."

"Why would he do that?"

"I guess she'd threatened him. I don't think she would really
have blackmailed him. He was her boss for one. And she loved him.
But my guess is that she was desperate enough to throw out a threat
about telling his wife. She'd been having an affair with him for about
four years now. She was too savvy to think he'd ever leave his wife
and marry her. Well, she must've been, mustn't she?"

Cordy opened her eyes wide and turned her palms upward,
begging off from an unanswerable question, then she nodded, urging
him to continue.

"The boss," he went on, "he's a big enchilada in the garment
district. Father of three with a house in Port Jefferson. He wasn't
going to marry a black woman who works in his showroom no matter how nice she looks or how good she is in the sack. She must've
known that. I guess she was content with the limo and the trips to
the Bahamas once a year. Oh, and he took her to Korea and Taiwan
too. Business trip to inspect factories there. There were payoffs.
Then she found out he had someone else, so even the illusion of
being the mistress was gone. What else does she have? It doesn't take
Billy Graham to tell you that disco, pills, fashion, and an occasional
holiday on an expense account isn't exactly a belief system. Ah, shit,
I'm really getting depressed."

She put her arm around his neck. "You helped to save her life,
Cliff."

"So where's my laurel wreath?" He seemed to smile because it
was expected of him. "It was purely accidental that I came home
early. And all the way down to the hospital I just kept thinking
about Gielgud."

"I know. You told me."

"Gielgud is eleven years old," he said gloomily. "In cat age
that's older than I am."

"Gielgud is too mean to die young, Cliff. And you're not desperate like Sylvia. You like your work. You have lots of friends."

"How do you know I have lots of friends?"

"You must. I know you must."

"Hey, here you are, having to comfort me"—he smiled and disengaged himself—"and you're the one who's really been dumped on.
You don't even know Sylvia and you've just been in New York for a
short time and you've already been in on a burglary and an at-

tempted suicide. Course, if you're a writer I suppose it's all grist for the mill."

"I hadn't thought of that. I did finish the Roxanne book. I'm sorry you weren't here to celebrate with me."

"Did Mr. Wonderful ever call?"

"Nope. Can't figure it out and I've stopped trying."

"Liar." He put down his cup and lifted the cat onto his shoulder.

"Look, I came here to work and I have worked. I came here to get an agent and it looks as though I've got that too. And on the first try."

"Hey, that's great."

"Yes. I felt real up for a while. You, my man, look dead beat."

"I am. I guess Gielgud and I best toddle upstairs. You're right, of course. I'll have to call her parents before I go to bed."

He turned at the door and kissed her cheek. "You've gotta believe me, Cordy. Last summer the only bad thing that happened in this building was that a water pipe broke and the rents went up."

"I believe you, Cliff."

"You won't give us bad press when you go back home?"

"Who would I tell?" She made a face at him and shut the door.

She did not wash up the cups, or even clean her teeth. With the instincts of a true survivor, she stripped off her clothes and fell into a deep, dreamless sleep the moment her head hit the pillow.

The Chrystallis office was in a warehouse on 29th Street, but since there was a Madison Avenue entrance to the building Chrystallis used the Madison Avenue address. Cordy finally found her way in and gave her name to the muffin-shaped woman in the cubicle marked RECEPTION. The woman pressed a button to announce that "one of our authors is here" and went back to chewing her pastrami sandwich. Cordy settled herself on a worn purple love seat next to the cylindrical ashtray and looked at the "Chrystallis Makes Your Dreams Come True" display on the purple wall. In the center of all the book jackets showing nubile maidens in various states of ecstasy was a photograph of a hefty woman with sausage curls being embraced by a mustachioed man who managed to look dessicated and oily at the same time. Cordy was reading the caption—"Mrs. Martha Acuff of Boulder, Colorado, meets Prince Ivan Romanoff'"— when a man came through the door marked PRIVATE. His shirttail was dangling and, despite the air conditioning, he was sweating profusely.

"How do you do. I'm Cordelia Simpkins Tyre."

"Of course you are." He rubbed his right hand on the seat of his pants and offered it. "I'm Maggie's replacement. Pleasure to meet you. Maggie thought you were a real find. I see you haven't disappointed us." His head bobbed at the manuscript in her hands. "And what's your next? Another adventure of Celeste?"

"It's Roxanne."

"Sorry."

"Don't be." Her eyes flitted over the Esmeraldas, Angeliques, Desirées, and Auroras on the wall. "I can see where you'd get confused."

"I'd like to show you around the offices but—"

"No, that's quite all right. I have a summer cold and I'd really like to get on home."

"Before you leave I want to tell you that we're starting a whole new line with more explicit sex. So you can go wild on the next one. Women's lib, you know."

"Is the format changing too? Or the plot line?"

"Uh-uh. Same old story." He grinned with enthusiasm. "Just more explicit sex. Not promiscuous, you understand. The heroine always has to be in love."

"But of course," she smiled with a touch of sarcasm. "About the rest of the advance, when can I expect to get it?"

"Check'll be in the mail next week," he assured her. And dangling the carrot of ego gratification just in case it wasn't, he added, "We're starting to put a picture of the author on some of the books and you're just the sort of author we want to show. I mean, the readership doesn't want to know that Jennifer Mae Dupree is a sixty-year-old queen from New Jersey. A beautiful woman like you— Hey, send me a snapshot and I'll see what I can do."

"It's been a pleasure to meet you, Mr. . . .?"

"Fishbein. Joe Fishbein."

"Mr. Fishbein. And I'll be looking for the check."

"Oh, Miss Simpkins Tyre, you're forgetting the manuscript. Hard to give it up, I expect. It's rather like having a baby, isn't it?"

"I did get fatter while I was writing it," Cordy said as she handed over the box. "But otherwise, no. It's not at all like having a baby. Thank you, Mr. Fishbein. Bye."

While waiting for the elevator she tore open a Handi-wipe and cleaned her hands. "Tacky, tacky," she laughed. And then: "Dear Abigail Pinkston Silverstein, please deliver me from the ranks of Chrystallis."

She had promised herself a reward, so she took the bus to Bloomingdale's. A family of German tourists pushed her through the revolving doors and past the jewelry counter. She moved aside to let them pass, then stepped into the crowd again, dodging out-of-work actresses who offered to douse her with perfume samples and moving around customers transfixed in front of TV screens showing mini-commercials of new products. She tried on a picture hat she couldn't afford, then wandered downstairs to the lingerie department. A diaphanous lavender nightdress, the sort Lupton would have liked, caught her eye. She took it from the rack and walked a few steps toward a mirror; but before she'd even caught sight of her reflection she thought, Who would you be getting this for?

"Did you want some assistance?" a salesgirl asked. She shook her head, put the gown back on the rack, and wandered off in search of the elevators. Her skin felt prickly and her bladder was full. There didn't seem to be enough oxygen in the air, though the women around her, fingering merchandise, taking out charge cards, studying themselves in mirrors with preoccupied expressions on their faces, didn't seem to notice.

Once, when she was about four and the family had been vacationing in Beverly Hills, she'd lost control and peed on the floor of a dressing room at Robinson's while waiting for Lucille to make a choice of dresses. She could remember the simultaneous terror and release she had felt crouching in the corner while the urine ran down her leg, staining her white sock. Lucille, mortified, had threatened never to take her shopping again. But that punishment, which had seemed more like a reprieve, had been forgotten soon afterwards. It was really amazing when she stopped to think how much of her childhood had been spent in department stores. She had to get out. But she had to buy something first, otherwise the detour would have been in vain. She decided she couldn't deal with going up to the fourth floor ladies' room. She hurried to the cosmetic counter, grabbed a bottle of bath oil, paid for it, and hurried to the exit.

On the street she acted like a native, dashing from the curb to signal a cab, pretending not to notice the man standing on the same corner with his arm raised, and barking out her address as soon as she'd flung open the door. Her bladder was about to burst. She was vastly relieved that the driver made no attempt at conversation.

As she let herself into the front hallway, she stopped by the mailboxes, hoping for a letter from Nonnie or one of Jeanette's drawings. An elderly black couple came out of Sylvia's apartment. The man, who had an oddly shrunken look, closed the door while the woman, more robust, dressed in Sunday best complete with flowered toque, stood to one side. The slow, methodical manner with which the man turned the locks suggested years of civil service. Cordy could imagine him rising at seven, taking his sack lunch to the Post Office or the Department of Motor Vehicles, counting the dollars that would pay for the orthodontist or the new refrigerator, and looking forward to retirement. The woman had the corseted behind and overseeing eye of a serious churchgoer. She had probably spent a good deal of the housekeeping money on Clorox, starch, and encyclopedias. She had prayed that her daughter would go to college, join a sorority, marry a responsible man, and produce grandchildren whose photographs she could put on the mantelpiece next to the vase of silk flowers and the portrait of Martin Luther King Jr.

As they passed her, the man raised his hat but kept his eyes on the floor. The woman tilted her chin up a fraction and looked Cordy in the face, her mouth twitching in an embarrassed smile, her eyes sharp, ready to defend. Cordy said, "How do you do. Isn't this heat something?" and raced up the stairs.

Cliff had slipped a note under her door: "Sylvia pulling out of it O.K. Parents have arrived from Philly, so don't be alarmed if you hear noises from downstairs. I'm off to New Haven *avec* Gielgud. You're such a Georgia peach you make me wish I was straight. Thanks for being here. Love, Cliff."

She pulled her clothes off, poured a generous capful of oil into the tub, and turned the faucets on full. It was impossible to think of what she might say if she met those simple, distraught parents again. Impossible to think of them downstairs, lying under the white satin covers on Sylvia's bed, turning their eyes away from the nude photograph, the mother praying, the father wondering where he'd gone wrong. She settled into the tepid perfumed water and closed her eyes. You're turning into a real Blanche DuBois, taking baths to calm your nerves, she thought. The weekend yawned before her. She didn't want to succumb to coffee and naps and watching the neighbors out the window. And morbid, meandering thoughts of loneliness and suicide. She wanted sunlight and salt water and pleasant, light conversation, even if her budget couldn't afford it.

She called and left a message on Maxine's machine. Yes, she would love to take her up on the offer to come to the Hamptons for the weekend.

Chapter XII

"So Ken—Ken Ebbleman—you know him," Maxine insisted as she veered off the Long Island Expressway toward the Hamptons exit.

"No. No, I don't," Cordy said softly.

"But you *must*. He played at Wimbledon last year. He does the commercials for Adidas. So anyway, Ken Ebbleman . . ."

Cordy swept her hair back from her neck and looked out the window. She might have known that her admission of ignorance would do nothing to staunch the flow of Maxine's chatter. Maxine had been rattling off a telephone directory of celebrities ever since they'd left Manhattan. The fact that Cordy had not heard of and wasn't particularly interested in any of the people Maxine was gossiping about did not deter her. She gasped incredulously at each of Cordy's confessions of ignorance, insisted that she *must* know the party in question, then gushed on, rarely completing a sentence, constantly interrupting herself to add verbal footnotes about brand names, tax brackets, or the marital status of her subjects.

"I don't follow tennis much, Maxine. Do you mind if I roll down the window?"

"You don't? That's too bad. *Everyone* plays tennis. Anyhow, Ken got absolutely freaked at the Trash and Bash party Mel threw on his courts," she rushed on, breathless and anxious as a wounded messenger who must impart vital information before death seals his lips forever. "Ken's been having a casual thing with Ginny, but he started coming on with Estelle—Estelle works for Norma Kamali, so she always has the most wonderful clothes—I mean, who else wears a couple of thousand dollars' worth of outfits in a single weekend?"

"I'm sure I don't know," Cordy demurred, her hand still poised on the window button. "Would you mind if—"

"Estelle was with Josh—Josh Middlemass?—he's a VP at Texas Instruments, mid-thirties, never been married—and when Ken started hitting her on the ass with his racquet she pretended to get mad. So she jumps over the net! And then she picks up the bucket of ice the Moet is sitting in—I swear, Estelle has absolutely no inhibitions . . ."

Cordy pressed the window button and took a deep breath. The rush of air served to muffle Maxine's voice, but didn't do much to relieve Cordy's claustrophobia. From the moment they'd met and Maxine had appraised her with that look that said she was pretty enough to be accepted, but not so overwhelmingly beautiful as to be unfair competition, Cordy had been fighting an intuition that she didn't like Maxine. Now, after two hours in her company, she was sure of it. It was bad enough that she'd made the mistake of paying for a weekend she wasn't going to enjoy, what was even worse was that she felt some irrational need to have Maxine like her. Why, she wondered, did this garrulous, superficial woman have the power to make her feel odd, overweight, and out of touch?

". . . and so he asked me if we'd met last year at Cannes, and I had to say no. I should've been at Cannes last year—I had a deal to promote this indie film about mud wrestling—well, it wasn't really about mud wrestling—that was just a symbol of female degradation—but the budget wouldn't stretch, so I didn't get to go. But I'm going this year. I had a thing with this guy who works for Gianni Versace, so I can stay with him. Speaking of movies, I hope you get to meet this Australian movie star who was at Mel's last week. He's such a hunk. I mean a hunk! Sexist, of course, but we don't make 'em like that anymore. So when I get to Cannes . . ."

Cordy smiled. Maxine might have been one of Chekhov's Three Sisters crying out to return to Moscow, so great was her need to get to Cannes. But then, Maxine was the sort of person who would always imagine a place she'd never been, or almost any place in Europe, to be infinitely superior to any place she'd actually lived. A sudden illumination, like the increase in light after a break in the current, blazed up in Cordy's mind: Maxine reminded her of her mother. Maxine, with her tousled hair, heavy jewelry, and short shorts, affected a style that was worlds away from Lucille's girlish gentility, but they were sisters under the skin. Whereas Lucille was a slave to the "right thing," Maxine was captive to the "in thing." Lucille would have fluttered about a "man of consequence"; Maxine blurted out a prospect's income and panted after "hunks." They both looked at any other woman as competition. Their concerns, values, and topics of conversation were really the same. And underneath all the chatter about celebrities, sumptuous dinners, and dazzling parties was the same anxiety, the same desperate fear of having missed out.

". . . and served Iranian caviar, which, as you can imagine, is just about impossible to come by anymore, because he still has import connections in the Middle East."

"That must've been wonderful." She had no idea what Maxine had been saying, but now that she'd made the connection, she knew that it wasn't really necessary that she listen. As long as she tossed in the occasional impressed or approving remark, Maxine, like a dog who yaps habitually for treats, would be satisfied.

"Oh, it was! Mel's parties are absolutely the best. Now"—Maxine waved vaguely to her right—"if we'd taken that turn we'd have gone to Bridgehampton. There's Bridgehampton, East Hampton, and Southampton—not to be confused. Bridgehampton has one bar that really jumps, at least on the weekend, but it's not nearly as upscale as . . ."

As Maxine started into her elliptic social rating of the towns, Cordy sniffed for sea air and looked at the shops on the main street. They were quietly expensive, and sold mostly leisure goods. It was, she decided, a sort of Yankee Hilton Head. They turned off the main street into a residential district. The houses, set well back from tree-lined streets, were old enough and architecturally tasteful enough to meet Nonnie's standards and must once have been inhabited by retiring, influential people.

"I always miss this turn because of all these trees," Maxine said as she ground the gears into reverse. "Wouldn't you think that since they have such great lawns they'd take those trees down so everyone could see?"

"No more than I'd think a woman with a good chest should go topless," Cordy said, but Maxine was too intent on backing up and turning into the circular drive to pay attention.

"Oh, shit," Maxine cried, motioning to the sprawling, neglected lawns. "This looks like Lubbock in September. I told Estelle to turn on the sprinklers. Now we're going to have to hire someone to come and spruce it up if we want to have that garden party next week."

She jumped out of the car, tugging the skimpy shorts away from her crotch and reaching into the back seat to get the shopping bag from the De Laurentis food emporium. "Grab your stuff and let's go in the back way."

Cordy took her books and bag and followed Maxine past banks of dry shrubbery to a flagstone terrace. A woman, basted, plucked, and almost as naked as a chicken, lay sprawled on a lounge chair.

"Estelle, this is Cordy. Cordy, Estelle."

Estelle said hello without any apparent movement of the jaw.

"Estelle's a writer too. She free-lances in all the major magazines. She did about fifty articles last year—dating, sex, the job market—but her specialty is marital communication. You might have seen her series with Dr. Enzio Block on how to keep a marriage together."

Cordy smiled. "I didn't read it, but I probably should have." She looked down at the weeds poking through the flagstones, then raised her head, trying to see into the dark lenses of Estelle's wraparound glasses. "Did you manage to?" Being looked at without seeing the viewer's eyes always made her uncomfortable.

"Manage to what?"

"Keep your marriage together," Cordy laughed to show the question was a joke instead of a rude inquiry.

"I've never been married."

"Then how did you . . . I guess Dr. Block did the research."

"Not Enzio," Estelle drawled. "He specializes in singles, and he hasn't put pen to paper in fifteen years except to write a prescription or a check. He just gave me six months free therapy for the publicity value of quoting him. Barter is in."

"Cordy's staying at Maggie Brocksen's place. You know Maggie," Maxine prompted. "Used to be at that schlock place Chrystallis, but now she's on the Coast with this big producer Murray—oh, what is his name?"

"Eisen," Cordy volunteered.

"Yeah, Murray Eisen. How could I forget! An actress I know had a thing with him. He's had three long-running series, in fact his series last longer than his marriages. He did—"

"Could you show me where to put my things, please," Cordy

interrupted before Maxine could get started on Murray Eisen's credits.

"Sure thing. Shit, Estelle, you might at least have remembered to turn on the sprinklers," Maxine said as she started toward the house.

Estelle, too languid even to shrug in earnest, raised one shoulder a fraction of an inch.

"It's been a pleasure meeting you, Estelle," Cordy said. "I guess we'll have a chance to get better acquainted while—"

"Cordy's from the South," Maxine explained, as though excusing her mannerliness. "Where's Ginny? I didn't see her car in the drive."

"Her car's in the shop."

"Oh, no. That means I'm the taxi service." Maxine jerked open the back door, then looked back at the yard. "Shit, Estelle, you could have remembered to turn on the sprinklers!"

Cordy followed her past a pantry and into a beautifully equipped kitchen. There was an open hearth, butcher-block tables, walls covered with hand-painted tiles, and two sinks filled with dishes and scummy water.

"I swear they need a house mother," Maxine fumed as she yanked open the door of the refrigerator. It was bare except for a carton of cottage cheese and a couple of bottles of Perrier. Maxine shoved in the shopping bag and spun around to the sinks. "Damn it! Ginny's supposed to do the dishes and Estelle's supposed to take care of the yard. I mean, I'm the one who's going to have to forfeit the deposit if the place is pigged up."

"I don't mind helping with the dishes. I've had so much takeout food since I've been finishing up the book that it would be a novelty to clean up after a real meal."

"This kitchen was in last October's issue of *House Beautiful*," Maxine said with the rehearsed crispness of a tour guide. "The owner, Maxwell Webster, designed it himself. The tile was imported from Mexico City and the marble pastry slab is from Italy. Maxwell is in Aix-en-Provence this summer. He and his wife just broke up. Come on, let me show you your room."

Maxine paused in the hallway long enough to check herself in the mirror, sucked in her stomach, and started up the stairs. "Ginny! G-i-n-n-y."

A woman in khaki bermudas and a button-down shirt came to

the landing toweling her hair. "You don't need to use your cattle-call yell, Maxine. I heard you come in." She smiled and nodded at Cordy. "I guess you're the new share. I'm Ginny Everett."

"And this is Cordy Tyre," Maxine said before Cordy could introduce herself. "Cordy's a friend of Maggie Brocksen. Maggie's an assistant producer to Murray Eisen out on the Coast. Ginny is in the executive training program at Chase Manhattan Bank."

"Which is not a hell of a lot to brag about." Ginny offered her hand. "Please don't worry about the dishes, Maxine. I'll do them as soon as I blow-dry my hair. I was too hung over to tackle them this morning. Besides, we're not having anyone over tonight. Estelle and I thought we'd go back to the Laundry for drinks before we eat, and if we don't meet anyone there we can just grab some burgers on the way home. You know we're both on a diet."

"What about Ken? Did you make it up with Ken?" Maxine wanted to know.

Ginny started away as though she hadn't heard the question, but turned at the bathroom door. "I hope Ken Ebbleman gets a case of herpes," she said with a tight jaw, "'cause with an ego like his, nothing else is going to put him out of commission."

Maxine laughed and pushed open the door nearest to her. "This is your room, Cordy. I hope it's O.K. You won't be in here much. We go out all the time—parties, bars, the beach."

The minute she stepped into the room, Cordy knew that Maxine's promise of riotous social activity was meant to compensate for the accommodations. Sports equipment was stacked in a corner, posters of KISS, Reggie Jackson, and E.T. covered the walls. On the bureau next to the bunk beds she saw the detritus (hairpins, a spent tube of sun screen, and a copy of the *Village Voice*) of the last "share," who had obviously decided that she could find a more attractive trysting place than the bedroom of an eleven-year-old boy. Cordy put her things on the bed and walked over to the window. "How far is the ocean?"

"Couple of miles. You couldn't walk there."

"Could I borrow that bike I saw on the back porch?"

"That belongs to the Websters' kid. I think it's too small for you."

"In that case, I think I'll rest for a while."

"Don't worry, we'll go to the beach tomorrow. Would you like to slip into your swimsuit and sunbathe with Estelle?"

"I don't think so."

"Oh, you Southern belles! Of course you're right. Sun is just ruinously aging for the skin. So rest. I'll knock on your door around six to give you time to get ready. You'll love the Laundry."

"I'd just as soon fix some supper here at the house."

"You can't. I mean, there isn't any food, and I can't go grocery shopping now. I've got a tennis lesson at three and it's two-fifteen already. You'll love the Laundry. Lots of guys hang out there. That's where we met Mel."

"Can I get something to eat there?"

"Sure. But the prices are stiff. Listen," Maxine added with the hint of an apology, "Ginny will be out of the bathroom in a minute. There's a sauna in there. Saunas are great for cellulite."

"I think I'll just rest." Cordy stretched out on the bed and closed her eyes. She wondered if she'd have to start snoring before Maxine took the cue to leave.

"O.K. I'll leave you alone. Traveling can really tire you out, can't it?"

"Traveling was the least of it," Cordy muttered as Maxine shut the door. She shoved the nubby plaid pillow under her head and closed her eyes. Her stomach rumbled. A laugh gurgled in the back of her throat. There was nothing for it but to laugh when expectations had been so quickly and so thoroughly dashed. The negative part of having an active imagination was that her mind invariably leapt forward, creating exciting possibilities, then reality always brought her up short. She'd done that with Sean and now she'd done it with her holiday weekend. As she opened her eyes and looked around the boy's room, she wondered which of the parents had custody. With a pang, she remembered Jeanette's room in Chicago. She could see herself smoothing the ruffled bedspread, arranging the china-faced doll Lucille had sent from Paris and the frog with one eye that had been Jeanette's favorite ever since she was teething. An aching need to hold Jeanette in her arms came over her. She wondered if Lupton had been in that room since they'd left.

Unable to rest, she picked up her book and read until the repeated banging of doors, shouts of hurry up, and the sound of the car backing out of the drive convinced her that she was alone in the house. She undressed and went into the bathroom. After sweats in the sauna, icy showers, and a shampoo, she felt her spirit move back into her body. She was whole again. Like a turtle she could carry her home on her back.

The front door slammed. She heard the other women arguing

over who was going to use the bathroom first. She had timed her occupation of the sauna perfectly. She slipped back into her room. Standing naked near the window, she watched the clear blue of the sky darken over the tops of the trees, and as she pulled on her underpants the sharp expectancy of a summer night in a new town took hold of her. While zipping up her blue cotton dress and piling her hair onto her head, the tingling expectation of quest, the surge of curiosity seized her again.

"Cordy, are you ready yet?" she heard Maxine yell.

Running downstairs into the living room, she saw what looked like the photography session for three trendy but diverse magazine advertisements. Ginny, sitting straight-backed on the couch, her hands folded in her lap, might have been waiting to take notes from a visiting professor. She had changed her khaki bermudas for a khaki skirt and button-down blouse with monogrammed pocket. Her hair was combed back behind her ears, her face was seemingly devoid of makeup. She had a fixed, unnatural freshness of eye and smile that made Cordy's facial muscles ache just to look at her. Maxine, in high contrast to Ginny's Preppy persona, was standing near the fireplace jingling her keys and wearing yet another skimpy outfit, her wrists bound with leather-studded jewelry that matched the dog collar around her throat. Her hair looked as though she'd just come in from a hundred-mile ride on the back of a motorcycle, and her thick makeup completed the pseudo-hooker, James-Dean-with-tits image. Estelle, dressed in aqua silk lounging pajamas, her long brown hair smoothed and turned up at the edges, was moving around the room touching the furniture with a proprietary air. Judging from the haughty expression on her face—which had just the right amount of cosmetic improvement—she had already become, at least in imagination, the Hostess/Wife of a multinational executive.

It was, Cordy thought, beyond understanding. Ginny, Estelle, and Maxine seemed to have made a conscious effort to divest themselves of any hint of intelligence or individuality. They were all educated and sophisticated. They earned their own livings. Yet they were ready to go out hunting for "the boys" just as surely as any fourteen-year-old she had known who'd doused herself with White Shoulders, slept with curlers in her hair, and squealed at touchdowns.

"Ready to go?" Maxine asked, as though Cordy's appearance had put a real doubt into her mind.

"Just a minute, please. I forgot something."

Cordy bolted upstairs. She needed a talisman to ward off any impression that she might be one of the hunting party, and to that end she rummaged in her overnight bag for the case in which she carried her jewelry. Muffled sounds of annoyance were already reaching her from the lower floor as she found her wedding ring. She pushed it down onto the pale band of flesh that a decade of wear had left on her finger.

"Cordy, are you coming or what?" Maxine yelled. "'Cause if we don't get there before seven-thirty we'll have to stand at the bar."

"Perish the thought," Cordy muttered and raced down the stairs.

Except for the sheets and towels decoratively draped from the ceiling and the exorbitant prices, the Laundry might have been an overcrowded bus terminal. There were too many bodies in too small a space for the air conditioning to do any good, and the decibel level made it impossible to hear, because most of the patrons, like Maxine and Estelle, talked at a pitch that was designed to attract attention. The conversation at their booth was mostly about plays, movies, and food, but since it was constantly broken off while the other women's eyes circled the room in feverish search, there was no point in even trying to follow it.

"Do you think we could go and get something to eat soon?" Cordy asked after she'd finished her second piña colada.

Estelle frowned. "It's only nine o'clock. If you're hungry why don't you order something here?"

"Cordy's right," Ginny said. "This place is yesterday's newspapers. Why don't we go on over to P.J.'s?"

"No. We have to give it another half hour," Maxine said sternly, as though Cordy and Ginny were buck privates who wanted to desert their posts. "*Then* we'll go over to P.J.'s."

"Would you mind giving me the keys to your car, please?" Cordy asked.

"But you can't sit in the parking lot!"

"I just need a breath of fresh air."

Keys in hand, Cordy shouldered her way to the exit, saying excuse me over and over again, though nobody seemed to acknowledge it.

At the door, a man in a jogging outfit looked her up and down. "I know it's cliché, but haven't we met some place before?"

"No, we haven't."

"But you're familiar," he insisted.

"Oh, no I'm not," she smiled and pushed past him.

She got into the back seat of Maxine's car and locked the doors.
Drawing her skirts over her legs, she put her head on the armrest
and tried to get comfortable. She had almost fallen asleep when she
heard the tapping of knuckles on the window.

"Cordy! Cordy, open up. We've heard about a party over at
Mel's place," Maxine announced triumphantly.

She blinked and opened the door.

"You've got those statistics wrong, Ginny," Estelle said as she
crawled over Cordy and arranged herself in the back seat. "I read
those statistics in *Savvy* and it's one hundred and twenty-eight
women to every one hundred eligible men."

"Not if you break it down by age, education, and professional
status," Ginny corrected. "Then it goes much higher. Something
like half a man for every woman."

"There's a saying in my part of the country," Maxine told them
as she turned on the motor. "'Better a share in gusher than a hundred percent of a dry well.' Point is, you've got to think of yourself
as outstanding, capable of beating out the competition."

"Oh"—Ginny laughed—"I thought you were counseling having
an affair with a married man."

"Statistics don't matter," Maxine overrode her. "When I took
that seminar on how to be successful, the one thing they stressed
over and over again was self-confidence. Self-confidence! Remember
that. There'll be a lot of new men at Mel's tonight. You know Mel
always entertains as though he was the reincarnation of the Great
Gatsby."

"Mel's got style," Estelle agreed.

"No. Mel's got money," Ginny said.

"Will Mel have food?" Cordy asked.

"There'll be everything you want there," Maxine assured her.
"Everything."

Fifteen minutes later, as Maxine squeezed her car into a place
between a BMW and a Rolls, Cordy saw that for once Maxine had
not been exaggerating. Except for a twelve-foot satellite dish antenna
sitting in the middle of the floodlit lawns, this really might have been
the Gatsby estate. Mel, Cordy had learned in transit, was a computer engineer who'd struck it rich when he'd started his own company. He was, Estelle had explained, one of those nerds who'd had
his head stuck in a book and had played with computers instead of

girls until he was thirty and was now trying to make up for lost time.

Nerd or not, he had enough manners to be standing at the entrance, under the tall white columns, ready to greet all comers. He was a slight man with unruly hair and yellowish skin. As Maxine flung her arms around his neck and shrilled, "Mel! I'm so glad to see you. Why didn't you tell us you were *en maison* tonight?" Cordy stood to one side and studied him. Even if she hadn't been told about him beforehand she would have spotted his type immediately. He was the man whose social discomfort was almost entirely camouflaged by his understanding of his social utility. He was the man who picked up the check.

"You know Estelle and Ginny." Maxine disengaged herself and wiggled her shoulders. "And this is Cordy Tyre. She's from Georgia and she thinks we Yankees are inhospitable because we don't feed her enough."

"Oh, surely"—Mel took a step toward her—"let me correct that misapprehension immediately. The victuals are—" Another gaggle of partygoers were crossing the lawn.

"Not to worry, Mel. I know my way around. I'll show Cordy where everything is." Maxine led the way into the house, pausing on the top step of the atrium to survey the crowd. "Oh, my God! There's . . ." She darted off before Cordy could even hear the name of the man who'd elicited the yelp.

"The powder room's this way," Estelle said as she turned and disappeared down a corridor.

Ginny had also disappeared.

Cordy paused long enough to plot a route through the atrium. She could see a terrace and what looked to be tennis courts through the french doors at the far end. The food would probably be on the terrace. She moved around the periphery of the crowd, smiling when looked at but staying her course until she'd finally arrived at a table laden with pasta, salads, salmon, caviar, duck, fruits, and cheeses of every description. She piled her plate with a not indecent amount and looked around for a place where she might sit, observing but unobserved. The potted palms near the grand piano, where a man with a bald head and half-closed eyes was crooning Noel Coward, seemed the best bet. Munching her herb bread and gorgonzola to the strains of "Someday I'll Find You," she noted the number of beautiful people in the room. At one point she spotted Ginny, smil-

ing up into the face of a ruddy blond in tennis togs, and hoped for
Ginny's sake that he wasn't the feckless Ken Ebbleman. A little later
on, as she chewed on the duck and the piano player gave an intense,
almost tearful rendering of "The Boy Next Door," Ginny stood a
few feet away from her but didn't seem to notice her. Estelle was
smoothing her hair back and imploring a man with very large ears to
"please explain what infinite gain differential amplifiers *do*, not that I
could possibly understand." She couldn't see Maxine, but occasionally she could hear her laughter. She was looking at her almost
empty plate and contemplating going back for seconds when Ginny
shouldered her way over and sat down next to her.

"May I?" Ginny said, pointing to a remaining cherry tomato.

"Oh, please. It's just that I haven't had anything since breakfast
and—"

"You should get some Dexatrim from Estelle. She always has a
cache."

"But I was hungry."

"Yes, that's the trouble. When you're hungry you want to eat."
Ginny sighed, as though appetite like death and taxes was an agony
to be endured. "Are you having a good time? Seen anything you
like?"

"I like the duck."

"No, I meant . . ."

Cordy licked her finger. Was it worth it to say she knew what
Ginny meant?

"Do you see that guy across the room? The one with the terrific
legs? That's Ken Ebbleman."

"I thought it might be. I saw you talking to him."

"We made it up. Sort of. I mean, it's like Estelle says, men are
so insecure these days that you just dare not ask them for any sort of
commitment. You have to learn to interface without crowding the
man's space, to keep in touch with your own needs but realize that if
your needs are rejected it's really the other person's problem . . ."
Ginny peered through the fog of cigarette smoke and posturing
bodies with a slightly bewildered look on her face. ". . . and know
that anger can be creative if— I don't believe it! That's Jonathan
Edwards. I'm just sure it is."

"Which one?" Cordy asked. There was a limit after all to antiso-
cial behavior.

"The one in the dungarees, with the longish hair. The one

who's dressed like a cab driver. Oh, Jonathan Edwards is just so brave."

He was lounging against a wall. A tall, thin man with arms that looked as though he might lift weights. His hair was beginning to recede from an already high forehead. His mouth, which was also thin, was moving, and the semicircle of people surrounding him seemed to think that whatever he was saying was outrageously funny, but his eyes looked past his audience, shifting around the room, fixing on one thing and then another. Just now they stopped on Cordy.

"It *is* Jonathan Edwards," Ginny whispered. "Oh, I'd love to go up and introduce myself, but I don't suppose he'd remember me. He was a professor of mine about seven years ago when I was at Bard. That was before he was famous. No, there's no way he'd remember me. I was in his creative writing class and I wrote this short story and—I'll never forget—when he handed it back he'd written 'bullshit' across the top in bright red ink. I've been in love with him ever since."

The ways of love are indeed strange, Cordy thought; even a scatological rejection could spark some people's desire. "Then he's a writer," she said, her interest piqued.

Ginny's brows lifted. "Jonathan Edwards! Why he won the Hobart Medal for literature last year. For *Galatea*."

"Oh, yes, I think I've heard about it. But I haven't read it. What's it about?"

"About? Well, it takes place on this island off the coast of Maine, or maybe it's Nova Scotia. I forget which. These awful trappers are trying to catch this stag, but that's not the main plot." Ginny bit her lip, pricking remembrance, and started again. "It's about this writer who has given up on Western civilization and he's left the world, so to speak. This young girl turns up at his cabin. She may be his illegitimate daughter, she may be the actual embodiment of the Muse, or she may just be a figment of his imagination. Anyhow, she's pregnant but she won't have an abortion, so the writer takes her in and has an affair with her. Then this younger man turns up. The younger man may be an actual flesh and blood rival, or he may be the incarnation of the writer's former self—you know, his younger, more idealistic nature. So they—"

"They have a triangular affair."

"So you have read it."

"No. Just kidding."

"But they *do* have a ménage à trois. There's a lot of sex in the book. That's where Edwards really shines. He's very graphic, but he preserves a pure lyricism throughout."

"Both lyric and graphic. Sounds interesting," Cordy smiled, glancing up to see if Edwards was still looking at her. He was.

"I can't tell you how many girls at Bard were hooked on him," Ginny went on. "But he had this wife—typical academic wife—you know, ponchos and the wrong haircut. I've heard that he's left her since the book came out, but I can't imagine it's because of his success. He's not that sort of person. He's real, you know what I mean?"

"Yes, he looks real." She couldn't keep her eyes from drifting to his, but when their eyes met, he turned away, downing the rest of his drink. He must have made another witty remark, because the group in front of him fell about themselves with laughter. But instead of looking pleased with his performance, he seemed to draw back almost as though someone had insulted him. Strange man, Cordy thought popping a cherry tomato into her mouth.

Jonathan Edwards put his empty glass on a passing tray and asked for another. The woman in front of him—a wiry creature tanned to a deep brown that was usually seen on the other coast—was laughing, a high chee-chee laugh, lips drawn back into a grimace. She reminded him of a spider monkey. But just a second ago, when he was recounting how he'd told the department chairman to shove his $17,000-a-year job, he'd felt as though he were the babboon and his audience were the zoo visitors. Which side of the cage was he on? He'd only had three drinks. Or was it four? In any case, this next would be his last. Then he'd go home. Or more accurately, he'd go to his editor's summer place, complete with writer's shack.

How the hell could anyone be expected to write in a room that had a chintz couch and a view of the ocean? It had been a year and a half since *Galatea* had come out. He'd accepted a whopping advance for the next book, but so far, the next book was two loose-leaf binders in a file cabinet and the black notepad in his hip pocket. One of life's little ironies. When you got to the point where they'd buy anything, you didn't have anything to sell; just as when you got to the point where you had your own money people started goddamn *giving* you things. Rent-free summer houses and the like. But what the hell, he had to admit that he liked it. Sometimes, mostly when he was under attack, he even felt he deserved it.

A year and a half ago, when he'd first started to be invited to parties like this, he'd felt a positive exhilaration. No more tucking his shirt into his baggy corduroys, leaving the pretty baby-sitter, and dragging Katherine to some ramshackle faculty apartment where he ate chips and dips and drank cheap wine, talked about the kiss-ass faculty chairman, fumed over the *New York Review of Books,* and flirted with some woman who had a spot of baby food on the front of her sweater. The pleasure he'd felt when he and Katherine had gone to buy the first new suit he'd had in ten years! Sure, he'd acted like some surly kid who was being fitted up for his bar mitzvah, but he'd seen himself as attractive, maybe for the first time in his life. And not just attractive to spoiled eighteen-year-olds who knew nothing about anything, but to intelligent, beautiful, selective people who might want to warm themselves at the bonfire of his success. Of course it's superficial, he'd explained to Katherine, but social life by its very nature was superficial. Provided you saw it clearly, worldly success could be fun. A roller-coaster ride. It wasn't as though he were a callow youth.

Katherine, practical Katherine, had only seen the award as a sum of money. She'd gone along to the first three or four months' worth of receptions and dinner parties but then she'd started to beg off. He'd had to admit that he didn't mind going alone, her presence being something less than a comfort. She didn't seem to enter into the pleasure, the *joke* of the thing. She watched with that cool analytical eye—the very eye that had attracted him because of its objectivity and intelligence, but now seemed coldly dissecting. Katherine was not impressed. She was, and always had been, supportive, but she would not be impressed, and in his forty-third year, the Hobart laurels on his receding hairline, he wanted just the opposite from a woman. And, to give himself credit for at least trying to keep the marriage together, he had told her as much.

The world would have it that he had left Katherine. The truth was that Katherine had taken the children and gone to visit her mother in Massachusetts, where, though there was no real talk of a divorce, she had remained. She seemed perfectly content to weave bedspreads, can vegetables, and serve on the local committee for a clean environment. She simply didn't understand that rather than being sucked in by his celebrity, he understood that the limelight didn't shine often or for so long that he could afford to, or even wanted to, ignore it. Christ almighty, the most recent winner of the Hobart Award had been announced just two weeks ago. *Tempus fugit* and all that.

And it wasn't as though he didn't have an increasingly jaundiced view of those who fawned over him. Why, he wouldn't even have come to this party tonight except that he couldn't get comfortable in that froo-froo shack. Restless and bored, he'd brought himself along for a few drinks. But he wasn't wholly here. Part of him was back at the shack, thinking if not working. He was detached. Even scornful. Surely it was all right to be here if he maintained an attitude of scorn.

He took a gulp of his new drink, his eyes passing over the heads in front of him to the blonde sitting across the room. There was something about her that reminded him of Katherine. Not a physical resemblance (she was younger and decidedly prettier), but the way she seemed to look out of herself, guarded, but then again maybe just shy. Definitely not chic, the way she was chowing down like that, popping the food into that pink, full mouth. And those tits. What a place to rest your weary head. Arms a shade too plump, the milkmaid sort that inspired sonnets in another century. And those masses of blond curls. They'd look dazzling in the sunlight. He tried to remember the opening lines of "To His Coy Mistress." Christ knew he'd taught the damned thing enough times.

"So give us a tiny hint, Mr. Edwards. What's the next book about?" the monkey woman wanted to know. "And don't say, 'It's about three hundred and fifty pages.'"

"It's about getting laid," he said ingenuously. "And now if you'll excuse me . . ." The clot of admirers hooted as though he were Robert Benchley and Groucho Marx rolled into one.

"I don't believe it." Ginny's nails dug into Cordy's arm. "He's coming over here." She got to her feet. "Mr. Edwards, it's such a surprise to see you! I don't suppose you'll remember me, but I was in your creative writing class at Bard about six years ago. I think I got more out of that class than I did out of my entire four years of college."

"And what did you get out of the class, Miss . . . ?"

"Everett. Ginny Everett. You see, you're still the same man: someone says something and you ask them what they mean. You're worse than my shrink. I just meant that I enjoyed it, I guess."

"Ah, yes, the pleasure principle of education. I know it well.

Though I'm inclined to think that ridicule is the best inducement to learning. Would you agree?" He turned to smile at Cordy.

"I can't rightly say," Cordy shrugged, conscious that he was interested in her and feeling a mix of pride and vulnerability. "I wasn't in a very serious or receptive frame of mind when I went to college."

"Where did you go?"

"To Georgia Tech. My husband was going there on a football scholarship an' I sort of trailed along."

"Cordy's from Georgia," Ginny put in.

Cordy raised her eyebrows. "I wish you wouldn't introduce me like that."

"But you are from Georgia."

"I know it. But when I'm introduced like that people make the silliest remarks. Jokes about magnolias or peaches . . ."

"Looking at you, I can see why they might." A corner of Edwards' mouth curled.

". . . or else they sidle up with racial jokes they think I'm going to laugh at."

"Which you don't?" Edwards wanted to know.

"Which I don't, Mr. Edwards." Cordy gave him her "I'm sweet as pie but don't press me" smile. He studied her face as though he was trying to commit it to memory.

"Congratulations on *Galatea*, Mr. Edwards," Ginny said.

"Call me Jonathan."

"Yes, congratulations," Cordy echoed.

"What did you think of the book—ah, Cordy is it?"

"I must confess I haven't read it. I'm sorry."

"Don't be. I have now reached the very pinnacle of literary success, those lofty heights where the public knows about me, has even developed an interest in my personal life, but feels no obligation to read me."

The pianist had finished his lament for "The Boy Next Door" and was hammering away at "Mad Dogs and Englishmen."

"Where are y'all from?" Edwards raised his voice over the music.

Cordy couldn't tell if he was mimicking her accent, asking both she and Ginny, or if his tongue was slurred from liquor. "Savannah," she said offhandedly, handing her plate to a passing waiter.

"That's different. Savannah's a port city. Any port city, even in the Deep South is subject to all sorts of outside influences."

"But we try not to be unduly influenced by them," Cordy smiled.

Edwards laughed and turned, wrapping his knuckles on the piano. "How's about playing 'Georgia on My Mind' for this little lady?" The piano player, grateful for any attention, shifted into the verse of the song. Edwards held out his arms. "Shall we dance?"

"I don't believe there's enough room."

"I don't dance anyway, but I'll make room for us to move from foot to foot," he said, placing his hand in the small of her back and guiding her a few steps. Onlookers moved out of their way. Cordy turned to see Ginny giving her a nod of approval. They almost bumped into a man who was demonstrating tai chi, but he sidestepped them with a graceful movement. Edwards drew her closer to him, his chin grazing her cheekbone. His after-shave—Vertiver was it?—was the same one her father used. She held herself stiffly, conscious of her breasts against his chest. The noise of the room seemed to recede, becoming only a background for the aching melody of the song.

> Georgia, Georgia, the whole day though,
> Just an old sweet song keeps Georgia on my mind . . .

She closed her eyes, the better to feel the other people looking at them. So what if she was being egotistical, she was relishing the attention. It was almost as though he'd picked her lucky number out of a hopper and cried out "And the winner is . . ."

> Georgia, Georgia, a song of you
> Comes as sweet and clear as moonlight
> through the pines . . .

Alidia had taken her to a Ray Charles concert once. The blind Charles had been led to the piano, where he sat, legs flailing to some internal, seemingly uncoordinated rhythm. Then he'd found the exact beat and rocked into it hard, carrying the entire whooping and swooning audience away with him. Alidia had burst into tears.

She could feel Edwards' breath, warm and moist, on her hair, but she couldn't seem to get the movements of his body. Oh, the ease with which she and Lupton had danced together. With the slightest touch Lupton had guided her through dips, twists, and turns. And when they'd danced to rock and roll, the way he'd moved toward her, his hips swiveling in that slow, insinuating grind. She pressed herself closer to Edwards. She was more than willing to follow if only she could sense his lead.

> Other arms reach out to me,
> Other lips smile tenderly,
> Still in peaceful dreams I see
> The road leads back to you.

"What are you thinking about?" Edwards asked.

"A concert I went to back home. I don't know what it is, but this whole summer I keep going back over my past."

"Perhaps your present isn't fulfilling enough," he whispered suggestively. He moved his head back to see the curve of her cheek, the white soft skin of her neck. Goddamn it she was pretty. He'd had a lifetime of fantasies about beautiful, willing women, but during the last year when reality had actually started to conform to his imaginings and a parade of lovelies had been literally within his grasp, he had found himself taking it quite calmly. Too calmly in fact. The result was that his fantasies had become more lurid, but he didn't seem to be able to live up to the reality. Perhaps if he could cut down on his drinking . . . Perhaps if he could take her out to the garden and get some air into his lungs . . . She was compliant, that much he could tell. He'd had a sense of mastery as he seized her. But now that he was actually holding her, his body had a strange sensation, as though her breasts were making indentations in his chest, and malleable as she seemed, her body was actually molding his. "Time," he found himself saying somewhat sententiously, "may be something we invent to stop everything from happening at once."

She nodded, wondering if Jonathan Edwards had a pithy aphorism for every situation. He probably did. She had never been with a famous intellectual before, it was bound to be challenging and a bit intimidating. The music stopped.

"Have you seen the gardens yet?" he asked.

"Oh, Jonathan, there you are." Mel, the host, was shouldering his way toward them. "I see you found Miss—"

"Tyre," Cordy volunteered.

"Or Miss Tyre found you. I'm sorry to interrupt, but there are some friends on the terrace who've been bugging me to introduce you."

Jonathan sighed, "You're so smart with your computers, why don't we just get my responses to all the standard questions and feed them into a program? Because if one more person asks me what hours of the day I work I might get violent."

"O.K. I'll tell them you're busy."

"No. I know how to sing for my supper. Where the hell are they?"

"On the terrace, but if you don't want to . . ."

Jonathan took Cordy's hand. "If this lovely lady will come with me," he said as he started to move toward the terrace, "I'll go. And if you could, Mel, have the waiter bring me another scotch on the rocks. Georgia, what'll you have?"

"Bourbon."

"I should have known."

As soon as she was introduced to the people on the terrace—a woman who described herself as an "avid reader" and her husband, who manufactured winches—Cordy slipped into a lounge chair. Being married to Lupton had given her plenty of practice at being the celebrity's consort. She knew when to fade into the background. Edwards, drink in hand, accepted the woman's compliments on *Galatea*, then turned on her. "If you're an 'avid' reader, then you should find a better adjective to describe yourself. 'Avid' reader is like 'bearded' demonstrator or 'avowed' Communist. It's a cliché." Cordy thought the remark was rude, but instead of being insulted, the woman smiled, as though Edwards had just given her a tip on the stock market. "And are your winches strong enough to hoist the wenches, or do you get hoisted on your own petard?" he teased the husband. The man laughed heartily. A few people drifted over to join the conversation or, more accurately, to listen, for Edwards dominated. He took another drink, which made him even more voluble. Cordy was amazed at the depth and range of his knowledge. He could seize on any topic, had a decided opinion on every subject; and the way he used words, as though they were tools or weapons, was impressive. He hammered, pried, shaped, and cut with them, glancing at her occasionally to make sure she was taking in a witty remark or agreed with a point he'd made. She was, for the most part, very entertained, but glad that she had chosen to be on the sidelines.

She had nursed her second bourbon down to a single melting ice cube when she noticed that the composition and tempo of the party had changed. The crowd had thinned out. Those lucky enough to have found a likely prospect had broken off into pairs and stood in corners, heads close together, arms draped, negotiating the next move. The man in the lounge chair next to hers had passed out completely. Waiters were picking up glasses and plates. A few die-hards who were determined to have a fun time had taken to the lighted courts, where the soft thup-thup of tennis balls was interrupted with shrieking excuses that they were too drunk or too stoned to play. Even the music sounded tired.

"And why shouldn't a book just be a book?" Edwards was asking. Without pausing, he went on to answer his own question. "It should be. I remember a high school teacher of mine saying a book was like a ship: It should take you anywhere. But since publishing has been taken over by conglomerates and is run by accountants and lawyers, the whole mentality has been corrupted. What does some guy who figures out cost overruns for Gulf and Western know about literature? He's only interested in whether a book can be turned into a TV show and whether the TV show is enough of a blockbuster to produce T-shirts and toys." He glared at the four or five people who were standing around him as though they were personally responsible for this turn of events. Cordy nodded. He looked so pained and frustrated that she was inclined to sympathize with him, though from the little she knew she couldn't see where he had personally been victimized. She turned her eyes back to the tennis courts and saw Maxine, looking the worse for wear, moving unsteadily toward her.

"Do you know it's almost midnight?" Maxine crouched next to her and whispered. "If you don't have something going here it's time to go home."

"Where's Ginny?"

"Last time I saw her she was hiding in the bathroom."

"And Estelle?"

"She disappeared with Ken Ebbleman about an hour ago. That's why Ginny's in the bathroom. C'mon, let's get this show on the road."

Cordy put her drink on the table next to her and started to get up.

"Hey, Georgia, where do you think you're going?" Edwards wanted to know.

"It's late and—"

"I'll take you home. Just let me finish this drink."

"See you at the house," Maxine said, as though Edwards' invitation automatically signaled Cordy's acceptance.

Cordy stood up uncertainly. Edwards was bound to be more interesting than Maxine's postmortem on the party. She asked for directions about getting back to the house. Maxine reeled them off and walked away.

"And what's your next book about, if I may be so bold as to ask?" the avid reader wanted to know.

Edwards drained his glass. "It's about a feminist who survives the Holocaust, goes to Beverly Hills, opens a boutique, and sleeps with a C.I.A. agent who happens to be a millionaire. Does that cover all the bases? Georgia, are you ready to go?"

Cordy nodded, smiling an apology at the woman, not altogether sure that she wanted Edwards to take her home, but taking his arm and following him back through the atrium. The piano player was picking out "Good Night, Ladies" with one finger and fluttered his free hand in farewell as they passed.

There were only a dozen or so cars parked at the end of the drive. Edwards pulled open the door of a VW bus. "I hate this car," he muttered. "This car has been out to get me ever since I bought it twelve years ago. I'm going to trade it in and get myself a sports car. God, I can't stand parties. I know they bring out the worst in me. I'm like the kid who didn't make it to the varsity team so he sits on the bench being sarcastic."

"But you were the celebrity," she said as he took her hand to help her up into the cab.

He looked at her with gentle curiosity, as though she, out of the entire herd, was the one who held some hope of deliverance. "What say we take a spin down to the beach?"

"It's kinda late."

"We won't take long. Then I'll take you home."

She'd looked forward to being at the beach even more than she'd wanted to be with people, and if that meant going at one in the morning, so be it. "All right."

He parked the car at the end of a road near some beach houses, but made no attempt to get out. Peering through the darkness, she could see silvery dunes and hear the steady pounding of the surf. She wanted to walk, look at the watery moon, feel the sand beneath her feet, and cleanse her lungs with the salty air. Instead she sat very still, listening to Edwards' continuing monologue and studying his face. Despite the sharpness of his features, he had a melancholy look, as though he was searching for something he'd given up hope of finding. She thought his conversation somewhat self-indulgent and the way his eyes did one thing while his mouth did another unnerved her, but she had to admit that she was impressed. He was a successful master of a craft in which she was the humblest sort of novice.

After a time he too seemed to be calmed by the sound of the waves. He put his arm around her, pulling her to him. His hand dangled over her shoulder, almost touching her breast. She felt as confused as when she'd been taken to the movies by some boy who might want to cop a feel.

"So are you divorced or what?" he asked, moving so that their legs touched from knee to thigh.

"I'm separated. I'm even separated from myself."

"But also from your great big football-playing husband."

"He doesn't play football anymore," she said quietly.

"So why did you run away to this part of the country?"

"I write"—better to tell the truth and face his derision right now—"romance novels. Or at least I used to. I came up here to find an agent. I thought it was going to be real difficult, but I got lucky. So now I'm going to try something a bit more challenging." Her words sounded so tinny to her own ear that for a moment she forgot the proximity of his hand to her breast. "The book I'm working on now—"

"Ah, romance novels. The folk tales of the true female psyche. An interesting genre. I was thinking of teaching a class on them."

This wasn't the response she'd anticipated. She turned her face to him, wanting to continue the conversation, but his hand had now dropped to fondle her breast. Her nipple stiffened under the brush of his fingertips and she dropped her gaze. What if he were another Sean Heandy? The notion of being chosen and then discarded was more than her emotional traffic could bear. But her body was responding all by itself, without asking permission. "I knew the minute I saw you that you weren't one of those ambitious career types. Ah, the times are out of joint," he breathed, "so many of the

nymphs have turned into Valkyries." He gave her breast a squeeze
and she looked at him in surprise before he buried his face in her
neck, gasping as though he'd just dived into the surf. Feeling the
tingle and moisture between her legs, she wondered if he would suggest going back to his place or try to take her here in the car. Her
arms felt their way up to his and locked around him. As she arched
herself into him he bit her neck. Had they been further along in the
rough and tumble, the bite might have been pleasurable; just now it
caused her to wince. The risk of being on an unknown beach with a
stranger flashed through her mind. What if Edwards' lovemaking
was as cruel as his words? How should she respond to his next
move?

But she didn't have to respond, because he drew away, threw
his head back and intoned, "'Had we but world enough, and time,/
This coyness, lady, were no crime.'"

She couldn't imagine what he was talking about, since her actions had been anything but coy.

"God!" he laughed, slapping the steering wheel. "I've been trying to remember the beginning of that poem all night."

"I know"—she released her tension by joining him in the laughter—"isn't it just awful when you have something goin' round and
round in your head and you just can't take hold of it?"

"Worse than you know, Georgia," he muttered, his voice both
tired and angry. "Worse than you'll ever know."

"It's that I'm not enjoying your company," she said after a
pause, "but I'm feeling awfully tired."

"Really that tired? Have you got a headache too?" he teased in
another sudden mood change, his hand reaching to give her knee an
avuncular pat. "All right. I'll take you home." He said it with gentlemanly resignation, as though she'd just fought off his advances but
he knew how to be a good sport about it. "Christ, I've got another
goddamn soirée to go to tomorrow night. I mean tonight. I don't
know when I'm ever going to get any work done."

"Couldn't you just send your apologies?"

"Impossible. A movie producer who's taken an option on the
book has invited me. It would make my life a hell of a lot more
pleasant if you'd go with me."

"I'd be happy to," she said, relieved that the proposition she'd
expected had been scaled down to an invitation.

The next morning, as an audaciously brilliant sun poured

through the windows, Cordy surfaced from a convoluted, highly erotic dream. She opened her eyes and quickly squeezed them shut, trying to recapture the Samurai warrior who was lifting her legs onto his shoulders with exquisite grace and gazing at her with a calm but purposeful expression; but the posters of E.T. and Reggie Jackson kept intruding. She cupped her hand over her pubic bone, a quizzical expression coming onto her face. Samurai lover. In a cave. She dressed in a hoop skirt *sans* panties. Curious. But even real life was curious. A year ago she would never have dreamt of being in the Hamptons and going out with a famous writer.

She threw back the sheet and went to the window. It was a glorious day for the beach, though she suspected Maxine wasn't up yet and that it would be midafternoon before they got there. She pulled on a pair of underpants and a T-shirt, opened the door, confirmed that no one was about, and went downstairs. She was rummaging in the kitchen cabinets trying to find a can of coffee or at least a jar of instant when she heard the back door slam. "Morning," Ginny smiled, perching herself on a chair. There was a puffiness around Ginny's eyes that suggested she might not have taken Ken Ebbleman's defection with complete equanimity. "Do tell, Cordy. What happened with Edwards? I didn't expect to see you here this morning."

While improvising a paper towel into a filter and pouring the last of the can of coffee into it, Cordy repeated as much of Edwards' conversation as she could remember.

"But what else happened?" Ginny pressed. Cordy could tell from her expression that Ginny thought she was keeping the really juicy parts of her adventure from her.

"I was so sleepy I really don't remember. He said something about man's alienation from Nature, but that was in German and I don't speak German. And he quoted that Andrew Marvell poem."

"'To His Coy Mistress'? Oh, he taught that in freshman poetry. How could you do it? How could you play coy and take the chance of being hard to get with Jonathan Edwards?"

"I wasn't playing hard to get. He was just quoting the poem." She poured the boiling water over the few spoonfuls of coffee. "Do you think we can get to the grocery store today?"

The door to the hallway swung open and Maxine, shielding her eyes, came in. "Did I smell coffee?" she asked, lowering her hand. Last night's mascara was smeared around her lids, giving her the look of an angry raccoon.

"Not much of it," Ginny said. "We'll have to go to the market."

"I did the shopping last week. You guys go and I'll pay you my share when you get back. Oh, shit, I feel awful. I feel lower than whale manure."

Cordy poured an equal amount of coffee into three cups. "If you'll give me the car keys and tell me where the market is, I'll go."

"I should think Ginny would be the one who'd want to get out of the house," Maxine said pointedly. "Unless she wants Ken to come downstairs and catch her in that ratty nightshirt."

Cordy put down her coffee. She had no idea that Ken Ebbleman and Estelle had been brazen enough to nest in the upstairs bedroom. Ginny drew her feet up onto her chair and started to pick the polish off her toes. "How did you plan it, Cordy? I mean, what was your strategy with Edwards?"

"I didn't have a strategy. I was as surprised as you were when he started talking to us."

"It's the Southern accent," Maxine asserted. "Men think Southern girls are hot and scatterbrained. That, and her wedding ring. Men always get turned on when they think a woman belongs to another man."

"I don't *belong* to anyone," Cordy said.

"You see"—Maxine yawned—"women fall into two categories: doormats and cuff links. Doormats"—she gave a vague nod in Ginny's direction—"are to walk on. Cuff links are to put on his arm to show how rich he is."

"I expect you learned that in one of your Success Seminars," Cordy said coolly.

"Nope. Life observation. God, I'm wasted this morning. I'm taking this coffee back to bed. Maybe we'll hit the beach this afternoon."

Cordy swallowed the last of the coffee and got up to rinse her cup, anxious to get upstairs and dress before Ken Ebbleman appeared. But as soon as Maxine had gone she couldn't help herself from asking, "Don't you mind, Ginny? Don't you mind about Ken and Estelle being upstairs?"

"I used to live in a coed dorm," Ginny shrugged, then secured her lower lip with her teeth and said more softly, "Of course I feel badly. But I know I shouldn't."

"How do you know that? I mean, I'd be throwing a tizzy."

"It's my fault. You see, I really want to get married. I hate playing around, so I get clutchy. It was probably my need for a premature commitment that drove Ken away."

"I know what my grandmother would say." Cordy was emphatic. "If you want to get married—which I'm here to tell you is not always the most blissful state—then you don't set yourself up as part of a harem. It makes it too easy for men."

"But how can you say no to some guy without running the risk of losing him to someone who'll say yes? And if you want him, isn't it hypocritical to say no?"

"I don't know." Cordy opened her hands in a appeal to be let off the hook. "You probably know more about his game than I do. But I do know one thing: It was tacky of Ken and Estelle to come back here."

"What exactly does tacky mean?"

"Tacky is . . . tacky. It's plastic slipcovers, or bad-mouthing your kin, or letting the roots of a dye job show. Or"—she flustered—"or not having coffee in the house when you know you're going to have people to visit."

Ginny reached for her hand. "Don't mind Maxine. She's had a lot of disappointments this summer. She was just being bitchy. I know that Edwards picked you up because he genuinely liked you. And"—she smiled again, eliciting trust—"I know it would be tacky to ask for details, but he must be a wonderful lover."

"Could I have the keys to your car? I really have to go get something to eat."

After doing the grocery shopping, Cordy drove around looking for a bookstore. She knew that she would have to plow through several volumes of theater and social history, as well as books on the fashions of the times and diaries of Fanny's contemporaries, if she was to do a good job on her book, but she couldn't resist taking time off to read *Galatea*. Maxine had left a note on the kitchen table saying she was spending the afternoon in bed recuperating, Ginny was nowhere to be found, and Ken and Estelle were sunbathing and playing kissy-face on the terrace, so she went up to her room and started to read.

By five o'clock, when she stopped to get ready for her date, she had almost finished the book. Edwards was a master stylist. The way he stacked up the words was awesome. But she was thoroughly confused by the plot. It was, as Ginny had hinted, impossible to figure out who Galatea was. She was no mere creature of flesh and blood. She had a madonnalike devotion to maternity, but her flip side was an obsessive need to gratify men with oral sex, the instances of which were steamy, elegiac, and so numerous that it was sheer bad luck that she'd ever gotten pregnant. But, Cordy thought as she came out of the shower and put on her blue dress, it was simplistic in the extreme to think of a writer's work as merely autobiographical. Edwards was no more the idealistic woodsman who was the hero of his book that she was the simpy Roxanne.

Wanting to be ready the moment Edwards arrived, Cordy went downstairs. She peeked into the kitchen to see Ginny, her eyes hidden behind dark glasses, doing the dishes while Maxine gave her a pep talk. She tiptoed into the living room and settled on the couch. The doorbell rang almost immediately, and Estelle, wearing a robe and carrying her purse, ran downstairs calling, "It's for us." She paid the delivery boy, walked by Cordy without a word, and ascended the stairs bearing Mr. Ebbleman's pizza as though it were the Holy Grail. Moments later Maxine, her arm protectively draped around Ginny's waist, came in to announce that they were going to see *Octopussy*. They'd just backed out of the drive when Cordy heard Jonathan's car.

The party was much like the one they'd been to the night before. She stood or sat by Edwards' side, feeling the envious glances of the other women and the polite sexual interest of the men, while Edwards, again the center of attention, held forth on any topic that entered his mind. He compared the shift to a technological society to the upheavals of the Industrial Revolution, wondered aloud about the difficulties of adapting novels to the screen, expressed his preference for nouvelle cuisine and Regency architecture. Again she was impressed by his mental acrobatics and flattered when he acknowledged her with "How am I doing?" looks or inquired about the freshness of her drink. But afterwards, as they drove back to the house, he seemed spent and almost tongue-tied. He turned off the ignition and drew her to him, fondling her in that way that was by turns casual then rough. Perhaps, she thought as he pinned her to the door and buried his face in her breasts, the surroundings were not conducive to anything but clumsy foreplay. She considered inviting him up to the room, but changed her mind when she thought of the bunk beds and posters. Out of half-closed eyes she saw the light go on in the living room and pulled away, pushing her half-exposed breast back into her dress. "Oh, did I make a mistake staying here," she whispered. "I feel as though I've been cast in some movie called *Dormitory Dolls.*"

"Then let me rescue you. I'm driving back into the city tomorrow. I can take you home."

"You know I came out here to go to the beach and I've never even seen the beach," she sighed. "And I've been so uncomfortable. Sure. I'd be grateful if you'd give me a lift back."

"But that doesn't mean I'm going to let you out of my clutches." He stroked his finger across her collarbone. "I want to see a lot of you, Georgia. A whole lot of you."

Chapter XIII

The omens were auspicious when Cordy returned to New York. There was a note from Cliff saying that Sylvia's parents had persuaded her to come home for some "rest," a letter from Nonnie, and, much to her surprise, two messages from Sean Heandy on the answering machine. She played the tape back several times, listening for the nuances, relishing even this electronic capitulation. The first message was matter-of-fact: He was sorry he'd missed her and left his number. The second had a more repentant tone: He'd been thinking about her but had been busy with work. When could they get together? She could sense that her lack of availability had made her more desirable. "You can go fry ice, Heandy," she talked back to the machine. "I have more important things to do with my time than wait on you." She had another date with Jonathan Edwards that very evening. Edwards, who, despite the pressures of his celebrity, had found time for her. Edwards, who, despite his acid tongue, was gentleman enough to want to get to know her before he took her to bed. And she had her own work to do. She had intended to go to the library that afternoon, but decided to go shopping and have her hair done instead. Tomorrow, she vowed, she would get back to her research. She would end her New York trip in perfect balance: working during the day and enjoying herself at night.

Edwards had other plans. He had no intention of confining himself to the evening hours. He wanted to take her everywhere and show her everything. In addition to the round of dinners and parties at night, he set aside the afternoons for her cultural improvement. He took her to the Cloisters and explained the symbolism of the Unicorn tapestries, insisted that they go to a series of *film noir* at the Museum of Modern Art and the retrospective at the Guggenheim. She began to wonder when he ever had time to get any writing done. Sometimes he was a bit condescending in his self-appointed role of mentor; but, she convinced herself, while her reference books lay unopened on her desk, that this was the sort of opportunity she couldn't pass up. She was meeting the famous and the near famous. She was seeing New York, really seeing it, from tatty brownstones near Columbia University where people still sat on the floor and passed bottles of cheap wine while they discussed literature and philosophy, to elegantly eccentric SoHo lofts where the cocaine was plentiful and even Edwards' voice was drowned out by New Wave rock.

But no matter where they went they always ended up on Maggie's couch. Edwards fondled, bit, and pinched her. He nuzzled her breasts. He partially undressed her. Sometimes he quoted poetry. But there was no chance he would cost her another dry-cleaning bill. In the mornings she woke up groggy and irritable, wondering what had been so important that it had kept her up until three in the morning. But she always woke up alone.

Her initial relief that he hadn't rushed her into bed gave way to doubts about her own attractiveness. Was she too plump, too aggressive, too passive? Did she smell bad? It was out of the question that she should inquire about any of these things directly. She decided to be patient. She tried, ever so gently, to find out about his background and his marriage, hoping to piece together clues to the trauma that had incapacitated him. She thought of breaking it off entirely, but the memory of lonely nights in the apartment made her feel like a kid who'd been quarantined with mumps. She thought of saying, "Let's be friends, but please no more kissy games," but decided that would be too cruel.

How, she wondered, had she ever been romantic enough to deny all of her experience with men and assume that Edwards was delaying sex because he wanted to get to know her? Not wanting to crush his ego by mentioning the dreaded word "impotence," she found herself drawn into an insidious game, pleading fatigue, headache, or upset stomach in order to break off their frustrating sessions on the couch. And Jonathan, innocent Jonathan, would stuff his shirt back into his pants and bid her a doleful good night as though he were the injured party.

Edwards' public behavior did nothing to disabuse people of the notion that he and Cordy were having the affair of the season. The way he touched her—his hand lingering on her hip bone or brushing her hair back behind her ears—gave the subtle but definite impression of sexual intimacy. She could never find a polite way of discouraging these gestures, but allowing them made her feel as though she was an unwilling conspirator in another deception.

During the middle of their second week together, Jonathan had taken her to another dinner party. She found herself, yet again, in the equivalent of front row center, this time in a Jacobean chair with a view of the East River. The maid was passing after-dinner drinks, and Jonathan was holding forth on the shortcomings of the Rockefeller Foundation. A man with a shock of prematurely gray hair and engaging blue eyes was watching her. When she followed the hostess into the solarium to see the bonsai collection, the man followed, waited for the hostess to leave, and promptly engaged Cordy in conversation. After a brief chat he asked for her phone number. She paused for a moment, realized there was nothing disloyal in accepting the request, gave him the number, and drifted back to her appointed seat in Jonathan's audience.

Despite the hostess's objections, Jonathan signaled that it was time to go. He drew Cordy to his side, draping his arm around her shoulder and nipping at her ear. The man who'd asked for her phone number was standing a little distance from them. When he heard Edwards say that he'd love to stay but Cordy was so tired that she "hadn't been able to open her big brown eyes this morning," he gave Cordy a sly cheat-to-cheat smile and took the hand of the woman standing next to him. Cordy saw that they were wearing matching rings.

"I really do have to get up early tomorrow," Cordy said as she and Jonathan reached the door of her apartment.

"Not even one lil' ol' nightcap?"

"'Fraid not. I have to get to the library when it opens. I have overdue books that I haven't even opened yet and I just can't stand to look at myself in the mirror unless I get something done."

"I thought we New England types were the ones plagued with guilty consciences," he drawled as he put one arm on the doorjamb. "You Southern belles are supposed to be exempt. You may feel a bit of remorse if you take that extra helping of dessert"—he pinched her behind—"but never guilt and surely not about work."

"Jonathan . . ."

"All right. I'll excuse you tomorrow, but how about going back out to the Hamptons with me for a few days? My editor and his wife are finally coming out to the house. You should meet them."

"I am sorry, Jonathan, but I really can't." She gave him her sweetest smile and got out her keys. She could imagine it now: the speculation and innuendo that would result if she and Jonathan had separate rooms, or three sleepless nights, if not an outright confrontation, if they didn't. She would come to the breakfast table, and the host and his wife would smile knowingly, seeing the bags under her eyes as the ravages of wild indulgence. "I really can't."

"Don't pull the rug out from under me."

That Jonathan Edwards had uttered a cliché without even commenting on it amused but saddened her. "I wouldn't do any such thing," she said, studying his face. Poor Jonathan, hiding out in the lofty watershed of his contempt, able to talk about every subject except the one that most concerned him. She turned her eyes away and put the key in the door, afraid that her face would betray her knowledge of the very private secret of this very public man. "You know I'm fond of you Jonathan, but I really do have to get some work done."

"All right"—he nodded, instantly jaunty—"I'll excuse you from going, but I'll be back in town Tuesday afternoon."

She felt a vast relief as she got into bed. The night was cool enough to have the windows open, and as she was drifting off to sleep she heard a couple coming down the street. Though she couldn't hear the exact words of their conversation, the tone of it was warm and lilting. Their voices overlapped, dipped into whispers, and rose to laughter; their intimacy was as sweet as a breeze across a lake. Summer lovers. More than envy, she had a sense of deprivation as she heard them pass. She watched the shadows of the tree on the wall, groped for the clock radio, let her fingers verify that the alarm button was on, then rolled onto her side, drawing her legs up to her chest.

"Big Apple time is eight forty-five. This is All News Eighty-eight. You give us twenty-two minutes, we'll give you the world." The announcer's voice roused her from her dead-man's-float position. "Fat chance," she groaned, fumbling for the switch. As she got to her feet and reached for her robe, she noticed that Maggie's desk

calendar hadn't been flipped for two weeks. Groggy, she turned the
pages and realized that she had a scant ten days remaining in New
York. Her time out of time, her island of freedom, was soon going to
be lost. And she'd been wasting time worrying about Jonathan Edwards, listening to lectures about obscure French movie directors,
being dazzled by introductions to people whose effect on her life was
no more illuminating than playing with a twenty-five-cent sparkler
on the Fourth of July. As she showered and dressed she felt an
urgency so vibrant and impatient that it was almost sexual. "Hit the
streets," Cliff had instructed her, and as she opened the front door to
the building, sniffed the potent combination of garbage, flowers, and
car exhaust, she was grateful to be alone. Her mind never, but
never, functioned at peak performance when she was with anyone
else, particularly a man. In the presence of men she sucked in her
stomach, smiled too much, worried about her makeup, and asked
silly questions. Men simultaneously intimidated and glorified her,
swung her between the extremes of adoration and contempt.

   She got onto the bus and found a seat near the rear, studying
the other passengers and making up stories about their lives. She felt
that she understood what made this one's mouth sag with resignation, sharpened that one's features with curiosity, or etched lines of
bewilderment in the forehead of another. She was so sure that her
observations were correct that when she got up to leave she was
tempted to ask the woman sitting near the door if it was true that she
was divorced, thirty-seven years old, had no children, watched educational television, and had three whiskey sours before dinner.

   After spending several hours at the theater collection at the Lincoln Center library, she came out into the afternoon heat, bought
some souvlaki from a street vendor, and wandered up Central Park
West. Passing the Museum of Natural History, she decided to go in.
The marble walls and high ceilings of the front hall were cool relief
from the sun-baked streets. She strolled into a semi-darkened room
where stuffed tigers, antelope, bears, and lions stood out from
artfully painted backdrops. A troop of children about Jeanette's age
were being shushed and counted. When the teacher ushered them
out of the room Cordy followed. They bypassed the bird collection
and went into the hall of insects.

   The teacher grouped them in front of a display case and tapped
the glass. "This is the dragonfly. Remember last week when we were
studying the dragonfly? And what did we learn about them? James?"

James looked down at his scuffed Adidas and muttered, "They're water insects."

"That's right," the teacher encouraged. "And what else do we know? Janet?"

"The females are called nymphs."

"That's right."

"How do they . . . you know . . ." a girl with a freckle-sprinkled face wanted to know.

"She means copulate," the precocious Janet explained. Her classmates erupted with giggles and uncontrolled hoots. The teacher tried to quite them with a wave of her hand. "The dragonfly's adaptation to life in the air extends to mating," she said, her voice as measured and aloof as the narration of a documentary. "Dragonflies mate in the air. They fly together in tandem. As they mate they appear to be a single insect. Both the male and the female fly forward simultaneously, and in such a position that all four pairs of wings operate independently and without interference. Any more questions? If not, take your partner by the hand and come quietly—I said quietly. Joseph, do you want to go and sit in the bus while we finish up here?" Joseph had stretched his arms and was waving them up and down, much to the delight of the freckle-faced girl. "If not then you'd best control yourself. Come on now children, let's go."

Cordy moved a step closer to the glass case and studied the long, slender bodies and filmy wings of the dragonflies. An idea for the book sprang into her mind. She knew that when Fanny's husband Pierce had taken her to his plantation on Butler Island, Fanny often escaped the oppression of the big house by rowing through the Altamaha delta. Much to the scandal of other planters' wives, Fanny sometimes took up the oar herself. Cordy would write a scene in which Fanny rowed through the lush, steamy waterways. The boat's crew would be singing one of the songs they had made up about Fanny's "wire waist"; and Fanny, watching the dragonflies gliding in tandem, would see in their airborne coupling all the freedom of movement and sense of equality that was lacking in her own life.

Cordy had the sensation of being watched. She turned to see a dark-skinned young man in a seersucker suit, a Nikon dangling from his neck. He moved his head quickly, making it all the more obvious that he'd been looking at her. She went through the archway toward what she thought was the exit, but found herself in a room full of birds. Trying to locate a floor map, she paused next to a fearful-looking vulture.

"This is your national bird, is it not?"

The young man was by her side. Thinking that he was making some sort of political joke, she replied curtly, "No, it is not. Our national bird is the bald eagle. If you ask one of the guards I'm sure he'll direct you to it."

"I am very sorry." The apology came out in a heavy, caressing accent she couldn't immediately identify. He bowed slightly, sensing that he had offended but at a loss to understand how, and stepped closer to the case. "Ah, yes. This is identified as a buzzard. Buzzards are birds of prey, and they do not soar, am I correct?"

"I think they just swoop." She smiled, looking at him more closely. He couldn't have been more than twenty years old. He was just about her height, so his liquid dark eyes, with brows that were thicker than her own but had the same fine arch, looked directly into hers. His black hair was neatly slicked back from his forehead and his lips had the curved delineation of Roman sculpture.

"Forgive me of observing, but you seem to be alone." He spoke very slowly, either summoning his courage or searching for the correct phrase with which to introduce himself. "I am also alone. I have come to see the museums of New York City. Would you wish to accompany me to the Hall of Gems?"

"I am sorry but—"

"Perhaps the lava of Pompeii would interest you."

"No. I was just looking for the exit."

"Then may I escort you?"

"No harm in that."

By the time they'd found their way out, he was suggesting that he walk her home.

"My name is Rafael Quidillo," he announced as they waited for the light to change. "I am from Caracas. Caracas is in Venezuela."

"Yes, I know. Are you a student?"

"Yes, I am a student, but at the Sorbonne, which is in Paris."

"Yes, I know that too."

"Parlez vous français?"

"Sorry, no. What are you doing in New York?"

"I have come to visit my father, who is doing business in Washington, which—"

"—which is the capital of the United States," she teased.

"Exactly," he said with deep seriousness, then smiled quickly, exposing a set of perfect teeth. "I apologize that I have only textbook English. I will visit my father in three days' time, but until then I am obliged to visit all cultural attractions of New York."

"That can get to you after a while. I know." She started across the street. "Well, Rafael, I hope you enjoy yourself."

"May I buy you a fruit drink or a Coca-Cola? Or perhaps"—he caught up with her and added shyly—"perhaps you would prefer some cocktail."

"That's very kind of you, but I must go home and work." The scene of Fanny watching the dragonflies was floating in her mind and she was determined not to be distracted.

"If you are otherwise engaged," he said with impeccable if stilted courtesy, "then perhaps I may be permitted to call upon you at a more appropriate time."

"You are remarkably persistent." She stopped and shook her head.

"Persistence, I believe, is not incompatible with courtship in your country. Here a man must be persistent because the woman may exercise free will in her choice of a partner."

"Free will is a very complex concept, Rafael, and I don't have time to discuss it now. I'm on my way home."

He moved a few steps in front of her, almost dancing. "I am not doubting the veracity of your words. American women are known to be forthright. They are also known for their independence and, if I may say, for the beauty of their legs."

She stopped and laughed out loud, then moved on, but at a much slower pace. It was such a lovely afternoon, and so far her aimless activity had stimulated and pleased her. She volunteered where she was from. He launched into a discussion of William Faulkner, Tennessee Williams, and Flannery O'Connor. When she told him that O'Connor's birthplace was just a few blocks from her grandmother's house he said her townspeople must be honored to have such a celebrated citizen. "Oh, no. I once heard my mother say that she felt sorry for O'Connor because she was an old maid. Old maid," she explained, seeing his brow crease, "is a woman who's never married."

"But surely this is of little importance in a woman of such abilities," he suggested. "Surely it is only in a backward culture where such a judgment would be made."

"I'm sorry to tell you that you're wrong. Women who aren't married are thought of as being eccentric or undesirable."

"But this is most strange."

"Yes, but that's still the way things are. Listen, Rafael, I've enjoyed talking with you, but this is the block where I live, so I must say goodbye." She put out her hand. He slipped his own under hers, started to raise it to his bowed head, then straightened up and clasped it tighter, but did not shake it. A prickly current of electricity went up the flesh of her arm. A lock of his hair had fallen onto his forehead and she wanted to push it back, let her fingertips trace the dark brows and linger on the beautiful line of his mouth. "Did you say you're going to Washington in a few days?"

"Eastern Airlines, Flight 630. Tuesday morning."

"Why then I suppose you might come by. Say tomorrow afternoon, around one o'clock. We could have lunch together."

Rafael arrived at five minutes to one the following day bearing a coffee table–size book of Monet prints and a bottle of cabernet sauvignon. He carried a list of restaurants torn from the *Cue* supplement and read it to her as she uncorked the wine. When she handed him his glass he sniffed and sipped with the cool manner of a connoisseur, then grinned. "May we crash the glass? Symbolically. As I have seen a Russian student in Paris do."

"You're on," she agreed. Four dollars and a trip to the store seemed a small price for his enthusiasm.

He closed his eyes as though he had climbed a high diving board and couldn't bear to see the water before he plunged, then swallowed the contents, dashed the glass to the floor and reached for her. His kiss was inexpert and so persistent that she had the feeling of being in a breath-holding contest. When they finally came unglued she couldn't help a sputtering laugh from escaping.

"I did not do it artfully?" he asked.

She brought her hand to her mouth, afraid she had offended, but his expression was one of curiosity with no hint of defensiveness. She took his chin in her hands and brought his mouth to hers, letting her tongue move in tender exploration. "I see," he whispered as he released her.

"And now, Rafael, I think we'd best go out and have some lunch."

"If you wish to be taken to lunch, then of course I will take you.

But as I look into your eyes, I do not think that your real wish is to be taken to lunch."

"No," she admitted, smiling at the persuasiveness of gentle honesty. "I do not really wish to be taken to lunch."

He took her hand, picked up the wine bottle, guided her around the glass on the floor and into the bedroom. She started to take off her blouse, but he whispered, "Please allow me," finished unbuttoning it, slipped it from her shoulders and stood shaking his head in wonder. They slid onto the bed. When she was naked he rolled from her and stood up, undressing himself, methodically folding his clothes and placing them on the chair. His body, smooth and muscular, without chest hair, reminded her of a statue of a warrior prince. He was eager and as patient as a young engineer learning the parts of a complicated machine; and she lay back guiding his hands, helping him to rouse her to a peak of high, relaxed intensity, then guided him into her. She felt the surprise, absurdity, and complete involvement of a dream state. Minutes later his solemn vigor was released in a brief, sharp cry.

When his breathing had calmed, she asked him if he had ever been with a woman before. He nodded a swift affirmation, then turned his head to look into her face, admitting that the women had been "professionals, which is something entirely different." She said she could see as to how it might be, smiling at his combination of sophistication and naivete. "But I will try again. Like the kiss," he insisted.

"I think you'll have to take time out," she said, rising onto her knees and reaching for the wine on the desk.

"But why?"

"Not for me. For you." She sipped the wine and contemplated the typewriter. Tonight she really must . . . Rafael was on his knees behind her, his hands locked onto her hip bones, pulling her to him. She had forgotten the continuous ardor of a very young man. The time-out suggestion was unnecessary. "Slower this time," she whispered.

"Of course. Every time slower. Slower"—he was easing in— "until everything stop. Everything."

Afterwards, as they lay toe to toe and hip to hip, she had a sensation of floating, acutely aware but content to let herself drift. Through slit eyes she admired the wash of sunlight on the wall and the contrast of Rafael's dark legs against the peach-colored sheets.

His body was still slick with perspiration, and he squirmed as she slid her hand down his chest, over his belly, to let her fingers rest on the spot where the taut flesh of his leg joined his groin. "My sweetheart girlfriend," he sighed. He rolled onto his stomach, turned his body around and slithered down her length. Kissing her instep, he pulled himself around to face her and placed her feet on his shoulders. "This I saw once in a book belonging to my uncle." He smiled. She smiled back, locking his image into her brain so that she would see him as she felt him, then closed her eyes.

Around six o'clock he announced that he would have to go. He was deeply apologetic about not spending the night with her, but he was staying with the family of the Venezuelan consul and was expected for dinner. He didn't seem to believe her when she said she didn't mind, but it was the truth. The afternoon had been idyllic and she didn't want to spoil it by finding out if he snored or hogged the bed, didn't want to wake up puffy-eyed and needing to brush her teeth. She asked if he wanted to take a shower, but he said that he would "carry the aromas with me." She kissed him goodbye, told him she would see him the following day, then showered and went straight to the typewriter.

If her attention wandered it was only to relish the serendipity of their meeting. A brief affair with a virile Latin princeling was the closest she would ever come to the plot of a romance novel. The difference being that she wouldn't confuse her desire with love. This was love in the afternoon, an entirely different thing, the sort of dalliance enjoyed by the very rich. Secret, transitory, time out of time, with no past and no future. Just present pleasure. And Lupton's imagined rage or Lucille's violent disapproval added just that soupçon of the forbidden, making the whole encounter that much more exciting.

The next day he arrived with a picnic basket from Ruelles, the Columbus Avenue place she had pointed out yesterday. They made love, showered together, and ran, still dripping, into the bed, where they sat cross-legged eating mangoes, pears, and sourdough bread washed down with wine. Rafael became pensive. "Too much happiness can rip the soul," he informed her. He had treasured the fantasy of making love to a beautiful American ever since his childhood, but it seemed this fantasy was commingled with some sense of betrayal. He had, he explained, grown up as a citizen of the international community, but lately he had developed a sense of obligation to his homeland and culture. He had become critical of the American influence in his nation's politics, and this was causing a rift with his father that he feared was irreparable. She listened until his consternation drove him into a combination of English, French, and Spanish that was totally unintelligible to her.

I wonder what he'll be like in ten years. A man to be reckoned with, I'm sure, she thought. But she reached out to stroke his hair and said lightly, "It's an identity crisis, Rafael. I'd like to tell you it's a passing phase, but I'm going through something like it myself. But"—she pushed him back into the pillows and started to tickle him—"why are you so serious? I can't understand half of what you say."

"You are right, Cordy." He said her name as though he were rolling it around in his mouth, tasting it. "Now we will talk only with bodies."

On Monday afternoon he arrived without food or drink and in a state of depression that had put purplish shadows around his eyes and made his lower lip slack. Instead of folding his clothes, he let them drop to the floor and stood looking at her, his eyes moist and sorrowful. No amount of teasing about the drawings in his uncle's book of erotica could rouse him to playfulness and he made love with the bittersweet solemnity of leave-taking. Afterwards he sat on the edge of the bed rolling and unrolling his sock and picking at a small cut on his knee. He straightened his spine and a glint of purpose came into his eye. "I will tell my father about you. I will explain that you are the subject of my heart and ask for permission to take you to Paris with me until I've finished my studies. Then we will go back to Venezuela. There will be difficulties but—"

"Rafael, you mustn't even think of such a thing. Our . . . our meeting like this—it's just"—she tried to find the right word—"it's an interlude."

He looked at her incredulously. "Don't you love me?"

Of course he had said that he loved her when they were in bed, but she had taken the words as the passion of the moment. She looked around the room. "You are very young, Rafael. You are only what? Twenty-one? Twenty-two?"

"Nineteen," he said sternly.

"Oh. Only nineteen."

"But in these matters it is of no importance, because of love."

"It isn't that I don't care for you. You've made me very happy but . . ." This was a turn of events that she had in no way anticipated. She was touched, tenderly sympathetic, but slightly annoyed.

"But you don't love me?"

"I'm very fond of you."

"How could you welcome me to your bed if you have no love for me?"

"Rafael, please. We met at the museum—we've only known each other for three days."

"This is time enough. I think you are still loving your hateful husband."

"Please don't spoil things by being jealous." She reached to stroke him, but he pulled away. She was sorry she'd told him about Lupton the day before. "If I'd known that this was going to upset you—"

"I am not upset!" He jerked up and stood at the foot of the bed. "I am with broken heart. 'Upset' is a little word appropriate to when one misses a bus or gets a bad mark on an exam."

"Yes. You are right. You must forgive me for not understanding, but you too must try to understand."

"Understand that we are lovers without love? This I know with a professional woman, but—"

"Now wait a minute." She gathered the sheet around her. There was something ridiculous about having an argument while you were stark naked. "Yesterday you said how grateful you were to come to bed with me. I was grateful too. You gave me a lot of pleasure, so don't spoil it now by being insulting."

"So you prefer pleasure without love."

"I don't need the illusion of love for it to be pleasurable. If you're honest with yourself you'll admit that you don't either."

"What is this talk of honesty? No one is lying. Just very bad misunderstanding. You have made me most unhappy. If you don't want me then I will leave you now." He pulled on his pants and turned away from her.

Oh, Lord, she thought, just my luck to have a romantic interlude with a real romantic. Though given his age and character, his tenderness and inexperience, indeed all the things that had attracted her to him and made her feel safe, she might have figured as much. And here she was, acting like any male philanderer saying, I want your body but I don't want to have to deal with your emotions.

"I didn't say I didn't want you, Rafael. Please, don't spoil this last afternoon together. Come back to bed. Ah, come." She reached for his hand, but he stepped aside, buttoning up his shirt. Was it possible that he was willing to forgo one last session of saucy questions, eager responses, and shimmering joy because she wasn't in love with him? "Oh, well"—she let the sheet drop and lay back on the bed, knowing that if he just looked at her his resolve would melt—"if you want to cut off your nose to spite your face." He turned, his brow furrowed at the unknown expression. "It means don't do something self-punishing," she explained.

"I do not punish myself," he said seriously. "You punish me. You have broken my heart." He took his jacket from the floor and left the room. As she heard the door open she ran after him. He stood, his head bowed, his hand on the knob, then slammed the door shut and took her into his arms. "I know from books—not my uncle's book which is just positions, but from other books—there is no balance in love. In love one person always wants more. The lover and the beloved. Which is better, Cordy? Tell me which is better."

"I don't know," she said softly. "I don't know."

There was no time to get back to the typewriter after Rafael left, because she knew that Jonathan was going to call. The prospect of being with him, having to listen to his endless talk, talk, talk, was about as appealing as a cross-country ride on a Greyhound bus. But if she didn't answer the phone he might drop by. So unless she wanted to turn off the lights and go to bed at sunset, she'd better answer the phone. How had she managed to get herself into this position? When she'd been a girl and had scheduled two dates in a single day it had been fun, proof of her popularity. Now she felt like an attendant at a revolving door. And the time it took. Time waiting, time preparing, time doing the postmortems and then hatching new strategies for the next encounter. She was acting out all the stories she'd heard while growing up—of Sue Ellen, who *said* she was going to Italy to study voice, or Suzanne, who *claimed* to be going to New York to get into advertising, when everybody knew that they were really leaving Savannah so that they could go hog wild in a place where nobody knew them. But at least those girls knew what they were about. They'd set out to have a fling, while she had geared her whole life to male attention without even being conscious of it. She'd compensated for Sean's lack of interest by taking up with Jonathan; made up for Jonathan's impotence by enjoying herself with Rafael. And at the bottom of each encounter was the desire to get even with Lupton. As if Lupton could know or care. Yet she had given him more power to direct her actions than she'd given over when she'd actually lived with him.

The phone rang and she heard her recorded message. "You have reached 358-4604, if you wish to leave a message please talk after the beep." She felt like hiding in the closet when she heard Jonathan's voice; "Pick up, Cordy. It's me." All she had to do was say a direct no, but when he asked to come over she found herself complaining about premenstrual cramps in a voice so coy that she might have been doing an imitation of her cousin Flora whose entire life was centered around trips to the gynecologist. Instead of being put off, Edwards said he would drop by with some Chinese food.

"Would nine o'clock be all right?" she asked, thinking that if she could start the evening late and end it early she might be able to get through it without too much misery. Tonight she was determined to break off the relationship entirely. The excuse that was the most effective—that she was in love with another man—couldn't be used, but she would tell him she'd upped the date of her departure.

Jonathan arrived with a bottle of scotch, a sackful of Chinese food, and a copy of *The Elements of Style,* from which, he suggested, Cordy might benefit. He poured himself a drink and sat down on a kitchen chair while she spooned the oysters with black beans and prawns with chili sauce onto plates. Though she had no appetite, she ate slowly and methodically. It was all she could do to sustain a nodding interest in Jonathan's talk, and she needed some activity to occupy herself. Jonathan continued to drink but barely picked at his food. Three days in the sun had tanned his face to a ruddy bronze, but instead of making him look healthy it only emphasized the wintery expression of his eyes. As though sensing her lack of interest, but not even considering the option of drawing her out, he redoubled his conversational efforts. He became fidgety, lit two cigarettes at once, and began to talk faster but in an increasingly desultory manner. By the time she had finished eating he had gone through his evaluation of Yeats, his theories about addiction, predictions about the future of marriage, and a critique of his weekend hostesses' culinary abilities. "And how about you, Georgia? What have you been doing with yourself?" he asked finally.

"I've been in the house mostly. In fact I'd love to take a walk."

He reached across the table and took her hand, licking her fingertips with a show of tender lasciviousness. "I thought we could spend a quiet evening at home."

Her mind clutched at possibilities for entertainment. TV? She wouldn't dare suggest it. Maggie's record collection? A definite no. Music would only be an interruption of his conversation or provide background for another tussle on the couch. Why hadn't she had the guts to say no in the first place? Disengaging her hand, she carried her plate to the sink, catching a glimpse of the half-empty bottle. "Hadn't you better have some more to eat," she suggested. "Booze on an empty stomach—"

"Why is it that you can't know a woman more than a week before she starts playing Mother?"

"I don't think I was doing that, Jonathan. It's just that I'm concerned about—"

"Don't be," he snapped. "Reform isn't in your line. Now come on over here, Georgia, and sit on the old man's lap."

"Jonathan, I really don't feel like . . ."

He lurched up and put his arms around her, pulling her backwards onto the chair with such an awkward movement that they would have landed on the floor had she not grasped the table to steady herself. He was growling playfully, but there was a clumsy determination to the way he was handling her. She felt a flicker of panic. What if he turned really nasty? He must have been drinking before he came and she had seen intimations that he could be a mean drunk. Should she try to humor him or would it be safer to try to get him out of the door before he became completely unmanageable? She pushed his hand away as he fumbled with the zipper of her jeans, struggled to her feet, and rocked backwards, bumping into the refrigerator.

His arms dropped limply to his sides. He laughed, shaking his head. "'What three things does drink especially provoke?'" he intoned, "'Marry, sir, nose-painting, sleep, and urine. Lechery, sir, it provokes and it unprovokes; it provokes the desire, but takes away the performance.' Do you know what that's from?"

Catching her breath, she shook her head, her mouth forcing a smile but her eyes wary. Whether the drink was the reason for his impotence or the other way around was a moot point and one that she had no desire to investigate or even discuss. "I'll put some coffee on." She zipped up her jeans and filled the coffeepot, sneaking a glance out of the corner of her eye. He had bunched his hands into fists and was rubbing them into his eye sockets like a cranky child. Easy does it, you can manage this, she told herself. Pour some coffee down him, ask him his opinion about something while he's digesting it, feign cramps, and get him the hell out. But as he lowered his fists, she saw his reproachful, assertive expression, and her confidence wavered again. "Why don't you go rest on the couch? I'll bring you the coffee soon's it done."

"You remind me of my wife. Ever told you that?"

"I guess if you live long enough everyone reminds you of someone else. It doesn't mean they're actually alike. More probably it means you're carrying a lot of people around in your head. Have I ever told you 'bout my grandmother Nonnie? Nonnie's a walking encyclopedia of people. I swear she knows everythin' about everyone for four counties," she gushed with nervous vivacity. "Jonathan, you do look done in. Why don't you go in and rest a bit?"

"Yes, ma'am. You tell me what to do and I'll do it." He blinked, lumbered to his feet, walked a few steps, turned to retrieve the bottle, and went into the living room.

She was pouring the water into the filter when the phone rang, but she decided not to answer it. She heard her recorded message, the beep and then a voice she didn't recognize immediately. "Cordy you were right about the way I behaved."

Oh, Lord Jesus, it was Rafael! Boiling water scalded her hand as she slammed down the kettle. She dashed toward the living room as the voice continued: "But you are still my sweetheart. I love you. I will never forget this weekend all of my life. I love you. Goodbye." Click. Too late, she switched the off button. She looked at the red welt on her left hand.

"So you were in the apartment most of the weekend, were you, Cordy? I'll just bet you were," Jonathan said, his voice pained and accusatory. For a split second she felt so trapped that she was tempted to outright denial. Then possible explanations, excuses, and apologies flashed through her mind. "I've burnt my hand," she said quietly. "I need to put some butter on it." Without turning to face him, she went back into the kitchen.

As she searched the refrigerator shelves for a cube of butter, she heard him come into the kitchen. The butter had dropped to the bottom shelf and she knelt on the floor to retrieve it.

"Would you like to explain this to me?" he asked in the reasonable, disappointed tones of a counselor asking a star scholar why she had flunked out of school.

"No. No, I wouldn't," she muttered.

"So you couldn't come to the Hamptons with me, but you spent the weekend in the sack. Is that right? What was he? A Frenchman? Some little Italian you picked up?"

Crouching, fixing her eyes on the leftover hunk of Gorgonzola that was hardening on the middle shelf, she pulled the wrapper from the cube of butter. In the past weeks she'd been so busy keeping up with the content of Jonathan's speeches that she'd never fully appreciated the range of his vocal instrument. A regular Laurence Olivier he was. Since the wheedling questions hadn't worked, he was now shifting into the accusatory tones of a prosecuting attorney.

"Jonathan, please. There's no point—" She bit her lip, partly to stop herself from saying, You're drunk and I can't talk to you, partly because the burn on her hand was starting to smart.

"Why don't you put some of that butter into your mouth and see if it will melt?"

"I don't have to put up with this. I don't have to act out this little drama just because you want to. Let's forget it."

"I can see why you were married to an athlete. You're quite a little sexual athlete yourself, aren't you?"

"You have no right to—"

"Tell me about this guy you were with all weekend."

"Jonathan, this is ridiculous. We've only been seeing each other for a couple of weeks. You can't talk to me as though I was your property. I didn't ask you what you were doing this weekend," she added, more than willing to mollify him with the pretense that she had been blind to his problem, "so I don't expect you to ask me either. Could we please just forget about this? I'll make you some coffee and we can call it a night."

"Aren't you the charming hostess? Aren't you so polite? Aren't you the hypocritical bitch?" he hammered at her.

Rage as potent as volts of electricity brought her to her feet. "Now just a minute, Big Daddy. I'm not going to take your preaching anymore. You know nothing about me, because you've been so busy talking an' impressing me and everyone else within earshot that you've never thought to ask. I've listened to you, let you preach to me and teach to me as though I was one of your schoolgirls. And I've let you make me a part of your show, but let me tell you something about hypocrisy: I may come from a part of the country where people pretend they're not doin' what they shouldn't be doin', but until I met you I didn't know about pretending like I was doin' something I wasn't. So don't come at me with your accusations and your complaints, because I won't take it. I'm free, white, and twenty-one, and I won't *take it!* Not from you or anybody."

His mouth automatically opened for rebuttal, but the drink had clouded his brain. Glazed, he studied the whiteness of the refrigerator door until his mental gears linked into place. His eyes sharpened. "Free? Freedom is a relative concept to which you undoubtedly haven't given much thought. Twenty-one you surely are," he said as cuttingly as if she had been a dowager. "And *white?* My dear, Georgia."

Her face flushed with shame. "I don't know why I said that," she cut in. "A stupid expression. I said it in anger. It's like you calling me a bitch. I know you didn't really mean that. So couldn't we just . . ." She held her hand out to him before she realized that she was still holding the cube of butter.

His face was smug but wary, as though he understood that he had caught her off guard and his victory could not be sustained. "Oh, but I did mean it, Georgia. I did."

"Then I guess you'd best leave."

"Yes, I suppose I'd best. Good luck with your 'romances,' Cordy." He was quite pleased that he'd been able to come up with that final retort as he lurched toward the door.

Even the brightness and heat of the sunlight couldn't raise her from the bed the next morning. She tossed about, willing herself back into sleep, but when that eluded her she settled for the semi-conscious drowning woman's parade of faces. Nasty Maxine had been right: Jonathan Edwards must've spotted her that first evening, must've known that she'd gone through a decade of being the celebrity's wife, playing quiet and playing nice. Must've sensed that she was insecure about her relationships with men.

At noon she rose to eat the leftovers and toss away the cartons. She fixed a pitcher of iced tea and swore that she wouldn't retreat to the bed until she'd completed at least four pages. The first hour at the typewriter was absolute hell, but then she forgot herself while writing about Fanny's farewell appearance at Covent Garden. Fanny was plucking flowers from her girdle and throwing them to the cheering audience, when the phone rang.

"Cordy? Cordy, are you there? O.K. This is Maggie."

She dived for the phone and switched off the machine. "I'm here, Maggie."

"Hiding out, huh? I hope you're working."

"I am. Sort of."

"Thanks for the letter. I can't tell you how proud I am that you lassoed Abigail Silverstein."

"Thanks. I wouldn't have even gotten an appointment if it weren't for you."

"Rest easy, child. I only help the friends I know will succeed, and it puffed up my ego to have her agree with my assessment of you. So how's it coming?"

"I don't know."

"Haven't had time for work, huh? I heard from Maxine. She said you'd captivated *the* Jonathan Edwards. Guess you're scoring on all fronts. That's one of the reasons I called. I figured you were having such a great time that you might like to know you could stay for another month. In fact, you can stay indefinitely."

"What do you mean I can stay indefinitely? Aren't you ever coming back?"

"Ever, never. I never say never. Fact is"—a short soft chuckle came from the other end of the line—"fact is, I'm getting married."

"You're what?"

"You heard it. I have to."

"Have to?"

"Not pregnant have to, circumstantial have to. See, I made the mistake of sleeping with Murray. Literally sleeping with him, just for comfort like, and then . . . Oh, I might as well begin at the beginning. You know I've been staying at Murray's while I've been looking for an apartment, right? It's a fantastic place, but it was all screwed up. You know, nothing in the frig but bean curd and dacquiri mix. Well, that's Murray for you. So like a good house guest I started straightening things up—a flower arrangement here, a supply of staples there. Fixed a meal once in a while so he didn't have to call the caterers when people came over.

"Anyhow, two weekends ago Murray's oldest kid comes to visit. Jeremy—that's his name—is a real basket case. Spoiled, fooling around with drugs, can't begin to know the value of a dollar, though part of that's Murray's fault. Murray keeps giving Jeremy these cross signals, like 'You're my kid and you're going to get all the things I never had,' then he turns around and bawls him out for being spendthrift. Hey, hold on a minute, will you, Cordy? I want to get a cigarette."

Cordy smiled as she shifted the phone to her other ear. When Maggie talked about Murray or Jeremy, her tone—matter-of-fact, slightly annoyed, but protectively affectionate underneath—already marked her as a family member. "So what was I up to?" Maggie asked. "Oh, yeah, so I stayed up late talking to Jeremy and then I went into Murray's room to try to make peace between them. In the course of the discussion I got into bed with Murray. Sex was the farthest thing from either of our minds, but Murray's so overworked he only listens when he's lying down. Finally we fell asleep, but somewhere between darkness and dawn, with that Malibu surf threatening to wash us all away, it was clutch and grab. I was willing to consider it a dream. I even tried to sneak back to my own room before he regained full consciousness, but he's asked me to marry him and I can't refuse."

"Can't refuse?" Cordy laughed.

"Hey, be realistic. What's my position going to be if I've slept with my boss? That's very sticky. I'm too old to play that game. Six months from now I could lose him and the job simultaneously, and I can't afford that. The smartest thing is to marry him. That way if we break up at least I won't be unemployed. You know, Cordy, picking a husband is like picking a tomato: You feel as many as you can and choose the least damaged of the crop. Hold on again, will you? Someone's on the other line."

"I don't know what to say," Cordy said when she heard Maggie on the line again.

"Just say, Mazel tov, because I think it's going to be all right. Murray and I are very comfortable together. We've been friends for a long time. Next time you get married, my advice is to marry a friend."

"I'm still married, Maggie."

"That's right, so you are. So what's the word? Do you want to stay on in the apartment? You could bring your little girl up, you know. Put in a loft bed or something. I don't care. I'm not going to give up the apartment, but I won't be coming back for a long time so—"

"That's very kind of you, Maggie, but—"

"O.K. I know I can't rush you. Think it over and call me back. I think you ought to stay. You've really pulled yourself together. You're working, you've got a famous boyfriend—and that's only the one I've heard about—and you've got a New York apartment. You're going great."

Cordy held the phone away from her ear, shaking her head. "Well, Mazel tov, Maggie," she said at last. "I'll talk to you in the next couple of days."

Gielgud, who'd already begged his share of the clam linguini, licked his paws while Cliff pushed back his plate and poured the last of the Soave into Cordy's glass.

"Here's to Maggie," he said for the third time. "Of all the possible scenarios I'd worked out for her, marriage to Murray Eisen wasn't even on the list. I'm really happy for her, you know. But I can't help feeling deserted. I don't know what I'm going to do without a friend downstairs. Won't you—"

"Cliff, my bags are packed. I'm leaving tomorrow morning."

"Change your mind. I even promise to baby-sit Jeanette if you bring her up here."

Cordy shook her head. "I'm just not cut out for city life."

"What are you talking about? One burglary, one attempted suicide, a couple of rotten affairs—all in a two-month period—I'd say you're a natural."

"A natural," she scoffed, and took another swallow of the wine, though she knew she'd already reached her limit. "I was scared. I was lonely. And as far as men go; Sean I rushed into bed and then felt I'd been taken advantage of; Jonathan *did* take advantage of me and I couldn't even see it or do anything about it; and then Rafael—"

"Now don't say that wasn't fun."

"But I hurt his feelings. And fun"—she sighed—"is that the best we can hope for?"

"Next thing I know you'll be saying you want to be back in Grandma's days with a month of Sunday buggy rides before the first kiss, and then a proposal."

"No. But it'd be nice to stretch the meeting, anticipation, sex, and disillusionment cycle out over a little more than a week."

"O.K., O.K.," he said, coming around the table and putting his hands on her shoulders. "So let's talk about the book."

"That's what everyone here does. They sweep their personal life under the rug and worry about their career."

"That's so you can afford a shrink when you reach your midlife crisis. How're you going to go back to Dullsville Savannah after you've lived in the Big Apple?"

"You New Yorkers are so provincial," she laughed. "You're always ready to put down parts of the country you've never even seen." There was no use trying to describe the longing she had for familiar places and people, how much she'd missed Jeanette and Nonnie, how vital it was for her to have roots and a sense of belonging. "I'll come back, Cliff. You know I'll come back. But right now"—her voice was reedy and wistful—"I need to go home. Yes," she said with more determination, "I want to go home."

Chapter XIV

Cordy sat in the Atlanta airport waiting for the connecting flight to Savannah. She shifted about in the plastic bucket seat trying to get comfortable. Her palms were clammy. The crotch of her jeans was too tight.

When the plane had lifted off from La Guardia her spirits had risen with it. Despite fears, loneliness, and emotional upset, she'd achieved what she'd set out to achieve. And she was going home again; this time with a sense of accomplishment. But somewhere in midflight her head began to ache. She cursed herself for not turning down that final glass of wine. She counted the money she had left. By the time they'd touched down in Atlanta, her accomplishments seemed to have shriveled into something that could be disposed of in a ten-minute dinner conversation. All she had was the opportunity and obligation to write the Kemble book. Apart from that she had no idea of what she was going to do with herself.

The businessman sitting directly opposite checked her out, then opened his briefcase and shuffled through his papers with a self-absorbed air that was designed to attract her attention. The woman sitting next to her was, she could feel, poised and ready to pounce on any opportunity to "pass the time of day." Cordy fixed her gaze on the vivid green astroturf, determined to avoid eye contact. If you met strangers' eyes, they invariably wanted something. Being in

New York had taught her that. Or perhaps, she mused as she crossed and uncrossed her legs, her time there alone had just made her more aware that beneath the banal requests for directions, a hand-out, or the time of day, were the deeper pleas for human contact, approval, or affection.

The woman's plump braceleted arm jostled on the curve of her seat, but Cordy pretended not to notice. She turned her head toward the window and looked out at the gray umbilical cord leading to the plane.

"'Scuse me, are you a Savannahian?" The slow sussurating question, the warming familiarity of the accent, caused Cordy to turn her head and nod.

"So'm I." The woman, all curls and jewelry, beamed at her. "But my son and his wife have moved up to Cleveland, so I have to get up North a couple of times a year if I want to see my grandchildren." She batted a thick fringe of mascara. "I'm Mrs. Scott."

Cordy nodded again, resisting the impulse to give her own name. She shifted in her seat and turned her head away, and for a moment it seemed that the woman was going to respect her reserve. Then, determined to break through, she jiggled her bracelets and touched Cordy on the arm. "I surely do wish the airlines had more direct flights back home, don't you? This waitin' around always tries my patience."

"You know what they say," Cordy shrugged. "If you die in Savannah, they'll reroute your body through Atlanta 'fore they bury you."

"Isn't it the truth!"

"We think of Savannah as a big city, but in many respects it's still a small town."

"Why I wouldn't say that." Disapproval stretched the woman's lips into an even wider smile.

"Of course, it is a city," Cordy conceded, softening her affront to regional pride without gracing it with a smile. If she gave any further hint of friendliness, she'd be in for a show-and-tell of grandchildren splashing in a backyard pool, an explanation of the charms on Mrs. Scott's bracelet, or, worse yet, an inquiry about people they might know in common.

"Let's see"—Cordy looked at the clock over the check-in desk—"we have another thirty minutes before the flight. I do believe I'll walk on over to the shops and buy somethin' to read. Can I get you anything?"

"I'd love to say yes to an Almond Joy, but I swear I must've gained ten pounds this visit. My son Timothy is an architect an' he's doin' *very* well, so he squires me around to all the restaurants."

Cordy got up and pulled at the legs of her jeans, hoping she could escape without having to hear details of Timothy's rise to power or Cleveland's four-star restaurants. The plea beneath the chitchat—"Tell me they'll miss me"—was already apparent from the anxious pale eyes and the vertical crease between them.

"You might could pick me up a package of gum if you're going to the stores," Mrs. Scott went on, unwilling to let her go. "I do believe that chewin' gum helps with the flight sickness, don't you?"

"Yes, ma'am. So they say. Juicy Fruit?"

"That'd be just fine. An' you just leave that overnight bag right here. I'll be glad to watch over it for you."

"Why thank you. I 'preciate that."

The businessman lifted his head long enough to give Cordy's rear end a brief, approving nod, then turned back to his papers. She walked to the center aisle and made her way through the crowd. It had been a long time since she'd seen so many baby buggies, leisure suits, and Army haircuts. She found the gift and book store and edged past the candy, trinkets, postcards, and pennants of Georgia Bulldogs toward the rear. Ignoring the magazines (recipes, fashions, and furniture for the girls; bosoms, buttocks, and sports for the boys) and turning her back on the wire rack where Passion, Love, and Ecstasy beckoned in vivid script, she was surprised to see a large section of books by, for, or about women.

It was a dizzying array of advice, confession, warning, and promise. Close to the top, studies of depression, abortion, and rape. A little further down, credos of competition and greed. Big Business. Tiffany's. Non-Stop Sex. At eye level, beneath the success manifestos, hints on how to seduce, understand, and hold on to a man. And on the bottom shelf, the dust-gathering nitty-gritty: histories of feminist fighters, statistics on poverty in older women.

The titles whined, shrieked, nudged, reasoned, and exhorted her to action. She picked up one book and then another, looking at the photographs: the snazzy, hard-eyed glamour girl; the gray-haired psychologist with the ample tell-mother bosom; the mother of three still playing Prom Queen with the help of a soft lens. And the jacket copy: first daughters were tortured achievers, but had greater orgasmic capacity; sexist enculturation began in the crib; career and child rearing were incompatible; career and child rearing were *not* incompatible; stay in the home; leave the home; this way stultification; that way loneliness; stress could be dealt with; guilt could be overcome; and with great effort and constant vigilance, dependency, that most common and most hideous of all bugaboos, could be vanquished. It was all here. Everything from how to find a job to how to find your clitoris.

She resented it. She hated being tugged first one way and then another. She didn't want to have to think about what it meant to be a woman every living moment of every day. She *was* a woman, damn it. Though just now, androgyny seemed to be the only real liberation. She wanted to pull the whole shitty mess down and light a bonfire.

"'Sugar and spice and all things nice,/That's what little girls are made of.'"

The man standing next to her thumbing through a copy of *Penthouse* was looking at her strangely. She was about to open her mouth and ask him what the hell he was looking at when she realized that she was already muttering. Quickly replacing a book, she walked to the cash register. She picked up a package of Juicy Fruit and a copy of a local newspaper. Just now, it would be a relief to read about hurricanes, guerrilla activities in Central America, and the machinations of OPEC.

"Miss? Oh, miss, you're walkin' away without your change."

She turned, scooped the bills and coins from the counter, and walked across to the ladies' room. She joined the line of women waiting their turn to get into the stalls. Opening the newspaper at random, her hands shaking, her eyes fell on an advice column:

Dear Dr. Cummings:
    I have been having an affair with a man for about a month. I'm very broke and the birth control is costing me money. I'd like to ask him to share the expense, but I don't feel that I know him well enough to talk about money. What should I do?
                                                        Signed, Confused.

The girl standing behind her tapped her on the shoulder and indicated a vacant stall.

Coming out, she brushed her hair and fished in the bottom of her purse for a lipstick. Her hand touched the disk of birth control pills. Today was the first day of a new cycle. She stood staring at the spotless tile. She took the disk, wrapped it in the newspaper, and tossed it into the trash receptacle.

After washing her hands, she pushed back her cuticles with a paper towel and walked out.

She slept contentedly for most of the flight. Mrs. Scott, who had fortunately been seated further toward the rear but was moving up and down the aisles in her never-ending search for conversation, nudged her awake just before the safety belt sign was flicked on.

Blinking down at the brownish red earth, the green tops of trees, she had another spurt of woozy anticipation. Jeanette and Nonnie would be there to meet her. There would be hugs and kisses, too many questions, struggles with the baggage, and then she'd be home again. For one evening at least she would enjoy a happy-ever-after reunion.

Coming down the ramp, she saw not Nonnie but Lucille. With her flowery sun dress, suntanned legs, and pink-tinted glasses, Lucille might have been her older sister. She was holding Jeanette's hand. Jeanette was noticeably taller, well into the bean-pole stage. With her hair drawn back and her body poised for a run, her resemblance to Lupton was startling.

"Mama! Oh, Mama! You're here." Jeanette broke free and hurled herself against Cordy's legs.

"Jeanette. Jeanette, Oh, my girl," she cried, swooping her up and kissing her. "I've missed you. I've missed you so much."

"You're too big to be pouncin' on your mother like that, Jeanette." Lucille smiled. "You'll hurt her back." She circled Cordy's waist and offered her cheek. "It's good to see you. How was the trip?"

"Fine. Just fine. It's good to be home."

She half expected Lucille to reprimand her for her slovenly clothes, but Lucille smiled again, her eyes brimming with sentimental welcome. "I love your new blouse, honey. What is this, a Japanese print?"

"Yes, I got it at Altman's."

"Well, you look very bohemian. I guess that's the way a writer's supposed to look, isn't it?"

"Did you sit near the window?" Jeanette asked. "Did you save one of those little bottles for me?"

"I didn't have a drink, so I didn't get a little bottle. But I do have a present for you."

"What is it? What is it, Mama?"

"It's . . ." Cordy pressed her lips together and rolled her eyes.

"I know. I know," Jeanette cut in, delighted with her mother's predictability. "It's a surprise."

"Sure enough, it's a surprise," she laughed, hugging her again.

Lucille turned her head this way and that in a show of flustered helplessness. "I suppose that we'll have to get your luggage."

"Yep, I guess we will. I think it's over to the right."

She took Jeanette's hand and led the way. A quick glance over her shoulder showed Lucille rooted to the spot, hand to throat and head tilted, as though she expected someone to notice her distress and rush to her rescue. Assuming she would recover herself and catch up, Cordy walked on.

She was hoisting one of her bags from the rotary pickup when Lucille came to her side. The businessman Cordy had noticed at the Atlanta airport was in tow.

"This is Jimmy Nelson, Cordy. You remember his sister Laverne?"

Cordy smiled and stepped aside as he took the bag from her. He helped them out to the car, which Lucille had left in the no-parking zone right in front of the entrance, and after a flurry of thank-yous they were off.

Jeanette sat between them, clutching Cordy's hand and buzzing with stories about day camp, swimming lessons, and her hermit crab. Opening her mouth wide, she showed where she'd lost a tooth. "Nonnie told me to tie a string around it an' put the string around a door handle and she'd pull the door shut, but I wouldn't do it." She winced at the horrible suggestion, nuzzled into Cordy's breast, and in hopes of getting another fifty cents from the tooth fairy started jiggling the tooth next to the gap.

"I thought Nonnie would come to the airport," Cordy said.

"She was plannin' to come, but then she remembered that she'd asked some people over to the house. I tell you, Cordy, Nonnie's mind! I don't mean to say that her mind's goin', just that she seems to have waived all obligation to let other folks know what's goin' on in it. I surely hope she's discharged her social obligations by the time we get back. Daddy's comin' over around six with a mess of crabs, and we're all going to have dinner together."

"Good. Then I'll save all my stories till dinnertime. You're look-ing real pretty, Mother. How've you been feeling?"

"Why thank you, Cordy." The reflexive smile flashed and dis-appeared. "I . . ." Lucille released a hand from the wheel and waved it, as though to preface her next remark, then, seeming to lose the thought, she blinked and checked the rearview mirror.

Cordy pulled her sunglasses down from her head and looked at her. The little tension lines around her mother's mouth were obvious now. Lucille adjusted the rearview mirror and looked into it again, as though she feared someone was giving chase. And you talk about Nonnie being preoccupied, Cordy thought. Lucille must be going through the change. But Lucille was always going through or strug-gling to get over something.

"Have you talked Daddy into that European trip yet?" she asked when the silence had gone on for a full five seconds.

"I've been having so much fun with Jeanette visiting us," Lucille said, as though she hadn't heard the question. "Course, she stayed out on the boat too long the other day. Got her face all blistery, didn't you, honey?" She turned to look at the child as she changed lanes. "Jeanette, don't be worrying your tooth like that. Your Uncle Jake's got a whole other year before he'll finish dental school. Oh, by the way, Cordy, Jake Junior called the other night. Tuesday—no, it must've been Wednesday. He was so sorry he'd missed you."

"Mother," she said quickly and as gently as she could, "I think that's the turnoff comin' up."

"Oh, Lord, so it is."

Cordy gripped Jeanette's shoulder and looked around, ready to blurt out another warning as Lucille turned swiftly from the wrong lane. She was too concerned with Lucille's erratic driving to pay much attention to the conversation for the rest of the trip. As they came down the ramp from the highway she could see the spires of St. John's, the dome of city hall, and the ugly square blocks of the Hilton and the Hyatt nestling in the sea of green. It was a lazy, hot Sunday, and there was hardly any traffic on the streets. After the crowds in New York, it looked like a ghost town.

She gave a silent thanks for her safe return as they pulled up in front of the house, then, grabbing Jeanette's hand, she flung open the door and ran up the steps.

"Nonnie! Nonnie! I'm home."

"Cordy, darlin'!" Nonnie hurried out of the library, pausing on the threshold long enough to turn back and utter, "Gentlemen, if you'll excuse me," then came forward, her hands fluttering up to either side of Cordy's face. She drew it forward and kissed her on both cheeks, then took her hand and walked her toward the back of the house. "You're looking real perky, darlin'. It's so good to have you safe home. I am sorry that I'd forgotten I was havin' company. I know it's an inopportune time," she continued sotto voce, "but I'd be so pleased if you'd come on in an join us for a spell."

A light-skinned black man of about Cordy's age came out of the library, met Lucille at the door, and asked if he might help with the luggage. Before Nonnie had a chance to make any introductions, Lucille was leading him out the door.

"What about the present, Mama?" Jeanette asked.

"I'm sorry, honey, but I'll have to talk to Nonnie and her visitors for a bit."

"Awww, can't we open it now?"

"Let's just don't . . ." Nonnie began.

"And say we did," Cordy finished the sentence for her, laughing.

"But you just got home, Mama." Jeanette twisted her mouth in disgust.

"Jeanette, you know what I've told you," Nonnie said. "No girl ever got results usin' a whiney lil' voice like that."

Cordy knelt and wrapped her arms around Jeanette's waist. "I'll tell you what. The present's in the side pocket of the white overnight bag. Maybe you and Grandma can open it while we're talking."

"And can I sleep with you tonight?" Jeanette pressed, seeing she was on a winning streak.

"Why I wouldn't have it any other way." Cordy squeezed Jeanette's bottom and got to her feet.

"O.K. It's a date," she cried, grabbing the overnight bag and bolting up the stairs.

"See, she's bright as a daisy," Nonnie nodded. "I'll tell you all 'bout her shenanigans after supper."

The front door opened and Lucille and the man came in.

"I do thank you so much, Mr. Redding." Nonnie moved forward. "I've introduced you to Mrs. Simpkins already, and this is her daughter, my granddaughter, Cordelia Tyre."

He offered his hand. While Cordy was smiling back into his

perfect teeth, Nonnie turned to Lucille. "We have some business to talk, Lucille. Would you care to join us?"

"I think not. Where did Jeanette go?"

"She's gone upstairs to her bedroom, Mother. I told her she could unwrap her gift."

"I believe I'll go and keep her company. Thank you, Mr. Redding."

"And now." Nonnie took Cordy by the elbow and guided her into the library. An elderly black man in a worn navy suit got to his feet and inclined the dome of his knobby head toward them.

"Do forgive us for deserting you, Mr. Justice. I know you remember my granddaughter, Cordelia."

He pushed his wire-frame glasses further up onto the bridge of his nose and bowed. "I surely do. Why yes, I remember when you were born, Mrs. Tyre."

"And Cordy, I know you remember Mr. Justice."

Cordy nodded, though the man was only vaguely familiar, and that, she felt, was from photographs.

The table was set with what she recognized as Nonnie's medium-important hors d'oeuvres: pickled okra and crackers topped with creamed cheese and pepper jelly. Several brochures and what appeared to be the mimeographed minutes of a meeting were next to the pitcher of iced tea.

"Before we recommence, may I serve you somethin' else to drink."

"I wouldn't mind a light bourbon," Cordy said.

"Mr. Justice?"

"I'm content with my tea, thank you."

"And you, Mr. Redding?"

"Perhaps some white wine with a little soda water, if you have it." He smiled, flashing the perfect teeth again, waited for Cordy to take a place on the couch, then sat down, crossing his long legs and shooting the cuffs of his linen shirt. Everything about him bespoke urbanity and controlled charm. Even the choice of beverage—he wasn't a teetotaler, nor was he inclined to strong drink—seemed to have been thought out. Cordy decided he must be running for public office.

"I do apologize for disrupting your homecoming, Mrs. Tyre," he said in a mellifluous voice. "I understand that you're returning from New York."

"Yes."

"I was at Princeton last summer, using their library for some research. I had an opportunity to get into the city on weekends, and I must say I often miss the excitement of New York."

"Yes, it is exciting."

"There are, of course, many drawbacks to it. A certain constriction because of the overcrowding and the pressures of a hectic lifestyle."

Nonnie handed the drinks around, took her usual place in the wing-backed chair, and said, "I know that your time is precious, Mr. Redding, so I think we'd best resume our discussion," in a polite but firm manner that put an end to the pleasantries. "So"—she opened her hand as though offering him the floor—"you seem to know a good deal about the Black Heritage and Restoration Association."

"I'm attempting to educate myself, Mrs. Hampton. Of course, I feel like a Johnny-come-lately. It's people like Mr. Justice here who've laid the foundation and deserve the credit." He nodded diplomatically in the direction of the older man. "However, I'm sure that the project will be a success."

"Getting people to loan money at varying rates of interest, securin' the matchin' funds, makin' a start—all those things, I grant you, are the beginnings," Nonnie said. "But success means payin' back the money on time, makin' sure that restoration doesn't turn into gentrification, an' keepin' those folks who've lived there all their lives in a better neighborhood at rents they can afford. The real estate speculation is already well into the Victorian district. It's already eaten into the old black neighborhoods. You've got slumlords, Yankees with ready cash looking for a place to retire, a general expansion outward from the Historic district—that's a lot to contend with, Mr. Redding. The city has changed and it's gonna change more, an' getting a whole city to change in the direction that pleases us, why that's a formidable task, Mr. Redding. Formidable." She took a sip of her drink, blotted her lips, and gave a soft, placating laugh. "You must forgive me. I'm afraid the subject stirs me to oratory. Now Mr. Justice has told me so much about you that I'd enjoy hearing you tell a lil' bit about yourself. Were you not born here in Savannah?"

"Oh, yes, ma'am. Right over on Taylor Street."

"An' you've been back how long?"

"Goin' on five years. You see, after I'd . . ."

Nonnie adjusted the pillow behind her back. She already knew most of what he was going to say, and what she didn't know she could guess. He was a local boy who'd gone North to college, perhaps, she guessed from his stature, on a basketball scholarship. He'd gotten his degree, in political or social science she would judge, though he didn't say, and he had gone on to graduate work at a more prestigious university.

Taking up her fan, she noticed the liver spots on her hands and reminded herself to repeat the application of lemon and cucumber juice. She missed part of his resume while she was examining her skin, but he continued, dropping letters—HUD, CETA, SNAP— as fast as a first-grader who'd just learned the alphabet. She tried to listen more carefully, but now he was peppering the air with all those silly new words. He said "interfacing" when he meant talking, "deprived socio-economic groupings" instead of poor people. He discussed "supportive infrastructures" when talking about committees he thought would back him up. When he said something about "the considerable element of the unpredictable which must invariably be taken into account," he lost her completely. She went back to her examination of the liver spots.

Why did educated young people persist in messing up the language like this? Now he was talking about "relationships." People these days were always talking about relationships. The word was all-inclusive, used to describe everything from a torrid love affair to how you treated the clerk at the corner grocery store. And worse yet, they talked about "*working* at relationships," as though all human commerce took place on some new level of Dante's Inferno, some ill-lit factory where concessions were manufactured and appeasement was packaged. Words like Love, Duty, and Loyalty seemed to scare people these days. Yet they also seemed to be equally put off by the hard compromises of a real deal. So they "worked at relationships." Still, she couldn't blame Sam Redding for being a child of his times. He was a smart young man, and if she didn't really concentrate on his words, his voice was mellow and, at the lower registers, had a strength that passed for conviction. Cordy, she noticed, was nodding at him as though she understood everything he was saying.

She studied Cordy closely. Her investment in Cordy's New York trip had yielded dividends. She was still wearing clothes that looked like she'd been called in from doing the gardening, but her hair, fingernails, and makeup looked fine. Her big brown eyes were lively and attentive, and she was sitting up straight, proud of her fine bosom, instead of hunching her shoulders the way she did when she felt bad about herself. She didn't yet have real presence, but she was well on her way to being a beautiful woman, not just a sexy girl. She would, Nonnie was sure, mature into a fine writer, a woman of property, though perhaps she would have to spend long stretches of her life alone. That was why it was so important that she be here now, taking an interest in the affairs of the community. It was *vital* that she cared about the lives of others. That could make her a phoenix. Otherwise she'd end up like a molting Bird of Paradise—peckish with dangling tail feathers. Like Lucille.

Sam Redding had stopped talking. Nonnie put the fan down and turned to Mr. Justice. The sunlight had turned the lenses of his glasses opaque, and she was annoyed that she couldn't see his eyes.

"And have you succeeded in getting Mr. Lavenel's endorsement?" she asked.

"You know Kevin Lavenel." Mr. Justice moved to the edge of his chair, spreading his hands with an energetic movement. "Kevin's not a man of . . . strong conviction."

"No," Nonnie muttered. "That he's not. Not hardly like ol' John Lavenel at all."

"John Lavenel was a quiet man, but he was a gentleman. He showed considerable courage. Well you remember," Mr. Justice said.

They clucked their tongues simultaneously. Cordy and Sam Redding shared a tolerant smile.

"I felt," the older man continued, "that if we could go to Kevin and tell him that you were willing to endorse Sam, why he'd come round."

"Oh, yes. Surely." Nonnie's eyes twinkled. "Then Kevin would talk to—"

There was a thudding down the stairs. Jeanette stood in the doorway holding her arms wide, displaying the bright red T-shirt with a glittering apple and "I Love New York" printed on the front.

"Mama, I've wanted one of these T-shirts for so long. An' I love those stickers you brought me too."

"Jeanette"—Cordy motioned her to her side—"I think you'd best say excuse me for interrupting conversation."

"'Scuse me."

"Why that is a beautiful shirt," Sam Redding grinned at her. "If my little girl saw that she'd pack me onto a train right now and send me to New York to get her one."

Jeanette, always susceptible to masculine attention, giggled and turned her head into Cordy's shoulder.

Nonnie got to her feet and extended her hand to Mr. Redding. "I do thank you for comin'. Mr. Justice has ridden before you like a good messenger. You should be very grateful to have such a man on your side."

"Indeed I am, Mrs. Hampton." He took her hand, then turned to Cordy. "I believe I saw another suitcase in Mrs. Simpkins' car. I'd be more'n happy to bring it up before we go."

"I would appreciate that," Cordy said, leading the way to the door. "What part of New Jersey were you staying in? Princeton itself?"

"No, Hopewell."

As soon as the front door closed, Nonnie reached over and touched the sleeve of Mr. Justice's suit.

"Well, Amos, what do you think?"

"I think he can win the election. You know I wouldn't be bringing him here to ask for your endorsement if I didn't think that."

"I know that. But is he the best man for the job?"

"He's the best we have now." His forehead puckered into ebony creases.

Jeanette sat back in the sofa pillows licking the cream cheese off a cracker. She was very quiet, because Nonnie and Mr. Justice were talking like they were telling secrets and she didn't want to be told to leave the room. Mr. Justice took Nonnie's arm and they walked over to the window, turning their backs.

"I know you favor Andrew to run, Amos, because Andrew's a man of ideas, but I do believe he's more of a teacher than a politician. He's better off to stay in the classroom. I expect Sam Redding is just too dapper for your tastes, is that it?"

Mr. Justice shrugged his sloping shoulders.

"Looks never hurt a politician," Nonnie went on. "There's still lots of silly ladies who'll vote for a man who's well fitted out. It's what they call charisma on the television."

"I hate to think we've fallen on such times that appearance is qualification for public office."

"And Redding is ambitious. He may want to run off to the state legislature in another couple of years, but I see no harm in that. It means he'll try to prove himself now."

"I came by to convince you, remember?" His chuckle ended in a long sigh. "It's just that I remember. I remember back when we really had to fight. The folks who were intimidated, made so scared they were afraid to open their doors at night, and that young man who had his head bloodied at the lunch counter. Course, it wasn't near as bad as it was in Mississippi or Alabama."

"No, no. *We* pulled together."

"A *few* of us pulled together," he said firmly. "And I'll never forget that first election. Folks standin' in the rain for hours—old people, young bucks, women with babies on their hips—standing in the rain for hours, determined, proud to have the privilege to vote. These young folk, they didn't live it. They don't understand what we went through."

"Now, now," she commiserated. "We've all got troubles. It's not just your people. The whole notion of struggle and sacrifice is, I'm sorry to tell you, in sad decline. We must persevere, Amos."

Jeanette wet her finger and picked up the crumbs she'd dropped on the sofa. Nonnie sounded tired and sweet, like she did when she told the stories and poems at nap time. Nonnie and Mr. Justice didn't say anything for a long time. It almost looked like they'd fallen asleep standing up or were playing statues. Then Nonnie touched Mr. Justice on the arm again, touched him the same way she touched the gold statue of the naked lady and the dogs that sat on the mantelpiece. The statue Nonnie loved so much she always dusted it herself. "You can tell him I'll endorse him, Amos. I'll send a check round to you this week."

"Just your name on the literature would help, Nonnie."

"No, no. I put my money where my mouth is. Besides"—she walked to the table and picked up a brochure—"I think I'd like to see some changes in this. Course, I wouldn't dream of interfering, but we might could make the language a bit more punchy. I'll jot down a few notes and send 'em along with the check."

As the front door opened, she stepped back and offered her hand. "Do come again, Mr. Justice," she said in a louder voice. "It's always a pleasure to visit with you." Now she noticed Jeanette and nodded for her to come to her side.

Jeanette swallowed the last of her third cracker and got up. "It's a pleasure to meet you, Mr. Justice."

"Why thank you, Miss Jeanette. You get Mrs. Hampton here to take you for a ride so you can give everybody the pleasure of seeing your pretty new shirt."

"Mr. Redding is waiting in his car," Cordy called from the hallway. "Please excuse me, Mr. Justice, I have to go upstairs for a minute."

"Goodbye, Mrs. Tyre. I'll show myself out, Mrs. Hampton. And thank you."

Jeanette watched him walk out in that slow, jerky way old people had, as though they were walking on rocks.

"How did you meet Mr. Justice?" Jeanette asked as Nonnie gathered up the glasses.

"Oh, that's a long story."

"But tell it."

"Let's see," Nonnie set a glass down and touched her finger to her lips. "When I first moved into this very house, a long, long time ago, right after your great-grandfather and I were married, Amos Justice was a lil' boy 'bout your age. Yes, he 'bout came up to my waist. His mother did the laundry for Mrs. Walters next door."

"Where the Bradshaws live now?"

"Yes. An' Mrs. Walters' carriage house was right next to our carriage house, so's when I was out in the garden Amos and I would talk. He used to drag a lil' wagon with the fresh laundry in it an' after he'd delivered the laundry he'd sit in the wagon an' I'd lean over the fence and we'd talk. Then much, much later, when he was full grown and I was already a grandma, we helped each other."

"How did you help each other."

"Now that is a long story, an' one you're still too young to understand. C'mon and help me carry these things to the kitchen. You know your granddaddy's goin' to be here soon. An' he's goin' to bring us a mess of crabs and oysters."

Cordy came in and took the tray from Nonnie. "Let me help you clean up."

"Where's Lucille?"

"She's takin' a nap."

"I declare, that girl can get more tired out with the least amount of activity than anyone I know. Run on in, Jeanette. Don't be eavesdropping."

Jeanette took the plate that was being handed to her and left, wondering how it was that sometimes she could be invisible and other times they noticed the minute she was in the way.

"I know what you mean about Mother," Cordy said. "She seemed so preoccupied today when she picked me up. Has she been all right?"

"She's just been herself, only more so."

"It's hard for her. She hates the thought of aging."

"Well, who doesn't?" Nonnie said decisively. "Growing old is no fun. Your joints creak, you don't feel as peppy, you forget things, though that, I s'pose, could be a blessing if you could learn to do it selectively. I know Lucille's miserable, but lots of folks get miserable. Difference is Lucille makes the people round her miserable too. You've got to eat what's set on your plate, otherwise you'll go hungry. Anybody who's lived through hard times will tell you that. Lucille's never really known hard times, so she has to invent them. But I don't want to be talkin' 'bout Lucille. I want to hear about you. Come on out an' tell me all 'bout New York. You said you got to go to the theater. Now tell me, what did you wear? Not those raggle-taggle things you're in now, I hope."

It was an even better party, Jeanette decided, than the parties with the candles and the silver dishes. Grandpa Jake brought in big drippy buckets and a bottle of champagne. And there was no tablecloth to worry about spilling on. Mama just put newspapers down on the kitchen table and Grandma Lucille put the bucket in the middle for the shells. Nonnie took out the big white pot and started it to boil. She got to sit on Grandpa Jake's lap and strip the leaves from the corn ears and play with the yellow silk. Grandpa Jake played a game with her, opening the oysters as fast as he could to see if everyone could eat them even faster. And they did. Then he got up, because he'd forgotten the champagne, and opened the bottle with a pop. Nonnie told her to close her eyes in case the cork jumped at her, and Jake poured the champagne into everyone's glasses, even hers. The only thing that could have made it better was if daddy was there.

"Here's to my lovely daughter, who's made us very proud," Jake said, raising his glass. "To Cordy's return and to her book contract."

"I don't have a real contract yet, Daddy," Cordy protested.

"But you will," Nonnie assured her. "You said that Silverstein woman was real nice. Did she give you her word?"

"She was sweet as she could be, but she can't give her word, because she may not be able to find a publisher who's interested,"

Cordy explained, trying to impress them with the precarious nature of the business. "But at least I've seen the last of a tewky lil' place like Chrystallis. I'm just going to try to put it all out of my mind until Mrs. Silverstein calls. Right now, I want to keep on working. But just this second I don't even want to think about that. I just want to eat some more. Daddy, open me another oyster, please."

Jake put down his champagne and took up the knife, wielding it with expertise.

"But weren't you just terrified to go out alone?" Lucille asked. "The stories I've heard. And the movies I've seen. Muggings, burglaries!"

"No, I didn't see anything like that," Cordy lied. "And I wasn't alone all of the time."

Lucille rested her elbows on the table, put a hand to her mouth, and sucked in her cheeks. Her eyes said, "I've already guessed the worst, so please don't sully me with the details."

"Course she wasn't always alone," Nonnie said. "That Maggie introduced her to her friends and she went out to that resort with them. And she had that neighbor upstairs—"

"Clifford."

"She had that Clifford upstairs to look out after her."

Lucille put a restraining hand on Jake's as he reached for another ear of corn and turned to Cordy, her eyes glittering with suspicion.

"Nothin' romantic, of course," Nonnie jumped in. "Clifford is . . ." She raised her hand and turned it this way and that.

"He's what?" Jeanette asked.

"And speakin' of friends, Cordy, Alidia Tatterns called to see when you'd be back. I invited her over to the house for a drink."

"An offer she couldn't refuse, I'm sure," Lucille said.

Cordy paused, oyster shell in midair. It was still difficult for her to guess who Nonnie would find acceptable and who she would burn in the swift flame of her inexorable judgment.

"That poor girl," Nonnie clucked, collecting the crab shells and tossing them into the bucket. "Why her complexion is enough to make her pull down the shade and lock the door forever. I swear her cheeks look like someone just stamped her with a waffle iron. There must be somethin' some plastic surgeon can do about that."

"I don't think she has any money," Cordy explained.

"It's a tragedy, it surely is. 'Cause she's got these eyes that are just like emeralds, an' she's smart as a whip."

"If drivin' a car into a tree and runnin' away from home constitutes intelligence, why then I guess she could qualify," Lucille said.

"Oh, Mother. She drove that car into a tree about a hundred years ago," Cordy said impatiently. "She was only 'bout seventeen at the time."

"She drove a car into a tree?" Jeanette asked, but no one paid any attention to her.

"She's always been a troublemaker," Lucille persisted.

Jake, still eyeing the corn but taking another oyster instead, shook his head. "Her daddy had lotsa capital to start with, but he threw it all away. He was always a day late an' a dollar short. Can't say I think very highly of him."

"Course you don't," Nonnie said.

Cordy leaned back, draining the juice from a shell. Nonnie would get into a debate now, for the heredity-versus-environment question was one of her favorite topics. Nonnie tended to make people she didn't like responsible for their own fate; but since she'd taken a fancy to Alidia (or perhaps chose to champion her because of Lucille's disapproval), she would undoubtedly come down on the "blood will tell" side of the question. It would take decades for science to catch up with Nonnie. Nonnie was sure she knew more about the damaging effect of "strange" second-cousin's genes than any team of Harvard researchers knew about their fortieth generation of mice.

"The girl never had a chance," Nonnie said emphatically. "Her mama was crazy to begin with an' her daddy wasn't too much better. After the mama died—an' I expect it was from drink 'cause Bernice's uncle worked for the trash collection at the time an' he told Bernice he like to have to hire an extra man when he went by the Tatterns', just to cart away the bottles—Alidia was tossed round from one relative to the other. Her daddy'd take her for a bit an' pet her like crazy, then when she got in the way, he'd ship her off to someone else. An' before that, the mama was always sneakin' up the backstairs. An' a woman who carries on like that—an' she wasn't a young woman either, so's there was no excuse . . ."

Lucille pressed her fingertips to her temples. "Mama," she said with pained condescension, "I do wish you'd lower your voice."

Nonnie flushed. She knew she'd gotten carried away and was talking too loudly, but it was humiliating to have Lucille correct her like that, as though she'd gone senile or something. Lord help her should she ever reach the day when she was dependent upon that one. She turned and reached for Cordy's hand and said, almost in a whisper, "Alidia has called twice, so soon's you get the chance you should give her a ring."

"I surely will."

"I think I'll put on a pot of coffee," Jake volunteered, putting his arm around Nonnie's shoulder. "Or would you care to finish up this champagne? It's imported."

"I don't care much for bubbly wines," Nonnie said coldly. "Maybe that's because I've never been to Europe."

"You could go to Europe any time you wanted," Jake said. "Every time I see old George Naughton he's talking about wanting to take you."

Jeanette stopped stacking the oyster shells in a pyramid. "It's true, Nonnie. Mr. Naughton showed me these pictures of castles and he told me he wanted to take you to see them."

"It would be a wonderful opportunity for you, Nonnie," Cordy encouraged. "There's no reason why you couldn't go."

"Ya'll seem to forget that I am in business. I have that restoration goin' on over on Henry Street, that en-tire block of apartments being fixed up on Gwinnett."

"Surely it wouldn't matter if you left for a month or so," Cordy pressed. "Remember when you used to recite, 'Oh, to be in England now that April's there'? You could spend your eighty-fifth birthday in London."

"Perhaps you're worrying about traveling with a man you're not married to," Lucille teased. "But George has even hinted to Jake that he'd be willing to marry you."

"Willing to marry me! Willing, did you say? Oh, you do make me laugh."

Lucille raised her eyebrows. "At your age I should think you'd be flattered."

"I don't see why I should be flattered by an offer where I know I'd be gettin' the worst of the bargain. George is a man who's had a heart operation. He doesn't need a wife, he needs a nurse. Now that he's reachin' the end of his life he'd like to be nursed with some degree of affection—an' that I have for George, that I do have—but I wouldn't put m'self in the position of being his nurse just to have the honor of being called a wife and maybe gettin' a trip to Europe an' being the recipient of his will. I'm not that full of vanity. Or desperation. Besides"—her voice dropped—"I don't love George Naughton. I like him to the point of worry, and I guess y'all think that concern should pass for love at my age. But I know what love is. And I don't love George Naughton."

Cordy looked down at the table and felt her eyes water. She had thought, even hoped, that time would wear away unfulfilled long-ings and passionate affections, but here was Nonnie talking about love with purity and conviction.

"Well, I guess that settles it." Jake got down on one knee, beat his chest, got up, and turned away in a pantomime of the rejected suitor. "The lady doth decline the offer."

The tension broken, everyone laughed as though they'd heard the best joke in years.

Jeanette was so happy she couldn't stop her giggles. The laugh-ter kept rippling out of her. She wanted to pick up the shells and fling them all around the room, but she knew that would be babyish. "Nonnie can't go away with Mr. Naughton," she hiccoughed. "Non-nie can't go away with Mr. Naughton because Nonnie loves Mr. Justice."

The laughter stopped. Grandma Lucille looked at her as though she *had* flung the oyster shells all around the room. Cordy looked down at her fingernails, and Grandpa Jake cleared his throat and felt in his shirt pocket for his cigar, even though there was lots of food left on his plate.

"I think that will be enough, Miss Jeanette," Nonnie said as though she was real mad. "You'd best go up and draw your bath water and get into bed."

Jeanette's lower lip trembled. She looked up at Cordy, hoping the hateful order could be rescinded, but Cordy just reached over, patted her on the knee, and whispered, "Go on up, darlin'. I'll be up real soon to help you with your bath."

"Quick, march," Lucille ordered.

Jeanette slid from her chair and ran out of the room.

"She didn't mean anything," Cordy said. "She probably just noticed that Mr. Justice was a friend and . . . She's only a child."

"Well, she'd best start to learn what she can and cannot say," Lucille said. "The very idea . . ."

Nonnie was on her feet, stacking up the dishes. "I know she didn't mean any harm, but she does have this habit of talkin' out wherever she is. Why just the other day I took her to Morrison's cafeteria and—"

"She didn't do anything wrong," Cordy insisted. "How a seven-year-old child is supposed to comprehend race relations . . ." She looked from one closed face to the other. "Oh, *excuse me*," she said angrily, throwing down her napkin and walking out of the room.

It was her fault, she told herself as she ran upstairs. She had gone off and left Jeanette to her family. She had given them the right to order Jeanette around, subjected her to their prejudices and their demands. The floor of her stomach dropped, leaving her with a nauseating feeling of guilt. She had deserted her child, left her without the comfort of mother or father, abandoned her to the indulgences and commands of three adults who couldn't even get along with each other.

At the bathroom door she listened to the rush of water and the softer, hiccoughing sobs. She knocked and went in. Jeanette was sitting on the toilet in her underpants. She had taken her barrettes out, and her hair fell onto her mottled face. Despite her flat chest with the pale dots for nipples, she looked as miserably distraught as any woman who'd just been abused by her lover.

"Why you must've dumped that whole box of bubble bath in here." Cordy made her voice as light and teasing as she could as she saw the foam inching up to the rim of the tub. "You've got a thimbleful of water and a mountain of soap in here, sugar." Turning off the faucets and crouching between the tub and the toilet, she tried to take Jeanette into her arms, but Jeanette arched and wrenched herself away. Seeing the heaving, stiffened little body, she was reminded of the only time the child had been seriously ill. Jeanette had had a bronchial infection the first winter they'd been in Chicago. Lupton had been away from home, and she had stayed up, night after night, walking, rocking, praying, driven to the outer reaches of panic.

She sat back on her haunches, tears stinging her eyes. "Oh, Jeanette! I'm sorry. I love you. I love you more than anyone in the whole wide world."

Jeanette, rigid with rejection, did not even seem to hear her.

"You don't have to take your bath if you don't want to," she rattled on. "Just get into your nightie and come downstairs and say good night. There's watermelon for dessert."

"I . . . don't . . . want . . . it," Jeanette sobbed. "And I'm never comin' downstairs. Never. They're all so mean."

Cordy reached up, smoothing Jeanette's hair back from her blistered forehead, and the child gave way, clinging to her, bursting into another series of sobs. "I . . . want . . . my daddy. I'm not going to bed until I get a call from my daddy. It's Sunday night and Daddy—"

"All right. All right," she soothed, though the plea made her feel utterly helpless. "Stop crying and we'll call Daddy. And after we've talked to Daddy, we'll go and get into bed together, 'cause Mama's very, very tired, and I know you're tired too."

"I'm not . . . not tired," Jeanette protested.

"All right. Shush, now shush."

She rocked her back and forth, smoothing her hair back and kissing the soft skin of her shoulders. She was in such a miserable position, squeezed between tub and toilet, that her legs began to ache. She got up, took a washcloth, held it under cool water, and wiped Jeanette's face. Jeanette sat, spent and silent, as Cordy wet the cloth again and pressed it to her own eyes. What a homecoming this had turned out to be.

"O.K., sugar, just get ready for bed, please." She pulled the plug out of the tub and wiped her hands while Jeanette struggled into the nightdress. "All right, let's get you into bed."

"But you said I could call Daddy."

"Yes,"—Cordy laughed, willing to admit when she was whipped
—"you can call Daddy."

They moved along the hallway in a conspiracy of silence. There was a faint clatter of dishes and voices coming from the kitchen and in a moment, Cordy knew, an emissary of peace—probably Jake— would come upstairs. She flicked on the bedroom light and reached for the phone.

"Quick now. Do you want me to dial?"

"No. I know how." Jeanette had passed through the eye of her emotional hurricane. The puffiness under her eyes had already started to go down and she looked almost smug as she punched the buttons of the phone. Cordy pushed aside the contents of her overnight bag and lay back on the bed, closing her eyes.

"Daddy, it's me. How come you didn't call me tonight? . . . Uh-huh . . . 'cause I had to tell you my tooth came out. I was going to keep it and send it to you, but I sold it to the tooth fairy instead. . . . Uh-huh, Mama came home. She came on the plane. . . .

Uh-huh." She cupped the receiver and whispered, "He wants to talk to you."

When Cordy didn't move, Jeanette ran to the bed and grabbed her arm. "Hurry up, it's long distance."

Cordy struggled to her feet and crossed to the phone. She picked up the receiver but couldn't bring herself to speak.

"Cordy, are you there?"

"Yes."

"So you're back. Why didn't you call? I've been real worried about you."

"No need. I've been just fine." She hoped she'd hit the right tone: curt and businesslike. She didn't want to burst into tears again.

"How did it go in New York? Did you get an agent?"

"I'm very tired now, Lupton. I'll write and tell you all about it. There is something . . ." She saw Jeanette leaning against the bed, ears perked and eyes sharp as a professional matchmaker's, and thought better of asking Lupton about the check he was supposed to have sent.

"There's no need to write me, Cordy. I'm comin' down."

"Wait a minute."

"I'm takin' some time off from the store. I've got it all worked out. I would've told you sooner, but Nonnie wouldn't give me your New York number."

"Listen, Lupton. I just this minute got back. I've got a million things to do."

"I have to come down anyway. My mama hasn't been feelin' too good and I promised her I'd visit."

"Oh."

"Naw. That's not the real reason. I am gonna see her, but the real reason is to see you. We can't go on like this any longer."

Her lips twisted into a wry smile. "'We can't go on like this'? You taken to watching daytime TV since I left?"

"Hey, girl," he laughed, then dropped his voice to a more seductive tone. "I've got to see you. We've got to talk, now don't we?"

"I guess we do."

"I'll be down next Saturday. I'll call and let you know the details. That all right with you?"

The mere hint of her concession had brought his voice back to booming confidence. She drew in her breath. "I'll talk to you later, Lupton. Jeanette wants to say good night."

Jeanette was already by her side, ready for her turn. Cordy walked back to the bed and sat down. "Hurry up, Jeanette," she mumbled as she put her head in her hands.

"Daddy, it's me again. . . . Uh-huh. . . . Guess what we had for dinner tonight, crabs and oysters. . . . Sure I'm a good girl."

Cordy took her face out of her hands long enough to gesture for Jeanette to hang up, but she was dancing from foot to foot as though she had to urinate and twisting her hair around her finger. Giving up, Cordy sank back onto the bed. The handle of her overnight bag jabbed her in the shoulder, but she didn't move. He'll turn up in a week, she thought. He'll turn up and give Jeanette some dimestore trash and she'll think he's hung the moon. And before he tells her goodbye and tells her to hang up the phone he'll ask her how much she loves him and she'll say what Lucille said to Daddy Lonnie and what I said to Daddy Jake, she'll say . . .

"A hundred, million, thousand bushels and forever and ever, amen."

Chapter XV

It was a muggy, sunless day, muting the colors in the square to the greyish-green of the Spanish moss. A black woman of indeterminate age sat on one of the benches munching a sandwich and gazing, placid as a Buddha, at the threatening sky. Cordy stood by the wing-backed chair and watched for Lupton's car.

The wisps of a dream she'd had last night floated in her mind, elusive as shadows. In the dream she'd had to climb through the window of a college lecture room. Someone had barred the doors against her. Once she'd gotten into the room, she'd been tied to a chair and given a blue book. Guards stood around her desk watching to make sure she didn't cheat. The other students were writing furiously, but she realized in panic that she didn't even know what the subject was.

A few drops of rain spat at the window. She smoothed the skirt of the gauzy yellow dress Bernice had ironed and Nonnie had hung in her closet this morning. Nonnie had also put fresh towels and talcum on the dresser, hints that Cordy must, out of pride, look her best. So here she stood, curried and combed, knowing that her only preparations had been cosmetic.

Seeing Lupton again. She'd played the scene so many times and with so many variations that its present reality escaped her. She had imagined him shamed and imploring, while she, no longer the crazed bitch who'd shrieked and slugged him, would be all cool justice, dismissing his entreaties with small, controlled gestures. "I'm sorry Lupton," she would say, with a smile that might be seen as superior if it were not for its lingering sadness, "but you see, it's too late." Then again, she'd imagined them holding each other, awash with acceptance. He would try to speak. She would touch his mouth with her fingertips, her wedding ring shining, her eyes telling him that yes, they could, they must, try again. Between these melodramatic polarities, she couldn't even think of how she would greet him.

A distant bass note that might have been from a ship in the harbor but was more likely thunder sounded. The woman on the bench put her sandwich into her lap and slowly opened a black umbrella. A man with his hands in his pockets came around the base of the monument. He had an easy, rolling walk, but his head was bent low and his shoulders were hunched, as though he expected the heavens to open up and deluge him.

She drew her breath in sharply as she realized it was Lupton. She'd forgotten that his bad leg bothered him in rainy weather, and since he didn't like to admit that it slowed him down, he transferred some of the pain to his neck and shoulders.

Tenderness stabbed her in the back. She could see his face as it had been in the hospital, right after the accident. Doctors muttering their mumbo-jumbo over him, soothing him with irrelevancies: "Of course, you won't be able to play football again, Mr. Tyre, but in all other respects you can lead a normal life." A normal life? When his only talent had been taken from him, when his future had just been obliterated? And she had muttered mumbo-jumbo too, trying to convince him that their marriage was a wonderful consolation prize, bestowing her egotistical "let me kiss it better" comforts. Why hadn't she had the wisdom to shut up? The pain was his, uniquely his. Perhaps Susan's claim to his affection was something very simple. Perhaps Susan had just known when to shut up.

She pressed her forehead to the window, eager to get a better look at him. As though he sensed being watched, he stopped and raised his head. She stepped back, but not before noticing that he had a beard. Lupton with a beard. Completely out of character. Not that she could presume to know Lupton's character anymore.

She opened the front door as he was reaching for the bell.

"Looks as though you just made it before the downpour."

"Hey, girl." He was startled, but made a quick recovery into his I-can-lick-the-world smile. "How y' doin'?"

"I'm fine. Just fine. Come on in."

She stepped to one side. He moved past her, then waited to see which room she was going to usher him into. She moved to the library, then, thinking perhaps the library was too formal—after all, he wasn't a stranger—she turned, almost bumping into him. He yielded. She paused. They started forward simultaneously, almost colliding again. "My turn to curtsy, your turn to bow," she laughed nervously. He nodded and stepped back, as genial as if he'd just been introduced to an attractive blind date. They stood and stared at each other, smiles melting. The patter of rain seemed to deepen the silence of the house.

"You're looking good, Cordy," he said gently, almost in a whisper. "Lost a little weight, haven't you?"

"Uh-uh. I'm just about the same. But you . . ." Her hand wanted to reach out and caress the beard. "I never thought I'd see you with a beard."

"Just got too lazy to shave."

"I always thought you'd look good with a beard, but you said no, remember?"

The pause lasted a full five seconds.

"Where's Jeanette?"

"Nonnie took her out for lunch. I thought we should talk."

"Sure, sure." His hands opened in agreement, then dropped to his sides. "Could I take you to lunch? We could go down by the river. Or, better yet, let's drive out to the beach."

She closed her eyes. The beach had been one of their favorite haunts—salty flesh of near-naked bodies, sunsets with vast horizons, and in the off-season, dark Atlantic waves crashing, thoughts of infinity, windows fogged with heavy breathing. No, not the beach. Stay on familiar territory. Keep busy. Give him attention without blinding him with it. "The weather's too bad for the beach. Bernice left a pot of red rice. I know you like that. C'mon into the kitchen."

His mouth shaped as though he were going to whistle, but he let out a low sigh. The smell of the house had hit him. Every house had its own unique smell and this one came back to him, strong as a blow to his solar plexus. Salty, sweet, and citrus it was. Floor wax, flowers, ham and biscuits, Cordy's perfume, and that lemony oil Bernice rubbed into the furniture.

"This house. Damn me, I'd forgotten all about this house. It's a goddamn shrine, isn't it?"

"I wouldn't say that."

"I mean— You know I'm no good with words. That's your job."

Her head dropped a few inches at this acknowledgment.

"I meant," he continued, "that I always liked this house. Seems strange not to have Nonnie to open the door. I always knew Nonnie didn't cotton to me one little bit, but she always opened that door so nice." The old lady had had months to fill Cordy's head with "I told you sos", that much he could guess. And Cordy standing here now, her backbone straight as though she were in corsets and her neck stretched tall like that, oh, he could see the old lady in her all right. Deep-chested, hardheaded women with delicate ankles and mean tempers.

He ducked his head in an effort to get her to look at him. "I always liked those big ol' family dinners she had. Never had anything like that in my life. You know how my family is: bunch of individuals who sorta look alike and only call on each other when they're in trouble. Hell, you couldn't really call 'em a family."

"I 'spect it was hard for your mama to try to keep everyone together after your daddy left." No, she would not be drawn into any sympathy for Lupton's deprived childhood. She turned abruptly, catching a glimpse of them in the mirror. Mirrors and mirrors and mirrors. A hall of mirrors. Would Jeanette's character be blighted by the loss of her daddy just as Lupton's had suffered from the loss of his? "Let's not stand around in the hallway."

It was gloomy enough to warrant turning on the kitchen light, but she moved straight to the refrigerator. She was so rattled that she had to keep her mind on one task at a time.

"Here, let me help you." He was right behind her, close enough to smell her just-washed hair. She straightened up, struggling with the heavy iron skillet.

"No. I can manage." She swung the refrigerator door shut with a movement of her elbow, feeling clumsy in her self-sufficiency. "So, you got in last night. Did you stay at a motel?"

He stationed himself near the sink and looked out on the garden. His throat was as dry as if he'd had a hangover. "How's Jeanette doing?"

"She's been fine. Better than I'd expected. Of course she misses you. I want to thank you for calling her every Sunday. I think we both have to make an effort to let her know that our disagreements have nothing to do with her. Children take these things upon themselves, you know. They feel guilty and personally responsible when their parents don't get along and . . ."

She was off and running now, reciting all the things she'd read in those child psychology books. He studied the garden, trying to remember the name of that flower that didn't grow up North. Cordy had shown him all the flowers when they were first dating. She'd teased him when he couldn't remember their names no matter how many times she'd told him. Her voice had always been soft and teasing in those days. And her body, though it had actually been firmer, had seemed to have a more yielding quality. He like to melt into her those days, though his tenderness always deserted him when he took hold of her. She didn't give way easy, but damn it, when she did . . .

"Those lil' pink and white flowers, what're they called again?" he asked in a dreamy voice.

"They're camellias, Lupton. Want a beer?" She sounded like a waitress at rush hour now.

"Sure. Sure." He turned to her, watching her put the silverware and the cloth napkins on the table. Susan didn't own any cloth napkins. Sometimes he and Susan ate off paper plates. "I'm glad Jeanette's fine. You know I—"

"Yes. Yes. I know you love her. I never doubted that."

"Thanks." He took the can of beer and moved away from the window to straddle a chair. "Yeah, I got in last night. Stayed over to Jeff Long's place. 'Member him?"

"How could I forget." Jeff Long. Bullet-headed, sassy with the girls. Right guard on the high school football team. Reached his full growth, which unfortunately was too small for college ball, when he was sixteen. Jeff was the sort of guy who thought it was cute to burp out loud. He and Lupton had raced cars together and gotten drunk together, not, as far as she could recall, with any joy, but to retch and stagger in some male rite of passage.

"He works at a body shop over to Victory Drive now. Wife's named Sherri. You wouldn't know her."

He popped the lid of the can and took a long swallow. He'd been damned lucky. He might have made the mistake of marrying someone like Sherri. Sherri had had a damned fine body when she was sixteen. Now, she'd gone stringy, wore rollers in her hair, and had no patience with her kids. The thought of ending up with such a woman, living in an apartment with phony wood paneling, and eating off paper plates, made his throat go dry again.

"Yeah, ol' Jeff was my best buddy. He used to be a tough son of a bitch. 'Member the night we won the state championship? Christ, what a game he played. Course, it's never the same after high school. In high school you knew the people who were cheerin' for you."

"How's the business going?" she said quickly, wanting to staunch the regret that was seeping into his voice. She put the bowls of steaming rice on the table and took her seat. "You didn't send me any money for Jeanette last month and. . ."

She said it offhandedly, but he shriveled just the same. He was glad she hadn't turned on the light. The dimness of the room seemed protective. "I've got the check for you right here in my pocket. Needed the money last month to pay off some bills. I owed the newspaper for some advertising an' they wouldn't do any more on credit. Figured I needed to have some sort of spread in the paper for the Labor Day sale. You know how it is with advertising."

She didn't know. They had never talked about business until it was going so badly that he'd had to talk about it. But, she thought, sipping her beer, that was her fault as much as his. Lipton had taken it as a point of pride to bring home the bacon and she'd let him. She'd never really asserted herself or tried to establish a real partnership with him. If only she'd been able to persuade him to come back to Savannah it might have been possible, with the help of her family connections and the collective memory of his football triumphs, for him to have a moderate success. But she mustn't slide back into "if onlys" or "it might have beens."

"Now, I figure this year"—he ignored the rice and cracked open another can of beer with Rotary Club bravado—"if the economy picks up . . ."

His mouth was moving, telling her about loans and advertising campaigns, but she couldn't pay attention to his words. She still knew this man. His ambitions were vague, no stronger than morning fogs that burned away with the brightness of the sunlight. He could take charge of a situation only when it demanded direct animal reflex. This was the thing that had made him a fine athlete and a vigorous lover. But physical courage, team spirit, and the ability to follow orders were not qualities that could help him anymore. There was no outlet for his courage, no framework for his camaraderie, no coach to tell him what to do. He had to invent his days now, wheedling for loans, deciding when to advertise, supervising inventories. And being the boss tired him; planning confused him. He had few business contacts and fewer real friends. The shopping mall in a

Chicago suburb would always be alien turf. Pity, that saddest and most pathetic kind of love, was rising in her like a tide. To stop her hand from reaching out to caress the unfamiliar beard, she picked up her spoon. Yes, she knew this man. Nothing could obliterate those years together, flawed though they were.

". . . and I've got the lease for another two years, so the rent can't go up."

She'd intended to confront him about the loan he'd taken from Jake, but now she couldn't bring herself to mention it. "I've found an agent and I think I have a good opportunity of selling another book," she said, wanting to share happy news for a change.

"So you went up and played hardball with those smart-assed Yankees, did you?"

He laughed too loudly. His locker-room laugh, his third-drink laugh. The one that always grated on her. It had been more of a burden than she could have imagined when she'd realized, a few years into the marriage, that they didn't share the same sense of humor. Lupton liked teasing and taunts and, in his more relaxed moods, windy stories. The whimsey and verbal jokes that appealed to her couldn't raise a chuckle from him. This difference in tastes had been a strain on their affections.

"Yankees aren't any smarter than we are, Lupton. Don't get into that trap of Southern inferiority."

"Are you kiddin'? I'm proud to be a Southerner. Always have been."

"It's absolutely amazing to me," she said as airily as if she were still at some cocktail party in Greenwich Village, "how much those old cliches still exist." Then, realizing how condescending she sounded, she confessed, "I was scared to go up there. It was hard for me to leave Jeanette. Harder still for me to be alone."

"I'll bet you weren't alone all the time."

"That," she said, while echoes of Sean's promise to call, Rafael's vows of undying love, and Jonathan's accusation that she was a "sexual athlete" darted through her mind, "is none of your damned business."

"I guess it is my business. You're still my wife."

Indignation popped and fizzled, short-circuiting the tenderness she'd felt only a moment before. "I suppose you're still seeing Susan."

"Your affairs are off limits, but mine are up for grabs, is that it?" he said, his eyes narrowing for combat.

"You were talking about me as though I was still your wife."

"You are still my wife! You become a womens'-libber or somethin'? Think it's all in *your* power to dissolve the contract? In the eyes of the world and in my eyes you're my wife!"

"I left off being your wife," she overrode him, "because you didn't want me to be your wife anymore."

"That's not true. I've always loved you." He chewed his lower lip, then repeated the vow softly, as though it were a magic incantation.

"Sayin' and doin' are two different things," she said angrily. A bubble of heartburning acid rose to her throat. Her sinuses clogged. The twitch in her right eye signaled a headache. She had promised herself that she'd stay calm and resist recrimination, yet here she was sounding like a first-grader who'd caught a playmate cheating at checkers. She'd allowed the conversation to get off the track, though just now she couldn't remember what she had wanted to talk about. Bank balances, late checks, secret loans?

She got to her feet and snapped on the light. "Was Susan pregnant?"

"No." He blinked in protest against the sudden illumination. "It was a false alarm."

She made a sound—half snort, half groan—and wondered if Susan was Machiavellian enough to raise a false alarm in hopes of getting Lupton to commit himself. Then again, it was possible that the strain of the affair might have caused real menstrual problems. The prohibitions and limitations of loving a married man—no telltale scratches or love bites, please, Lupton's watch on the bedside table ticking off her appointed time, the quick washing of his genitals to get rid of her smells—may have destroyed the delicate balance of Susan's hormones. Plot, hysterical pregnancy, or legitimate miscalculation—any one was a possibility. Lupton wouldn't have a clue, that much she knew.

"Tell me about Susan," she said, feeling the muscle in her eye jump again.

Lupton hesitated. He crushed the empty beer can, aimed it at the trash can, and missed. He didn't know what to say. Making a clean breast of things might be the way to Cordy's forgiveness. Then again, it might be a trap. There was no way to know how to deal with a woman's plea for honesty. You could start out with straight talk and then find yourself enmeshed in nets. When women asked for honesty they usually meant that you should tell them what they wanted to hear.

Cordy moved from the doorway, picked up the beer can, and deposited it in the trash; then she turned to him. She seemed calm now, staring at him with a level but unescapable gaze. He decided to give at least a censored version of the truth.

"She just came by the store one day," he said. Susan was not the sort of girl he'd notice in a crowd. She was angular, in fact, with a boyish walk and little breasts with big nipples that poked at the cloth of her shirt. Except for the nipples, not his type at all.

"She was the one who came on with me." Directly and, so it seemed in the beginning, entirely without complications. He'd called to tell her that her broken tennis racket had been restrung. She'd invited him to bring it to her apartment. It had been the first open proposition he'd had since he'd screwed around when the team was on tour, though that, being a group enterprise with strict laws of protectionism honored by both his teammates and the sports groupies, didn't count as cheating. He'd told Susan up front that he was married, but she'd said she was lonely. Because of her job she never met guys over eighteen. Susan didn't seem beautiful enough or sure enough of herself to make any demands or cause any trouble. And the vague notion that she might be a lesbian intrigued. Why, it had seemed almost impolite to turn down a lonely girl with passably good legs. "She's single," he added. "She's a PE teacher at Memorial High."

Cordy grunted, discarding images of nubile teenagers and sleek divorcées, and framed a picture of a muscular beauty with close-cropped hair. Susan would be streamlined and lithe, the sort of girl for whom cellulite and stretch marks were no more of a threat than a tropical disease would be for an Eskimo. She crossed her arms over her breasts, her hands clutching her shoulders, and the sides of her mouth twitched in a self-deprecating smile. Here she was, the Grand Inquisitor with a sinus headache. She hated this picture of herself, but she couldn't stop herself from asking, "Are you still seeing her?"

"Once in a while," he said miserably. "But it's nothing serious. She knows I wanta get back with you." He had tried to break it off with Susan when Cordy had run out on him. He'd told her in no uncertain terms that he loved his wife and child. But Susan's pride wasn't sufficiently offended to make her show him the door. Instead, she'd seemed to accept her secondary position with good grace. There was no ranting and raving from good ol' Sue. Not a single nasty scene. She'd commiserated with him; she'd told him how sorry she was that she'd caused him so much trouble. Frustrated by the balancing act he felt the two women had forced him into, feeling lonely, he'd slid back, a night at a time, into accepting the dinners Susan dished onto the paper plates and the comfort of her somewhat bony body. It was only temporary, he'd told himself. A man had to rest his head somewhere. But lately it had really started to get strange. He'd found himself thinking about Cordy when he was with Susan. Even when they were in bed. It was crazy to be fantasizing your wife in order to have sex with your girlfriend. And there was something else: Beneath Susan's sportsmanlike acceptance was a very real tenacity. If Cordy came back to him, Susan would throw in the towel; but if there was a divorce, Susan very definitely expected to be the next Mrs. Tyre. It was a trap from which he dearly hoped Cordy would rescue him.

"I don't love Susan," he assured her. "You're the one I want. You're the one I need."

She didn't doubt his sincerity. There was a pleading in his voice that reminded her of a child begging for Mama to make it better, the same plea she'd heard in her own voice when alone, in extremis, she'd cried out for help. Pity, jealousy, fear, and even a low hum of desire were all calling in her now, barely stifled by the old anger. And she was tired. Bone-aching, near to giggling tired.

"Cordy? Darlin'? What's the matter? Your face has gone all ashy."

"I have a terrific headache." She raised her hand to her forehead as though to demonstrate the truthfulness of what she'd said.

"Can I get you somethin'?"

She didn't object when he came to her, circling her with big, protective arms. She touched the beard. It had an almost electric bristle but was silkier than she'd supposed. A few white hairs shone amidst the brownish blond ones. Lupton getting gray! She closed her eyes and rested her cheek against his, giving way to the familiar smell and feel of him. Once, many years ago, looking at the fiftieth-anniversary photo of Nonnie and Lonnie, they had joked, as all young couples do, about growing old together. Lupton had said that she would outlast him, and she had protested and then cried, saying that she could never survive the loneliness. "Time," Jonathan Edwards had said, "is something we invent to stop everything from happening at once." She had made a great circle, back to the house in Savannah, but in that intervening decade she'd made an investment. Her investment had been in Lupton and in their marriage. An affair was a present-tense thing, but a marriage was a promise; it encompassed the past as well as the future.

If she divorced him, she would start out all over again. Ten years older. And alone. No home of her own, no real income, no one to scratch her back or make her a cup of coffee when she was tired.

She would be depriving Jeanette of a father she loved and needed, and she would have to assume the sole responsibility.

She had a toehold, but no more, on a career she didn't quite believe in.

She had Jeanette.

She did not have this familiar body to curl next to in the animal death of sleep.

"Lupton," she might have cried if only she could have summoned the energy. "Oh, Lupton."

He was patting her back, burping her like a baby, saying, "Shush, shush . . ."

The rush of sibilant comfort, so unlike him, threw her into such a division of feeling—wanting to trust, fearing to trust—that she thought she was going to vomit.

She wrenched herself away, diving for the sink. Putting her head down, she felt the sweat break out on her face. She gulped great drafts of air. The smallest trickle of bile came up from the region of her heart and lodged in the back of her throat. She gagged, but couldn't bring it up. She tried again, and the strangling sound rose and changed into something like laughter. So this was the reality: neither proud rejection nor passionate acceptance, just an overwhelming and disgusting need to throw up.

Lupton was now a vague, hovering presence, but she distinctly heard the front door open.

Jeanette's feet were racing along the hallway.

"Daddy! Daddy! Are you here yet?"

Oblivious, and at the same time preparing to enter the scene of reunion, Cordy reached for a glass and filled it with water. It tasted sweet and, by some amazing grace, quelled her nausea. Composed, lips parted, she turned to see Jeanette being lifted high into the air, then brought down hard, her legs wrapping around Lupton's waist.

Nonnie was standing in the doorway, a smile of welcome set upon her lips, her eyes as blank as the windshield of a car.

"How's my girl?" Lupton laughed, tossing her up and down.

"How's my number-one girl? You've got so big I hardly recognize you!

"Daddy"—Jeanette pulled back, her eyes wide—"you've got a beard! When did you get a beard?"

"You know what they say, darlin': 'A kiss without a mustache is like a day without sunshine.'" He nuzzled his chin into her neck, sending her into shrieks of ticklish delight.

How Cordy got through the next fifteen minutes—the itinerary of Lupton's visit to his mother in Jacksonville, the search for Jeanette's lost toothbrush, the instructions to good behavior, and the final embrace—she would never know.

She found herself standing on the front veranda, Nonnie at her side. She watched Lupton and Jeanette cross the square. Lupton was holding the umbrella Nonnie had lent him, sheltering Jeanette from the drizzle. Jeanette trotted by his side, toting Cordy's overnight bag, her face upturned.

And then they were gone.

"Well, I never . . ." Nonnie pried Cordy's hand lose from the ironwork railing and guided her through the door. "Don't think it didn't take all m' strength to stop from namin' him what I know him to be."

They stood by the potted plant, the door firmly shut behind them.

"When he started into all that poesy 'bout how he missed y'all, I had to restrain m'self from physical abuse. 'Root hog or die,' I wanted to tell him."

"Not now," Cordy whispered, one hand reaching to the banister, the other fluttering in a feeble attempt to stop the chatter.

"Cordy, I tell you—"

"*Not now.*"

Cordy mounted the stairs, knelt before the toilet as though it were an altar, and finally brought up the shameful effluvium of anger and disgust. She staggered to her bed.

It was dark outside when she woke up. She felt her way downstairs, beckoned by the light in the kitchen. Nonnie was at the table, a bourbon in one hand and a copy of the *Georgia Gazette* in the other.

"I see here where the Transportation Comissioner is callin' for improvements on the Islands Expressway," Nonnie said matter-of-factly. "And Cordy, turn the fire on under that skillet will you? Bernice like to kill us if we don't finish up that rice tonight."

"Are you still using Claxton and Braun for your attorneys?"

"Course I am. I'd as soon change my religion as change from Claxton and Braun. Though"—Nonnie touched her finger to her lips and creased her brow—"I did change my religion, didn't I? Changed it three times, an' may do so again. You know I was raised up Methodist, married Episcopalian, then—"

"Good," Cordy interrupted, looking straight ahead. She supposed she never would honestly be able to say that she'd come to a decision. Decision implied judgment. She hadn't been in enough control to judge. But at a precise moment—as she'd gripped the edge of the sink and pulled herself up from the bathroom floor, breaking the nail on her right index finger—she'd known that it was all over. Reconciliation wouldn't mean harmony; it would mean acquiescence, and acquiescence wasn't in her nature. She might play at it, but underneath, seeing Lupton's failings as clearly as she did, she would become the leader, not a partner. She'd known that though love remained there was no energy behind it. That despite the desire to forgive, there was no real forgiveness in her heart. That if he came home an hour late she would never fully believe his excuses. That she didn't like his laugh. "I want to get their number from you. I'm going to divorce Lupton."

Chapter XVI

"I declare," Nonnie said, tilting her head upwards, "the people who fixed up this apartment ought to be prosecuted." She stood in the middle of the unfurnished room, her arms held closely to her sides, as though she was afraid to brush against the slightly grubby walls. "Why they dropped these ceilings and put up this tacky cardboard stuff is beyond all comprehension."

"The view is pretty," Cordy offered, motioning toward the large magnolia outside the window.

"That's not a view, that's a tree."

"All right, it's a tree, but it's pretty."

Cordy looked around for another positive thing to point out, but apart from the low rent, the tree was the only attractive feature of the place. The living room was smaller than she'd remembered it to be, and the paint job, which had looked pristine enough when she'd inspected the apartment the night before, showed itself to be slapdash in the brighter light of day. "Two hundred and sixty dollars is a good price for a two-bedroom," she said firmly.

"This is no two-bedroom. That lil' cubbyhole you showed me in there is nothin' mor'n a trunk room. The original floor plan, before they chopped it up like this, must've had what you're callin' the living room as the bedroom, and what you're callin' the bedroom as a dressin' room. An' that lil' trunk room—"

"Whatever it was, it's big enough for a single bed," Cordy interrupted. It was exasperating that Nonnie should act as though she was making this choice because she lacked taste, instead of acknowledging that she was doing it out of necessity. "Jeanette kind of liked the fact that the room was small. She said it was like a playhouse."

"Well, yes," Nonnie drawled, restraining herself from the obvious rejoinder and walking into the bathroom. "How's the water pressure?"

"I didn't check it," Cordy confessed.

She followed and watched as Nonnie turned on the faucets and flushed the toilet, hoping that no comment would be made about the sliver of soap that had been left in the gummy dish, or the stain of mildew around the base of the tub. A few hairs had been swept into one of the corners, and the sight of them filled her with disgust. She thought of the sauna, sun lamps, and marble-topped sinks in the main bathroom of the Chicago house. This place, with its institutional green tile and gold-striped wallpaper, wasn't much of an improvement over the apartment she and Lupton had shared when they were students. Of course she hadn't minded it then. She'd been playing house for the first time and she'd been confident of their upward mobility. In those days a cheap apartment was transitory, the sort of place you could make jokes about years afterward when you were surrounded by tasteful luxury.

The toilet continued to run as they walked back into the living room.

"Who all are your neighbors?" Nonnie asked.

"I don't know. I saw a woman in a white uniform going upstairs, so I guess she's a nurse. An' the agent told me that the man who lives downstairs works for the gas company. Look"—Cordy flung her hands out—"I know it's not ideal, but a lot of places won't take children and I have to get settled in somewhere. I haven't done hardly any writing since I've been back and I'm starting to get the jitters."

"Now don't be too hard on yourself. You've been in a turmoil about the divorce, an' you've been gettin' Jeanette settled into school an' all."

"There are always excuses for not doing things," she said irritably. "Always."

"Now just wait a minute." Nonnie took one of her hands and squeezed it. "Why don't you stay on with me for another three months? That block of apartments I'm doin' over on Gwinnett will be ready then, an' you know they're a lot nicer than this."

"Of course they're nicer. And they'd be more than twice this rent and"—she took her hand away and raised it in protest—"I'm not about to take one at a reduced rate. You've already put out over two thousand dollars to send Jeanette to Country Day, an' you've talked me out of taking a part-time job so I can work on my book. On top of that, you've given me money to take that history class at Armstrong College. I can rationalize all the tuition money, but I've got to draw the line here. It's not that I don't want better, Nonnie, but I have to learn how to make it by myself."

The continuing gurgle from the toilet seemed to orchestrate her frustration. Turning quickly, she went back into the bathroom and jiggled the handle. She supposed she'd have to pick up one of those awful do-it-yourself books. Folding her arms, she prayed for the surge of water to stop, for if it didn't, Nonnie would be at her side again, full of dire predictions about the plumbing. Perhaps she'd made a mistake in moving back to Savannah. There was help here all right, but with its concomitant and continual interference. Nonnie was always ready with a handout, and the worst part of it was that she was tempted to accept even more money and kid herself that it was a loan, though she had no notion of when she could pay it back. When she'd told Jake and Lucille that she planned to get the divorce Jake had offered assistance, but she'd lied and said she was solvent, because she couldn't help but think of the money Lupton had borrowed as a mutually incurred debt. Lucille, who customarily exhibited a contempt for money and spoke of it only to say that there was never enough, seemed to believe that all of Cordy's problems would be solved if she got a good divorce lawyer.

"It's the ball cock," Nonnie called out. "You've got troubles with the ball cock."

"The what?" Cordy laughed, suppressing her impulse to make a pun.

"The ball cock on the toilet. It needs to be replaced."

Mercifully, the water stopped running. Cordy went back into the living room to see Nonnie bent forward scrutinizing the fireplace.

"Cordy, I do believe you could make this functional again without too much trouble." Nonnie straightened up and smiled. "An' I've checked the floors. If you sanded them and put down a couple of throw rugs it'd be a whole lot better than this shag carpet. Ray Stokes is a good handyman. I could send him over to help you."

"I'll fix the toilet, and I might sand the floors and repaint the walls, but I'm stopping there. I don't want to restore the place, I just want to make it livable."

"Whatever you say, darlin'. You know I don't want to interfere," Nonnie said demurely, walking back to the window. "This here tree *is* pretty, and I believe the foliage is thick enough that you wouldn't have to put up draperies if you didn't want to." Even though the place gave her gooseflesh, Nonnie had determined not to find fault now, because she knew that her objections were not wholly aesthetic. The fact of the matter was that she hated to see Cordy and Jeanette go, though she knew it would be selfish to hold Cordy back from independence. Having them in the house had given a lively rhythm to her days. It had been good to plan menus and help Jeanette with her hair and her homework. She had liked sitting and sharing a drink and a chat with Cordy; and it had been so much easier to fall asleep knowing that someone else was in the house. Loving people from a distance was all very fine, but sharing meals and hugs, problems and jokes, that was the daily contact that really mattered. If you were involved with the struggles and pleasures of others, you couldn't become too absorbed in your own aches and pains. She bent forward to retrieve her purse from the floor, then straightened up when she felt the crick in her back.

"Hand me my purse, will you Cordy? What are you plannin' to do about furniture?"

"It'd cost far too much to have the furniture shipped from Chicago," Cordy said, not mentioning that she had called Lupton and asked him to send only her clothes and her hope chest. "I thought I'd go through the carriage house this afternoon and see what I can find."

"Surely. I believe there are some rugs an' chairs out there, an' there's Grandmother Hampton's ol' dining-room table, though there's a crack in it an' some of the leaves are missing. But you just root around an' take what you want. I can tell you now there's no decent mattresses. You can take the single one from upstairs for Jeanette, but you'd best buy one for yourself. If you don't spend money on a good mattress, you'll end up spendin' it on a chiropractor."

"Oh, yes, I know," Cordy said. A lifetime of homilies—don't close the windows when you go to sleep; don't run with a stick in your hand; don't wear panty hose because your privates can't breathe; feed a cold, starve a fever, ran through her mind as she opened the front door and waited for Nonnie to finish her tour of inspection.

"An' I guess you'll need some good readin' lamps," Nonnie said, turning in a half circle and wagging her head.

"Uh-huh. Don't you worry, I won't ruin my eyes by doing close work without a good light. But I've got to hurry along now, Nonnie. You know I've got that appointment with the lawyers and I have to go home and change."

"Course I know you have an appointment," Nonnie's eyes twinkled as she passed her. "Didn't I make it for you?"

You surely did, Cordy thought, because you were afraid I'd back out. She locked the door and smiled as she watched Nonnie wobble down the stairs on her high heals.

"Do you want me to drop you somewhere, Nonnie, or are you coming home with me?" she asked as she opened the car door.

"You can just take me on over to Elizabeth's on Thirty-seventh. I believe Joan and Lethia are having lunch there today and I think I'll join them," Nonnie answered as she settled into her seat. She had spoken to Lethia only yesterday and already knew that Lethia's luncheon conversation would be no more than an update on how Beauregard had reacted to his distemper shots. And Joan would prattle about her gardening or what Phil Donahue had said this morning. Still, it was important that she meet her friends for lunch. During the last months she'd broken her pattern of luncheon appointments and she'd sent her excuses to countless committee meetings. But now that Cordy and Jeanette would be moving out, she knew she'd have to make an effort to resume her old routines. Meetings, obligations, appointments—that's what she'd need now, sure as a child with a bellyache needed a dose of cod-liver oil. She would call Amos Justice and tell him that she'd take a more active part in Sam Redding's campaign for alderman; she'd set her alarm in case she was tempted to loll in bed in the mornings; she'd make sure to have a new book on her bedside table at night. She would get by. The skills of solitude were sad skills, but they were skills nonetheless.

"What did you say, Nonnie?"

"I don't think I said anything." Or did I? she wondered.

"Are you feeling all right?"

"Lordy, don't tell me I'm so loquacious that you think I've fallen ill if I'm silent for a mere five seconds," she laughed. "I was

just keepin' my mouth closed, working up my digestive juices. I do
so enjoy going out to lunch with the girls."

Cordy showered, put on her makeup, and went to the closet. As
she took the white suit from the hanger, she sighed and turned back,
hoping to find something else to wear but knowing she wouldn't.
She'd worn the white suit to every important date during the last
three months, and it was beginning to feel like a uniform. The suit
was out of season now, and though it was still spotless, it seemed
stained with associations. What had once struck her as elegantly simple now looked dowdy. Zipping up the skirt, she felt sulky and put
upon. Her own good looks, her father's, and then her husband's
pride in seeing those looks shown off to advantage had fostered an
extravagant streak in her that she had only become aware of once the
flow of money had dried up. As she surveyed herself in the mirror
she wondered how long it would be before she could enjoy a real
shopping spree. She'd made up her mind to sell her mink coat as
soon as it arrived from Chicago, but as she considered what she must
do with the cash—rent and deposits, utilities, shoes for Jeanette,
tires for the car, a mattress and refrigerator, and, most importantly,
a new electric typewriter—her dreams of indulgence floated away
like a handful of balloons that had been released into the wind.

"I'll think about it tomorrow," she shrugged, picked up her
purse, and hurried downstairs. She wasn't looking forward to the
meeting with the lawyer, and thought perhaps she could fortify herself with a quick visit with Alidia.

During the past weeks, Alidia had become her chief source of
comfort. Alidia listened without offering too much advice and saved
Cordy's sense of humor from atrophy. She had not expected a closeness to develop between them. In fact, she had called Alidia more
out of politeness than interest when she'd returned from New York
and felt some trepidation when she'd accepted Alidia's invitation to
visit. She'd anticipated a chaotic scene—tabletops scared with rings,
dishes sitting in greasy water, or, worse yet, a leftover boyfriend
sitting in a messy bed—but the apartment showed an order that
Alidia was incapable of bringing to her emotional life. The tabletops
and floors were polished, and the furniture, though sparse and inex-
pensive, was well chosen. Except for some explicit Japanese erotica
and a set of canisters marked not SUGAR, FLOUR,and RICE, but UP-
PERS, DOWNERS, and QUAALUDES, the place was almost conventional. And Alidia herself seemed calmer. She had a job as a

barmaid now, and though she complained that the tips were lousy she said she liked the customers. The bar was a neighborhood dive and gave her plenty of opportunities to hear the gossip she claimed to abhor but obviously enjoyed. But the biggest surprise was finding out that Johnnie, the soldier they'd met that night in the bar, had graduated from pickup to live-in lover.

Though these changes seemed to put Alidia in better spirits, Cordy felt them to be superficial: being a barmaid was one in a series of jobs, just as Johnnie was sure to be one in a series of lovers. Alidia's major problems—her troubles with her family, her low opinion of herself, and her drinking habits—remained unchanged. Because of Johnnie's presence, she seemed to brood less about her family and, again because of Johnnie, she was more likely to supplement her liquor with marijuana or cocaine. Cordy worried about her, but knew that any expression of concern would be laughed off. Alidia had an almost impenetrable system of defenses. She was always eager to point out her addictions and shortcomings, thereby taking the sting out of any criticism.

Whatever the alchohol and drugs were doing to Alidia's nervous system, those who chose to be with her had to accept the combination. Some may even have been grateful for the mix. Alidia drunk was not a woman you'd want to cross. The drugs seemed to soften her more violent outbursts and mute her angry diatribes. Cordy, who had no time or inclination to go out drinking with her, was never exposed to this side of her personality, and she was careful to time her visits so that she wouldn't have to run into Johnnie. The combativeness Alidia had shown toward him that night in the bar had apparently been bested by Johnnie's sexual blitz. Alidia now claimed that Johnnie was "sweet," though Cordy couldn't be in his presence without feeling a bristling tension that came close to fear.

Cordy opened the iron gate and let herself into Alidia's backyard. The barbecue grill was covered with plastic, clay pots and garden implements were stacked neatly against the brick wall, but there was no evidence of cultivation. Alidia didn't have the patience to nurture anything. She was the original "black thumb" she said. Yet she had a remarkable patience with children. Jeanette was crazy about her. Though that, Cordy suspected, was because Alidia was in many respects a child herself.

Alidia's voice was wafting out of the kitchen window. Her tone was both mournful and defiant, a perfect combination for the old slave song.

"Massa kill a big ol' duck,
Give us peoples the bone to suck.
Ain't I right?"

Cordy stood still and listened through several verses, marveling at her friend's talent. Alidia showed talent in all the arts. She could sing, dance, paint, and, Cordy was sure, she could write if she put her mind to it. The chances were that she wouldn't, or couldn't, put her mind to anything, Cordy thought sadly as she knocked on the door.

"If you're a good ol' boy with a case of booze an' a bunch of roses, then come on in."

Cordy opened the door. "And if I'm not?" Alidia was standing at the ironing board, a can of beer in her hand. She had recently dyed her hair black and styled it like a silent movie vamp. Her matchstick legs stuck out beneath a pink slip and her face was smeared with a clay mask, making her eyes an even more vivid green. Several men's shirts, pressed to a fine crease, hung on the door of the refrigerator.

"You're doing Johnnie's ironing?" Cordy asked. She was still amazed at Alidia's swings from self-assertion to subservience. "Hell, I never ironed Lupton's shirts."

"That's why you've been cast off, girl. Don'tcha know you're s'posed to stir the greens, iron the clothes, keep your mouth shut, an' make the slats in the bed go bampety-bam, elseways your man will desert you?"

"That must've been my mistake."

"We poor folk got to iron our own clothes. Don't have no mammy to do for us. How come you're all gussied up?"

"I'm going to see the lawyer, didn't I tell you?"

"Oh, yeah, now I remember. Day of Wrath and Judgment. I can see you're all pasty-faced underneath your blusher. Sit down for a spell."

"Don't mind if I do." Cordy lifted a stack of clothes from a chair and sat at the table. "I'm just a nervous wreck. Nonnie helped me to make up a list of questions to give the lawyer, and I swear I'm going to have to read them off, otherwise I won't know what to say."

"Don't you worry. It'll be *beaucoup* easy. Lupton's not contesting and he's not fighting you for custody. I'll bet he'll go along with everything. But sure as God made lil' apples you'll have to chase him for money."

"Please," Cordy said, putting her head into her hands, then lifting it to force a smile. "I've got to admit it wounded my pride some that he took my decision so easy. It amazes me. I know if I'd said yes we'd still be married. Can you imagine leaving the whole course of your life in someone else's hands like that?"

Alidia shrugged her bony shoulders and took a swig of her beer.

"It's very human, Cordy. Very understandable. Directing their own lives, responsibility . . . it's just a weight for most people."

"Anyhow, I didn't come here to talk about Lupton," Cordy said, though she knew that one of the reasons she liked being with Alidia was because she could indulge herself in talking about him. "Jeanette's the one I'm really worried about. She didn't say much when I told her I was getting the divorce, but I'm waiting for the storm to break. She's like that, you know. She seems to have a fear, almost a delicacy, about emotion. She won't talk. She keeps everything bottled up inside and then, whammo, she throws a real tantrum."

"Wonder where she gets that from." Alidia opened her eyes wide, arching her brows and causing the mask to crack on her forehead.

"But I know she blames me for the divorce. I said all the right things, assured her that we both loved her but that we couldn't get along, so we'd decided not to live together."

"And?"

"She was very stoic, almost resigned, like some damn diplomat who's negotiations had failed. Then, when I asked her what she was thinking, she said she supposed the divorce meant that she wasn't going to get a baby brother or sister. But last night, when I was tucking her into bed, she told me that Daddy had told her the *he* wanted us all to live together again. So I guess she thinks it's my fault."

"I don't think there's much you can do about that."

"Nor do I. So why the hell do I feel so guilty? I lay awake last night turning it every which way in my mind. I shouldn't feel guilty. But I do. There's nothing to be done for it. And worse than guilty, I realized I want Jeanette to understand *me*. The more I'm alone with her the more I treat her like an adult. That's just not fair."

"Are you going to take the apartment?"

"Yeah. I'm going through Nonnie's carriage house this afternoon to look for furniture. Want to come over before you go to work?"

"I'd love to. I'm going to finish up this ironin' and take a shower. This mask I have on my face promises to give me a complexion smooth as a newborn baby's backside. Sure you don't want to stay around for the miracle?"

"Uh-uh. I've got to go." Cordy rose to her feet. "Well, thanks for listening."

Alidia wrinkled up her nose. "I wasn't any help. Maybe when you get into your own place things will slow down for you. And maybe you'll find some guy to take some of the loneliness out of the nights."

"The only guy I'll be looking for is one who knows something about plumbing."

"Don't you miss sleeping with someone?"

"That's a dumb question. Of course I do. I've got Jeanette to consider too, y'know. I can't be draggin' guys in."

"I just go crazy when I have to sleep alone. I mean it, I just go crazy! What about Johnnie's friend Carl? Remember him? He's always asking about you. That man is the genuine article, Cordy. He's sweet as home-baked bread."

"Oh, Alidia. Please."

"He comes over here sometimes, just sits in the kitchen an' talks to me about gettin' himself a farm. I mean, he's solid."

"Damn it, you're sounding like Nonnie."

"O.K., O.K. Run on an' get yourself a divorce, girl. Good luck."

Cordy was almost out the back gate when Alidia stuck her head around the door and shouted, "Think of it like goin' to the dentist for surgery. Just start countin' backward from a hundred and when you wake up you'll be a free woman again."

"One hundred, ninety-nine, ninety-eight," Cordy called out as she walked to the car.

The offices of Claxton and Braun were so much a part of the landscape of old Savannah that it would have been deemed both tasteless and unnecessary to have a sign larger than the seven-by-ten-inch brass plate mounted next to their front gates. As Cordy crossed the lawn and stared at the pillars of the portico, she had a sense that she was about to enter a museum instead of going to see a lawyer. The mansion had been built by a wealthy cotton factor, or trader, prior to the Civil War and had later been occupied by Union troops. Some long-gone Claxton, a banker she believed, had bought and renovated the place around the turn of the century. It had subsequently passed on to his son, and the son of that son.

She pushed open the heavy door and entered the large foyer. Mahogany paneling rose to the height of the french windows. Above the paneling was a collection of gilt-framed paintings of men in declamatory poses with threatening skies, horses, and cannon in the backgrounds. A glass-fronted display cabinet containing antique documents was set on one side of the central staircase, and a waxen-faced older woman sat behind a desk on the other. The thick oriental carpet absorbed Cordy's steps as she approached the desk; and, mindful of the enveloping silence, she lowered her voice to a respectful whisper. "I'm Mrs. Tyre. I have a two o'clock appointment."

"Ah, yes." The woman smiled gratefully, as though she'd been stationed there specifically to await Cordy's arrival. "Mrs. Hampton's granddaughter." She gestured toward the bank of leather chairs placed in close formation next to the windows. "If you'll be kind enough to take a seat, I'll tell them you're here."

Cordy sat down and removed her gloves. The woman whispered into the intercom, then sat back smiling in the same grateful but somehow pitying fashion. She knows why I'm here, Cordy thought, and tomorrow morning all her friends will know, and some of her friends will tell their friends and . . . She gave the woman one final tight smile and turned to examine the painting above her head. The artist had a talent for landscape—the darkened sky, puffs of clouds, and wind-racked trees were well rendered—but the central figure, a general with saber drawn, looked almost smug, oblivious of the bodies that littered the battlefield.

"Yes, he must've been a sadistic ol' bastard," a man's voice whispered.

She had not heard anyone approach, and was even more surprised that the man should have guessed her thoughts so accurately. "Yes, I wouldn't have wanted to be a private in that one's army," she said, turning to see a face that was both instantly recognizable and unfamiliar. "Oh, my goodness, Clay!"

He bowed slightly, a smile barely moving one side of his mouth. "Won't you come upstairs to the office."

She followed him up the staircase and down another carpeted hallway into a room with a monumental fireplace, walls of books, and a desk whose surface shone like a midnight lake. He indicated a chair and took his place behind the desk. "It's wonderful to see you again, Cordy."

"Why, it must be at least ten years. I thought you were in England."

"I was. And it's more like twelve years. I didn't know you were back in Savannah until your grandmother called me last week."

"Well, I've been up in New York part of the time."

"Yes, I know."

She toyed with the clasp of her purse. She wanted to pick up a paperweight and hurl it across the room. The very idea that Nonnie would try to play matchmaker at a time like this filled her with rage. Damn! It was enough that she had to deal with a divorce, now she'd have a former boyfriend as her lawyer, and god only knew how many sordid details Nonnie had already poured into Clay Claxton's ear. She determined to have it out with Nonnie tonight.

"I'm sorry we have to meet under such"—Clay opened his hands, then deciding that he didn't know enough about Cordy's circumstances to characterize them, let his hands drop onto the desk— "under these circumstances."

"I am too. Though I'm grateful for your assistance. I hope there aren't going to be any difficulties with the divorce. I don't anticipate any."

Since she seemed determined to drop all pleasantries and conduct the meeting as though they were strangers, he put on his glasses and picked up a pen. "Let me just start with some standard questions."

He had difficulty taking his eyes away from her. Even though she was nervous and, he was sorry to note, not altogether pleased to see him, she looked wonderful. Her large brown eyes with the finely etched brows were glittering, almost as if she were angry. Her throat, soft as a flower petal, arched from the collar of her suit in a deliciously subtle line, and as she undid the buttons on her jacket and sat back, her breasts, which had had that ripely mature look even when she was sixteen, moved invitingly in the silk blouse. He cleared his throat and started to make notes.

"You were married in Chatham County, correct?"

"Yes," she said, though of course he knew that already. He'd had a crush on her ever since they'd been fourteen, and even when he'd gone off to Andover she'd been the first girl he'd called when summer vacations rolled around. She'd never told him directly that she'd become engaged to Lupton, but the news must've traveled fast, because he'd stopped calling her just days after the announcement. He'd left for Yale, perhaps a few weeks ahead of schedule, when she'd married, though his parents had included his name on the gift card that had come with a silver tray.

"The date of the marriage?"

She drew the slip of paper from her purse and told him the date.

"And you've been back in residence in Chatham County for six months?"

"Not quite."

"Yes, you've been in residence for six months," he corrected.

She nodded, assuming that there was some jurisdictional regulation about residency.

"Your husband is not going to contest, is that correct?"

"No. I mean, yes, he's agreeable."

She continued to answer his questions but watched him carefully, trying to take in the changes that the last dozen years had brought to him.

As a very young man, Clay had shot up before he'd filled out. He'd had tremendous drive and agility when playing basketball and he'd been a surprisingly good dancer, but when he wasn't performing some action that required specific coordination, his movements had been positively embarrassing. He was always ducking his head or wondering what to do with his hands. His skin, like Alidia's, had gone through violent eruptions, and though all the girls said he was handsome, Cordy had only felt annoyance when his devotion was pointed out to her. He couldn't make conversation. He'd constantly violated the unwritten law not to discuss "deep" subjects. When others were joking about football scores or parties, Clay'd talked about history or national politics. She'd secretly enjoyed talking with him, but she'd almost resented her attraction, because it seemed preordained. Everyone in her family, most especially Nonnie, had said that Clay was perfect. What they meant was that the Claxtons, even for the lofty Hamptons, were the very pinnacle of the social ladder.

So even when Cordy had felt the stirrings of reciprocal affection, she'd guarded against it. Clay was too serious and far too shy to make out with a girl just for the hell of it, and a prolonged open-mouthed kiss might start a momentum that would overwhelm them both. Clay would declare himself; she would accept. She'd have the wedding of the decade and two sets of precious family silver. But she would never have the chance to break out of the social strictures. Sex would be legitimate, endorsed, blessed. And Clay's discussions of Thomas Jefferson or Judge Brandeis were no match for a drunken skinny-dip or a wild ride; and his tender control couldn't compete with the excitement of being crushed by a very confident football hero.

Yet, as she looked at him now, she had to admit that of all the people she'd known, none had been so improved by the passage of time as had Clay Claxton. Even under the suit, she could see that his body had filled out with a rangy musculature. The acne had left a very slight pitting on his cheeks, giving a rugged quality to a face that might otherwise have been, with its full mouth and molded nose, a mite too handsome. His eyes behind the glasses were tired from so much close work, but they were a distinct and arresting gray.

"No stocks or bonds? No property other than what you've already mentioned?" Clay asked. He felt a bit of a phony posing the question, since Nonnie had called the day before to tell him that Cordy would probably minimize the seriousness of her financial situation so she, Nonnie, was depending on him to take a firm hand in money matters. Now, watching Cordy study the slip of paper in her lap, he was ashamed that he'd gloated, if only momentarily, because her hulk of a husband had left her high and dry. Cordy, his Cordy (for he had thought of her that way for years), was in trouble. He wanted to get up from the desk, take her in his arms, and tell her that everything would be all right. Instead, he threw his shoulders back, raised his arms to his head, and stared at the bookcase.

He could still remember sitting at the dinner table and hearing about her engagement to Lupton Tyre. Not wanting his parents to see how upset he was, he'd forced himself to eat while his mother had debated the merits of a silver tray over a crystal decanter as a wedding gift. At the end of the meal, almost gagging on a peach cobbler, he'd announced that he would go up to New Haven early and spend a couple of weeks with his roommate's family. How could she do it? he'd asked himself over and over again. How could she marry that Neanderthal?"

On the train going North, in the hotel room he rented until the semester began, in the bar where he sat alone and sullen, knocking back glass after glass of flat beer, the question had persisted. He was sure he knew Cordy better than she knew herself. Of course he'd seen how she acted in company, flirting and carrying on with that silly life-of-the-party vivacity, but he knew her other side. When they'd been alone she didn't just listen, she asked questions and expressed opinions; they argued and laughed together. "How can she marry him? What will they ever *talk* about?" he'd asked disdainfully, though Cordy and Lupton struggling through a moronic conversation was not the image that plagued his mind. He'd cursed himself for being such a prig, for masking his shyness with intellectual superiority, trying to woo her with discussions about history while his mind was full of hot-house fantasies straight out of D. H. Lawrence.

His depression had been so deep that he'd almost flunked out of law school that semester. Then he'd taken up with Stella, a girl in his torts class, and for the first few months of their affair, swept along by the pleasures of steady consummation, he'd almost convinced himself that he was in love with her. Fortunately, Stella had been wise enough to see that he wasn't. In fact she had pointed this out to him, with considerable sang froid, shortly after he'd told her about "this girl back home that I used to date." After Stella, he'd taken up with Chris, then . . .

Cordy was shaking her head. He picked up his pen and started to take notes again. "So the division of property will be relatively simple."

"Yes. Lupton seems to agree to everything. I don't want any of the furniture except the hope chest Nonnie gave me. I expect that when he sells the house he'll sell the furniture too and we'll divide the profits equally."

"The real estate market is depressed now, especially in that part of the country. What provisions for support will you demand before the sale of the property?"

"He has been sending some child support, but not much. And the checks have been erratic. But to tell you the truth, I don't see that he can do much better. His business is in real trouble. I know that for a fact, because it was already in trouble last year."

"I don't suppose you have any income tax statements or papers showing the real condition of his business?" She shook her head again. "Then why don't I call and have a talk. It sounds as though things are reasonably amicable between you."

"I wouldn't go that far. After all, I am divorcing him."

"Exactly. So it'd be best if I hammer out the settlement. I'm not saying you shouldn't talk with him, but you'd best leave the financial questions to me."

"How long will it take?"

"That depends on how quickly we can come to an agreement, but once we've filed it will be very quick. Within about thirty days."

"Thirty days. I see." Her mouth went dry even as her palms started to perspire. Thirty days.

"Yep, Section 30-102, Paragraph Thirteen. It's very easy to get a divorce these days," he said somewhat sadly. "After thirty days the marriage will be irretrievably broken."

"Irretrievably broken"—mere legal words, yet she saw a precious vessel being dashed to the ground: fragments, jagged pieces, shards, atoms.

There was a tap on the door and a pretty young girl with a bow in her hair put her head in. "Excuse me, Mr. Claxton, but did you want me to hold your calls?"

"Yes, Mary. Please don't interrupt until I'm finished talking with Mrs. Tyre."

Cordy swallowed. In thirty some days she wouldn't be Mrs. Tyre. She would only be Jeanette's mother, Nonnie's granddaughter, a woman who hoped to have her name on the jacket of a book.

"May I pour you a brandy, Cordy?"

She shook her head and took up the piece of paper to make sure she'd covered all the points, but she was afraid she was going to cry. It was the last thing in the world she wanted to do, especially in front of Clay Claxton.

"Yes, I would like some brandy. I didn't think I wanted any but—"

"Woman's privilege to change her mind." He grinned, got up, and crossed to the cabinet. "And a man's too."

He handed her the snifter and sat on the side of the desk, his pants legs pulled taut over his thigh muscles, his arms wrapped around his chest. She raised her eyes to his hands, looking for a wedding ring.

"Don't worry so much, Cordy. The divorce sounds relatively simple. I don't mean the emotional aspects, just the legal ones. Nonnie told me you've written a couple of books and that you're starting on another one."

"Yes. Yes, I am. If I can ever settle down again."

"I was pleased to hear you're writing, but I wasn't altogether surprised. I always knew you'd do something."

"I don't see how you could've predicted that. I don't think I had a serious thought in my head between the ages of fourteen and—" she smiled and shrugged—"and last month."

"Maybe I remember you better than you remember yourself."

"And how have you been?" she asked, reserve melted by the warmth of his confidence.

"Oh, I'm fine. I've only been back in Savannah for about eight months myself, and just between us, I'm not sure whether or not I'll stay."

"What did you do after law school?"

"I went to Cambridge University. Figured I should do at least one thing that hadn't been laid down by the last four generations. I liked it there. I almost didn't come back. I was going with an English girl and I toyed with the idea of staying on. I suppose it's true to my heritage that I'd be an incurable Anglophile, but I thought I'd better come home before I made the final decision. I don't think it's too egotistical to say that I'm both qualified for and interested in a broader spectrum of the law than I'm likely to practice in the family firm. If I don't move back to England I'll more'n likely move to Atlanta, talk my father into setting up an office there, expand the practice. Savannah seems small to me now. I expect it does to you too."

"Yes. Though I find that I still have a strong love-hate relationship with it. I guess love-hate relationships come easy to me."

He gave her a slow smile and took the empty glass from her hand. They looked at each other for a full thirty seconds before she got to her feet.

"I can't help staring at you," he said. "It's still a shock to see you after all these years."

"I felt the same way when I saw you, though I'm afraid I didn't act very pleased. The circumstances, as you say, are not the best."

"I'll give you a call within the week," he said as he walked her to the door. "Or perhaps you'd like to get together for a drink before then. Not business, just to talk about old times."

She almost said yes, but drew back in the nick of time. Her life was far too complicated, she was too emotionally raw, to go through the maze of old associations.

"The next few weeks will be very tight for me. As a matter of fact, I'm running late now. I have to pick my daughter up from school and then I'm going through Nonnie's carriage house to find some furniture. I'm moving into my own place next week."

"If I can be of any help . . ."

"Perhaps after I've settled in. Thank you again, Clay. It was good to see you."

*   *   *

Alidia held the padlock steady while Cordy tried to put in the key. Jeanette stood nearby in the shade of the sagging wisteria trellis, shifting from foot to foot and sucking on the end of her ponytail.

"The key's going in but it won't turn. I think the lock is rusty," Cordy said, bending down to study it.

"Here, just give it a yank an' it'll open," Alidia advised, turning back to smile at Jeanette. "Excitin' isn't it? Like we're pirates going after buried treasure."

Jeanette took the hair out of her mouth, pressed her lips together, and nodded. She'd earned another fifty cents from the tooth fairy and had decided not to smile until her new tooth grew in. But it was hard not to, because she was excited. She'd asked Nonnie to let her explore the carriage house lots of times, but Nonnie had said, "Let's just don't and say we did," like she said when Jeanette asked for ice creams before supper or wanted to stay up and watch TV. Jeanette guessed there must be something special inside the little house. She knew that people had carriages before they'd had cars and wondered if perhaps there was still a carriage in there.

"Here we go." Alidia gave the door a final pull and it creaked open.

Jeanette drew her breath and followed them. It was dark and hot inside and it smelled funny, like a birdcage mixed with those white flakes Cordy put into winter clothes when she packed them away.

"Go stand near the window till we find the light," Cordy told her. "There's junk all over the place an' you're likely to trip on something."

Jeanette moved cautiously to the square of dusty light. She couldn't imagine how Nonnie could own a place so dirty. The windows were streaked and had cobwebs on them and there were flies on the sill. She touched one of the flies to make sure it was dead, then poked at the spiderweb. Bernice had told her that in old times, before there were Band-Aids, people put spiderwebs on cuts to stop the bleeding. She wrapped some of the web around her finger and wiped it in the pocket of her jeans.

"Here, I think I've found it." Alidia was jumping up, reaching for the string that dangled from the ceiling. She jumped again, laughing, and a single bulb flicked on, throwing a yellowish light onto the incredible jumble.

Jeanette stood very still, her eyes wide in amazement. There were chairs and tables, picture frames, mirrors, stacks of books and dishes, flags, chests big enough to hide in, and they were all thrown higgledy-piggledy like her toy closet back in Daddy's Chicago house. There were wonderful things and scary things. Things she'd never seen before. A statue of a man fighting a lion, a wheelchair made out of hard straw, a big red flag with bright blue crisscross and stars, and hanging next to it another flag that said MASONIC LODGE. There was a bicycle dangling from the rafters, and a broken chandelier. Cordy and Alidia were squeezing through furniture, moving things around, and talking with each other, so it was almost as good as being here along. She opened a little umbrella made of lace, then found a lampshade, all silky, with beads at the bottom, like the skirt of the doll George Naughton had bought for her at the County Fair. There was a cabinet with a big horn on top of it, and on the horn a picture of a little dog with his ear cocked to the horn. And a thing shaped like a lady, but with no head, arms, or legs.

"Mama, how come we have this thing like they put in the store windows?"

"That's a dressmaker's dummy, sugar. That was Nonnie's shape, an' the lady who made her clothes fitted them onto that."

"There's about a four-piece place setting in this box," Alidia called out, "if you don't mind eating off plates with hunting dogs on 'em."

"I want to have a plate with a dog on it," Jeanette said, crawling over a suitcase to get to Alidia's side.

"What do you think about this dining-room table, Alidia? Even if I take out the leaves it's still banquet size."

"They sure built things to last in those days, didn't they?" Alidia moved a chest out from under some cardboard boxes and, perching on the side of the chair that had lost its rushing, lifted its lid. "Oh, Cordy, come and look at this stuff. You could open a boutique."

Cordy shifted a bag of golf clubs and squeezed past the dining-room table to kneel next to the chest.

"Just look at this black sequined cloche," Alidia sighed.

"Put it on, Alidia. Put it on," Jeanette urged.

Alidia squashed the hat onto her head and tilted it over one eye.

"An' looky here"—Cordy rummaged in the chest—"hand-crocheted baby sweaters, a receiving blanket and . . ." She lifted out a package wrapped in tissue paper and carefully folded back the top layer.

"Is it a doll dress?" Jeanette wanted to know.

"No. It's a christening robe."

Cordy put her hand underneath the delicate lace. The letters W.L.H. were embroidered on the yoke. "This must've belonged to Uncle Wade. He was Grandma Lucille's big brother. He died before you were born, Jeanette. In fact, he died before I was born."

"And get a load of this." Alidia held a pair of bloomers up to her waist and danced around. "Positively antediluvian! An' all these lil' buttons down the side. A girl really had time for second thoughts before she got down to the buff in those days."

"What does that mean, ante—"

"Antediluvian? It means before the deluge, sugar. Before the flood."

"What flood?"

"The flood in the story in the Bible. Noah had to build an ark— that's a great big boat—an' he had to take two of every kind of animal."

"Oh, yeah. I saw a cartoon about that," Jeanette said.

"An' look here." Cordy held up a yellowed program. "It's a dance card dated 1918. It's from the pavilion out at Tybrisa. That must've been the year after Nonnie and Lonnie got married. Lord, can you imagine being married for almost sixty years!"

"I probably won't even live to be sixty," Alidia said with the little barking laugh, reaching into the chest again. "Oh, Cordy, Cordy, this is exquisite." She lifted out a beaded vest. Her hands palpated it ever so gently, so that even in the dim light the amber, jet, and crystal beads shimmered and danced. "You must ask Nonnie if you can have it. A year from now when you're invited to the Telfair ball, you simply must wear this over a black satin strapless dress."

"I don't think I'll be going to any Telfair balls, but oh, it is lovely," Cordy breathed, hardly daring to touch it.

"If you get to have that, do you think Nonnie would give me the christening dress for my doll?" Jeanette asked.

"No, Jeanette, an' you mustn't ask her. That isn't a plaything. It has special memories for Nonnie. In fact, I don't even think we should mention finding it."

Cordy wrapped the tissue paper around the tiny garment and placed it back in the chest.

"Listen," she said, getting to her feet and dusting off her pants, "this here treasure hunt is a hell of a lot of fun, but I've got to get down to finding some furniture. What do you think about the dining-room table, Alidia? Is it just going to dwarf everything else in the room?

"Sure it is, but it's fine-lookin'. I'd take it if I were you."

Nonnie appeared in the doorway, her figure silhouetted by the fading afternoon light. She shielded her eyes with her hand and advanced a few steps.

"Now just look at you girls," she clucked, taking in Alidia's sequined hat. "I send you out here to get down to come serious business an' here you are playin' house. Alidia you look for all the world like Theda Bara. If you want that silly ol' hat, you take it, 'cause it'd look ridiculous on anyone else. Bernice has made some lemonade. C'mon into the house and have some. You too, Jeanette. Leave your mother with a few minutes of solitude so's she can think in a straight line for a change."

"O.K. Y'all go on in and I'll join you in a minute," Cordy said.

"Thanks for the hat, Nonnie." Alidia walked over and put her arm around Nonnie's waist, then motioned for Jeanette to join them.

Cordy closed up the trunk and sat on it, looking around. The anger she'd felt toward Nonnie just a few hours ago seemed to float away on the motes of dust and sunbeams that danced near the window. A feeling of sadness came over her as she surveyed the motley bits an pieces, trash and treasures of other peoples' lives. From this she'd pick and choose to begin her new home, though the pieces would not suit her little apartment any more than the ideas of christenings, balls, the Bible, and fiftieth wedding annivesaries fit her solitary modern life.

"Cordy, is that you?"

"Yes. Alidia?"

"It's me. I absolutely *have* to talk to you."

Alidia's voice was both breathless and demanding, but since Cordy had come to expect her friend's melodramatic presentation of fairly commonplace events she was not alarmed.

"I'm just going out the door, Alidia. We're packin' up some things for the move tomorrow, so I was just going to drive over to Wall's to pick up some ribs," Cordy stalled. "I could give you a call tomorrow."

"You say you're goin' over to Wall's? I'll meet you there."

"O.K. I'll see you in the parking lot in about fifteen minutes."

Cordy grabbed up her keys, called down the hallway to let Nonnie and Jeanette know she was leaving, and shot out the front

door. It was coming on to nightfall and the sky was coral and
golden, fading into blue: a southern sunset at its most spectacular.
She wondered as she hurried down the steps if she would ever find
the time to sit and relish the beauty around her, or if she would
always be dashing about fulfilling one obligation while neglecting
another. Fanny Kemble had written about the Southern sunsets in
her journal, and Cordy made a mental note to start one of the chapters with a rapturous description of their beauty. That was, she
thought as she slammed the car door, if she ever got around to writing the book. In her impatience, she ground the gears as she pulled
away from the curb. She would, she vowed, deal with Alidia's problem sympathetically but swiftly. Then she'd come home, eat dinner,
finish the packing, read to Jeanette, and put her to bed; and, come
hell or high water, she'd write for at least two hours. So what if she
woke up grouchy and exhausted? She'd probably wake up that way
even if she did get eight hours' sleep.

She pulled up behind a new beige Volvo and waited for the
light to change. The light turned to green, but the Volvo didn't
move. She almost sounded her horn, but cursed and reached for the
antacid pills on the dashboard instead. She could see in a flash that
the couple in the Volvo were out on a date. The woman was sitting
midway between the passenger door and the driver, equidistant between new and old intimacy, talking and fluffing her hair. The man
seemed less involved in the conversation but was at least interested
enough not to be paying attention to the light. Cordy turned her
head to look out the window. Better to be Zen and contemplate the
sunset than to get impatient with this scene of flirtation and afflu-
ence. But then she did a double take. The man had turned to look at
his date and she saw his profile. It was Clay Claxton.

He drove off without noticing her.

Thank god I didn't sound the horn, she thought as she stared
after them. She could imagine Clay sitting over a bottle of wine,
relishing the view of the river as he told the girl about the glory of
the Thames or the beauty of her hair. "Just remember, Clay Claxton, I knew you when you had acne and were too gawky to make a
pass," she muttered.

The car behind her honked.

You have absolutely no reason to be upset because you saw
Clay Claxton going out on a date, she lectured herself as she ground
the gears again and jerked forward. But she felt older and more tired
because she'd witnessed it.

She drove a few more blocks until she was on the fringe of the black neighborhood and pulled into the vacant lot in front of Wall's. Wall's was black capitalism at its most primitive: a stucco house with a single strip of red neon over the slant of roof and another strip of green neon over the door, a place where women cooked up home-made ribs and deviled crabs over an open hearth and served them up to paying customers three nights a week. Alidia's Chevy was no-where to be seen, so she got out, bought the ribs, and then got back into her car.

The aroma of the ribs was making her mouth water. She was just about to open the paper bag and sneak a taste when Alidia pulled up, started to get out of her car, then reached into the glove compartment to take a hip flask.

"Damn it, don't think you're going to turn this into a drink and gab session," Cordy mumbled to herself.

"You want a swig?" Alidia offered as she opened the door.

"No. No, I don't," Cordy said impatiently. "Nonnie and Jeanette are waitin' supper. I can't stay long."

Alidia got in, unscrewed the flask, and belted back a quick one. Cordy didn't even try to keep the look of disapproval from her face.

"What is it, Alidia? Did you have a fight with Johnnie?"

"No." Alidia shuddered and put the flask between her legs.

"Then what is it?"

"I don't know how to tell you this. In fact I don't even know if I should tell you this."

"Come on, Alidia, what is it?"

"Do you remember Jacques Haur?"

Cordy tried to put a face with the name. "Yes, I know him. That is, I met him at my parents' house. So what?"

"He tries to tell people that he owns horses and stocks an' all. Maybe he does, for all I know. But his money comes from dope. He's been runnin' a boat up the coast for about a year now. He's a big-time dealer. I know"—she stopped to take another swig—"be-cause Johnnie buys from him and then sells it out at the base."

Cordy wiped her hand over her face and sighed deeply.

"No, no, wait." Alidia screwed the top back onto the flask and turned to her, demanding her attention. "The last time I saw Jac-ques—oh, it must've been a coupla weeks ago—he was talking about how he had this fancy woman on a string. I didn't connect it—well, I mean, how could I ever connect it with—"

"I love you Alidia, but you're tryin' my patience. I don't care about Jacques Haur an' I don't care about the dope traffic an' I don't care about—"

"I didn't connect him with Lucille. With your mother."

"My mother? Why would you connect him with my mother?"

"Your mother is having an affair with Haur."

"What?" Cordy could barely countenance the accusation enough to question it.

"I didn't put any of it together until today. Johnnie had talked me into drivin' over the Haur's place on Hilton Head. Johnnie thought the cops were after Haur, because he was supposed to pick up some stuff from Haur on Monday and we've been trying to call his house ever since then. Haur always delivers. I mean, he's had some big deals with Johnnie—"

"What the hell's this got to do with my mother?" Cordy accused her. She was dumbfounded, unable to figure out what was being said, yet she felt a stab of filial protectiveness that constricted her chest and stiffened her back. She stared at Alidia, looking for some evidence of drunken malice in her face, but Alidia seemed calm, as though she was marshaling evidence and waiting for Cordy to be quiet so that she could speak again.

"Anyhow, Johnnie heard that the cops were makin a sweep, an' he thought maybe Haur had ducked out with his cash. So he talked me into going to Haur's place. I went over there this afternoon, an' just as I was comin' into his drive I saw your mother pull out."

"It couldn't have been my mother."

"It was. I saw her real clear. When a woman almost runs you off the road—"

"Did she see you? Did you talk to her?"

"No. She was absolutely freaked out. Thank God I was sober, because otherwise I swear we would've run into each other and we'd have killed each other. I called out after her an' then I looked at her car as it drove away. It was your mother, Cordy. I know it was."

"But that doesn't prove . . ."

Alidia took another swig out of the flask. "I don't know what all is goin' on. But your mother is involved with Haur somehow. An' I think she's this woman that he was talkin' about the last time we saw him. He said she was married, an' older, an' lived in—"

"That's the most ridiculous thing I've ever heard!"

"I know it sounds crazy. I know it does. But it flashed on me so clear when I saw her today. She was a mess, Cordy. She wasn't makin' no social call. She looked like she'd been crying, an' she almost plowed into my car. I'm not lying."

Cordy grasped the wheel and put her head on it. There was no use in questioning Alidia any further, for Alidia had presented whatever evidence she had. She had drawn a preposterous conclusion from her near accident, so the simplest course of action was to seem to take her accusations seriously but to disregard them entirely. And yet . . . Alidia did not lie. Alidia told the truth even when it went against her. If she said she wasn't drunk, she who all too readily confessed to her weakness, and if she said she'd seen Lucille . . .

"You know I never liked your mother," Alidia said quietly. "I don't know why I'm tellin' you this, because I might be wrong. But I felt I should tell you. Jacques Haur is slime. He's a dangerous man. Let me put it this way: If this were the sixteenth century, Jacques Haur would be a grave robber. If your mother's screwin' around with him, she's way out of her depth. He's on the fast track. You'd better warn her."

"How can I?" Cordy lifted her head from the wheel and laughed. "I mean . . ." She fixed Alidia with a defiant and disbelieving glance. "Alidia, my mother is fifty years old!"

"Hey, I gotta get to work." Alidia opened the car door, then turned back to look at her. "You know, for someone who's as smart as you are, you've got these incredible gaps of understanding. Dollars to doughnuts, your mother's been havin' an affair with Jacques Haur."

Chapter XVII

What she remembered most vividly was that dreadful animal on the road. If it hadn't been for that dog, Lucille was sure, none of it would ever have happened.

The sun pricked and bled through the bedroom curtains, trapping her in a fetid cave. Straining her ears, she thought she could hear Jake puttering around in the kitchen, closing the refrigerator door with care, so as not to disturb her. But that was not possible. Nothing from the kitchen could be heard at this end of the house. It was that she could sense his presence and knew without doubt what he was doing, what he would do. In another twenty minutes he would pad down the hallway, crack open the door, and ask if he could get her anything. And she would groan and turn, feigning disturbed sleep, and tell him she needed nothing. What she really needed was to know what had happened to that dog, to make sure that it was buried, though it was too late for that now. Some neighbor out for a walk would have discovered it. The A.S.P.C.A would have been called. Or perhaps it was still there, for though she had gone to the house at the end of the road many times after that awful afternoon, she had always been careful to take the other route.

She had known from the very beginning that Jacques didn't love her. And somewhere, submerged in the deepest part of her being, the part that broke through in the waking sweats, she had even known that he didn't like her, that he had considered her a plaything. But it would have been impossible for her to admit that. Even now she shied away from the blinding evidence, that she had been fascinated, flattered, and exploited, while Jacques had barely gone through the motions of pursuing her. After the party at his house, when they'd stood on the dock, he had come by the house only once, and that, by his own admission, had been because he'd happened to be driving by and had noticed that Jake's car wasn't in the drive. She could still remember his hands dangling from the patio chair as she'd served him drinks, and the feline, almost feminine, way he'd draped himself against the door as he'd left, saying, "I'll be home Wednesday afternoon. A lazy lady like you should like the afternoons."

That particular Wednesday, perhaps because she'd taken two Valium instead of one when she'd gone to bed, she'd had great difficulty waking up. She'd had two cups of coffee with her juice. She'd bathed and worked out in front of the full-length mirrors. Twisting, bending, and counting, she'd hummed to the bossa nova beat. But the seldom heard voice of her libido hissed, insisting, "If not now, then when?" She'd turned up the stereo, then snapped it off, and as a last exercise of the will she'd called up Ellen Hamilton to say that she'd changed her mind and, yes, she'd love to make a fourth at bridge that afternoon. Ellen had made her suffer for the late acceptance by reminding her that a fourth was needed only because Patty Brown had been called away to attend the birth of a grandchild.

Ironically, for there was no hope of keeping her mind on the game, Lucille had played well. Taking the small winnings as a sign of deliverance, she'd wanted to keep on.

"Oh, dear, I couldn't possibly," her partner, Ruth Sheppard, had yawned. "Buzz and I got that new X-rated channel on our cable and we stayed up real late last night watching I won't begin to tell you what. Besides, I'm having drinks with our C.P.A. I'm thinking of buying a part interest in that lil' boutique over at the Gallery of Shops."

"You're going to learn about bookkeeping?" Elizabeth Salter asked, running her fingers through her thick gray hair.

"No"—Ruth laughed—"I'm just going to learn enough to make people think I've *actually* learned about it. I don't have the patience to really bother with all those figures."

Ellen gathered up the cards and reached for the sherry decanter. "Oh, don't let's talk about balance sheets," she complained. "Tell me about the X-rated movie. Ralph is so mean, he just won't let me turn on that channel. It's the late news, and the stock market quotations, and then he insists on turning off the set."

"I'm not sure I'd want to watch an X-rated movie," Elizabeth Salter said, almost to herself. "That sort of thing embarrasses me."

Ruth reached into her purse for her compact. "That's just because we were brought up with all those movies where the couple kissed, the music swelled, an' then the camera went up to the sky or showed a fireworks display or somethin'." Her little finger whisked away the lipstick that had caked at the corners of her mouth.

"Oh, I used to go see those old movies every week of m' life when I was a girl," Ellen laughed. "I was 'bout seventeen years old 'fore I realized you didn't get pregnant from kissin'."

"Thank god we're almost past the point of worrying about gettin' pregnant," Ruth said, snapping the compact shut.

"So I should think we'd be past the point of watchin' X-rated movies," Elizabeth said tartly. "It isn't that I think they're *morally* wrong, but"—a smile flickered at the corner of her mouth—"the idea of watching instead of . . . you know."

"Oh, 'Lizbeth"—Ruth reached to pat her hand—"you watch the Olympics even though you can't run or jump or anythin', don't you?"

"Are you sure you don't have time for another game?" Lucille interrupted. "It'd give y'all a chance to win back some of your money."

"No," Elizabeth said firmly, rising from her chair. "Even if Ruth could stay, I couldn't. I'm leading the discussion at my Institute for Learning class tomorrow, so I want to get to the library."

"*Chacun à son gout.*" Ellen sighed, removing the plate of little sandwiches. "Though how you can take an interest in soil erosion on the Georgia coastline is beyond me, 'Lizbeth."

"It's good to keep your mind active," Elizabeth said.

Ellen and Ruth exchanged glances: Elizabeth would never let you forget that she used to be a schoolteacher.

"I'll help you with these dishes," Lucille offered.

"No, no. Nothin' here to worry 'bout," Ellen insisted. "Next week 'Lizbeth and I'll win it all back from you, don't you worry."

Lucille had tucked the fifteen dollars she'd won into her wallet. Since her car was blocking the drive, she'd been the first to leave.

She had taken the long way home. Driving along the dirt road, the tape deck playing, the air conditioner protecting her from the waves of shimmering heat that rose from the hood of the car, she'd

had the sensation of being hermetically sealed. Tonight after supper—she would make scampi and garlic bread, never mentioning the
cholesterol—she would talk to Jake. She'd tell him about her bridge
winnings and confess to having squirreled away five hundred dollars
of the housekeeping money. If she presented it in the right atmosphere, Jake would laugh and see her nest egg as enterprising rather
than secretive. Then she'd tell him about this new plastic surgeon in
Atlanta who, she had it on good account from Ellen, was first rate
even if he was a Filipino. Wondering how long it would take the
swelling under her eyes to go down after the surgery, she reached
forward to slot another cassette into the tape deck when, thud, a
bouncing thing caught somewhere in the underbelly of the car.

She'd slammed on the brakes. The car skidded, sending up
clouds of dust. There was another thud as the object bounced free of
the tires. Then a high-pitched whining. She'd scrambled out. The
heat hit her full in the face. Bird caws and insect sounds crept out of
the woods, assaulting her. She looked around, but could see nothing.
For a moment she thought that some tiny but necessary cog of her
mind had slipped its gears, spinning her imagination out of control.
She turned, ready to get back into the car. And then she saw it,
lying between the front wheel and the fringe of weeds. A scrawny
dog, a mongrel, its tongue distended, pink and obscene, its hind legs
jerking in spasms. She bent closer, hand reflexively reaching down,
then retracting from the dirty fur. There was no sight of blood, not,
at least, for those interminable moments as she crouched, then
straightened up, wondering what to do. But then the rhythm of its
back legs slowed and stopped. Its front paws clawed at the earth and
the smallest trickle of blood came from its mouth. Its eyes rolled and
focused on a large rock that lay by the side of the road.

The cassette was still playing, something with an even beat and
too many saxophones, like the band at the country club, but the
insect buzz seemed to overwhelm the music. She reached into the
dashboard, turned off the motor and sat down, staring at the dead
thing by the side of the road. It was surely dead now, though she
daren't go close enough to examine it. She hadn't seen it run out of
the woods, so how could she possibly be responsible? She should
drive to the next house and call someone, though she wasn't sure
who. The creature had no identifying tags, and the way its ribs
stuck out from its chest she was sure it was a stray that had had to
forage for its food. It was dead now. Never again would it sniff or

couple, run in the woods, rummage in garbage cans, or sleep in the sun.

She took a copy of *Town & Country* from the back seat and started to rip it apart. A sheaf of papers in her hand, she edged toward the body, dropping the pages, one by one, to cover it. A clump of weeds was clutched in its front paw. With the toe of her high-heeled sandal she nudged it off the road. She kicked off her sandals and flung them into the back seat, then sat, arms draped on the steering wheel, head on hands, until she'd stopped shaking.

The pebbles of the drive cut into her feet as she walked to Jacques Haur's front door. He answered the bell almost immediately, as though he'd been lurking behind it waiting. He was barefoot and wearing a loose-sleeved robe that had symbols she didn't recognize down the front. His cheekbones shadowed the hollows around his mouth, and the pupils of his eyes were sharpened to tiny pinpoints of intention. She said his name just once, and that seemed to loose her last shred of control.

It was not at all as she'd imagined it would be. The first climax, and by far the most powerful one, had been when she'd presented herself at the door knowing that she just didn't care. Didn't care how she looked or what she said or what they did. Later, there had been another moment of abandonment—his body moving in hers or hers in his, it didn't matter so long as the eclipse was total. And then a dizzying fatigue, as though she'd been caught in a riptide and thrown up onto the shore.

It was deathly quiet. The ceiling fan circled above. His gaping mouth was still stuck to her neck. His body, which had thrust with steady, machinelike precision a moment before, became an alien, oppressive weight.

He shuddered and heaved himself off of her. There was a moment's respite—a moment's only—when the fan blessed her perspiring flesh and she felt if not at peace then sufficiently stunned to accept it as such.

She'd heard the toilet flush. She'd propped herself up and contemplated the stark room and the banal vulgarity of finding her underpants and putting on her makeup. When he'd turned on the shower, she'd hurried to dress, unwilling to face his judgment.

By the time he came out of the bathroom, again wrapped in the strange robe, she was already prepared to go.

They had not even kissed goodbye.

Yet she had gone back. Every Wednesday afternoon for the next five weeks.

He had shown her affection only once—the last time—and now she understood that it had been by design. As he was plowing into her, he'd grabbed her chin and commanded that she look into his eyes. Even at that moment he had not assumed a real personality for her, but he had established the force of his presence and an admonition that he would have to be dealt with. And afterwards, instead of taking his shower, he'd sat on the edge of the bed, his back to her, his hands dangling between his legs. For the first time she'd noticed a scar beneath his left shoulder blade. The puckered streak of violated flesh had made him seem more frightening than vulnerable.

When she'd asked what was wrong, he'd straightened, as though offering his back to her touch. "Lucille," he had said, and again she was surprised, because it was the first time he had used her name. "I don't know, Lucille. I'd just like to get away from it all. Do you s'pose we'll ever be able to take a weekend together? Just a weekend?"

Flattered, touched, she'd whispered that it would take some doing but that she supposed she could arrange it. He'd taken her hand and kissed it, then lay back next to her, caressing her absently. She'd asked him to tell her what was wrong, half expecting some confession of love. "I'm in a lil' trouble," he'd said hoarsely. "Nothin' serious. Just that it's making me preoccupied." She'd assured him that he could trust her, that she was hardly in any position to violate his confidence. He'd closed his eyes and told her about it. He'd dropped some money gambling. He was expected to pay it back the following day. He'd called the bank in Virginia, but the bank officer who knew him was on vacation, so the damned bureaucrats at the bank required that he send a written authorization before they would wire the funds. She suggested that he just explain this to his creditors, but he gave a sour laugh and said that apparently she didn't understand his position. His "creditors," as she called them, were not the sort of men who accepted excuses. He'd hinted that they were dangerous. "If you could see your way clear, just for a couple of days, till the cash gets down from Richmond . . ."

It was all he'd have to say. She wanted to help him, wanted to bind him to her with gratitude if not passion. Yet when he'd mentioned three thousand dollars, she'd been stunned. She'd wanted to back out, but felt that she couldn't. Her pride depended on an appearance of generosity and autonomy.

She'd taken the money out of the savings account the next day and dropped it by his house. He'd kissed her as she'd given it to him and asked if she wanted him to come by her house to return it, or if she would prefer to wait until their usual time the following Wednesday. She'd said she'd wait.

She'd felt particularly beautiful that Wednesday. Their intrigue had prickled her skin with excitement, flushed her with triumph. It was all so simple. It was having it all. A grateful lover and a husband who could not be hurt, because he would never find out. Not that Jake had ever really known her. Jake only knew the docile, inexperienced girl who'd married him; he couldn't know a wild, hot woman who was capable of taking risks. She would simply watch out for the next bank statement, which would show the withdrawal and redeposit, and she would destroy it. The month after that, there would be no record of what she'd done. Then she and Jacques would plan their weekend together.

She had fairly skipped to his front door, tapping it gently with a dat-dat-da-dat-da, dum-dum. When he didn't answer she rang the bell. Then standing back, she felt the pulsating heat of the day, the prestorm restlessness in the air that sucked the breath out of her lungs and made her heart race. The shades were drawn, making the windows seem sightless, dead. She brought her hand to the middle of her chest to calm the pounding of her heart, then turned and groped her way down the steps. Blundering to the back of the house, thrusting aside the sticky vines and overgrown bushes, she stumbled up onto the veranda, reached for the handle of the mesh screen, and yanked it back. She exerted an equal pressure on the door, but it refused to open. She fell backwards, losing her balance. She called his name, at first unsteadily, in whimpers. But even before she began to pound on the door and shriek, she knew that he was gone.

She must have been whipped by an overhanging branch as she'd run back to the car, because there was a little gash on her neck. And as she'd careened down the road, dust billowing into the air, she'd almost had a head-on collision with a white car. The driver had yelled, "You stupid bitch," as she'd swerved and driven on.

She could hear Jake moving in the hallway now. She knotted her fists and pounded her belly, groaning into the pillow. She wondered if there were enough sleeping pills left in the bottle to release her from this agony of fear and humiliation. The idea was compelling, for at least in the final act she would be fully conscious of her victimization. Though, she thought with sudden clarity, Jake had been a victim too, if he but knew it.

The doorknob turned slowly. Through the fringe of her lashes she could see the outline of Jake's body.

"How y' doin', darlin'?"

"Mmmm, er . . . what?" She turned onto her side, pulling her legs up toward her chest. "Don't worry, Jake. I'll get up soon."

"No need. Just wondered if you needed anything."

"No. No." She turned her mouth into the pillow, wishing him gone, but he came forward, standing over her. She knew he would not turn on the light without asking if it was all right to do so, and, fortunately, it was now too dark for him to see her face.

"You know," he started, then stopped.

He could see only the barest outline of her body, but she seemed to be crumpled up, curled against some heartless attack and not just the pain of a migraine. If he could find a way to comfort her she might unwrap the self-protective arms and move aside to make room for him.

He craved her affection now as he had once craved her breasts and her thighs and his joyful release between her legs. She had never needed it as much as he had. But then again, she had never denied him, though sometimes her indifference was even worse than rejection. On balance, even acquiescence was sweet if you really loved the woman.

Remembering the years when she had yielded to his insistence, he sat on the side of the bed, forcing her to move over. He placed his hand on the hard curve of her hip bone. Perhaps if he had been a more artful lover he might have roused her more fully. But in the beginning his appetite had been so intense, and his knowledge of female anatomy so limited, that he was overcome with domineering tensions. There had been only a few before her, prostitutes mostly, and that one brief affair in Nuremberg with Elsa. Elsa of the broad shoulders, unshaved legs, and ice-blue eyes. Elsa, who had actually cried out for it.

"You know," he began again.

He had failed Lucille somehow. He had known it from the first. From those honeymoon days that had been put aside for lovemaking. And he had tried to make up for his failure with houses and gifts and holidays. A piece of jewelry had been an apology for his inconsiderate vigor; a vacation had been an atonement for, as well as an excuse to exercise, his lust. Then, in the years when the children were growing up, the lovemaking had taken on a certain assumed regularity, as necessary as a healthy diet, but not something you howled at the moon about. And his one fall from grace—that two-month affair he'd had with his associate's secretary, some twelve years ago—in retrospect that had been no more than an attempt to revive his powers. It had been as coarse and transitory as those jokes about putting an old bull in a new pasture. It had never, even for a moment, made him question his love for Lucille.

"You know . . ."

"What is it, Jake? That's the third time you've said 'you know.' an' I don't." Her voice was tremulous and she shifted further away from him, almost as though she were afraid.

"I'm goin' to miss Jeanette," he said in a cracked voice. "I know she was a handful, but it kinda took me back to when Cordy and Jake Junior were kids. And you know somethin' else, Luce? Just now, sittin' out on the patio, I realized something. I've always dreaded the twilight. Seems as though my vision goes at twilight. I just can't help getting melancholy. Maybe that's why I'm so interested in charting the stars. The stars seem so far away, but when I can look at 'em through the telescope, they get close and more hopeful.

"And another thing I've been thinkin'. . ." He reached over and pulled the rucked housecoat down to her ankles, then brought his own legs up onto the bed. "I don't like being retired. I don't like it at all. How would you feel 'bout my starting to work again? Not full time. I prob'ly couldn't find full-time work if I tried, and I know I wouldn't want to be gettin' up to the clock anymore. But there's construction starting up, an' I have some contacts. There's always a need for a good consulting engineer. I believe I could get some consultation work. In fact, I know I could."

"If you think you want to do that, then I think you should," she said softly, getting up. She walked slowly to the bathroom and switched on the light, shielding her eyes. "I'll just take my bath, then I'll fix supper."

"You don't have to. We could go out if you like."

"No. I'd rather stay home."

He had expected some remonstrance, or at least some discussion. His going back to work would scuttle the plans she'd made about going to Europe. Perhaps, he thought, easing back, folding his arms beneath his head, it had been unfair to spring the idea on her when she had a headache and probably wasn't listening properly.

He could hear the bath water running now, and he could imagine her taking off the robe, testing the water, and pouring in that perfumed oil that lingered for hours. He could remember the times when she'd prepared herself for bed while he waited, hard and ready, ears tuned to the gurgle of water going down the drain. He suspected she enjoyed her preparations more than she enjoyed the act itself. But she wasn't preparing now any more, than he was waiting sharp with anticipation. Still, he wished she hadn't closed the door, as though the bathroom was her refuge. And he wished he hadn't been left alone with his thoughts.

Lucille knelt by the tub, still in her robe. She dipped the sponge into the water and squeezed it, dipped it again.

The money had to be replaced. She'd gone through all possible sources in her mind. She might tell Ellen and Elizabeth that she'd overspent her charge cards, and she could add in the secret stash of housekeeping money. But no, that didn't add up to three thousand dollars. If she approached Ruth . . . One by one she crossed names off the list. All save one. Nonnie.

She turned the hot water on full blast, holding her hand underneath it until she winced with pain. Going to Nonnie would be the most terrible reckoning she could think of, but in a perverse way its very horror had an odd fascination. She had tried to measure herself with Jacques Haur and she had plummeted only the depths of humiliation and despair. Now she would have to appear before the most terrible throne of judgment to beg for mercy and reprieve.

Chapter XVIII

As the chimes in the lobby of the Civic Center signaled the beginning of the performance, the crowd reluctantly broke off conversations. Men checked their vests for tickets, women smoothed coiffures. There was a general movement toward the doors of the auditorium. "Evenin', Eugenia. Evenin', Bill. Wonderful to see you." Nonnie smiled and waved to a passing couple before turning back to look at George and Cordy. Then her hand came back to the throat of her black velvet dress; she worked her tongue around her teeth and set her mouth into a thin line. "I suppose Lucille is going to stand us up."

Cordy looked down at her hands. The lobby of the Civic Center was the last place she wanted to be. Late that afternoon, when Lethia had called Nonnie to say she had an attack of neuralgia and wouldn't be coming, Cordy had impulsively offered to come. Her sympathies were most readily engaged by people who didn't ask for sympathy, so when she'd seen Nonnie packing up Jeanette's things and insisting that she didn't mind being alone, she'd volunteered. And she wanted to see Lucille. All day long, as she'd supervised movers, unpacked dishes, tacked sheets up to windows, and fixed the ball cock on the toilet, her mind had kept coming back to Alidia's accusation. She'd dismissed it as preposterous a dozen times, and just as many times she'd been alarmed by its possible truth.

"I'm sure Mother will be here," she said, drawing her gloves onto hands rough from scrubbing the bathroom. "I spoke to her this afternoon." Lucille had sounded normal during their conversation, or at least she had answered Cordy's questions about how she was feeling in that characteristically laconic, distant tone. But, Cordy thought, if she could actually see Lucille, she might have a further clue. But what sort of clue? Lucille wasn't likely to turn up with a scarlet A embroidered on the front of her Oscar De La Renta gown. She scanned the almost deserted lobby, then faced Nonnie again. "Let's wait another few minutes."

"No, ma'am," Nonnie said firmly. "It's bad manners to walk into a concert after it's already started. I'm not about to go traipsin' down the aisle after that foreign conductor who came all the way from New York has taken his bow. Callin' attention to yourself like that is just rude." She took a few steps toward the auditorium door, then stopped, opened her beaded purse, and brought it close to her nose.

"I've got the tickets," George reminded her. " 'Member you gave 'em to me in the car?"

"Then get them out, George. Get them out. I declare, you're worse than Jeanette. Look how you've gone and rolled up your program like that an' gotten print all over your hands. How're you going to know what they're playin' if you don't have your program?"

"I won't live long enough to read it. I swear this collar is goin' to garrote me before intermission," he grumbled, wedging a finger between the folds of his neck and the collar of his dress shirt. "I wish you hadn't insisted on me wearing this. I don't see too many other men wearin' black tie."

Nonnie snapped the purse shut and shook her head. "Talking about what other people do is the poorest excuse for conduct I ever heard. A tuxedo is proper attire for the symphony."

Cordy looked down at the carpet and tucked her tongue into her cheek to avoid smiling. She wouldn't dare tell Nonnie that formal dress was more a sign of provincialism than sophistication or that the sprayed hair and fur wraps she'd seen tonight were out of fashion.

"I simply don't understand you, George," Nonnie went on. "You worked so hard to get a symphony in town, but it's like pullin' teeth to get you to come."

"I didn't work for anything. I wrote a check. An' I only did that 'cause you wouldn't stop fussin' at me. You acted like a bird in a dust bath. 'Savannah's got to have a symphony,' you kept saying; made it sound about as important as having indoor plumbing."

"Now, now"—she touched his arm—"I promise you'll enjoy yourself once you've settled in. It's Brahms's Fourth. Nice and restful and a beautiful melody. Just think of the waves on the ocean."

They took a few more steps to the door. The young man put his hand out for the tickets. Cordy turned her head to the vacant lobby. George started to give up the tickets, then stopped to examine them as though they were a poker hand. "Tell you what—you ladies go on in an' I'll wait for Lucille. She's bound to be along soon and we'll join you at intermission."

"No you don't, George. I know you. You'll hang around waitin' for them to set up the refreshment table."

George stuck out his jaw, releasing another bulge of imprisoned flesh from his collar. "Don't be foolish, Nonnie. It's not like you can get a real drink here. All they have is Co-Cola, an' that white wine reminds me of cat piss."

"Come on in with us. Lucille thinks she's so important the whole blessed orchestra has to wait on her. Let 'em close the doors in her face if her manners aren't any bettern'n that."

Applause, soft as a shower but quickly rising to the sound of hail on a tin roof, came from the auditorium. The ticket taker darted forward and closed the doors.

"Wait, here she is." Cordy motioned to the far end of the lobby. Lucille, resplendent in a long rose-colored evening coat, was crossing the carpet as slowly as if she'd been leading a cortege.

"This is no time to be doin' your Jackie Kennedy imitation," Nonnie muttered under her breath. "Hurry up, Lucille!"

"I am so sorry," Lucille whispered as she reached them. "I decided to drive in by myself and—"

"Can't you see it's already startin'? Come on in," Nonnie ordered.

"I thought I'd spend the night at the house, Nonnie. That is, if—"

"Will you hush!" Nonnie nodded for the ticket taker to open the door, then reached for it herself.

The applause had stopped. The conductor, as though he had eyes in the back of his head and could see the procession headed for the fifth row, stroked his baton and waited. Nonnie, all innocent dignity, slipped into her seat first. George, smiling back at the multitude of upturned faces, motioned Cordy in next. For a split second, as she moved past him, she thought he might give one of his campaign salutes. He took Lucille's elbow, helping to settle her into her seat, then took his own place on the aisle. The conductor raised his baton. As the first slow, sad strains of music washed over her, Cordy took off her gloves and knotted her perspiring hands together.

At the pause between the third and final movement, Cordy looked to her left, then to her right. Nonnie had fallen asleep. Only the high collar of her dress prevented her head from nodding onto her chest. Lucille, lips tight, might have been sitting for her portrait. George, knee jiggling, had worried his program to tatters. If he was listening to anything it was his own internal drummer.

See no evil, speak no evil, hear no evil, Cordy thought. A gust of laughter inside her threatened to escape and blow her away to social disgrace. But a moment later, as the fourth movement began and she continued to study Lucille out of the corner of her eye, her laughter evaporated.

She had watched her mother at countless concerts, watched her arrange herself in her favorite pose—hand to cheek with little finger extended to frame a half smile, or hand to shoulder, caressing her skin in that satisfied, distracted way that was designed to draw attention from already distracted men in the audience. Tonight Lucille's behavior was decidedly strange. She sat bolt upright, hands clutching the armrests so tightly that her rings stood away from her fingers. Her neck was pulled out of her shoulders, strained into knotty cords. The fine cheekbones seemed more pronounced, and her eyes, artfully shadowed and fringed as usual, had hollows beneath them. Through her own fatigue, Cordy sensed her mother's greater exhaustion, for what could be more laborious than a life of keeping up appearances? If she was having an affair—and now Cordy was convinced of it—it was causing her more pain than pleasure. She couldn't understand why Lucille would take such a risk. She wouldn't have been surprised if Lucille had developed a crush on an entertaining hairdresser, but the fact that she was bedding down with a vicious drug dealer was beyond understanding.

Lucille's notion of sexy was consumer sexy, advertising sexy, essentially passive. Sex was how you looked, not what you wanted. It was being adored and flirted with, not having a gut-churning need that might destroy your life, because if her father discovered her mother's adultery . . . The gust of air that had been laughter came through Cordy's nostrils in a snort. Adultery, indeed. Such an old-fashioned, Biblical word. A word that she would never use except in relation to her parents. Just this afternoon she'd imagined her father, all punishing indignation when he discovered her mother's betrayal.

The vision had given her some satisfaction. Now, looking at her mother, she felt a strong stirring of protectiveness. Lucille was bone china, brittle and fragile. If Lucille went to the edge of things, she would tip over and shatter. Cordy wanted to take her mother's hand and press a reassurance into it, to say, "Don't let Daddy find out that you've been naughty, because he'll punish you." And, as the orchestra played on to the final notes of confidant resolution, she covered Lucille's hand with her own.

Lucille drew her hand away almost instantly. If she'd felt the touch, she'd taken it as a cue to applaud.

Nonnie jerked awake. "Didn't I tell you you'd enjoy it?" she called across Cordy and Lucille to George.

George was on his feet, ready to use the standing ovation as an opportunity to be first up the aisle. "'Member we saw Adler and Florence Welk before the show an' we said we'd see them at intermission," he boomed over the applause.

Nonnie gathered up her skirts. "You come on out with us, Lucille. The Welk's were askin' after you."

"I'll just wait here if you don't mind," Lucille said softly.

Cordy stood up and guided Nonnie over to George. "I think I'll wait too. I want to talk to Mother."

"Suit yourselves." Nonnie dismissed them, took George's arm, and started up the aisle.

"I do love Brahms, don't you?" Cordy asked. When Lucille continued to stare into the mid-distance, she tried again. "I thought the violin section was particularly fine."

"Yes. They were fine."

"Are you feeling all right, Mother?"

Lucille's hand floated up, then dropped back to clutch the armrests. "Just the highway was crowded on my way in. You know how I hate to drive alone in the dark."

"If you're planning to spend the night at Nonnie's, why don't you come on over tomorrow afternoon? I have classes in the morning, but I've moved into the new apartment and—"

"I know you've moved. I talked to you this afternoon, didn't I?"

"Just . . . I thought now that I'm back home for good, an' we haven't even talked about my New York trip really . . ." Cordy stammered.

"Yes. I can imagine your New York trip," Lucille said dreamily.

"We could get together. Just you and me." Should she interject the question now? Laugh and say she'd heard the most improbable gossip?

"We will get together, darlin'. Just now I'm having the bedroom repapered and I just don't have time to turn around. I'm only staying in town because there's a decorator I want to visit with."

"But I need to talk with you. You seem so . . . preoccupied." Preoccupied. A bland word, a safe word, the sort of word Lucille's presence always seemed to force out of her mouth. But she couldn't say more. Intermission at the symphony was hardly the time for confrontations. But then it was never the appropriate time with Lucille. Countless visits over the years had ended in the same duet of complaint and regret: "Why didn't we have time to talk? Next time we'll really talk."

Cordy sighed. There would never be more than the promise of communication between them. Never. "Did you like the Brahms?"

"Mmmm."

"How's Daddy?"

Lucille turned her head slowly. "He's fine. Why wouldn't he be fine?" She studied Cordy's face. "I do believe I'll take a trip to the little girls' room. And you should come too, honey. You've eaten off all your lipstick."

"I'll just stay here. The bathroom's always so crowded."

"Has Lupton sent you any money yet?" Lucille whispered as she got up and smoothed her skirts.

"Yes," Cordy lied. "Everything's fine."

"Good, good, darlin'. I'll see you in a minute. What is the second selection tonight?"

"Ravel's *Bolero*. As I recall, it's only about twenty minutes long."

"It like to ruin the entire evenin' for me, racing down the aisle like that," Nonnie complained as George drove slowly down the deserted moonlit streets.

"Now, now," George said, "we got in 'fore it started and we stayed for the whole thing, so stop fussin' about it."

"An' then she sat there lookin' like she was the chief mourner at a state funeral. I swear I don't know how I raised that one. George? I say George, why didn't you turn on Bull Street?"

"Thought I'd take you ladies to the DeSoto for a drink."

"Now how can we do that with Lucille comin' over to the house? Cut on down Abercorn to Harris, then . . ."

Cordy put her legs up on the back seat. And down Harris around Madison Square, cross Jones, check to see if Mrs. Webster's lights are still on, get to Monterey . . . The same pattern through the same streets with the same people. She might just as well have signed herself into an old age home.

"I'll bet she didn't even ask you how you were doing, did she Cordy?" Nonnie went on.

"Yes, yes she did," Cordy answered tiredly.

"I'm surprised she could take her mind off herself long enough to inquire. That one thinks the whole world revolves around her. When she shuts her eyes she thinks it's night. Why lookie there"— Nonnie moved closer to the window—"there's Pat Epworth reelin' out of Pinkie Master's Saloon! An' Janellen told me he'd joined A.A." She turned and peered into the back seat. "You're very quiet tonight, Cordy."

"I was just thinking about a book I was supposed to read for class tomorrow."

"Oh. Who was that girl Clay Claxton was with? I don't believe I ever saw her before."

"I don't know who she is. I only saw them as they were getting into his car and he didn't have time to introduce her."

Please shut up, Nonnie, just please shut up, Cordy thought as she tilted her head trying to catch a glimpse of the moon through the trees. A full moon. A lovers' moon. And the sun would come up tomorrow and the moon would come out tomorrow night whether or not her mother was playing around with Jacques Haur. It was none of her business. She would put it out of her mind. So what if Mama, after solicitous inquiry about Daddy's golf game and cholesterol count, slipped off for an afternoon screw? So what if her idealization of Mama and Daddy as the loving, ever-faithful couple had to be tossed onto the dustpile of old myths? So what? But, Cordy resolved, if once more, just once more, Lucille started in on her about how to be the perfect wife, or came on with any of her hypocritical drivel about sex, she would let her know that she'd seen through the entire pitiful game.

"Maybe Clay didn't want to introduce her," Nonnie persisted. "I don't think she's a Savannah girl."

"No. He probably got so bored he's started importing them," Cordy said.

"I only meant that I don't believe I've made her acquaintance. An' I didn't like the way she had her hair all frizzed out like that."

"That's the style," George informed.

"Might be the style, but it's not a pretty style. A woman's got to choose the styles that are right for her. Now I was thinkin' tonight, Cordy, that you would look your best in a dress that was cut away at the neck. Not so low that you're givin' it all away, just—"

"You surely would, Cordy," George grunted. "An' I can tell you I'm not going to the symphony again 'less I get to sit next to a pretty woman in a low-necked dress. There's nothin' to look at at these symphony concerts."

"Oh, George," Nonnie laughed.

"It's no threat to the community just to take a look. It's 'bout all I'm good for now."

"An' I thought greediness and gluttony were your only remaining vices. Now you're tellin' me you're goin' in for Peepin' Tom."

"That's not a Peepin' Tom, that's a voyeur. A Peepin' Tom is—"

"Will you look at that!" Nonnie interrupted. As was her habit when she approached Monterey Square, her entire attention was now riveted on the house. "Bernice like to think she's working for the stockholders of Southern Bell. Every light in the house is blazin' away. George, there's a parking place. There, next to Miz Elkin's Cadillac. Back up. Then we'll all go in for a nightcap."

"I'm just going to run up and get Jeanette and take Bernice home," Cordy announced.

"Not even one lil' drink? You don't want to talk to your mother?"

"I can't. I told you I've got to read a book for class tomorrow."

"Damn this collar," George wheezed as he twisted his head to judge the distance between the parked cars. "You come on in an' join us, Cordy. It's not right for a pretty woman to study too hard."

"Yes, I'm sure Bernice won't mind stayin' on for a bit, Cordy."

"What's this class about anyhow that it's so important?"

"The class," Cordy said rapidly and with a decided edge, "explores the nature of Southern society. The contradictions of a basic hedonism coexisting with fundamentalist religion, and the resulting hypocrisy. The lack of rigorous intellectual debate, the graciousness and tradition and the underlying violence and meanness, the myth of the Southern belle and her equally mythical counterpart, the happy Negro buck, both of whom were expected to be sexless except for procreation within their own race, which, of course, helped to promote the rape myth, though most Southern ladies ran about as much

risk of violation as they risked being struck by lightning . . ."
Breathless, she sucked in enough air to conclude the diatribe. ". . .
an' even pretty woman study, George, because even pretty women
have to earn a living, and no, I don't want to see my mother."

"George, watch out!" Nonnie cried. "You almost grazed Miz
Elkin's fender."

"And that's what they're teachin' at Armstrong College these
days?" George demanded, turning off the ignition.

"Anything goes at a college, George," Nonnie informed him.
"It's the spirit of free inquiry that makes for a good college. An'
Cordy, maybe you'd best not come up if you have things to do. I
expect Bernice is feeling like she's wants to be goin' home."

"I'll hurry on in," Cordy said as she got out. "And thanks so
much for driving us, George."

Cordy raced up the stairs and into the front parlor, where Bernice was sitting on the sofa, Jeanette's head and arms curled in her
lap. "I figured you'd be along directly," Bernice yawned. "Mr. Ted
Koppel gonna interview the South African ambassador an' I sure do
want to be home to see that." She stroked Jeanette's head. "C'mon,
sugar. C'mon now. Mama's home."

"I'm in a hurry too, Bernice. I'll just carry her if she doesn't
wake up."

"She's comin' to, aren't you, baby?" Bernice encouraged, propping Jeanette's body up. "Don't want to wake her up too fast. It's
bad for the heart."

But Jeanette, with the revitalization unique to a seven-year-old,
was already awake and whinning. "Can't I stay the night in my old
room, Mama? Can't I?"

"No. And please put your shoes on now, 'cause I'm in a big
hurry."

"You're always in a hurry. Why can't I stay?"

"You heard me," Cordy snapped, reaching down to button
Jeanette's cardigan. "Come on now. I'll give you a piggyback to the
car."

"Don't you be doin' that, Cordy," Bernice advised. "She be too
big for that now."

"I am not too big. My Daddy—"

"You big enough to fuss with me, big enough to want to stay up
and watch TV shows, you big enough to walk. C'mon now." Bernice stood Jeanette on her feet. "I be gettin' my coat, an' I'll meet
you in your Mama's car."

Cordy laced Jeanette's shoes and took her hand. "You'll get to sleep in your new bed tonight. Won't that be exciting," she said with forced enthusiasm. They'd reached the front door just as Nonnie and George were opening it. There was the round of kisses and good-nights. Nonnie suggested that there was half a pie in the kitchen that Cordy was welcome to take, but Cordy, her patience strained to the point of teeth grinding, hurried Jeanette down the stairs and said she'd pick it up tomorrow. As soon as they got into the car, Jeanette slumped against her and closed her eyes. Cordy watched Bernice and Nonnie lingering at the door. "Come on," she muttered to herself. "It's not as though you won't see each other in ten hours." But the two women continued to talk. From the closeness of their heads and the way they took turns bobbing them, Cordy supposed that Nonnie was nattering about Lucille. Then, as she heard a car approach, Bernice raised her head, disengaged herself, and lumbered down the steps.

"Here's your mother just about to pull up, but I guess we'll miss her," she said with a twinkle, climbing into the car and putting her arm around Jeanette. "Please peel on out from the curb like they do on those cop shows Cordy, 'cause I don't want to miss Mr. Koppel."

"Just a tad," George said, offering his glass.

For once Nonnie took him at his word and poured a niggardly portion from the bourbon decanter. On his first drink, George had wondered aloud who Cordy's professor at Armstrong might be. On his second, he had mentioned a friend on the Board of Trustees and said he thought the man had a right to know what was going on in the classrooms. She knew that if he had a third he was likely to start up about Cuban agents infiltrating and filching money from the State of Georgia.

"Oh, I'm about played out," she said, putting the stopper back into the decanter and wandering over to her wing-backed chair. In case that wasn't enough of a hint, she slipped her feet out of her high heels.

"Do you s'pose Lucille is comin' back down stairs to say good night?"

"She's been actin' so crazy tonight I can't tell you what she'll do. Puts me in mind of an old dog my daddy had. Used to whine to go out of doors, but when you opened the door it'd hang its tail, look mournful, and settle back down on the mat."

George drained his glass and stood up. "Then I guess I'll be movin' along."

"I'll see you at the Review Board meeting tomorrow," she said, trailing after him to the door with her shoes in her hand.

"I always forget just what a slip of a thing you are without your shoes." He looked down at her. Her diminutiveness called forth long-buried feelings of his own strength and desire to protect her. "You looked real pretty tonight, Nonnie. Real pretty. We could have a fine time seeing Europe together."

"Why, Mr. Naughton"—she laughed—"I couldn't be compromising my reputation by traveling with you."

"I know you better, Nonnie. If you want to do a thing you don't hardly consider what it's goin' to mean to your reputation. But"—he stretched the ruddy folds of his neck and cleared his throat—"if there's some other way for us to arrange it that's more suitable to you . . ."

"Dear George," she said as she opened the door, "you'll have to forgive me, but I'm about to fade away right here in front of you." It would have pleased her some to hear George try to get his tongue around a proposal, but she liked him well enough not to put him through the embarrassment of making an offer she was bound to refuse. She fingered her pendant, smiled, and touched his arm. "Let's table it for another meeting."

"All right then." He sounded wounded but somewhat relieved. "Good night."

"Mind you don't scrape Miz Elkin's fender," she called after him. Then, closing the door: "I thought he'd never leave."

She started back into the parlor to turn off the lights, but paused, hearing Lucille's tread on the stair. "Why you're still all dressed up, Lucille. I thought you'd gone up to get ready for bed."

Lucille descended to the bottom step and halted. "I have to talk to you."

"We can talk tomorrow," Nonnie yawned. "Didn't you say you're going to the noontime organ recital at Christ Church?"

"No. I have to talk to you now."

"Don't you see me standin' here? Talk on. But make it snappy if you don't want to be carryin' me upstairs."

Lucille took another step. "I'll like to go sit in the parlor."

"Then let's go sit in the parlor." The pouches under Nonnie's eyes constricted as she studied Lucille for a moment before turning into the front room, crossing to her favorite chair, and dropping her shoes onto the carpet. She had thought Lucille's woebegone appearance might be the prelude to an apology, but now she could see that something more important—a request or a disclosure—was in the offing.

Lucille paused again on the threshold. "I think I'd like another drink."

"Then for pity's sake fix yourself one. I would have poured you another, but seein' as how you're so abstemious I didn't think to offer."

Lucille helped herself to the bourbon, took a sip, but did not turn around to face her.

"Well, what is it, Lucille? You're actin' like some young'un who's taken out his violin for the company but has to be begged into playin' it," Nonnie said impatiently.

When Lucille finally spoke she did so so softly that Nonnie was not sure she'd heard her properly. Instead of asking her to repeat herself, Nonnie played the words back in her mind: "I need to borrow some money." Nonnie settled further back into the chair and waited.

"I said I need to borrow some money. I don't know when I can pay it back, but I will pay it back and I don't ask you favors very often, but the favor I want to ask"—the words were tumbling out, bumping into each other—"the favor is that you give me the money without askin' me any questions."

"Don't be foolish, Lucille. You don't think I'm about to loan anybody money without knowing what it's for, do you?"

"I only wish—"

"Wish on a chicken bone, sugar. You tell me how much, an' you tell me what it's for, an' most likely I'll give it to you. Though I don't see why you can't get it from Jake. Unless you've been actin' like a high roller with those lazy women you play cards with. Lucille? Lucille, please turn round and look at me. Whatever's the matter with you?"

Lucille turned, her face twisted into a mixture of anger and resentment. "You're my mother. Why can't I come to you for help? I remember when you loaned Vivian's husband fifteen thousand dollars for that stupid lil' business out in Arizona and—"

"That was about a hundred years ago, an' I don't see what that's got to do with you."

"It's just that . . ." Lucille turned pink, gaggged with frustration, and flung her arm out, spilling part of her drink on her dress.

"All right. All right. That has nothing to do with me." She put the drink down and moved to the couch to sit, then lurched forward, her head bent. "I gave some money to a man. I didn't intend to give it to him. It was a loan he promised to pay back within the week. But he's left town. I don't know where he's gone . . . and . . . and . . ." Her head bent lower still, until it touched her knees. Her shoulders were shaking. "Oh God. Oh, God. Oh, God."

"What man?"

Lucille shook her head from side to side, trying to ward off the question. The intonation Nonnie gave to "man" showed that she had already guessed that he was no mere friend.

"I said, 'What man?'"

"You don't know him. You'll never know him." Lucille threw her head back, her tear-strained face defiant. "His name is Jacques Haur, if you must know. And I was in love with him."

Nonnie touched the whorls of her fingertips together and stared out the window. "You slept with this man. This Jacques Haur. You gave him money. And now you want me to give you the money so that Jake will not find out."

Lucille stopped sobbing long enough to gulp in more air. Was it possible that she was going to pass through the eye of this storm without so much as a reprimand? Here was Nonnie, touching her fingertips point to point, the way she did when she was plotting a business deal, talking so calmly that Lucille might have asked her a question about interest rates. No, it wasn't possible. Nonnie was holding back in order to prolong her torture.

"How much? How much did you give him?"

"Three. Three thousand dollars."

Nonnie's breath whistled out of her. "And you don't know where he's gone?"

"I'll get it back to you. I promise I will. I just—"

"How do you 'spose you're going to get it back to me? Out of your housekeeping money? What possessed you? My god, girl, what possessed you?" Nonnie demanded, rising to her feet.

"I don't know. I don't know. If I knew I'd tell you," Lucille sobbed. She felt as though she'd been taken to some emergency room and instead of helping her staunch the blood that was oozing out of her the head nurse was demanding that she remember her Social Security number or her insurance company. "I know I was wrong," she cried. "I know I was crazy. But I have to have the money. I have to put it back into the account before Jake sees it's missing."

"Does anyone else know about it?"

"I don't know. I haven't told anyone. But Jacques . . . I don't know. I don't know him well enough to guess."

"You don't know him well enough to guess, but you were sleepin' with him? My God, how could you take such a risk? You think you've gelded your husband to where he's goin' to pay for your gigolo?"

"He wasn't a gigolo. You make it sound like . . ." Lucille twisted away and staggered to her feet. "Oh, I should have known better than to ask you for anything. I should have known you couldn't understand."

"I understand this much: Even if you get the money, if your husband finds out about this he'll divorce you. I know that man. He won't take it. What will you do then, huh? You, who are less able to take care of yourself than any person I've ever known. What will you do if Jake finds out?"

"Please don't lecture me," Lucille whimpered. "Please."

"Hush your mouth! Don't you yell at me. I am your mother and you will not yell at me."

"I'm not yelling. Can't you hear that I'm not yelling?" Lucille cried in a voice so strained and pleading that despite its softness it had the intensity of a scream. "Just help me. Help me. But don't, *please* don't lecture me. I just can't stand it anymore. You're always above reproach. As though you're never been tempted by anything in your entire life. You always do the right thing. You always say the right thing. Always! Every time you open your mouth it's with some cute little joke or story that says the right thing and makes everyone else feel bad."

"I have never said I—" Nonnie's mouth gaped, stunned by the vehemence of the unexpected attack.

"But you do say it," Lucille spat. "Maybe not with your mouth but with every gesture you make. The world according to Eunnonia Grace! You have never doubted yourself, have you, Mama? Even when you were young you didn't, and now that you're the old queen bee . . ."

Nonnie had to grip her hands together to stop herself from slapping Lucille's contorted face. "You act like a child," she said with steely rage, "so I s'pose it's natural you think like a child. You've always been so busy lookin' in your mirror you've never seen anyone else. An' let me tell you, Lucille, you've had a charmed life. A blessed life. You've never had to worry 'bout where your meals were comin' from. You've never lost a child or had a love go sour on you. You've never dealt with illness that dragged on so long you prayed to see someone you loved put into that grave so's you could have some peace—"

"An' you resent it, don't you, Mama? You resent it that I haven't had to go through hardships." Lucille's mouth twisted into a bitter smile. "You wanted me to walk three miles to a one-roomed schoolhouse just like you did, wanted me to clean the peas from my plate 'cause children in China and Macon were starvin'. Wanted me to have a husband who liked his golf and his TV better'n he liked me. Oh, you've got your pride, haven't you, Nonnie? An' you love your pride better'n you love your grits. An' one thing you pride yourself on is bein' so open-minded. But your mind is shut up tight. And what have I done that a million women don't do every day? What? Except that I did it on your territory 'stead of runnin' off to New York to do it."

"You leave Cordy out of this. You don't know the first thing that's happenin' to that girl, because you've never cared to know. An' don't come at me 'bout havin' an open mind. I've opened my mind so many times I've felt the wind rush through an' shake my brains loose so's I thought I'd never get them back into the pan. You s'pose openin' my mind means I'm going to condone your cheatin' on a man who still thinks you hung the moon?"

She was breathing hard and could feel the palpitations of her heart, but now that she could see Lucille starting to cringe she would not stop until she had said her piece. "And don't you come to me trying to twist this thing around as to how I don't understand you. That's hog swill, sugar. I understand you and I understand this situation better'n you do: You are a spoiled woman. Worse, you are a foolish one. And in your boredom and your foolishness you run round creating problems you expect other people to solve. You end up payin' some no-count for what he had between his legs.

"An' don't tell me you did it out of love. You prob'ly didn't even do it out of lust. You did it out of vanity. And now you want me to bail you out. And if I do, I say if I do, Lucille, it'll be because I don't want Jake to be hurt, not because I have any sympathy for you." Her temples were swelling and pounding and her eyes seemed ready to pop out of her head. Gasping, she felt her way back to a sitting position, throwing her head back.

"Mama? Mama, are you all right?" Lucille whispered hoarsely, moving forward, crouching down next to her and staring up into her face. "Oh, Mama, please. Please." She pitched forward, gripping Nonnie's legs.

Nonnie saw spots before her eyes. She could feel Lucille's head thrust against her knees, bone against bone. If only she could catch her breath and still the pounding in her chest.

"Mama. Mama. Please help me," Lucille whimpered, her fingernails piercing Nonnie's calves like tiny electrodes. "I'm so scared. I'm so unhappy."

Nonnie's hand found Lucille's head and began to move on it, stroking it in time to her own labored breathing. This was the child who had stayed on, but the one who was, and always had been, furthest from her. Why did this head feel like an alien thing when she had pushed out of her own body?

"I'm so scared, Mama. I feel so lonely all the time. And I'm afraid Jake's going to die and leave me all alone and I . . ."

The self-pity in Lucille's voice stilled whatever groping desire Nonnie had to understand. "The old queen bee" Lucille had called her, but now Lucille was cringing on the floor, thinking only of herself again, begging for help. Nonnie reached down and pried the hands away from her legs. Grasping the arms of the chair, she rose to her feet. "If you can suffer to hear one more word of advice from me," she said, "I might say that it's not the best idea to attack the character of someone you're wantin' money from." She stepped around the crumpled body and moved to the doorway, where she paused without turning around. "I will write a check in the morning and leave it under the silver tray. I am very tired and I'm going to bed. Please remember to turn off the lights."

Nonnie closed the door to her room. Though her heart was still pumping wildly it didn't seem to have the force to circulate her blood. Her hands and feet were like ice. Without turning on the light, she reached into the bottom drawer of the bureau to find an old pair of bed socks she'd knitted for Lonnie. Her joints ached as she pulled the nightdress over her head, and as she stood near the bed braiding her hair she almost sank to her knees before remembering that she had abandoned the habit of prayer after Wade's death.

Why Lucille had done such a thing was beyond all understanding. Why the woman had gone out seeking her own destruction, and to the tune of three thousand dollars! And she was no green girl. Lucille was a grandmother herself. So how could she, Nonnie, be held responsible in any way?

The sheets were cold. Tomorrow she would ask Bernice where she'd hidden the hot water bottle. Blinking at the moonlit branches of the chinaberry tree, she tucked her hands into her armpits and hoped that sleep would overtake her swiftly and completely. What sort of a low-life scroundrel could that Jacques Haur be? If she knew where he was hiding out she'd have a mind to take a buggy whip to him. She squeezed her eyes shut and turned onto her side. As her hand went up to her throat, she discovered that she'd forgotten to take off her pendant, but her fingers were so stiff that she dared not fiddle with the clasp.

Three thousand dollars! Why it was enough to put a down payment on a house. No, she corrected herself, she was being fuzzy-minded. Three thousand dollars might have been a down payment on a house twenty years ago. It wasn't all that much nowadays. But there was no use pretending that it wasn't going to rankle, no use pretending that she wouldn't bristle like a porcupine whenever she thought about it. Still, she tried to calm herself, it would never happen again. This insane affair was the desperate act of a desperate woman. It was the last round up. She would give Lucille the money and that would be the beginning and the end of her motherly responsibility. She had never understood Lucille and she never would. Lord knew she had treated all her children with equal care, but a kudzu vine didn't grown into a rose bush no matter how well you tended it. So it was better not to think about it. Better for everyone.

Her thumb, moving back and forth on the soft gold of the pendant, felt a tiny dent. Lucille had put that dent there, light-years ago, when she was teething. She had been rocking her to sleep and reading at the same time, and Lucille had reached up, grabbed the pendant, and bitten into it with one of her three teeth. The memory was as sharp as if it had happened yesterday. Sharper, for yesterday's memories were like yesterday's bills, troublesome but already vague. It was the old memories that survived, alive with minute and painful detail. She could still see the dewy skin of Lucille's baby arm, reaching and yanking, still hear the squeal as she'd pushed the arm away and set Lucille onto the dark green linoleum of the kitchen floor.

She rubbed her feet together and shifted about in the bed. No matter how devoutly she wished for it, sleep would not come easily tonight. She opened her eyes again. The moon had gone behind the clouds. Though she could still hear the branches scratching against the windowpane, the chinaberry tree was dark. Against her will she began to sift and weigh and sort, her thoughts going back and further back to the year of Lucille's conception.

There had been unseasonal rains and one bad hurricane in the summer of 1934, but to her it had been a wonderful summer, at least the most wonderful summer since 1929. The Hampton clan, believing itself to be of such lofty stature that its fortune could only be affected by a direct act of God, had been shaken to its very roots by the Depression. Lonnie and his brother had fought to hold on to the business and the property, but in '31, they'd been forced to cut production at the mill down to three days a week. Lonnie, whose romantic dreams of Progress had taken on an almost Yankee pride in acquisitiveness, had retained a tradition of loyalty and personal responsibility toward his employees. He had cried the day he'd had to let most of them go. Later, he'd tried to unload some of the Hamptons' land, but finding the market glutted, he ended up turning it over to the hapless tenants and urging them to dig a living out of it if they could.

Even Lonnie's mother Ettie had cracked under the strain, going from a smug assurance that things would get better into a petulant bewilderment when they did not. Finally, after having heard the word "revolution" uttered in her own front parlor (albeit by a friend of Lonnie's who was the worse for drink and, when pressed, had only the foggiest notion of what he might rebel against), Ettie Payne Hampton had sought her answer in religion. From the pulpit she had been assured that this evil Depression, like Reconstruction, Populists, Bolsheviks, and the boll weevil, had been hurled as a direct punishment from the hand of God.

It was no surprise to Nonnie to find that Mother Hampton's impressive carriage was more the result of boned corsets than of real spine. She did not mind when Ettie began to lock herself in her bedroom, where presumably she made her views known to the Lord and occasionally humbled herself enough to ask for his intervention. Ettie's retreat left her free to run the house as she saw fit, without interference or imputations that the bobbing of her hair was directly related to the decline and fall of the social order. Nonnie had less of a desire to understand the general collapse than a need for some action that would prevent her and her children from falling into the poverty she had known in her own childhood. There was still food in the larder and whiskey of a cheaper brand in the liquor cabinet, but things had gone from bad to worse and there was no telling what was up ahead. There was much to be learned from a sting of misery, but after a time deprivation only sapped energy and wore away the will for change.

With the election of Mr. Roosevelt things had turned around, not just for the city but for the whole country. Something would finally be done. Something would be done about the gaunt-eyed men who wandered the roads, the swarms of terrified depositors who shook their fists at locked bank doors, the dust-colored children of sharecroppers who fed from a sack of flour and a hunk of fatback. And Nonnie held great expectations for change in her own life. Her deliverance too was at hand. The most intense period of maternal responsibility was over. Constance, the youngest, would go into the first grade in the fall. The long years of tending to infants—the daily grind of coaxing spoons into mouths, checking bowel movements, combing hair, and wiping noses—were coming to an end. Even with the help of Lonnie's Mammy Lily, it had not been an easy task. But now she would not have to leave the bedroom door open to be instantly responsive to a cry in the night. Now she would have time to read and visit. Time to make herself pretty.

And then she found herself pregnant again.

Lonnie, sensing her unhappiness, tried to humor her with little gifts and extra attentions, but no hank of cloth or passing caress could ease her frustration. Her other pregnancies had never, until the final weeks, interrupted the steady rhythm of their lovemaking, but this time she began to think of the pleasures of the bed as a trap. She and Lonnie had always been lovers. They had joked about the idea that a woman should yield to her husband out of a sense of duty, so when she had first turned away from him in bed Lonnie's pride had been too great to settle for mere submission. But as the weeks went by, he became more insistent. Once when she was undressing he came up behind her, scooping her hair up onto her head and nibbling at her neck. When she'd pulled away, he'd grabbed at her, circling her waist and pulling her against him. "There's no use lockin' the barn door after the horse is out," he'd teased, thrusting his free hand between her legs. She had struggled free, hissing that his barnyard joke suited his nature just fine. Then she had thrown a bottle of bath salts at him. A few nights later, turning in her sleep, she'd felt the hardness of his buttocks, groped his half-erect privates, and moaned for him. Their relations returned, more or less, to normal, though her moments of greatest desire now tended to come when she was semiconscious. Sometimes, when she was bathing or dressing, she noticed that Lonnie looked at her belly with a sheepish, almost guilty expression.

For the first five months when she was carrying Lucille she had refused to wear maternity clothes, but then she'd had to go out to the carriage house and unpack the smocks she hadn't given away to Lily's daughters. The children were delighted by the prospect of a new brother or sister, but when her pains had started she had felt none of the joyful "At last!" she'd had with her other deliveries, but only a resigned "Here I go again." She had weaned Lucille after a few months and eased her into the routine she'd established for the other children, a routine she now performed with less anxiety, but also with less devotion. Responding dutifully to the habitual distractions and interruptions, she had left the pampering to the rest of the family. Lonnie was smitten with his new baby girl. "We wouldn't give up till we got it right," he would beam when friends pointed out that Lucille had inherited the best features of both parents. Even Mother Hampton was softened by the sight of the golden curls and dimpled skin, and she indulged the child with dolls, music boxes, ribbons, and dresses. Lucille never lacked an audience, and she developed a precocious understanding of the needs of that audience.

At three she knew how to lisp a nursery rhyme, twist a ringlet around her finger, and curtsy. She understood that being a dainty good girl who smiled all the time would get her a hug or a licorice stick. And like anyone who is constantly called upon to perform, she became temperamental, voraciously addicted to approval, and deeply concerned with her appearance. By the time she was five, in her new Easter dress and bonnet, she had shied from Nonnie's embrace, saying she didn't want to be mussed. Nonnie had turned away, hiding the sting of rejection, while the family, intuiting a moment that would be turned into a standing joke, had laughed. "Luce doesn't want to be mussed," Wade would tease a decade later, passing Lucille in the hall and ruffling the hairdo she'd primped for a half an hour to achieve. Sometimes, pricked by concern, seeing the vulnerability and the envy that lay beneath Lucille's preening, Nonnie would try to talk to her. But it was too late. To the teenage Lucille, she was little more than a wardrobe mistress and a custodian. Anything she said was interrupted as a criticism.

Nonnie sat up in bed and wiped the water from her eyes. To tell herself that she had treated all the children equally was a comforting half-truth. It denied the importance of willing arms and a tender eye. Sins of omission were sins just the same, and the shameful truth was that she had never loved Lucille as she had loved the others.

The moon had come out from behind the clouds. She got out of bed, padded across the carpet, and opened the door without making a sound. Feeling her way down the passage, she turned on the hall light next to the room where Lucille was sleeping.

She tapped gently on the door. When there was no answer, she called, "Are you all right, Lucille?"

After a time she heard a voice that might have come from the bottom of a well: "I'm fine."

"Can I get you anything?"

"No. No. It's very late. Please go back to bed."

Chapter XIX

Cordy folded her arms across the typewriter and rested her chin on her hands. "Oh, Fanny," she asked, as though Fanny herself had been standing beside her, "why did you marry Pierce Butler?" She had been working on a section where Fanny, now mistress of the Butler plantation, had become a sort of intermediary between her husband (whom she now called Mr. Butler) and the slaves—particularly the female slaves. Fanny had discovered that Joe, one of the slaves, was going to be given as a "present" to a departing overseer, who planned to take him to Alabama, and in her effort to save Joe's wife and children from the agony of separation, Fanny thought to buy the family herself. Cordy tipped her head from side to side to ease the crick in her neck and picked up Fanny's diary:

> . . . a long chain of all my possessions, in the shape of bracelets, necklaces, brooches, earrings etc. wound in glittering procession through my brain, with many hypothetical calculations of the value of each separate ornament, and the very doubtful probability of the amount of the whole being equal to the price of this poor creature and her children; and then the great power and privilege I had forgone of earning money by my own labor occurred to me, and I think for the first time in my life, my past profession assumed an aspect that arrested my thoughts most seriously.

Why Fannie—a glittering theatrical success who earned her own way, had a multitude of suitors, and was a fierce Abolitionist—had chosen, against the advice of friends and family, to marry Pierce Butler, a plantation owner who by all accounts was Fanny's intellectual inferior, was still a mystery. It was true that Pierce had pursued Fanny for a long time, but it didn't seem likely that mere persistence would have worn down such a self-willed woman. Fanny must have succumbed to Pierce because of the contradictions in her own passionate nature.

Cordy bit her cuticle and decided she would have to go back and rewrite the proposal scene. She had originally set it at a party in a Philadelphia mansion and she was pleased with her description of the banquet and the women's beautiful clothes, but she knew she would have to ditch it. Instead she would set the proposal in the late afternoon with Fanny and Pierce riding alone in the countryside. Told from Fanny's point of view, the descriptions of Pierce's stallion would mingle with a description of Pierce himself—a confusion that might well have taken place in Fanny's mind—to show Fanny's blind and overwhelming sexual attraction for the man.

She got up from the typewriter, poured herself a cup of cold coffee, and went to the refrigerator to get milk. Jeanette's drawing of a Pilgrim shaking hands with an Indian was taped to the door of the refrigerator, reminding her that it was only a few days to Thanksgiving. September had gone into October; October had slipped into November; but since she counted completed pages instead of dates it was easy to lose track of time. The only significant event in the past three months had been when she'd gone to court for the divorce. Apart from that it had been a steady round of housekeeping and going to classes. (A young man who sat next to her had asked her out for coffee, but she'd declined. A woman about her age had invited her to a Parents Without Partners meeting, but she had winced at the very idea of joining a herd of displaced wives.) She had eaten Sunday dinners at Nonnie's and gotten together with Alidia a couple of times a week. And she had been writing the book. The possibility that she might not sell the book was so fearful that she had to suppress it in order to keep going.

Sometimes when she had trouble sleeping she wondered if this would be the measure of her days; for try as she might, she couldn't envision any future self. Living without a man for any period of time seemed unthinkable. Living with one in the way she'd lived with Lupton was even more impossible. And she was determined not to let her hormones or her ego push her into any time-wasting, messy affairs. She would just slog on, a day at a time, using the cards Fate had dealt her as she used the hand-me-down furniture. She had joked with Alidia that if anyone asked where she lived she would tell them Limbo Lane.

As she poured the milk into her coffee mug, she heard the mailman at the gate. Eager for an excuse to leave the apartment, if only for a moment, she went downstairs. In the mailbox, along with a telephone bill and a flier from Citizens for Clean Air, was a fat envelope from Claxton and Braun, which, she knew, contained her divorce decree. She weighed it in her hand as she mounted the stairs, then threw it on the kitchen table. After staring at it for a time, she went to the bathroom. Coming back into the kitchen, she stared at the envelope again, reached, then drew back her hand. Wrapping her arms around her breasts, she went into the living room, where she paced back and forth like a prisoner in an exercise yard. "You are acting crazy," she said to herself. But instead of opening the envelope she sat on the couch and looked out at the magnolia tree. When the phone rang she jumped.

"Cordy, it's me, Alidia. If you're not busy I thought I might come over."

"Alidia! Oh, yes, Alidia. Please come over. I just got my divorce papers and I don't . . ."

". . . don't know whether to shit or go blind. Congratulations I'm shopping over at Piggly Wiggly. I'll be there in ten minutes."

When Alidia came up the back stairs, Cordy took the grocery bag from her arms and handed her the envelope.

"You mean you haven't opened it yet? Jesus, woman, you're crazier than I ever thought you were." Alidia walked past her to the living room, ripped open the envelope, and let it flutter to the floor. "Cordy. Please. Sit down before you fall down. Go on, sit." She gave Cordy a little shove onto the couch, then rocked back and forth, hooking one thumb into her armpit and holding the papers at arm's length. "Here comes d' judge, here come d' judge." She mimicked an old man's quavering voice. "Here comes d' plaintiff, Cordelia Simpkins Tyre, and the defendant, Lupton L. Tyre—boo, hiss, boo.

"'The plaintiff is a resident of Savannah, Chatham County, Georgia, and has been a resident of the State of Georgia for more than six months prior to the filing of this action'—oh, you fibber, you. 'Plaintiff and defendant were lawfully married'—and blah,

blah, blah." She flipped the pages until she reached the last. "Here comes the good part: 'that the marriage contract heretofore entered into between the parties be set aside and dissolved as fully and effectually as if no such contract had ever been made and entered into.'

"Easy for you to say, Judge!" Alidia threw the papers onto the couch, then grabbed Cordy, hugging her and pulling her to her feet. "Yippee! When did you get it?"

"About a half hour ago. I kept batting it around like a cat with a ball of wool, but I just couldn't open it. Clay called a couple of days ago and offered to bring it over . . ."

"Wouldn't he just."

". . . but I told him to put it in the mail."

"What's the matter with you? Why so glum? I'm here to celebrate. Let's drink a toast to your freedom." Alidia smacked a loud kiss on both of Cordy's cheeks and ran into the kitchen to get the bottle of Jack Daniel's Cordy kept under the sink. "You know there's one great thing about being a drunk," she called out. "I never have to worry about a reason to drink. I drink when I'm unhappy; I drink to celebrate my happiness. There's always a reason."

Cordy folded up the divorce papers. She'd almost begged Alidia to come over, but she now had a perverse desire to be alone.

"Cordy, please, don't get all moony. Remember what happened to Lot's wife when she looked back." Alidia handed her a shot of neat bourbon and raised her own glass. "That's the only lesson I ever took from the Bible: Don't look back."

"I'm not looking back. I'm looking forward. I got a call from Abigail Silverstein the other day. The proposal was turned down by the first publisher she sent it to."

"So what? Even I know that's the rule rather than the exception. What about that letter she wrote to you where she said the new chapters were even better than she'd hoped they'd be? She's a professional. She has no reason to string you along. As long as she's hanging in there with you, you'll have to keep the faith."

"Please, no exhortations to keep the faith. I've had a large and unexpected dose of spiritual encouragement lately."

"Who from?"

"My mother, believe it or not. If I recall my childhood accurately, the only time she ever wanted to go to church was to show off a new dress. But she's taken on a very religious cast of mind lately. Last time she visited she told me she was going to pray for me."

Alidia drew her feet underneath her and gave her barking laugh. "Ah, circumstance gives birth to virtue once again."

"She seems quite sincere about it," Cordy mused.

"I guess it's easier for her to pray for you than to make any emotional or financial contribution to your success. But we were talking about the book."

"And Lupton hasn't sent the child-support check. He told Clay he'd put our house on the market, and I sure hope he sells it soon. But if he doesn't, if I don't get half of the proceeds from that, I don't know . . . Maybe I should start looking for a job. I am a good typist."

"Bite your tongue. You're a writer, not a typist."

"If I'd stayed on with Chrystallis I could have churned out three or four books a year, and even if it was for peanuts—"

"Ridiculous. Staying on with Chrystallis would be like staying on with Lupton. I know you're going to make a living at this. Trust me. I have acutely sensitive intuition about everyone but myself and the man I'm sleeping with. And those pages you let me read last week, they were really good. Ah, shit, Cordy, wipe that smirk off your face. Would I lie to you?"

"You might."

"True, I might. But I'm not. You can't be Lot's wife about the book either."

Cordy put her glass on the coffee table, looked around the room at the unmatched furniture, and drifted over to the window. "I know it's important to keep going. Not just for myself but for Jeanette as well. If I keep writing I can be at home when she gets in from school, and that's important to me."

"Oh, you poor single mothers, y'all have such guilt you make Judas Iscariot look lighthearted."

"You don't understand," Cordy snapped. "You've never had to be responsible for a child."

Alidia's eyes, over the rim of the glass, registered surprise rather than hurt. "I'm not a mother, becaue I'd be a lousy mother. And I'm not a wife, because I've been a lousy wife. But—"

"But you're a wonderful friend. Alidia, please forgive me. I don't know what the hell's the matter with me. I don't know why I'm lashing out at you."

"Not to worry," Alidia shrugged, averting her eyes. "You're already forgiven. It's always easier to forgive a friend than a lover.

That's one of the things I wanted to tell you: I've broken up with Johnnie."

Cordy opened her mouth, trying to phrase a response. She wanted to say "Thank god," but Alidia's relationship with Johnnie was built on *Sturm and Drang*. Tomorrow they might be reunited, and Alidia wouldn't thank her for her expression of relief.

"Go ahead and say it, Cordy. I know you're glad."

"Not glad exactly. I mean, I only care about how you feel."

"Don't be coy. I'm always attracted to rotten men. You know it. I know it—or at least I know it afterwards. So, I'm leaving town."

"Wait a minute. Wait a minute. Does one follow from the other? I don't care about Johnnie, but I do care about your leaving town. Why leave town? For how long? I mean *why?*"

"Johnnie wants to stay in the apartment, and I don't want to fight him about it."

"But it was your apartment to begin with," Cordy said indignantly.

"For chrissake, I'm not married to him. I can split up with him without arguing over property. That's all marriage is anyway, a property agreement."

"That certainly isn't true. Marriage is—"

"You're still a romantic, Cordy. The trouble with being a romantic is that reality can never measure up. Never. Anyhow, I don't care about that damned apartment. I've lived in a hundred apartments. Probably I'll live in a hundred more. It's not just that Johnnie's starting to get violent. Hell, I knew he was a good ol' boy the first night I met him, and I know good ol' boys start slapping you around when they can't think of what else to do."

"Johnnie hit you?"

"But I like good ol' boys. And what's the big deal? You told me Lupton hit you."

"Only at the very end."

"That's my point. That's when you know it's the end. But don't you understand. I have to leave now. The only thing to do is to make a clean break."

"Alidia you're not making any sense."

"I'm not claiming to. So, let me tell you. Carl's driving back to Iowa to visit his folks, and I'm going to drive with him. Carl's told me so much about the farm and all that I'm really looking forward to seeing it. He says the sky meets the earth out there and just being there makes you feel clean."

Cordy couldn't tell if Alidia was whipping herself up about the trip in order to blot out the pain of another affair gone wrong or if she truly loved the ongoing adventure of herself more than she could love any place or any man. "You can't run away from yourself, Alidia," she cut in, though even before she'd completed the sentence she knew how trite she sounded.

"Want to bet? I want to get out. I want to go. I want to be on the road again." As if to demonstrate her need, Alidia got up and started to move around, waving her arms expansively. "I want to sleep in tacky motels, eat at roadside diners, and talk to truckers. I want some guy in a bar to tell me his life story—his *real* life story— because he knows he'll never see me again. That's when I feel the old adrenaline pump, Cordy, when I'm traveling. For me, living life is more important than making something of myself. I don't know how to make something of myself. But when I embrace the chaos—"

"And you accuse me of being a romantic! You're much more of a romantic than I am. Embrace the chaos, my ass."

Alidia was standing with her legs set apart. Her stance, her ruined skin and clipped hair gave her a hard-boiled look, but her thin outstretched arms and wild eyes still roused something in Cordy that was close to admiration. Against reasoning and jugment she loved Alidia. With no one else did she have such a sense of equality, such straight-shooting criticism, such easy give and take. "You know, Alidia," she muttered, "sometimes I wish I were more like you."

"When we hit that highway, when I'm driving at night and see that center line going on into— What did you say? You wish you were like me? That's really funny. I've always wished I were more like you. You're not just going to improvise your life, you're going to plan it. I know you're a little screwed up now, but you'll start planning it again. I kinda envy that, but I just can't do it. You know in a way it's easier for me than it is for you. I knew real early on that I'd never fit into any of the old molds. But you expected to fit. You thought you were gonna live the same sort of life your grandmother and your mother lived. And you're just now finding out that you can't. My life is crazy, but it's closer to what I expected it to be; but you're having to go through all this stuff about making your own money and finding the right man and—"

She stopped. Though Cordy's face was impassive, two tears rolled down her cheeks in perfect symmetry. "Oh, Cordy, I'm sorry. Oh, Cordy, stop, please stop. I can't stand it. I don't mind howling and screaming, but weeping—I can't stand real weeping. I can't

stand it when the water just comes out of your eyes like that and you
don't make a noise." She knelt on the floor and looked up at Cordy's
face. "This is the saddest. Girl, you don't even know it, but you're
really depressed. It's the divorce papers, isn't it?"

"No, it's not the divorce. I can't seem to figure out . . . I don't
know what it's about. I don't know how I feel about the divorce
papers. I guess I'd thought they would give me a sense of finality. I
guess that was stupid, but I'd hoped— You know when you were a
kid and you were about to have a birthday and you thought that
when you woke up on the morning of your birthday that you'd be
different, grown up or something. And then you woke up and you
were just the same. I'm not making any sense, am I?" Cordy sniffled
and wiped her nose with the back of her hand. "What am I doing? If
Jeanette wipes her nose with her hand I always correct her. Oh,
Alidia, I'm going to miss you something fierce."

"You make it sound as though I'm about to die," Alidia
laughed. "It's not like I'm never coming back. You know me. I go in
circles." Her voice dropped lower, mournful and fluttering as a
dove's. "Great circles. I'll always come back. I'll come back just to
spite them. Come on now, take a sip of your drink."

"I don't want a drink. I have to keep working this afternoon."

"All right then, I'll take it. " Alidia tossed off the shot of bourbon and shuddered. "And I'm not going to hang around and interrupt your work. Just pour me another quick one while I run down to
the car and get my blues records from the trunk. I'm going to give
you my collection."

"I don't want to take—"

"Then consider them a loan. A guarantee that I'll come back.
Think that I'm just leaving them with you for safekeeping. Now"—
Alidia got to her feet, put one hand on her hip bone, and wagged her
finger—"I want you to study these blues, Cordy. Get down and
really learn to love them. And I'll tell you how to do it. You turn out
the lights. You put on your grubbiest old robe. You put the bottle
on the floor next to you and you swig from it, 'cause you're just too
blue and too tired to wash a glass. Then you put on the record and
you wallow. I mean really wallow, girl." She lurched and wiggled
and drew down the corners of her mouth. "And you wallow so
much that pretty soon you see how damned ridiculous you are." She
moved her bottom from side to side, getting closer and closer to the
floor in a duck walk, and wrapped her arms around her head. "And

then . . . and then . . . you laugh. You laugh at yourself 'cause none of this basket-weaving therapy crap works for us serious cases."

Cordy sniffled, and in spite of herself her laughter went up like a kite in the wind. Alidia had given her much the same demonstration about the meaning and uses of the blues when they'd been teenagers. It wasn't until she'd been alone at Maggie's that she'd started to appreciate what Alidia had meant.

"You see! It works. You're laughing. Now I'm going to run on down and get the records. I tell you, you ought to be glad to see the back of me. My leaving town is going to cut your liquor bill by at least twenty dollars a month. But you know what? I'm going to miss you something fierce too. And don't worry about not feeling final about your divorce. You'll wake up one morning and you'll really know that it's all over. And you'll feel great about it. You'll feel really free. 'Cause you need a man to live *with*, Cordy, but you don't need a man to live."

The finality Alidia had predicted did not come about in quite such a liberating way.

A few nights later, when she got home from her parents' house, Cordy showered, put on her robe, poured herself a drink, and turned on Bessie Smith's *Empty Bed Blues* album. It had been quite a day. Her mother had insisted that they all come to Hilton Head for Thanksgiving dinner, but when Cordy, Nonnie, George, and Jeanette arrived, Jake explained that Lucille wasn't up to fixing the meal and said that he was taking them out to a restaurant. Nonnie was peeved. Taking a holiday dinner in a restaurant was, to her, tantamount to admitting the breakup of the American family. The fact that the menu was in French further increased her aggravation. The meal was so interminably long that Cordy could see the carved-ice turkey that graced the buffet table start to melt. When the desserts finally arrived and the waiter had trouble igniting Lucille's cherries jubilee, Nonnie looked smug; but when he finally succeeded she clasped her hand to her throat and said she'd come to eat, not to be immolated. She was aghast at the one-hundred-and-sixty-dollar bill, but insisted on picking it up. While she and Jake were arguing over who was going to pay, George slipped the waiter his credit card.

Cordy hoped they would drive back to Savannah after the meal, but Jake talked George into watching a replay of the football game on the Betamax. Nonnie and Jeanette went for a walk, Lucille took a nap, and Cordy sat alone in the living room thumbing through the latest issue of *Vogue*, trying to block out the sound that drifted from the TV room, and wondering what Lupton was doing. Finally, after Jake and Lucille put up an argument about why Jeanette should stay the night, Cordy relented, left Jeanette behind, and crawled into the back seat of George's car. On the way home, Nonnie talked so continually that she didn't seem to notice that George had some difficulty differentiating the brake pedal from the accelerator.

Cordy played "Rainy Day Blues" for the fourth time but didn't sense that any humor was going to lift her gloom. She was about to go to bed when the phone rang. It was Clay.

"I just took a chance on calling you, Cordy. I didn't think you'd be home. I tried you yesterday afternoon but you were out."

"I wasn't out, I just wasn't picking up the phone." She'd been working on the proposal scene and it hadn't been going well. "You know what it's like when you're working alone. You long for someone to interrupt you but you're annoyed when they do."

"What is it now, relief or annoyance?"

"Neither. I'm not working. In fact, I'm getting ready for bed."

"May I drop by? There's something I need to discuss with you and I promise I won't stay long."

"Sure, come on by."

As soon as she'd hung up she started into the bathroom to put on her makeup. "This is ridiculous," she said to herself as she reached for the eye shadow. It was ten o'clock. She was tired. She'd already washed her face, yet here she was getting ready to paint it again, like some rodent that had been conditioned in a behaviorist's laboratory. Electric shock: little mouse turns left in maze. Man coming over: Cordy paints her face. She pushed her makeup case aside, brushed her teeth, pulled the sash of her robe tighter, and turned off the bathroom light.

"You look far too energetic to have come from a family dinner," she said when she opened the door to him. He was dressed casually, in jeans, an open-necked shirt, and deck shoes, and his sunburned face had an "all's right with the world" grin.

"No, missy, I just left the big house. But I was out sailing most of the day, so they had to take me as I came. Wasn't it a great day?"

She admitted as to how she hadn't noticed the weather and offered him a drink. He followed her into the kitchen. While she picked half-formed ice cubes from the tray and cursed the old refrigerator, he looked over the reference books on the table and asked how her work was going. He was genuinely interested in what she was writing, but it was difficult concentrating on her answer. He'd caught a faint smell of toothpaste when she'd opened the door, and though peppermint had never had an aphrodisiac effect on him before, he was sniffing for another whiff of it. Toothpaste/bedtime/sex. A homey and intimately appealing train of associations. The last woman he'd had an affair with had made a real production of going to bed. She had worn cutsie nightdresses and perfume so heavy he'd never been able to enjoy the natural smells of her body. As far as he could recall he'd never seen her without makeup. He'd enjoyed the slick-magazine fantasy of it the first time, but soon found her lack of spontaneity a bore. He liked the way Cordy looked now, all bundled up in that long robe with the V neck, so that only her fine ankles and bare feet, her throat, and the slightest swelling of her breasts showed. She looked simple, almost chaste, but there was that naked body underneath. With a single easy movement he could undo the sash, slide the robe from her shoulders, let it drop to the floor, and finally see and caress her body. He was glad her back was turned now, because his arousal was getting beyond the mental stage. God almighty, he thought as he got up and wandered into the living room, I'm like a fourteen-year-old kid on a bus. But it was a damned waste of a natural resource for Cordy Simpkins to be going to bed alone.

He averted his eyes as she handed him his drink. "Listen, Cordy, there's something I have to talk to you about," he said as he settled on the couch.

She started to sit beside him, then decided on the armchair. "Shhh. Just wait till this record's finished."

He took his glasses off, put them on the coffee table, threw his head back, and listened. She liked the fact that they were comfortable enough to sustain a silence without embarrassment, but as with many sustained silences, she began to feel their physical presences more acutely. He was thoroughly relaxed now, his arms draped over the back of the couch, his head tilted so that she could see the line of his jaw, his nostrils and cheekbones, but not his eyes. His legs were sprawled, his jeans pulled tight on his thighs and crotch. She tucked her feet underneath her and wrapped her arms across her breasts. She might, she thought, have found some middle ground between making herself up or slopping around in her robe. With her straggly hair and shiny face she must look like a neglected housewife.

"Yeah, I like that song," he laughed when the mournful crooning had come to and end. "One minute she's begging her lover to
please be kind, the next she's threatening him with physical violence."

"I don't think that's emotionally inconsistent."

Though her cheeks were dimpled, her eyes were aloof as though
he, simple clumsy man, couldn't begin to comprehend the contradictions of the human heart. He started to tell her that he really like the
song and that his remark hadn't been sarcastic, but then he stopped.
She would get to understand his tone in time. Just now he was trying to figure out why she'd asked him to listen to something she liked
and then evaluated his reaction as though it were some sort of test.
Not that he cared. He was so taken with her that all of her moods
came as a revelation. He liked watching the expressions on her face,
whether they were angry or merry. Nothing she could do could in-
timidate him now. He was far too curious to be intimidated.

She was telling him about the song, and he was thinking about
something he'd heard once that had always stuck with him: Human
beings were the only animals that made love face to face. He imagined her face above him, below him, side by side. Yes, he'd look at
her face when he made love to her. He'd keep his eyes wide open.
And he bet she would too. When she was finally ready to go to bed
with him it would be without games, seduction, or pretensions.
They would look at each other and their eyes would flash the same
urgent message: I want you and you want me. Completely. Now.

"Cordy, you're aware of all the nuances of the song, but you
told me you didn't even notice the weather today. How come? It
was one of the best days we've had all year."

In reply she hunched her shoulders, then let them drop. The
neckline of her robe fell another inch or so away from her breasts.

"I know you got the final papers. Did that depress you?" he
asked.

"Why should that depress me? I initiated the proceedings,
didn't I? It's over. Lupton can live his life and I can live mine."

He wasn't sure he believed the self-possessed toss of her head.
In his judgment, Lupton was not, and never had been, worthy of
her love, but love was often the reflection of the passions of the lover
more than the worthiness of its object.

"If I seem out of sorts," she continued, "it's just because I'm
missing Alidia. And I'm trying to recuperate from a national holiday. It's"—she paused, then grunted softly—"families."

She described the meal in the French restaurant and the drive home. The fact that he responded to her story so readily increased her enjoyment in the telling. Soon they were talking in a sort of shorthand, discussing people they knew in common. "And you," she asked, "do you mean to tell me you just slid through and had a wonderful time?"

"Not entirely. You know my folks."

"Pillars of Savannah society. I'm surprised they'd let you in the door without your coat and tie."

"They're not so stiff in private. In fact I've always thought they had a sort of hysterical charm. I grant you there were a couple of times today when the scales tipped on the hysterical side, but I know how to time it now. I was only there for supper, and I was in a tolerant mood. I'd had a great day on the water. I felt so good about the way I handled the boat today that I've decided to enter her in the Charleston regatta next year."

"Yes, you said you'd had a good time."

"Good time isn't the word for it. I was high. When I started out this morning there was very light air. I couldn't tell which way it would shift or if it was going to shift at all. Then early afternoon it picked up." He bent forward now, moving his hands—she had never noticed how well formed his hands were, powerful yet almost elegant—shaping his enthusiasm. "A terrific fifteen-knot breeze out of the southwest. I was sailing close-hauled and I knew I could fetch the island in one tack. She was footing beautifully. When she's balanced she almost sails by herself, I just have to be sensitive to her. It's not like anything else. . . . I have the sense of command, but it comes from feeling where the sea and the wind and the boat will let me go. When she . . ."

She was almost starting to feel jealous of the boat. The words he was using—luffing, billowing, beating, reaching—created a simultaneous languor and excitement. She crossed and uncrossed her legs. The downward throb of arousal consumed almost all of her consciousness.

". . . so she told me where she wanted to go and I just kept pointing her, taking advantage of what was happening. Goddamn it, it's fine, Cordy. A perfect combination of effort, skill, and instinct. Just"—his eyes held hers—"just beautiful. Promise me you'll come out with me real soon."

"I promise. Just as soon as I finish this next chapter."

"How long will that be?"

"I can't tell. But I have to keep at it." She pulled the robe tighter around her throat. As badly as she wanted him, she was afraid of the moment of decision. Stories of lonely women going to bed with their divorce lawyers flitted through her mind. What if they made love and he took it as a casual thing? Was a romp, however memorable, worth the risk of destroying years of friendship? They were intimate now, but afterwards . . . "What was it you wanted to tell me?" she asked.

"It can wait," he said impatiently.

"No, tell me. You said you had something to tell me and I want to hear." Her intuition was guiding her like a radar screen tracking a target. She knew he must've heard from Lupton.

"Hey . . ."

"No," she said, softening her insistence with a laugh. "I bet you heard from Lupton. And I want to know. After all . . ." She had almost said, "After all, I'm his wife."

Clay got up and walked to the mantelpiece, crossing his arms on it. The mention of Lupton's name had shattered the moment. He had come over to talk to her about the call—well, actually the call had been an excuse to see her—but now, when things were so ripe, when he knew that all he had to do was reach out . . . Still there was no point in forcing things. That wasn't how he wanted it.

"I suppose he called about the child support being late," she prodded.

"No. He wants to work out a deal about the equity in the house because he's decided to keep it, at least for the present. He's getting married again and—"

"What?"

"Yeah. I admit that piece of information rocked me back some. He's sure not wasting any time, but under the circumstances—"

"He called you to tell you he was getting married? He called *you?*" Her head was moving slowly from side to side and her eyes were bulging. "After all these years he called you! He's not just gutless, he's insane. He hasn't know her but— It is Susan, I suppose? Did he tell you that?"

He shrugged, disgusted. "I believe he mentioned that name."

She was so indignant, so quickly and thoroughly enraged, that his coolness was an affront. She got up from her chair and started pacing the room, her head still shaking, her mouth gaping open as anger, frustration, and shock struggled to express themselves. "He was here the first goddamn week in September asking me to go back with him, and now, three months later—three lousy months—he's getting married to Susan. And he calls and tells you!"

"Calm down, Cordy."

"Calm down! Don't you tell me to calm down. That cowardly bastard. I could kill him. I could kill him!"

"About a half hour ago you said you didn't care what he did with his life," he reminded her.

She turned her head swiftly, looking at him as though he insulted her.

"But," he added lightly, "we agreed that emotions don't have to be consistent, and I guess you're giving a demonstration of that."

Her stare hardened, as though she regarded him as the enemy.

"Why are you so upset, Cordy?" He asked the question slowly, as though he really wanted to know, then turned to the mantelpiece. "O.K, O.K. Never ask a question for which you don't already have the answer. I learned that the first year of law school. I do have the answer—or at least part of it. But"—since they were discussing the settlement and since he was her lawyer, he reverted to his professional demeanor—"I don't think Lupton's marriage will appreciably affect your financial situation. I'll do everything I can to guarantee that it won't. I'll make sure he lives up to the letter of the agreement. In fact, it might even be to your advantage if he can pay you the equity in the house now instead of putting it on the market. Apparently his future wife has a job—though she's pregnant and won't be able to work much longer—but her parents are going to help them out so—"

"Clay, will you please shut up. I don't want to talk about the equity in the goddamned house. I don't want to talk about Susan's dowry or her pregnancy or Lupton getting another handout from somebody's parents. I just . . . just . . ." Her hands shot out, assertive yet pleading, then her fingers curled into a fist and she punched the back of the armchair. He put his hands on his hips and looked into her face. "I know you're mad, Cordy. But don't take it out on me. I don't like being told to shut up. I don't blame you for being angry. You have a right to be angry—but at Lupton, not at me. I don't intend to pay Lupton's dues."

"I'm angry at all of you. All of you . . . men!"

"Ah, well, if it's that diffused, if I only have to take my bitty portion of an anger that goes to fifty percent of the world population, then I guess I can take it."

"Don't be sarcastic, Claxton. Don't make fun of me."

"I wasn't making fun of you. I was just trying to get you to lighten up."

"He treats me like this and you tell me to lighten up? Jesus Christ!"

"All right. Tell me what I can do to make you feel better. You want to talk about it? You want me to fix you a drink or put my arms around you? Or do you just want me to watch you shove the furniture around? I'm up for any of it."

She looked at him, ˅ ary, suspicious, acutely aware of the hive of contradictions buzzing within her. He put his hands on her shoulders. "I'll try to allow for your current prejudice against men if you'll try to suspend judgment in my particular case."

She almost gave way to the pressure of his hands until a smile that she saw as too knowing curled his lips.

"I guess I'd like to be alone," she said after a pause, not turning away but stiffening herself.

"You don't have to tap-dance for me, girl. I don't mind your being angry. I just don't want it to be directed at me unless I've provoked it."

"We are not born anew with every dawn, Claxton. And I think it's damned egotistical of you to think that this has anything to do with you."

"Ah, Christ." It was absurd that the desire and the openness they'd shared such a brief time ago could be so quickly destroyed, but he knew that she was too angry and too proud to accept anything from him. "What a waste," he said quietly, dropping his hands.

She understood what he was saying, but her thoughts were already back with Lupton. And Jeanette. She could imagine herself trying to explain to Jeanette that she was going to get the little brother or sister she wanted, but not in the way she'd wanted it. "That's life, Jeanette. Even when you get what you want it's not exactly as you'd dreamt it would be."

She was furious to think of Lupton taking money from Susan's parents, even if some of it would ultimately come to her. What a mess. A fleeting "Oh, sister, if I could tell you what I know" sympathy for the future Mrs. Tyre was overtaken by another thought: If Susan had been, or had thought she was, pregnant twice within the space of a year, then perhaps Susan knew what she was about. Perhaps she was so eager to have a child that she was aware of the compromises she was making. Perhaps Susan had a very clear idea—

clearer than her own had been until the last year—that she would have to direct and support Lupton.

She looked up to see Clay heading for the door. Another man walking out. She squashed the impulse to run after him. "What did you say, Clay?"

"Nothing."

"I'm sorry. I'll see you out."

"No need. Feel free to call any time you like."

She slumped down onto the couch after he'd left, lost in thought. Lost: wanting, strayed, absent, bereaved, cut off, unredeemed. Easy enough to knock the furniture around, but how long could a tantrum last? Besides, it was her furniture. Her lousy hand-me-down furniture. She thought of the antique bedstead, the Regency chair, and the sideboard with the leaded glass that were in the Chicago house. She didn't want any of them, but she despised the idea of Lupton and Susan using them. Then she compounded her rage by chastising herself for being petty. What the hell did she care about furniture? There were larger considerations here: the nature of love and illusion, cowardice and betrayal. That's right, you silly bitch, be an idealist and end up without a pot to piss in or a window to throw it out of.

It was ironic that having yearned for a sense of finality, for something that would make the divorce seem real and truly separate her from her past, she was bewildered and resentful now that it had been presented to her. But that was it: It had been presented to her. Once again she was reacting to Lupton instead of acting herself. What did she really care if Lupton was getting married? What did she really care what he did with his life? Rationally, she didn't care. And yet . . . She felt as though she'd been hit and she wanted to hit back. If she didn't hit back her anger would turn inward and destroy her, not in any immediate way, but with a slow sapping of her will, a shriveling of her sense of self. With a distant, chilly intuition—she had never realized just how cold intuition could be—she knew that revenge was not only impossible but beside the point. Lupton would do himself in. Perhaps he already had. But it was necessary for her to act. To *do* something.

Around one o'clock in the morning she got up from the couch, made herself a pot of coffee, and sat down at the typewriter. Pasted on the wall next to a list of words she constantly misspelled and the injunction not to use too many adjectives was the quotation "The doors of fortune open outward and must be stormed from within."

She burned her tongue on the coffee and got up, drawn toward the window. With some difficulty she raised the cracked and blistered frame, secured it with a piece of wood she kept there for that purpose, and put her head out. It was blissfully quiet. She couldn't imagine how she'd survived the impertinent disruptions of police sirens, transistor radios, and traffic all that time she'd been in New York. Above the tops of the trees a dark, mysterious sky with just a few large stars. Looking first right and then left at the moonlit buildings, she saw a single light burning in a house far up the block and felt a kinship with whomever that other night creature might be. "Now, Fanny," she whispered into the clear moist air, "just come and stand behind me and whisper in my good ear."

"But I like cream cheese and white bread," Jeanette protested, one hand propping up her chin, the other toying with a fork and pushing the scrambled eggs around the plate.

"But you've taken it for lunch two weeks in a row. It's not very nutritious. Why don't you be more adventuresome? At least let me put the cheese on wheat bread and put some of these alfalfa sprouts on it," Cordy ventured, holding up the package of sprouts and smiling at it with the unnatural enthusiasm of a TV saleswoman.

"You can put them on if you want to, but I'll just pick them out."

Cordy tossed the package of sprouts into the sink. Surely one of the worst things about being a divorced parent was being on the lookout for the disagreeable traits of the ex-mate in the child. Jeanette had Lupton's pigheadedness as surely as she had his nose and his rangy legs. And lately she'd started to exhibit another of his characteristics: Instead of arguing, which Cordy preferred, since she could exert her authority when reason failed to prevail, Jeanette had taken to a "You go your way, I'll go mine" attitude that was impossible to meet head-on. Cordy couldn't tell if this withdrawal was part of the normal patterns of growth or if Jeanette was still punishing her for the divorce. She decided to back down on the issue of wheat bread and alfalfa sprouts—perhaps Jeanette found some security in eating the same lunch day after day—and pulled her chair up to the table.

"Come on now, drink this orange juice," she cajoled, taking the fork and pushing the eggs onto it. "Remember when I played the mama bird and you played the baby bird?" Easy days those. She'd been no madonna when Jeanette was a baby, but once Jeanette had started to walk and talk, they'd enjoyed each other tremendously.

"I'm not hungry."

Cordy dropped the fork back onto the plate. "All right. I guess you'll eat when you are. But I can promise you one thing, Jeanette: You're not going to get any junk food."

"I understand. Can I leave the table now."

"*May* I leave the table now."

"Yes, you may," Jeanette laughed as she got up, throwing her arms around Cordy's neck and kissing her with buttery lips.

"Go on then, get your books. I don't want you to miss the school bus."

Cordy went back to the sink and finished fixing the lunch. Even the sound of the tinfoil being ripped from the box jangled her nerves. Ever since Thanksgiving she'd been working until three or four in the morning; and though she relished the heady feeling of solitude that being up in the wee hours gave her, the little sleep she was able to snatch before the alarm went off left her edgy and impatient.

Once she'd gotten Jeanette off to school, she ate the cold eggs— not because she wanted them but because she didn't want to waste them—and did the dishes. She drank another cup of coffee, but still felt groggy. By eleven o'clock, when she realized that she'd read the same paragraph in her history text three times, she put aside her resolve to stay up so that she might go to bed early and get back into sync with Jeanette's schedule, and she wandered into the bedroom. The air was polluted with the sulphurous fumes from the upriver paper factories, so she shut the windows and pulled the heavy drapes. The draperies, unearthed from a trunk in the carriage house, were far too grand for the apartment, but they provided a comforting darkness even in the middle of the day. Without taking her clothes off, she crawled into the unmade bed.

The first time the phone rang she thought it was the alarm. By the time she'd propped herself up, it had stopped ringing. She'd just settled back into bed thinking how peaceful life must've been in the days before any fool had the power to disrupt your privacy just by putting a dime in a slot, when the ringing started again. "All right, I give up," she cried, racing into the living room and being assaulted by the sunlight. "Hello. Nonnie? Is it you?"

"No, it's Abigail."

She was about to tell the caller that she'd dialed the wrong number, but the voice continued. "Is this Cordy? Cordy?"

"Yes, it's me."

"This must be a bad connection. You sound very far away."

"No. I'm here." She cleared her throat, thought about saying she'd call back, but remembered her phone bill.

"I hope you're sitting down . . ."

Not damned likely, since it had just taken all her strength to get to her feet. She didn't want to admit that she'd been sleeping at twelve-thirty in the afternoon.

". . . because I've got some great news for you. We've got an offer on the book. It was a mistake for me to submit the proposal and that one sample chapter. But it's O.K. Those new chapters have cinched it."

Now she did stagger into a sitting position. "That's nice." Her voice sounded bland.

"Listen to these figures and tell me what's acceptable. You have three possibilities with an inverse ratio of up-front advance money to royalty percentages. I think Maggie told me that you need cash right now, so you may want to settle for the lesser royalty and the larger advance. On the other hand . . ."

When Abigail had finished talking, Cordy had no idea what she'd heard. She cursed herself for sounding like a cretin, then asked Abigail to repeat the figures. Still confused, she had the presence of mind to say that she'd think it over and call back in a hour. Abigail told her to make it two, because she was going out to lunch. Fortunately Abigail hung up before Cordy broke down and shouted, "You've saved my life." She went into the bathroom and splashed her face with cold water. And when she'd convinced herself that she hadn't fantasized the whole thing, she leapt into the air yelling, "I don't believe it!" time after time. Six thousand dollars! Or five or seven, depending on which deal she took. No, it was going to be six. Middle of the road: neither foolishly adventurous nor foolishly timid. Needing affirmation of her decision, she called Nonnie, but Bernice said that she was out at the nursing home and wouldn't be back until late afternoon. She called Clay—having good news was a nice excuse for contact—but the secretary told her that he'd gone to London for the week. There was no help for it. The decision was completely hers.

She was relatively calm until she picked up the phone to call Abigail, then she thought she might upchuck the tuna-fish sandwich she'd eaten while she'd walked around the kitchen mentally paying off her bills. Abigail congratulated her again and gave her an estimated date when she would receive the contract and the first part of the advance before she was interrupted by another long-distance call. "Sorry," Abigail apologized as she came back on the line. "So, I guess we have everything straight now?"

"Yes, fine. Straight. Thank you."

"Stick with it, Cordy. Remember I told you that I don't particularly like historical books, but I've really enjoyed reading this one. You've got a great future ahead of you. Now if you have any other questions . . ."

"There is one other thing, Abigail. I'd like the name on the contract and the book to be Cordy Hampton, not Cordelia Simpkins Tyre."

"Fine. You've got it. I'll be in touch. Congratulations again."

She was amazed at herself. She'd had no idea that she was going to change her name. It had just popped out. But then Alidia always said that people lived lives of dust because they stifled their impulses. "Cordy Hampton." She said it softly, turning it over, trying it on. When she was even younger than Jeanette she'd wanted to create her own name. Esmeralda she'd thought to call herself. But Lucille had told her that names were given and could not be changed until a girl got married. And the discomfort she'd felt when she'd first been addressed as Mrs. Tyre. She'd always thought of Mrs. Tyre as being Lupton's mother. "Cordy Hampton," she said again. It wasn't true that "a rose by any other name would smell as sweet." There was a powerful magic in names. "Rose is a rose is a rose." She remembered walking in Nonnie's garden while Nonnie named the flowers, the butterflies, and insects, and how the very namming had made these things more real to her, as though she somehow possessed them. "Cordy Hampton." She repeated it again and smiled.

Chapter XX

Nonnie woke before dawn. "C'mon now girl, get these here bones in an upright position," she muttered, though this morning, being Christmas morning, there was no need to urge herself out of the warm indulgence of the bed. She wanted to get up. There were a million things to do. She threw back the covers, swung her legs over the side, and slipped her feet into her slippers, pleased at the ease of her movements. Some mornings the body failed you, but others it was right there doing your bidding just as it was supposed to. She padded to the closet and pulled on the light, reaching past the satin hangers with the little bags of sachet attached to them to take her old blue and white housedress from the hook. She wouldn't take time to fix her hair now. Later, after she'd dressed the turkey, made the breakfast, and put everything in order for the dinner, she'd come up and change. She wound her braid around her head and secured it with pins, wincing with indignation as she felt the arthritis in her hands.

She tiptoed down the hallway and descended the stairs. The Christmas tree in the parlor had permeated the hall with the scent of pine; and she stopped, her hand on the banister, sniffing and staring at the milky blue that came through the fanlight above the front door. As she opened the door and looked out at the square the chill air hit her like a splash of cold water. The streetlamps were paling out in the dawn light, the birds were starting to sing, but not a soul stirred. She took a deep breath and pushed her hands into the sleeves of her cardigan. This had always been her favorite time of day. For most of her life it had been the only time when she was completely alone and could take the time to feel. She'd learned to think her own thoughts while she did the household accounts or wrote out a grocery list, but feeling demanded a certain privacy and a certain leisure. Years ago, before they'd started putting milk in cardboard cartoons, she'd been tuned to the sounds of the milkman, and while Lonnie and the children slept she'd collected the bottles from the back stoop, sliced the bacon, set the table, and still had time to linger at the kitchen window to watch the beauty of the morning.

She walked back to the kitchen and shut the door behind her. The turkey was so big that she staggered as she lifted it from the refrigerator to the table. She pinched the flesh and gave it a pat of approval and put on the water for coffee. She brought out the cutting board, tested the knife, crumbled the cornbread she'd made some days before into the enamel bowl, and took the vegetables from the bin. The kitchen was so quiet that she could hear the crunch as she bit into a piece of celery. She pulled a captive strand of celery from the back molar that had always been a trap, and washed her hands, grateful that she'd never had to replace her real teeth with dentures. The smells of the onions sautéing and the coffee perking made her feel so content that she started to hum. As she cleaned the giblets, the first rays of the sun began to filter through the trees, and she stood transfixed watching its lemony light gloss the leaves and change the color of the tiles on the roof of the carriage house from a brownish gray to a warm terra-cotta. Hearing a noise in the passageway, she turned quickly and almost guiltily to the door. Bernice, her head still wrapped in her kerchief, her hand holding the front of her old brown coat together, beamed at her.

"Merry Christmas, Miz Hampton."

"Oh, Bernice! You like to scare me to death. What are you doin' here? I told you not to botner comin' by, didn't I?"

"I hope the Lord bless you with more Christmas spirit 'fore the day is out," Bernice said indignantly, taking off her coat.

"Merry Christmas. Merry Christmas. Just that you startled me. I was deep in thought an' didn't figure anyone else was up yet."

"I come by 'cause it's like a crazy place at my house. Childrens up an' rippin' open packages at four in the mornin'. Yes, ma'am," Bernice shook her head. "It's Angela's fault. Last night lil' Lloyd want to know what time was Santa Claus comin', an' since Angela wants to get them all off to bed she says Santa Claus gonna come at midnight sharp. Bless me if lil' Lloyd don't set the alarm clock for four in the mornin'. That boy's but eight years old an' already smart as a snake. Told me last week he don't even believe in Santa anymore, but Angela goes an' spends all her salary to get him a video game just the same. There be no peace in my house this mornin' and maybe never again. So I come on by. I'll help you with the fixin's, then go on back once it calm down an' get m'self ready for church."

Nonnie chuckled sympathetically. Bernice was always feuding with her daughter Angela, who, according to Bernice's lights, played fast and loose with her money and was lax with the children. "Shall I pour you some coffee?"

"I 'spect I shouldn't, but I 'spect I will."

"Is your bladder troubling you again? Coffee won't help a runny bladder, Bernice," she cautioned as she took down another cup.

"Don't I know it? But I can't wake up 'less I smell the coffee." Bernice settled her haunches into a chair and started to spoon sugar into her cup. "An' how come you're up so early?"

"Got to get this bird into the oven."

"You must be tired. Everyone comin' in on you like this, you couldn't have put your head on the pillow 'fore the cock crowed."

"Just barely, but I feel fine. Got all my chicks about me last night. Vivian an' her grandson Billy came in the afternoon, then Jake and Lucille carried Jake Junior an' his girlfriend over for supper, then 'bout ten o'clock we went over to the airport and picked up Constance and Phillip. I like to fall down when I saw Jake Junior. He's got a real bush of a mustache. Seems like when he went off to dental school he was still as hairless as a Chihuahua."

"What's his girl like?"

"She's just like a vanilla pudding. Got real mild features and a nature to match. She's going to be a dental technician, so I 'spect if Jake Junior starts his own practice she'll be helping him out. She comes from Augusta. Nice family. I believe I know her aunt."

"You want me to shell the peas or peel the potatoes?"

"I'll bring you the peas. Just keep sittin'."

"An' Vivian. How's Vivian?"

"You stay on till she gets up. I know she wants to see you."

"I'm gonna. I want to see her too."

"You won't recognize her. She's a full axe handle across the behind."

"No!"

"Yes, yes she is. I never thought Vivian would go to flesh, but I guess since Joe's died she don't care as much anymore. I'll have to get onto her about it. She's too young to think the table is her only pleasure in life. Her skin's all leathery too, though she says she can't do much about that 'cause of the Arizona weather. Had herself written up in the Tucson paper. All about her cactus garden and her tryin' to start the opera out there. The clipping's around here somewhere." Nonnie put down the knife, started to wipe her hands, then shrugged and went back to slicing some carrots. "Well, she'll find it for you. Oh, I meant to soak the fruitcake again first thing an' it slipped my mind. Will you get the brandy from the cabinet? The cakes are in the pantry right next to the pies. An' don't be upset when you see your sweet potatoe pie's already been cut into. I tried to keep Billy out of it, but you can't keep a thirteen-year-old boy away from a pie."

"So how many in all are you fixin' for?"

"Let's see. Lucille and Jake, Jake Junior and . . . what is her name again? It's something sweet-sounding . . . anyway, Jake's girl, Vivian and Billy, Phillip and Constance—"

"How's Constance?"

"Pretty as a picture. I think Phillip's pouting some 'cause she dragged him down here and he wanted to stay with the grandchildren, but Constance is fine."

"An' who else?"

"Lonnie's brother John, and Winetta—"

"You s'pose he's ever goin' to marry that woman?"

"Only time John will need a minister now is when he's on his deathbed. He's been seeing Winetta ever since Clara died, an' that's got to be fifteen years. If it doesn't come to a boil in the first year, I figure it can go on simmering till the cows come home." Nonnie shook her head, wondering if Cordy would continue to ignore Clay Claxton until the crucial moment had passed her by. "Then there's John's son Curtis, an' Cousin Cissy, George Naughton, and of course Cordy and Jeanette. Hamilton and Flora said they'd drop by *after* they go to the Hyatt. You know how Hamilton likes to throw away money just to prove he has it. So that makes—now, I counted them up last night—"

"Seventeen." Bernice drained her cup and got up. "What you plannin' to do about breakfast?"

"I'm not plannin' anything. I'm not going to all this trouble fixing dinner to have people so stuffed with breakfast they're not going to be able to appreciate the meal. I was just going to throw a hunk of cornbread, a cup of coffee, and maybe an egg at whoever put their face in the door, but since you're here I guess you could whip up a batch of biscuits."

"First I'll put them leaves in the dining-room table. They's too heavy for you to be liftin'. Then I'll get the brandy."

"While you're in there take a look at those poinsettia plants sittin' near the window. Both Joan and Lethia gave me one. I'm going to take one to old Cora Masters when I go over to the nursing home, but you can have the other if you like."

"I'll take it sight unseen. Carry it to church with me." Bernice moved quickly to the door, wanting to finish the chores so she could get back and hear the rest off the gossip before she and Nonnie were interrupted.

Cordy drove up to the house around noon. "Now put your shoes back on and carry those slippers into the house," she told Jeanette as she turned off the ignition. "They're called house slippers because you wear them in the house. They're not made for outside."

"I'm just going to run up the stairs in them."

"Let's not bargain. Take them off, please."

Jeanette reluctantly took off the pink satin slippers with the little pink bows and put them back into the box. Of all the presents she'd received, the slippers, a gift from Lucille, were her favorite. Cordy had confined herself to buying things that Jeanette needed— a book bag, tennis shoes, pajamas, and a robe. Jeanette had not been taken in. She knew a necessity masquerading as a gift even if it was wrapped in fancy paper.

"That's a good girl. No sulking now, just go on in."

"Will Billy be there to play with me?"

"I expect he will be there, but Billy's a big boy. He might not want to play."

"Wait. I have to put on my lipstick." Jeanette held on to the dashboard, grabbed the rearview mirror, and twisted it to her. Reaching into her purse, also a gift from Lucille, she took out the Bubble Gum Lipgloss, pursed her lips, and smeared the goo on.

"Come on, Mama. What are you waiting for?"

"I'll be in in a minute. You run on."

Cordy watched as Jeanette raced up the stairs and opened the front door. Even during Lupton's first season with the Bears, when expensive gifts had been as plentiful as holiday party invitations, she'd always returned, at least in memory, to the house on Monterey Square. She'd thought with a sentimental nostalgia of the crowds of relatives around the table, the huge bowls of eggnog, and the Christmas tree ornaments that dated back to before her birth. But now that she was back home again, she still felt mildly depressed. A predictable and interminably long day of forced merriment stretched before her. People would gorge themselves and talk about their diets. Someone was bound to get sick. Someone else was bound to drink too much. The conversation was bound to veer into one argument that would never be allowed to come to a boil but would be watched as carefully as a simmering pan of milk. Her divorce would be the hottest item, though nobody would discuss it outright; instead, she'd be hauled into corners and questioned about how she was holding up. But there was no escape. She couldn't plead work, illness, or prior commitment. Not on Christmas day.

As she opened the front door a delicious mix of aromas—roasting turkey, ham, cakes, pies, and pine needles—tickled her nose and made her mouth water. "Merry Christmas," she said as she entered the kitchen. "Where is everybody?"

"Your folks haven't come yet, and I sent the others off for a walk. Let 'em work up an appetite and keep out of my way," Nonnie said as she slid a knife around the edge of a cake pan.

"Merry Christmas, Cordy." Bernice looked up from the sink. "I'll be needing some more salt for this wash, Miz Hampton. These greens are all buggy."

"Why are we having greens for Christmas dinner?" Cordy asked.

"Because Vivian requested them," Nonnie said, shaking salt into the rinse water.

"May I help?"

Just sit and have yourself some coffee, then I'll put you to work. You can make the white sauce for the onions."

"Or cut up the oranges for the ambrosia," Bernice added.

Cordy looked around. Every surface was covered with pots, pans, plates, and food. "How many are coming? Looks like you've got enough to feed an army."

"Seventeen," Nonnie said, looking off into the pantry, where Jeanette had wandered. "Jeanette, soon's as you get a cookie *in* your hand you're gonna get a slap *on* it. Don't be fooling with those cookies."

Jeanette drew her hand away from the plate. "I wasn't taking, I was just touching."

"I'll explain how one can lead to the other before you start courting," Nonnie laughed.

"Seventeen people," Cordy said. "Who all—"

"Seventeen ain't hardly no number to be flustered about," Bernice shrugged. "Remember the time we fixed for— How many was it, Miz Hampton, thirty or forty? That be the year everyone came home. Oh, we've had some big dinners in this house."

"Was that the year Jake Junior got sick and threw up right onto the dining-room table?" Cordy wanted to know.

"No, sugar," Nonnie corrected. "The time Bernice is talkin' about was when we were still setting a separate table for the children out here in the kitchen."

"Please, Nonnie. I don't have to eat in the kitchen, do I?" Jeanette cried.

"No, you won't have to. That was when we had litters of children underfoot."

"People don't have litters. Only animals have litters," Jeanette said. "My science teacher said—"

"I do wish you had someone to play with, Jeanette. Why don't you go over to the Crawfords' an' get Katie to show you her presents."

"She won't want me. She's got brothers and sisters to play with."

"Tell you what," Cordy suggested. "I'll call over to her house and see if she'd like to have you. Or maybe you could bring her back here."

Jeanette followed Cordy into the hallway and waited, sullenly expectant, while Cordy secured her an invitation to visit.

"Don't go spoiling your appetite by eating candy canes," Nonnie called from the kitchen. "I'm going to be watchin' you at dinner, and if you don't eat your vegetables—"

"Jeanette, you've got those slippers on again," Cordy said. "I told you—" But Jeanette had already run out the door.

Cordy sat down at the table. Nonnie cleared a space and set a sack of beans and a colander in front of her. She snapped the beans slowly, because it was obvious that Nonnie and Bernice didn't really need or want any help. "Men work from rise to set of sun, but women's work is never done," Nonnie said as she decorated the ham with pineapple slices.

"Ain't it the truth," Bernice agreed, but they moved with the pleasure and relaxation of an old vaudeville dance team. A flicker of Nonnie's eyes brought an ingredient from Bernice's hand. Bernice opened the oven; Nonnie basted the turkey, her wrinkled face creasing into a smile of satisfaction. Nonnie got the heavy cream from the refrigerator; Bernice had already plugged in the beater. The soft patter about other recipes, other Christmases, dead or absent relatives, marked their rhythm like a metronome. As Cordy stood at the sink washing up pots and looking out at the garden, she knew this preparation would be the best part of the day.

Finally Bernice packed up the poinsettia and one of the pecan cherry cakes and fetched her coat. At the same time the front door opened and Lucille, Jake, Jake Junior, and his girl Taffy came in. They'd just finished taking off their coats when Constance, Phillip, Vivian, and her grandson Billy returned. There was much bustling and greeting in the hallway and appraisals of appearance and the weather as people shifted about from room to room.

"Why don't you come and help me set the table," Constance asked, taking Cordy's hand. "I think I remember where everything is kept, but I may have forgotten."

"Everything is just where it was an' where it's supposed to be," Nonnie told her. "The silver's on the sideboard, and don't forget to put a pad under that tablecloth."

As soon as they were in the dining room, Constance pulled the door to. "I wanted to help this morning, but Nonnie just about threw us out of the kitchen. She's like a general drawing up a battle plan when she fixes these dinners. Now, where does she keep the tablecloths?"

"Second drawer down. The pad's in there too."

"I guess you've gotten reacquainted with everything since you've been back home."

Here we go, Cordy thought. She's leading up to the divorce.

Constance held the cloth to her chest and smiled. "Cordy. Little Cordy. How have you been girl? How have you *really* been?"

"I'm fine, Aunt Constance. I'm just fine."

"I must say you look it. You look better than I've ever seen you, and that's the truth."

"You look well too." Constance was a handsome woman, but her style obscured her resemblance to the Hampton family. She had long ago taken on the protective coloring of Phillip's family of Boston Brahmins and in her tailored drab olive dress, burgundy low-heeled pumps, with her clipped ear-length silver hair and minimal makeup, she was unmistakably a Northern matron.

Cordy put on the pad and stood, hands extended, waiting to catch the end of the tablecloth as Constance unfurled its billows of lace. "I can't tell you how happy I am that I convinced Phillip to come down home," Constance said as she smoothed the wrinkles out of the cloth. "I expect you're glad to be back too. When you're going through a crisis it's family you rely on, no matter what your feelings about them. I've tried to get Stephanie to come and stay with us." Her voice dropped. "I guess I can tell you, Cordy. Stephanie and Frederick are getting a divorce too. We're just sick about it. Of course she has her degree, but she hasn't worked in years and . . ."

The strongest memory Cordy had of Stephanie was from two decades ago when Jake and Lucille had taken her on a visit to Boston and she'd seen snow for the first time. Stephanie had pushed her into a snowbank. Since then she'd seen Stephanie only a few times, though she'd been shown the usual graduation/wedding/christening photos; and Lucille had kept her informed of how much money Stephanie's husband was making.

"Please don't mention it to anyone," Constance went on. "I don't want to spoil anyone's holiday by bringing it up."

"I won't tell anyone," Cordy assured her, opening the box of silver.

"And Phillip isn't well either. He has to have a gall bladder operation in another three weeks. And I'm going to convince him to retire from the bank afterwards. But there's no reason to bring that up either. It would only get Nonnie upset."

Cordy began to count the silverware into seventeen sets. Oh, my god, she thought, by the end of the day I'll be privy to more secrets than I'll know what to do with. Were all families like this? Did they all have a show of togetherness while individual members went on with their own interior lives and nursed their own secrets?

Constance fingered a serving spoon and held it up to the light. "My, this is lovely. I wonder if that old story is true, about Grandmother Ettie's mother sewing the silver into a mattress during the Civil War."

"I don't question family myths," Cordy laughed. "Every truth changes in the telling. Whenever any family tells a story from its past it always has the air of high romance, and I expect it's full of just about as much bunk."

"It wasn't until I had children of my own that I ever questioned anything I'd been told in this house." Constance looked around her with an affectionate but superior air. "But my generation was more naive. We expected we'd do things the same way and live the same way. Now people enter into marriage holding divorce as an option. How can any marriage work if you go into it thinking that you'll be able to get out? Nowadays everyone wants his or her own way. There isn't such a thing in marriage." Cordy picked up a napkin and polished a spot on one of the butter knives. Despite Constance's preachments, Cordy knew that her aunt was very adept at getting her own way. Constance sighed and laid down the spoon, but continued to stare at it. "I've always wanted to ask Nonnie to leave the silver to me. It's the only thing I want from here. I suppose it would be tasteless of me to ask her about it. I mean, one can't talk to an eighty-three-year-old woman about her will. If she were sixty or seventy it might be permissible, but—"

"We all proposes, Nonnie disposes," Cordy said, having to smile at her own joke, because Constance had taken up another piece of silver and was examining it with an expression of mild greed. "But if you want to mention it, why don't you? You'd be surprised at Nonnie. There's hardly anything she isn't willing to talk about."

"That may be true for you. But you're right about her intuiting things. Last night she asked me about what was wrong with Billy."

"Is anything wrong with Billy?"

"He has a learning disability. He's run away from home twice. That's why he's living with Vivian. Vivian seems to be the only one who can handle him, but you can see it's too much for her. She doesn't complain, of course, but she stuffs herself with food to ease the frustration."

Cordy drew in her breath and counted out the butter knives. Constance walked around the table lining up the forks. "But enough about everyone else. I want to talk about you, Cordy. We're all just as proud as we can be, with your writing and all. Do tell what this book you're working on is about. Nonnie is bragging that it's going to be just grand."

"It's a novelization of the life of Fanny Kemble. Do you know who she was?"

"I'm afraid not."

"Well," Cordy began, "Fanny's aunt was the famous trage-dienne Sarah Siddons. It seems her whole family was talented . . ." She saw nothing wrong in pandering to whatever theories of inher-

ited abilities Constance might have as long as she could keep her
from further probing and preaching.

"And which of you gentlemen is going to carve this here turkey?" Nonnie looked around the table. At quarter to three, when she
was almost ready to serve, John Hampton, his girlfriend Winetta,
and his son Curtis and daughter Cissy had not yet made their appearance; and Nonnie had threatened to start without them. But
they'd arrived in the nick of time, so now that everyone was here she
determined not to spoil her triumph by dwelling on their poor manners.

"I'll carve," George Naughton volunteered.

"No, George, you're a guest." His smile was so benign that it
must be intoxicated, and she couldn't risk an accident just to flatter
him. "Jake," she said, handing him the knife, "you're the nominee.
So before y'all start tellin' Jake what part of the turkey you want,
let's raise our glasses in a toast."

"Wait. We should say grace first," Lucille said. "Jeanette, why
don't you give us the blessing?"

Heads bowed as Jeanette squirmed and lisped the blessing.
Through downcast eyes, Cordy looked at Lucille. Lucille had chosen
to wear a velvet pantsuit and white lace jabot, which automatically
excluded her from kitchen service. Her contribution to the day's activities was going to be of a spiritual nature.

"Thank you, Jeanette. That was very sweet," Lucille said.

"Rolly, rolly round the table, fill your belly while you're able,"
George laughed. Though she hadn't taken a bite, Lucille pressed her
napkin to her lips.

"C'mon now, start passing the dishes before everything gets
cold," Nonnie ordered.

"That's the blessing of the chef, and that's the only blessing I'm
interested in," announced Cousin Curtis, who hadn't gone to church
since his affair with the organist had been discovered. "I'm not going
to play shy. Cissy, pass me those yams and marshmallows."

Everyone laughed and started to talk at once, so it was impossible to hear more than snatches of conversation. Preferences, requests, and compliments about the food mingled with the rich
aromas. Jeanette asked for gravy to make a bird's nest in her mashed
potatoes, and Nonnie jumped up and scurried to the kitchen to get
the forgotten gravy boat. Uncle John, who'd had so many bourbons
that his face was as expressionless as a boiled egg, shook his head as

his girlfriend Winetta spooned dressing onto his plate. "Just eat a lil' somethin' Johnnie," she begged, pursing the lips she still painted in a cupid's bow.

Cousin Curtis caught Cordy's eye and rolled his own to heaven. Phillip declared that his doctor had forbidden him both cranberry sauce and ham. "Don't you know that popular opinions about food, sex, and child rearing change fashion faster than the length of women's skirts," Vivian told him, loading her own plate with turkey, ham, greens, yams, potatoes, beans, Jello-O salad, and biscuits. "If you want advice about food, ask a waiter, not a doctor." Jake set down the carving knife and wagged his finger at Lucille. "Don't try to restrain me today, woman. Caution is not appropriate to a feast."

Nonnie, now that she was up, refused to sit down. She circled the table, urging second helpings and carrying platters to and fro. Taffy, Jake Junior's girlfriend, was so busy looking at him that she dropped a creamed onion on the table. At Nonnie's insistence, Cordy took a small second helping of ham, though the sheer volume and richness of the food had taken the edge off her appetite. She sipped her wine (Nonnie had wanted to serve coffee with the meal, but Lucille and Constance, joining forces for once, had managed to convince her that coffee with the meal was déclassé) and studied the faces around the table.

These were her people. This was her bloodline. She felt the pull of affections that went back to her earliest memories but also a sense of estrangement. Familiarity bred prejudice, and she doubted her ability to see any of them clearly. Yet she sized them up as she had no recollection of having done before.

Here was her father talking about mutual bonds with Phillip, his right hand poised with fork in midair while his left automatically reached around her mother's chair. Her mother's very indifference seemed to have secured his habitual devotion. Perhaps a man deprived of but constantly seeking a passionate response from his wife was the only good husband. That wasn't something she wanted to believe, but it was certainly something that she had observed—and not just with Jake and Lucille.

But a cool wisdom would never do her any good, because she knew that no matter what the practical problems, she would leave a man for whom she had no passionate response. That strain of pride and independence she'd inherited from Nonnie. And it was apparent in Aunt Vivian. With her shelf of a bosom, her tiny ankles and wrists, her thick, unmanageable hair, Vivian was almost a caricature of the Hampton women. Vivian was intelligent, sometimes even witty, though her character was too self-indulgent to permit any channeling of these talents. Though Vivian's appetites were now focused on food, Cordy was sure Vivian must have had a few affairs. Cordy could remember some knock-down-drag-outs between Vivian and her husband, a wildly handsome ex-musician whose lack of business sense had been a strain on the Hampton coffers. It seemed natural that Aunt Vivian would end up in Arizona. She could be as prickly and juicy as a cactus, and she loved to turn her face to the sun.

Constance, on the other hand, was more wily and conservative, with a sharpness of eye, an acquisitiveness and ability to adapt, but no craving for anything out of the ordinary. Had they lived in more violent times, Constance would have curtsied and negotiated with General Sherman to spare the city; Vivian would have greeted him with a pitchfork, just to show what side she was on; and Lucille would have cried and fainted dead away. Cordy herself might have been torn between all three responses.

"In my opinion, Phillip . . ." her brother was saying. Cordy noted that he'd dropped the "Uncle" and was now addressing Phillip as an equal. Jake Junior's impending graduation from dental school and engagement to Taffy had been his final rites of passage. Now he too uttered opinion as though it were fact. Taffy nodded her pale apricot-colored head and looked at him with adoring, myopic eyes. Cordy, being his older sister and knowing that Jake Junior had never given serious thought to anything except the scores of the Georgia Bulldogs, was under no obligation to listen. Though she loved him, she rarely thought about him and never worried about him. As Lucille's indisputable favorite, he'd grown up with a sense of entitlement and a reach that matched his grasp. His self-confidence, his very normalcy were comforting to Cordy, as was his physical presence.

Last night he had hugged her and whispered, "I'm glad you got rid of Lupton, Sis. He was never good enough for you." She'd been somewhat surprised, because Jake Junior had had a worshipful attitude toward Lupton, or so she had believed. Now that she was divorced, he wouldn't even question her decision. In this unexamined loyalty he was like everyone else in the family. Despite squabbles and secrets, they closed ranks against anyone who'd hurt one of their own.

Jeanette was trying to cut up her ham and was spattering

pineapple sauce on the tablecloth. Cordy reached over to help her, but Winetta had already left her seat and was cutting the meat into bite-sized pieces and talking to Jeanette. Cordy smiled her thanks and Winetta smiled back. Knowing she was invited only because Nonnie was liberal-minded, Winetta was grateful for any crumbs of acceptance. When she was a girl, Cordy had heard Winetta described as Uncle John's "fancy woman" and had imagined a florid seductress with a pushed-up bosom and a gardenia behind her ear. She would never forget her surprise on being introduced to the anxious, patient creature with the stiff lacquered hair who broke out of her timid silences only to offer her assistance. Nonnie had said that Uncle John was so contrary that he wanted a motherly type for his mistress.

Cordy reached over and stroked Jeanette's forehead and noticed it was hot. She asked her how she was feeling and Jeanette muttered a dignified "Fine, thank you." She supposed Jeanette's usual exuberance had been dampened by the presence of so many strange adults, and felt sorry for her being an only child. When she'd been Jeanette's age she'd sat at the kitchen table with a slew of other children. Unguarded, except by Bernice's tolerant eyes, they'd mushed food, licked fingers, fought over the wishbone, and thrown dough balls at each other.

George Naughton's audible burp signaled a change in the tempo. Plates were pushed away; chairs were pushed back. Groans of overindulgence and gentle sighs of gastronomic surrender rose into the already turgid air. Constance, saying something about missing the beauty of snow, got up and raised a window. Cousin Cissy giggled and declared that she would have to let out the waistband of her skirt. Nonnie said that no one could really appreciate the desserts without an intermission and told Jeanette and Billy to go into the parlor and play checkers. With the smile of disorientation that Cordy had initially mistaken for shyness, Billy took Jeanette's hand and left the room. Uncle John took out his cigar and lit it, oblivious of Nonnie's glare when he put the spent match onto his salad plate. The cigar's pungent odor reminded Cordy of the time Uncle John had taken her onto his lap and she, sensing more than avuncular interest, had struggled against his kisses. She had hated his big yellow teeth ever since then.

"No, no, Mama, you sit!" Aunt Vivian was up, pressing Nonnie into her chair at the head of the table with affectionate determination. "You fixed the dinner and you sit. The girls will help clear and make the coffee."

"I'll be glad to help," Taffy volunteered.

"I remember when we were little," Lucille sighed as the other women began to pick up the plates. "We always had the dinner served and the help always cleared up afterwards."

"Nobody keeps full-time help anymore," Constance told her.

"I don't need more help," Nonnie said emphatically. "Bernice more'n keeps things running around here."

"I wonder why you stay on in this house," Phillip said, loosening his tie. "Even with Bernice, it's bound to be too much for you, rattling around in all these rooms. And the heating and air conditioning bills alone—"

"I use the fireplace in the cold weather, an' I open the windows an' have the shade trees in the summer," Nonnie said.

Uncle John coughed a cloud of smoke. "I remember when Lonnie wanted to sell. Had a coupla prospective buyers too."

"I can tell you that when I retire, Constance and I are going to get out from under. Buy a condo and really start living," Phillip continued.

"Does it look to you as though I haven't been livin'?" Nonnie inquired.

"I know what Phillip means," Constance came to his defense. "Of course the place is lovely—there's no denying that. There's also no denying that it's impractical for a single, elderly woman. These big houses—they were designed for another time."

"Well, surely," Cousin Curtis put in. "Late Regency period, to be exact."

"I meant," Constance overrode him (she had always found Curtis flip and not nearly so witty as he thought himself), "another time sociologically. People had bigger families then. And," she added pointedly, "there were always a couple of unmarried relatives hanging on. Several generations lived in one house. People didn't shunt their senior citizens off to nursing homes."

"If you mean old folks, say old folks," Nonnie butted in. "Don't give me any of this senior citizens bunkum."

"What was so dreadful about those days?" Winetta asked timidly.

"If you'd ever had to live with your mother-in-law"—Vivian laughed, popping an olive into her mouth—"you wouldn't have to ask. But there's more reasons than practicality for holding on to anything. Where would we all gather if we didn't have the house? I personally wouldn't want to care for it, but I'm glad it's here."

"But I know what Phillip means," Jake Junior said. "In an age of nuclear power it's strange to be thinking about chopping wood for a fireplace."

"Maybe chopping wood *is* better," Cordy said. "We don't have any real notion of what the hazards of nuclear power are. And too many Southern states have become dumping grounds for—"

George Naughton chuckled. "Since Cordy's been in New York she's opposed to everything. New York spun her head around and put it on backwards."

"That's got nothing to do with it," Cordy remonstrated, but then she shrugged. There was no point talking to George Naughton.

"I agree with Cordy," Vivian cut in. "The risks of nuclear power have been well documented. Why look what happened at Three Mile Island. If you aren't concerned with peoples' health, George, just think about what happened to property values."

A babble of voices, each struggling to express its view, rose in a cacophony that blasted the after-dinner underwater calm.

"Oh, please," Lucille pleaded, "let's not start fussin' at each other about nuclear power. That's not what I call dinner conversation."

"You think the only fit dinner conversation is about the dinner itself," Jake Junior teased, taking Lucille's hand.

"This house," Nonnie said in a voice so commanding that everyone turned to the head of the table. "This house has been Hampton property for over a hundred and twenty years. Have you no sense of the importance of that? This house is going to be on the tour of historic homes next April, an' I don't much care what any of you think of it or want to do with it. Long as I'm alive it will be preserved."

"It's a beautiful house. One of the most beautiful I've ever seen." Phillip tried to placate her. He was backed up by a general chorus of agreement.

Lucille put her fingertips to her temples. "There's no argument here, Mama. Don't try to turn this into an argument."

". . . the best cook in the entire state of Georgia." Jake's voice trailed after Lucille's in a dying fall.

"I know there's no argument," Nonnie said quietly, rising from her chair. "No argument at all. But if y'all don't mind, I'm goin' up to my room for a lil' rest. I'll be down to serve the desserts in another hour."

The veneer of amiability cracked, if not shattered, a momentary pall fell on the table as Nonnie left the room. Vivian, quickly stepping in as second in command, suggested that everyone retire to the parlor and she would serve the coffee there. The men withdrew, the women scurried back and forth to the kitchen.

Alone in the dining room, Cordy took the crumb catcher and silver brush from the sideboard and started to sweep the tablecloth. Jake Junior, now puffing one of Uncle John's noxious cigars, came in. The way he smiled at her made Cordy think she was in for another unsoliciated revelation.

"Hey, sweet sister, how'd you like to help your brother out?"

"Any way I can."

"Taffy and I have decided to skip dessert. I sure would appreciate it if you'd loan me the keys to your apartment. You know how Mama is. She's insisted that we use separate bedrooms at her house. I was going to have it out with her, but Taffy felt embarrassed, so—"

"Say no more. My purse is in the kitchen. I'll go get it and slip you the key."

She passed Lucille and Constance in the hallway, carrying trays of coffee. The TV set had already been switched on in the parlor, effectively putting an end to any more topical discussions, though George Naughton's voice was heard to boom over a jeans commercial. In the kitchen, Vivian and Winetta were scraping dishes and loading them into the dishwasher. There were platters full of leftovers and smeared silverware all over the place. "Don't think I'm dodging the clean-up, Aunt Vivian. I'll be right back," Cordy assured her, though the sight of the turkey carcass and the congealed gravy made her feel as though she'd never want to eat again.

Jake Junior was smoothing his mustache and pacing back and forth. She handed him the keys. "Taffy's waiting out in the car," he said conspiratorially. "If anyone notices we're gone, just tell them I've taken her on a sightseeing tour."

"You'd best make it a quickie." She winked. "Nonnie'll send a search party out after you if you're not back to praise the coconut cake."

As soon as she re-entered the kitchen, Aunt Vivian caught her eye. "Let's get these decks cleared in a hurry, Cordy. Then I want you to come sit with me. I think we ought to take some time to have a little talk."

Nonnie slipped off her shoes, undid the neck of her dress, and stretched out on her bed. The sky was already beginning to darken, and if she could have her way she would have taken a bath and gone to bed that very moment. She was almost giddy with exhaustion; and since she'd seen them all, embraced them, listened to them, fed them, and sized up how they were doing, she wished they'd all disappear.

They'd be scattered all over the house and garden now, like children at recess, but they'd regroup for the sweets and later still for the leftovers, the drinks, and the good-nights. Jake Junior and what's-her-name would be off looking for some corner to pet in. Cordy would make some excuse to leave early, probably saying she had to get back to her book. Lethia had said that Cordy was involved in the "creative process," but as far as Nonnie was could see, the girl was just getting more ingrown, sitting back and watching people as though she was always taking notes. Vivian seemed all right, happy in a slatternly sort of way, though she did have that young Billy on her hands; and Billy, poor boy, was marching to the beat of a much slower drummer. Phillip didn't look too good either. His color was bad and the way he kept talking about what he was going to do when he retired was a sure sign that he had a health problem he didn't want to face. Still, Constance had a firm hand on the rudder. Constance couldn't count on any help from her children, but she was financially secure.

And Lucille . . . She didn't want to think about Lucille. Except for a measly hundred-dollar check that had come in the mail, Lucille had never mentioned anything about the affair with Jacques Haur. There was no way of knowing what was going on with Lucille, but somewhere between a prayer and a face-lift, she figured Lucille would pull through.

Shutting her eyes, Nonnie crossed her ankles, careful not to muss the skirt of her good silk dress. She had counted her chicks and appraised their needs. Next week she would talk to old man Claxton and make a few changes in her will. Old man Claxton would look at her funny, though at the retainer she was paying him she didn't feel he was entitled to anything more than a smile of gratitude, and he would bring the will up to date. That was the most she could do:

Feed them, love them, study them, and make her plans accordingly.
The Christmas get-together had served its purpose.

A shaft of light from the hallway made her stir. "Nonnie, may I
come in?" she heard Jeanette ask, though the child had already come
to the side of the bed. "Mama says if you don't want to get up can
we serve the desserts, 'cause more people have come and I've been
waiting for the cakes for a real long time."

"I guess I drifted off. Oh, it's already dark outside, isn't it.
Climb on the bed and let me see you."

"But it's dark."

"I already know how you look, so I can see you in the dark."

"You're like a cat, Nonnie. Cats can see in the dark," Jeanette
whispered, hoisting herself up onto the bed and taking her hand. "I
like to feel your skin, Nonnie, 'cause it's like Play Dough. It wiggles
all around."

"That it does, sugar. That it does."

"I ate all my vegetables, did you see? So what's for dessert?"

"There's coconut cake and rum balls and three kinds of pie and
divinity. Bernice made us some peanut fudge. And there's pecan-
cherry cake and . . . oh, my, another Christmas coming to an end."

Clay Claxton had turned the key in the ignition, but he didn't
move his car. It was almost midnight and the airport parking lot was
all but deserted. He'd been traveling since early morning and was
bone tired. Still, he didn't move. He watched the couple who were
standing some fifty feet away beneath the arc light decorated with a
plastic Christmas wreath. He'd noticed the guy on the flight. It had
been hard not to notice him, because he was wearing red-checkered
pants, a sports jacket that wouldn't button over his paunch, and his
haircut looked as though someone had put a bowl on his head and
whacked around it with a blunt knife. Poor slob, he'd thought. Now
the guy was backed up against a camper, and a woman with peroxided
hair and an equally unfortunate choice of clothes was tickling him and
reaching into his breast pocket. After a playful struggle to the accompaniment of a country-western tune that blasted out of the camper,
she extracted some trinket. The guy made a lunge for her and they
wound their arms around each other. They didn't kiss. They just held
on tight, swaying slightly beneath the arc light. And who's callin' who
a poor slob, he thought as he drove his Volvo toward the ticket booth.

New Year's Eve was four days away and he'd accepted several
invitations. If he turned up alone he'd be out of place and have to

face all that "eligible bachelor" crap. Of course, he could ask Michelle to fly in from Atlanta, but that meant she'd want to stay for the entire weekend. She'd loll around his apartment wearing his robe and talk about her most recent psychological "breakthrough." No. Michelle was out. Perhaps Jill . . . No, not Jill either. To hell with resolutions; he was going to call Cordy. After the scene on Thanksgiving night he'd vowed not to call her. If she ever got her act together she could damned well call him. But she probably didn't have a date for New Year's and he wanted to be with a woman who would do him proud, a woman he could talk with. "Bullshit, Claxton," he muttered as he pulled onto the highway, "you just want to see her."

Though Cordy and Clay had the breeding and the looks to be the perfect social couple, it was obvious to everyone who watched them that they wanted to be alone. At the first party of the evening, as they sat at the table eating the traditional Hoppin' John that was supposed to bring good luck, they didn't seem to notice the people around them. Later, at Judge and Mrs. Cavanaugh's house, Cordy chatted with other guests, but her eyes were on Clay. Clay listened while the judge explained a new regulation governing international shipping, but his leg jiggled with impatience. They excused themselves as soon as it was politely possible to do so, saying that they were going to a restaurant a friend of Clay's had just opened.

Clay took the longest route to get there because he wanted to hear more about Cordy's book contract. They lingered in the car, oblivious of the merrymakers carousing along River Street, while Cordy asked about his trip. (She was curious to know if he'd seen his old girlfriend while he was in London, but only asked about his business and the shows he'd seen in the West End.) Clay's friend Mike Petrokins finally put an end to the conversation by putting his head in the window and asking why they hadn't come inside. They followed him to the restaurant, but after twenty minutes of deafening disco, flashing lights, and a mob whose collective will was aimed at drunken oblivion, they pushed their way to the exit.

"It's Alison and Kevin's place next," he told her as they got into the car. "They should be a bit more civilized."

"I don't think there is such a thing as a civilized New Year's Eve party," Cordy said as she moved to the far side of the seat. "Maybe we could just go back to your place."

He'd considered suggesting that himself, but had thought better of it, knowing that he couldn't trust himself under those circumstances. The evening had convinced him that he wouldn't mind courting her for a long time, but when he made his move he wasn't going to take no for an answer. "I don't have much to drink," he stalled.

"Not even a bottle of cooking sherry?"

"I don't cook."

"It doesn't matter. I've had enough to drink already. In fact"— she smiled mischievously—"I'm a little high."

"O.K. We can drop by my place. At least we'll be able to toast the New Year without being mauled by a bunch of drunks. After that we'll go to Kevin and Alison's place." No, he would not even touch her. He wouldn't want her to wake up and feel remorse because she'd been tipsy.

"Hey, we'd better hurry up. It's almost midnight."

When he pulled up to the curb on the quiet, dark street they could already hear horns honking in the distance. "Guess we missed it," he said, helping her out of the car. It seemed a bad omen, evidence that they would always be doomed to miss the main event, that their timing would always be off. "Well, Happy New Year, Cordy." He put his arms around her and kissed her lightly, then started to release her. To his surprise she clung to him. She had made up her mind when he had called and asked her out that she wanted him. It was a purely physical thing. And this time she would give herself without any emotional complications.

"This beaded thing you're wearing looks kinda fragile," he said, drawing back.

"Oh, I found it in Nonnie's trunk." She followed him up the pathway, trying to fathom his aloofness.

He unlocked the door and turned on the light. A leather couch, a large oak desk, and a stereo were the only pieces of furniture. Cartons of books were stacked against the walls. "That's as far as I got with the interior decorating." He nodded toward a nineteenth-century seascape that was mounted above the desk. "Make youself at home. What would you like to drink?"

"A light bourbon and water. Where's the bathroom?"

"Through the bedroom. Over there." His voice was husky. He turned quickly and walked out of the room.

She stood in front of the bathroom mirror trembling slightly. Her indicision lasted only a moment. Then she lifted the beaded vest over her head.

"Cordy, where are you?" He paused on the threshold of the bedroom, drinks in his hands. The bathroom door opened and he saw her silhouetted against the light. She was wearing only the black strapless dress. Her hair was down. Her feet were bare.

He moved to the bed and set the drinks down on the night table without taking his eyes from her. It wasn't how he'd thought it would happen. He hadn't told her how much he cared about her; she had made no admission of affection to him. "Oh, Christ," he said, "come on over here. Now."

Chapter XXI

"We don't have this style shoe in a triple A, Mrs. Hampton, but if you're taken with it I'll be glad to special-order for you."

As Nonnie moved her feet in the shiny teal-blue shoes, an illustration from a children's book came to her mind. She couldn't recall if she had owned the book as a child or if she had given it to one of her own children, but she could almost feel the heavy glossy paper and she could see the picture in minute detail of Cinderella seated next to the hearth while the prince fitted the glass slipper onto her foot. What she'd liked best about it was the frog with the expectant but sorrowful grin perched next to Cinderella's hand. Perhaps the shoe-store owner, Mr. Knowles, with his bulging eyes and mouth that almost stretched from ear to ear, had put her in mind of the frog.

"Would you like to special-order, Mrs. Hampton?"

"I'd buy them in a heartbeat if you had them in my size, Mr. Knowles, but I guess circumstances is going to rescue me from impulse. I think I'll pass. Sorry to trouble you."

"No trouble at all, Mrs. Hampton. You're one of our best customers and we're always glad to see you."

"I had no mind to be shoe shopping today, but when I passed your window these caught my eye. It's been a long time since I've gone dancing, but I guess shoes will always be my greatest weakness."

She slipped her feet out of the shoes and looked down. There was that hateful bunion protruding from the big toe of her left foot. It had been there for years, but the sight of it always shocked her, always made her feel as though someone else's foot had been attached to her leg while she wasn't looking. It was one thing to get up in the morning and approach your face, knowing that a strange old woman was going to stare back at you, and over the last few decades she'd accustomed herself to the alien image caught by chance in a store window, but this foot with the bunion simply wasn't hers. She shoved it into her navy-blue pumps.

Knowing that business was bad, she lingered at the door to ask after Mr. Knowles's family and noticed a large leather bag of the sort she'd carried diapers in. The bag would be perfect for Cordy's books and papers.

"I do believe I'll take this here bag."

Mr. Knowles gave her a smile that was a mite more genuine than the one he'd given when she'd decided not to buy the shoes and asked the salesgirl to write up the slip. Nonnie leaned over the counter to check the girl's calculations. Shopping was such a chore these days. The salespeople were so careless you wondered what they'd learned in school. As she put the sales slip into her purse, she noticed the date: March 12. It had a significance she couldn't put her finger on. Was it someone's birthday that she had forgotten? Did she have an appointment she'd neglected to keep?

She shrugged and stepped out onto Broughton Street, pausing to admire the display shoes that had drawn her into the store, then she started toward the intersection. For a Friday afternoon there wasn't much activity on the street and most of the shoppers were black. She wasn't sure if they came out of habit, or because some didn't have cars to get out to the shopping centers, or out of some sense of territoriality, for this was where they'd sat down at the dimestore lunch counters. The street was starting to look pitiful. The clothing store next to Mr. Knowles's Red Cross Shoes was all locked up, with a sign in the window saying it was relocating out at the Mall; the old movie theater was closed up too, and across the street she could see some young bucks hanging around that nasty place where they had the pinball machines and video games.

She made a mental note to call Amos Justice and ask how he

was coming with the Youth Employment Program, and she planned
to speak her piece about the revitalization of Broughton Street at the
next realtors' meeting. She'd have to be careful not to show her prejudice about the Mall, but she couldn't stand the place. All those
smelly parking lots, Musak piped in at you so you couldn't hear
yourself think, so many big stores you never got to know the owners
by name, that big box cut up into four little boxes that they dared to
call a movie theater, and all those young people lolling around as
though they had nothing in the world to do with their time. And all
of it enclosed, so that you couldn't tell what time of day it was or
what the weather was like.

She looked up at the brilliant blue skies with scudding clouds.
As she waited for the light to change, she heard a piercing, helpless
wail and turned to see a boy of about three, miserable ooze pouring
from his nose and eyes, being shaken and told to keep still. She was
tempted to say something chastising to the mother, or at least try to
explain to her that a child's pain was worse than any other, because a
child had no sense of past or future and was so utterly dependent.

The cry of a sick child always pierced her heart. Her little
brother Benjie had cried like that. Poor little Benjie, burning up with
the fever that finally consumed him. March 12, 1911. That was the
date of Benjie's death. And about five years later, when Nonnie was
just sixteen, her mother had died on March fifteenth. She would
never forget how raw the weather had been, as though the heavens
had opened up to weep with her. November seventh was when Tabitha had died. And July fourth was Lonnie's last day. She had never
known the date of Wade's death. The "missing in action" notification
had come months before the final word. There were only three hundred and sixty-five days in the year, and she could mark as many of
them with death dates as with birth dates. More than sadness, she
felt a sort of emptiness that made her weary.

The light turned green and she crossed the street. It was two
o'clock and she'd had no lunch, but since she hated to eat alone, she
decided she would walk by the river before she dropped by the
building on St. Julian Street to check up on Mr. Dozier and his
boys.

She crept crablike down one of the steep cobblestone stairways
going down to the waterfront. It was foolishly vain of her to persist
in wearing high heels when so many of the city's streets were uneven, but there was something about sensible shoes that always
made her feel poor.

"New shoes, new shoes,
Pretty pink and blue shoes,
That's the sort I want.
But flat shoes, fat shoes,
Wipe-them-on-the-mat shoes,
That's the sort I'll get."

She laughed at herself. She must be going soft in the head, singsonging old rhymes.

A Japanese cargo ship was heading out to sea. One of the sailors was throwing something, bread she supposed, into the water and the gulls dipped and glided after it. A chilly breeze brought out her goose bumps as she walked gingerly over the trolley tracks and to the railing. She raised her arm and waved farewell to the sailor and he waved back. How her imagination had flown the first time she had seen a ship. She had read *Treasure Island* and told her mother that she wanted to be a sailor, but Mama had said that girls couldn't be sailors. Yet water had always been associated with escape in her mind. Here on the bluff Lonnie had proposed to her and that had been her escape and her adventure.

She left the railing and sat down on a bench, wanting to stretch out, close her eyes, and let the sun warm her face. Instead she sat upright holding her gift to Cordy and her purse in her lap. Memories of the past were pulling at her so strongly today that it seemed silly to resist them. Giving way would be like setting down a burden, like resting.

The night had been warm, but here on the waterfront a breeze had ruffled her hair and swirled the skirts of her gingham dress that still smelled of soap. They had walked and talked. Lonnie had kissed her. She could remember the kiss more totally than she could remember her wedding night, for the kiss held the seeds of all future surrenders. The kiss had made the promise. Lonnie had taken her in his arms. She had acknowledged the necessity of refusal only briefly. Then she had parted her lips and let him find the soft, wet secret of her mouth. She had kept her eyes closed even after he had opened his, and she could feel his gaze on her. She had kept her eyes closed and willed him to propose and save her from a future that held only loneliness and dreams if she chose not to marry, or early aging and drudgery should she accept a proposal from one of the mill hands. When she'd opened her eyes and seen him staring into her own with a tender curiosity as well as a surprise at her passionate response, she had known that her wish would come true. He was too honorable to take her and cast her aside.

She wanted him to know that she would be a partner for all of his dreams as well as a mate for his bed. So she took his arm and they started to walk again, she inquiring about his plans for the future, asking him how the Armistice would affect the cotton market. Yes, the kiss had held the seeds of that June night, months after their marriage, when Lonnie had persuaded her to take off their night-clothes and they had made love completely naked . . . or that night after they'd been told of Wade's death.

Years of petty differences, misunderstandings, complacency—the banality of the everyday—had all but obliterated even the memory of tenderness or desire. They had held each other for comfort only; but then the anguish, the loss, the desperate knowledge of mortality, had brought them together with a hunger so unexpected and violent that the next morning as they sat at the breakfast table, a middle-age couple in carpet slippers, they had averted their eyes from one another in embarrassment.

And when she's nursed him through his long decline, saliva drooling from his mouth, his eyes giving little hint of recognition, let alone the appreciation she yearned for in order to keep her strength up, when she'd interpreted his slurred words for the relatives and visitors, oh, she could remember how those relatives and visitors had looked at her, seeing her as the good wife who honored her pledge "in sickness and in health." But no mere pledge could have bound her to such servitude had she not remembered those crucial turning points and the promise of that first kiss.

She shivered and wrapped her arms around herself. Her foot had fallen asleep and her fingers felt numb. As she inhaled the smell of the river, her mouth watered for shrimps. She decided to go by the fish store and buy some before she went to check up on Mr. Dozier's boys.

Cordy was fixing supper and Jeanette was sitting at the kitchen table doing her homework when the phone rang.

"Cordy, this is Bernice. I hope I'm not troublin' you, but I'd like for you to come over if you could."

"Is anything the matter?"

"It's Miz Hampton. Seems like she crawled up on some ladder

at one of the buildings that's being fixed up and she fell down and cracked her head. Mr. Dozier had to bring her home in his car."

"Is she badly hurt? Have you called the doctor?"

"Now you know how she is about doctors. That's why I'm calling you. She says it's nothing but a little knot, wouldn't even lie down when she first come home. Later she admitted as to how she was feeling giddy and went up to her room, but she swears she won't have no doctor. I stayed on, thinking she would wake up, but now it's getting dark—"

"I'll be right over."

"I figured you could maybe talk her round. You know she won't stand no one being bossy with her, but at her age it seems to me she ought to have that knot looked at."

Cordy took the liberty of calling Dr. Skinner but only got his answering machine. She left Nonnie's number, bundled Jeanette into the car, and drove over. Bernice had fixed a supper tray and said she would sit in the kitchen with Jeanette while Cordy took it upstairs.

"Nonnie? Nonnie, it's me, Cordy. May I turn on the lamp?" Cordy set the tray on the dresser and tiptoed to the bed. Nonnie stirred but did not answer.

"Nonnie, are you asleep?"

"Not anymore. You just woke me up, didn't you? Would you mind telling me what you're doing over here? No, you don't have to tell me. Bernice has been busybodying around and getting everyone riled up. I told her . . ." The rest of the sentence became garbled in a yawn.

"Nonnie, I'm turning on the lamp. I want to look at your head."

"There's nothing to look at," Nonnie said impatiently, blinking at the light, her hand going up to touch the back of her head. "Didn't even take a gash. An egg, that's all, a little old lumpy egg-size thing. And I tell you how it happened. I tried to point out to Mr. Dozier where one of the painters had done a sloppy job. Dozier pretended not to see it, so I had to crawl up on this fool ladder to point it out, and either me or the ladder wasn't steady.

"Now Dozier's so mad at me he's threatening not to do business with me anymore. Says his insurance won't cover old ladies climbing up on ladders. It used to be when you hurt yourself people asked how you were, now they fuss at you about their insurance premiums. Well"—she propped herself up on one elbow, her eyes sharp with indignation—"I told Dozier that *I* may not want to do business with *him* anymore if he's going to carry on in such an ungentlemanly fashion. I expect the real reason he got mad is because I was right. You should have seen the island that painter left. It was the size of your hand. Anyone God gave eyes to could have seen it."

"I've already called Dr. Skinner's office and he wasn't in. But when he calls back I know he's going to say we should go over to the hospital and have your head X-rayed. So why don't we just get in my car and drive on over there now."

"You're the one who needs to have your head examined if you think I'm rushing over to the hospital for a little lump. And what's that there tray doing on the dresser?" She knitted her brows in disapproval. "I'm perfectly capable of coming down for supper if I feel like eating, which I don't. But since you and Jeanette are here, I might as well bring myself downstairs and share your company. Have you eaten yet?"

"No, but that's not important. Nonnie, I wish . . ."

Nonnie was already struggling to the side of the bed. "If I didn't have a headache before, I'm sure going to get one now if you don't stop badgering me. Just reach me those slippers, will you? This arthritis will spoil my sweet nature yet." Cordy put the slippers onto Nonnie's feet and followed her out of the room. "I bought you a present today, Cordy. I was going to put it away till your birthday, but . . ."

Nonnie took only toast and tea at supper. Bernice, who was still lingering in the kitchen, noted her lack of appetite, but before she could offer it as proof of illness, Nonnie fixed her with a reproachful stare. Since it was Friday night, Cordy said that she and Jeanette would sleep over and she sent Bernice home. Nonnie was too grateful to raise an objection, and she was too tired to protest when Jeanette took her by the hand and led her to the TV, but some time later, when Mr. Dozier called, she perked up and told Cordy to thank him for his concern, say she was feeling fine but was in no mood for conversation.

"You always put me to bed, Nonnie, but you're sick tonight so I get to put you to bed," Jeanette told her when the late news came on. Nonnie allowed herself to be led upstairs.

Cordy sat alone in the parlor. Nonnie appeared to have been tired and a bit shaken up, but apart from that she seemed normal. In all probability the fall and the bump on the head were nothing to be alarmed about. She would give Dr. Skinner another call in the morning. Since she saw the hopelessness of trying to get Nonnie to visit his office, she wanted to persuade him to drop by, though even Skinner's urgings would not be enough to get Nonnie to the hospital if she didn't want to go. She sighed, turned off the lights, and started up to bed.

Jeanette was sitting on the topmost stair sucking on the end of her ponytail. "I've put the patient to bed," she whispered, her voice full of the melodramatic pity of a TV hospital show but ringing with triumph that she had been able, at least in play, to order Nonnie around. "Do I have to take my bath tonight?"

"No. I guess you could skip it. Come on now, I'll tuck you in."

"Nurses don't get tucked in. And you know what, Mama? I don't have any pajamas here, so I guess I'll sleep in my nudy."

"All right," Cordy helped her up and smacked her bottom. "Sure you don't want me to tuck you in?"

Jeanette shook her head, kissed Cordy's stomach, and ran into her room. Cordy took a deep breath and walked to Nonnie's door. The bedroom was dark. Nonnie's head had almost disappeared into the white of the pillows. Her eyes were closed, but she turned her palm upward, inviting Cordy's touch. "Do you want to borrow a nightdress, sugar? Sit with me a minute. Sit and let me thank you for going to all this trouble. It's not that I need you here, but it's always nice to have your company. Now sit and tell me how you are, how you really are, not just the tewky little everyday stuff."

"I'm fine, Nonnie. You're probably fine too, but I do wish—"

"I am fine. And are you pleased with how you're coming on the book? How's Fanny?"

"Fanny's fine and I'm almost two-thirds of the way through. It's up and down. I'm pleased one day, disgusted the next. I have an awful lot to learn and sometimes I get discouraged, but I guess that's the nature of the beast."

"But look how far you've come, Cordy. Look how far you've come. You'll be able to earn your own way, and that'll do you the world of good. And"—she tilted her head coquettishly—"how are things with Clay?"

"Just fine. We're good friends."

"More'n friends, surely. When he came by the house last week I saw the way he was looking at you. And I've seen you give more'n just a sisterly glance in his direction. If I can see a spot a painter's left on a ceiling you can bet I can see that. He's ripe to get married,

Cordy. If you don't pluck him off the tree he'll fall into some other woman's lap."

"Nonnie, please. No matchmaking. Not every relationship has to end in marriage. We're getting along just fine as it is."

"I'm not going to say any of those nasty things 'bout a man not buying a cow if he can get the milk for free—"

"I think you just did," Cordy interrupted.

"But you are spending a lot of time with him. You're making an investment. And if you're making an investment you might as well have a contract."

"Nonnie, that's so bourgeois." Cordy stifled a yawn, but at the mention of Clay a ripple of pleasure went through her, and it wasn't just thoughts of past and future pleasures of the bed. They'd made jokes about their "compatibility" from the first, enjoying lusty animal sex while steering clear of "emotional complications." But last week a subtle but definite change had taken place. They'd kissed a million times, pressed lips onto each other's shoulders, arms, genitals, legs, and backs. But this particular kiss . . .

They'd come back from an afternoon on the boat. Jeanette had already taken the picnic basket and was ambling up the dock. Cordy was tying the rope to the mooring and Clay crouched next to her watching. "Hey, you've really gotten the hang of that now," he'd complimented her as he tugged at the knot. He took her hands to help her up. They'd risen in a single fluid movement, looking into each other's eyes, and then their lips had come together. The kiss was given and received down the length of her body, from the top of her newly washed hair to the tip of her canvas shoes, every inch of her alive to the direct sensation of contact, his penis pressing into her belly, her nose tilted to the side of his, smelling the salt and sun on his face, every sense willing, ready to merge. And then they had looked into each other's eyes, offering a wordless promise. There was such a pledge in that kiss that it had frightened her. She dared not trust it. And yet . . .

"I can see you're not paying any attention to me, Cordy, so go on to bed and I'll see you in the morning."

"Sorry. I guess I'm tired," she said as she patted Nonnie's hand and got up.

"One last thing," Nonnie continued as Cordy started to leave. "It's no good for a woman to come to a man unless she's got her own dignity."

"I guess not," Cordy yawned again as she backed off.

"But you don't want dignity to stiffen into pride. You know I was at Lethia's for lunch last Wednesday and I noticed how sorry she's gotten since she's been living alone. Talks about her aches and her pains all the time, and persnickety! I just moved one of her little what-nots from her chiffonier and she acted like I'd changed the structure of the universe." Cordy put her hands on her hips and shifted her weight onto one foot, wondering what the arrangement of Lethia's treasures had to do with her. "People kinda shrink when they live alone," Nonnie went on. "They get set in their ways so's they lose their elastic. After a while they can't change."

"I don't live alone, Nonnie. I live with Jeanette."

"You know how fast that child is growing? I can see the changes from week to week. Another ten years, maybe even eight, she won't be needing you anymore."

"I can't see ten years ahead. And there's lots of good things about living alone too, Nonnie. Privacy, time to think—"

"Loneliness comes to all of us soon enough, Cordy. Soon enough the world will be depopulated of most of those you've loved most. But the worst kind of loneliness is not being able to trust. If you have your dignity you can trust. You must."

Cordy stifled another yawn. "Yes, I know."

"Long as you know. Good night darlin'."

Toward dawn Cordy heard a crash. She bolted up, pulled the sheet around her, and rushed into the hallway. The bedside lamp was on in Nonnie's room, but the bed was empty. She checked the adjoining bathroom, hurried to Jeanette's door, then stood shivering, her ears pricked, until she realized that the noise was coming from downstairs.

When she opened the kitchen door she saw Nonnie, still wearing her nightdress, standing at the sink and greasing one of several large baking pans.

"Nonnie. What in heaven's name are you doing?"

"Don't know if three pans will be enough," Nonnie muttered to herself.

"What do you think you're doing?" Cordy asked again, exasperation creeping into her voice.

"That's easy to see, Ettie. I'm making cornbread." Nonnie turned, her mouth pursed with impatience, her nostrils flaring; before her glance softened admiringly. "Cordy. What a sight you are with your hair all tumbling down like that. Why, your shoulders are prettier than my statue on the mantelpiece."

Cordy shook her head. "You're making cornbread at five-thirty in the morning?" she asked with a helpless laugh.

Nonnie joined her laughter, looking down at the spilled corn-meal and the piece of eggshell that floated in the bowl of buttermilk. She couldn't imagine who'd made such a mess. Her merriment changed to soft perplexed chuckles, then dipped into shy self-consciousness, and finally rose into a relaxed, good-humored aware-ness of a joke at her own expense. "I guess it is a little early in the morning," she said sheepishly.

"Why don't you go on back to bed? If you want cornbread I'll make it later, and," Cordy added, slowing her speech and talking as firmly as if she were making a bargain with Jeanette, "if I make the cornbread then you have to agree to visit Dr. Skinner."

Nonnie wiped her hands down the front of her nightdress and nodded. "I like Joe Skinner. Yes, I'll see Joe."

"Good. Now come on up to bed, and have yourself a good rest."

As Cordy helped her into bed and drew the covers up to her neck, Nonnie stared into her face until her gaze seemed to lose its focus. Her eyes glimmered with the milky, expectant look of an in-fant's. Her mouth opened and turned up in a fatuous, almost simple-minded smile before her eyes focused again. Then, as Cordy stroked the wisps of hair back from Nonnie's wrinkled forehead, Nonnie reminded her that the oven ran hot, so she would have to set it twenty-five degrees below the desired temperature.

After cleaning up the mess in the kitchen Cordy sat drinking cup after cup of coffee, until Bernice arrived. She told Bernice about Nonnie's behavior, but Bernice said that once or twice before she had come to the house to find Nonnie cooking in the early hours of the morning. "It don't mean she's gone silly, just years and years of doin' like that, she sometime slip and makes it her pleasure again," Bernice explained. They went upstairs and saw that Nonnie was resting peacefully, her chest barely rising but a soft snore coming from her open mouth. "Best let her rest," Bernice advised. "Sleep be better'n a doctor for our pains. You go on home and change your clothes, Cordy. I think she be fine."

"I have to drop Jeanette off at a Brownie cookout at noon, but by then I should have reached Skinner and persuaded him to come by. She's agreed to see him."

"That's good. You start forcin' an ol' person like they was a child, it make them a child."

When Cordy returned in the early afternoon, she was in another quandary. Dr. Skinner's nurse had told her that he was playing in a golf tournament at Hilton Head but suggested that his new associate would be glad to visit. Knowing Nonnie's reaction to a strange doctor who'd barely passed his thirtieth birthday, Cordy anticipated another session of delicate negotiation.

Bernice was sitting by Nonnie's bedside reading her Bible. She told Cordy that Nonnie had still been feeling nauseated at lunchtime and had come back to bed immediately afterwards.

"It's not normal for her to be so tired like that," Cordy whispered. "I'm going to wake her up and drive her to the hospital."

"What we gonna do, Cordy, pick her up and carry her?"

"She was disoriented this morning. I know she was. If I take a really firm tone with her, I think I can get her to come. Nonnie?" Cordy raised her voice and came closer to the bed. "Nonnie, can you hear me?"

A faraway voice echoed in Nonnie's brain. Who was that calling her? Who wanted to pull her away from the seashore where she was enjoying herself so? She didn't want to answer. It was so lovely here with the children, crowds of them, not just her own Wade, but many children, black and white. She sifted the sand and it formed cakes in her hands, cakes that puffed up and baked in the sun. There were so many mouths to feed that she was afraid of spilling, afraid of it seeping away. She looked up and saw Lonnie sitting out in his boat. It must be that Lonnie was calling her. He put down the oars and tilted his straw hat back on his head, smiling and raising his arm. She could see the arm close. Suntanned it was, bulging against the damp cloth of his rolled-up sleeve. She stood up, raised her skirts above her knees, and began to roll down her stockings. As she reached the water's edge, he turned the boat and started to row further out. The water lapped against her legs, deliciously warm. Up to her knees she was now, so that she had to raise her skirt still higher, and she became afraid. But then he motioned for her again, his eyes teasing her fear. The water would not be too deep. He extended his arm as though inviting her to dance. Further and further she waded. Her feet left the sandy bottom and she was engulfed. Floating in the luminous shining water, her whole body washed clean, and behind her eyes the glowing orb of the sun.

"Nonnie?" Cordy brought her face close enough to feel the issue of warm breath. "Nonnie," she said more sharply, gently slapping her hands. Cordy raised her head and met Bernice's eyes which were as wide and shocked as her own. She put her arms around Nonnie and tried to lift her out of the pillows, while Bernice flung back the covers.

"I do believe she's wet the bed," Bernice whispered. "She's never done that before. Miz Hampton, oh, Miz Hampton." Bernice's arms entwined with Cordy's and she cradled Nonnie's head against her breast. "She passed out, Cordy. I believe it's her time. I believe she gonna go."

"Don't you say that," Cordy almost shouted.

"We best call the doctor again an' leave her be. She want to go in her own bed I know."

"Be quiet! She's going to be all right. She's just got a little bump on her head. Now hold her while I go call the ambulance. She's not going to die!"

Through the lobby doors of the emergency waiting room the sky was changing from a streaked coral into a placid deep blue. The two women sat motionless, oblivious of the couple sharing a bag of peanuts from the snack machine and the fat man in work clothes who paced in front of them biting his nails.

"It's almost dark. I'm gonna try to give your folks a call, again," Bernice said. "Unless they're staying out for supper, they'd be coming on home by now."

Cordy swept her hair back from her face as an acknowledging gesture, and Bernice rose to her feet and walked off in the direction of the telephone.

"Mrs. Tyre?"

Cordy looked up into the bloodshot eyes of the doctor.

"Mrs. Tyre, could you come into the conference room with me?" He turned abruptly, walked down the hallway, his shoes squeaking on the buffed linoleum, and pushed open the door to a boxlike room with green walls, a Formica-topped table, and several plastic chairs. Closing the door, he motioned to her to sit, then he turned away from her gaze, crumpled a Styrofoam cup, and tossed it into a wastebasket. "Mrs. Tyre," he began again.

"She's dead, isn't she?"

"Yes, ma'am. I'm sorry to have to tell you that your grand-mother passed away a few minutes ago. She died of a subdural arachnoid." He cleared his throat, watching her. When she did not move he went on. "That is, the blow to her head started an internal hemorrhage. The blood oozes slowly from the ruptured vessels, almost like a web. Arachnoid is after the word 'spider.' She had apparently gone into a coma early this afternoon. I am very sorry, but there was nothing more that we could do."

"No. Was she . . ." The question choked. What was she going to ask? What answer could possibly be given? Her eyes blurred as she studied a heart with initials that had been scratched into the tabletop; and then, as though she'd been hurled through space, the floor of her stomach dropped.

"She was absolutely not in pain. She went very peacefully. I'm not just saying that to comfort you, Mrs. Tyre. It was just as though she went to sleep."

"But she won't wake up." Cordy's arms dropped between her legs and her head fell to her chest. "Oh, god, oh, god, oh, god," she said softly, over and over again so that the words began to sound like gibberish, some incantation in a forgotten language. Then, like a rope that she could clutch to stop herself from plummeting further into the abyss, obligations, arrangements, the necessity of notifying people, came into her mind. She held onto the edge of the table and got to her feet. "Thank you, doctor." She looked at his white coat. A tiny speck of blood near his nameplate absorbed her attention. "Thank you so very much. And now if you'll excuse me, I must tell my friend Bernice and . . ." She got to the door and stopped again. Some half-formed questions floated into her mind and then submerged. He opened the door for her and stood aside.

Chapter XXII

The breeze from the marshes was brisk enough to sway the moss on the overarching trees, but the warmth of the sun and the insistent unevolved hum of insects gave the afternoon a feeling of drowsy remembrance. Strange, Cordy thought, that a crowd so large could be so quiet that the caw of a bird and the sound of the doors of the hearse being opened were sharp and distinct. She took Jeanette's gloved hand and stared down at her hair, which looked particularly alive and gleaming. From the corner of her eye she could see the pallbearers setting the casket on the dirt just outside the fence of the family plot. Lifting her head, she looked past those gathered around the gravesite to the multitudes that lined the pathways almost down to the marshes. There must have been a few hundred people—friends, neighbors, distant relatives, business associates, church members—faces she knew but had trouble recognizing out of their usual context—the mailman, the owner of the shoe store—all the people Nonnie had known, and perhaps because of the eulogies in all the papers, some people Nonnie had never even met.

Scanning the faces, she realized that she was looking for Clay. She thought she'd seen him just moments before getting out of a limousine with the mayor. If she could just see his face and have him look back at her in that intimate, knowing way, as though he understood just what she might be feeling (even though she didn't know what she was feeling herself), how reassuring that would be. Her skin felt itchy under the new black dress. She'd bought the dress in a hurry, not really noticing that it was too tight across the bust. Now she rounded her shoulders to stop the front buttons from pulling. The aroma of the honeysuckle and verbena, smells she usually loved, seemed sickly sweet. Her stomach growled. She realized that she'd had nothing but coffee all day, and it had left a sour taste in her mouth.

She blinked against the sun and turned her eyes to Lonnie's headstone. "And now abideth faith, hope, love, these three; but the greatest of these is love." The open grave where Nonnie would lie was crowded so close to Lonnie's that she had an image of a couple sleeping in a single bed. Nonnie would be the last to be laid to rest in the Hampton plot, but, she reasoned, most of the family had gone from Savannah. They were scattered all over the country. Some, Vivian's oldest son, for example, had lived in Germany for years. They did not come together for marriages and births anymore. Most did not even come for burials. The majority of her cousins had only wired flowers, and a few store-bought sympathy cards had already arrived. But Uncle Phillip and Aunt Constance had flown in. Phillip stood just outside the rusted iron gate, Constance on one arm, Vivian on the other, and Cousin Stephanie stood behind them looking sullen. And there, near Great-Grandmother Ettie's headstone, was Uncle John. His splotchy face registered an indistinct but definite fear, as though the notion of mortality had just come upon him. Cissy held on to his elbow, using her other hand to secure her broad-brimmed hat against the breeze. Winetta, in close proximity, still seemed to be alone, her silent tears disappearing into the soft grooves of her cheeks. Joan Witherspoon and Lethia Grant, in dark suits that probably smelled of mothballs, stood side by side like unused book-ends. And Cousin Curtis and his lover were over there near the big oak tree. They stood close together so that their shoulders and hands might touch accidentally.

As the minister sidestepped the clods of earth mounded at the side of the grave, Cordy heard a loud gasping sob. She looked behind her, past her father's shoulder, to see George Naughton, tears flowing from his shocked, protruding eyes. He passed his hand over his mouth, felt in his breast pocket, and looked about helplessly. A black woman with a cold, wizened face, his housekeeper Cordy guessed, moved to his side and pressed a crumpled handkerchief into his hand. Deeply embarrassed, he buried his face in it, his shoulders still heaving in spasms of grief. Cordy felt her father's hand come to

rest on her shoulder and moved ever so slightly to acknowledge his
touch. Jeanette sneezed, drew her hand away from Cordy's long
enough to wipe her nose, then looked up apologetically, eyes wide.
Cordy squeezed her hand and glanced across at her brother. Jake
Junior looked stoic and slightly awkward. Taffy was blubbering and
shaking her head in the sort of public display that made Cordy want
to slap her. She guessed Taffy hadn't gone through too much suffering if she could make such a show of it and decided she didn't much
like her future sister-in-law.

The minister reached the head of the grave and waited for all
movement to stop. An even deeper hush fell on the crowd. As he
opened his mouth to speak, Cordy looked to her immediate left
where Lucille was standing. The upper part of Lucille's face was
hidden beneath the veil of her hat. Her lips were bloodless and trembled uncontrollably, though Cordy had seen her take two Valium
just before they'd left the house. Cordy felt for her hand and took it
in her own, where it stayed, unresponsive as a piece of wood. She
sighed and exerted a gentle pressure, but Lucille's hand did not respond to her touch.

The day after Nonnie had died, when she and Lucille had been
making preparations for the funeral, they'd had one of those violent,
painfully inappropriate but absolutely predictable arguments that
erupt between family members in a time of crisis. Lucille had insisted that the Episcopal minister be invited to perform the service.
Cordy had insisted that Nonnie would have wanted the Unitarian
minister. She was convinced that Bernice would back up her choice
and against Lucille's wishes she had telephoned her. Bernice said
there was no cause for argument, because shortly after Lonnie's
death Nonnie had made a list of instructions for her own funeral.
She said she was sorry for not mentioning it sooner and told Cordy
she would find the instructions underneath the paper lining of the
middle drawer of Nonnie's bureau.

The list was exact, detailed, and even humorous. Fox and
Weeks were to be the funeral directors. There was to be no viewing
of the body, because "I won't want people looking at me when I
can't look back at them." The only memorial service was to be at the
gravesite at Bonaventure Cemetery. It was to be conducted by the
Unitarian minister and he was to limit his remarks to five minutes. A
reception was to be given at the house following the burial. Plenty of
food and liquor should be served, but not in the good crystal. There
were to be no flowers except those cut from her own garden, but

those who wished to send flowers should be instructed to make a contribution in kind to the King Tisdale House, a tiny black-history museum in a Negro neighborhood.

This last request had given Lucille an uneasy intimation of what the further disposition of property might be. "We have enough on our hands without calling all over town to let people know about Nonnie's eccentricities," she said. Cordy had bristled, saying that she saw nothing eccentric about any of Nonnie's instructions and that there was no question but that they must be obeyed.

"Of course," Lucille had answered, "we will do as Nonnie tells us. As always. And maybe when we've laid her in her grave the Lord will be permitted to direct her as she has always directed us." Lucille's tone was resigned rather than bitter and she'd had a sad smile on her face. Had Cordy not been so tired, so utterly miserable and so full of regret (she had neither gotten Nonnie to the hospital in time to save her, nor had she allowed her to die in her own bed), she might have been able to let the remark pass. As it was, she cursed and said that if the Lord could run the world half as well as Nonnie had run her life then things wouldn't be in such a piss-awful mess. When Lucille had upbraided her for not talking like a lady, the emotional dam had burst, and she'd poured out years of frustration, anger, and hurt. She couldn't remember just what she'd said, but she'd just about said it all. She'd called Lucille self-centered, coldhearted, and hypocritical—in fact just about every nasty thing she could lay her tongue to—and had been on the verge of spitting out the final crushing accusation about Lucille's affair with Jacques Haur when Lucille had collapsed in a torrent of tears, sobbing that Cordy was being cruel and that she'd loved Nonnie more than anyone would ever know.

At the mention of Nonnie's name, Cordy's fury had given way to a deep shame, not so much for what she'd said, but that she should have said it at such a time. She was vastly relieved that she hadn't lost control so completely as to mention the Haur affair. She apologized and asked Lucille's forgiveness. Lucille cried that she hoped Cordy would suffer the same ingratitude and abuse from Jeanette as she was suffering from her. After rushing to the bathroom to wash her face and repair her makeup, she'd again rejected Cordy's apology and said they'd best "just forget the whole thing." They'd gone on with the plans for the funeral. But from the way Lucille had acted toward her during the last few days, Cordy knew that her outburst was far from forgotten.

"As Hesiod said," the minister began, "'Before the gates of excellence the high gods have placed sweat; long is the road thereto and rough and steep at first; but when the heights are reached, then there is ease, though grievously hard in the winning.' Eunnonia Grace Hampton . . ."

A rivulet of sweat ran down Cordy's back. She straightened her spine, feeling the front of her dress pull tight across her breasts, and stared straight at the minister as though to remind him of the five-minute time limit Nonnie had requested. The quote from Hesiod would undoubtedly lead into a speech about struggle and the formation of character and a life well spent, but what did a Greek poet have to do with Nonnie? It was better than quoting the Twenty-Third Psalm, but nothing anyone could say really meant anything. Not that she doubted the minister's sincerity, she just wanted him to stop. She didn't know how she was going to endure the crowds of people who would come back to the house and try to comfort her by saying what a wonderful woman Nonnie had been. More than anything, she wanted to lie down in a dark, cool room and have Clay hold her hand without talking.

". . .Eunnonia Grace Hampton molded her life into one of hard-won excellence. Her notion of excellence did not have to do with fame or artistic achievement or monetary gain. It had to do with the business of living, with human relations . . ."

Cordy looked at her mother. Lucille was restraining the trembling of her lips by moving them in silent prayer. Cordy squeezed her hand again, but Lucille was too numbed by chemicals or too concentrated on her prayers to feel the touch. The deepest part of her has always been closed off and it always will be, Cordy thought. But she had been wrong to call Lucille a religious hypocrite. Lucille prayed and she prayed fervently. Though she would never have a real faith, would never pray out of awe or joy or gratitude, as Bernice was able to do, she did pray. She prayed out of distress and helplessness, like a child importuning a parent. She prayed to ask for things. Watching her, Cordy felt a strange reversal of roles. It was as if she'd become Lucille's mother.

"Those of us who knew this great lady stand witness to the fact that her humanity was deep, wide, and generous. It flowed like a river to her family and beyond, touching the lives of all she met. She struggled to improve the lives of all the people in this community just as she worked, worked tirelessly, to improve its beauty. For she understood how one's physical surroundings enhance or destroy the natural yearning for beauty inherent in the souls of men and women. She was, in fact, very much like this city which she loved so much: gracious, graceful, and generous, firmly rooted in a past but with a vision of the future . . ."

A river or a city, Cordy thought impatiently, just pick one metaphor and stick to it. She was breathing shallowly, through her mouth, because the smell of the flowers was making her feel dizzy. Her gaze wandered to the large group of blacks standing behind the hearse. There was Sam Redding, now Alderman Redding, and a light-skinned well-groomed woman who must be his wife, their heads bowed in a respectful if conventional pose of mourning. And Bernice, surrounded by a slew of children, all scrubbed and dressed in their ice-cream-colored Sunday best. Bernice was wearing a beaded black pill box hat that had once belonged to Nonnie. It looked frivolously small on her large head. Cordy wanted to meet her eyes, but Bernice's eyes were closed. She was swaying back and forth ever so slightly, her lips parted in a radiant smile, her hands resting on the shoulders of a fidgety little boy. Amos Justice, fierce and angry as an old soldier, was at her side, his back ramrod straight. He stared directly at the coffin, his eyes boring into it, his lips pulled into a thin, determined line. Amos Justice will miss Nonnie as much as anybody will, Cordy thought, closing her eyes. Her eyes felt swollen and gritty, as though she'd been crying for a long time. But she hadn't been crying. She'd wanted to but she hadn't been able to.

Even before she became aware of the fact that the minister had stopped speaking, she sensed some movement on the periphery of the crowd. The soft buzz of human voices superseded the buzz of the insects. Her shoulder tingled strangely as her father took his hand away. She felt a film of sweat on her forehead, indeed all over her scalp, so that her hair seemed to be standing away from it. Lucille disengaged her hand. She blinked her eyes open. Vivian was shaking hands with the minister. Constance, Phillip, and Stephanie had already started to walk away. Car doors were slamming and she heard a motor start up. Jeanette tugged at her hand but she ignored it, turned around, and reached for George Naughton. "Are you all right, George?"

George shuffled his feet and looked down. An artery was pounding in his temple and his eyes were still swimming with tears.

"You're coming back to the house, aren't you George?"

"I don't think so, Cordy. I—"

"Oh, do come. I'd like it so much if you did," she reassured him. "You don't want to be alone now, George. Besides, I need your company."

"Well, if you need me to be there, Cordy . . ."

"I do. I do."

He nodded and walked slowly away as though he weren't sure which car he'd come in.

Jeanette tugged on her hand again, and she bent down to hear her whisper, "Please, Mama. I'd like to stay to the end. Until they"—her voice quavered—"until they bury her."

"No, darlin'; they'll do that after we're gone."

"But I don't want to leave her."

She brushed Jeanette's lips with her own and wiped the tears from her cheeks. "No. No. Come on now. Lots of folks are coming back to Nonnie's house, and I need you to help me."

"Like a waitress? Can I give out those sandwiches?"

"Yes. You can be a waitress."

Jake Junior touched Cordy on the elbow. "We're all ready to go," he said and started to guide her over to the limousine. Her father, Lucille, and Taffy were already inside. She could hear Taffy saying, "She's up there looking down on us. I just know she is. I could hear her voice so clear just now and it was saying, 'Don't cry anymore. I'm up here with the angels now.'"

Cordy drew in her breath. It was going to be a long ride home.

"I've brought my car. Would you like to drive back with me?"

"Oh, Clay," she said before she'd even turned around, "I was looking for you but I couldn't find you."

"Can't we go with Clay, Mama? Can't we?" Jeanette begged.

"I guess so," Cordy said softly, tilting her head to one side and looking up at him. Jake Junior had already gotten into the limousine. "I'll just tell—"

"I'll tell them." Clay took a few steps toward the car, then turned, reached for her hand, took it almost surreptitiously, and brought his face close to her ear. "'I want to hold your ha-a-and,'" he crooned the Beatles' lyric under his breath. "Listen, Jake"—he raised his voice and moved off to lean on the door of the limousine—"this looks pretty crowded so I'm going to take Jeanette and Cordy along with me. We'll see you at the house."

They sat in Clay's car with the air conditioning turned on until most of the crowd had dispersed. Jeanette pressed her forehead to the back window and stared at the men from the funeral home who were waiting patiently around the coffin. Clay simply held Cordy's hand and said nothing. The silence was as refreshing as cool water after a long thirst. Cordy undid the top buttons of her dress and began to feel that she could breathe normally again. As Clay started up the engine and the car bumped over the rutted dirt road, Cordy smiled to herself and said, "Don't let Taffy pull your teeth."

"What's that?" Clay asked.

"I said"—she started to laugh—"I said . . . It was something that Nonnie said." She could barely get the words out for laughing now: "'Don't let Taffy pull your teeth.'"

She remembered the conversation almost in its entirety. It had been the day after Christmas and she and Jeanette had gone over to Nonnie's to have their first supper of leftovers. She had asked Nonnie's opinion of Taffy, and Nonnie had said, "I expect Jake Junior's taken with her, and in a couple of years from now, when he's not, she'll still be able to hold on to him. Compromise is always easiest for people who don't know they're making it. She'll suit him just fine. But between you an' me an' the lamppost, Cordy, I'm just as glad they'll be living in Augusta. That girl's too sticky to have around more'n twice a year. I ought to embroider a little sampler for your brother to put in his office. It'd say 'Don't let Taffy pull your teeth.'"

"That's the worst pun I've heard in years," she'd groaned when Nonnie had said it. Now she couldn't help herself from uncontrollable laughter.

"I don't understand what you're laughing about, Cordy," Clay said, though his lips were already turning up in an empathetic smile.

"It's just something Nonnie said about my brother's . . ." She gasped, sucked in her breath, and spelled out the word "fiancée," then held her hand to her chest to calm herself. "She said . . ."

Jeanette pulled off her gloves and put her thumb into her mouth. She didn't like the way Cordy was making those mixed-up sounds, so that she couldn't tell if she was laughing or crying.

Cordy continued to sputter, shaking her head, laughing. If only she could tell Nonnie what Taffy had said about her being up in heaven with the angels. How Nonnie would have snorted at that one. How Nonnie would have . . . she passed her tongue over her lips and tasted the salt of her tears. Oh, how much she would miss Nonnie! There were certain confidences, dreams, and jokes that were uniquely suited to Nonnie's ear. No other person would do.

But just imagining Nonnie's response sent her into another peal of laughter.

"All right." Clay chuckled with her. "I get it now. I get it now."

"I don't get it," Jeanette piped up.

"You're not supposed to," Clay assured her, still chuckling. "You know, Jeanette, I was watching you during the service and I've got to tell you how proud you made me, standing next to your mama and acting so grown up like that."

Jeanette, blessed with Clay's approval, smoothed her skirt and stared out the window. She knew they were burying Nonnie now, and she planned to come back, just as Nonnie had taught her, and water the plot so that a rosebush would grow.

"You all right, Cordy?" Clay asked. "Do you want me to pull over?"

"No. No, I'm all right," she answered, wiping her eyes. "We'd better hurry on back and attend to the guests. Later . . ."

"Yes, later."

Chapter XXIII

The house on Monterey Square had been, the woman from the Historical Society assured Cordy, one of the most popular attractions on the tour of homes. "And you're such a brave little thing"—she sighed, seizing Cordy's hand as Cordy was inching toward the door, ready to bid her goodbye—"honoring Eunnonia Grace's commitment to us when it's been but a month since she was taken to her heavenly rest."

Cordy smiled and took another step. "Yes. Thank you."

"You can be right proud of yourself. Everything was just as Eunnonia would have wanted it."

"I'm not sure she would have wanted that television crew barging into the dining room."

"I blush about that. I really do. Not that it was my responsibility to clear it with you. That was Lethia Grant's obligation. But her dog's been feeling poorly and I guess she was just so worried she forgot."

"Well, it's done now. No harm. Good night."

"Don't forget to watch the news," the woman called over her shoulder as she gripped the iron railing and went slowly down the stairs. "And thank you again for everything."

Cordy stepped back into the parlor. Considering the fact that a few hundred people had walked through it during the course of the day, it looked remarkably undisturbed. The Hepplewhite chairs were in their place, as was the velvet footstool. The eighteenth-century English prints of hares and partridges that had never seen this part of the world looked down with bright, disinterested eyes. The hairy-pawed feet of the Empire sofa rested on the polished floor, content never to reach the Isfahan rug that was only inches away. The windows were still raised and the draperies open, framing the gathering dusk in the square. Diana, one arm raised, her breast pulled into a high, indestructibly youthful curve, cavorted with her hunting dogs. There were a few indications that the room had been on display: vases of flowers on the officer's desk as well as the coffee table, the PLEASE DO NOT TOUCH sign Bernice had insisted on placing next to Diana's bare feet, and the "conversation piece" Bernice had unearthed from the carriage house—a gold birdcage, circa 1880, containing a lifelike finch that, when wound up, warbled and fluttered its wings.

Cordy slipped her feet out of her high heels and sank into the wing-backed chair. Though the day could be counted a success, she felt strangely sad. There had been something about the way in which people had moved about, their voices muted and respectful, their movements constrained, that had depressed her. It was as though they'd thought they were in a mausoleum. When one of the visitors had looked up furtively when Cordy had seen her touching a medallioned panel on the library wall, Cordy had said, somewhat impatiently, "It's been around for over two hundred years. I don't think it'll break."

She looked around the room and closed her eyes. She simply couldn't believe that the house now belonged to her. Each day since she'd learned the contents of the will she'd tried to digest the fact and to come to some decision about it. Much as she loved the house, it was almost a burden to know it was her property. Unlike the other grandchildren, she had not been given money; and though the value of the house far exceeded their bequests, she had no notion of whether she could even afford the taxes and maintenance. Besides which, receiving the property seemed to have alienated most other members of the family from her. She supposed that she was extremely naive not to have anticipated such a reaction, but was appalled nonetheless.

There had been considerable consternation when it was found that Nonnie had left one of her houses in the Victorian district to the Black Heritage and Restoration Association, and it was generally felt that her generosity had slipped into eccentric beneficence when it was disclosed that Bernice was to get a sizable monthly stipend to be administered by the bank; but the fact that Nonnie's fortune was greater than any of them had supposed and that they would all receive amounts in excess of what they'd anticipated softened annoyance toward these bequests. It was Cordy's receipt of the house that excited envy, and only Jake and Aunt Vivian were exceptions to the general ill-will.

True to his nature, Jake either didn't see or chose not to acknowledge the undercurrents of jealousy and suspicion. He stated that it was only natural that Cordy should get the house, since she had the most affection for it and no one else would think of moving to Savannah. Uncle Phillip bristled at that one, saying that now he and Constance were retiring they had many options. They didn't like the New England snow all *that* much. Aunt Vivian said, cryptically but not unkindly, that the will was exactly what she'd suspected it would be. She pointed out that in addition to the bulk of the estate, which was divided among the three daughters, with smaller amounts given equally to all grandchildren save Cordy, and educational trust funds set up for the great-grandchildren, Nonnie had selected items that were completely appropriate to particular individuals. Constance was to get the silver, while she, Vivian, was allowed to take any paintings or carpets she chose. Lucille would receive most of the jewelry, save individual "remembrance" pieces to be given to Joan, Lethia, and Cousin Cissy. The bourbon decanter and matching glasses, along with a small locket, went to George Naughton; and Winetta was to have Nonnie's silver vanity set.

But Constance had passed a remark about Cordy returning to Savannah "in the nick of time," as though Cordy had come back to ingratiate herself. Taffy had said it was so nice that Cordy was going out with Clay Claxton and asked if Clay wasn't an associate of the firm that had drawn up the will. Taffy had masked her insinuation with such a vapid stare that it had taken Cordy a full beat to recognize its outrageous insult. Even Jake Junior, who'd probably had an earful from Taffy, had said that Nonnie was "doddering" at the Christmas dinner. "You'd be doddering if you had to fry yourself and egg," Cordy had snapped, "let alone prepare a meal for the whole tribe."

But the worst reaction, because it was no reaction at all, had come from Lucille. She'd behaved as if she had not heard that particular part of the will, had asked Cordy no questions about her plans, and had maintained a gruelingly polite and chilly distance.

Despite Cordy's continued attempts at reconciliation, Lucille remained aloof, almost as though she was afraid of being slighted. Yet
just today Cordy had felt an understanding sympathy for her
mother.

Some of the women from the Historical Society had worn long
skirts and affected bits and pieces of period costume. Lucille had
arrived in a cream and pink turn-of-the-century ensemble that was so
finely made and tastefully authentic that she seemed to be an apparition from another time. There had been a particular moment—mid-
afternoon when the sun was streaming through the fanlight above
the entrance—when Cordy had passed through the hallway and had
been struck by her mother's beauty. Lucille was standing near the
umbrella stand greeting the guests and asking them to sign the register. As usual, she was meting out her civilities, extracting more attention than she bestowed. Cordy could see that her courtesies were
an extension of her grooming rather than any true generosity of
spirit, and yet she was transfixed by the delicate curve of Lucille's
cheeks and shoulders, the graceful movements of her hands, and the
shape of her perfect mouth.

It was sadly ironic that the most beautiful women were the first
to notice that they were aging. Lucille, Cordy remembered, had
started to worry about it when she was in her early thirties, but her
awareness had not called forth talents or revived aspirations that
might have helped her through the rest of her life. Given the longev-
ity of the Hampton women, Lucille was probably just past the halfway mark, and yet it was all over for her. Cordy felt a catch in her
throat. She had known the heady power that came from the ability
to attract—the marvelous distractions of being admired and desired.
Perhaps because she was not as beautiful as Lucille, perhaps because
she had been born in a different time, perhaps because her sexuality
had been gratified and she had reveled in men's physical beauty as
much as they had in hers, she had not been lured into the drowning
pool of vanity. It would always be a mystery to her that Nonnie,
who had helped her to understand the necessity of courage, humor,
and compassion, had failed to inculcate any of those characteristics
in her own daughter.

She had thought of going up to Lucille and telling her just how
lovely she looked. Instead, she had continued into the dining room,
where Lethia and Joan, seated at either end of the table, were pouring tea. Almost tripping over the ganglia of cords the television crew
had strewn on the floor, she'd stood behind the blinding lights and

watched, amused, while the director, a young woman in jeans and an Army-issue shirt, ordered Lethia to pick up the plate of cucumber sandwiches one more time and *smile* as she handed it to the guest. She had taken the director aside and said, "I don't mean to tell you your business, but I think you'd get a great shot if you filmed the entrance. The fanlight above the door is one of the architectural features of the house, and there's a woman standing beneath it—she's wearing a cream and pink dress and she's incredibly beautiful." The woman nodded, wandered into the hall, came back, and called, "Fred, Jeffrey, you want to set up for some shots in the hallway." The crew moved unceremoniously around the guests. Lethia looked somewhat crestfallen that she'd failed her screen test. The cameraman, passing the table, took a couple of cookies and shoved them into his mouth.

As she'd watched one of the crew hold a light meter up to Lucille's face and saw Lucille give him her most radiant smile, Cordy had felt her throat catch again. As unobtrusively as possible, she'd moved through the crowd and mounted the stairs to the bedroom. She sat down on the bed, opened her purse, and reread the letter she'd received from Alidia the previous day:

The sky *did* meet the earth in Iowa. And it was clean. Too clean. This comes to you from Alaska. We're on the Kuskokwim River now. Carl and me, that is. We're great traveling buddies. I've got a job in a bar. The salary's outrageous, but so are the prices. Carl's still looking for work. He thinks he might like to be a salmon fisherman and I think I'd like to bankroll him. I'm glad I'm seeing this place before they screw it up completely. The pipeline ain't gonna work and the natives are starting to commit suicide now that they've got afternoon TV. Savannah seems worlds away—slow and decadent—at least for the present. You, my pet, are neither. *Non carborundum illegitium*, which loosely translated means, "Don't let the bastards wear you down." Love to Jeanette, Nonnie, and Fanny. Miss you, Alidia.

Cordy heard Bernice's carpet slippers scuffing down the passageway. Bernice appeared at the door. She'd taken off the black dress with the white cuffs and collars she'd chosen to wear during the day and was back in her loose floral print.

"I guess that woman from the Hysterical Society's done gone."

Cordy laughed. "Bernice, I wish you wouldn't call it that. After you told me that last night I swear I almost slipped and said it to the woman's face."

"Kitchen's all cleaned up, so I sent that girl who came to help on home. Would you like me to fix you a drink?" Bernice was a teetotaler herself, but she liked to pour for others.

"I can fix one myself."

"I've got some coffee perkin' out in the kitchen. You want to come sit?"

"Sure."

Cordy poured herself a bourbon and carried it out to the kitchen. She opened the freezer and got some ice.

"There's nothin' 'cept some of those little leftover fancy sandwiches and a few hunks of cheese. Been nothin' in that refrigerator since I cleaned it out. Looked sorrowful bare when I come in this mornin'. But you'd better help yourself to what's there. You haven't eaten anything since you've been in my sight today, and you know how your bowels are goin' to get if you don't eat."

"I'm not hungry. Besides, Clay is coming over in a bit. He'll take me out to dinner if I want."

"He is obliging, that young man. And not so stuffy like his mama and papa be. He's a real gentleman."

"Yes. Yes, he is," Cordy agreed, plunking the ice cubes into her glass and drawing a chair up to the table.

Bernice stood next to the stove studying the steady plop-plop in the dome of the percolator. When she judged the coffee to be done, she poured herself a cup and sat down. She looked into Cordy's face. "You're feelin' poorly, aren't you? Have you had a chance to get any more of your book done?"

"Sure. I'm keeping at it. I'm into the final chapters now."

"Been typing away most part of a year, haven't you?"

"I'm getting there. And I'm going to keep on. If I stopped now it would be like driving across country to Los Angeles and stopping in Bakersfield."

Bernice heaped another spoonful of sugar into her cup. She didn't know where Bakersfield was. "I been thinkin', now that I'm not working, I could go visit my son in Jacksonville. I know I'd best go, but I can't seem to get my suitcase packed. Angela's childrens need me, though she say they don't. . . . One thing an' another . . ." She licked her finger and rubbed a speck on the table. "Don't know what to do now that I'm not workin'."

The clock ticked on. The purr of the refrigerator motor was suddenly audible in their silence.

They sat divining each other's thoughts until, finally, Cordy rested her head in her palm and decided to give them voice.

"I can't believe it, Bernice. I still can't believe it."

"She be happy right now seeing us do the things she'd want us to do."

"I don't believe that, Bernice."

"I know," Bernice said calmly. "I've been prayin' for you to find the faith." She took a sip of her coffee, wiped her lips, and smiled. "Miz Hampton, she was like that too. Didn't have no faith in the Lord. Thought He'd deserted her sure when He took Mr. Wade. She went on all those years doing the right thing with no confidence at all that she was bein' tested. But the Lord is mighty pleased at the way she took the test. The Lord will reward her righteousness."

Cordy took a long swallow and said nothing.

Bernice folded her arms across her pendulous breasts, her forehead creasing with the effort of trying to comfort a nonbeliever. "The Lord blessed her in the way she went—peaceful like that," she continued. She didn't want to push Cordy, she just wanted to show her the good. "Miz Hampton been through bad illness with Mr. Hampton. I come in here some mornings see her still sitting up in that chair near his bed, her eyes all but floating in her head. Yes, it was a blessing that she left so swift and easy."

Only the ticking of the clock and the soft tinkle of ice as Cordy swirled her glass intruded on another long silence.

"An' think about the joys she had in livin'," Bernice continued. "Not too many folks have eyes that see so clear or mouths that taste with such pleasure. And smell! When that woman put her nose into a flower or a cookin' pot it like to make you sing just to see her. She was present in spirit for all her days."

Cordy stood up quickly and walked to the window. "I can't think of living here, Bernice. I just can't."

"Then I s'pose you'll have to sell it," Bernice answered calmly.

"How can I sell it? She gave it to me. She wouldn't want me to sell it."

"That's right, she gave it to you. If she want you to do some special thing with it, she'd've told you. Don't you think a woman like Miz Hampton—a woman who had her own special way of putting butter on a hunk of bread—would have left you instructions if

she'd wanted you to have instructions? No'm. She give it to you
'cause she want *you* to decide what to do. She's dead and we've got to
figure out our own way of doing things."

The logic of what Bernice was saying made Cordy feel more
confused, since it offered not a solution but a greater range of options. Apart from all the practical questions, she felt a swarm of
contradictions—between her will and her work, her need for perma-
nence and her desire for change, her need to uphold traditions without letting them become her jailer. She was not a rebel like Alidia,
but neither did she wish to capitulate to the tedium of being part of
the small but arrogant oligarchy of Savannah society. Somehow, living in the house would expose her to that. Of course, she *could* sell
the house. She'd have plenty of money then. So much money that
she wouldn't have to think about working. She could travel or . . .
She sighed and shifted her feet, already bored with herself because
she knew that no matter how she tried to think things through, this
decision, like all major decisions, was already being made by instinct
and would present itself at a particular moment. Her legs felt itchy.
She lifted up her skirt and rolled down her panty hose. As she
turned and bent to the floor to slip them off her feet, she saw that
Bernice's shoulders were shaking. She came around to her side,
ready to put a comforting hand on Bernice's arm, and saw that she
was chuckling. "What is it?" she asked, an empathetic smile already
curling her lips.

"It's that cage with the fine singing bird. The one I put in the
parlor today. That belong to your great-grandmother Ettie Payne.
Brought it back from Paris when she was a slip of a girl. Miz
Hampton, she hated that thing so much she wouldn't give it house
room. Said anything in a cage was no fit toy. I expect she didn't like
it because—" Bernice broke off, sealed her lips together, and then let
them open into a mischievous grin that showed her gold tooth. "But
I always thought it was fine. So I went and pulled it out of the mess
in the carriage house. And the folks did like it, didn't they?"

Cordy nodded, though her opinion of the piece was closer to
Nonnie's and she'd only allowed Bernice to show the cage because it
delighted her so. Bernice brought her hand down on the tabletop
with a gently assertive thud. "See, we don't have to be doing everything according to Miz Hampton's lights. She was contrary in this
one thing: She loved folks who stood up, folks who had spine. She
just didn't always like it when they stood up to her."

"You know it's ridiculous for me to be thinking of living in a house like this when I don't hardly have the money to pay for my apartment," Cordy said.

"I think some folks get successful 'cause they sticks their necks out an' then they have to make money so's their necks won't get chopped off. I mean, you wouldn't stop your writing, would you?"

"I may not want to stay in Savannah all my life," she shot back. The tempo of the conversation had changed, as though they were now bouncing a ball between them.

"What you gonna do? Go rovin' all around the country?"

"I haven't told you about my stay in New York. O.K., it was a mixed bag, but some very exciting things happened."

"Movin' and movin'. My husband had it like a disease."

"And there's plenty of places apart from New York."

"My Angela's got the same kinda restlessness. And Clarence— he just have to run off to Detroit."

"A house like this. I mean, Phillip was right, it is sort of a white elephant. It's like monogamy . . ."

". . . I just don't understand the need of it."

". . . great ideal, but impractical."

"If'n I couldn't wake up and see that vine on my neighbor's fence I'd feel so strange. Peoples think you seen something once you see all of it. That don't speak much hope for—" Bernice's eyes shot up to the clock. "Oh, Lord," she said, pressing both hands on the edge of the table and propelling herself into an upright position with a speed that was, for her, unusual. "I've got but thirty minutes to get home so's I can watch the TV."

"My god, Bernice, you're an addict, you know that?" Cordy cried, but Bernice was already gathering up her vinyl purse and the shopping bag that held her good black uniform.

"We're goin' to be on," Bernice said, hurrying into the hallway. "This house is going to be on. Did you forget it?"

"Oh, yes, I had." Cordy moved after her. "Do you want me to drive you home?"

"No, ma'am. I want to walk and I can get there on time. They'll be talkin' all international and state first, but if I move fast I'm bound to get there on time. We'll be 'human interest.' At the end, y' know. Don't forget"—she opened the door and called back— "Channel Three. Bye, Cordy."

Cordy went back into the kitchen, put Bernice's cup and saucer into the sink, and went to the refrigerator to put more ice into her glass. She didn't want to watch the TV show. She couldn't bear the thought of part of their lives being shown, however fleetingly or glamorously, to an audience of strangers. She wanted to get quietly intoxicated. Not drunk but intoxicated. The former meant "overcome, out of control"; the latter "greatly excited and rapturous." She rested her head on the refrigerator door and smiled at her pleasure in these subtle differentiations. Despite the losses of the last year she counted herself a very fortunate woman. She had found her work. She had the privilege of learning the craft of writing, of weighing words and feelings. She was a storyteller, and the pleasure of reading and writing would be with her until the end of her days.

She walked to the telephone, relishing the stillness of the house and the feel of the polished wood floors on her bare feet, and dialed Clay's private line at the office.

"Clay?"

"Yes." He was still wearing his professional voice, measured and distant.

"It's me."

"Hi, girl." His tone changed to one of anticipation. "Is the coast clear? Did anyone try to lift the crockery?"

"You wouldn't have believed it. It was like Grand Central Station. These television people came and you should've seen Lethia Grant. Once the cameras started rolling she was like some cuckoo that came out of a clock. Served up those cucumber sandwiches with exactly the same movement three times in a row, but couldn't coordinate the smile with the handling of the plate. I can't tell you about it, I'll have to show you what it was like. And Bernice unearthed this bird cage from the carriage house and—"

"Talkin' about the carriage house, I was thinking that you could clean it out and convert it into a writer's office."

"I don't know. I've never thought about that."

"Listen, I'll finish up here and take you out to dinner."

"Would you mind if we just stayed home? Maybe you could pick up some pizza or crabs or something."

"Fine. I'll be there in about thirty, forty minutes."

She went into the parlor and headed for the wing-backed chair. She was grateful that Clay was coming, yet it was good to know that she would have this time alone. She looked out the window. The lamps had not yet gone on in the square. The azaleas were in full bloom, the crimsons and pinks disappearing into the darkness but the white blossoms doubly distinct, luminous in the twilight. And the largest oak, the one that had been Nonnie's favorite, was both serpenting down toward the rich Southern earth and twisting its branches upward to the sky.

Cynthia Peale is the pseudonym of Nancy Zaroulis, she is the author of many successful novels. She lives outside Boston, and is currently at work on the third book in her Beacon Hill Mystery series.

MURDER AT BERTRAM'S BOWER

Agatha Montgomery, the proprietress of
Bertram's Bower, a home for 'fallen
women', is considered a saint by all who
know her. Agatha's brother, the Reverend
Randolph Montgomery, also lends his
considerable reputation to his sister's
efforts. But when two residents are
brutally murdered on successive nights, it
will take more than saintly reputations to
save the Bower from scandal. Agatha's
childhood friend, Caroline Ames, con-
vinces her brother, Addington, to conduct
an unofficial investigation. There are
suspects aplenty, and the case becomes
even more complicated when disturbing
rumors begin to circulate about the
Reverend . . .

A murder mystery in Victorian Boston.

Books by Cynthia Peale
Published by The House of Ulverscroft:

THE DEATH OF COLONEL MANN

CYNTHIA PEALE

MURDER AT BERTRAM'S BOWER

A Beacon Hill Mystery

Complete and Unabridged

ULVERSCROFT
Leicester

First published in 2001 in the
United States of America by
Doubleday
New York

First Large Print Edition
published 2002
by arrangement with
Doubleday
a division of
Random House Inc
New York

British Library CIP Data

Peale, Cynthia
  Murder at Bertram's Bower.—Large print ed.—
  (A Beacon Hill mystery)
  Ulverscroft large print series: mystery
  1. Large type books
  2. Detective and mystery stories
  I. Title
  813.5′4 [F]

ISBN 0–7089–4697–6

Published by
F. A. Thorpe (Publishing)
Anstey, Leicestershire

Set by Words & Graphics Ltd.
Anstey, Leicestershire
Printed and bound in Great Britain by
T. J. International Ltd., Padstow, Cornwall

This book is printed on acid-free paper

For
Katherine

1

Boston: the January thaw, 1892. A watery gloom hung over the city like a shroud.

Day after day of heavy, relentless rain had threatened to submerge the new-filled Back Bay, and the miniature lagoon in the Public Garden had overflowed its banks. On Beacon Hill, streams of water pounded the brick sidewalks and cascaded down the narrow streets, splashing women's voluminous skirts, splattering horses with mud up to their blinkers. People clung to their firesides, waiting for winter to return.

In the South End, Officer Joseph Flynn of the Boston police was making his rounds. He had been on the force for less than a year, and he was eager to do well in this job which until recently would not have been given to an Irishman like himself. When he saw the shape on the ground halfway down the alley behind West Brookline Street, he paused. Because it was night, and very dark in that district, he could not immediately tell what the shape was. A heap of refuse, he thought, or a pile of rags. Or, at worst, some drunken tramp from the nearby railroad yards.

Still. Best be sure. On the lookout for rats, his bull's-eye lantern sputtering in the rain, he stepped carefully along.

When he came to it — to her — he could hardly believe what he saw. He had witnessed some serious mayhem during his brief time with the force, but he had never seen anything like this. Half crouching, holding his lantern close, he stared at her for a long moment.

Dear Mother of God. What monster had been at work here? He felt his stomach heave, and he heard the anguished cry torn from his throat. His lantern clattered to the ground. Suddenly overcome, he fell retching to his knees. Then he vomited onto the dirty, rain-soaked snow.

2

'I will put Matthew Hale next to Harriet Mason,' said Caroline Ames. Her pencil hovered over the sheet of paper on which she had written names around a diagram of her dining room table. 'He is so terribly shy with women, and Harriet can get conversation out of a lamppost.'

Dr. John Alexander MacKenzie had been struggling through a life of Lincoln highly recommended by the clerk at the Athenaeum. Now he laid aside the heavy volume and rose to knock the ashes of his pipe into the grate where simmering sea coal warmed the parlor at No. 16½, Louisburg Square.

'Might she not frighten him?' he said, smiling down at her. She'd given him permission to smoke when he'd come to live here several months before, and he'd been grateful to her — for that, and for much else.

She was a pretty woman of some thirty-five years, a little plump, with fair, curly hair caught up in a fashionable Psyche knot and frizzy bangs partially covering her wide, smooth forehead. Her eyes were brown, her mouth a vivid rose, and although her cheeks

3

were tinged with pink, he was almost certain that she did not use face paint. She wore a high-necked long-sleeved dress of soft gray, plainly made and slightly out of fashion because of its bustle. Her only ornament was a mourning brooch for her mother.

She had been fussing over this dinner party for weeks, and now it was nearly upon them. Although MacKenzie had been invited to it, he hardly cared about it — only to the extent that it was a worry for her. When she had first announced her intention to have it — 'For Nigel Chadwick, who is coming from London, and every hostess in Boston is maneuvering to get him to her table!' — he had thought the effort would be too much for her. She had been wounded by a bullet in the shoulder the previous November, and while she had healed well, her normal strength and vitality had been slow to return.

And, too, he thought darkly, she was not an ideal patient, too quick to take up her multitudinous activities, many of which were good works. Only that morning she had been summoned on an errand of mercy for the Ladies' Committee at her church, and to his chagrin, she had gone.

'It is my turn to go, Doctor,' she'd said.

He had protested as much as he thought he dared, for he was only a boarder, after all. 'In

4

this weather?' he'd said.

'They wouldn't ask me unless it was important. I know this family. The committee has been working with them for months — since last summer, in fact. The woman is an excellent person who is trying very hard to keep the family together. I must go — but to ease your mind, I will take a herdic.'

He'd offered to go with her himself, or even in her place, but she'd refused, allowing him only to go down to Charles Street at the foot of the hill to find a herdic-phaeton for her and bring it to the door. These were small, fast cabs unique to Boston, whose strong, agile horses darted about the city at all hours.

Now, safely home once more, she'd been struggling for the past half hour with the seating for her party.

'I don't think so,' she said in answer to his question. 'Harriet isn't a frightening kind of person, just very chatty.'

'Then by all means,' he said, 'you must seat her next to him.'

She looked up at him, returning his smile. He was stockily built, not much taller than herself, and a few years older (she'd turn thirty-six in May). He had graying hair, a broad, honest face adorned by a not too brushy mustache, and kind, wise eyes. She'd

5

liked him from the moment he had presented himself the previous September, bearing a note from Boston's most famous surgeon, Dr. Joseph Warren. MacKenzie, a surgeon himself with the army on the western plains, had taken a Sioux bullet in his knee; after the army doctors in Chicago had informed him that he must lose his leg, he had come to Boston, to Dr. Warren, to see if he could save it.

Warren had done so, and had recommended his neighbors across Louisburg Square, Addington Ames and his sister, Caroline, as a place for MacKenzie to board at not too great an expense while he recuperated.

The Ameses' elevator, installed for their late mother's convenience, had been a great help, particularly in the first days after his operation, when he was confined to his room on the third floor at the back of the house. Margaret, the all-purpose girl, had brought him his meals, and Caroline herself had come up once or twice a day to see how he did. Eventually, when he could hobble about, he sat by the window and enjoyed the view: down over the crowded rooftops of the western slope of Beacon Hill to the river, and to Cambridge beyond. On fine days, all the autumn, he enjoyed the sunsets, and as he recovered further and could go downstairs in the elevator, he had enjoyed the Ameses' company as well. He had become, he thought, not so much a paying boarder as a friend. Now, in the winter, he could not imagine a life apart from them. From her.

He moved to the bow window that overlooked the square. Its lavender glass was old, original with the house. Caroline had told him that it had been imported from Europe; imperfect, it had turned color when the sun first struck it. Her grandfather, a China trader and one of the first proprietors of the square, had been too thrifty to replace it. It gave the trees and shrubbery in the central oval an eerie, purplish cast; MacKenzie still wasn't used to it. This day, rain lashed against the panes, making him glad to be indoors. He'd heard about the vagaries of the New England weather before he'd come, but rain in January seemed very odd indeed.

A tall, cloaked figure was striding through the downpour. In a moment more, he had passed beneath the window and they heard him coming in.

Caroline brightened. 'There! That will be Addington. He is probably soaked to the skin — I can't imagine why he felt he needed to go to Crabbe's in this weather.'

Her brother was a devotee of Crabbe's

7

Boxing and Fencing Club down in Avery Street, beyond the Common. He went there nearly every day, sometimes very early in the morning after a night of stargazing. He kept a telescope on the roof of the house, but for the past several nights, the thaw, with its clouds and rain, had made stargazing impossible.

They heard him stamping in the vestibule, and after a moment he slid open the pocket doors to the parlor. He was a tall man, whippet thin, with dark hair combed straight back from his high forehead, dark, deep-set eyes in a long, clean-shaven face, and a pronounced nose. Ordinarily he was self-contained, not given to displays of feeling; just now, however, they saw from his expression that something was obviously amiss.

'What is it, Addington?' Caroline asked.

'Bad news, I am afraid.' He carried a folded newspaper, which he gave to her. 'Look at this.'

As she opened it, MacKenzie saw that it was an 'Extra,' and he caught sight of the bold black headline: MURDER AT BERTRAM'S BOWER!!! And in slightly smaller type: VICIOUS CRIME!!! WOMAN'S BODY FOUND IN ALLEY!!!

Caroline quickly scanned the page. They saw her amazement — then shock, then

8

horror. Deathly pale, she looked up at them, while the newspaper dropped to her lap.

'May I?' said MacKenzie, taking the paper and reading: Last night a young woman, Mary Flaherty, a resident of the well-known home for fallen women, Bertram's Bower, had been murdered in a South End alley not far from the Bower. A brutal crime; robbery not a motive; Deputy Chief Inspector Elwood Crippen of the city police stated that 'the crime was probably the work of a deranged person.'

'I am sorry, my dear,' Ames said to his sister. He advanced to the fire and took up his customary position, one slim, booted foot resting on the brass fender. 'I know that Agatha is your friend.'

Agatha Montgomery was the proprietress of the Bower.

'I must go to her at once, Addington.'

'In this downpour? Surely she will be distraught, distracted — '

Just then Margaret knocked and announced lunch, putting a brief end to Ames's protest. But as they spooned up their leek and potato soup, and ate their minced beef patties and boiled beets, Caroline explained to Dr. MacKenzie about Bertram's Bower.

'It is a most worthy establishment, Doctor.

And, unfortunately, a necessary one. Agatha takes in girls who — well, they are girls of the street, if you follow.'

He did.

'If Miss Montgomery felt the need to speak to you,' Ames said, 'she would have sent you a telegram.' He eyed his plate warily. He did not like beets.

'Not necessarily. She was never one to ask for help, even when she most desperately needs it. It is her brother, remember, who does all the fund-raising.'

She turned to MacKenzie. 'Agatha has been a friend of mine since we were children, although she is a few years older than I. The Montgomerys grew up around the corner on Pinckney Street. When Agatha was seventeen, her father went bankrupt. She never had a coming-out. She started Bertram's Bower about ten years ago, when an uncle left her a small inheritance. Now she and her brother, the Reverend Randolph Montgomery, support the place from donations.'

'You go there regularly,' MacKenzie said. Caroline had recently resumed most of her schedule: church meetings, Sewing Circle, Saturday Morning Reading Club, and, of course, the Bower.

'Yes. To teach the girls to read and write, and to sew and do fancy embroidery. They

10

come to the city in search of work, and if they cannot find it, or if they find it and are then dismissed, they end up on the streets.' She shuddered, and her brother frowned at her.

'Not a suitable place for you, Caroline,' he said. 'You know I have never approved of your going there.'

'If Agatha Montgomery can devote her life to those poor creatures,' she replied with some spirit, 'surely I can give them one afternoon every other week.'

She turned to MacKenzie again. 'She is very strict with them, of course — and of course she must be. She must maintain the highest moral standards. The girls violate the rules at their peril, and well they know it. But they know, too, they are fortunate to be there, because a girl from the Bower can almost always find decent employment when she leaves. Agatha's reputation for high standards guarantees that. At first, when she had just opened the place, she used to go out at night, searching for girls on the streets. Can you imagine? She would talk to them, persuade them to go with her. She keeps them for three months, usually. Feeds them, gets medical attention for them at Dr. Hannah Bigelow's clinic. And she recruited all her friends — her former friends, that is — to teach them.'

11

'Did you know this girl — the one who was — ah — '

'Mary Flaherty? Yes. Not well, for she already knew how to read and write when she came to Agatha, and she could sew a pretty seam. She was a lovely girl, bright and hardworking. You could see she wanted to advance herself in the world. And in fact Agatha kept her on when her three months were up, employing her as her secretary.'

Her eyes held MacKenzie's in a steady gaze. 'Sometimes I think the work that Agatha Montgomery does over there in the South End is more important than all our charity fairs and sewing for the poor and Thanksgiving baskets of food that the church gives out. We play at good works, but when our hour or two of service is done, we return to our comfortable homes. Agatha lives her charity, she works at it twenty-four hours a day. It is her life. Oh, dear, she must be devastated!' She turned to her brother. 'And think of the harm such a scandal will do to the Bower's reputation, Addington. No one will want to volunteer, donations will fall off — they might be ruined because of this!'

'The Reverend Montgomery is a skilled fund-raiser,' Ames replied. 'I don't imagine this incident, unfortunate as it is, will crimp his style.'

'Unfortunate!' she exclaimed. 'Is that what you call it?'

'Unfortunate — yes. Hardly a scandal. It is not Agatha Montgomery's fault if some deranged person — as your friend Inspector Crippen put it — has murdered one of her girls.'

'Do not call him my friend, Addington.' She shook her head. 'If Inspector Crippen has charge of this case, they might never find the man who killed Mary.'

'True. But a random killing in the night — if it was random — is a difficult thing to solve.'

'All the more reason for me to go to Agatha and see what I can do to help.' Her face, ordinarily so gentle and sweet, hardened into lines of determination as she added, 'So, yes, Addington, I am going to go to her. And I am going to try to bring her back here with me. She must be in a terrible state. It will do her good to get away, even just for overnight. We can put her in the front room on the fourth floor.'

'You are not forgetting Wednesday evening,' he cautioned, referring to her dinner party.

For a moment it was obvious that she had done exactly that.

'Oh — no, of course not. I have things fairly well in hand, and even if Agatha does stay until tomorrow, that is only Tuesday. Will you come to the Bower with me, Addington?'

'I would prefer not to.'

She accepted the rebuff with only a slight tightening of her lips. 'Doctor?'

'Well, I — Yes, of course.'

MacKenzie sighed to himself. He'd become accustomed to a nap after lunch. But now Caroline Ames, for whom he had come to have feelings that went far beyond casual friendship, was asking him for help. He could not possibly refuse her.

'Good,' she replied. 'We will go at once.'

Since it was obvious that nothing would deter her, Ames threw up his hands and set off in the rain once more to find them a cab. Shortly they heard the horse's hooves on the cobblestones outside, and Caroline and the doctor, stoutly protected against the weather with waterproofs, galoshes, and her capacious umbrella, bade Ames good-bye.

He stood at the parlor window and watched through the lavender glass as the narrow black cab wobbled its way to the end of the square and turned down Pinckney Street. It was early afternoon but already growing dark. What state Agatha Montgomery would be in — or what tale of horror Caroline would bring back to him — he could only imagine.

It was a bad business, this murder. Nothing for a lady like Caroline Ames to be involved in.

3

In the cab, MacKenzie glanced at his companion. Beneath the brim of her dark gray bonnet, her face was strained and pale. Her hands in their black kid gloves were clenched in her lap, and although her gaze was directed toward the passing row upon row of redbrick and brownstone town houses that lined the streets, he doubted that she saw them. He cast about for some comforting thing to say to her, but he could think of nothing. For the time being she was estranged from him, and he acknowledged to himself that the very fact of her concern for her friend was part of the reason he had come to care for her: She was a woman of tender sensibilities, kindness and goodness personified, just as all women were supposed to be but were not.

Soon they crossed over the Boston & Providence railroad tracks and passed into the South End. This was a district much like the Back Bay and built around the same time, thirty-odd years before, but as it was literally on the wrong side of the tracks, it had quickly fallen into shabby disrepair. Its handsome buildings had been cut up into apartments, and, worse, single rooms for rent; many of them had deteriorated through years of neglect. As the cab rolled by, MacKenzie saw more than a few disreputable-looking characters who would never have ventured onto Commonwealth Avenue or Beacon Street or the Ameses' place, Louisburg Square. But he noted, too, a number of churches. There must be some kind of faithful flock existing hereabouts, he thought.

Bertram's Bower, on Rutland Square, was one of a number of matching brownstones that curved around a small oval 'square,' a kind of miniature Louisburg Square. Here MacKenzie could see that some effort had been made to keep property values up: The high iron fence that encircled the little oval was intact and free of rust, the brass door knockers on the houses were brightly polished, the doors themselves freshly painted. Someone — Agatha Montgomery? — had seen to it that this little enclave, at least, would not succumb to decay.

They alighted, MacKenzie paid the driver, and sheltered by Caroline's umbrella they mounted the tall flight of steps to the Bower's door. He lifted the knocker and brought it down sharply twice.

It was opened by a frightened-looking

young woman in a white bib apron over a plain dark dress.

'Yes, sir?'

'Hello, Nora,' Caroline said.

'Oh! Miss Ames! I didn't — ' She broke off, obviously embarrassed.

'Is Miss Montgomery in?' Caroline asked. She smiled at the girl, whom she knew from her embroidery class.

Nora hesitated. 'No, miss,' she said, not meeting Caroline's eyes.

'You mean, she is, but not to visitors?' Caroline said gently.

Nora nodded.

'Well, I imagine she will be in to me — to us,' she corrected herself.

Nora's eyes slid unhappily to MacKenzie.

'This is Dr. MacKenzie,' Caroline added. Standing on the stoop, they were getting thoroughly wet, and with a graceful gesture that waved the girl aside, she stepped into the vestibule, and MacKenzie, shaking out the umbrella, followed.

'Oh, but, miss — ' Nora began, looking more frightened than ever.

'Never mind, dear,' Caroline said. 'I'm sure Miss Montgomery will see us.'

She moved into the dim, bleak front hall, MacKenzie close behind. Two meager gas jets on the wall by the stairs provided the only illumination, hardly sufficient on this dark day. The place had an institutional smell: a combination of cooking odors, strong lye soap, and an indefinable smell that was the odor of many human bodies crowded together. But it was oddly silent, he thought. Surely now, at mid-afternoon, a place like this should be buzzing with activity? Or perhaps not; perhaps the girls were at their classes, and the noise and chatter would come later, when they were released.

'I will just go and see — ' Caroline began, when suddenly, from the back of the hall, a woman appeared. She was middle-aged, of middling height, with a mannish look to her — broad shoulders, short, thick neck, and a coarse-featured face.

'I told you not to admit anyone!' she snapped, addressing the now thoroughly cowed Nora. Then, seeing Caroline, she caught herself. 'Miss Ames,' she said, but hardly in a welcoming tone.

'Matron Pratt,' Caroline replied easily. 'I have come to see Miss Montgomery. This is my friend, Dr. MacKenzie.'

As Matron Pratt flicked her cold gaze over him and instantly dismissed him, his greeting died on his lips.

'She's not in,' Matron said.

'She isn't? Oh, dear, I am sorry.'

Just then they were aware of a movement at the top of the long, narrow flight of stairs. A young woman — another resident of the place, obviously — had started down, but when she saw Matron Pratt, she stopped.

'One demerit, Slattery!' snapped the matron.

'But I was just — '

'Back to your class! Or I'll give you two!'

Stifling a sob, the girl retreated.

Caroline tried again. 'Mrs. Pratt, I know what a difficult time this must be for you, but I wanted to see Agatha, just for a moment.'

'She's not fit to see anyone, Miss Ames.'

'So she is here?'

'Yes.' Matron Pratt's cold gray eyes never wavered as she met Caroline's anxious gaze. 'But she's in no condition to see you. The police have been all over the place, all morning. I swan, I don't know how we are supposed to get on with our business here, with them poking and prying.'

'Yes,' murmured Caroline, aware that Nora was edging away from them toward the stairs. 'But if she could see us, even for a moment — '

'Cromarty!' snarled Matron Pratt. 'You were told not to allow anyone in! Two demerits!'

Nora stared at her, appalled. 'But, Matron — '

'You heard what I said! Get back to class now, or I'll make it three!'

As Nora scrambled up the stairs, they saw a female coming down, and this time she did not flinch and flee at the sight of Matron Pratt.

'Agatha!' Caroline exclaimed, relieved to see her friend at last.

The proprietress of Bertram's Bower peered down at them, squinting a little, as if she could not see clearly. She moved aside to let the luckless Nora pass, and then descended slowly, clinging to the banister; once she seemed to stagger, but she caught herself before she fell.

'Oh, Agatha! I came as soon as I heard the news.' As Miss Montgomery reached the bottom of the stairs, Caroline seized her hands. 'And I have brought my friend, Dr. MacKenzie,' she added.

He advanced and held out his hand. Miss Montgomery did not seem to see him at first, but then she took his hand — hers was icy cold — and mumbled a greeting.

She was as plain a woman as he had ever seen, with graying hair parted in the middle and pulled back severely into a knot. Her face was long and rather equine, with a prognathous jaw and thin lips; her complexion was muddy, and her eyes were a watery color that he could not put a name to.

He chided himself: This was not some would-be debutante, but a woman in severe distress whose looks hardly mattered. And so he spoke to her gently, and said he hoped they were not intruding.

She did not seem to understand him. Shock, he thought; shock and stress, and very little sleep last night, more than likely.

Matron Pratt hadn't moved, but her rather threatening presence did not deter Caroline.

'Dear Agatha,' she said, 'can we not sit someplace and talk for a bit? I could use a cup of tea, and — '

Suddenly Miss Montgomery came back to them. 'You must pardon me, Caroline,' she said with an attempt at a smile. 'I — we — have been — most upset.'

'Of course you have,' Caroline replied warmly. 'I came as soon as I heard the news. I could hardly believe it.'

'Come,' said Miss Montgomery, 'we will go into my private room. And, yes, tea is a good idea. Matron, would you have one of the girls bring us a tray?'

Glowering, Matron Pratt pinched her mouth into an even tighter line than before.

'You should rest,' she said. MacKenzie wondered at her tone: Was she in the habit of ordering Miss Montgomery about?

'I have done that,' Miss Montgomery replied. 'And now I will take tea with Miss Ames. And her friend,' she added.

She led them past a door labeled Office and back along the hall. At the end was an arched doorway that gave onto a good-sized dining room, empty now, the long tables laid with places for the next meal. Opposite was an unmarked door, which Miss Montgomery opened.

'*Oh!*' She stopped short, nearly causing Caroline to collide with her. Then she advanced slowly into the room — a small, chilly parlor — and Caroline and MacKenzie followed.

A young woman had risen from a chair by the window. She was of medium height, plain — homely, even, and with her eyes reddened by weeping. In her dark dress and white apron, she was obviously a resident of the Bower. Caroline recognized her, in fact, as one of the girls in her Thursday afternoon sewing class. She nodded at Caroline, but she addressed herself to Miss Montgomery.

'Excuse me, miss,' she began. 'I know I shouldn't be here — '

'No, Brown, you certainly should not,'

Agatha Montgomery replied grimly. 'Whatever are you thinking of?'

'I'm thinkin' of Mary, miss.'

They were — had been — roommates, Caroline remembered.

'We are all thinking of Mary,' Miss Montgomery replied a little more gently. 'But you should not be breaking the rules — '

'I just wanted a word with you, miss.'

Caroline knew this girl, Bridget Brown, as dutiful and humble, the way Bower girls were supposed to be, and never one to make trouble. She was amazed that Bridget had the gumption to stand up to Agatha Montgomery like this.

'As you see, I am occupied just now,' Miss Montgomery said. 'So go back to your class, and if Matron sees you and tries to give you a demerit, tell her I said you were to be let off this once.'

But Bridget was not so easily disposed of. 'I need to speak to you, miss,' she said. Although her eyes were cast down in a properly subservient attitude, her voice was steady and determined.

The proprietress of the Bower stared at her for a moment as if she were weighing something in her mind. Then: 'You may come to see me before supper,' she said. 'But for now, you must return to your class.'

Uncomfortably aware that she, too, was probably breaking one or another of the Bower's many rules, Caroline stepped forward and put her arm around the girl to lead her away. 'Dear Bridget,' she murmured, 'this is a terribly difficult time for you. I came here today to see if I could do anything to help Miss Montgomery' — they were in the hall now, and walking toward the stairs — 'but if I can do anything for you, as well, or for any of the girls here, you must let me know.'

Bridget stopped and stepped away from her to face her. 'I don't know how I could do that, Miss Ames, seein' as how we aren't allowed to use the telephone.' She nodded toward the instrument on the wall by the office door.

An indisputable point. 'What did you want to ask Miss Montgomery?' Caroline said.

Bridget bit her lip. Then: 'I wanted to ask her — somethin'.' Bridget's eyes flashed up at Caroline; then she looked down again.

Something private, obviously. Caroline didn't know the girl well enough to press her further.

'All right, Bridget. As she told you, you may speak to her later. But before you go back to class, I want you to promise me that you won't leave the Bower until the police catch the man who — who killed Mary.'

Bridget had gone very pale. 'You mean, because he might get me too?'

'Yes. That is exactly what I mean.' Caroline did not want to frighten Bridget more than she was already frightened, but she felt it was necessary to speak so, to keep her safe. 'He might get any of you,' she added. 'So you must stay here. Will you promise me that?'

'Can't stay in all the time, Miss Ames. You could go crazy, stayin' in this place.'

'Well, then, promise that you will go out only in the daytime — and not alone! You must always go with one or two other girls.'

Bridget gave her a last, imploring look. She was crying again. Caroline thought she was about to say something more, but then, without replying — without promising what Caroline had asked of her — she turned and ran up the stairs. Poor thing, Caroline thought. She is grieving for her friend, and neither Agatha nor I can be of much help to her.

Agatha Montgomery's parlor was furnished in what looked like cast-off items — probably from some of the same benefactors who supported the place, Caroline thought as she rejoined the other two. Miss Montgomery motioned her visitors to sit on a worn horsehair sofa, while she took a wooden rocking chair.

'I apologize for that intrusion,' she said. 'Thank you, Caroline, for dealing with her. It was good of you to come. In my experience,' she added with some bitterness, 'people often turn away at the first sign of trouble.'

'Dear Agatha, can you talk about it at all?' Caroline said gently.

Miss Montgomery shook her head. 'It is very hard,' she said, and they heard the catch in her voice.

'Yes. I know it is. But if you could — '

A rap on the door, and a girl came in bearing a tray. No hot-water jug, Caroline noted; the tea was already brewing in the pot, then. When Miss Montgomery did not move to pour, she rose and did so herself.

'Here,' she said, handing a cup to her friend. 'This will do you good.'

Miss Montgomery took a few sips of the steaming brew and then, seeming somewhat revived, set her cup and saucer back onto the tray.

'You knew Mary,' she said.

'A little. She was always in the office, so I didn't see her much. A slightly built girl, with brown hair and a pretty Irish face?'

'Yes.' Miss Montgomery grimaced as if she were in pain. 'Yes, she was pretty. And very slight indeed — seriously underweight — when we took her in. In fact, she was near death. She had pleurisy, and she could not draw a breath without agony. Under our care, and with Dr. Hannah's help, she revived.'

'Dear Dr. Hannah,' breathed Caroline.

'But even as sick as she was, I could see right away that she was different from the others,' Miss Montgomery went on. She paused to take a handkerchief from her cuff and dab at her watery eyes. 'She was really quite bright, and surprisingly well spoken. She was about nineteen or twenty, but she seemed younger — hardly more than a child.'

'And so after she had stayed her three months — ' Caroline prompted.

'I asked her to stay on, to be my secretary. I had been managing without one, but the work never lets up, and I really thought I could not go on unless I had help. I asked Randolph about it, of course, because he oversees the budget and I needed his permission to pay Mary a small salary. It wasn't much — not nearly what she was worth.' Miss Montgomery paused again and thought for a moment, lost in her memories.

Then she went on. 'Eventually, Randolph came to see what a good investment it was. He even came to the point of offering to buy us a typewriting machine. All the most forward-looking businesses use them, and she was eager to learn. He'd bought her an instruction manual, and she was studying it. Oh, she was a wonderful girl! I cannot understand why — '

She broke off, and there was another pause. MacKenzie shifted uncomfortably on the hard sofa. Undoubtedly because of the weather, he thought, his knee had begun to ache.

Miss Montgomery began to speak again. 'Last night, even though it was Sunday, Mary said she would work in the office to bring the account books up-to-date. Matron had gone to her regular Sunday evening religious service over on Columbus Avenue — with a Mrs. Mary Baker Eddy, do you know her? — and I was at evening prayers at Trinity Church in Copley Square. Miss Cox had come in to mind the girls, as she does when both Mrs. Pratt and I are out.

'I got back shortly before nine. The house was quiet. I did not see Matron, but I did not expect to because her Sunday evenings generally last until ten. Miss Cox gave her report — all was well, she said — and I said good night to her and she left. All the girls were asleep upstairs — or in their rooms, at any rate. The office was dark, so I assumed that Mary had finished her work and had gone to bed.'

She paused, as if to gather her strength.

They waited silently, caught up now in the drama of her story.

She went on: 'So, seeing nothing amiss, I went to my room at the top of the house. I never heard Matron come in, and I was asleep when the policeman came. It was Officer Flynn, our neighborhood patrolman.'

She drew a ragged breath, and when she spoke again it was haltingly, as if she were having to force out the words. 'Matron came to wake me at once, of course. She said he wanted me to go with him. He would not tell her why, but somehow I knew it was some terrible trouble.

'I dressed as quickly as I could, and we hurried over toward Warren Avenue. As I came near, I saw three or four carriages — police vehicles, and a long black wagon. There were lanterns and torches, so that the place was brightly lighted. Over and over again, I asked Officer Flynn why he had come for me, but he would not tell me. Yet all the while, I knew — not that it was Mary, but that it was one of our girls, and some harm had come to her.'

Her voice broke then, and with a great shudder she put her hands over her face while she choked back her sobs.

Caroline made small soothing noises to

comfort her, and MacKenzie waited, uncomfortable as men always were in the presence of women's tears. Perhaps she should not go on, he thought, but as it was not his place to suggest it, he trusted in Caroline's judgment as to how much more emotional turmoil her friend might be able to endure.

Miss Montgomery, somewhat recovered, went on: 'There was a crowd gathered at the entrance to the alley behind West Brookline Street. When I reached it, I saw another little group halfway down, four or five men and something lying on the ground. It was covered with some dark drapery, a blanket perhaps. When I approached the men, one of them spoke to me and introduced himself as Inspector Crippen.'

'Yes,' Caroline interjected. 'I know him.'

'You do?' Miss Montgomery seemed momentarily surprised — startled out of her grim recital.

'Yes. My brother — but never mind that. Go on. You were in the alley with the police?'

'Yes. It seemed that I had been summoned because a body — and that is what it was, a body — had been discovered by Officer Flynn. At first he thought it was a bundle of rags, but then he saw a shoe protruding and he realized it was the body of a woman. He recognized her as one of our girls. So he sent

31

for help, and they told him to fetch me to give positive identification.'

Her voice trailed off, and for a moment her face went slack with the memory of what she had seen. Caroline pictured it: the dark, the rain, torches and lanterns flickering in the raw night wind, the little circle of men's faces peering down at the girl's body. And poor Agatha, called out on such a dreadful errand . . .

'She had been badly cut up,' Miss Montgomery went on. 'Her dress was slashed to ribbons. Underneath it I could see her terrible wounds. The rain had washed away her blood, but the puddles by her side were dark with it. I never thought a human body could contain so much blood. Oh, it was horrible! Horrible! That poor girl! She didn't have an enemy in the world. Unless it was someone from the streets she came from, someone from her past. Or — some madman.' Piteously, she looked at Caroline. 'Yes, it must have been that. Some madman. Some lunatic, killing poor Mary and not even knowing who she was.'

'Obviously, anyone who would commit such a crime — such a savage crime — was not in command of his faculties,' Caroline replied. She did not want to seem callous, but — 'Agatha, do you have any idea why Mary went out last night?'

'No. None.'

'It is very odd, don't you think? Since she had said she would work in the office, and she was such a dependable girl?'

'Yes. It is odd. I can't think why — '

'And Miss Cox never mentioned that Mary had gone out?'

'No. She had the girls in Bible study' — a weekly undertaking, Caroline knew, mandatory for all residents but not, apparently, for Mary — 'and when she left, she would have seen that the office light was not on, and she would have thought — just as I did — that Mary had finished her work and gone to bed.'

Caroline cast a warning glance at MacKenzie. She didn't want him tattling to Addington about what she intended to say next.

'Agatha, perhaps we can help you. To find out why Mary left. To talk to the girls, perhaps, and ask — '

'No.' Suddenly Miss Montgomery stopped weeping. She made a final swipe at her reddened eyes, blinked rapidly, and took a deep breath. 'No, Caroline, it was more than kind of you to come, but you have your own affairs to tend to. The police will manage well enough, I imagine.'

'Yes, but — '

'No. I insist. You must not trouble yourself anymore.' She stood and walked to the window, moving stiffly, as if her bones ached, thought MacKenzie. In her dark, shapeless dress, lacking a bustle or nipped-in waist, lacking any kind of ornament, she seemed even taller, more gaunt than before. 'It is still raining hard,' she said. 'I will send one of the girls to fetch a herdic for you.'

'Then at least come to us for the night,' Caroline persisted. 'It would be no trouble at all. We could put you on the fourth floor and we have the elevator so you will be spared the stairs — '

'No.' Miss Montgomery turned to face them, and now MacKenzie saw what he had not seen before, the strong-minded female who had brought this place — this refuge for fallen women — into being. 'No,' she repeated less vehemently. 'You must go home, and I — I must deal with matters here.'

Caroline made one last try. 'Surely Mrs. Pratt can deal with any emergency — any further emergency — and she can send a telegram to you at our house if you should be needed.'

'You do not subscribe to the telephone?'

'No. We have talked about it, but — no, we do not.' So far, Ames had won, and a subscription had not been taken.

'Well, then,' said Miss Montgomery, as if that settled the matter: If the Ameses had no telephone, she could not possibly stay with them. With somber courtesy, she held out her hand to MacKenzie. 'Good day to you, Doctor,' she said. And to Caroline: 'You have been more than kind to come. But now, if you will excuse me, I must see to my girls.'

4

MacKenzie's shattered knee, operated on in late September, had healed well until November, when his recuperation had had a temporary setback in the business of the death of Colonel Mann. Now, in January, he still occasionally awoke in the morning to find that his knee had stiffened, making it difficult to navigate the stairs.

On those days he went down to breakfast in the elevator. Like all machinery, it made its own peculiar noises. He had come to expect them whenever he stepped in and pushed the brass handle either right or left, depending on whether he wanted to go up or down. Now, on the morning after his visit to Bertram's Bower, when he pulled shut the grille and grasped the handle to push it to the left, down, there was a heart-stopping pause — a hesitation that had never happened before. He was just about to let go of the handle and step out, when the elevator started its descent. But its soft moan and wheeze sounded different this day: more strained, somehow.

Nevertheless, since he had started to go

down, he had to keep his grip on the handle or he would stop between floors. So down he went, past the second floor, where he could have alighted had he had second sight.

When the cab had just passed the second floor, the machinery shuddered to a stop. Here between floors it was gloomy despite the leaded glass skylight that topped the shaft; the cab's brass grille all around allowed a little more light to come from the stairwell. Still, it was pretty dim.

Worse, the elevator, great convenience though it was, was a space no bigger than four feet by four feet, and perhaps seven feet high. It was a small space to be confined in, particularly for someone like himself, who suffered from a mild form of claustrophobia.

This is a pretty pickle, he thought. After a moment, not knowing what else to do, he called, 'Ames! Are you there?'

He heard Ames come out of the dining room and into the first floor hall. 'Halloo! Was that you calling, Doctor?'

MacKenzie could hear him clearly; had Ames been on the stairs, he could have seen him through the grille.

'I'm afraid the thing has gotten stuck,' he called. 'I'm not sure what to do.'

'Don't do anything! You might disrupt the machinery and go crashing down. Damn!

Caro's down in the kitchen with Cook. Just wait a minute — '

It was Caroline who was the elevator expert, since she had had to learn the idiosyncrasies of the thing in the course of attending to her mother during that lady's illness. She had given MacKenzie a thorough course of instruction not only on how to operate it but also on its little quirks.

He tried to remember, now, precisely what she had said. 'If you feel it start to shudder too badly' (he thought she'd said that) 'you must grip the handle — so — and pull it neither left nor right but toward you. And if it starts to drop too quickly, push this button' — a large white ceramic thing above the lever with the word BRAKE embossed upon it. Installed next to it was what looked like an oversized red china doorknob that she had made no mention of, or if she had, he had forgotten what it was. 'And if it stops altogether — I mean between floors, where it is not supposed to — then do — '

What? He racked his brain. Her other instructions he thought he remembered, but this most crucial one he could not recall.

He stood frozen in fear. What if the damnable thing dropped straight down to the basement, collapsing into a crumpled heap of brass and wood? He did not dare to touch either the handle-lever or the big white ceramic BRAKE button. He contemplated the large red — for emergencies? — knob, but he was even less inclined to touch that unknown. He could only stand stiffly, his knee throbbing, and wait for his rescue.

'Hold on! Don't panic!' called Ames. He was on the stairs now, right outside the cab. He himself never used the elevator; he didn't trust it, and incidents like this only confirmed his suspicions. 'We'll have you out in no time. Are you all right?'

MacKenzie said he was, although in truth he was not sure.

'Good. Good. Now I am going to go down to the kitchen and fetch Caroline — ah! There she is now.'

And he pounded down to the front hall, calling to his sister as he went.

In a moment she was there, speaking to MacKenzie from the stairway; he could see her through the grille. She gave him the crucial instruction — the one he had forgotten — and in no more than a minute or two he was safely downstairs.

'What a fright!' Caroline exclaimed as he emerged, shaken, from the elevator cab. 'My dear Dr. MacKenzie! Such a dreadful experience! Thank goodness you don't have a weak heart! I am going to write out all the instructions for every conceivable occurrence, and post them inside the elevator so this will never happen to you again.'

Flexing his knee a bit, he assured her that no harm had been done, and they proceeded into the dining room. He heard the dumbwaiter thumping and creaking in the back hall, and then Margaret appeared bearing the breakfast tray. What he needed, he thought, was a cup of strong black coffee to repair his nerves; the oatmeal that was their standard fare except on Saturdays, when they had bacon and eggs, seemed singularly unappetizing just now.

The morning *Globe* lay at Ames's place at the head of the table, and MacKenzie could see a bold black headline. Now Ames picked it up, started to hand it to his sister, and then hesitated.

She had seated herself and was pouring his tea. 'Here you are, Addington. Why — what is it? What is wrong?'

'More bad news for Miss Montgomery, I am afraid.'

She put down the teapot and stared at him. 'Oh, no. What is it?'

'Another girl from the Bower has been killed. And in the same way.'

'Oh, *no*.'

MacKenzie thought he heard tears in her

voice. For the moment she'd forgotten him, so he poured his own coffee. After a few sips, he felt much better.

She put out her hand and Ames gave her the newspaper. Rapidly she scanned it, uttering little exclamations of dismay as she did so.

'This is terrible, Addington.'

'Did you know this girl?'

'Bridget Brown. Yes. She was in my Thursday class. She was quiet, never offensive. In fact, we saw her yesterday afternoon. Do you remember, Doctor? She was the girl who wanted to speak to Agatha. I made her promise she wouldn't leave the Bower after dark — and never alone. But she must have gone out, after all, and — ' She broke off, trying to acknowledge to herself the horror of what had happened.

Then: 'Oh, poor Agatha! After all these years, when she has worked so hard to make the Bower a respectable place — '

'It is not her fault that some madman is loose in the district, Caroline.'

'No. Of course it isn't. But you know how people are. After this, when they think of Bertram's Bower they will think of these hideous crimes. They won't stop to consider — Oh, Addington, this will be the ruination of the Bower! People will never support it if it

41

is associated with scandal like this. Agatha will have to give it up, and all her years and years of good work will have been for nothing!'

'From what you told me of your visit to her yesterday, she seems to be holding up fairly well.'

'Yes, but that was before — before this second death.' She stared at him with anguished eyes.

He put out his hand and she gave the newspaper back to him. Watching her across the table, MacKenzie could see that she was struggling to contain her tears. Absently, he began to pull at one end of his mustache, a habit he had when he was unnerved.

At length, composing herself, she rose, helped herself to oatmeal, and returned to the table where, MacKenzie was glad to see, she began to eat. After a moment she said, 'Addington.'

'Yes?' He did not look up at her. According to the *Globe*'s account, Deputy Chief Inspector Elwood Crippen was assuring the public that the perpetrator of these atrocious crimes would soon be caught. People need have no fear for their safety, but in the meantime, while the hunt was on, he cautioned them, particularly females, to avoid walking alone at night in the South End.

Crippen. He felt a little shiver of distaste as he called up into his mind's eye the image of the officious little policeman. Caroline was right: Crippen would bungle this case for certain. Too quick to make an arrest, too quick to jump to unfounded conclusions . . .

'Bridget Brown was Mary Flaherty's roommate,' Caroline said.

He looked up. 'I beg your pardon?'

'I said, 'Bridget Brown was Mary Flaherty's roommate.' '

'Are you sure?'

'Of course I'm sure! Otherwise I wouldn't say so. Don't you think that is significant?'

He thought about it. 'It might be, yes.'

'And what did she want to speak to Agatha about, I wonder.' Her face suddenly became animated. 'Addington, we must help Agatha. Really we must.'

He contemplated her from beneath his dark brows. His look was stern, but MacKenzie thought he saw in it some hint of apprehension.

'And how are we to do that?'

'I don't know. How would I know? You can go to the Bower — go to Inspector Crippen, for that matter. Offer to help him.'

'He does not look kindly on my help, Caro. You know that.'

She waved her hand in irritation. 'Nonsense. He is often mistaken, but he is not a fool. If you can save him from making a serious mistake — as you have done twice before — '

'And do not forget Cousin Wainwright,' Ames added. That worthy, a cousin on their mother's side, sat on the board of police commissioners. He was jealous of the authority of the police and did not welcome unasked-for assistance from outside the ranks.

'Oh, Cousin Wainwright!' Caroline exclaimed. 'He cannot possibly object to your talking to Inspector Crippen, or even visiting the Bower.'

'Caroline, we cannot intrude ourselves into this case,' Ames said flatly. He handed the newspaper to MacKenzie and rose to get his oatmeal from the sideboard.

His sister made no reply, but MacKenzie noted her rather alarming expression. Had he been asked to describe it, he would have said that it was one of mulish stubbornness. It did not quite fit with his image of her as the Angel of the Hearth, compliant always to the wishes of her older brother.

Ames returned to the table and began to eat. Caroline watched him for a moment, and then she said, 'Remember Agatha's father, Addington.'

'What about him?'

44

'Don't you remember that our own papa thought very highly of him? They were friends for years.'

'Yes. I know.'

'And before Mr. Montgomery went bankrupt, I believe I am right when I say that one time he helped Papa through some business difficulty. I don't know the details — Mama did not either, but she once told me — '

'Caroline.' Ames had stopped eating, but he still held his spoon. 'Listen to me.'

'Yes, Addington, I am listening,' she said, but her expression did not change.

'There have been two atrocious murders over in the South End. Both victims were residents of Bertram's Bower. The police have begun their investigation. I have no doubt that soon enough they will find their man. You and I' — and here he spoke with unusual sternness — 'have no business interfering.'

'How can it be interfering, simply to — '

'None,' he snapped. 'As regrettable an affair as this is, it is none of ours. I would ask you to remember that.'

For a moment she held his gaze; then she looked down at her half-eaten oatmeal congealing in its dish.

'I have no time today or tomorrow,' she said at last, 'because of my dinner party. I cannot even attend Sewing Circle this morning. But after tomorrow evening I will be free to — '

'Don't say it,' he warned, scowling at her.

'I will say it. Agatha is my friend. I have known her all my life. I work at the Bower two afternoons a month, as I have done ever since she started it. I have watched her build the Bower from a rented apartment into that entire house, which they were able to buy because of her brother's skill at fund-raising. That was a tremendous achievement, to buy that place. Think of it, Addington — think of how they have worked over the years. And now Agatha is in trouble. Through no fault of her own, but serious trouble all the same. What would you have me do? Turn my back on her? Refuse to help her?'

'Of course not, but — '

'Then you agree that I must do what I can.'

'You must do nothing, Caroline. I forbid you.'

She lifted her chin. Not an Angel of the Hearth, MacKenzie thought, but a warrior princess from some ancient myth. He had admired her tremendously from the day he'd met her, and never more than at this moment.

'Of course, what I can do is very little,' she went on as if she had not heard her brother's last words, 'compared to what you might

46

accomplish. I — well, you know how people hate pushy, forward women. Agatha herself has often been accused of being forward, but really it is just her sense of mission that drives her. While I — well, I have never had much to be pushy about, have I?'

'Fortunately,' Ames muttered.

For a long moment she contemplated him. Then: 'I really do think you should go to see Inspector Crippen.'

'And tell him what?'

'You don't have to *tell* him anything. But you might *ask* how the case is progressing.'

'And what about Cousin Wainwright?'

'You probably won't see him, but if you do, send him to me. I will deal with him.'

Ames could not repress a smile. He was four years older than she; he could remember the day she'd been born. From that day, he had been brought up to care for her as a gentleman should care for his sister, to protect her, cherish her, keep her from all that was sordid and vile in the world. He had done so as well as he could. It was not his fault that she had inherited the family stubbornness and, worse, its stern New England conscience that sometimes prompted her to act rashly for what she considered good cause.

'All right, Caroline.' He shook his head. 'I will go to see Crippen, and for your sake as well as Miss Montgomery's I will try not to antagonize him too greatly.'

5

Half an hour later, Ames and MacKenzie made their way along Louisburg Square to Mt. Vernon Street and up Mt. Vernon to Joy. The rain had stopped during the night, but still the morning was damp and gray, the air filled with the sour salt smell of the sea. The redbrick town houses that lined the way, with their shining black or white doors, their brass door knockers, their shuttered windows, did not glow today as they did in the sun. The city had an air of grim expectation, as if it waited for the thaw to pass and winter to return.

'He'll be annoyed,' said Ames, lifting his hat to a woman passing.

'I imagine he will,' MacKenzie replied. He had met Crippen the previous autumn and had not liked him — not least because the man had seemed to want to pay suit to Caroline Ames.

'Still, Caroline is right,' Ames went on. They trod carefully along Joy Street, down the steeply sloping sidewalk that led to Beacon; the bricks were slick with the wet, and often uneven. 'She is very loyal, my sister.

And it is true that Agatha Montgomery has devoted her life to her flock over at the Bower. It is too bad that it might all come to nothing now because of some madman.'

They came out to Boston Common, dull and dreary on this dull and dreary day, tall, leafless elms lining the walkways, the grass dead and brown and patched with soot-blackened snow. Few pedestrians were about. There was skating on the Frog Pond in winter, but now the ice had melted and signs were posted warning would-be skaters away. Beyond the treetops, the tall spire of the Park Street Church rose into the pale gray sky.

They walked up the hill past the gold-domed redbrick State House, and down again past the forbidding brownstone exterior of the Boston Athenaeum. The morning traffic was heavy, carts and wagons and carriages and herdic-phaetons all jostling for passage. At the foot of Beacon Street, they had some difficulty, but then they were across, passing the oddly truncated King's Chapel and mounting the broad granite steps of the ornate Second Empire City Hall, going through the tall oak double doors and entering the hushed, thrumming atmosphere of the city's municipal offices.

They went up to the second floor, down a corridor, and into Crippen's lair.

'Not in, sir,' said the young man guarding the inner office door.

'Really?' said Ames. 'And when might he be?'

'Not for a while, I'm — '

The door opened and Crippen appeared. 'Davis, did you find — Ah! Mr. Ames!'

He had been frowning at first, but now, seeing Ames, a smile spread over his ugly little face, and he held out his pudgy hand, its fingers stained with nicotine.

'Good morning, Inspector.'

'And to what do I owe this pleasure?' Crippen said, shaking Ames's hand vigorously. He was short and plump, nattily dressed in a rather common way in a brown checkered suit, yellow vest, and a cravat in a particularly hideous shade of green. His watch chain, stretched across his paunch, looked as though it needed a few extra links. Although his clean-shaven face looked young, and was surprisingly unlined for a man in his position, his hair was gray.

MacKenzie, understanding that their dislike was mutual, did not offer to shake Crippen's hand.

'I merely wanted a word,' said Ames.

'Ah! A word! Come in, come in.' Crippen was all smiles, forgetting what he had been about to ask his clerk.

MacKenzie followed Ames into the inspector's crowded little office, and they seated themselves on rickety wooden chairs before the overladen desk.

'It's about these murders over in the South End,' Ames began, removing his hat and gloves and placing them on his knees.

'The South End,' Crippen repeated.

'Yes. The girls from Bertram's Bower.'

'Bertram's Bower,' Crippen repeated.

You are stalling, MacKenzie thought, and that means you have made no progress in the case.

'A couple of Irish streetwalkers,' Crippen said. 'I don't see — '

'The proprietress there is a great friend of my sister's, and as you can imagine, she — Miss Montgomery — is extremely distressed.'

Crippen pursed his lips. 'And well she should be, Mr. Ames. Well she should be. But we'll have the matter cleared up quick enough, seeing as how she's got a likely suspect under her own roof, so to speak.'

'You don't say. Under her own roof?'

'That's right. Of course, we can't make an arrest yet, haven't got our case complete. But we have it well in hand, Mr. Ames. You can tell your sister I said so.' Suddenly, alarmingly, he leered at them; a revolting sight, MacKenzie thought. 'And how is she? Recovering well?'

'Perfectly well, thank you.'

'I am going to call on her one of these days, you know.'

'You are welcome at tea any afternoon, Inspector.'

'Is that so? Well, now, I just might turn up sometime. You can tell her that too.'

Ames cleared his throat. 'About your suspect, Inspector?'

'Ah. Yes. Well, we must bide our time a bit. He'll come walking into our arms one of these days, and sooner rather than later, I should think.'

'Indeed? But he must be some kind of madman, if the newspaper accounts were correct. Have you found the weapon?'

'Not yet.'

'Some kind of knife — '

'Yes.'

'There must have been a good deal of blood, from what I gathered from the account in the newspaper.'

'Not really. There was severe mutilation of the lower abdomen, true enough, but — '

'Like the first girl, the night before,' Ames interjected.

Crippen frowned. 'How did you know that? It wasn't in the papers.'

'As I told you, my sister is a friend of Miss Montgomery's. She went to the Bower yesterday afternoon, as soon as she saw the news. How did you manage to keep it from the early editions, by the way?'

Crippen grunted. 'With difficulty, Mr. Ames. With difficulty. Those newspaper fellows would run over their own grandmothers to get a story ahead of the competition. Anyways, where was I?'

'You were saying there wasn't much blood. Because of the rain, I take it.'

'Right. It was cats and dogs all night — and the night before as well. And besides, the fellow knew his business. He strangled 'em — garotted 'em — before he cut them up. So they didn't bleed as much as they would have otherwise.'

'And the knife was some kind of hunting knife, or fish fillet — ?'

'From what we can tell, in both cases it was a blade about one inch wide, six inches long. Probably a common kitchen knife. The Bower's cook says just such a knife is missing.'

'But no idea who might have taken it?'

'Not yet.'

'And it would be easy to dispose of.'

'That's right. We searched the alleys thereabouts, and the train yards, but I doubt

54

we'll find it. My guess is, by now it's at the bottom of the Charles.'

'You have spoken to the residents of the Bower?'

'Naturally. I myself interrogated a dozen — ah — females there, and my men questioned everyone else.'

'And what did you conclude?'

'Nothing, for the moment. These things take time. We don't want to arrest the wrong person and have the right one get away, now, do we? I will tell you one thing, however. Mind, it's strictly against the rules — but you say you are acquainted with Miss Montgomery? And her brother also, the Reverend Randolph Montgomery?'

'Yes. You have questioned him?'

'He was here earlier. He gave us some interesting information.'

'About — '

'About an Irish boy who works at the Bower.'

'Oh? And what did he say?'

'That it would be well to keep an eye on him, the Irish being what they are. And considering what the medical examiner has just put on my desk' — he lifted a sheet of paper and let it drop again onto its pile — 'the Reverend Montgomery may be right.'

'Why?'

'One of those girls was in the family way.'

'You don't say. Which one?'

'Mary Flaherty.'

'The first one to be killed.'

'That's right.'

'How far along was she?'

'About three months.'

Ames thought for a moment. The police department's medical examiner was a thorough, meticulous man, a swamp Yankee from Worcester. He'd been with the department for nearly twenty years, and Ames knew the police took some pride in the fact that Boston had been one of the first cities in America to have its own forensic physician. 'That is, of course, very interesting,' he said, 'and in a way it might simplify the case.'

'Precisely.'

'You suspect the Irish boy was — ah — intimate with her?'

'Yes.'

'Do you have any information about her other than that she was a resident of the Bower? Anything about her family?'

'No. Most of them are from out of town, those — ah — women. They have no family here.'

'Well, then, what about her friendship with the second girl — Bridget Brown?'

'How do you mean?'

'They were roommates.'

'I know that.'

MacKenzie detected a note of irritation in the inspector's voice, as if he thought Ames was wasting his time by giving him information that he already had.

'My men are right on top of this case,' Crippen went on, 'but even so, we have a good deal to see to otherwise. That North End gang, for instance. We've been tailing them for the past three years. They don't know it, but they are about to be brought to heel.'

'I am glad to hear it,' Ames replied easily, and, in an aside to MacKenzie: 'The inspector refers to a gang of roughnecks, Irish boys. What do they call themselves, Inspector? The Copp's Hill Boys? Yes. They are a scourge upon the city, and we will be well rid of them. They have nothing to do with this case — right, Inspector? — but still, we will be happy to see them gone, once and for all.'

Not for the first time, MacKenzie noted that when Ames spoke of Boston, he did so in a proprietary way, as if the city were his own personal responsibility, as if it needed him to tend to it, to keep it running smoothly. It was not surprising, he reflected, given that Ames's ancestors had been among the first settlers of the place, centuries ago, when they'd come over on the *Arbella* with John Winthrop. Caroline had told him that an Ames had lived in Boston ever since, and had been able to show him on a map exactly where.

'But to come back to the Bower,' Ames went on. 'The second victim — Bridget Brown — was not — ah — in a similar condition?'

'No.'

'But killed in the same way.'

'That's right. Garotted, then cut up.'

'Were there signs of a struggle?'

'Now, that's an odd thing, Mr. Ames. No sign at all. She was lying in a puddle — the drains in those alleys aren't kept as clean as they should be — but flat out on her back.'

'And what do you make of that?'

'That she was killed elsewhere and dumped in the alley.'

'I see.'

'Usually in violent killings like these, you get some indication that the victim tried to defend herself. Superficial wounds on the hands and arms, and so forth. But since they were both strangled first, we didn't have that here.'

'And what do you deduce from that?'

'Hard to say. I remember four or five years ago — not my case — a woman killed her husband over in the West End. Big brute of a thing, he was. She got him quiet by using chloroform on him first, to put him unconscious before she finished him off.'

'And did you find any trace of chloroform on either of these girls?'

'No. But it's hard to find that anyway. It evaporates quickly, leaves no trace. And with all the rain to wash it away — but it's a possibility. 'Course, since he strangled 'em, he didn't need to chloroform 'em as well, did he?'

'It would seem not,' Ames said. He stood up. 'You have been very helpful, Inspector. We will not take up any more of your valuable time — '

'Wait!' Crippen exclaimed. 'I almost forgot. One more thing. Have a look at this. If you hadn't come in, I'd have brought it around to you myself.'

He pulled out a drawer from the oak file cabinet behind him and extracted something. Handing it to Ames across the desk, he said, 'Damned strange, isn't it?'

It was a sheet of rough paper, creased where it had been folded. Upon it were pasted cut-out, printed letters. Ames read:

VPZRYPMOHJYROHJYDJSTQYRAAMPPMR

'Well?' said Crippen impatiently. 'What do you make of it?'

'Nothing, for the moment,' Ames replied, handing the paper to MacKenzie. 'What is its provenance?'

'Beg pardon?'

'I mean, where did you find it?'

'Oh! Yes, that's important. We found it on Mary Flaherty.'

'Ah. She was clutching it?' But no, he thought, the rain would have disintegrated it.

'In the pocket of her skirt.'

'And you have put your cryptanalysts right onto it, I assume?'

Crippen threw him a disdainful glance. 'There's no money in the budget for cryptanalysts, Mr. Ames. That's why I thought you might like to have a look at it. You told me once that a lot of your friends over the river know strange languages. I thought perhaps you might recognize this, or that one of them might.'

'That is possible,' said Ames. 'I will certainly have a go at it.' He took out his small Morocco leather notebook and, retrieving the paper from MacKenzie, copied the letters.

'And if you can make anything of it — ' Crippen said.

'Certainly, Inspector. I will notify you at once. I have your permission to show this to Professor Harbinger? He is a brilliant linguist, among his other talents.'

'Does he know Gaelic?'

'Gaelic? I don't know. Why? Ah! The Irish connection.'

'That's right. Well, see what you can do with it, in any case. If it isn't Gaelic, it may not be of any use to us.'

6

A short while later, on Newspaper Row at the foot of School Street, Ames and MacKenzie walked along until they came to a narrow doorway that gave onto a steep flight of stairs. At the top, down a corridor, Ames opened a door whose lettering announced the BOSTON LITERARY JOURNAL. MacKenzie knew the place, had been here before: It was the office of Ames's good friend, the proprietor of the publication, Desmond Delahanty.

'Desmond!' Ames exclaimed as they went in. They were in a small, cluttered office with every surface piled high with papers that looked like manuscripts. Behind a desk, one foot slung on its littered surface, sat a man with very red hair worn long over his collar, and a mustache whose ends drooped down near his jawline.

'Ames!' Delahanty replied, equally enthusiastic. He rose, threw down whatever it was he'd been reading, and held out his hand. 'And Dr. MacKenzie — good to see you.'

He was slightly shorter than Ames but equally thin, with bright blue eyes, an Irishman's beguiling smile, and a brogue to match. MacKenzie had known Irishmen in the army, but never one so charming.

'What brings you slumming?' Delahanty said with a grin. 'D'you want to make me a present of some literary endeavor?'

Ames snorted. 'Hardly. I want to exploit you, Desmond — and your connections.'

'My connections?' Delahanty looked around in mock puzzlement. 'And what might those be?'

Ames did not reply at once. He picked up a neatly bound periodical from one of the tables and waved it at his friend. 'The new issue?'

'Dummy copy. And only a month late.'

'Anything good in it?' Ames was a subscriber; every now and again he found something interesting.

'A story by a young lady that isn't bad.'

'Not the young lady with the illegible handwriting?' Ames said, smiling. Delahanty was often besieged by hopeful scribblers, male and female alike, whose persistence mounted in inverse ratio to their literary talents.

'No.' Delahanty rolled his eyes. 'I haven't seen her since before Christmas, thank God. I think I finally managed to discourage her. Told her to take up some other interest, like decoupage or Berlin needlework.'

Ames laughed, but then suddenly he sobered. 'I have a more serious business, Desmond,' he said. 'The murder of the girls at the Bower.'

'Ah.'

'Miss Montgomery, the proprietress, is a friend of Caroline's.'

'I see.'

'Caroline holds to the belief that one must help one's friends when trouble comes. And so now she has it in her head that we must help Miss Montgomery by attempting to . . .'

To what? Find the madman who had murdered, in the most hideous fashion, two of the Bower's girls?

Crippen's ugly little face rose up in his mind's eye, and he went on. 'To find who might be responsible for the deaths. Crippen is heading up the investigation,' he added as if in explanation.

Delahanty nodded. 'Your sister is a loyal friend.'

'Loyal — yes. And perhaps rather foolish. But she maintains that if the murderer is not caught — if, God forbid, more girls are killed — the Bower will suffer.'

'Yes. Well, she is right about that, I'd say. And of course my fellow journalists hereabouts make as much sensation as they can out of such matters. Anything to sell their rags.'

'Both those girls were Irish, Desmond.'

'That they were.' Delahanty's eyes were suddenly cold.

'We visited Inspector Crippen just now over at police headquarters, and I had the distinct impression that he has not put their deaths at the top of his agenda.'

'Because they were Irish girls,' Delahanty said. He glanced at MacKenzie. 'To be Irish in Boston, Doctor,' he went on, exaggerating his accent, 'is to be less than human. It is the NINA effect. I'm sure you've seen it. 'No Irish Need Apply' — a motto found in every help wanted advertisement, every position listed at every Intelligence Office — '

Ames held up his hand. He had been friends — good friends — with this particular Irishman since they had met five years before. He did not need yet another of Delahanty's sermons on the iniquities of Anglo-Saxon Boston.

'Yes, Desmond,' he said. 'I imagine that is so — because they were Irish girls.'

Delahanty waited.

'And so,' Ames went on smoothly, 'I thought perhaps — I don't suppose you knew them yourself, but I thought perhaps you might know someone who does. Did,' he corrected himself.

'I might.' Delahanty nodded. 'Yes, in fact,

I'm sure I do. My friend Martin Sweeney runs the Green Harp Saloon down on Atlantic Avenue. He knows nearly every Irish family in Boston.'

'Crippen believes the girls came from elsewhere.'

'Even so. They may have had some connection to the Irish community here, and if they did, Martin will know of it — or he will know of someone who does.'

'Excellent. What do you say to lunch at Durgin-Park, and then perhaps you will be good enough to introduce us to this Martin Sweeney?'

Delahanty looked around his cluttered little office. 'I don't — '

'Oh, come on, man,' Ames said, reading his friend's thoughts. 'It will do you good to get out for a bit. And if you have lunch at Durgin-Park, you won't need to bother with dinner. Unless they've shortened their portions since the last time I was there.'

The Durgin-Park Market Dining Rooms opposite the Quincy Market were always busy at noontime: men from the neighboring financial district, seamen on leave, traveling salesmen — 'drummers' — in town for a little recreation. There was no individual seating here; customers sat at long, communal tables and suffered the slings and arrows of the outrageously rude waiters whose insufferable manners were part of the attraction of the place, as Ames had explained to MacKenzie on their first visit some weeks before.

This day, the place was crowded as always, the waiters as harried and rude as ever as they dashed back and forth from the kitchen bearing platters of Yankee pot roast and boiled scrod and Indian pudding. The noise precluded any further conversation about Bertram's Bower or anything else, so Ames and his companions devoted themselves to their food — a bargain at fifty cents for the pot roast, less for the scrod — and in good time, well fed, stood outside once more in the busy Haymarket.

'Shall we call on your friend Sweeney?' Ames asked Delahanty, stepping out of the way of a farmer's wagon navigating the straw-strewn cobblestones. Behind them, the domed granite market building loomed into the rainy sky. Directly in front of them was the redbrick Faneuil Hall with its gilded cricket weathervane; farther on was Scollay Square and its notorious, illicit entertainments.

Delahanty waved down a herdic, and soon they were making their tortuous way through the city's narrow, crooked streets. The horse was balked at almost every corner, and more than once they heard the driver cursing, not at his horse but at the malign Fates that seemed to rule the city's traffic.

At last, however, they came to the waterfront, the neighborhood of Sweeney's saloon. It was only mid-afternoon, but the early winter darkness was fast coming on. In the rain, the street-lamps, sparsely spaced out, gave off a pale, ghostly glimmer. Faint gleams from the cab's sidelights glistened on the wet cobblestones, and the odor of the sea filled the air. Over the clop-clop of the horse's hooves came the melancholy clang of bell buoys in the harbor. Gone was the cozy residential neighborhood of Beacon Hill, the bustling streets of downtown. MacKenzie could see only the black hulks of warehouses and chandleries, the grim establishments of any working waterfront. Opposite the long row of their forbidding exteriors were the wharves and docks, and the bowsprits of fishing smacks tied up prow to street, arching over the heads of the occasional passersby on the sidewalk. Every so often they saw the dimly lit sign of a place like Sweeney's.

A little hush fell over the crowd as they entered, and MacKenzie was made uncomfortably aware that he and Ames, at least, were aliens.

'Martin, my friend!' Delahanty cried as he

led the way to the long, polished mahogany bar. Behind it stood a tall, stout, gray-haired man wearing a spotless white shirt with sleeve garters, and an equally spotless white apron over his trousers. He nodded at Delahanty, but he did not smile.

'Desmond. It's been a good long while, man, since you've shown your face to us.'

'Yes, well, I have a demanding profession that never lets me rest. But today I have brought you two new customers. Gentlemen, what is your pleasure?'

Ames and MacKenzie, introduced to the barkeep, ordered Guinness Stout, and Delahanty did the same. As they made themselves a little place to stand at the bar, talk rose up around them again; still, MacKenzie had the uncomfortable sensation that they were being watched. Like explorers coming into a native village, he thought, we are indelibly marked as outsiders.

Delahanty, however, proved to be a man of two worlds, comfortable in both. In a little while he had chatted up his friend to the point where the saloon proprietor, poker-faced at first, actually gave Ames and MacKenzie a small, grudging smile.

'Oh, yes,' he said. 'I know Bertram's Bower.'

'Do you indeed?' said Delahanty. 'Might

69

you know anyone there who could be of assistance to Mr. Ames?'

Sweeney observed them for a moment, his smile vanished. Then: 'I know a lad who works there. A handyman, like. Jack of all trades. He comes here nights to help out, when he can.'

Delahanty's thin face brightened. 'Does he indeed? And who might that be?'

'Garrett O'Reilly. I've known his ma since she stepped off the boat, and that was twenty-five years ago if it's a day. Used to know his da as well — a good friend of mine, Jim O'Reilly was — till he died, two years ago now. Left his missus with eight little ones younger than Garrett. The lad's worked for Miss Montgomery over to the Bower since Jim went. The missus thought it was a bad influence on him, but they needed the money, so she's let him stay. He had th'infantile paralysis when he was just a little lad, so he's a bit lame, no good to th'army, or on the docks hereabouts neither. So when the Reverend Montgomery and his sister, Miss Agatha, offered him a handyman's place, he was glad enough to take it. His ma is always worried he'll take up with one o'them women, but I guess he's kept clean. I've not heard a bad word about him, an' I would'v' if any was bein' said. Talk to him, tell him you

70

spoke to me. He might know somethin'.'

'Will he be here tonight?' Ames asked.

Sweeney shrugged, expressionless. 'Don't know. He doesn't keep a regular schedule. He might be, might not.'

'Martin,' said Delahanty, 'did you happen to know either one of those girls?'

'No,' Sweeney said. 'I don't say that I don't know one or another of 'em over there from time to time. There's good Irish girls enough who've fallen by the wayside, or been ruined through no fault of their own. But those two — no, I didn't know 'em.'

'But you'll keep an ear out for us, will you?'

'That I will.' Sweeney nodded once, emphatically. Ames felt that he was a man of his word, and that once he had accepted your friendship, and given his own in return, he was your friend for life. 'I hear a good deal one way and another,' Sweeney added.

Ames produced his card. 'A note to this address will always reach me.'

Without looking at it, the barkeep tucked it into his shirt pocket. 'All right,' he said. 'If someone's taken it into his head to kill Irish girls, I want to help put a stop to it right enough. But talk to Garrett. He'll know something the police haven't picked up, or I'm an Englishman.'

He turned away to tend to business, for the

place was filling up now toward the end of the day.

'Shall we wait for this lad?' Ames asked Delahanty.

'I can't stay — not tonight. I must dress for dinner at Mrs. Gardner's.'

A smile of understanding passed over Ames's face, and to MacKenzie he explained: 'Mrs. Gardner — Isabella Stewart Gardner, of the New York department store Stewarts and the Boston Lowell Gardners — has the most artistic and literary circle in the city. She is a noted collector — not only of objets d'art, but also of talented young men like Desmond here.'

'None of your blarney now,' Delahanty said, laughing. 'The next time she gives one of her big 'crushes,' Doctor, I'll have her secretary send you a card. Addington is invited regularly, but he never comes.'

'A waste of time, those big turnouts,' Ames said brusquely.

'But you won't get better food this side of Paris, my friend.'

Outside, it was full dark now, and still raining hard. A carriage light came bobbing toward them along the broad cobblestone street: a vacant hansom. They hailed it and climbed in.

Carefully, because she was a little on edge, Caroline lifted the china teapot, poured the hot amber liquid into one of her second-best cups, and handed it with its saucer to her guest.

'It is so kind of you to call, Cousin Wainwright,' she said. 'I'm sure Addington will be home any moment now.' For there was no need to maintain the pretense that Cousin Wainwright had come to visit her; it was Addington he wanted to see, and she had a good idea why.

On the other hand, she had promised Addington that she would deal with Cousin Wainwright, and she felt duty bound to do so now, while she had him to herself. The only problem was, Cousin Wainwright had a firmly settled opinion of woman's place, and interfering in a murder investigation was not it.

He was a tall, fat, balding man with none of the family looks. He stared into the depths of his cup as if he were looking for tea leaves to read. He seemed uncomfortable, she thought, far too large for the chair he had chosen, which was a delicate Empire piece with fluted legs and a worn brocade seat. Caroline hoped that his trousers were not damp, else the brocade would be ruined.

Ordinarily at ease in any social situation, for the moment she was at a loss. She hadn't seen Cousin Wainwright in ages — not since her mother's funeral well over a year before — and in any case, whenever she had seen him over the years, she'd never known quite what to say to him. He was stern and straitlaced, a man of impeccable rectitude, who had single-handedly brought about great improvements in the Boston police force. This had included the hiring of a few Irishmen, somewhat lessening the tensions between the reigning Yankee class and the huge numbers of Hibernian immigrants. 'Paddies,' they were called, after St. Patrick, the patron saint of their benighted island. So many Irishmen were arrested, day after day, that the long black police wagons that carted them off to jail had become known as paddy wagons.

'And how is your boy, cousin?' Caroline asked a little too brightly.

'Well enough.' Wainwright's boy — a boy no longer — was in his third year at the College, which was what Brahmin Bostonians called Harvard.

'Enjoying his studies?' she added, feeling slightly desperate. Try as she would, she could not summon up an image of the lad.

'I shouldn't think so,' Wainwright said, looking up at her at last. 'But I told him he had to stay on, and so he will.'

'Oh, yes, you are quite right to tell him — '

She broke off as she heard the clatter of hooves outside, and prayed silently that it was a cab bringing Addington home at last.

'There he is,' she said as she heard his voice and MacKenzie's in the front hall. Cousin Wainwright took a quick sip of tea and set down his cup. As he stood, Caroline glanced apprehensively at the brocade. It looked quite dry.

The pocket doors slid apart, and Ames and MacKenzie came in. 'Well, Caro, we have had a most interesting — ' Ames began. For a moment, Caroline thought he looked startled at seeing their guest, but he quickly assumed his usual sangfroid.

'Cousin. Good to see you,' he said, advancing to shake Wainwright's hand. He introduced MacKenzie, and the men settled themselves. Caroline handed around tea, while MacKenzie helped himself to a piece of Sally Lunn cake.

There was a little silence. Then Ames, never one to flinch from an awkward moment, said, 'I visited your place this morning, cousin.'

'So I understand.' Wainwright scowled at him.

'Things seem to be going fairly well, wouldn't you say?'

'Well enough — if we can be free of outside meddling.'

Oh, dear, thought Caroline. So it was going to be an unpleasant encounter after all. Well, it couldn't be helped. And Addington was certainly capable of standing up to anyone, even Cousin Wainwright.

'Oh? Who has been meddling?' Ames asked. His face was bland and smooth, but Caroline thought she saw a hint of amusement in his dark eyes.

'I shouldn't think you'd need to ask that,' Wainwright said. 'Inspector Crippen — '

'Good man,' Ames interjected.

'Yes. He is. And he doesn't need civilians coming in to interfere — '

'Oh, now, I wouldn't say it was interfering, simply to pay a call — '

'That is exactly what it was,' Wainwright said. His jowly face had taken on a pinkish color, which made the contrast with his starched white shirt collar all the greater as it cut into the folds of his neck. 'Interfering with police business. I cannot understand why you believe that you can manage our affairs better than we can manage them

76

ourselves. Hah? Why is that?'

Ames bit back the sharp retort that sprang to his lips: because Crippen works hind foremost, deciding upon the solution to a case and then finding evidence to fit it. 'I am not trying to manage anything,' he said.

Caroline was proud of him. Ordinarily he did not trouble to hide his irritation, but at the moment he was hiding it very well.

'Then why did you take up an hour of Crippen's time this morning?' Wainwright demanded.

'It was more nearly fifteen minutes. Did he complain?'

'What with the Copp's Hill Boys ripe to be got,' Wainwright went on, 'and now these murders over in the South End — '

'It is my fault, cousin,' Caroline put in. She knew she shouldn't interrupt, but she had to deflect his anger before it boiled over with who knew what consequences for poor Agatha Montgomery.

Sharply, he turned to look at her; he seemed to have forgotten her existence. 'What?'

'I said, it is my fault that Addington went to see Inspector Crippen. I urged him to do so.'

'And why did you do that, pray?'

'Because Agatha Montgomery, the proprietress of the Bower, is a friend of mine. She grew up just around the corner on Pinckney Street. She has been the heart and soul of the Bower ever since she started it, and it seemed to me that with these dreadful murders, she stands to lose it all. People will no longer support the Bower if scandal attaches to its name, and poor Agatha would be — '

'And what does that have to do with Crippen?' Wainwright demanded. His face was redder than before, and he was blinking rapidly, as if her putting herself forward in such an unladylike way had unnerved him.

'Why — I asked Addington — and Dr. MacKenzie too — to pay a call on him to see if they could help him in his investigations. It was not meant to be an interference — or meddling, as you put it. It was meant to help. The sooner we — you — find the person who killed those girls, the less danger the Bower's mission will be ruined.'

Wainwright looked baffled. 'You think that Addington can outwit the police in a matter like this?'

Caroline lifted her chin, and her face took on the look of steely determination that MacKenzie had come to recognize.

'It is not a question of outwitting anyone, cousin,' she said. 'It is a question of helping

78

Agatha. And if Addington — or even if I — can assist her in any way, we intend to do so.'

Wainwright's jowls, bright red now, flapped like a turkey's. 'You!' he exclaimed, fixing her in his hard little eyes. 'You don't mean to tell me that you would involve yourself in a murder investigation!'

'Yes,' she said. 'I do mean to tell you exactly that. If any of us here' — her gaze swept over her brother and MacKenzie — 'can do anything at all to help Agatha in this terrible affair, we will do so. And I might add, cousin, that it would not be the first time that Inspector Crippen owed us — owed Addington — a debt of thanks. You will remember the business at the Somerset Club — not to mention the death of Colonel Mann — '

'Enough!' Wainwright shot to his feet, startling them all. He stared down at Caroline, momentarily speechless with outrage. 'I did not come here to listen to such drivel,' he said at last. 'I came here to warn you — all of you — to stay out of this business once and for all. I would advise you to heed that warning. Good day to you.'

And before she could answer, he stalked out of the room, pulling the pocket doors shut behind him with unnecessary force.

They heard him in the vestibule, and then the front door slammed and he was gone.

'Well!' Caroline said, managing a little laugh. 'I certainly didn't keep my promise to you about dealing with Cousin Wainwright, did I, Addington?'

'Don't worry about it.' He emptied his lukewarm tea into the slop dish, poured a fresh cup for himself, and stood at his accustomed place before the fire. 'He will calm down soon enough. I suppose Crippen complained to him, although I must say, Crippen seemed happy enough to see us.'

'What did he say?' Caroline asked. 'Did he tell you anything useful?'

'Yes, as a matter of fact, he did.' Briefly, Ames recounted what they had learned. MacKenzie was shocked when he spoke so matter-of-factly about Mary's pregnancy, but Caroline seemed neither shocked nor surprised at that particular piece of news.

'Agatha has had to deal with something like that before,' she said. 'There have been at least two girls who have had to leave because they were in the family way. One of them, I believe, was already *enciente* when she came to the Bower, and the other — well, they have pretty close supervision, but some of them manage to evade it all the same. You have met Matron Pratt, Doctor, and you can see for yourself how strict she is. She must be, under the circumstances — strict, and always vigilant. Agatha went through two or three matrons before Mrs. Pratt came to her, and none of them was satisfactory. Those girls need a good, strong hand to guide them, and whatever else you may think of Mrs. Pratt, her hand is very strong indeed.'

MacKenzie nodded. 'Too strong, do you think?'

'Why, how could she be too strong? It is a houseful of girls — there are twenty at least, and sometimes more — many of whom have never had proper guidance in their lives. And she has only three months to guide them, don't forget, before they must go back into the world, with all its temptations and possibilities for error. Even if she must sometimes seem unfair — the way she did yesterday, for instance, with that poor girl who answered the door — I have no doubt that she has the best interests of the girls at heart.'

MacKenzie was not so sure about that, but he let it pass.

'Look at this, Caroline,' Ames said then. He took out his pocket notebook and showed her the jumble of letters he had copied in Crippen's office.

'What is it?' she said, staring at it.

81

'Some kind of note found on Mary Flaherty's person. It wasn't written — it was letters cut out and pasted together.'

'How very odd,' she said, handing the notebook back to him. 'Some kind of code, or cipher?'

'Yes. Crippen thought it was either that or some esoteric language. But it isn't any language I've ever seen. And so much for Cousin Wainwright's pique,' Ames added. 'Crippen was planning to come to me for help, so I don't see how Wainwright can object if I call on him, in turn, to find out what he knows.'

Caroline met MacKenzie's eyes and smiled. 'Did you have an interesting day, Doctor?'

'Indeed we did. And not the least of it was our excursion down to the waterfront.'

'The waterfront! Why did you go there?'

MacKenzie deferred to Ames, who told her of their visit to the Green Harp Saloon.

'Garrett O'Reilly!' she exclaimed. 'Yes, I know him. I see him sometimes when I go to teach the girls. He's a good boy, very dependable.'

Ames contemplated her. 'Is he the kind of boy, do you think, who would — ah — get Mary Flaherty in the family way and then murder her to keep her quiet?'

She went a little pale as she set her cup and saucer onto the tray. 'No, I don't think he is,' she said.

'Crippen seems to think he might be,' Ames replied.

At that, she blazed up. 'Then Crippen is wrong!' she said vehemently. 'Again! He was wrong before, and he is wrong now! Why, Garrett O'Reilly is a perfectly wonderful boy, Addington! He is as nicely mannered as any young man over at the College — better, in fact — and bright and capable. I cannot believe he is involved in this business. Oh, dear! And Inspector Crippen will arrest him, and he will charge him with the crime — '

'Crimes,' Ames interjected. 'There have been two deaths, remember.'

'Yes, and all the more reason to believe that Garrett had nothing to do with them! Why would he kill Bridget if it was Mary whom he — '

Her vocabulary failed her, and she broke off as a knock came at the pocket doors.

'Excuse me, miss,' said Margaret, looking in, 'but Cook is wanting to speak with you about the dinner.'

She meant, Caroline knew, not tonight's repast, which would be something plain and easy to prepare, but the dinner for the following night, when a dozen people were coming to meet her 'lion,' the British journalist. Caroline had thought every detail of the menu was settled, but apparently not.

'All right, Margaret. I'm coming.' And when the maid did not immediately withdraw: 'Is there something else?'

'Yes, miss. When I took out the big serving platter, I found it cracked right through.'

The potted grouse, thought Caroline. Potted grouse was heavy — too heavy to risk a disaster. Fortunately, they had twenty-four hours to repair the damage.

'The recipe for china cement is in my household book,' she said. 'I will be down directly, but you can begin to prepare it. Beaten egg white, quicklime — and it will need some old cheese, well grated.'

The maid withdrew. She'd been with them for more than ten years, with never a day off more than her half-Sunday every other week. When she'd asked permission to visit her sister in Fitchburg, Caroline hadn't had the heart to refuse. She was to take the train on Saturday night, and somehow they'd survive until she returned.

'I must go to Cook,' she said to the men, 'before she works herself up into a state. And tomorrow is hopeless. I must be here all day, getting ready. A hired girl is coming in to help, and the pastry cook arrives at dawn.

And you, Addington — '

He smiled at her, understanding. 'I will be well out of your way as soon as I finish breakfast. And Dr. MacKenzie will be with me.'

'You will go to the Bower,' she said, and it was not a question.

'Yes, Caro. I — we — will go to the Bower.'

7

At breakfast the next morning, Caroline sifted through her letters — the bills went first to Addington, although she was the one who dealt with them in the end — and extracted one, a thick pale blue envelope with a stamp far too beautiful to be American.

'At last!' she exclaimed, smiling. And, at MacKenzie's quizzical glance, 'From Val in Rome. I haven't heard from her since she sent me that one brief note just after she arrived. Oh, I do hope she is having a good time! You don't mind if I read it, Addington?'

He waved a hand at her, his face hidden behind the morning *Globe*. MacKenzie made do with his oatmeal, resigning himself to a breakfast without conversation, but, after a moment Caroline said, 'Listen to this, Addington!'

Ames put down his paper. 'What?'

'Val and her set have taken up with the crowd that visits the artists' studios, and they go two or three times a week to the museums. They even went to Florence last week. I am so glad she went abroad after that horrid episode with George Putnam. His mother passed me in the street the other day and cut me dead.'

Their cousin Valentine, recovering from a broken engagement, had fled to Italy for the winter. She had invited Caroline to join her in the spring, in the South of France, but MacKenzie, realizing his selfishness, hoped Caroline wouldn't go.

'Good,' said Ames, returning to his newspaper. But after a moment he put it down with a small *tsk!* of irritation. 'They are bungling it,' he said.

'Crippen?' MacKenzie asked.

'Of course Crippen. Who else? He promises the public that the killer of the Bower girls will be apprehended 'swiftly' — his word. Meanwhile he promises — as he has done for weeks now — that the Copp's Hill Boys will be behind bars any moment.'

Caroline left off reading Val's letter and tucked it back into its envelope. She was too busy to fully savor it. Tomorrow, she thought, when I have more time.

'You are going to the Bower this morning, Addington?' she asked.

'Since I promised you that I would — yes.'

'I've been thinking,' she went on.

At once he was on his guard. Caroline, thinking, was always problematical.

'I want to invite Agatha for this evening,'

she said. 'And her brother.'

'Really? Are you sure that would be wise?'

'Yes, I am.'

'Won't people think it odd for a woman in Miss Montgomery's situation to show herself at a social occasion?'

'But that is the point, Addington. It is important for people to see that she has not been banished — that the people who have supported the Bower have not turned away from her. Don't forget that Imogen and Edward Boylston are coming. He sits on the Bower's board of trustees.'

He grunted, still skeptical.

'So I will write a note to Agatha,' Caroline said, 'inviting them both, and if you would deliver it to her — ?'

Ames rolled his eyes and retreated behind his newspaper once more, and Caroline met MacKenzie's glance with a little smile of triumph.

Half an hour later, Ames and MacKenzie made their way down the steep slope of Mt. Vernon Street to Charles. Pedestrians hurried by, tilting their umbrellas against the rain, while delivery boys and errand boys hurtled past, dodging in and out. Over all rose the strong odor of the sea and the ever-present smell of horse dung.

They found a herdic in front of the S. S.

Pierce grocery store, and at last, with a crack of his whip, the driver found a way clear and they set off.

'As Caroline says, Miss Montgomery is a most admirable woman,' Ames said. He did not look at MacKenzie as he spoke but gazed out at the row of brick and brownstone town houses along Beacon Street.

'Yes, she seems to be.' MacKenzie put a hand on the seat to steady himself as they took a sharp corner at Arlington.

'And unfortunately, her work at the Bower is sorely needed,' Ames went on. 'Down near Crabbe's, at certain hours of the evening, it is becoming impossible to walk twenty paces without being set upon by some poor drab in search of a customer.'

Ames's wide, thin mouth drew down in an expression of distaste, and MacKenzie had a brief mental glimpse of the austere, proud and proper Bostonian who was Addington Ames being accosted by a woman of the streets.

They crossed the railroad tracks near the Boston & Providence station and came into the South End. A newsboy was crying a late edition at the corner of Columbus Avenue: 'Read all about it! Bertram's Bower! Vicious crime!'

'The journalistic community seems to be

89

making a good profit out of this affair,' Ames said sourly.

'That is their business, I suppose,' MacKenzie replied. He had a memory of his landlord threatening bodily harm to a prying reporter, two months before, in the case of Colonel Mann.

At length the herdic turned into Rutland Square and they alighted at the Bower. As Ames paid the driver, MacKenzie looked up at the tall brownstone. All the blinds were drawn, giving it the look of a house of mourning — which it was. No wreath adorned the front door, however. Probably they did not deem it wise to draw attention to themselves, he thought.

They mounted the steep steps, and Ames lifted the knocker and brought it sharply down.

No answer.

He tried again, but still no one came. Just as he raised his hand to try a third time, the door flew open, and they were confronted by the forbidding figure of Matron Pratt. MacKenzie had come to think of her as a dragon matron, hostile to all outsiders.

'No visitors allowed,' she snapped.

'I beg your pardon, madam,' Ames said, 'but we are not visitors in the usual sense of

90

the word. I am a friend of Miss Montgomery's. Is she in?'

Over the past four months of his acquaintance with the Ameses, MacKenzie had learned that Addington Ames could be curt to the point of rudeness, but he could also be the image of controlled, ever so slightly condescending courtesy, as he was now.

Matron Pratt looked them up and down as if they were the most disreputable type of interloper — traveling salesmen perhaps. 'No, she is not!' she snarled, and before Ames could speak again, she slammed the door in their faces.

'Well, Doctor, it seems that we are not welcome here,' Ames said mildly. He was not offended, or even surprised, at Matron Pratt's behavior. He'd never met her, but he'd heard a good deal about her from Caroline.

'Shall we try again?' he said, once more lifting the brass knocker and bringing it down hard.

Instantly, the dragon matron confronted them for a second time. 'I said — '

'We heard what you said.' Ames braced his hand against the door to prevent her from slamming it shut. 'I understand that you are in crisis here,' he went on. 'I simply want a brief moment with Miss Montgomery, and I promise you — '

'What is it, Mrs. Pratt?' came a voice from within.

As the dragon matron turned, they could see beyond her the tall, angular figure of Agatha Montgomery.

'They want to talk to you,' Matron Pratt said.

'Who does?' Miss Montgomery advanced. 'Oh — Mr. Ames.'

'My sister would have come again herself,' Ames said, 'but she was unable to. So she asked me — us,' he corrected himself, 'to come instead, to inquire if there is anything we can do to help.'

Miss Montgomery shook her head. 'She is very kind to worry so about us,' she said. She seemed about to say more, but she was interrupted by the sound of a crash from the rear of the house, followed immediately by a loud wailing.

Miss Montgomery turned to Mrs. Pratt. 'Matron, will you — No. Never mind. I will go myself.' She left them and hurried back along the hall.

Ames took this opportunity to step into the vestibule. Matron Pratt stared at him in amazement. Obviously, thought MacKenzie, stepping close behind, she is not accustomed to having her dictates opposed. Ames shut the outer door, and then he moved into the hall and MacKenzie followed. The place seemed as deserted as it had been the day before, and it carried the same institutional smell. They would never rid themselves of that, MacKenzie thought; probably the girls carried it with them when they left.

'You are trespassing!' snapped Matron Pratt, recovered from her astonishment. 'I will call the police!' There was a telephone on the wall outside the office door.

'Please do,' Ames said smoothly. 'They are friends of mine. I would be delighted to see them.'

Miss Montgomery was approaching them from the back of the hall. 'It was an accident,' she said distractedly, as if she were speaking to herself. 'Coughlin dropped some plates.'

Matron Pratt narrowed her eyes, no doubt calculating the cost of the breakage, MacKenzie thought.

'Now, Mr. Ames,' Miss Montgomery said, 'you wanted to speak to me.'

'If you can spare the time.'

'At the moment, I cannot. But Matron will help you, and then perhaps I can — '

'I have the schedule to attend to,' Matron Pratt protested.

'Yes, well, that can wait,' Miss Montgomery said.

A look passed between them. Then Matron Pratt said nothing more, merely muttering an assent and opening the door to the office. 'In there,' she said sharply, but then, as if she remembered something: 'I haven't had my paper returned to me!' she called to Miss Montgomery.

They heard the reply: 'I have already spoken to everyone except O'Donnell and Fletcher. You might question them yourself, Matron, at the noon meal.'

Matron Pratt slammed shut the office door and turned to face the visitors. Her face was rigid with anger, and her mouth worked for a moment before she spoke.

'They are thieves, here, along with everything else,' she said then.

'Thieves?' Ames replied. 'How do you mean?'

'I mean, they steal things!' she snapped.

'You have lost something?' Ames asked.

'No! I didn't lose it! Someone stole it! My tract — one of my papers from my Sunday evening meetings.' As she came into the room, she flexed her broad, thick hands.

'And you think that one of the — ah — young women here has taken it?'

'I don't think it! I know it! How else could it disappear?'

Surely, thought MacKenzie, the 'Mrs.' in

Matron Pratt's name was a courtesy title, for what man would marry such a harridan?

She went to the front windows and peered out from behind the blind. 'There he is again,' she said.

'Who?'

'One of those newspapermen. They are like a plague, worse than the police. They haven't left us alone for a moment.'

She came back to them, but she did not take a chair. Neither, therefore, did they.

MacKenzie looked around. It was a fairly large room, linoleum-floored, with a good-sized desk facing the door. Rows of oak filing cabinets and glass-fronted bookcases lined the walls. On the bookshelves, neatly arranged, was a set of what looked like account books, each with its year stamped in gold on its spine. On the desktop were stacks of bills and correspondence, an in box and an out box, a glass pen tray and two bottles of ink, a sheet of green blotting paper — fresh, unmarked — and a tall spindle impaled with a thick stack of notes. The top one had the notation: 'Mr. Boylston, 10 A.M.'

'What do you want?' Matron Pratt said abruptly, addressing Ames.

'I want — if possible — to help.'

She surveyed him for a moment, and he surveyed her back. 'That's what we try to do

95

here,' she said. 'We try to help. *Them*,' she added, casting her gaze upward; they took it to mean the young women housed on the upper floors.

'Indeed,' Ames replied. He felt a fleeting moment of compassion — no more — for Elwood Crippen, forced to deal with this gorgon and not having the option, as Ames did, of walking away from her if she did not cooperate.

But he would not walk away, he thought. The more this woman defied him, the more he wanted, perversely, to pry from her some small item of information; he would keep at her until he did.

'And I am sure that you do help them,' he added.

She glared at him. 'The ones as want to be helped,' she said. 'Some don't.'

'How do you mean?'

She shrugged her massive shoulders, which were encased in a black dress of some cheap-looking stuff. 'A lot of them just take advantage of *her*, if you ask me.' She meant Agatha Montgomery. 'They know they can get fed, and get to a doctor if they need to — and most of 'em do, as you can imagine — and rest a bit from their labors, if you take my meaning. We give them a little vacation here, and then out they go, back where they

96

came from, looking for men to make their living off of.'

'You mean they do not take the employment that they might get after their — ah — lessons here?'

She threw him a glance of contempt. 'If a girl gets work in an office for four or five dollars a week, she won't think that's such a grand thing, will she? When she can make that much in a night — on her back.'

MacKenzie had never heard a woman speak so crudely, and he was mightily offended by it. Ames, however, seemed not to notice — or, if he did, not to mind. 'Yes, well, I take your point,' he said. 'But about the two girls who — ah — Mary Flaherty and Bridget Brown?'

Matron Pratt sniffed contemptuously. 'Brown was humble enough. Never caused trouble. Did her work.'

'And Mary Flaherty?'

Instantly, a look of pure malice crossed the matron's face. 'I couldn't say.'

'Was she well liked?'

'By some, I suppose.'

'But not by you?'

'I couldn't say,' she repeated.

'Try. Could you tell us anything about her?'

'I've already told it all to the police.'

'Even so.'

Again the woman's heavy shoulders rose in a shrug. 'She was getting above herself.'

'You mean because of her position as Miss Montgomery's secretary?'

'Yes. She gave herself airs.'

'In what way?'

'About the typewriting, for one thing.'

'How do you mean?'

'The Reverend Montgomery said he was going to buy a typewriting machine for the office. He bought her a manual so she could start to learn about it. And when she talked about it — and she did talk about it till you were sick of hearing her — it was always 'When I get my typewriting machine.' Like that. With her nose in the air, as if learning to pound away on one of them things was going to make her all of a sudden better than the rest of us.'

Ames nodded. 'So perhaps some of the girls resented her?'

'Yes. 'Course they did.'

'Did you?'

It was a thrust that went home. Her mouth twitched, and she clenched her hands again.

'It isn't my place to resent any of the girls here.'

He let it pass. 'Was there anyone in particular who disliked either Mary or Bridget?'

'Brown — no.'

'But Mary Flaherty?'

She frowned. They waited. She wants to tell us, thought MacKenzie, but she cannot quite bring herself to do so.

'Verna Kent,' she said at last. 'Miss Montgomery expelled her last week,' she added.

'Because?'

'She was a thief. I told you, we have our share of them here.'

'What did she steal?'

'One of Flaherty's petticoats. Flaherty found out about it and told Miss Montgomery.'

'Did this girl admit it?'

'She could hardly deny it, could she, when the petticoat was found under her mattress?'

'So then?'

'She was angry with Flaherty, of course. She went after her — right here in the office. A terrible scene she made. She went for Flaherty's throat, crying that she would kill her. I hauled her off,' she added.

'And then she left?'

'Yes.'

'And you saw nothing of her afterward?'

'I didn't, no. But the next day, when Flaherty went out, Kent was waiting for her over on Warren Avenue. She went after her again — set right on her. Lucky for Flaherty there was a policeman nearby.'

'And the girl was arrested?'

'Yes.'

Easy enough to check, he thought.

'Do you know where she is living now? Assuming that she is not in the lockup.'

'On Chambers Street, in the West End.'

'Did Mary have any other enemies that you know of?' Aside from yourself, he thought.

Matron Pratt shrugged. 'I don't know about enemies, but she didn't have many friends. She thought too well of herself, if you can imagine it. And she was far too free, coming and going. I don't know why Miss Montgomery allowed it.'

'How do you mean?'

'She didn't keep to a schedule like the others. She'd work here in the office at night, and then she'd go out during the day. She had to run her errands, she'd say. Errands! I ask you. And often enough she'd go out at night, too, without signing out. Where was she going at all hours? Aside from everything else, it isn't safe for a girl to go wandering about in this district. I guess she learned that lesson in the end,' she added with grim satisfaction.

'Did you ever speak to her about it? About

her comings and goings?'

'Oh, yes. I spoke to her all right. But she never thought she had to listen to what I said. 'Never you mind about me, Mrs. Pratt,' she said. And gave me such a look! I'd have taken a switch to her if I could. The little baggage! Well, she went out one last time, didn't she? And she never came back.' Her face had taken on a gloating expression that Ames found repulsive.

'Did you see her go?' he asked.

'No. Sunday night is the night for my meetings over on Columbus Avenue. I go out at a quarter to seven every week.'

'And you return when?'

'Not before ten.'

'I see. Was Sunday visiting day, perhaps? Were there any visitors to the house that day — anyone strange, I mean, whom Mary might have met? Fathers of the other girls — brothers or uncles perhaps?'

'No men!' she snapped.

'No men visitors? None at all?'

'Men are the cause of all their troubles, Mr. Ames.' Matron Pratt's face had darkened into an expression of pure hate.

'But surely — '

'Men are vile creatures through and through. I should know — I was married to one of 'em once.' A sneer had enhanced her expression, so that she looked more forbidding than ever.

'Surely there are some men in the world of whom you approve,' Ames said. 'The Reverend Montgomery, for instance.'

'Not him either.'

'But he comes here, does he not?'

'Yes,' she muttered darkly.

Against your wishes, MacKenzie thought.

'All men are worthless if you ask me,' she added. 'And so are the girls who go with them.'

MacKenzie felt slightly ill in the face of this woman's implacable animosity toward all his sex.

There came a tap at the door: one of the girls, come to announce that Miss Montgomery would see the gentlemen now.

In her private room at the rear of the house, Agatha Montgomery sat in her rocking chair before the low fire. At her murmured word, the two men sat opposite her on the same worn horsehair sofa where MacKenzie had sat with Caroline two days before.

'It is good of you to see us,' Ames began.

Miss Montgomery inclined her head. She looked somewhat more composed than before, but still there were lines of tension around her mouth, and a haunted look in her pale eyes.

'You should not have troubled yourself, Mr. Ames.'

'As I said, Caroline wanted us to. And — ' He reached to his inside jacket pocket and withdrew the envelope containing his sister's note. 'She invites you to dinner this evening — you and your brother. She is entertaining a 'lion' from London, and she thought he might amuse you.'

She did not at first seem to understand what he said. 'How . . . kind.'

'You will come?'

'I — I don't know.'

'Just a dozen or so people, a congenial company. She thought it might — ah — divert you a little.'

'Caroline has always been a good friend to me, and now she still — ' She broke off, thinking. 'All right, Mr. Ames. Yes. We will come, and please thank her for her thoughtfulness. She has always, over the years — I remember when my father — well. That was a long time ago, was it not?'

She fell silent, staring at her hands clasped in her lap.

Then Ames said: 'Miss Montgomery, can you tell us anything about the second girl who was killed?'

'You mean Brown.' She did not look at him.

'Yes.'

She shook her head. 'No. Nothing. She was a good girl, quiet, obedient. I thought that when she left us, she would have no difficulty in finding a position — a decent position — to support herself.'

'Was she from Boston?'

'No. Fall River.'

'No family locally?'

'Nor in Fall River either, as far as I know.'

'I see. And no enemies?'

'No. She was far too inoffensive to have enemies, Mr. Ames.'

'Did she have any particular friendships here?'

'Only Mary.' She used the girl's Christian name, he noted. Was that significant?

'So Bridget would have been upset about Mary's death?'

'Oh, yes. She was very upset. She — ' Miss Montgomery pressed her lips together, as if she were trying to keep back what she had almost said.

'Yes? She what?' Ames prompted softly.

'She . . . went out. In the late afternoon, after her sewing class. She came to me to ask permission, and of course I refused it. How could I have agreed to let her go out after what had happened to Mary only the night before?'

104

'But still, she went.'

'Yes. I remonstrated with her — '

'You mean you argued.'

Ames had a mental image of poor Bridget, inoffensive, humble, arguing with Agatha Montgomery. The girl must have had a very good reason indeed to defy her, never mind wanting to leave the safety of the Bower.

'Yes. But short of physically restraining her, I could not stop her. After she left, I thought that perhaps she wanted to go to church — to find a priest perhaps.'

'So what did you do then?'

'I followed her.'

'And did you ever find her?'

'No. I went all the way to the cathedral, but I never saw her.'

'Did you go in?'

'Yes. She wasn't there.'

'So you came back?'

'Yes. It was raining hard.' She shivered as if she were still cold and wet, as she must have been last night, hunting for Bridget Brown through the dark streets of the South End.

'And when she didn't return?'

Miss Montgomery's gaunt face crumpled for a moment, then she regained control. She met Ames's eyes steadily as she said, 'I will tell you frankly, Mr. Ames, it is not unheard of for one of our girls to go missing. I was frantic, but of course I could not let it be seen. The girls were upset enough, what with Mary's death.'

'You did not think to notify the police?'

Miss Montgomery looked a trifle abashed. 'I cannot go to the police every time one of our girls fails to turn up for supper. I would have gone, yes — if, say, in a day or two she had not come back.'

She pressed her handkerchief to her eyes as if to forestall her tears.

Suddenly restless, Ames stood up and began to pace the little room. He thought of Crippen's revelation that Mary had been pregnant. Did Miss Montgomery know that? It was too delicate a question to put to her at this point, he thought; if he went too far beyond the bounds of good manners, she would refuse to talk to him altogether.

But the coded note — yes, he could ask her about that.

She stared at the copy he'd made. 'I have no idea what this is.'

'Or who could have sent it?'

'No.'

'Did Mary receive the Bower's mail?'

'Yes. She dealt with it every day.'

'So we cannot know if this was sent to her through the mail or if someone here' — she looked up at him sharply — 'gave it to her.'

'Who would do that?' she said. 'Anyone here who wanted to send a message to her could simply speak to her.'

'Then, for the moment, at any rate, we must assume that this was sent to her from outside. So even if Bridget had no friends or family in the city, Mary probably did.'

Do you know, he thought, watching her. Do you know that Mary had someone who was more than a casual friend, someone who had put her in the family way, and then, very possibly, killed her to silence her?

Miss Montgomery handed back his pocket notebook. 'Did the police have any idea — '

'No. None. Inspector Crippen asked me to look at it because he thought I might be able to translate it.'

'And can you?'

'No.'

She blinked several times, as if absorbing what he said, and then she stood up.

'I must thank you again, Mr. Ames, for being so kind.'

She was dismissing them. No, he thought, not yet.

'I wonder if we could impose on you a little further, Miss Montgomery.'

She'd put out her hand to bid him

good-bye, but now she took it back. 'Yes?' she said warily.

'I would very much like to see Mary and Bridget's room.'

She hesitated. 'I am afraid that isn't possible.'

'Because — ?'

'Because — it isn't clean.'

'But that is nothing. Clean or not, it doesn't matter. I simply want to see it — just for a moment.'

Still she hesitated. As she looked down at the tips of her worn boots protruding from beneath her dark skirts, she seemed to be waging some internal struggle. MacKenzie wondered if she, like Matron Pratt, harbored a dislike — a hatred, even — toward men.

At last she gave in and looked up at Ames. 'All right. If you insist.'

She led them out and up the stairs. As they went, MacKenzie glanced behind, down to the hall. He saw the office door cracked open, and he knew that their progress was being observed by the dragon matron.

It was mid-morning; some of the Bower's residents were in the second-floor hall, changing classes. MacKenzie noted that all of them, dark or fair, tall or short, looked more or less the same, and not only because of their plain dark dresses and white aprons.

108

They all had a look of defeat about them, he thought, and in girls so young — most of them did not look more than in their early twenties — such a look was painful to see.

Now, catching sight of the two strange men, a few of them stifled little cries of alarm, and all of them looked frightened. MacKenzie had a sudden urge to speak to them, to reassure them that he and Ames meant no harm, but of course he could not.

Miss Montgomery led them on, up to the third floor. She stopped before a door numbered 37. Without knocking — for who would answer now? — she turned the knob and pushed open the door.

The room was dim, the blind at the single window pulled down. Only a little light from the gas fixtures in the hall penetrated to the interior. Then Miss Montgomery turned up the gas by the door and suddenly the room was filled with a harsh, bleak illumination.

They saw a bare linoleum floor; two cots, both neatly made; two night tables; two small bureaus topped with basins and ewers; one small bookcase. A door ajar halfway along one wall showed the presence of a closet. Over one cot hung a lithograph of Jesus; over the other, a small crucifix. Not clean? thought Ames. Despite Miss Montgomery's objections, the room looked as if it and everything

109

in it had been freshly scrubbed and polished.

He stood still for a moment, looking around. 'Do you know what the police took with them, if anything?'

'No.'

He went to the closet door and opened it: a small, shallow space. A few items of clothing hung from hooks; on a shelf were two flimsy cardboard hat boxes.

He turned back to the room as if he expected something — some telling thing — to announce itself. But the room was as anonymous — as unrevealing — as a vacant room in a cheap hotel.

He went to the bookcase, which held perhaps a dozen volumes. He took each one and flipped through its pages to see if something might fall out — a note, a clipping, anything to tell him something about the two girls who had shared this barren chamber.

'Did the police examine these?' he asked Miss Montgomery.

'Not that I saw.'

A few dime novelettes; a book on etiquette; a *Life of Jesus*; a cheap edition of *Little Women*; the memoirs of Mary Livermore, who had been a nurse during the Civil War. This last bore an inscription: 'For another Mary, from one who admires her very much, in the hope that it will inspire her to be a good girl.'

He held it out to Miss Montgomery. 'Do you know who gave her this?'

She looked at it. 'No.'

'Were you aware that she possessed it?'

'No.'

'So you do not know whether she brought it with her when she came, or — '

'She didn't do that. She came — ' Her voice roughened, and she cleared her throat. 'She came with no more than the clothes on her back. And those we disposed of immediately, since they were not fit to wear.'

He glanced at the inscription once more and then returned the book to the shelf. He opened the bureau drawers, riffled through the contents of each one. Nothing. Remembering the tale of the stolen petticoat, he turned first to one cot and then to the other and slid his hand underneath the thin mattresses. Nothing there either.

Miss Montgomery stood like a sentinel at the hall door, watching him. When Ames finished, having found nothing, MacKenzie thought she looked secretly pleased, as if to say, I told you so.

'Thank you,' Ames said to her. 'As you said, there is nothing here to help us.'

'No.'

'One more thing,' he said.

She had started to turn down the gas, but now she stopped.

'Yes?'

Sooner or later, MacKenzie thought, she will have had her patience tested long enough, and we will be asked to leave.

'You have a boy who works here. Garrett O'Reilly.'

'Yes?'

'Might we have a word with him?'

'How did you know — '

'We heard of him yesterday from a mutual friend.'

A look of distaste came over her face, as if she thought that such an association, even at one remove, was not proper for a man of gentle birth like Addington Ames.

When she did not answer, he said again, 'I would like to see him for just a moment. He works here regularly, I believe. Might he be here now?'

'I am not sure. I will ask Matron.'

'You will ask Matron what?' said the man who had suddenly appeared in the doorway.

8

He was tall, though not so tall as Ames, and stylishly dressed in a dark brown coat, finely tailored, with a velvet collar and bright gold buttons. Across his pale yellow waistcoat stretched a heavy gold watch chain ornamented by several talismans. He wore a fine gray silk cravat, and his feet were shod in shining leather boots that looked expensive. His thinning, pale brown hair was long at the sides, with impressive sideburns, and brushed back over the crown to give a luxurious, bouffant effect. In one hand he carried, incongruously, a half-eaten sweet roll.

Miss Montgomery, startled at first, went rigid. Then, when she realized who had come, her face assumed a look of loving pride — adoration, even, thought Ames — that seemed unsuited to her. She gazed greedily, hungrily, at the newcomer, as if his presence gave her some much-needed emotional nourishment.

'Randolph! I never heard you on the stairs.'

For a moment, he ignored the two men. As he looked into his sister's eyes, he laid the flat of his free hand against her sallow cheek in a gesture that was oddly intimate.

'How are you, my dear?' he said softly.

'I am all right. And you?'

'You needn't worry about me. As long as I know how you do, I shall be fine.'

Despite his dandyish appearance, it was his voice that captured attention: a rich and mellifluous voice, a true preacher's voice. He must be impressive in the pulpit, thought MacKenzie; he must sway his congregation as the wind sweeps over a wheat field. He was intrigued. The Reverend Randolph Montgomery was very different from the preachers he had known in the Mid-west, and was probably very different too, he thought, from most of his brother ministers in Boston.

'And what was it you were going to ask Matron?' the reverend asked his sister again.

'If Garrett has come to work today.'

'Ah. Garrett. I have not seen him, but then, I have been in the kitchen with Cook this past half hour.' He smiled at Ames. 'Mr. Ames, how are you?'

Ames introduced MacKenzie, and the reverend offered his left hand. An odd handshake, MacKenzie thought, letting go at once.

'I am a bachelor, living solitary,' the reverend continued, 'so I have taken it upon myself to make friends with Cook here. She is a kindly soul. She often feeds the folks hereabouts who come begging at the kitchen door, and she feeds me up very faithfully as well.'

And, indeed, he looked sleek and well fed, MacKenzie thought, far more so than any of the Bower's girls.

'I am acquainted with your sister, Ames,' Montgomery went on. 'Is she well?' His handsome face showed a courteous smile, but his eyes were chilly. Handsome, but weak-looking, MacKenzie thought, with not quite enough chin and the eyes a trifle too close together.

'Yes, thank you.'

'And you have come here because — ?'

Still those chilly eyes, despite his smile.

'Caroline was most distressed at the news of your trouble.'

'You mean the death of two of our girls.'

'Yes.'

'And so she wanted you to come to offer help?'

'Yes.'

'It is very kind of you.' The reverend contemplated Ames for a moment. 'I cannot imagine what you could do for us, but I am grateful to you — and to Miss Ames — for your concern.'

But you do not seem grateful, thought

115

Ames. You seem — what? He could not put a name to it, but he felt very strongly that the reverend did not want him here.

'But why are you here in Mary's room?' the reverend went on. 'Surely the police have done a thorough job of searching it.'

'I told them that, Randolph,' Miss Montgomery said quickly. 'But they insisted — '

Did I insist? wondered Ames. Yes, I suppose I did.

The reverend arched an eyebrow. 'Do the police approve, Mr. Ames?'

'Of my coming here? I have no idea. But when I visited Inspector Crippen yesterday, he made no objection to my helping in a general sort of way.'

'A general sort of way,' the reverend repeated. 'I see. Well, then! If the good inspector has no objection, I can hardly object myself. In fact — ' He moved away from the threshold, down the hall toward the stairs, and they followed, Miss Montgomery closing the door of Mary and Bridget's room behind her.

'Why not come along to the rectory, where we can speak without interruption?' the reverend said over his shoulder as they began to descend the stairs. 'It is not far, and I can offer you some small refreshment.'

Garrett O'Reilly, it seemed, had not been

seen at the Bower that day, and so shortly Ames and MacKenzie found themselves outside in the rain once more, accompanying the Reverend Montgomery to his rectory three blocks away.

This proved to be an imposing mansion house made of stone like the church next door. A wrought-iron fence surrounded a small front garden whose few winter-dead plantings were half covered in dirty, icy, rain-pelted snow.

The reverend opened the gate and led them up the path to the door, where, beneath the cover of the porch, he shook the water off his umbrella, closed it, and produced his key.

'You won't find me standing on ceremony,' he said as he ushered them in. 'I am a plain and modest man, and I live the same.'

You are neither plain nor modest, thought Ames, but as he looked around, he saw that the reverend spoke the truth — about his house, at least.

The wide entrance hall beyond the vestibule was barren, no pictures on the walls, not a stick of furniture. Their footsteps echoed on the bare tile floor as they followed the reverend into the parlor. Here they saw a worn, threadbare carpet, a sagging serpentine-backed sofa, and three ancient upholstered chairs. Several straight-backed wooden chairs surrounded a large round table in the center of the room which was laden with books, newspapers, periodicals, and a messy pile of manuscripts.

A bachelor's place, indeed, thought MacKenzie, and he had a brief, poignant memory of the welcoming parlor at No. 16½ Louisburg Square, with Caroline Ames giving them tea, and a sea-coal fire simmering on the hearth.

Here, a few charred sticks of wood lay cold in the grate. The reverend threw off his overcoat, tossed it onto a chair, and bent to put in a handful of kindling. As he touched a match to it, a small, inadequate flame appeared.

Then he turned up the gas, and they saw even more clearly than before that this was — in contrast to the man himself — a place that looked most desperately poor. The plush upholstery on the sofa was worn down to the nub, the seats of the chairs were lumpy, and a film of dust covered every surface. Better to leave the lights low, thought Ames as he and MacKenzie seated themselves at the table.

The reverend swept off the clutter, dumped it onto the sofa, and said, smiling, 'Do you know, Doctor, someone told me about you only the other day. Addington Ames has taken on a boarder, my friend said — a veteran of the Indian wars in the West. So already you are acquiring a little reputation here in Boston, which, despite appearances, is a village at heart, full of gossip.'

MacKenzie did not know how to reply to this, and so he said nothing, but merely nodded.

'And your bad knee?' the reverend went on.

'Healed well, thank you.'

'Good. I am glad to hear it. Nothing so tiresome as not being able to get around. I get around myself a good deal, as you can imagine.' He chuckled, inviting them to share this glimpse of his busy life.

'Now, what can I offer you?' he went on. 'I have sherry, or a drop of Scotch whisky. It's a bit early in the day for stimulants, I grant you. Or if you would prefer tea, I can whip down to the kitchen to put on the kettle.'

They declined any refreshments. Ames took out his pocket notebook and opened it to the page that held the copy of the coded note. 'Have a look at this, Reverend,' he said. 'Crippen can make nothing of it. Your sister couldn't either.'

'What is it?' Montgomery took it and squinted at it so that MacKenzie wondered if he needed reading glasses but was too vain to produce them in front of strangers.

'It is a copy of a note that was found in

119

Mary Flaherty's pocket on the night she was killed. Some kind of code, obviously. Crippen thought it might be some foreign language, but it isn't that.'

The reverend gave it a final glance and handed the notebook back to Ames. 'I have no idea what it is,' he said dismissively.

Ames watched him for a moment. Then: 'You knew Mary Flaherty.'

'Yes.'

'How well?'

Montgomery smiled with what MacKenzie thought was rather irritating condescension. 'Fairly well, I suppose. As well as anyone did. She was — how shall I put it? She was a very inspirational kind of girl.'

'How do you mean?'

'I mean, when you looked at her, you saw the real possibilities — the very real hope and promise of what Agatha is trying to do. Here was a girl' — his rich baritone rolled over them — 'who had been on the streets. I will not mince words: Mary was selling herself to any man who would buy. Agatha found her, took her in, healed her in body and spirit — a task in which I had some small part — and let her see that her life need not be one of shame and degradation. Under Agatha's care, Mary — and many like her, make no mistake — blossomed.

The world was no longer for her a place of fear and violence and foul disease and miserable death. In fact — '

'Do you know of any enemies she might have had?' Ames broke in. 'Or the other girl, Bridget?'

'No.' The reverend shook his head slowly, thinking about it. 'Well, there was the business of the girl who was expelled a week or so ago — '

'Yes. Matron Pratt told us about that.'

The reverend allowed himself a small smile. 'She is a perfect dragon, is she not? But she is a strong right arm to Agatha. She lacks a certain finesse, it is true, but I do not believe Agatha could operate the place without her, as rough and ready as she is. Before she came, Agatha had a difficult time of it, maintaining order. But now Mrs. Pratt keeps a steady hand — '

'Do you think that this girl — the one who was expelled — might have been angry enough to kill Mary?'

'I don't know.'

'She threatened her — accosted her in the street.'

'I know she did. But still, it seems highly unlikely, don't you think?'

'Yes. Particularly in light of the fact that a second girl was killed also, and as far as we know, the girl who was expelled had no quarrel with her.'

'Correct. No, I think — ' Montgomery pursed his lips. 'I think, if you are looking for a more likely suspect, Mr. Ames, that you might look in the direction of one Fred Brice.'

'And who is that?'

'He is a young man who sells typewriters. He brought a machine to the Bower one day last fall to give us a demonstration. So that Mary could see it, you understand, since she was the one who would be using it.'

'And — ?'

'Well, he made Mary's acquaintance, of course. And I must say, anyone who met Mary — any likely young man, I mean — was quite liable to fall in love with her. She was a very pretty girl, was Mary.'

'And did he? Fall in love with her, I mean.'

'Oh, I think so. Yes indeed. He came around quite often after that, Agatha told me. Several times he came when I was there — I am in and out, you know.'

'You are the only male whom Mrs. Pratt allows regularly on the premises,' Ames remarked.

'The only — well, yes. If you put it like that.'

'Aside from Garrett O'Reilly.'

'Aside from — yes.'

'You warned Inspector Crippen about him.'

The reverend's eyebrows rose. 'Did I?'

'So he says.'

'Yes, I remember now. I did pass that along to the police.'

'And did you also pass along the fact that Mary was in the family way?'

There was a little silence while the reverend absorbed it. Then: 'Really?' He seemed surprised.

'Yes. Really. According to the medical examiner.'

'You don't say.'

'And so if this typewriter salesman was in love with Mary — '

'Yes. I see what you mean. Very possibly he was — ah — the man responsible — '

'And very possibly he did not want to make an honest woman of her, so to speak. You are certain he was infatuated with her?'

'He seemed to be. Matron spoke to me, once or twice, about what a nuisance he was, always hanging about, sending Mary notes and so forth.'

'Given her attitude toward men, I am surprised she allowed him entry,' Ames remarked. 'And as for notes, we saw none in Mary's room.'

'I doubt she would have kept them. She had — how shall I put it? — higher aspirations than Fred Brice.'

'How do you mean?'

'I mean that Mary probably thought that even a likely young man like him was not good enough for her, although to be Mrs. Fred Brice might not be such a bad thing for a girl from the Bower.'

He laughed, but without sound. MacKenzie thought it an unnerving sight.

'At any rate,' the reverend went on, 'and I was not present to witness it, you understand, I was told that on Saturday last — '

'The day before Mary was killed.'

'Yes. On Saturday last, Brice came to the Bower and made one hell of a scene with Mary. You didn't hear about it? Agatha was not there either — we were together, as a matter of fact, at a convention of Presbyterians over at the Mechanics' Hall — but Mrs. Pratt certainly was. Brice found Mary at work in the office and made some kind of proposal to her, apparently. Things worked up into a very loud and acrimonious argument. Finally, Mrs. Pratt threw him out — literally. She is quite strong, as you may have noticed.'

'Have you told this to the police?' said Ames.

'Yes.'

'So you think this typewriter salesman, rebuffed in his advances to Mary, worked himself up into a murderous passion, not at the time, but — what? — more than twenty-four hours later?'

'I have no idea, Mr. Ames. I am merely trying to be helpful.'

'Yes. Of course. Well, now you have given us another person who held a grudge against Mary, but neither this typewriter fellow nor the girl who was expelled had any grudge against Bridget Brown, as far as you know.'

'Right.'

Ames leaned forward in his chair, resting his elbows on his knees. 'What do you think, Reverend? Have you any notion of who might have killed those girls?'

The reverend looked away as he considered the question. 'Not really,' he said at last, meeting Ames's eyes again.

'But — ?'

'But you know as well as I do, this district is not what it was when it was built, some forty years ago now. This district went from brand new and as elegant as the Back Bay to what it is now, a place where some streets are handsome and well kept and some are not. We have — how shall I put it? a rather more — ah — diverse population than what you have up there on Louisburg Square or on

125

Commonwealth Avenue. You should see the stream of Irish who pass through in the summertime on their way to the Braves' ball field off Walpole Street alongside the railroad tracks. And all year round we have tramps, hobos — all kinds of riffraff. Oh, yes, we have quite a problem here with the transient and homeless population.'

'Some of whom come begging at the Bower's kitchen.'

'Yes.'

'One of the cook's knives is missing.'

'Yes, she told me that,' the reverend said.

'It may be relevant. Probably it is, in fact. Do any of these — ah — transients ever bother the Bower's girls?'

'Not the ones whom Cook feeds, one must assume. But the others? Indeed they do.' The reverend frowned, remembering. 'They ride the rails, you know, back and forth between here and who knows where — Springfield, Albany, a number of places. Looking for work — or for handouts. When they are here-abouts, they prowl the neighborhood and beg. They are most annoying — and dangerous. Several times over the past few years they have accosted girls from the Bower. Only the other week, an inebriate tried to — well, fortunately she got away. Two girls were raped last year, however.'

'By the same man?'

'Yes.'

'And was he caught?'

'Yes.'

'A drifter?'

'That is correct. He drifts no more, however, since he was sentenced to a term in the state prison over in Charlestown.'

'So he is not our man in this case.'

'It would seem not.'

'And there have been no further assaults since his arrest?'

'Except for the one that was averted, none that I know of — and I would know, of course. Very little happens at the Bower that I do not know about. Agatha — and I speak in all modesty — Agatha relies upon me, as of course she should, in most matters concerning the running of the Bower, quite aside from financial details.'

Raising the money to run the place is hardly a detail, Ames thought.

'You helped her draw up the rules?'

'I did. I saw no reason why such a worthy enterprise should be deprived of Christian counsel.'

'Of course.'

There was an awkward little silence. The reverend looked around the room as if he were seeking some new topic of conversation.

Ames cleared his throat, but the reverend did not seem to notice; now he was studying the large gold ring that he wore on the small finger of his right hand.

That's the end of it, Ames thought; he'll give us nothing more. He cast about for some way to keep the conversation alive, but before he found it, the reverend spoke again.

'You have been very kind, Mr. Ames, to trouble yourself about this wretched business.'

'Yes, well, as I said — '

'I understand — your sister encouraged you.'

Caroline. 'That reminds me, Reverend. Caroline is holding a dinner this evening for Nigel Chadwick — do you know him? He is a London journalist touring America to promote his latest book. I took a note from her, just now, to Miss Montgomery, inviting you both to join us this evening — if you will forgive the lateness of the invitation.'

The reverend blinked. 'Indeed? How very kind.'

'Will you come?'

'Why — yes. I — we — will be happy to join you.'

But he did not look happy, MacKenzie thought; he looked puzzled.

'Caroline thought it would do Miss

Montgomery good to get away from the Bower.'

'Yes, I imagine it might.'

The reverend got to his feet. Now, at last, the interview was definitely over. He started toward the door, and Ames and MacKenzie followed.

'I am sure that in a matter of days,' the reverend was saying, 'the police will have brought this distressing matter to its conclusion. I have every confidence in them,' he added as they came to the vestibule. 'Inspector Crippen is one of their best men, don't you agree?'

The front door was open to the pelting rain. Ames stepped out and rescued his umbrella from where he had left it on the porch. 'Yes, I do,' he said with a small smile that Montgomery did not return. 'That's what troubles me — that Crippen is one of their best. Good day to you, sir.'

★ ★ ★

In the herdic-phaeton, Ames let out an exasperated laugh. 'A smooth customer, is he not, Doctor?'

'The Reverend Montgomery?' MacKenzie shook his head. 'Yes, indeed. But very effective for the purposes of the Bower, I imagine.'

'Yes. I am sure he is that. They don't run that place on a pittance, and from what Caroline tells us, they exist entirely on what he can bring in. I can just see him, making his case to a parlor full of ladies, any one of whom is wearing a piece of jewelry that would support the Bower for an entire year. Did you happen to notice the pages on his table?'

'No.'

Ames grunted. 'I couldn't be sure, but I thought the handwriting matched the dedication to Mary Flaherty, written in a book in her room.'

'Really?'

'Yes. But I could hardly steal a sheet to make sure, and beyond that, I don't know what good it does us. Or not at the moment, at any rate.'

He fell silent, brooding. The cab made its way through the rain-drenched streets, past the Boston & Providence railroad station, down Charles Street between the Common and the Public Garden. Perhaps the reverend had been right, he thought; perhaps Crippen, for all his faults, would be able to catch the man responsible for the Bower murders. Perhaps he, Addington Ames, did not need to involve himself further.

And yet . . . Caroline's reproachful face

rose up in his mind. She was right, of course. Agatha Montgomery did the city much good with her refuge for fallen women, and he and Caroline should do what they could to help her, even indirectly, to keep the place going. As it would not, if the scandal grew.

'He was filled with helpful suggestions about a possible suspect, was he not?' MacKenzie said, jarring him out of his reverie. 'Drifters, hobos, baseball enthusiasts — not to mention the typewriter salesman and the Irish lad. And yet, despite what he said, I would put my money on that dragon matron.'

'What? The estimable Mrs. Pratt? Why do you say so?'

'I can't give you a particular reason. But she seemed so filled with anger, so — resentful, is that the right word? — so resentful of the girls, and particularly Mary. Do you not think it odd that a woman like that, so bristling with hostility, would seek employment in such a place?'

'But you heard what Caroline said, and the reverend also. Mrs. Pratt does her job and does it well. Besides which, she claimed to be at her religious meeting on Sunday night. Do we know if she was at the Bower on Monday, when the second girl was killed? I agree with you, Doctor. The woman is hardly a sympathetic figure. Whether that makes her a murderess, I doubt we can say.'

At Beacon Street, the herdic suddenly lurched as the driver took his opportunity and whipped his horse across, along Charles Street to Mt. Vernon. Rapidly, they went up the hill and came into Louisburg Square, and then they were home; a tall, redbrick, swell-front town house, with lavender-glass windows and a shiny black front door, fanlight above it and a brass door knocker in the shape of a humpbacked sea serpent — a reminder of the origins of the Ames family fortune, rather depleted now, when Ames's grandfather had been one of the foremost China traders in the city.

Ames paid the driver and they mounted the small flight of granite steps, scraped their boots on the iron boot-scraper beside the door, and went in. The odor of spicy pea soup greeted them, and in the next moment Caroline appeared from the dining room.

'Addington! I am so glad you're home. Margaret is just serving lunch. And this came.' She held a small yellow envelope: a telegram.

Hanging his cape on the hall tree, Ames took the telegram and opened it as he went into the dining room.

'Well?' she said, seating herself at her place

at the table and ladling out his bowl of soup. 'What is it? Something to do with Agatha?'

'I don't think so.' He read it again, just to be sure. And it was only a few words after all:

Can you call this afternoon stop.
Serena Vincent

Serena Vincent.

He tucked the telegram into his breast pocket and waited until his hands were steady before he lifted his soup spoon. Suddenly, the dreary day had brightened, a fact that had nothing to do with the weather.

'What is it, Addington? Or is it something personal?'

The soup was thick and hot, one of his favorites. 'It is Mrs. Vincent. She wants to see me this afternoon.'

Instantly Caroline froze. MacKenzie understood her reaction. She was wary of Mrs. Vincent: a notorious — and very beautiful — actress who had once, some years earlier, been a member of the Ameses' social circle. But she'd been caught out in an adulterous affair and disgraced, divorced by her husband, her name never mentioned again in proper Boston households. Instead of having the decency to commit suicide, or at the very least to move away, she'd stayed on in the city and made a successful career for herself on the stage. Only last fall, after not having seen her for some years, the Ameses had made her acquaintance once more.

'Why?' she said, more sharply than she had intended.

'I have no idea. I assume that I will discover why when I go to see her.'

Caroline forced herself to change the subject. 'How did your morning go at the Bower, Addington?'

He shrugged. 'Not as badly as it could have, I imagine.' And he told her of their interviews with Matron Pratt and Agatha Montgomery.

'You saw Mary's room! I am surprised that Agatha let you do that.'

'Yes, well, perhaps she is more upset than we know. At any rate, there was nothing helpful to be seen there. And then the reverend came — '

'He did? How did he seem?'

Ames glanced at MacKenzie. 'What would you say, Doctor? He didn't strike me as being terribly distraught.'

'No,' MacKenzie agreed. 'But then, all these men of the cloth are disciplined to hide their feelings, wouldn't you say?'

'Hmmm.' Ames thought about it. 'Perhaps.

At any rate, he assured us that Inspector Crippen and the police are perfectly capable of apprehending the man responsible for the murder of the Bower's girls, and he has every faith that they will.'

Caroline made a little moue of distaste. 'Do you mean he asked you not to involve yourself?'

'Yes. I would say he asked exactly that.'

'But you won't stop — '

'No. Not yet, at any rate.'

'Did you deliver the invitation to dinner?'

'Yes. They will come.'

Ames wiped his mouth with his napkin and pushed back his chair. Serena Vincent, he thought. He was eager to be out of the house and on his way to see her. More eager, perhaps, than was prudent.

'Can I be of assistance to you this afternoon, Miss Ames?' MacKenzie asked.

'Oh — no, I don't think so. But thank you.'

Ames paused. 'In that case, Doctor, perhaps you would like to hunt up Verna Kent? A girl who was expelled from the Bower last week,' he explained to Caroline, 'and who threatened to harm Mary Flaherty.'

MacKenzie nodded with what he hoped was sufficient enthusiasm. 'Yes, of course.'

Margaret appeared in the doorway. 'Cook says to come, miss. The boy from S. S. Pierce hasn't delivered the order, an' the aspic isn't takin' right either.'

As Caroline rose and hurried out to see to this latest domestic crisis, Ames said to MacKenzie, 'We are well away from here, Doctor. I wish you luck.'

And I you, MacKenzie thought.

9

At Serena Vincent's fashionable apartment
hotel on Berkeley Street, the concierge,
forewarned, ushered Ames in and directed
him to the elevator. As the uniformed
operator clanged shut the door, Ames realized
that he was sweating a little, and his heart was
beating fast.

Stop it, he told himself as the brass and
mahogany cage rose slowly upward. She is an
actress: beyond the pale. The fact that her
husband had been far too old for her, and,
worse, a mean and vicious man; the fact that
her punishment — banishment from Boston
Society — had turned into a kind of victory
for her; the fact that since he'd met her the
previous autumn she had lived in his dreams
— all of those facts were irrelevant. No
woman could be an actress and still be
thought of as decent. By rights, he should
think of her only with contempt.

But that was not the way he thought of her:
not at all. He was honest enough to admit it,
to himself if to no one else. The last time he'd
seen her, in the fall, she'd been jailed in the
Tombs, dressed in prison garb which did

nothing to lessen the impact of her stunning beauty. He remembered how he'd briefly put his hand on her shoulder and felt her warmth through the cheap, flimsy cloth.

The elevator stopped, the door clanged open, and he stepped out into the thickly carpeted hall. He was admitted by the maid, a middle-aged woman who, as he knew, was more duenna than maid. She took his hat and gloves and Inverness cape, and then she showed him into the parlor, where Serena Vincent awaited him.

She rose as he entered. She was tall for a woman, some years younger than himself — about thirty, he thought — with auburn hair and wide, greenish eyes set in a stunningly beautiful face. He realized with a little pang that he'd forgotten just how beautiful she was, and how could he have done that? She wore some kind of tea gown of grayish-green silk, with — apparently — no corset or, indeed, undergarments of any kind to encase her voluptuous figure.

'Mr. Ames,' she said, advancing and giving him her hand. He caught a whiff of her scent — something French, no doubt. 'How kind of you to come.'

Her voice was low, with a husky, sensuous undertone, but as he knew, she could project it seemingly without effort to the last row of the second balcony.

'Not at all,' he said. He was relieved to hear that his own voice sounded steady, reassuringly normal.

A small Yorkshire terrier on a silk pillow by the fire lifted its head and growled softly at the intruder, but at a word from its mistress it subsided.

She motioned him to a chair and took a seat opposite on a brocade settee. He was conscious of not knowing what to do with his hands; he still heard his heart pounding in his breast, and he wondered if she could hear it too.

'I have read in the newspapers about the trouble over at Bertram's Bower,' she began. She spoke with grave formality, as if the moment of closeness — intimacy, almost — between them in the Tombs had never happened.

'Ah.' So it was not some personal thing, then, that she'd wanted him for. He felt a small stab of disappointment.

'And since you were so helpful to me last fall, I thought perhaps, since it is Inspector Crippen who is in charge of the investigation — '

She didn't need to say more. It was Crippen who had arrested her — mistakenly — for the murder of the infamous Colonel

William d'Arcy Mann.

'I understand.' He smiled at her. Looking at her was like looking at some glorious work of art created by an artist who specialized in sensuous femininity.

'I wonder if you do.' She did not return his smile. 'You are familiar with my story, are you not?'

Her story. Did he want to hear that? 'Yes, but — '

'I married foolishly, too young. Then I took a lover — yes, I admit it, I have always admitted it. And then my husband divorced me.'

'I don't see — you needn't go into it — '

'Ah, but I must, Mr. Ames. You see, when my husband banished me, it was without a penny. I had no money of my own. My own family would not have me back, not after the disgrace I had brought upon them. I was literally without a soul in the world to turn to. I had no place to live, no way to survive.'

The amazing thing was, he thought, that she said these things so calmly, only the shadow of remembered pain in her eyes to show that she spoke of her own disgrace, and not, say, that of some heroine in some play.

'It was Agatha Montgomery who took me in,' she went on. 'Does that surprise you?'

'Yes.' It did, very much.

'It shouldn't. I was as destitute as any of the girls she finds on the streets. I very likely would have been on the streets myself if she hadn't helped me.'

She paused, remembering. Then: 'It was a day toward the end of March. Just after lunch. I knew my husband had learned of my — indiscretion — but I didn't know the end would come so quickly. He handed me my hat and cloak, and a small valise with some clean undergarments and — always with an eye for detail — a bar of lye soap. He took me by the arm and literally pushed me out of the house. I remember that I stood on the doorstep, looking up and down Marlborough Street and wondering if I should throw myself under the wheels of the Green Trolley that was just passing by.'

She reached for an enameled box on the table beside her and took out a long, thin brown cigarette. 'Do you smoke, Mr. Ames?'

'No, thank you.'

But he sprang to his feet to light it for her with a match from a silver matchbox.

She inhaled deeply a few times, seemingly lost in thought. Then she went on: 'But even at that blackest moment of my life, suicide did not appeal to me. So . . . for the last time, I walked down the front steps of that house where I had been so unhappy. I walked and walked — I don't remember where. At last I found myself in front of a pawnshop over on Tremont Street in the South End. I realized that I did not have a dollar to my name, but I did have — I was wearing a pearl brooch. I went into the shop. The proprietor took my brooch and gave me ten dollars for it — can you imagine? It was a fine piece, worth much more. But it was ten dollars more than I'd had before, so I accepted it. I suppose I was still in a state of shock, too dazed to bargain with him for a better price. I found a rooming house that did not look too disreputable, and I took a room. For twenty-four hours I sat in that room, contemplating the wreckage of my life. At last I got up, I went out, and I found a café where I had a bowl of soup and a piece of bread — ten cents, coffee included.' Her mouth twisted in a bitter smile at the memory.

'As I was leaving, a woman came in. She was tall, ugly, very determined-looking. Yes — Miss Montgomery. She must have seen something in my face that led her to speak to me. She did not recoil when she learned who I was, as if merely to speak to me would soil her beyond redemption. She had heard of my scandal, of course — everyone in Boston had heard of it — but she did not judge me. She offered me a place to live — at Bertram's

Bower, yes. Do not look so surprised, Mr. Ames. It was a warm bed, a safe place, a place where I could gather my wits about me and think how to start my life over again, as I needed to do.'

'But — ' He thought of the sad, defeated girls he'd seen that morning; he could not picture a woman like Serena Vincent among them. 'How did you fit into the population there?'

'I didn't — not very well. The matron — this was before Mrs. Pratt — was a kindly woman, far too lax with the girls. So I was able to avoid the classes in reading and sewing, which in any case I hardly needed. I stayed in my room, mostly, for the brief time I was there. Miss Montgomery often came to talk to me. She helped me to see that I was, after all, a child of God like everyone else, and that even though I had transgressed, I was young, I could make something of my life.'

She stubbed out her cigarette in a china dish, and then she met his eyes with a somber look. 'I wonder, Mr. Ames, if you could understand me if I tell you that Agatha Montgomery is a kind of saint.'

Saints were papist things, not part of his own upbringing, which had been Unitarian.

'She is a truly Christian woman,' Mrs.

Vincent went on, 'a rare soul. She labors day after day with the outcasts of this world, with girls who would never be admitted to the decent homes of the city, not even as servants. She gives herself to them, she slaves for them, she rescues them from a life that is worse than death. I know she is hardly an attractive woman. Many people would call her unladylike, unfeminine. She is too driven to be ladylike. All people with a true mission in life are like that, I think — heedless of surface appearances, of the niceties of so-called polite society. She doesn't care what the world says about her, because she has her work to do, and she will do it, come what may.'

'You would like me to help her.'

'Yes. She needs help now, and I have very little faith — as you can imagine — that Inspector Crippen is up to the job.'

'You and my sister both,' he said, 'agree on that point.'

'And did she — your sister — urge you to involve yourself in the case?'

'To do what I can, yes. She feels that if this man — this murderer — is not apprehended quickly, the Bower will suffer scandal that will make it impossible for the place to continue, depending as it does on donations.'

'From the respectable people of the city.'

She made 'respectable' sound like a slur. 'People who would not allow any of Miss Montgomery's charges into their homes but who feel it their Christian duty to support her in her work. At a respectable distance,' she added with some bitterness.

He shrugged. 'Hypocrisy does not necessarily cancel out people's desire to do good.'

'No. It does not. But I believe your sister is right, Mr. Ames. People will not want to be associated with the Bower if this man — this killer — is not found quickly.'

She shuddered. Did she see herself, he wondered, night-walking the streets, as degraded as any girl whom Agatha Montgomery took in? But no, Serena Vincent would never have stooped to such an existence. True, it was scandalous of her to have gone on the stage, but at least it was not too unpleasant a life, and from what he saw around him, she made plenty of money.

Unless she had found a lover to support her. He hated to think that; forcibly he pushed the notion from his mind. She'd recently had a lover, he knew, but the fellow had killed himself last fall, and in any case he'd not been wealthy. Had she mourned him? Did she still? He couldn't tell. But she made a fine high salary at the Park Theater, where she was the resident star; she didn't need some man's fortune to live well. He thought that most women earning so much would have been coarsened — unsexed — by that fact, but she was not. Far from it.

'Do you — now — support Miss Montgomery in her work?' he asked.

'Of course. I give as generously as I can. I can hardly do otherwise, considering what she did for me.'

'Her brother does well at raising funds.'

'Yes.' Her face had suddenly gone blank.

'You know him?'

'I — yes. A little.'

'Do you' — it seemed intrusive, but he wanted to know — 'give your donations to him, or do you give directly to Miss Montgomery?'

'I give to her.'

Tell me more, he thought, but apparently, she was not about to. The moment passed; she was smiling at him.

'Well, then,' he said. 'Since not only my sister, but also the most acclaimed actress in the city, asks me to involve myself in the case, I can hardly do otherwise, can I?'

He was not accustomed to delivering gallant little speeches, and certainly not to a woman like Serena Vincent, but the words had come to him effortlessly, due, no doubt, to her somewhat intoxicating effect on him.

146

Yes. He felt intoxicated. He realized it — and realized, too, that he should probably take his leave. Allowing oneself to be intoxicated by any woman, but particularly by a woman like Serena Vincent, was a dangerous business.

But he didn't want to leave. That was the very devil of it: He would happily have stayed in this luxurious little bijou flat for as long as she would have him. Just to sit here across from her and watch her, and catch a whiff of her perfume, and listen to her low, sensuous voice — it hardly mattered what she said — was like some amazing gift.

Just then the maid brought in a tea tray, and so he did not need to take his leave just yet. He accepted a cup and allowed Mrs. Vincent to charm him further with a lively patter, her painful memories apparently forgotten, but all the while, as he watched her, he pondered in a small corner of his mind the story she had told him. Amazing, that she'd been so destitute, that she'd had nowhere to turn for help. She'd been born and bred a Boston Brahmin like himself, but in her hour of need, it had not been any of those folks who had helped her, but another castoff from that same cold, insular tribe, Agatha Montgomery.

' . . . and so, of course, we had to demand a

rewrite,' she was saying, her beautiful face illuminated with laughter just barely contained. 'No one — and certainly not I — could stand before an audience and say lines like that.'

'Of course not.'

There was a little pause. She set down her cup and clasped her hands — slender and long-fingered, the nails shaped to a perfect oval and buffed to a high polish (and who gave you that stunning emerald ring? he wondered; and what favor did you bestow on him who gave it?) — clasped her hands before her swelling bosom and said, in what he was sure was her best tragedienne's voice, 'Mr. Ames, I have never adequately thanked you for what you did for me in the business of Colonel Mann's murder.'

'No thanks necessary.'

'Ah, but I think they are. If you had not persevered — why, I might have been on trial for my life. And now I am asking you for help once more. I am shameless in my asking, because I ask not for myself but for Agatha Montgomery. If it were for myself, I would not ask at all — but you understand that.'

'Yes.' Lovely woman, he thought — and where would you turn, should you yourself ever need help again?

She rose, and he did also. 'It is late,' she

said, 'and I must get to the theater.' She walked to the door, opened it, and went before him into the foyer. The maid was nowhere to be seen, but Ames had the sense that they were being watched.

Mrs. Vincent took his things from the hall tree and handed them to him. When he'd thrown his cape around his shoulders and was reaching for his hat and gloves, she held out her hand to him and he took it. He felt the impact of her touch rocket through him. She fixed him in her lustrous eyes. 'If I can be of any help, you will tell me,' she said. 'I am tied to the schedule of my performances, but otherwise you can find me here.'

'Of course.'

'And you will let me know how you do?' She was holding his hand in both her own.

'Yes.'

His heart hurt a little when she released him. And then he was out in the hall, her door closed behind him. Too late, he wished he'd managed to say something more. As he waited for the elevator, as he went down and out into the street once more, as he stood on the sidewalk and gathered his wits, deciding what to do next so as to avoid returning home and getting in Caroline's way — during all that time he realized that he had the sense of having narrowly escaped some dangerous

149

episode. If he had stayed, if he had kissed her hand instead of merely holding it . . .

Stop it.

She had asked him for help. That was enough — for now.

The rain had lessened, but the chilly damp of the thaw still blanketed the city. He took a deep breath of the salty air and began to walk.

★　★　★

At No. 16½ Louisburg Square, Dr. MacKenzie alighted from the herdic. As always when he returned to this place, he felt his heart lift at the thought of seeing Caroline Ames. She would be busy now, of course, because there were only a few hours until her guests arrived, and he'd have no hope of a word with her, or a cup of late afternoon tea by the parlor fire. But still, he would know she was near, he would feel her presence in the house, making of it the home he'd never had, not since his childhood. And even then, that childhood home had not meant to him what this one did.

He took off his hat and gloves and hung his overcoat on the hall tree. His cane stood, unused, in the umbrella stand. He hated it, was glad he didn't need it any more. Caroline was just coming up from the kitchen as he went into the front hall.

'Oh! Dr. MacKenzie! I thought it was Addington.'

Her hair was disarranged, and a grease spot soiled her apron. The cuffs of her sleeves were turned up, revealing a smear of flour on one forearm.

'He has not returned?'

'No.' A frown creased her smooth white brow. 'I know it sounds selfish of me, but I don't like to think of him with that woman.'

He understood: For all her kind and generous heart, Caroline Ames, like all respectable women, was deeply suspicious of actresses. Even actresses like Serena Vincent, who had come from her own class.

'He will be back soon, no doubt.' He tried to sound reassuring. Despite her beauty, Serena Vincent was not the kind of woman he himself would ever be attracted to, but he did not yet know Addington Ames well enough to judge Ames's susceptibilities. The man had hidden depths to him, a romantic side to his temperament that MacKenzie had been surprised to discover: Only last fall, Ames had been scheduled to travel to Egypt, to the Valley of the Kings, on an archaeological expedition with one of his former professors at Harvard. The professor had broken his leg, and so the trip had been canceled.

Caroline had reverted to her immediate concerns. 'The blancmange did not come right,' she said, almost as if she were thinking aloud. 'And the hired girl cannot seem to understand that I do not want the napkins laid flat, but folded to stand straight, as I showed her — and she cannot master the folding.'

Suddenly she slumped against the wall. MacKenzie, alarmed, put out a hand to steady her.

'My dear Miss Ames, if you will allow me to speak in my professional capacity — you need to rest a bit. You are working yourself up into a nervous state over this dinner, and if I were your physician, I would order you to stop.'

She gazed into his kind, worried eyes and managed a smile.

'You are not my physician,' she said softly, 'but I know you are right. Let us have tea together, Doctor, and you can tell me of your afternoon's adventures.'

He slid open the pocket doors to the front parlor, and Caroline pulled the bellpull by the fireplace to summon Margaret. Then she sank onto the sofa and smiled at MacKenzie again.

'You see how reasonable I am, Doctor. Twelve people coming tonight, and yet I obey you because I trust your opinion.'

He heard the sound of hooves on cobblestones, and he went to the window to look out through the lavender-glass panes. In the gathering darkness, the bare trees in the little iron-fenced oval seemed like twisting arms ready to snatch the unwary interloper, and the shrubbery, shriveled in the winter cold, looked as if it hid goblins ready to pounce. The lights in the tall red-brick town houses across the way glimmered with the suggestion of sanctuary.

A four-wheeler clattered by. He gave himself a little mental shake. He reminded himself that aside from being reluctant to spend even the smallest sum on something (like a cab) that he found unnecessary, Ames was a dedicated walker. He roamed the city at all hours, loping in his long stride, thinking, thinking — about what? MacKenzie hardly knew. Ames was a man of many interests, most of them intellectual. In a way, although he had graduated from the College years before, he'd never stopped being a student. He was an autodidact, always studying some esoteric subject or other, a faithful patron of the Athenaeum, visiting his former professors across the river for conversations that lasted long into the night.

Margaret appeared with their tea, and

153

Caroline poured and offered MacKenzie his cup as he came back to her.

'And what did you discover this afternoon, Doctor?'

He settled himself into what had become his own chair, a Morris rocker. 'Not much.'

'You found the girl who was expelled from the Bower?'

'Yes.' He frowned at the memory.

'And?'

'I doubt she could have been responsible for the crimes. She was very ill — with pneumonia, I think.'

'She was bedridden?'

'Yes.' In a stinking room in a stinking tenement, although he would not tell her that. 'She was very weak, with a high fever. She did not want to talk to me at first, but then, when she realized what I was asking her, she vehemently denied any involvement in Mary Flaherty's death. It seemed unnecessary to ask her about the second girl.'

'Well, at least you have discovered that much — that she is one less person we need to consider.'

He caught the 'we,' and he met her gaze, which had suddenly turned defiant.

'Yes, Doctor. We. I know Addington does not want me to involve myself in this matter, but how can I not? Poor Agatha! I do hope she will come this evening. You're sure she said she would?'

'Yes. And the reverend as well.'

MacKenzie was torn. He understood — and applauded — her urge to help her friend. But her brother was right: Bertram's Bower was no place for a lady like Caroline Ames.

But he understood, as well, that despite her charming exterior, she was a woman made of stern stuff. Underneath her pretty coiffure lay a mind as keen, in some ways, as her brother's, despite the fact that it had never been educated beyond Miss May's School for Girls. And her character, too, was steely and determined, infused with a fierce sense of right and wrong. He knew that the Ames's formidable aunt Euphemia, who lived over on Chestnut Street, had been a stalwart in the fight for abolition decades ago before the war; some of her blood ran in the veins of this delightful woman before him now, and inevitably, it would find a way to announce itself.

She smiled at him again. 'You will think me strong-minded,' she said.

'Not at all.'

'Oh, yes. I can see it in your eyes. You think I am an Amazon, and at any moment I will start to agitate for the vote.'

He cringed a little. Given the opportunity, would Caroline Ames join the suffragists?

'No,' he said. 'I do not think that.'

She laughed at him. 'Well, to be perfectly frank with you, Doctor, I do not care if you do. But woman suffrage is not our problem at the moment, is it?'

Despite her laughter, her voice was strained. He watched her for a moment, and then he said, 'Miss Ames, do you not think you should go up to your room to rest for a while before you dress for dinner? I am sure that Cook has everything well in hand — '

'But I am not,' she retorted. 'Dear heaven, that reminds me — the blancmange! She said she'd do it over, and she sent down to the market for another two dozen eggs. I don't even know if they've come. Please excuse me, Doctor.'

As she sprang up, they heard the front door slam. Ames, home at last, thought MacKenzie. Well, that should ease her mind a bit.

She slid open the pocket doors.

'Addington! I am so glad you're back! Cook is in a temper, and we don't have our blancmange yet, and — '

She broke off. Through long years of experience, she knew better than to bother him with her domestic concerns; this was no time to begin.

156

She hesitated, torn between her need to tend to affairs in the kitchen and her desire to hear what he might have to report. And so when he came into the room, she followed him.

'Well?' she said. 'And what did Mrs. Vincent want?'

He accepted the cup of tea she handed him and took his accustomed place by the fire.

'She wanted what you want, Caro,' he said.

'How do you mean?'

Should he tell them the story he'd heard from Serena Vincent — her abandonment, her disgrace, her rescue by Agatha Montgomery? No.

'She is a strong supporter of the Bower,' he said.

'She is? You mean financially? I never knew that.'

'Yes, well, I imagine she and Miss Montgomery both wish to keep it quiet. Her money is not quite so pure as some.'

They heard the unmistakable note of sarcasm in his voice.

'And so she asked you to help?'

'Yes.'

Caroline struggled with it, and her better nature won. 'I am glad she did that. Good for her. I never would have thought that someone like Mrs. Vincent — '

'Had an altruistic bone in her body?' Ames finished for her.

She lifted her chin. 'No, Addington. That is not what I meant. What I meant was, she left the world of good works behind when she took up her life on the stage. I always think of actresses and artists and such as rather selfish, self-absorbed creatures. Which I suppose they have to be. I never would have thought of her as being concerned for women less fortunate than herself.'

'You call Serena Vincent fortunate? When she suffered disgrace that would have killed many women?'

'Yes, but she turned it to her advantage, didn't she?'

'Yes,' he replied softly. 'She did.'

There was a silence as he stared into the fire. Then MacKenzie said, 'I found that girl, Ames.'

'Ah.' Ames came back from his reverie and turned his dark eyes on his lodger. 'And did she confess?'

'Hardly. She was very ill. I doubt that she could have been up and about two or three nights ago.'

'Hmmm. Well, then, at least we have eliminated her. After I left Mrs. Vincent, I went across the river. I took the electric cars' — a new wonder, a marvelous improvement

158

over the horse-drawn omnibuses — 'to visit Professor Harbinger.'

'Your Egyptologist friend at Harvard.'

'Yes. I thought he might be able to tell me something about that very odd note that Crippen showed us.'

'And did he?' MacKenzie asked.

'No. It was like nothing he'd ever seen before. We went through all kinds of possibilities — a simple transposition code, the cipher wheel, the Vigenère Table, the St. Cyr Slide, a cipher square with a key word — '

'Excuse me, miss.' The pocket doors slid open to reveal Margaret, looking harassed. 'If you could come down — Cook's sayin' she's goin' to leave this instant, and the hired girl's takin' a fit — '

And so Caroline's moment of respite came to an end, and with an exclamation of alarm she hurried out.

10

They were fifteen that night around the shining mahogany table, and as Caroline surveyed her guests, she felt a sense of well-deserved triumph. It was going to be all right — more than that.

The hothouse flowers (expensive, but worth it), the tall candles glowing in her heirloom silver candelabra, the sparkling crystal, the china adorned with the Ames family crest brought over by her grandfather from Whampoa in '27, the silver epergne laden with fruit — yes, it was a picture-perfect scene. No hostess in the city could have offered a more elegant display of hospitality. She glanced at the portrait of that same grandfather gazing down at them from its place over the mantel. He'd been a stern man, very old when she was quite young and never given to showing his feelings, but he'd be proud of her tonight, she thought, if he were here.

The candlelight — so much more flattering than gaslight — glowed on the women's shoulders and, here and there, décolletage, and glittered on the discreet displays of jewelry, much of which, like Caroline's china and silver, was heirloom. Imogen Boylston was wearing her mother's pearls; Edith Perkins was almost too showy in a matched set of emeralds; Harriet Mason's grandmother's ruby earbobs dangled and sparkled every time Harriet uttered a syllable, which was frequently. As Caroline had hoped, Harriet had taken the shy Matthew Hale under her wing. He could hardly get a word in edgewise, but he looked enthralled at Harriet's ceaseless chatter.

The guest of honor, Nigel Chadwick, sat at Caroline's right. He was a small, fastidious man with pale hair and a closely clipped mustache. He wore gold-rimmed spectacles over his bright, canny eyes, and he spoke in a high-class accent that every now and then slipped into what must have been his native cockney. He had the air of a man touring the former colonies — ever courteous, and only occasionally condescending. Caroline could see, from the way her female guests hung on his words (the men were less enthralled), that she was having one of the triumphs of the social season. Her friends, she knew, would be envious for a time, but eventually they would forgive her, and as the evening slipped into legend, Chadwick's bons mots would be passed along, and embroidered upon, and everyone would say how clever Caroline Ames had been to snare him, and how beautifully she had carried it off.

The hired girl, looking smart in her black dress and white ruffled cap and apron, was handing around the salmon mousse. Caroline met the eyes of her friend Imogen Boylston, who lived in a grand house on Commonwealth Avenue and was known for her elaborate entertainments. That lady arched an eyebrow and smiled as if to say, congratulations.

Next to Mrs. Boylston sat the Reverend Randolph Montgomery. He seemed in fine form this evening, chatting wittily on any number of topics, always ready with a quip or a question, all the while devouring with gusto the food that was placed before him. His pomaded hair shone in the candlelight, his handsome face radiated goodwill, his demeanor was that of a man without a care in the world.

But as Caroline watched him, she thought, he knows these people here tonight hold his fate in their hands. He is putting up a good front, but all the same, he must realize the need to extricate the Bower from scandal as soon as possible, so that these people, and others like them, will continue to give generously to his appeals.

His sister Agatha looked less at ease. She sat down the table at Ames's left, next to Desmond Delahanty. She spoke very little and ate less. She should try to seem more tranquil, Caroline thought, to reassure people that she can bear up under the strain of the past few days.

Chadwick was talking about his adventures in America. 'I landed in New York — oh, two weeks ago now,' he said. 'And d'you know, I was delighted to see it in every bookshop. Amazing!' 'It' — his book, which he was assiduously promoting — was a slightly scandalous work about Queen Victoria.

'You people over here may have fought a war to separate yourselves from us,' he added, 'but I believe you miss us all the same. You can't seem to get enough gossip about the Royals.'

'Indeed, Mr. Chadwick,' chirped one of the ladies. 'Tell us something delicious about the Queen.'

He paused for effect. Then, with a conspiratorial smile: 'For one thing, she is extremely superstitious.'

A little murmur of excitement went around the table.

'Do go on, Mr. Chadwick,' chirped the same lady. 'Don't torment us — do tell!'

'She cannot tolerate a broken mirror,'

163

Chadwick said. 'And as for spilled salt — a catastrophe! And she lives in dread of certain dates of the month — the thirteenth, of course, but the fourteenth as well. Her beloved husband, Prince Albert, died on the fourteenth of December back in eighteen sixty-one, and' — another dramatic pause — 'only last week, on the fourteenth of January, her grandson Prince Albert Victor died.'

An audible gasp came from the ladies.

'Yes,' Chadwick went on. 'Very odd, is it not? But there is more, much more. I should refer you to my book, but — well, I can tell you this much at least. She is a confirmed spiritualist.'

A few of the ladies squealed with delight. The hired girl took away their plates and stepped aside for Margaret bearing Cook's potted grouse. Caroline, thinking of the mended platter, mentally crossed her fingers, but it was all right, it held.

Chadwick waited for Margaret to leave the room before he continued. 'She used to indulge in table-turning with Prince Albert — her husband, I mean. And after he passed on, she took part in spiritualistic séances with her Scots gillie, the notorious John Brown. He died some years ago, and I have not been able to determine whether she has since made

164

contact with him, wherever he is now.'

Chadwick basked for a moment in the admiration of his audience, but then, as if he feared giving away too much from his book, he turned the conversation back to his adventures in America.

'I have been to Philadelphia, to Baltimore, Washington — a strange place, that — and Richmond. I returned to New York for a few days, and then I made my way north, to your fair city.'

'And you return to London when?' MacKenzie asked, picking at his grouse. He'd never had it before, and he didn't care if he never had it again.

'Next week — from New York.'

'And how do you find us here in Boston?' asked Edward Boylston. He was a stout, balding man, a pillar of strength to the Bower, where, twice a year, he audited the account books.

'How do I find you?' Chadwick allowed himself a small smile. 'Why — very well. Very well indeed. You are so very — ah — democratic, don't y'know.'

Delahanty met MacKenzie's gaze and quirked an eyebrow. 'Democratic' was the last word he'd have used to describe this assembly of upper-crust Bostonians.

'I'm sending back a regular report to my

165

newspaper,' Chadwick went on. 'I want to give 'em a good sense of you. I've been to the theater in New York, I've visited reformatories and prisons, I saw a hospital in Baltimore, and tomorrow I am to have a tour of your medical school here at Harvard. I've gone to the big department stores in New York, and to Wanamaker's in Philadelphia. I saw your Congress in Washington — amazing, the oratorical powers of some of those gents. They could give our fellows in Parliament a run for their money any day. I even went to an auction when I first landed in New York. I have a weakness for eighteenth-century stuff, and they'd advertised a little Watteau for sale.'

'How fascinating,' said Caroline. 'Did you get it?'

'No, worse luck. I stopped just in time before I bankrupted myself. I never saw the fellow who did. He had a straw bidding for it. Someone told me later he was a Boston man, in fact.'

They felt that he was chastising them. Was he holding them collectively responsible for doing him out of that painting? wondered MacKenzie.

'We have many noted connoisseurs here in Boston,' Delahanty replied, smoothing over the awkward moment. 'If you have time, I'll take you to meet Mrs. Gardner over on

166

Beacon Street. She's been buying up half the treasures of the Continent, and she even has a smart young man to help her choose what is best. Her collection is a bit of a jumble, but you might find it interesting.'

Caroline threw Delahanty a grateful smile. In the little silence that followed, Matthew Hale, perhaps emboldened by the three glasses of wine he had drunk, leaned around his neighbor, the voluble Mrs. Mason, to peer at the reverend. 'Speaking of New York, Reverend, I saw a friend of yours there last week.'

'Oh?' replied Montgomery. He did not seem particularly interested.

'Yes, indeed. A most charming lady.'

Montgomery did not reply, but a wary look came over his face.

'And she had a most interesting secret to tell me,' Hale went on, smiling merrily now. He was flushed, and his eyes were shining brighter than Caroline, who had known him since childhood, had ever seen them.

'I don't think — ' Montgomery began, but Hale was too quick for him. He prattled on, chuckling a bit, glancing around the table to gauge the effect of what he said.

'She gave me to understand that she is your fiancée, Reverend. You sly dog,' he added, grinning broadly. 'I told her that half the

167

single females in Boston had set their caps for you. It was too cruel, I said, that you went to New York to find a bride.'

As Montgomery, for once, seemed at a loss for words, they were startled by the sound — and sight — of his sister choking. At once, MacKenzie jumped up and began to pound her on her back.

During this distressing episode, Ames noted that the reverend sat perfectly still, his eyes fixed on Matthew Hale. It was not a look of a man who has had his secret revealed but who doesn't mind very much. Rather, it was the look of a man who would like to murder the person who revealed it. Montgomery's eyes burned with anger, and he did not appear even to notice his sister's difficulty, eased now by Dr. MacKenzie's efforts.

'Well,' Hale said cheerily, oblivious of the effect of his revelations on the reverend. 'Is it true, sir? Will you soon be entering the sacred bonds of matrimony with that charming lady from New York? Or is she, shall we say, allowing her own hopes and desires to triumph over the facts of the matter?'

The Reverend Montgomery's face had gone from pale to pink to an odd shade of puce. He was clutching his fork in a death grip; had it been his wineglass, he would have shattered it. 'I — it is a personal matter, sir,' he managed to get out at last.

MacKenzie sat down. Agatha took a sip of water. Harriet Mason asked someone a question about the new exhibition at the art museum in Copley Square. Margaret returned bearing the next course — a melange of vegetables. And so, somehow — Caroline never remembered exactly how — they got past the moment that had threatened to ruin her party.

By ten o'clock they were finishing the blancmange, which had turned out splendidly after all. Fruit and cheese appeared and were consumed, and then Ames suggested that the men remove to his study for their coffee and port and cigars. A question had come up about ancient Athenian red-figured pottery; he could show them a very fine example, he said, that he'd picked up in Sicily several years before. The ladies, he added with a look at Caroline, could proceed into the parlor, where the men would join them shortly.

Everyone rose. Ordinarily, Caroline should have led the women first out of the room, but when she saw that Agatha had remained seated, as if the effort of standing were too much for her, Caroline asked Mrs. Boylston to take the ladies out. The men left, then, as well, and Caroline and Agatha were alone. When the hired girl looked in to see if she could clear, Caroline asked her to wait.

'What is it, Agatha?' she said. 'Are you all right? The evening went well, I thought, and I am so glad that you and the reverend could come — '

Miss Montgomery was visibly trembling. 'I do not feel well, Caroline. But as you say, it is very good for Randolph to be here. I don't want to take him home just yet. The men often have much to say to one another away from the women. If I could just lie down for a few moments . . . '

'But of course!' Caroline was alarmed. Her friend really did look ill, her muddy complexion pale, her eyes watering. 'I will take you up to my room — we will use the elevator — and you can rest for a bit. Should I ask Dr. MacKenzie to see you? He is very kind, and very wise, I think. Perhaps he could — '

'No — no,' Miss Montgomery gasped. 'I just need to rest for a bit — perhaps I laced too tightly.'

Caroline put her hand under Miss Montgomery's elbow to steady her, and as she did so, her eye was caught by a gleam of gold on the carpet.

'Why — what is that?' she said.

'What?' asked Miss Montgomery. 'Oh, goodness, it belongs to Randolph. He wears it on his watch chain.'

Despite her momentary faintness, she managed to stoop and retrieve it. Caroline had glimpsed it for only a second; she thought it was some kind of coin.

'It must have dropped off when he got up from the table,' Miss Montgomery said. 'I will give it to him later,' she added, opening her small, shabby reticule and slipping it in.

After Caroline settled Miss Montgomery upstairs, she returned to the front hall, where she paused for a moment. She heard a burst of masculine laughter. Good.

In Ames's study, the question of the vase settled, he offered port and cigars to his guests. One of them, a man whom Ames did not know well but whose wife was an associate of Caroline's in many of her charities, offered the Reverend Montgomery his condolences on the trouble at the Bower.

'It will pass,' the reverend said. 'With the good Lord's help,' he added.

Chadwick's ears had perked up. 'You and your sister have been the subject of the sensational reports I have read in your local news sheets,' he said to Montgomery.

'Yes,' the reverend replied slowly. He seemed not to want to discuss the matter.

'Do you think — but no, you wouldn't know that, would you? I was going to say, do you think the man is targeting your — ah — place specifically, or may these be random murders like our own case a few years ago?'

'Your own case?' Ames asked before the reverend could reply. 'You mean — '

'Yes. He called himself Jack the Ripper, but of course we never knew who he was really.'

'Never caught,' said someone.

'No.'

'I hardly think — ' the reverend began, but he was interrupted by Delahanty.

'Did you report on the case for your newspaper?' he asked the Englishman.

Chadwick paused before he replied. 'I did, yes.'

'And since the police never caught the man — never even came close — he is still at large?'

'At large? I am not sure about that. Let us say that he has claimed no further victims.'

'All of them in the slum district of Whitechapel — the East End of London.'

'Yes.'

'A curious fixation, was it not?' said the man who had first spoken. 'Not really killing at random, was he, since he always chose as his victims — ah — ladies of the evening, shall we say?' He smiled in an unpleasant way.

'Yes. Five women, possibly six. From

172

August to November, three years ago.'

'And then nothing,' said Delahanty.

'Right. It was as if he went away.'

'Or died.'

'Or died, yes. Or was incarcerated for some other crime. It was a baffling case. There were several suspects, each with his fervent adherents. A local butcher, some said. A demented barrister, some said, who killed himself just when the murders stopped — a convenient coincidence perhaps. Some people even thought that the murderer — and his victims — had some connection to the Crown. I touch on that aspect of the case in my book about the Queen. Her own physician had a very vocal claque supporting his nomination as the Ripper.'

'The Queen's physician?' said Ames. 'But that is extraordinary, is it not, to suspect such a man?'

'Sir William Gull, yes. Preposterous on the face of it, of course. There was a scurrilous story about one of the Queen's grandsons having some involvement with a woman, a child born, blackmail, et cetera. And because the victims were all — ah — extensively carved up, it has been held that the murderer knew something of surgery.'

'Or butchery.'

'Or butchery, yes. But may I ask, Mr. Ames

173

— does your killer here send notes to the newspapers the way the Ripper did?'

'No. Not yet, at any rate. But he — '

The reverend loudly cleared his throat. 'Do you think it necessary to burden our visitor with the tawdry details of a minor local case?' he said to Ames.

But the Englishman's eyes had lighted up, and he seemed eager to hear every detail of the murders at Bertram's Bower — to hear them from Ames, if not from the Reverend Montgomery, in the hope, perhaps, of learning some detail that the newspapers had not reported.

'The two women were both residents of the Bower, were they not?' he asked Ames. 'I should think that was of some importance.'

'It may be, yes.'

'And the police have no idea — ? Of course not. The police in Boston, no doubt, like the police in London, have far too much to do, and too few men to do it. Has the weapon been found?'

'No.'

'Not surprising. A knife is an easy thing to dispose of. Well, I will say this: One thing you can count on is that if the killings continue, as they probably will, there will be a public outcry. Even though the women involved are — ah — of the lower orders, as they were in

Whitechapel, there will be panic. Just as there was panic not only in Whitechapel but in all London. The idea of some lunatic stalking the streets and bent on brutal murder is simply too horrifying for the public to bear, no matter who his victims are. Two women dead already, and then a third, and a fourth . . . Oh, yes.'

'How do you mean?' Ames asked. 'Are you insinuating that — '

'I am not insinuating anything. I am stating flat out that a man who kills in this way will not stop at two. He will kill again.'

Not everyone in the room had been paying attention to the conversation with Chadwick, but now, suddenly, all eyes were on him.

'Why do you say that?' Delahanty asked.

'Because it is the nature of the beast. Consider: The bodies of these two women were found not far apart in the same district of the city — a poor district, yes? Although not the slum that Whitechapel is, I daresay. They were both reformed prostitutes. I would wager that some Boston man with a grudge against them, or women like them, has decided to start killing them. In some twisted fantasy of revenge perhaps — or in a hideously misguided attempt to rid the city of their kind. Unless — '

He smiled, not pleasantly. 'Unless our man

175

has come over here to America.'

There was an appalled silence.

'You mean — the Ripper?' Delahanty said at last. 'Here in Boston? But how could that be?'

'Easy enough. Quite a few people in London held to that view — that the Ripper had escaped. Never proven, of course. And so if you assume, as some people have, that the Ripper did not die, did not kill himself or meet with some disaster, and so eluded Scotland Yard's net, you can at least entertain the possibility that he may have bought passage away from London. Where? Anywhere. South Africa, India, the Orient. Or any city in America, Boston included.'

'That is absurd,' said Edward Boylston, frowning.

'Absurd?' Chadwick removed his spectacles, flicked a speck of dust off one lens, and replaced them. 'How is it absurd, sir?'

'Because the Ripper must have been mad, and how could a madman plan so rationally to make his escape?'

'Madmen's twisted minds can come up with diabolical, insanely logical plans,' Chadwick said. 'Madmen can decide upon a course of action quite as readily as you or I can. That course might be mad — probably will be, in fact — but it is a plan that can be

176

acted upon, and will be acted upon, just as you or I would act upon our own.' He waved a hand dismissively. 'But we gain nothing by idle speculation. What is needed in these tragic cases is evidence. And that, unfortunately, is the hardest thing to come by. Facts. Information. Physical evidence — those are the difficult things in cases like these. In any event — yes, I understand that it is time to return to the ladies — in any event, gentlemen, I will say to you once more: Your killer, whoever he is, Ripper or not, is not done with his work. He will kill again.'

On this dispiriting thought they joined the ladies in the parlor, and shortly afterward the evening came to an end. As the guests took their leave, MacKenzie stood with the Ameses in the front hall, saying good night. Then, his head stuffy with cigar smoke and too much port, he stepped outside and stood at the top of the little flight of granite steps, watching the last of the carriages make their way down the square, their red taillights blurred in the fog that had come with the dark. A damp night, with a raw, penetrating chill. Suddenly, he shivered, but not from the temperature. This is a night for murder, he thought. He remembered Chadwick's warning, and in his mind's eye he saw the shadowy, faceless man who had killed two of the Bower's girls, slipping from door to door along the dark, deserted streets of the South End, searching for another victim.

He turned and went back into the house, grateful that he had such a warm and welcoming refuge as No. 16 ½ Louisburg Square.

* * *

It was the middle of the night, and Caroline lay wide awake, listening to the bells in the Church of the Advent tolling the hours.

Addington had told her about Nigel Chadwick's prediction. She couldn't believe it. Another murder of another Bower girl was not possible — it would be too cruel for poor Agatha, who, on leaving earlier, had looked so exhausted and despairing that Caroline almost regretted having invited her. Perhaps the evening had been too much for her after all. Perhaps she would have been better off back at the Bower.

No. The Bower, now, must be a place of torment for Agatha. Every room in it must remind her of Mary. Poor Mary — a pretty girl who had wanted to better herself.

Who had killed her — and Bridget too?

Why?

Caroline turned over on her side, and then,

her mind racing, turned back again.

Who had killed Mary?

Was it the unknown someone who had sent that odd, coded note? Who would send a note like that? And why? And what was the key to the code?

Suddenly a thought blazed across her mind. After a moment, stunned, she sat bolt upright.

Could it be?

She slipped from her bed and turned up the gas, wincing in the light. On the bookshelf by the fireplace. Her own collection of novels by Diana Strangeways, England's premier lady novelist of sensation stories. Diana Strangeways was Caroline's secret vice. Caroline belonged to a Saturday Morning Reading Club, whose members read uplifting works to improve their minds: the poetry of Alfred, Lord Tennyson, the essays of Ralph Waldo Emerson. But no matter how much improving literature she read, she maintained her devotion to the thrilling stories annually produced by Miss Strangeways — tales of love and adventure and fabulous derring-do, whose heroines were always beautiful and strong-willed, the dashing heroes always handsome and gallant.

And always, there was a little trick to the plot — a secret, discovered usually by the

179

heroine in the nick of time.

Caroline was thinking of such a secret now as she took one worn volume from the shelf and then another. Oh, where was it? In *The Curse of the Wigmores*? In *The Second Lady Mandeville*? In *The Velvet Glove*?

Ah. She'd found the right volume at last. Heedless of the chill of the room, she sank down into the little rose velvet slipper chair by the cold fire and eagerly flipped through the pages until she came to it. Yes. There it was. Her heart pounding, she read it once, then again.

Perfect.

She'd not wake Addington now to tell him, but in the morning —

She thought she'd be too excited to sleep when she went back to bed, but she was wrong. She fell asleep at once and slept until her usual time to rise, which was seven-thirty. And when Ames came down to breakfast, she was awaiting him with her news.

11

'Miss Strangeways?' said Ames. He took his porridge from the tureen on the sideboard and came to sit at the table. 'Good morning, Doctor,' he said to MacKenzie, who was just coming in, and then, turning back to Caroline: 'I hardly think she will be of help to us.'

Caroline heard the disapproval in his voice. He had never actually forbidden her to read Diana Strangeways' novels, but she knew he thought of them as no better than trash.

Which, perhaps, they were — but such fascinating, such diverting and elegant trash that even if he had forbidden them, she would have found some way of surreptitiously continuing to read them, year after year, as they appeared regularly from across the Atlantic to a horde of eager, devoted readers in America.

'But just listen, Addington,' she said. She'd already tried to explain the discovery that she'd made in the middle of the night — the revelation that lay in the pages of one of Miss Strangeways' torrid, lurid narratives — and she'd botched it. He hadn't understood her at all.

He doesn't want to understand, she thought, because it is coming from Diana Strangeways, of whom he does not approve. Ridiculous. Pry open your mind, dear brother, and *listen*.

She tried again. 'Two lovers, Addington. From feuding families — like Romeo and Juliet. Forbidden to communicate with each other, they must contrive to do so secretly.'

He was scanning the morning *Globe*, hardly paying attention to what she said.

'So romantic!' Caroline went on, smiling at MacKenzie. Her eyes sparkled as she recalled the story. 'Miss Strangeways certainly knows how to make you want to turn the page. At any rate, the solution they — she — came up with was to provide each of them with a copy of the same book of poetry. Love poetry, of course. And they wrote their notes in code, using numbers. Page and line and so forth. Don't you see, Addington?'

He put down the newspaper, and now he was staring at her, his teacup halfway to his lips. He fixed her in his dark, brilliant eyes as if he would see through to her soul — as if he were trying to read in her mind something that even she might not know was hidden there.

'How do you mean?' he asked.

'Two people, working from the same — oh,

I don't know what to call it! The same key. Isn't that what a code is? Or a cipher? Or what if — what if, instead of a key, what if there were some kind of cipher machine? Like a telegraphy machine that sends the Morse code — ?'

'You must have been reading Jules Verne, Caroline, not Miss Strangeways. A machine? But Mary did not have a machine.'

'No, but she had the key to one, Addington. She had the typewriter manual. And would not such a manual have a diagram of the keys?'

Carefully, he put his cup back onto its saucer. He held her gaze still, his mind working furiously.

'Yes,' he said as if to himself. 'The manual for a typewriting machine.' And then, more forcefully: 'By God, Caroline, I think you've hit on something!'

She flushed with pleasure. 'It was not I, Addington, it was Miss Strangeways.'

'Then I am not only in your debt, but in hers as well. She will never know how she helped us. A typewriting machine! Of course!'

And before she could reply, he had leapt up and dashed out of the room; in another moment they heard the front door slam.

'Now where has he gone?' Caroline said to MacKenzie. Her porridge lay cold and congealing before her. She pushed it away. She'd eaten far too much last night to be hungry now.

MacKenzie didn't answer. He'd risen, too, and had gone through the hall into the front parlor, where he stood at the lavender-glass windows, looking out onto the square. A dull day, no rain yet but no sunshine either; he couldn't remember when he'd last seen the sun.

He caught a glimpse of Ames's tall, dark-clad figure across the square, pounding on Dr. Warren's door. After a moment, a maid let him in.

'Dr. Warren?' said Caroline when he returned to the table. 'Why Dr. Warren?'

'You have put into his mind the idea of a typewriting machine. No doubt he hopes that Dr. Warren will have one.'

'Ah. Of course.'

But Ames's hope was misplaced, as he reported when he came back not five minutes later. 'He didn't have one,' he said without explanation, as if he assumed they would understand. 'But downtown — yes. Are you finished with your breakfast, Doctor? Come along, then. Typewriting! And who of all the people involved in this case would have been familiar with a typewriting machine?'

'The salesman,' said MacKenzie.

'Right. Who had a nasty argument with Mary Flaherty the day before she was killed. And who — if my knowledge of traveling salesmen is correct — may have had a way with him, may have been accustomed to seducing the young women he met in his travels. Yes, Doctor? What do you think?'

'I think we'd better see if we can decipher the note before we jump to any conclusions.'

'Right again.'

They walked rapidly along the square and over the hill to the Common, where they cut across on one of the long paths. In no more than ten minutes they had arrived at Proctor & Moody's Stationery and Office Supply Store at 37 West Street. Proctor greeted them personally, all smiles, hoping no doubt for a good sale. His shop was a wilderness of paper, pens, pencils, bottles of India ink, bottles of glue, letterhead in all sizes (engraving extra), account ledgers, receipt books, blotting paper, green eyeshades, and all the other dozens of items necessary to the modern office.

'A typewriting manual?' he said, his face falling a bit. 'Why — yes. Right here. Perhaps you wish to buy a machine?' he added, brightening. 'They are very useful, very useful indeed.'

'No,' Ames replied shortly. 'Just the

185

manual, if you please.'

He flipped through the pages until he found what he sought: a diagram of the keyboard.

'What a devil of an arrangement,' he muttered. 'Why did they design it like this? Q W E R T Y — It makes no sense.'

'I believe it was done deliberately in that way so that the typewriter — the person who uses it — would not jam the keys,' Proctor offered. 'But it is not difficult to learn.'

'Yes, well, I have no intention of learning it,' Ames replied, fishing for his coin purse. 'But I will purchase this booklet. Ten cents? No — I don't need a receipt. Come along, Doctor.'

Shoving the manual into his pocket, he exited the store, MacKenzie following behind, and went along three doors to a small coffee and tea shop, still busy at this early hour. Settled at a table toward the rear, Ames took out his notebook, opened the manual to the diagram of the typewriter keyboard, and began to puzzle over the code. MacKenzie ordered coffee for both of them and waited.

'No,' Ames muttered, scribbling. 'It doesn't work. Damn! But perhaps — yes — perhaps this way — '

Their coffee came. Ames pushed his away and went on working. The shop was

186

overwarm. MacKenzie wanted to remove his coat, but he didn't want to make any movement that might distract his companion.

For some few minutes longer, Ames remained hunched over the materials in front of him, studying them intently, uttering little grunts of satisfaction — or frustration — as he looked from one to the other, made a note, looked again, made another note. Then he scribbled furiously.

'Yes,' he murmured. 'Yes, I think so.'

At last he gave a little cry, causing several of the other patrons to stare at him. 'Look here, Doctor,' he said. He slid his notebook across the table, narrowly missing MacKenzie's cup, and pointed to the open page. 'Look at this — and this! You see? Just as I thought.'

Just as your sister thought, MacKenzie amended, but he kept the notion to himself as he scanned Ames's printing:

COME TONIGHT EIGHT SHARP TELL NO ONE

'You see?' said Ames, his face alight with triumph. 'Mary Flaherty's death was no random murder — nor Bridget's either, I'll wager. Someone lured Mary to her fate. Someone who very cleverly composed a code that not many people would know how to

187

break. Look here — you see how it goes? It is the letter to the immediate right of the letter desired, so that C becomes V and O becomes P and so forth. He excluded punctuation marks — used only letters, which made it more confusing at first.'

'Very clever,' said MacKenzie. And indeed it was, he thought, depending as it did on such a relatively new and unfamiliar thing as the keyboard of a typewriting machine. Few people had ever seen a typewriter keyboard; almost certainly none of the girls at the Bower had seen one, except for Mary Flaherty. And it was not something that came readily to mind when one faced the task of solving a cipher. No wonder Professor Harbinger had been stumped. Undoubtedly, it would be years before the scholars at Harvard began to use the machines.

'Come on,' said Ames, scooping up his papers. 'I must show this to Crippen immediately!'

He proceeded up Tremont Street at a good clip, MacKenzie struggling behind. When the doctor reached the Parker House, he saw Ames just disappearing into City Hall; when MacKenzie finally arrived at Crippen's office, he found the two men deep in conversation.

'I don't see how this helps, Mr. Ames,'

Crippen was saying. He glanced at MacKenzie coming in but did not greet him, and returned his attention to Ames's pocket notebook, which he held open before him.

'But of course it helps, man!' exclaimed Ames. He paced nervously back and forth across the narrow space between Crippen's desk and the door. 'Don't you see? This note was sent to Mary Flaherty by someone who wanted to lure her away from the Bower, secretly, to meet him. At a time when she was supposed to be working in the office — '

'A romantic assignation,' said Crippen. 'What of it?'

'What of it?' cried Ames. He was nearly exploding with frustration. 'Only this — that Mary Flaherty was pregnant! And the man who sent that note — '

'And how do you know it was a man, Mr. Ames?'

'Because one thing we can be sure of is that no woman impregnated her. The note summons her to a romantic assignation, and who else would summon her in such a way except the man who was — is — responsible for her condition? And also because it is so clever a cipher. Far too clever for a woman to have devised.'

MacKenzie thought of Caroline Ames, and then he thought of Diana Strangeways, but he kept silent. This was not the moment to distract Ames in a discussion of the mental powers of the so-called weaker sex.

Crippen, exasperated, tossed Ames's notebook onto his littered desk. 'I am not arguing with your translation,' he said, 'just your interpretation.'

'Inspector, listen to me. There is a man named Fred Brice who sells typewriters. He is known to have struck up an acquaintance with Mary Flaherty. The Reverend Montgomery told us that Brice was probably in love with her. He is known to have visited her at the Bower on the day before she was killed. They had an argument. Are you telling me that you see no connection between those facts and the fact of this note?'

'I am.'

'But you said yourself, Inspector, when you showed it to me and asked me to look into it — '

'Yes, well, that was then. This is now, and the investigation has taken a different turn.'

'How so?'

Crippen shrugged. His ugly little face was closed — secretive. And stubborn, thought MacKenzie; he is a stubborn man, jealous of his prerogatives.

'I know where this case is going, Mr. Ames, and it has nothing to do with this note. What is more, I know how important it is that we move quickly. I have had word, this morning, from my superiors. They have warned me about a piece that is to appear in this afternoon's edition of the *Boston Star*.'

'A cheap penny sheet — '

'Cheap it may be, but it has the biggest circulation in the city. Its proprietors practice NewYork journalism here in Boston, and very successfully, I am sorry to say. And in this afternoon's edition, they are going to run an article saying, in effect, that we have Jack the Ripper right here in our midst. I know it sounds unbelievable, but it's going to stir up trouble all the same.'

Ames glanced at MacKenzie; each saw the thought in the other's eyes. 'Who wrote it?' Ames asked Crippen.

'A visiting Britisher. A fellow who has done some investigating of his own, apparently, into the Whitechapel murders.'

'Nigel Chadwick,' Ames said.

'I don't know his name. They didn't say. All I know is, that piece is going to cause a commotion. People are going to be upset — even more than they are already. Only last night, one of my men had to rescue a fellow over on Columbus Avenue from a pack of screaming women, claiming he was going to murder one of 'em.'

'And was he?'

'Of course not. He was a perfectly respectable fellow, just stopped a girl to ask directions of her, and she became hysterical.'

'You have ascertained where this man was on the night Mary Flaherty — '

'Yes, yes, of course. We checked him out. He was with his family in Dorchester, a dozen witnesses to attest to it. But about this newspaper piece, Mr. Ames. We have to move quickly, before the entire city gives way to panic. Not to mention the possibility of copycat crimes. I've no doubt we'll have at least one of those before we're through if we don't catch this fellow soon. I have to tell you, I don't think this business of the note moves us along at all. With all due respect — and I appreciate your help, Mr. Ames, don't think I do not — but with all due respect, I have a hunch we're going to resolve this case, and very quickly too. That young Irish fellow at the Bower — '

'Garrett O'Reilly.'

Crippen's eyebrows rose. 'You know him?'

'I know of him, yes. And you told us the Reverend Montgomery brought up his name.'

'Well, then. There you are.'

Where are we? thought MacKenzie, struggling to keep his expression free of the dislike he felt for the little police inspector.

'Look at it this way, Mr. Ames,' Crippen went on. 'We have already agreed that whoever put Mary preggers was in all likelihood the one who did her in, isn't that so? Yes. Now I ask you, who is more likely than that young Irish fellow to — ah — succumb to the temptations all around him in a place like Bertram's Bower?'

'Yes, but — '

'And, consequently,' Crippen went on; he was puffed up now, warming to his theme, 'if he succumbed, and if he then became frightened of being found out, what was more likely than he'd try to — ah — eliminate the person who could name him as her seducer? And consequently ruin him, hah? The sole support of his widowed mother, isn't he? Wouldn't like to be discharged from his place at the Bower, would he? Couldn't afford to be, in fact. So there you have it. I'm bringing him in anytime now. We'll soon see what kind of story he makes up to try to defend himself. One thing I'm sure of — he won't know anything about typewriting machines.'

Ames stared at the little inspector, his lips pressed together as if to forcibly stop some angry retort from spilling out. Then, quietly: 'I would ask you to keep an open mind, Inspector.'

'Open mind? Of course I have an open

mind, Mr. Ames. That's my job. You're leaving now? Just stop by my secretary on your way out, will you? Have him make a copy of that note. I'll put it in the file, even though I can't see what good it does us. But I thank you for bringing it.'

Ames looked dreadful, MacKenzie thought — angry, and deeply troubled. They waited for a moment by the secretary's desk while the young man copied the decoded note, and then they were out in the corridor once more, their footsteps echoing on the worn marble floor. Municipal employees hurried by, including a few young women in dark skirts and high-collared white shirtwaists, with celluloid sleeve protectors over their cuffs. MacKenzie hated to see them. Females who ventured into the working world would inevitably be coarsened by the experience; they belonged at home, Angels of the Hearth, presiding over their proper domestic sphere. Like Caroline Ames.

'I want to see Delahanty,' Ames muttered. But in Newspaper Row on Washington Street, Delahanty's office was empty. A note on the door instructed callers to go inside and make themselves at home; Delahanty would be back within the hour. Since there was no time noted, it was impossible to tell how long that would be.

They had been waiting for only ten minutes or so, however, when Delahanty appeared. At once he apologized for keeping them. 'I've had the devil of a time with my printer — I needed to go to his plant to make my corrections for the next issue. How are you, Addington? Any news? That was a nice time your sister gave us last night, even though I think that English fellow is off on the wrong tack when he talks about the Ripper coming over here.'

'Yes, well, listen to this, Desmond.'

As Ames proceeded to tell his friend of the interview with Inspector Crippen, MacKenzie saw the Irishman's face, ordinarily cheerful and bright, darken into anger.

'That man is a pox on the population,' he exclaimed. 'It's always the Irish, isn't it? We are responsible for every petty theft, every assault, every murder — '

'Can you get hold of the lad?' Ames interrupted. 'Send him a message — either at the Bower or at his home?'

'Yes. What shall I tell him?'

'What I told Martin Sweeney — that he must come to me if he has any trouble with the police. You must insist that he do so.'

Delahanty flushed a little, and he hesitated, biting his lip. He looked almost hostile. 'Now, why would a man like yourself, Addington, do a favor for an Irish lad? The Irish being the plague on the city that they are.'

'Not as much a plague as an incompetent police force. God damn it, Desmond! Do you think all of us are blind bigots?'

Delahanty shook his head. Suddenly, he seemed embarrassed. 'No, I don't. It is just that — well, I don't want to see an innocent lad hanged because he happens to have come from the wrong place.'

'Nor do I. Will you tell him?'

'Yes.'

Ames's face brightened. 'Will you come to the St. Botolph for lunch?'

Delahanty — educated, charming, 'literary' — was a member, thanks to Ames's sponsorship and over the objections of some of the older men.

'Not today, thanks. But — ' Delahanty put out his hand, and Ames took it. 'I beg your pardon, Addington,' the Irishman said, his voice a little rough. 'I did not mean to — '

'I know what you meant. Don't give it another thought. But do get word to that boy that he must come to me for help if necessary.'

'He might not want to. For a lad like Garrett O'Reilly, Louisburg Square is alien ground.'

'Nonsense. If his situation grows desperate

enough, Louisburg Square will seem a safe haven.'

It was nearly noon. In the street, boys were crying the early editions of the afternoon newspapers. All their high, shrill voices cut through the dank air like sharp little knives, but the *Star*'s boys were getting the most business: 'Read all about it! Jack the Ripper! Police stymied! Jack the Ripper here in Boston!'

With a muttered oath, Ames plunged through the crowd, threw down a penny, snatched up a paper, and began to read. MacKenzie, seeing the big black headline — JACK THE RIPPER HERE!!! — did the same. Heedless of the throngs swirling around them, they stood on the sidewalk and read the columns of badly set type that contained the poisonous drippings from Nigel Chadwick's pen:

. . . brutal evisceration . . . women of the streets . . . a faceless, nameless terror . . . a monster who, unsatisfied in London, has come across the sea to prey on the citizens of Boston . . . the beast will strike again, for his thirst, far from being slaked, only increases with the blood of each new victim . . . a warning to the gentler sex — do not walk at night, do not venture from the safety of your hearth . . .

'What rot,' muttered Ames. He looked around. All up and down the sidewalk, people were holding the same newspaper, reading, transfixed by Chadwick's reckless scribblings, glancing up with frightened eyes, murmuring in low voices to their companions, looking about them to see if, even now, the killer stalked them.

'Crippen was right to be concerned,' MacKenzie remarked as they started to walk. Jostled by the crowd, he bumped into a woman absorbed in the Ripper story. She started, threw him a frightened glance, and quickly moved away. Several men nearby glared at him threateningly.

Ames seized MacKenzie's arm and shouldered his way through the crowd. They turned up Bromfield Street in search of a herdic.

'Damn the man for his mischief,' muttered Ames.

MacKenzie was shaken. He'd seen the look in the men's eyes — fierce and hungry, hunters' eyes, eager to seize him and — what? Beat him? Lynch him perhaps? In any case, exercise some rough justice, frustrated that they could not catch the real murderer who now, thanks to the traitorous Nigel Chadwick, had terrified the city and would continue to do so until he — or someone supposed to be him — was caught.

12

Jane Cox lived in a threadbare apartment on Phillips Street, on the back, less affluent side of Beacon Hill. She was a small, neat woman whom Caroline knew only slightly, since they did not travel in the same circles. However, they had in common Agatha Montgomery and Bertram's Bower, and so Caroline was able to dispense with the formalities and get to the point at once.

'You didn't see Mary go out last Sunday night?' she said.

Miss Cox frowned. She sat perched on the edge of a Windsor chair with her hands clasped in her lap. 'No. I had the girls in Bible study in the reading room.'

'Which Mary was not obliged to attend.'

'No. She had' — Miss Cox's frown deepened — 'extraordinary privileges.'

'So I understand. So when you came in, she was working in the office.'

'I did not see her. I saw only that the gas was turned up — the door was ajar — and I assumed she was there.'

'You did not speak to her?'

'No.'

'And nothing unusual happened during the evening?'

'No. Nothing.'

Caroline shifted slightly on her chair. Her corset was too tight — it was always too tight — and her head ached after the excitement of the previous evening. Perhaps she should not have come out this morning, but she had been restless after Addington and Dr. MacKenzie left, and she hadn't wanted to stay in.

'And after Miss Montgomery returned, you passed the office on your way out, and it was dark?'

'Yes. I have told all of this to the police, Miss Ames, and I don't see — '

'I understand. And I don't mean to press you, but it is such a dreadful thing for Agatha — Miss Montgomery — to have to bear, and if any of us can be of any help to her at all — '

'I will not go there again until this man is caught,' Miss Cox said with an air of prim dismissiveness.

'Oh, but you must! It is very important that all of us stand by her — '

'And be murdered for our pains?' Miss Cox exclaimed. 'We do enough for her as it is. I hardly think that we need put our lives in jeopardy as well. I do not even want to leave here' — with a frightened expression she looked around the small, poorly furnished room — 'and walk to Charles Street, never mind going over to the South End. I will not visit the Bower again until they catch this man. No woman is safe on the streets of the city until he is behind bars.'

Caroline bit back the angry retort that sprang to her lips. People like Jane Cox — she thought of her as a sunshine patriot, a summer soldier — were too infuriating. Coward, she thought as she rose to take her leave. You can stay in this miserable little room for the rest of your life for all I care.

But as she descended the stairs and came out onto the street, she could not repress the thought that Miss Cox's sentiments were probably shared by most of the people — the good people of the city — who were connected to Bertram's Bower. Despite her own efforts of the previous evening, demonstrating her loyalty by inviting Agatha and the reverend to her home, most people would probably take the path of least resistance and turn their backs on Agatha while this terrible trouble persisted. Just as she'd foreseen.

This afternoon was one of her afternoons to teach at the Bower. Even more than usual, she looked forward to it. She'd speak to

Matron Pratt, she thought, and to some of the girls.

* * *

Lunch at the St. Botolph Club on lower Newbury Street was always more or less the same: some kind of soup, cream of pumpkin in season, clam chowder or consommé otherwise; some kind of overdone fish or fowl or meat, wet cod or dried-out chops; soggy vegetables; Boston cream pie or Indian pudding for dessert.

This day, the dining room hummed with conversation, as it always did, members trading gossip, trading family news and financial information. Ames and MacKenzie could hear the convivial voices as they came into the lobby, and through the open doors they could see the large communal dining table ringed with men.

Before they could go in, however, someone emerged from the members' room opposite.

'Ah! Ames! Have you a moment?'

It was Edward Boylston, who last night with his wife had attended Caroline's dinner party.

'Yes, of course. Doctor, would you wait?'

MacKenzie said he would, and set about studying the announcement board, where

202

there were often listings of some interest.

Boylston led the way to a quiet corner. He seemed upset, Ames thought.

'It's about the Bower,' Boylston said.

'What about it?'

'I had another look at the account books this morning.'

'And?'

'And something doesn't add up. I've had my suspicions for some time now, but — '

'How do you mean?'

'David Fairbrother told me last week what he'd given to the Bower in December. And on Monday, Harry Venn said he'd given — well, quite a large amount. But the books don't show it. They show something from both those men, but not the right amount.'

'You assume they were telling you the truth?'

'Of course. Why would they lie?'

Ames shook his head. 'No reason. What do you propose to do about it?'

'I don't know. I had planned to speak to the reverend, since he does the fund-raising, but in view of the trouble they have just now — '

'Yes. I understand. Well, perhaps you'd better wait until the police make an arrest in the murders.'

But this did not satisfy Boylston; he seemed

to want to say something more.

'You know the police, Ames.'

'Some of them, yes.'

'And your cousin — '

'Yes. Sits on the board of commissioners.'

'I've never had much to do with the police myself, thank heaven. So I didn't know — You see, Ames, I am wondering if this — ah — irregularity in the books has to do with that girl's murder.'

'Which one?'

'The first one — Mary Flaherty.'

'How do you mean?'

'Well, she worked in the office, didn't she? I used to see her there myself. She had access to the account books. What if she spotted something wrong and spoke about it to someone who didn't want it known?'

'If, as you say, a lesser amount was noted in the account books than was actually given, how would she have known that?'

'Hmmm. That's true enough.'

'I think you should wait for a few days,' Ames said. 'Let us see if the police can make an arrest in the murders, and then you can take your concerns to an attorney.'

'Yes. You're right. This is no time to start some new trouble over there. I must say, Miss Montgomery looked poorly last night. I suppose she takes it very hard, all this trouble. My wife thinks the world of her, you know.'

'As does Caroline,' Ames replied. Account books, he thought. Why hadn't he looked at them himself? But it wouldn't have done any good; he wouldn't have known the correct amounts to look for.

He parted from Boylston with a promise to meet again the following week, and then he joined MacKenzie and they went in to lunch.

MacKenzie examined the plate of soup that the waiter placed before him. Clam chowder. Well, that was all right; in his time in Boston, he'd grown fond of clam chowder. As he began to spoon it up, he looked around.

Desultory talk rose and fell. He listened for any mention of the murders at Bertram's Bower, but he heard none. The newspaper that carried Chadwick's poisonous article was not one these men read, and in any case, it had just come out; most of them would have missed it on their way here an hour or so earlier.

No, the murders of two poor girls over in the South End would not concern the members of the St. Botolph Club. Their lives were safe and secure, well removed from poverty and scandal — particularly now that the blackmailing Colonel William d'Arcy Mann and his scurrilous gossip sheet, *Town*

Topics, had been done away with. The men here had been glad enough of that, MacKenzie knew; some of them had paid up to the Colonel, and some of them, thinking Addington Ames had killed him, had congratulated him for doing so.

As the main course appeared — roasted fowl of some kind with cranberry sauce and mashed potatoes — a new arrival came in. He was of average height, neatly attired, with a high, domed forehead, a small beard, penetrating blue eyes, and a businesslike manner. Professors were popularly supposed to be absentminded and rather vague, but William James was just the opposite: precise, brilliantly focused, ever alert.

Ames nodded to him across the table. Professor James was just the man he wanted to see, and so, half an hour later, lunch over, the members scattered to their afternoon's business, he and MacKenzie and the professor retired to one of the club's private rooms.

'I must be in Cambridge at three,' James said, 'but yes, I have a little time. How are you, Doctor?'

MacKenzie said he was well enough. Although he had met William James several times, he was not yet accustomed to speaking easily to this world-renowned professor of psychology — a new discipline, not yet considered legitimate by many in the academic world.

'What is it, Ames? These murders over in the South End?'

'You know about them.'

'Yes.'

'My sister — ' Ames began.

'Has she recovered fully?'

'Yes, I think so.'

'Good. A nasty thing, a bullet wound. But you would know about that, Dr. MacKenzie, would you not? So what interest has your sister in these crimes, Ames?'

Ames told him.

'I see. Admirable. She wants to protect her friend and her good work.'

'Yes.'

'And she thinks her brother is the man to do it.'

'Yes.'

'She may well be right.' James smiled. 'So what did you want to ask me?'

'There is a rumor, scurrilously being spread in the newspapers today, that Jack the Ripper has come to Boston.'

'I know. I heard the newsboys as I came in.'

'As you can imagine, this irresponsible notion — that we have such a madman in our midst — has put considerable pressure on the police.'

'Of course.'

'And so I was wondering — I hardly know how to put it. Everyone describes the Ripper as a homicidal lunatic, and that is how they refer to this man here in Boston as well. What the public does not know, because the police have not released the information, is that the first girl who was killed was pregnant. So her condition might have been a motive for her murder.'

'But the second girl was not?'

'No. And because her death seems motiveless — '

'As far as you know.'

'As far as I know, yes. But if — I repeat, *if* — Mary Flaherty's pregnancy was not a motive, then the killings may in fact have been random acts committed by some madman. But he is not obviously mad, not raving and conversing with voices in his head, or he would instantly call attention to himself.'

'No,' James replied, 'I would think he is not that.'

'So what kind of madman are we looking for? Can you venture a guess — make some kind of hypothetical description of him?'

James sat back in his chair, steepling his fingers.

'It is an interesting question,' he began. 'And you — and your sister — have more than, shall we say, an academic interest in the answer.'

'Yes.'

'You would like a psychological profile of the man who killed those two girls — leaving motive out of it?'

'Psychological profile,' Ames repeated. It was not a term he had heard before, but it fit. 'Yes. That is it precisely. What is such a man like, Professor? In his mind — in his emotions — in his soul, if you will? A man who attacks women in the streets at night for no obvious reason other than that they have crossed his path?'

James thought for a moment. Then: 'I have no idea.'

At once he saw Ames's face drop with disappointment, and he added quickly: 'Which is not to say that I won't try to answer you all the same. What is this man like? Why, I would say that he is like the character in Robert Louis Stevenson's tale *The Strange Case of Dr. Jekyll and Mr. Hyde*. Have you read it?'

'No.'

'Fascinating. The great writers — the Greek tragedians, Shakespeare, Dickens — are very wise about the human psyche. I am not sure that I would classify Stevenson as the equal of Sophocles — I would not, in fact — but nevertheless, in that story, he created an unforgettable character, a man who could well be your murderer.'

'Or he could be Jack the Ripper,' MacKenzie offered.

'Or Jack the Ripper, yes.'

'So you are saying — what?' Ames asked.

'I am saying that he is probably a man who is someone like us. An ordinary man, showing no hint of the sickness within himself — a mental sickness rather than physical, and therefore sometimes difficult to see. A softening of the brain, perhaps, that like a recurring fever periodically erupts and drives him to violence.'

This is hardly helpful, Ames thought.

'In the story,' the professor went on, 'Dr. Jekyll becomes more and more deranged — and it shows physically. But that need not be so. This man here in Boston may well seem perfectly normal, whatever that is, with no change in his appearance. The change, you understand, being Stevenson's way of dealing with the mind-body relationship, his way of showing, externally, Dr. Jekyll's mental and spiritual deterioration. Caused by a potion — again, symbolic, used for dramatic effect. I would say that he — your murderer here — is probably fairly low-key. Inoffensive, mild-mannered. But underneath — yes, underneath he is a sadistic killer. It is possible that he gets sexual satisfaction from what he does. I gathered from the newspaper accounts that the girls were pretty badly cut up. Around the female organs? Yes? Well, that fits with what I am telling you.'

'So he could be anyone,' MacKenzie said uneasily.

'Yes.'

Ames gave a short laugh. 'Crippen will not be happy to hear that.'

The professor shrugged. 'That is his problem, not mine. I am simply trying to answer your question.'

'Of course. And do you think — since we are assuming that both girls were killed by the same man — might we assume also that he will find a third victim?'

'Or even a fourth or a fifth,' James replied.

'Like the Ripper, in fact.'

'Yes. Until somehow he is stopped.'

Which is what Chadwick said last night, Ames thought. 'The Ripper was never stopped — or not by the police, at any rate. The killings stopped, but the police never caught him.'

'Is there any record of such a case?' MacKenzie asked. 'Other than the Ripper, I

211

mean. A man who kills repeatedly for no apparent motive? Again and again — '

'Serially,' James said. 'One, and another, and another, and another. That is what I would call him, in fact: a serial killer.' The phrase had an ominous ring to it.

'The Ripper was that, of course,' James added. 'And I suppose Bluebeard would qualify, if he existed. Otherwise I know of no example, nor of any way to predict such behavior, much less prevent it. We have much to learn' — and here he smiled at them — 'about ourselves and our darker impulses, which we hide under the rather thin veneer of civilization.'

Much indeed, thought MacKenzie. And meanwhile —

Professor James stood. 'I must go. My students await me. But listen, Ames. If this man is caught — '

When, Ames thought. It must be when.

' — I would be glad of an hour's conversation with him.' James tapped his high, domed brow. 'To discover, perhaps, a little of how his mind works. Fascinating, is it not? The workings of the mind — a secret world, each man's mind hidden from every other. Good day to you, gentlemen. I hope I have been of some little help.'

13

That noontime, while Ames and MacKenzie were lunching at the St. Botolph, Caroline ate a hurried, solitary meal at home. Then, well protected against the elements in galoshes and waterproof and carrying an umbrella, she set off for Bertram's Bower, where, half an hour later, she was admitted by a girl she didn't know.

'Is Matron in?' she asked.

'Yes, ma'am.' The girl was a dark, bold-looking little thing with slightly protruding eyes. Almost at once she disappeared down the back hall.

Caroline knocked on the office door.

'Come!' was the brusque reply.

Matron Pratt sat at what had been Mary Flaherty's desk. She was wielding a pen, her brow knotted in fierce concentration.

'Good afternoon, Matron.' Caroline had never felt quite at ease in Mrs. Pratt's company, and she felt even less so now.

''Afternoon, Miss Ames.'

'How are you?'

'I'm well enough.'

'And the girls — how are they managing?'

213

A faint sneer crossed Mrs. Pratt's face. 'Not so saucy nowadays.'

'I was wondering — ' Caroline had approached the desk, and now she stood before it, as much a supplicant as any poor Bower girl.

'Yes?' barked Mrs. Pratt.

'I — I would like to talk to some of the girls. I'll start my class on their work, and then I'll have a little while free. Would that be permissible?'

Mrs. Pratt blinked. 'Talk to the girls? What about?'

'Why, about Mary and Bridget.'

Mrs. Pratt sniffed. 'I don't see what good that would do. They don't know anything they haven't already told the police.'

'Yes, but — ' Caroline's gaze strayed to the bookshelves as she struggled to find a way to make her case. A row of account books, a dictionary, a volume on deportment, and —

'What is that, Matron?'

'What is what?'

'May I?' Without waiting for permission, Caroline stepped to the bookshelf and slid out something that was little more than a pamphlet: an instruction manual for the Remington typewriting machine.

'This is what the Reverend Montgomery gave to Mary,' she said, 'so she could study it before he bought the machine itself.'

Mrs. Pratt regarded her with hostile eyes. 'Yes.'

'Has it always been kept here?'

'Mostly. Sometimes she took it up to her room to study it. Much good it did her.'

'I see.' Caroline slid the little pamphlet back into place. The coded note, she thought: And this might be its key. Just as — thanks to Diana Strangeways — she'd thought. Well, she'd have to depend on Addington to decipher it, as she was sure he would.

'As I was saying, Matron — I'd like to talk to some of the girls who may have known Mary and Bridget. Can you give me any names?'

Mrs. Pratt thought about it. Then, grudgingly: 'All right. They might not be so eager to speak to you, what with the police asking questions all over the place. But, yes, go ahead. Say I gave permission.'

'Mrs. Pratt — ' Had the woman been less hostile, Caroline would have seized her hand; as it was, she clenched her own hands into fists in an effort to strengthen her determination.

'You understand that we — my brother and I — are trying to help you.'

To her surprise, Matron Pratt's grim visage softened. 'I know that, Miss Ames. You're a good friend to Miss Montgomery. Not like some,' she added bitterly. 'And Lord knows she needs her friends now. She's built this place up from nothing over the years, she's given her life to these girls, and to see it all disappear, just because of some madman — Well. I made up my mind the day I came here, I would stand by her come what may. I know the girls think I'm too hard on them. Of course I'm hard. That's what I'm paid to be. I don't do it for them in any case.'

To Caroline's astonishment, the matron's eyes glistened with tears, and she paused for a moment to regain her composure. Caroline had never thought Mrs. Pratt had the smallest chink in her armor, not the tiniest soft spot in her adamantine heart. But she did: Agatha Montgomery.

'No, I don't do it for them,' Mrs. Pratt repeated. 'I do it for her. She gives herself night and day, works herself to the bone for them — and do they appreciate it? No. They come in here straight from the streets, and the first thing you know, they're complaining about me. About the discipline, about the fact that I make them keep clean and abide by the daily schedule and do their work — oh, yes, I know they don't like me. But do I care? Not a bit. I work for Miss Montgomery, not for them.'

Will wonders never cease? thought Caroline. I can never again think of you with dislike, Matron Pratt, not after this little confession.

'And you are indispensable to her, Mrs. Pratt. I'm sure you know that.'

'Yes.' Matron was her former grim self once more, all show of emotion gone. 'I am. And she knows it too. Now. You wanted the names of girls who knew Flaherty and Brown. You should speak to Quinlan — and O'Connell, I suppose.' She glanced at the large Seth Thomas clock on the wall. 'They should be in the reading room. You're taking your class today as usual?'

'Yes — yes, of course. I'll just start the girls on their work, and then I'll find — ah — Quinlan and O'Connell.' She hated Matron's use of last names only, but she supposed there was a reason for it.

Upstairs, she settled the eight girls in her class into their work. Nine, she thought; there should be nine. Bridget had been in this class. Her empty chair was by the window. As Caroline's throat tightened, she coughed, but the tightness didn't go away. The girls were working on the satin stitch. Most of them were embroidering handkerchiefs — little squares of cloth that Caroline had bought, cut to size, and brought to class. They had hemmed them, and now they were embroidering their initials.

'Go on with it,' she said to them, 'and I will be back shortly.'

They gazed at her with sad, wary eyes. Most of them had succeeded in learning the satin stitch, but in the larger world, when they left the Bower, success at anything would be chancy, she knew. She supposed they knew it as well. Poorly paid clerking in a store, even worse paid factory work — such would be success for them.

She left the classroom, closing the door behind her. She was on the second floor. The Bower was quiet, everyone at her assigned place. She'd need to look in on Agatha before she left, if only to make sure that her indisposition of last night had cleared up. But just now she wanted to find the girls who had known Mary and Bridget.

The reading room was at the back of the second floor. Its shelves were filled with mostly self-improving tomes: *A Young Woman's Guide; A Treatise for Young Ladies; Mrs. Smallwood's Manners and Morals*. Diana Strangeways would have no place here, thought Caroline, which was too bad. Her stories were sensation stories, yes, but at least they gave one some enjoyment; these stuffy preachings could

218

put a girl off reading for life.

A few young women were sitting at tables, books spread open before them. At least one, resting her head in her hands, seemed to be asleep. The girls Caroline sought were sitting side by side, whispering — something that was forbidden by the list of rules posted on the wall: no talking, no whispering, no exchanging of notes, no eating, no sleeping . . .

They seemed startled to see her, but then they recognized her as one of the good women of Boston who regularly came to teach them. And when she asked them to come with her, they promptly obeyed — glad, perhaps, to leave the reading room and its stultifying offerings.

Where to have a private word with them? They suggested the dining room at the rear of the first floor. It would be empty now, and they probably would not be disturbed.

Quinlan — that was Liza — was the more forthcoming of the two. She was brown-haired, plain, with a scar across her upper lip where once, perhaps, it had been split. She'd taken a penmanship class with Caroline several weeks before, and Caroline had liked her; she'd seemed bright, with a fair amount of gumption. Now, in fact, she showed a remarkable amount of spirit as she answered

Caroline's questions.

Yes, she remembered the fight between Mary and Verna Kent. Verna had threatened Mary — oh, yes. She'd screamed and yelled something terrible. Matron herself had had to forcibly put her out.

And then on the street — yes, Verna had found Mary the next day and had threatened her again.

'But in the end, she didn't actually do Mary any harm?' Caroline asked.

'No, miss.' Liza's eyes grew round as she considered the implications of the question. 'Do you think it was Verna who done it, miss? Mary an' Bridget both?'

'No. In fact, I am fairly certain it was not. We found Verna. She is very ill. I don't believe she could have been well enough to get up in the night and walk out into the pouring rain.'

Liza nodded, somewhat reassured.

Why? Caroline wondered. Because of the notion that it was, after all, some stranger who had done these terrible crimes rather than a girl who had lived among them? Yes: A stranger they could understand, menacing though he might still be. But to believe that a girl like themselves had killed someone she'd known at the Bower — that was too unnerving.

'Did you know Mary well, Liza?'

Liza shrugged. 'Some.'

'Katy? Did you?'

Katy was pale: eyes, hair, skin — all of it. She licked her lips nervously before she replied. 'A little, yes, miss.'

'And do you know if she had any enemies? Anyone who might have wanted to do her harm?'

Katy let out a nervous laugh. 'Nobody liked her much, miss.'

'Why not?'

'She was — ' Like the others, Katy had a vocabulary too limited to express herself well. 'Uppity, like.'

'You mean, she gave herself airs? Thought she was better than everyone else?'

Katy nodded, relieved to have been understood. 'That's it. Like she was too good for us. An' she used to say how she wouldn't be here for long.'

'Because she was going to find another position someplace else? Or — '

Katy's face twisted with the effort of remembering precisely. 'I think — well, she didn't come right out an' say it, but I think she had it in mind to get a husband.'

'Really? And did she say who he might be?'

Katy shook her head. 'No. But I heard her say' — she affected a high, mincing voice — ' 'I'll have a ring on my finger before long.

An' good riddance to all of you here.' '

She lifted her chin. 'I ask you, miss, who would marry one of us?'

Her simple question — the bleakness of it, the premise upon which it was based — wrung Caroline's heart. Who indeed?

'But you never knew who the man was? She never mentioned a name?'

'No, miss.'

'We didn't see much of her,' Liza offered.

'Because she worked in the office?'

'Yes.'

'And that was another reason she — ah — gave herself airs? Because she had that position?'

'Yes.'

Liza seemed to want to say more, but she was having trouble with it.

'Go on, Liza,' Caroline prompted.

They sat before her, eyes downcast. What is it that they are not telling me? Caroline wondered. And how can I persuade them to divulge it? She felt like a bully, but she pushed on nevertheless. 'Because she worked in the office for Miss Montgomery,' she said, 'and because — '

'Because of *him*,' Liza said very low.

'Who?'

The two girls exchanged a glance. Liza sniffled. 'I don't like to say, miss.'

'Oh, but you must tell me, Liza. If Mary knew anyone — any man, I mean — who might have wanted to do her harm — '

'Oh, I don't think that, miss. I don't think he wanted to do her harm. But she was friendly with him, like, an' she gave herself airs on account of it.'

'Who? Who do you mean, Liza?'

Again the two girls glanced at each other. Katy bit her lip, shifted uneasily in her chair.

'Himself,' Liza said then. 'The Reverend Montgomery.'

'Ah.' There was a brief silence as Caroline absorbed it. 'But of course — he promised her a typewriting machine, didn't he?'

The coded note, she thought. But no, that must have come from the elusive typewriter salesman.

Liza nodded. 'You'd never believe the way she carried on about it.' Her eyes were hostile, remembering. 'Oh, she was little Miss Princess, bragging about it. Who'd want one of them things anyways? *I* wouldn't! It would hurt your hands somethin' awful to use it.'

'But about the reverend,' Caroline said, steering the conversation back to more pertinent paths. 'She was friends with him?'

Katy threw her a sly glance — a glance far too knowing about the world and its wicked ways, Caroline thought.

'Maybe more,' Katy said. 'Maybe she was more than friends with him, if you know what I mean.'

Caroline struggled to keep her expression noncommittal. Mary was pregnant, the medical examiner had said; but surely not by the Reverend Montgomery?

'No, Katy, I am not sure I do know what you mean.'

Katy shrugged. 'Goin' out at all hours, an' where did she go, if not to him? I seen her once, comin' out of his place. She was all — like — flummoxed. But happy — she looked real happy. 'What'r' you doin' there,' I asked her, but she wouldn't say. She just got that look on her face, like 'That's for me to know and you to find out.' An' when he came here, just happenin' to run into him, always givin' him the eye.' She batted her eyes in an exaggerated imitation of a flirtatious look. 'Like that. 'Oh, yes, he's goin' to buy me a typewritin' machine. He's my special friend. He's such a handsome man, isn't he? An' a real gentleman.'

'That's the way she went on, miss. Enough to make you sick. As if a gentleman like the Reverend Montgomery would ever give her a second look.'

Liza had been troubled during this last, and now she said, 'But he did, didn't he?'

224

'Give her a second look, you mean?' Katy replied.

It was a dialogue now between the two of them, with Caroline watching on the sidelines.

'Yes. He didn't seem to mind, the way she made up to him.'

'I seen them one time when they didn't know I was there,' Katy said. 'I was comin' down the stairs, an' the office door was open a bit, an' they were standin' inside.' She giggled and flushed a little, and threw a half-ashamed glance at Caroline. 'An' he had his hand — oh, I daren't say it, miss. He had his hand *here* — ' And she gestured toward the insignificant swell of her bosom.

Really, thought Caroline, I do not believe this. The Reverend Montgomery may be no better than he should be, but surely he has some sense of decorum.

'She wasn't the only one neither,' Katy added.

'How do you mean?'

'I seen him once in the back hall with — what was her name, I can't remember. She's gone now. It was just after I came here, an' she was in her last week or two. I knew who he was because he talks to each of us before Miss Montgomery takes us in.'

'He does?' Caroline was surprised. 'I didn't know that.'

'Yes. We all have to have a private talk with him, like, beforehand.'

Times had changed, then, Caroline thought, from when Agatha roamed the night-time streets looking for candidates for her charity — girls who would immediately be taken in, fed, tended to, given a bed. Perhaps it was understandable that now she asked her brother to interview the girls first, since her reputation had spread, and there were so many more, it seemed, needing her help.

Or perhaps she hadn't asked him to do it. Perhaps he had insisted.

'So you saw him with a girl?'

'Yes.'

'And what were they doing, together there in the back hall?'

'He was — I don't know. She was pushin' him away.'

'And did she succeed?'

'Yes, miss. She got away from him.'

'And did he see you?'

A sudden look of fear crossed the girl's face. 'No, miss.'

'You hope,' Liza said.

'He didn't. I know he didn't,' Katy said firmly, but still she looked frightened.

Of course Katy could never have reported such an incident, Caroline thought. Who would believe it?

'What about Mary?' she said. 'Can you remember what happened on the night she was — on the night she died?'

'How d'you mean?' Liza asked.

'I mean, did anything unusual happen? It was Sunday — ' Only last Sunday; it seemed much longer.

They thought about it. 'The police already asked us,' Katy said.

'I know they did. But perhaps by now you remember something you didn't tell them. What did you tell them, by the way? Anything?'

'No, miss. Nothin' to tell. It was Sunday night, like you say. We had our supper. Matron went out to her service, like she always does.'

'And Miss Montgomery was out, too, so Miss Cox was in charge.'

'That's right.'

'Mary was working in the office.'

'Yes.'

'Did you see her go out?'

'No. We was at Bible study with Miss Cox, up in the readin' room, an' then we went to bed.'

'What time was that?'

'Well — ' Katy hesitated, working it out. 'The rest of 'em went up about half past eight. But I had to stay back with Miss Cox because I was bad.'

'Bad? How were you bad, Katy?'

She glowered, remembering. 'I laughed.'

'You laughed. At — ?'

'Samuel Two, eleven.'

'I see.' David and Bathsheba. Caroline smothered a smile herself. Jane Cox, lacking the character to be faithful to Agatha, also lacked a sense of humor.

'So you stayed behind with Miss Cox — '

'An' when I was goin' out, after a while, I saw Miss Montgomery comin' in.'

'And did you speak to her?'

'No, miss. I was goin' up to bed, an' I heard the door an' I looked down into the front hall. She came in all wet — soakin', she was. She had her bag with her' — her carpetbag, which she had carried, Caroline knew, for as long as she'd run the Bower. In former times, she would carry food in it, or shawls, or bottles of one patent medicine or another, to give to girls on the streets — 'an' she just stood there, like she was too tired to walk up the stairs. I didn't think she'd want to speak to me.'

'I see. Well, that was thoughtful of you, Katy. I imagine that she was exhausted, and what with the rain — '

'She was drippin', miss. I thought for sure she'd be taken with the pleurisy, but she wasn't.'

'All right. So much for Sunday night and Mary. Now, what about Bridget? Did you know her?'

'Some.'

'And? Did she have any enemies? Anyone who might have wanted to harm her?'

They couldn't think of anyone.

'And you saw her last — ?'

'Monday,' Liza said. 'She wanted to go out, an' Miss Montgomery didn't want her to.'

'No, of course she didn't want her to. But Bridget was disobedient, and she went out anyway?'

And learned the grim lesson: Disobedience brought swift and certain punishment. In Bridget's case, death.

'Yes.'

'Can you remember anything else about Bridget that day?'

Liza's glance wavered as she looked away.

'Well? What is it?'

'She — she an' Garrett — '

'Yes? What about Garrett?'

'He was pesterin' her, like.'

Worse than pulling teeth, Caroline thought.

'How do you mean, pestering her?'

'I don't know. I don't know what he said. But he said somethin' to her and she said, 'Leave me alone!' She was cryin'.'

'This was before she had her argument

229

with Miss Montgomery?'

'Yes. Just before.'

'Did you ever see them talking another time? Garrett and Bridget?'

'Yes, miss. Once or twice. I think — '

Katy's brow creased with the effort to articulate her thoughts.

'I think she was afraid of him,' she said at last.

'Afraid? Of Garrett? But why?'

'I don't know, miss.'

There seemed nothing more to be said. The two girls sat quietly before her, humble, deprived, rescued here temporarily by Agatha Montgomery but destined soon to go out into the world again to try to survive. Caroline felt sudden tears prick at her eyes, and she blinked rapidly to banish them. Crying would do no good — not for them, and not for Mary or Bridget either. It was information that was needed — and after all, these two had given her some of that.

She thanked them for their help and watched them as they rose and went out. For a moment she sat alone in the empty dining hall. All the tables were laid for supper, crockery and cheap tin flatware, row after row of empty places that soon would be filled with the Bower's girls taking their evening meal. The food at Agatha's was hardly lavish, but

Caroline knew it was nourishing enough, meat and potatoes and porridge and milk. Most girls, after their three-month stay, were considerably healthier than they'd been when they came.

Garrett. Why had Bridget been afraid of him? What had he wanted from her?

And who was the man Mary had spoken of? A man she'd thought might marry her — who could that have been?

Would a typewriter salesman take up with one of the girls from Bertram's Bower?

And as for the Reverend Montgomery — no, it was unthinkable. Surely Katy and Liza were mistaken about him.

It was time to talk to Cook.

The Bower's kitchen, a vast space taking up most of the basement, was in full battle mode as the evening meal was being prepared — mutton stew, from its pungent smell. In a far corner, by the back door, Caroline saw a man — dirty, dressed in rags — wolfing down a chunk of bread. As he saw her come in, he slipped out. Cook, who had no other name that Caroline knew, was berating one of her slaveys for not properly scouring the pans. Her broad red face was redder than usual, and her voice rained down on the unfortunate girl's head like so many blows. She broke off abruptly as Caroline came in.

'Good afternoon, Cook.'

''Afternoon, miss.'

'I was wondering — could I have a word?'

The woman hesitated, but then she relented. With a curt order to the slavey, she led Caroline into a small pantry at the back.

'Now, miss, what is it?' She stood facing Caroline, arms akimbo, her stout torso swathed in a vast white apron.

'Garrett?' she said when Caroline asked about him. 'No, I haven't seen him all afternoon. He was here earlier though.'

'Do you see him often?'

'Often enough.'

'Do you — might he have some attachment to one or another of the girls, do you think?'

Cook stared at her. 'Attachment? I don't know what you mean, Miss Ames. He's a good boy, minds his business. Miss Agatha was kind to give him work here, and he knows that,' she added grimly.

'You have been here — how long?' Caroline asked.

'Miss Agatha hired me from the Intelligence Office the first week after she set up here, and I've been with her ever since.'

'She is fortunate to have you,' Caroline murmured.

'I am fortunate to have her, miss.' Cook's face revealed nothing. 'She took me on when

I needed a place, I don't mind telling you. Not that I haven't worked hard for her. I always have, and I always will, because Miss Agatha is the best woman in the world and she needs all the help she can get.'

'Yes,' Caroline replied. 'She is. She does. And this dreadful business — '

'Hurts her. Yes. It hurts all of us. It hurts her brother too. Miss Agatha is a wonderful woman, and he's just the same — the best man in the world.'

'Yes, I — '

But Cook had warmed to her subject now and was not to be stopped. 'I feed him up, poor man. He comes in here nearly every day — he lives alone, y'know, no one to care for him. Get yourself a housekeeper, I say to him. Someone to look after you. But he won't — doesn't want the expense. Wants every penny he gets to go either to his church or to this place.'

But he doesn't spare himself on his wardrobe, Caroline thought.

'So he comes in here,' Cook went on, 'and we talk, and he gets something to eat. He's a fine man, a good worker for the Lord. And the Lord will reward him in the end.'

'I think all of you here will find your reward,' Caroline replied, 'if we can just get past this terrible business. Matron has told me — '

'That one.' Cook's mouth clamped shut.

'Mrs. Pratt? What about her?'

'I don't like to tell tales, miss.'

Oh, but do, Caroline thought. Tell me anything. Everything. What do you know, Cook?

'What about her?' she said again. 'She is very strict with the girls?'

'Well, she has to be, don't she? But it's different with her, isn't it?'

'How do you mean?'

'I mean — ' Cook struggled with it. 'I mean — she don't care about the girls here. Not the way Miss Agatha does, nor the reverend neither.'

True, Caroline thought. But please explain.

'Sometimes I think — '

'What? What do you think?'

'I don't like to speak out of turn, miss. But I s'pose you heard one of my best knives is missing. The police wanted to know all about that, I can tell you. I don't know, I said. All I know is, all my knives was here on Saturday night when I left — I spend Saturday night till Monday morning with my cousin in Brighton — and when I came in on Monday morning, one of 'em was gone. I always sharpen the knives before I go on Saturdays, lay them out in the drawer, each one in its place. So when I came in to work on Monday morning I went right to the drawer like I always do, and right away I saw someone had taken one.'

'No chance you misplaced it?'

'No, miss. I'm very careful with my knives. Have to be, don't I?'

'Yes. Of course you do. But are you telling me you think someone here took it? Someone at the Bower?'

'Well, who else?'

'I saw a man just now — a stranger. Men come to beg food here?'

'Yes.' Cook threw her a defiant look. 'I feed them when I can. I know what it is to be hungry.'

Not recently, Caroline thought, taking in the woman's ample girth.

'Could someone have broken in while you were away?'

'No. Not with Her Nibs up there keeping watch.'

'You mean Matron.'

'Snotty old bitch,' Cook muttered. 'Don't care a thing about these girls. Spends all her time smarming up to Miss Agatha — oh, I tell you, miss. We've had some run-ins, Matron Pratt and me. She comes down here, ordering me about like I was some kind of servant to her — which I'm not. Miss Agatha gave me full charge of the kitchen and there's no one can tell me what to do. But Matron comes down, tells me I'm putting too much food out. Too much food — too expensive, she says. Cut back, she says. But how can I do that? These girls need feeding up. They come in all worn down to nothing, I don't care that they've come off the streets, they're flesh and blood just like you and me. I'll feed them as much as I can, I says to Matron. Miss Agatha is the one to tell me if I'm spending too much on provisions, and she never has told me so yet. So go about your business, I says, and leave me to mine.'

Caroline nodded. 'Good for you, Cook.'

Cook leaned in close, and Caroline caught a whiff of liquor on her breath. 'You want to know what I think, Miss Ames?'

'Yes — tell me.'

'I think — ' Cook looked around, although they were quite alone in the pantry, well away from the activity in the kitchen. 'I think the police maybe should ask Matron a few more questions.'

'Why do you say that?'

'Because. She's a mean one, make no mistake. I heard — mind you, I didn't see it for myself — but I heard a while back she was saying she would beat one of the girls. Beat her, can you imagine? Lord knows she's as strong as a bull. And has a nasty temper to boot. Where was Matron on Sunday night, I ask you.'

'She was at her religious meeting, I believe.'

'Hah. Religious meeting.'

'And when Bridget was killed — '

'I don't know about Bridget. But on Sunday night — the night Mary was killed — Matron was coming back from her meeting, wasn't she? Could'v' done it then, couldn't she? Could'v' taken my knife on Saturday night or any time on Sunday, couldn't she?'

'Well, I — '

'I have to get back to work, miss. I don't know if I've helped you at all, but you just think about what I'm telling you, and see if it makes any sense.'

With that, she pushed open the pantry door and went back to the kitchen. As she did so, Caroline caught sight of a tall, thin youth in conversation with one of the slaveys.

He knew who she was, of course, and now he met her gaze and even smiled a bit as she approached. As always when she saw him, she was struck by his looks: He was extraordinarily handsome, with a wide brow, a strong jaw, black hair, and sapphire-blue eyes. He had, as well, a good, decent, intelligent look to him. She thought he was perhaps nineteen or twenty years old.

'Garrett.'

'Miss Ames.'

'How are you?'

'Not so bad.' As he edged away from the slavey and toward her, she saw and remembered his limp. Childhood meningitis, someone had told her; he was fortunate that he wasn't crippled altogether.

'Garrett, I was wondering — ' How to put it, that she was nosing about in the Bower's affairs?

She tried again. 'I was wondering if you — ah — ever had any dealings with Mary Flaherty?'

He'd been smiling at her — a bit too familiarly? — but now his smile faded, and as his finely chiseled features subtly changed expression, his eyes became cold. 'Dealings, miss? How d'you mean?'

'I mean — ' Well, what did she mean after all? She could hardly put it to him plainly. 'I mean, did you know her?'

'Yes, miss.'

'How well?'

'Not well. I knew who she was.'

'Did you ever speak to her?'

'Yes, miss. Now and again, I did.'

The Irish were reputed to be a mysterious race, hard to fathom. She didn't know any Irish well except for Desmond Delahanty. I should have asked him to accompany me, she thought; Garrett will never tell me anything on my own.

'But you weren't — ah — friends with her?'

What was it she saw in his eyes? Contempt? Surely not. 'No, miss.'

'So you wouldn't know about any — ah — particular friends she might have had? Apart from here at the Bower, I mean.'

'Particular friends? No, miss. I — ' He broke off, as if he'd been about to tell her something and had thought better of it.

'What, Garrett? Please tell me.' Do you know that Inspector Crippen suspects you? she thought.

'Well, I was goin' to say, I don't think she was a friendly sort of girl, if you know what I mean.'

'No. I don't.'

'Well — ' He lifted his thin shoulders in a shrug. He was wearing a faded, tattered jacket and mismatched trousers, but even his ragged clothing, even his extreme thinness (and why did not Cook feed him up along with the reverend and all the Bower girls and the occasional tramp?) could not detract from his striking good looks. In another lad, those looks might have made his fortune, but for him they were no help at all. Oh, Garrett, she thought, life is so very unfair. Help me to keep it from being even more unfair to you than it has been already.

'You mean, she gave herself airs?' Caroline asked.

'Yes.'

'Thought she was too good for most of the people here?'

'That's it. She never would have bothered with the likes of me.'

She'd have done better if she had, Caroline thought.

'You didn't like her?'

Again he shrugged, as if the matter were of no importance. 'I suppose I didn't. What of it?'

'Nothing. Nothing at all. And you weren't here on Sunday, of course.'

'No, miss.'

'You don't really have any contact with the girls here, do you?'

He looked faintly puzzled. 'No, miss. It's not my place to do that.'

'Of course not. So you don't know any of them particularly well, do you?'

'My ma would have my hide, miss. She thinks it's bad enough I work here. She says — ' A faint flush rose to his thin cheeks. 'She says they're bad, these girls.'

'So you've never become friendly with any of them?'

'No, miss.'

'You didn't know Bridget at all?'

'No, miss.'

'Never spoke to her?'

'No, miss.'

He was getting restless under her questioning; no doubt he wanted — needed — to be about his work.

'Thank you, Garrett. I won't keep you. Oh — just one more thing.'

He had turned away with a respectful nod to her. Now he stopped short, but he didn't turn back.

'Garrett?'

He faced her. 'Yes, miss?'

She was scrabbling in her reticule, where she kept a small store of useful pamphlets, timetables, and the like. 'Can you — could you just read this railway schedule for me? I seem to have forgotten my spectacles.'

He looked at the little scrap of printed paper she held out to him, but he didn't take it. 'I don't read, miss.'

She felt a little stab of astonishment even as his admission told her what she wanted to know. 'You mean, you can't? You never learned?'

Some people would have been ashamed to admit it, but he was not. He regarded her coolly, and with dignity.

'That's right, miss. Most of us don't, at home. Only Michael, in the primary school. He's learning.'

'I see. Well, thank you anyway, Garrett.'

'Yes, miss.'

As he made his way out of the kitchen, she watched him go. There was a settlement house in the North End, with classes in reading and writing English. Perhaps she could persuade him to sign up. His limp was one thing; not to be able to read was far worse.

Or perhaps he could read after all. Perhaps he'd lied to her.

As he'd lied about Bridget. Liza had said that Garrett and Bridget had had words — that Bridget had been afraid of him, had complained that he was harassing her.

Was that true? It must be true. Why would Liza make up such a thing?

So while Garrett might deny harassing Bridget — probably he would, in fact — why would he deny ever speaking to her at all?

14

'And you believe him, Caroline?' Ames asked.

'I don't know what to believe. But that he can't read — yes, I believe that.'

She sipped her tea, thought about taking an iced lemon cookie, and decided against. Her warm-weather wardrobe, such as it was, would never fit if she didn't lose ten pounds. She hadn't worn it last spring because she'd still been in mourning for her mother. Now, with the passing of another year, she was sure she'd have to take every single item to the dressmaker to be let out.

She had come home from Bertram's Bower half an hour ago, a little later than usual, and both Dr. MacKenzie and her brother had been quick to tell her they'd been worried about her. Never mind what she'd been able to learn at the Bower, Ames said, the city was a dangerous place just now.

'I saw a man being set upon in the Public Garden as we came home,' he told her. 'Poor chap — he'd stopped to ask a lady if he could assist her, and she started to scream about the Ripper. In no time, half a dozen men had tackled him. Lucky the fellow got away with his life.'

'Chadwick did us all a bad turn with his mischief-making,' MacKenzie said.

'He might at least have warned us,' Caroline replied indignantly. 'Do you know, Addington, I feel as though he — well, as though he betrayed us somehow. I mean, how could he come here to dinner, and sit among us all for the entire evening, and not warn us what he'd done?'

'He did warn us, in a way,' Ames said. He was standing at his usual place by the hearth; as he spoke, he stared into the simmering flames as if there he would find the answers that eluded him.

'How do you mean?' Caroline asked.

'Well, he told us about the theory that the Ripper had escaped to America. To Boston, in fact.'

'That is hardly the same as warning us that he was about to set the city on its ear and throw people into a panic. Really, Addington! The nerve of the man! To write such an irresponsible piece — and in that trashy newspaper.'

He half turned to throw her a smile. 'No, it isn't the same. But still, it gives Crippen something more to chew on. Perhaps it will deflect him from the Irish boy. Who else did you speak to at the Bower besides Garrett O'Reilly?'

She recounted her interviews with Matron Pratt, with Liza and Katy, with Cook. When she finished, they were silent for a time. Darkness had long since fallen; the shutters on the lavender-glass windows were closed, keeping them safe against the night.

Suddenly, involuntarily, Caroline shivered — so violently that MacKenzie, noticing as he noticed everything she did, took a crocheted afghan from the sofa and offered it to her.

'No — no, I am not cold, Doctor, thank you.' Just the opposite, in fact; what with the fire and the closed pocket doors, the room was uncomfortably warm. She wished she could unbutton the long, tight sleeves of her dress and loosen the high collar that, just now, threatened to strangle her; she wished she could be rid of her corset, remove the binding whalebone stays that constricted her waist.

And yet, so warm, she shivered — with fear, with dread of what the dark might bring. Yes, Matron was right to be strict with the Bower's girls, and tonight she must be stricter still. Tonight she must forbid them — literally on pain of death — to leave the safety of the Bower, to venture out into the shadowy, menacing streets of the South End, where lurked a nameless, faceless shadow of a man who had killed two of them already, and who might kill a third.

Like Jack the Ripper.

No. Impossible. It was too horrible even to contemplate — that here in Boston, this sane, safe, neatly compact and tidy little city, was harbored the homicidal lunatic who had terrorized all of vast, dark London three years before.

Ames approached the tea tray, took a brandy snap filled with whipped cream, and sat down. 'We had a talk with Professor James this afternoon,' he told Caroline.

She brightened. She liked Professor James, particularly since he had once confessed to her that he preferred the sensational novels of Diana Strangeways to the weightier works of his brother Henry.

'Was he helpful?'

Ames shook his head. 'I don't know yet, but it is always enlightening to talk to him all the same. If nothing else, it helps me to sort out my own thoughts.' He swallowed the last of the confection and sipped his tea. 'And in fact I have been thinking, Caroline' — when do you not, dear brother? — 'about what it is that connects those two girls, Mary and Bridget.'

He'd set down his cup, and now he ticked

off his points one by one on his long, slender fingers.

'Both were Irish. They were roommates. Is either of those facts pertinent to their death? Or — '

He cocked his head at her. His eyes were fixed on her, but she realized that he did not see her. He had the look that he wore when he was sorting something out in his mind — his clever, even brilliant mind. Caroline had long since accepted the fact that of the two of them, Addington was the brilliant one. She didn't much care. Brilliance in a woman would be a hindrance.

He was speaking and she was missing it.

' . . . the fact that they were both residents of Bertram's Bower? Is that what connected them?'

'I don't know, Addington.'

'No. Nor do I. But consider: If it is Bertram's Bower that connects them, then we must take into account not only the Bower itself, but its surroundings.'

Restless, he got to his feet and began to pace.

'But perhaps more to the point,' he said on his second turn back and forth from the shuttered windows, 'has it struck you that Agatha Montgomery is the only person we have encountered who seems to believe that

Mary Flaherty was a paragon of — well, I can hardly say virtue — but of many other admirable qualities?'

'You mean, Agatha was the only person who liked her,' Caroline said.

'Yes. That is exactly what I mean.'

'Perhaps Bridget liked her too.'

'Perhaps she did. But no one has told us that, and Bridget, now, cannot tell us either. So as far as we know, Mary Flaherty was heartily disliked by all who knew her.'

'I hadn't thought of that,' Caroline said.

'It might be significant, don't you think?'

He had paused by the fire, but now he started to pace again.

'Consider what we have,' he said. 'We have a number of people who disliked Mary Flaherty. The girl Verna more than disliked her, she threatened bodily harm to her. But in light of the fact that she is ill, unable to rise from her sickbed, I believe we can safely eliminate her from our speculations.

'Then we have the other girls at the Bower. Apparently none of them liked Mary, but we have discovered no one there who seems capable of carrying that dislike to the extent of murder.'

'Garrett?' murmured Caroline.

'Yes. Then we have Garrett O'Reilly. Whom

Crippen seems to have settled upon as his perpetrator.'

'But, Addington, he cannot — '

'I know. He cannot read, and so undoubtedly he did not concoct that ciphered note. Which in any case Crippen does not believe has anything to do with Mary Flaherty's death. But you have told us, Caro, that Garrett denied speaking to Bridget, while the two girls you spoke to insist that he did. So that leaves him with a cloud of suspicion hanging over him, despite Delahanty's and Martin Sweeney's vouching for him.'

'I don't believe that he is capable — ' Caroline began.

'Possibly not. But the cloud is there, and there it will remain until he is cleared. Now. Who else do we have to consider? Matron?'

'She is certainly strong enough,' MacKenzie offered. 'And filled with — how would you describe it, Ames? Hate?'

'Yes. She is that — filled with hate for the very girls who are in her not-so-tender care. But why would she do it? Why would she be moved to kill not one but two of them?'

'If she'd learned that Mary was in the family way, and thus might bring disgrace on the Bower, perhaps she thought to eliminate her.'

Ames snorted. 'And Bridget as well? That is

249

going a bit far, is it not, even for a woman like Mrs. Pratt. To risk not one but two murders, thus twice putting her own neck in jeopardy? I agree with you, the motive may have been there, but still. She is hardly a sympathetic figure, but whether she is a murderess — hard to say.'

'The typewriter salesman,' MacKenzie said. 'Remember that he had an argument with Mary the day before she was killed.'

'Yes. I think we cannot eliminate him — or not, at least, until we have a chance to speak to him. A traveling salesman already has points against him, given the reputation of the breed.'

Caroline shifted in her chair. Her shoulder was aching again, undoubtedly because of the weather. She'd ask Margaret to get her a hot water bottle tonight, and she'd retire early and read a Diana Strangeways in bed.

'We still don't know very much about Mary,' she said. 'Perhaps the person who killed her is someone we never heard of — someone from her past, someone with a longstanding grudge against her.'

'Yes.' Ames nodded. 'That may be our answer after all. But then, once more, we are left with the question of why that same person — if it was the same person — killed Bridget also. I am convinced that the two deaths are connected, so this hypothetical person must have known both girls. And they had different backgrounds, so they probably did not know each other before they came to the Bower. No, I do not believe that our man is someone from either girl's past. He is someone who knew them both here and now, and for whatever reason found it necessary to . . . eliminate them both. I believe absolutely that Mary's condition led to her death — someone wanting to get rid of incriminating evidence, if you will. Mary and her unborn child being the evidence. But the second girl . . . '

'Who may have known about Mary's condition,' MacKenzie offered.

'Yes. Probably she did. And so to silence her — '

'You are forgetting Nigel Chadwick's theory,' Caroline said. She heard the bitterness in her voice; she couldn't help it. All the triumph of her dinner party had vanished, replaced by righteous anger at Chadwick's betrayal.

'Jack the Ripper? Here in Boston?' Ames's mouth curved into a sour smile. 'An interesting idea, but despite all the journalistic to-do, not likely.'

'Why not likely?' MacKenzie asked. 'The

251

method is the same, the type of victim, the locale — '

'The South End of Boston is not Whitechapel, Doctor.'

'No. But still, it is the haunt of a number of dubious characters — riffraff off the rails, single men in rooming houses — '

'Some of the houses there are very fine,' Caroline said in a small surge of hometown pride. 'Just as fine as any in the Back Bay. It is just that — well, the district never quite caught on. And the population there is not all riffraff. There are a number of churches in the South End, and all of them well attended. Why, the Reverend Montgomery regularly preaches every Sunday to an overflow crowd. He is a splendid preacher, so they say; I've never heard him myself.'

The Reverend Montgomery. She hadn't told Addington all that Katy had said about him. It was hard to believe, but still —

'Addington,' she began.

'For the moment, I think we must continue to believe that the two deaths are connected,' he said. Something was nagging at the back of his mind, but he could not call it up. 'Or that Bridget knew something, perhaps, about the murder itself. The only other possibility is that she was murdered in copycat fashion to muddle the case. Which, I grant you, is a distinct possibility, but hardly helpful.'

Caroline tried again. 'Addington, about the Reverend Montgomery — '

'Yes? What about him?'

'One of the Bower girls told me this afternoon that he — '

But how could she say it? It was too awful to think about, let alone speak of in mixed company.

She'd caught his attention, however, and he stared at her, waiting, his expression one of wary anticipation.

'Yes, Caro? That he what?'

'I can't believe it. It is too grotesque — '

'Grotesque? What are you talking about?'

'Katy told me that she'd seen the reverend — oh, I don't know what to call it! *Molesting* seems too strong a word, but — she said she'd seen him with one of the Bower's girls — and with Mary too — behaving in a — an improper way. A too-familiar way, I mean. And she said — as I've told you — that Mary threw herself at him in a most forward fashion. She even saw Mary coming out of the rectory one time, looking — disheveled. And I wonder if — '

She broke off at the sound of the door knocker and, a moment later, Margaret hurrying to answer. Let it not be Inspector Crippen, she prayed.

The pocket doors slid open. Margaret appeared, followed closely by the bulky, imposing figure of Cousin Wainwright.

Caroline's heart sank. Cousin Wainwright might be even worse than Elwood Crippen. Undoubtedly he had come to reprimand Addington — to warn him once again to stay clear of this case. Her face felt stiff as she smiled at him. She'd promised to deal with him, and she hadn't. Well, now she would.

He greeted them with a brusque word and declined Caroline's offer of tea. Nor would he sit; he stood menacingly before them like a hanging judge.

'Good evening, cousin,' Ames said cordially, just as if their last interview had not been an unpleasant one. 'To what do we owe this — '

'No time for chitchat, Addington. I've just come from a meeting with the mayor.'

'Ah. And how is he?'

'Not good. I don't have to tell you why. This confounded notion that we have that Ripper fellow here in our midst has given him a bad turn. He's been literally a prisoner in his own office ever since that story came out today. Sheer speculation, I said, no need to panic, but every ward heeler in the city has been hounding him to take action. So he's putting the screws on the police pretty tightly, I can tell you.'

Wainwright's small eyes flicked from one to another of his listeners as if he might find the answer to his dilemma from one of them. As indeed he might, Caroline thought. Still, she was glad he hadn't heard their discussion of a moment earlier; they were no farther along than Crippen.

'Crippen tells me he has his suspect,' Wainwright went on, 'but if he's wrong, there will be what-all to pay. The Irish in this city have no love for the police as it is, and if Crippen railroads an Irishman to the gallows and then it comes out that he was mistaken — '

'Crippen will not railroad anyone, cousin,' Ames interrupted.

'Let's hope not. Have you seen him?'

'Not since this morning.'

'Hmmm. Well, I saw him not an hour ago. He is determined to make an arrest before the week is out, mistaken or not. He's a good man, Crippen, but sometimes a trifle — shall we say — overenthusiastic.'

'When it comes to the Irish,' Ames said.

'When it comes to the Irish, yes. I don't mind telling you, Addington, we have a delicate situation here.'

'To say the least,' Ames murmured.

255

'And tomorrow morning Crippen has scheduled a line-up. I'd appreciate it if you could come.'

'Really, cousin? But I thought you wanted me to stay out of it.'

Wainwright glared at him. 'So I did. But that was before this English scribbler stirred everything up with his foolish speculations. I can't understand the fellow, throwing a bomb into our midst like that. A Red revolutionist couldn't have done worse.'

Bomb-throwing revolutionaries were an ever-present threat, but mostly they operated in Europe.

'So you'll come to it?' Wainwright added. 'Tomorrow at ten in the Tombs.'

'Certainly. If you wish it.'

'I do. We can't put an end to this matter too soon, and perhaps, in the line-up — well, we will see. D'you know, on my way here I took note of people passing, particularly the women. They were afraid — terrified, even — and the men looked ready to riot at the drop of a hat. That's what one irresponsible journalist — '

'And newspaper,' Caroline put in.

'And newspaper, yes — what one irresponsible journalist and newspaper together can do. They can put an entire city into panic. Destroy the public's confidence in the police.

Give rise to vigilante justice, men being snatched up off the street and beaten — lynched, even. And we can't have it. Not while I sit on the board of commissioners.'

He drew himself up to his full height and stared at them as if they were personally responsible for the city's fearful state. And perhaps I am, Caroline thought guiltily. After all, I entertained Nigel Chadwick in this very house, not twenty-four hours ago. Did Cousin Wainwright know that? She hoped not. And if I had not held that dinner, perhaps Chadwick would not have felt emboldened to write his sinister little screed . . .

Cousin Wainwright was saying good-bye. ' . . . find out what you can, Addington. I was wrong when I warned you off the other day, and now I'm asking for your help.'

And with that he was gone, leaving the astonished little trio in his wake. As Caroline met her brother's eyes, she thought: Cousin Wainwright doesn't seem to consider that someone aside from Addington — herself, for instance — might also be of help in this case.

15

There were seven men in Crippen's line-up. Three looked harmless; two looked like the tramps they were; two looked thuggish, murderous, capable of any misdeed.

"Morning, Mr. Ames.' Crippen was even more puffed up than usual, strutting around the little room with its window looking onto the line-up. Present also were Agatha Montgomery, Matron Pratt, and three Bower girls.

'Good morning, Inspector. You have a couple of prize specimens today, I see.'

Crippen winked. 'Just a couple, Mr. Ames. Gives it a little interest, like.'

'Of course.'

Ames stepped to the back, to stand beside MacKenzie. Agatha Montgomery and the others from the Bower moved to the front, where they had the best view. The men in the line-up were sitting. Now Crippen gave the order, and more lights went up so the men's faces were brightly illuminated.

'Look front!' called a police functionary.

The men did, and then, as ordered, to the left and right.

'Stand!'

They stood. One of the thuggish ones was muttering to himself, but he broke off on a short command from the functionary.

Crippen turned to Miss Montgomery. 'Well, miss?' he said. 'D'you see anyone likely?'

She was peering intently at the line-up. 'No,' she murmured after a moment. 'I don't recognize — ' Her face was contorted as she scrutinized the seven men. 'I don't believe I've ever seen any of them, Inspector.'

Crippen grunted. 'You, miss?' he said to Matron Pratt.

She did not deign to look at him, but after a moment she said, 'Third one from the left. I've seen him once or twice.'

Crippen nodded and turned to the girls. 'Well?'

They were cowed, obviously intimidated. All their young lives they had tried to avoid the police, and now here they were, in a basement room next to the infamous Tombs, and the police were questioning them.

It was too much for one of them. She began to cry, bowing her head on the shoulder of one of her companions, who comforted her. 'There, Meg! Don't take on! You ain't done nothin', they won't hurt you.'

She meant, Ames understood, the police rather than the seven men in the room beyond.

'Come on, girls,' Crippen barked. 'We don't have all day.'

But they were useless. They stared, transfixed, at the line-up, but they were unable to say if they had ever seen any of these men lurking near the Bower or anywhere else.

After a moment Crippen gave up. He ordered his men to detain the man Matron Pratt had singled out, and to release the others.

'Now, Matron, can you tell us more? You've seen this man near the Bower?'

'I — yes.'

'When?'

'I'm not sure. Sometime in the last few weeks.'

'Lurking? Or walking past?'

'I — I think I saw him when I went to my Sunday evening meetings. Twice. Yes, I'm sure of it.'

'All right.' Crippen motioned to an officer. 'Let's have him upstairs. See what he has to say for himself. You're free to go, ladies. I'll be in touch if this fellow looks promising at all.'

As Miss Montgomery and Matron Pratt shepherded the three girls out of the room,

Crippen turned to Ames.

'Wait here if you want,' he said. 'I won't be a moment.' In less than five minutes he was back.

'Nothing,' he said. But he didn't look as disappointed as he might have, Ames thought.

'You mean, he denies being near the Bower?'

'I mean, he was pulled off the street this morning to fill up the places. He's a clerk at Goodwin and Hoar. He lives in Cambridge. Says he's never been near the Bower, and I believe him. Says he had nothing to do with the murders, he can account for his time both Sunday and Monday evenings. So there you are. We've released him.'

'Well, Inspector, I am sorry this little exercise turned out to be a waste of your valuable time.'

Crippen gave him a sly look. 'Not a waste, Mr. Ames. It was just a formality in any case. Some little sop to throw to my superiors — and the newspapers, who are on me now like a pack of jackels. Had to toss one of their men out of my office this morning, if you can believe it.'

'How do you mean, just a formality?' Ames asked.

'Why, I mean I'm getting closer to the man

responsible in this case — closer every day — and I put on this little show simply because my superiors told me to. I knew before we began that it was all for nothing, but there it is. You have to know how to play the political game in this business, Mr. Ames.'

'You mean you not only have to do your job, you also have to give the appearance of doing it.'

Crippen allowed himself a small smile. 'That's it. We have to look as though we're right on top of the matter. And we are, Mr. Ames. We are.'

'How so, if I may ask?'

'I am not at liberty to say.'

'I see. But — ' Ames leaned in to speak close to the little inspector's ear. 'I couldn't help but notice that you did not have a certain young Irish lad in that line-up.'

'Aha. Indeed I did not.' Crippen's eyes grew cold. 'Didn't need to, did I? I mean, they all know him at the Bower. Don't need to see him in a line-up to identify him, do they?'

Ames thought of Caroline's discovery that Garrett could not read. 'I wonder if we could impose upon you, Inspector, to have another look at that coded note? I'd like to see the original again.'

'I told you, Mr. Ames, that note has

nothing to do with this case.'

'Nevertheless. Are you returning to your office now? We would take only a moment of your time, I promise.' The Tombs had recently been moved to the basement of the new courthouse in Pemberton Square, not far from police headquarters in City Hall.

Crippen shrugged. 'If you like, yes, come along. I just need to speak to my sergeant and then I'll catch you up.'

Outside in the rain, MacKenzie said, 'Inspector Crippen stacks his deck, don't you think?'

'What?' Ames replied. 'Stacks his deck? Worse than that, I'd say. That line-up was no better than a charade. I will speak to Cousin Wainwright about it when we are done with all this. I shouldn't be surprised if they get a complaint or two, hauling men off the streets in that fashion.'

An omnibus lumbered by, and then another. Then came a break, and they made their way across. The air was damp and chill, heavy with the odor of horse dung and burning coal, and the muck underfoot had congealed into an icy mess that made walking treacherous. MacKenzie trod cautiously, careful of his newly healed knee.

'And another thing,' Ames went on as they

proceeded down School Street toward City Hall. 'I can think of someone else — another familiar face if you will — who wasn't present for that line-up.'

'Who?'

'The Reverend Montgomery.'

MacKenzie was taken aback. 'Surely you do not mean to imply — '

'I mean to imply nothing. I am merely saying that the more I think about that man, the more I suspect him — of what, I am not sure. But he is a trifle too smooth for my taste — remember what Caroline told us about him — and he had both the opportunity and the means to kill both Mary and Bridget.'

'And his motive?' MacKenzie asked.

But to this Ames did not reply.

At City Hall, the door to Crippen's room was closed. In the outer office, the harried-looking secretary blinked nervously and ran his hand through his hair as he explained to them that the inspector was not in at the moment, but if they cared to wait —

He glanced apprehensively at the corridor, from where they could hear footsteps and a man's voice — not Crippen's — raised in anger. Ames could make out a few words: ' . . . city in fear . . . panic in the streets . . . your responsibility . . . '

'It sounds as though our friend is in some

kind of trouble,' he murmured to MacKenzie.

Suddenly a rather shaken-looking Crippen appeared in the doorway. Behind him they glimpsed a tall, white-haired man who did not come in but went on down the corridor.

'Perhaps we should come back later?' Ames said to the little police inspector.

'What? Oh — no. Come in, come in.' Crippen was pale, his voice unsteady. Without looking at his clerk, he hurried into his office and Ames and MacKenzie followed.

'Trouble?' Ames asked solicitously.

'That was my chief.'

'I know. I recognized him.'

'He — '

'Wants results.' Ames nodded. 'I imagine he is feeling pressure not only from the mayor, but from certain of the commercial establishments. Eben Jordan and his like, yes? No one will come into the city to shop or do business if the public panic keeps up.'

'That's it in a nutshell, Mr. Ames. Public panic. They lean on him, and he leans on me. He has threatened to take the case away from me if I cannot make an arrest.'

'But you believe that you will — '

'Oh, yes.' Crippen's ugly little face was grim, his mouth set in a hard line. 'Just as soon as I — well, never mind about that. You wanted to see that note again, did you?'

'If you wouldn't mind, yes.'

'I have it here.' Crippen turned to the tall oak filing cabinets behind his desk. In a moment he produced the note and handed it to Ames, who studied it briefly before handing it back.

'Yes. Thank you, Inspector. I just wanted to refresh my memory.'

'But I told you, Mr. Ames, that note doesn't signify. It doesn't have anything to do with the case.'

'All the same, I — '

'And if you're going to go after that typewriter salesman, you can think again. He isn't in the city.'

Ames hesitated, mindful of Crippen's touchy vanity. 'Have you considered a night watch, Inspector? If people assume that the killer will strike again, I would think that public confidence would be bolstered by a show of force. A massive police presence in the South End, an operation for the next two or three nights, letting it be seen that you have put every available man on the job — '

Crippen shook his head. 'Every available man, Mr. Ames? But we are close to moving in on the Copp's Hill gang. I need every warm body I have for that, so where am I going to get the men for a display of force in the South End?'

He was sweating, MacKenzie saw. Disgusting.

'Well, now, that is a question,' Ames replied. 'You are being squeezed both ends against the middle. But I have every confidence that you will find a way. Come, Doctor.'

Outside once more, they made their way up School Street to Tremont. Across the way, at the Parker House, newsboys were crying their wares. 'Ripper in Boston! Police hunt killer! Public warned!'

'Damnation,' muttered Ames. He plunged across and, throwing down his coins, snatched up a *Herald* and a *Post*. As he turned away, his foot slipped on something.

He looked down. It was a printed paper, muddied and wet. Still, for the most part, it was legible. He picked it up.

★ ★ ★

That morning, while Ames and MacKenzie viewed Crippen's line-up, Caroline went to see her friend, Dr. Hannah Bigelow. She would be an inconvenient visitor, she knew, for mornings were Dr. Hannah's time to see scheduled patients. Nevertheless, Caroline told herself, this was not a casual call but something much more important. Since Dr.

Hannah treated the Bower's girls, it was possible she'd heard something that might be helpful. Probable, even, Caroline told herself, remembering what she'd heard about the Reverend Montgomery from Katy and Liza.

Shortly after ten she set off from Louisburg Square, walked briskly through the rain down the hill, and took the Green Trolley to Dartmouth Street, where she disembarked. Coming into Copley Square, she passed shouting newsboys, and she stopped.

Jack the Ripper. They were caterwauling about Jack the Ripper.

Feeling as though she was about to do something very daring, she approached a boy selling the *Post* and bought one. Her eyes scanned the page. She could hardly believe what she read. They were stating flat out that Jack the Ripper was in Boston. The morning *Globe* had carried an article about the Bower killings on an inside page, but nothing like this.

She stood as if rooted to the ground, hardly noticing when people jostled her to get a newspaper for themselves.

The Ripper. But surely Nigel Chadwick's article had been only speculation. Why had the *Post* — and the *Herald* too — taken up his poisonous fantasy?

She looked around. People were snatching

up papers, reading avidly. She started to walk again, past the foundation of the building that would be the new Boston Public Library. It would be a Renaissance palace, as fine as any building in Europe. Boston deserved such a palace of learning, a kind of temple to the arts. But what good would a grand new Renaissance palace do for a city forever stained by its association with the notorious, the black, evil Jack the Ripper?

But the Bower killer wasn't the Ripper. He couldn't be.

She passed the S. S. Pierce castle and came into the South End. Here she saw poor-looking women hurrying by, heads bowed; three or four men clustered at a corner. They eyed her, but at least none of them spoke to her or made rude noises the way men sometimes did.

By the time she came to Columbus Avenue, where Dr. Hannah's clinic was, her sides were hurting from her lacings, and she longed to take a deep breath. Perhaps the women of the Sensible Dress League had a point, she thought. The next time one of them offered her a pamphlet, she'd take it.

The clinic was housed in a tall brownstone that like all the others hereabouts had seen better days. The waiting room was full, as it generally was; the woman at the reception desk was someone Caroline did not know. She received Caroline's request to see Dr. Hannah with a cold stare. She would see, she said.

Caroline took a seat on one of the hard wooden benches along the wall. The room was warm, smelling of garlic and unwashed bodies. A few babes in arms wailed listlessly; one small girl of about five stood at her mother's knee and stared fixedly at the newcomer.

Poor mite, thought Caroline, what lies ahead of you except years and years of drudging work punctuated at frequent intervals — too frequent — by the arrival of yet another mouth to feed?

A door opened and Dr. Hannah's assistant came out. The woman at the desk spoke to her, glancing dubiously at Caroline as she did. The assistant, whom Caroline knew, nodded and beckoned.

'I'll just get Doctor a cup of tea,' she said when they were in the corridor. 'She needs a rest. She's been on her feet since six this morning, and the day isn't half over yet.'

Dr. Hannah's office was neat and spare, like the doctor herself. She came in at once, smiling to see her friend.

'Caroline! What a pleasant surprise.'

They greeted each other with a kiss and an

embrace. Dr. Hannah was a small, thin woman with graying hair and luminous gray eyes. She smelled of some chemical mix, and since she did not wear corsets, considering them unhealthy in the extreme, Caroline felt her body through the thin gray stuff of her dress, her bones quivering like a captive bird's. Quivering with fatigue, Caroline thought. She is working herself to a shadow here, and no matter how hard she works, or how long, her work will never be done.

The assistant brought in a tray of tea and biscuits, and Dr. Hannah, sinking onto a wooden chair, asked Caroline to pour.

'What brings you?' she said, smiling as she accepted the steaming brew.

'It is this business about Agatha's girls.'

'The murders?'

'Yes.'

Dr. Hannah arched a skeptical eyebrow. 'Don't tell me you are involved in that nightmare.'

'I have known Agatha since we were children. You know I go to the Bower regularly to teach. I don't have to tell you how important Agatha's work is. And now, because of this madman, she is in danger of losing everything she has worked for all these years. People will no longer support her — '

Dr. Hannah raised a hand as if to ward off

further expostulations. 'I understand. How can I help you?'

'I wondered — you tend to the girls there.'

'Yes.'

'And I thought perhaps you might have heard something, or — did you know Mary and Bridget? Agatha told me that Mary was quite ill when she came to the Bower. Did you treat her?'

'Yes, I did.' Dr. Hannah frowned, remembering. 'Sometimes I do not recall a particular girl — there are so many of them, you understand — but I do remember Mary. She was pretty and bright, and once she'd begun to recover her health, she was the kind of girl who — I hardly know how to put it. She was the kind of girl who seemed determined, after her bad start, to make something of herself. Of her life.'

'That seems to be the general opinion. You saw her — when? Months ago, when she first came to the Bower?'

'That's right, and for some weeks afterward.'

'But you haven't seen her recently?'

'No.'

'Nor Bridget either?'

'I can check the files, but I don't believe so.'

'And you don't know of anything that might help us — Addington — to learn who killed them?'

Dr. Hannah shrugged. 'You know as well as I do that girls like that — the girls who go to the Bower — are more vulnerable than your neighbors up on Beacon Hill.'

There was no censure in her words, and yet Caroline caught a faint hint of — what? Reproach? For Caroline and her well-off neighbors? No, not that, not anything so strong. But something.

'Yes, I know that.'

'And so they are often put in the way of — shall we say — unwelcome advances. Such girls are not treated with the respect that men show to what the world calls 'decent' women. I believe that most of the girls whom Agatha rescues — there is no other word for it — truly want to begin a new life. A decent life, away from the streets. But sometimes they fail. A man will try to press himself upon them, make advances . . . And the girls fall — or fail — all over again.'

'Do you think Mary welcomed such advances, assuming she had them?'

'Mary? I don't know. She might have. But she was obviously determined to rise in the world — as far as a girl like herself could rise, which might not have been very far.'

'She was expecting a child,' Caroline said abruptly.

Dr. Hannah stared at her. 'Are you sure?'

'The medical examiner said so.'

'I see.'

'So perhaps someone did press himself on her, as you put it. But not on Bridget. Poor Bridget was not the kind of girl who would have had many overtures.'

'And yet someone found it necessary to kill her too,' Dr. Hannah said.

'Yes.'

'Probably because she knew something that the killer — if it was one man and not two — could not afford to have revealed?'

'Addington thinks so. Perhaps she knew Mary's condition.'

'Yes.' Dr. Hannah met her eyes. 'And she may have threatened to tell — '

'Yes. Perhaps.'

Dr. Hannah swallowed the last of her tea and shook her head when Caroline offered her the plate of biscuits. She frowned and looked away, obviously working something out in her mind. Then she met her friend's eyes again. 'Do you know Agatha's brother at all?'

'The Reverend Montgomery? Why, yes, I do.'

'How well?'

'Not very. He came to dinner on Wednesday night, as a matter of fact, part of a group of a dozen or so.'

'Was that the first time you ever invited him?'

'Yes. As you know, I have not entertained for the past year and more, not since Mama's last illness. But before that — no, I'd never invited him. Why do you ask?'

'Because.' Dr. Hannah's expression turned hard, her eyes grew cold. 'I am going to tell you something I have not told before. I never thought I could tell it — not to you, not to anyone. Not even to the police,' she added bitterly.

'The police! What are you talking about?'

'I am talking about the Reverend Randolph Montgomery. He is widely admired, is he not, for his devotion to the Bower, for helping his sister maintain the place by his ceaseless fund-raising?'

Caroline felt a small warning tremor at the back of her mind. 'Yes,' she said faintly, 'he is.'

'And yet,' Dr. Hannah went on, 'perhaps he is not the paragon of virtue that he pretends to be.'

'Pretends to be? What do you mean?'

'I mean' — Dr. Hannah leaned forward, fixing Caroline intently in her gaze — 'that he is a fraud.'

'What are you talking about?'

'I am talking about the girls who come to

me here. They are filled with remorse, some of them — for their pasts, for what the world would call their shame. But some of them, seeking shelter and help from Agatha, are subjected to new shame, new degradation — and from the very place that is supposed to be their refuge.'

Caroline stared at her, dreading what would come next.

'He molests them,' Dr. Hannah said flatly.

'Who?'

'Whom are we speaking of, Caroline? The Reverend Randolph Montgomery. That paragon of virtue, that man of the cloth who parades himself before the world as a man of God, a man dedicated like his sister to the salvation of the outcasts of this city. Oh, yes, she rescues them all right. And then he moves in on them, preys on them — a bad pun, is it not? He prays for them, and with them, and then he preys *on* them. Poor things, they are terrified to tell. They confess to me only after I have built up their trust in me, and even then I must pry it out of them. They don't want to be dismissed from the Bower, you see. They are afraid that if they tell what he does to them, they will be thrown back onto the streets before their three months with Agatha are up. So they keep quiet, and it is not until I see signs of distress that have become all too familiar to me, and I begin to question them, that they tell me — about him.'

Caroline's heart was beating so fast that she found it difficult to breathe. Katy had told her this, and now Dr. Hannah was telling her all over again. The Reverend Montgomery — oh, but how could he? How could he betray Agatha like that?

'Have you spoken to Agatha about this?' she said.

'I tried to, once. She would not listen — would not believe me.'

'No, I imagine she wouldn't. Well, what about the police, then? Surely he is breaking the law, to — to molest them?' Caroline's knowledge of exactly what molestation might entail was scant, but it was enough for her to understand what Dr. Hannah meant.

'The police?' Dr. Hannah's voice was filled with contempt. 'And how far do you suppose I would get, complaining to the police? Who would believe me? Who would believe the girls from the Bower? The man is not a fool. He knows it is his word against theirs — or mine.'

'I can't believe it myself,' Caroline said, and then, seeing her friend's expression, quickly added, 'Oh, I didn't mean that. I do

277

believe you — of course I do. As a matter of fact — '

'What?'

'I spoke to two of the Bower girls yesterday. They told me that he — something like what you have just said.'

'Well, then.'

'But it is just so — so *dreadful*.'

'To think that the Reverend Montgomery uses the Bower as his own private hunting ground? Yes, it is dreadful, isn't it? But not so unbelievable, I think. Many men of the cloth are not the monuments to virtue they pretend to be.'

Caroline knew that Dr. Hannah did not go to church. Occasionally, in the past, she had invited her to her own church, the Church of the Advent, but Dr. Hannah had always declined. She had little time to rest, she said, and Sunday mornings were precious hours to sleep. Caroline believed that Dr. Hannah, in her own way, did the Lord's work, and so, after a few refusals, she gave up. Dr. Hannah's religion was her work, her work her religion. Caroline was sure God understood that even if her fellow mortals might not.

She sat silent for a moment, absorbing what Dr. Hannah had told her. Surely, she thought, there must be some way to stop him. He must be spoken to, admonished, warned

. . . But then she realized the truth of what Dr. Hannah had said. Who would believe it — that a man of the cloth, brother to one of the best-known and most widely admired benefactresses of the city, was in fact a monster of depravity?

No. She flinched from the vision of Dr. Hannah — or, worse, her own self — trying to make that case. Dr. Hannah was right. They would not be believed, and they would themselves become the objects of derision or, worse — scorn, calumny — oh, what to do with this most unwelcome information? Hearing it from Katy had been one thing, but from Dr. Hannah . . .

She would have to tell Addington, of course. But what would he do then? Go to Crippen? To other ministers? But Addington, like Dr. Hannah, was not religious; he had no friends and few acquaintances among the clergy.

Still, she was glad Dr. Hannah had confided in her. Where that confidence might take her she had not yet begun to sort out. She would tell Addington and let him deal with it; he would know what to do.

It was nearly noon when she left Dr. Hannah's clinic, and now, having walked briskly over to the South End an hour earlier, she felt too tired — too crushed by

279

the knowledge she carried away with her — to walk home. So she hailed a herdic-phaeton and sat limp and brooding as the little vehicle jounced along the rainy streets.

The Reverend Montgomery — a duplicitous, even an evil man. A man who turned one smooth, bland face to the world, and showed another to the poor, helpless girls in his and Agatha's charge.

What did it mean? What could it mean?

She peered anxiously out the cab's little window. They were nearly home; she felt the herdic tilt as the horse turned up the steep slope of Mt. Vernon Street. Suddenly, urgently, she wanted to unburden herself to Addington, and she hoped he would be home.

He was, and MacKenzie with him. They rose when she entered the parlor. As always, she was heartened by the smile on the doctor's broad, honest face, and by Addington's acknowledgment, a nod, a half-smile, that meant: Here you are safe again, Caro, and we are here to protect you. She didn't always *want* to be protected, but just now she did.

'How did it go?' she asked her brother, meaning Inspector Crippen's line-up.

He told her.

'But — ' She absorbed it. 'You mean he deliberately did not include Garrett because he has decided that Garrett is guilty?'

'It would seem so.'

'That is ridiculous. Yes, Margaret, we're coming.'

She led the way into the dining room, where their lunch awaited them: vegetable soup, a plate of cold ham, Cook's good whole wheat bread.

'And what have you been up to, Caroline?' Ames asked. He spoke not without a small tremor of apprehension. She was his own good, obedient younger sister who would never intentionally act to rouse his disapproval. Yet she had a way of following her conscience that sometimes led to trouble.

She told them about her visit to Dr. Hannah Bigelow, and what Dr. Hannah had told her about the Reverend Montgomery.

MacKenzie received this information with a muttered oath — 'damnable rascal!' — for which he instantly begged her pardon.

Ames was silent, his dark, brilliant eyes fixed on her. Then: 'We can assume that Dr. Hannah would have no reason to lie.'

'Lie? Of course not! Why would she lie?' She put down her soup spoon and met his gaze as she said softly, 'What are you thinking, Addington?'

'I am thinking that Crippen is about to make a colossal blunder.'

'One wonders what — or how much — Miss Montgomery knows about her brother,' MacKenzie offered.

'Dr. Hannah said she spoke to her about his behavior some time ago, and Agatha would not listen.'

'Of course she would not listen,' Ames said. 'Aside from everything else, it is her brother who keeps the place afloat financially.'

'Addington, really! You don't believe that Agatha would sacrifice those girls — the girls to whom she devotes her life — to her brother's lechery?'

'No. I do not. Not when you put it like that. But still, we must keep in mind that he serves her well.'

'So what if he does? At the same time, he undermines her work — violates it.'

'Yes.' Ames nodded. 'He does that also.'

'I would venture that Miss Montgomery cannot — literally cannot — bear to believe such things about him,' MacKenzie said. 'It is more properly the province of Professor James, this partitioning of the mind to avoid the pain of unwelcome knowledge, but from what little I know of human nature, I would say that in order for her to survive, she is compelled to deny her brother's behavior. For her to acknowledge it would be impossible.'

'Yes, I imagine it would be,' Caroline agreed. 'Her life's work — and at the very heart of it, a hideous rot. Oh, Addington, you don't think that the reverend had anything to do — '

'Yes. I do think he had something to do — with this case.'

It was the world turned upside down, she thought. The good man was bad, the shepherd of the flock was the wolf in sheep's clothing. She was still struggling with it, as she had been struggling ever since she listened to Liza's and Katy's revelations, when Ames pushed back his chair and stood up.

'What are you going to do, Addington?'

'I am not sure.' He was reaching into his pocket for his handkerchief, when his fingers touched the sodden paper he'd found on the street. He pulled it out.

'We must still fit this into the puzzle,' he said. He handed it to her.

'What is it? Oh — a Christian Science tract. Where did you get it?'

'It was lying on the sidewalk in front of the Parker House.'

'And how do you mean, fit it in?'

'The type,' he said. 'It matches exactly the cut-out letters on the coded note found on Mary's person.'

'But what — '

'I don't know, Caro. Not yet. Crippen refuses to listen to me, refuses to believe the note has anything to do with Mary's death. But I believe it does — and now that I have this, I believe it all the more.' He glanced at MacKenzie, remembering the doctor's suspicions of the forbidding female who guarded the girls at the Bower. 'We must keep in mind that Matron Pratt is a devoted member of this sect.'

'Where are you going now, Addington?' Caroline asked.

For he was going someplace, that was obvious. He hovered by the door, restless, preparing to take his leave.

'Out.'

It was raining still, but not heavily. The walk down the hill and across the Garden would be nothing; in less than a quarter of an hour he could be at the Berkeley Arms. It was early afternoon, too early for her to be at the theater. Unless she had some other engagement — at her dressmaker's perhaps — she might be at home. As if she held him by an invisible cord of memory — of desire — she drew him to her even as he warned himself away.

But yes. He would go to her. Ever since he'd spoken to her, two days ago, he'd felt

284

that she'd left something unsaid. And now, with this fresh information about the Reverend Montgomery, he was sure of it: She had something more to tell him after all.

16

'It is simply outrageous, Caroline,' said Aunt Euphemia Ames, 'that an entire city must be terrorized — *terrorized* — because of one man's behavior.'

A small, elegantly dressed figure, she tucked her hand more securely into Dr. MacKenzie's arm. The three of them were walking down through Boston Common to the Music Hall on Tremont Street, where Euphemia and Caroline had season tickets for Friday afternoon Symphony. Ordinarily, Euphemia's niece and Caroline's cousin, Valentine, accompanied them, but in her absence over the past several weeks, Dr. MacKenzie had agreed to go in her place.

'Yes, aunt,' Caroline said. 'I agree with you. It is outrageous. But — '

'Where are the police in this matter?' Euphemia went on impatiently. She was a formidable woman of some seventy-five years, tiny, intense, a terror to anyone who aroused her wrath and to many who did not. 'I am going to speak to Cousin Wainwright. It is intolerable that the police cannot apprehend this man.'

Caroline had a brief image of Euphemia speaking to Cousin Wainwright, and, worse, upbraiding Elwood Crippen. If Euphemia scolded Inspector Crippen, he would simply arrest Garrett O'Reilly all the more quickly.

'They need a little time, aunt — '

'Time! Don't talk to me about time, my girl.' Caroline would turn thirty-six in May, but to Euphemia she was and always would be a mere slip of a girl, giddy and heedless and needing a firm hand to guide her.

'In my day,' Euphemia went on, 'such a situation would never have been tolerated. Why, it is only because we have a man with us today that I agreed to go to Symphony. And I am not easily intimidated, as I don't have to tell you.'

She didn't. Over Euphemia's bonnet, Caroline and MacKenzie exchanged a smile. Euphemia Ames was a legend in her own lifetime, a fervent abolitionist in her youth, a perpetrator of lawless acts like shepherding escaped slaves along the Underground Railroad, one stop of which was on the back of Beacon Hill. Aunt Euphemia had been a scourge of all that was proper and sedate, and had never been intimidated in her life as far as Caroline could tell. It was strange to hear her now, going on about her fears.

As they waited to cross at Tremont Street,

Euphemia suddenly turned on her. 'I trust that Addington is not involved in this case,' she said. 'I know you have some connection to the Bower, Caroline, but that needn't mean he must get mixed up in it.'

For all Euphemia's lawlessness in her youth, she was grimly law-abiding now, the most proper of Bostonians; she had reared the orphaned Valentine with what Caroline had thought was far too heavy a hand. Nevertheless, Val had turned out splendidly, and Caroline seized upon her now as a way out of any discussion of Addington's activities.

'I had a letter from Val the other day, aunt,' she said brightly. An omnibus lumbered by, followed by two more and a steady stream of carriages and cabs following.

'And how is she?' Euphemia asked. 'I haven't heard from her in two weeks. I hope she isn't in with a fast crowd. You never know about those foreigners, but one thing you can be sure of is that they're not reliable.'

'Oh, she's very well. I think she's having a grand time.'

Having a grand time was not Euphemia's notion of the way to recover from a broken heart. 'There, we can cross now,' she said. 'Worth your life to go out these days. I never come downtown anymore.'

Safe across, Euphemia paused to settle her bonnet, which had come slightly askew. She cast a shrewd glance at Caroline. 'Someday, niece, you must tell me the real reason why Valentine threw over George Putnam.'

It was a shot intended to stun, and it did.

'Why — aunt — I believe that she — ah — '

'Never mind about it now,' Euphemia said. 'But he always seemed to me to be a perfectly good match for her. I grant you, he is a trifle dull, but there are worse qualities in a man than dullness. And his people are as steady as a rock. Not a weakness anywhere in that family tree. So why did she decide to create that little scandal by giving him back his ring?'

To avoid a larger scandal, Caroline thought, but she could never have said so. Euphemia knew nothing about Val's being blackmailed by the late, unlamented Colonel Mann, and let's keep it that way, Caroline prayed.

At the Music Hall, people were streaming in. In this crowd, Caroline did not see the anxiety abroad on the city's streets, for this was a solid Brahmin crowd, the Friday afternoon regulars, safe and secure in their tight little world. Not even the advent of Jack the Ripper himself could unsettle these folks.

Nodding left and right, for both she and Euphemia knew nearly everyone here, she led the way in. They settled themselves in their seats and began to peruse their programs.

MacKenzie stifled a sigh. Truth to tell, he was not overfond of classical music. Before he came to Boston, he'd never even heard any, and since he'd been to Symphony a few times with Caroline, he couldn't say he was any the better for it.

Except for the fact of her company: for that, he was very grateful. But the music — heavy, lugubrious stuff produced under the energetic baton of the Symphony's German maestro — no, he wasn't terribly fond of that. He preferred the martial tunes of John Philip Sousa, or the lilting melodies of the Waltz King, Johann Strauss.

As if on cue, the audience quieted. Herr Nikisch strode onstage, bowing to the applause that greeted him. He lifted his baton, and with a mighty crash of sound, the afternoon's concert began.

★ ★ ★

I will have you yet, Reverend, Ames thought as he strode down Commonwealth Avenue. He passed a woman he knew, tipped his hat to her, and kept on going. He seldom stopped

290

to chat, and just now he certainly would not do so. He needed to keep going lest his nerve — his steady, steely nerve — fail him. Ordinarily he was the coolest of men, always calm while others grew excited, always quiet and thoughtful while others chattered without thinking.

Now, however, he was disconcertingly unsettled.

He didn't need — he really didn't need — to see Serena Vincent again, and unannounced at that.

No matter. He was sure she had something more to tell — something important — and now, having geared himself up to it, he meant to find out what it was.

She did not seem surprised to see him. She wore a tea gown of flowing green velvet, and her glorious hair was not completely up. Seeing it halfway down her back was like seeing her partially undressed.

'Mr. Ames,' she said in her low, seductive voice.

She gave him her hand and let it linger a bit in his. Then, motioning him to a seat, she arranged herself gracefully opposite and smiled at him. 'And to what do I owe this unexpected pleasure?' The Yorkie was growling at him, and she snapped her fingers to quiet it.

He hesitated. Chitchat was not his style, and yet what did he expect her to say? Something rude — dismissive?

'I am sorry to trouble you again so soon.'

'No trouble. I was just reading manuscript plays. It is a tedious job at best, and this week's offerings are worse than usual. You have no idea how difficult it is to find good material.'

No. He did not.

'Might you try some of the classics, perhaps?' he ventured.

'You mean Shakespeare? Oh, but that is not my forte. Even the comedies are beyond my reach, I fear. His plays always seem to have — how shall I put it? Too many words.'

This was not Ames's opinion of the Bard of Avon, but he let it pass. He had not come here to discuss dramaturgy.

'About Miss Montgomery — ' he began.

'What is the news from the Bower?' she broke in. She seemed genuinely interested.

'Not very much, I am afraid.'

'And all this business about Jack the Ripper does not help, I am sure.'

'No. It does not. My sister entertained that fellow Chadwick at dinner on Wednesday evening, and his thanks to her was to publish that irresponsible piece in the *Star*.'

She did not quite smile at that. She was

wearing face paint, he was sure, but on her it did not look cheap and artificial but exactly right. Her beautiful eyes lingered on him, and he saw a question there beyond the one she had voiced.

'My cousin, who sits on the board of police commissioners' (and how pompous and stuffy that sounded) 'asked me at first not to involve myself in the case. But then, when he saw the degree to which the public has become exercised over the matter, he changed his mind and asked me to — ah — make such inquiries as I can.'

'That was very clever of him.'

He felt himself flush a little. 'And so, since you asked me also, I have come back today to say — '

'What?' She leaned toward him as if she wanted to help him sort out his thoughts. He had a sudden, startling glimpse of her bosom, and he felt himself flush more deeply.

'To say that when I spoke to you before, I went away with the sense that perhaps you had not told me all that you might.'

She lifted one exquisitely arched eyebrow. 'How very perceptive of you.'

'Then you do have something more — '

She sat back, and suddenly her beautiful face — the face that had thrilled a thousand male hearts — ten thousand — went blank.

'I am not sure that I do,' she said. 'Have something more to tell you, that is.'

'Because?'

She contemplated him. 'Because it is not the kind of thing you might believe.'

'I believe all kinds of things, some of them very strange.'

She went on looking at him. A man could drown in those eyes, he thought.

'Mr. Ames, you know this city as well as I do. Better, perhaps. You know what Boston people are like. They are a starchy lot, with very definite ideas about what is proper and what is not. I am living testament to that. No — you needn't make excuses, not for them, and certainly not for me. But what I am trying to say to you is that people believe what they want to believe. And here in Boston they want to believe that I am a — what? A loose woman, a woman who has gone upon the wicked stage, a woman who was cast out of decent society — oh, yes, I committed the sin of adultery, I do not deny it, but the fact that there were extenuating circumstances never seemed to have entered people's minds. They cast me out, and that was that. The fact that I have survived has probably offended some of them. Not that I care — of course not. But you understand what I am trying to tell you. People's minds are set in a certain way, and it is very difficult to change them.'

She paused to offer him a cigarette. As before, he declined; as before, she took one and allowed him to light it for her.

She inhaled deeply two or three times, staring into the fire. Over the murmur and hiss of the flames, he heard rain spatter against the window. He felt as if he were caught in the spell of some enchantress. Because it was this particular enchantress's spell, he did not want to break it.

'It is . . . the Reverend Montgomery,' she said at last.

He felt no surprise. It was almost as if he had known what she would say.

'What about him?' he asked, but he knew what she would say next as well.

'He is . . . a predator.'

'Yes.'

'You know that? How?'

'I — my sister has her own informants.'

She nodded as she tapped off the ash from her cigarette. 'If they told her that he makes advances,' she said, 'they have informed her correctly.'

'He made advances to you?' He felt a sudden stab of anger.

'Advances — yes.' She frowned at the memory. 'More like an assault. And most unwelcome, I can assure you.'

The sight of it in his mind's eye sickened him. 'When?'

'Years ago, back when Agatha took me in. I suppose he thought I was vulnerable — which I was, but not to him — and therefore, like all men of that kind, he made his move.'

'And what did you do?'

She smiled. 'I sent him packing, of course. Fortunately I was not wearing corsets at the time, and I had full freedom of movement. I gave him a knee in the place where he would feel it most.'

Such plain talk from most women would have appalled him, but from Serena Vincent it did not. Because she has been coarsened by her years in the theater, he thought, and therefore I expect her to speak coarsely? Or because she has paid me the compliment of speaking frankly, as if we were much better acquainted than we are?

'Did you tell Miss Montgomery?'

'No, of course not. She worships him. She would never believe anything bad about him. But when I read of Mary Flaherty's death, I thought of him at once. If he made advances to Mary, and perhaps more than that — do you know if she was in the family way?'

'Yes. She was.'

'Well, then, perhaps — do you not think

— the reverend may have been responsible for her condition?'

'I think it is quite possible. I even think it is possible that he may have killed her. Unfortunately, what I think and what can be proved are two different things.'

'And then there is the matter of the second girl,' she said.

'Yes. Even if the case could be made against the reverend for Mary's death, we would still need to account for that other one.'

'Unless she was killed by someone else, an imitation crime?'

'That is not likely, I think. I believe the same man killed both girls.'

She extinguished her cigarette. 'And I believe that you are correct. So what will you do now?'

'I don't know.'

She stood up, and he did also.

'I am glad to have seen you,' she said. 'I have been wondering, ever since I spoke to you the other day, whether I should have told you what I know about the Reverend Montgomery. It is almost as if you read my mind, coming here this afternoon.'

She was walking him to the door. When they reached the little entrance hall, he saw her maid hovering in the background. Mrs.

Vincent held out her hand and he took it.

'I cannot imagine what will become of Agatha if it turns out that the reverend is the man the police — and you — are searching for,' she said. 'I adore her, and her work is so terribly important. She must continue it. But to have that man by her side, supporting her with his fund-raising and yet betraying her in that dreadful way — it is a difficult thing, Mr. Ames.'

'Very difficult.'

'Good luck,' she murmured.

She had allowed her hand to remain in his, and now, for an instant, he gripped it so hard that her eyes widened in surprise as, reflexively, she tried to take it back.

At once he released her. She stood so close to him that he was nearly overcome by her heavy, sensuous scent. He didn't know what to do. He'd been in the act of leaving, but now, if he'd had one word from her — only one — he would have stayed.

And she seemed to understand that — his sudden, devastating need for her.

She lifted her hand and with her fingertips lightly traced the line of his cheek — an amazingly daring gesture far beyond the bounds of propriety. Deep within himself he felt his body — his very soul — respond to her touch. As delicate as it was, it nearly scalded him. She was looking deep into his eyes, but he could not read her expression.

'I will be thinking of you,' she said.

And I of you, he thought. But when he tried to speak, he could do no more than utter a curt — too curt — farewell.

In minutes he was out on the street once more. It was raining hard now; he looked for a herdic, but of course there was not one to be had, not in this weather.

It was mid-afternoon. Caroline and MacKenzie would not be back from Symphony for another two hours. Usually he wouldn't mind being at home by himself, but today the last thing he wanted was to sit in his study, his mind going around and around, picking over what Serena Vincent had told him, her words like a festering wound on his soul. And, worse, to remember the brief, intoxicating sensation of her touch — No.

He was on Boylston Street now, across from the Hotel Brunswick. He sheltered for a moment in the doorway of Boston Tech. Pulling out his pocket notebook, he flipped through the pages until he found the address he sought; then he set off again in the rain.

★ ★ ★

Fayette Street was a street of small brick houses, miniature houses really, set along its narrow length behind the Boston & Providence station. Here the air was thick with smoke, and the city sounds of horses' hooves and iron-rimmed wheels on cobblestone streets were drowned out by the cacophony of the engines, their shrill whistles, their ear-shattering snorts and *chuff-chuff-chuff* explosions of sound.

Halfway along, Ames stopped. Yes, this was it: the address he'd gotten from the fellow's employer. He yanked the bellpull and heard, faintly, the corresponding sound within. After a moment, the door was opened by a slick-looking young man in shirtsleeves and without a collar; a sparse growth of hair decorated his upper lip.

'Yes?'

'I am looking for Fred Brice.'

The young man looked him up and down. 'And who are you?'

'My name will mean nothing to him,' Ames replied coolly. 'Is he in?' He is you, he thought.

'He might be. What's it about?'

'Are you Fred Brice? We might speak more comfortably inside, if you could give me a few moments of your time.'

Ames had been standing on the narrow

granite stoop. Now he moved in, and the young man backed away.

'Say, mister, I didn't — '

'Just a moment or two is all I need.'

Ames pushed the door shut behind him. They were standing in the front hall of what appeared to be a boardinghouse; he could see a list of rules and regulations framed and hanging on the wall. The wallpaper was faded and stained, the air stale and reeking of burned potatoes. From somewhere above, he heard a woman's scolding voice.

The young man had assumed a belligerent look, but he made no further protest as he opened the door to a small parlor furnished in a cheap suite of horsehair sofa and chairs. The grate was cold, the air only marginally less offensive than that of the hall. Although the light was dim, the young man made no move to turn up the gas.

'Now,' he said, shutting the door. 'What's this about?'

'It is about the murder of Mary Flaherty.'

The young man's gaze wavered for a moment and then held steady again. 'And what does that have to do with you? Who are you anyway? The police? Let's see your badge, then.'

'No, I am not the police. You know about her death?'

'I saw it in the papers in Worcester. And your name is — '

'My name is Addington Ames. Although I am not the police, I am working with them.' A small untruth, not stretched too far.

'And?'

'You knew Mary Flaherty, did you not?'

'Sure. I knew her.'

'We have been told that you visited her at Bertram's Bower last Saturday, and that you argued with her.'

The young man's narrow eyes narrowed further. 'If you're trying to stick me with what happened to her, mister, you're barking up the wrong tree.'

'Oh? Why is that?'

'I don't mind saying I had a few words with her. She — Well, never mind about that. But I left for Worcester right after I saw her, and I just got back not an hour ago. So you'll have to look elsewhere for your man.'

'She was your friend,' Ames replied. 'And yet you seem remarkably unconcerned about her death. Considering the way she died.'

'Friend?' Brice sneered. 'Mary wasn't no friend of mine.'

'You became acquainted with her because you sell typewriting machines, isn't that so? And Bertram's Bower was in the market for one.'

'That's right.'

'You hadn't sold it to them yet?'

'No. Tight with their money, they are, over there.'

'But Mary bought a manual from you?'

'Yes. Well — she didn't buy it herself. The Reverend Montgomery was the one who actually paid for it. It was his idea to get them a machine.'

'Correct.'

'Look, mister, I don't know what you want of me.' In a nervous gesture, Brice wiped his hand across his mouth. Then, speaking more firmly: 'I had nothing to do with Mary's death. And when I left her on Saturday, I made up my mind I wasn't going to see her again.'

'Why?'

'Because. She told me to my face that I wasn't good enough for her. She had her sights set on someone better than me, or so she said. Can you believe it? A girl from the Bower, and she had her sights set above me? I have prospects, you know. I won't be a drummer for much longer.'

'Drummer' was the popular name for traveling salesmen, who, in their travels, tried to drum up business.

'Indeed,' Ames remarked dryly.

'That's right. I've got my eye on a share in

303

the firm. This time next year, I'll be pretty well set up if everything goes according to plan.'

Very little in life goes according to plan, Ames thought.

'Who was this person whom Mary spoke of?' he asked. 'Did she mention his name?'

'No.'

You are lying, Ames thought, but he kept silent.

'I don't mind telling you,' Brice went on, 'I was put off by the way she acted. Perhaps we had words — yes, I suppose you could say that. Words. We spoke sharp — of course we did. What d'you expect, when she gave herself airs like that?'

'But you have an idea of who the man was,' Ames replied. It was not a question.

Brice hesitated. 'I don't want to get into no trouble,' he said.

'You will be in very great trouble indeed if you withhold evidence in a murder investigation. Did you know that she was pregnant?'

At this, Brice's mouth dropped open, and for the first time, Ames saw fear in his eyes.

'Is that a fact?'

'You didn't know?'

'No.' Brice tried to pull himself together. 'Look, mister — '

'Who was the man Mary spoke of?' Ames persisted.

'It sounds foolish, what I'm going to tell you. She'd got way above herself, Mary did, and I told her as much. 'You'll come to grief in the end, my girl,' I said. But of course she wasn't about to listen to me. Who was I? Nobody, as far as she was concerned.'

Ames waited. After a moment, struggling with it, Brice burst out, 'All right! You want to know who the man was, I'll tell you. But you won't believe it. I didn't believe it myself. But she did, didn't she?'

'Who was it?' But he didn't need to hear the name; he already knew what Brice would say.

'It was the Reverend Montgomery.' Brice spoke sullenly, as if guarding himself against Ames's disbelief. When Ames merely nodded, Brice added more confidently, 'She thought he was going to marry her. I tried to tell her he never would, but she wouldn't listen. 'He'll have to,' she said. 'Why,' I said. 'Because,' she said, and she wouldn't say more. Now you come here and tell me she was in the family way. Well, I didn't put her there. And I'd be surprised if the reverend did. Him a man of the cloth, and her an Irish girl, and from the streets? Even as handsome as she was, and she was that, I don't mind telling you. A very fine-looking girl.'

He leaned in to Ames, speaking confidentially, one man of the world to another. 'Now, here's the way I see it. She got herself into trouble, see. And she went off loony, the way some girls do when they find themselves in that condition. And, being loony, she had it all settled in her mind that she'd get a fine gentleman like the reverend to marry her. Crazy, isn't it? I'd say you have to find the man who got her into trouble in the first place, and then you'll find the man who killed her.'

Yes, thought Ames. That is my notion exactly.

He nodded, then reached into his jacket pocket and took out his card. 'If anything else occurs to you, I can be reached here.'

Brice glanced at it, plainly impressed at the address. 'I'm off to Providence on Monday,' he said. 'But, yes. If anything else occurs to me.' He slipped the card into his trouser pocket. 'She wasn't a bad girl, you know.'

'No, I don't suppose she was.'

'She just had — ideas above herself, if you know what I mean.'

'Yes.'

'She didn't know her place, like.'

'I gather she didn't.'

Ames turned to go, but then he remembered something else — unimportant now, but something that should be checked all the same. 'Are you a Christian Scientist, Mr. Brice?'

'What's that?'

Ames shook his head. 'It doesn't matter.'

All the way back to Louisburg Square, as he thought about his conversation with Fred Brice, typewriting machine salesman, the young man's words echoed in his mind: *You have to find the man who got her into trouble in the first place, and then you'll find the man who killed her.*

17

It was Friday evening after dinner. In the parlor at No. 16½, Ames was sunk into his chair, his chin on his chest, lost in thought. MacKenzie had pulled a straight chair opposite Caroline's, and now he sat with his arms extended, a large skein of dark blue yarn looped over them. Her hands moved with amazing speed as she rolled the yarn into a ball, glancing at him from time to time, her soft brown eyes reflecting the pleasure she took from his company in this humble work.

And he saw something else there as well — a shadow of pain, of fear, that reflected the events of the past few days. This was not a normal, peaceful evening at home, and they both understood that. Their surface calm covered the knowledge of the brutal death of two girls from Bertram's Bower, and until the killer was found, no evening at home would ever be normal or peaceful again.

'Ah — just a moment,' Caroline said. She put down the rapidly growing ball and ran her fingers along the yarn. 'It is imperfect just here — you see how it is thick and then thin? I will just knot it — so — and then break it and knit it in when I get to it.'

'What will you make with it?' said MacKenzie. He never ceased to be amazed at her skill; only last Sunday she'd finished the third of a set of twelve petitpoint seat covers for the dining room chairs. They were the handsomest seat covers he'd ever seen (not that he'd seen many), and he couldn't imagine actually sitting on them.

'Oh — I haven't decided. A shawl, perhaps.'

But she had enough of those, and so did every female she knew. She'd thought of something a little more daring: a muffler for him. He needed a new one; his old one was very shabby. Probably it was army issue from when he'd first joined up, and never having had a wife or any other female to look after him, he'd never acquired another. Of course, a muffler was a personal thing, perhaps too personal. She'd have to think about it.

'There.' Rapidly, her hands moving so swiftly that he could hardly see them move, she finished up. He relaxed his arms and reached for his pipe.

'Now,' she said perhaps a shade too brightly. 'What would you like to do this evening, Doctor? Shall we read?'

His thoughts were far too unsettled to concentrate on reading. 'How about a game of draughts?' he replied. 'I beat you very soundly last week, if I recall correctly.'

She laughed. It was the kind of laugh a woman gives to a man when she knows he admires her.

'I was off my game, as you well know,' she said. 'Perhaps we should have a hand of vingt-et-un — but it is no good with only two. If Addington would play — '

She glanced at him. He still seemed oblivious.

'No,' she said. 'Addington is thinking. He won't want to be disturbed.'

'Dominoes, then?' said MacKenzie. He moved toward the cabinet where they kept their games and decks of cards. Most of them were well worn, relics from childhood. Like everything else in this house, the cabinet held the sense of a family who had long lived here, and would continue to do so for years to come. His own life had been constant moving from one place to the next, first with his widowed mother when he was a child, living on the charity of relatives, and then with the army, going from one post to another. He'd never had a proper home.

Until now.

Ames looked up, and Caroline, noticing, said, 'A game of vingt-et-un, Addington?'

'What? Oh — no, thank you. I want to walk a bit.'

Something in his eyes made her uneasy. 'Where, Addington?'

He felt, superstitiously, that if he told her, he would jinx it. On the other hand, probably she and MacKenzie should know where he was bound, just in case.

'I am going over to the South End,' he said. 'To the Reverend Montgomery's place.'

'You mean the rectory?'

'Yes.'

He hadn't told her about Serena Vincent's run-in with the reverend. Hadn't wanted to — hadn't been able to. In some odd way, he'd felt he was protecting Mrs. Vincent by not telling. She hardly needed protection, from him or anyone else, but still.

Randolph Montgomery. He felt his pulse quicken in anger. Respected, widely admired man of the cloth — and duplicitous predator, preying on helpless females. And what further crimes had he committed? Fornication? Rape? Murder?

Yes, what he knew about Randolph Montgomery sickened him, and yet he did not know enough. He needed to know more.

Over dinner, he had passed along what Fred Brice had told him about Mary

311

Flaherty's ambitions. Caroline had been appalled.

'Marry — the Reverend Montgomery? But that is ridiculous. The reverend would never marry a girl from the Bower.'

'Of course he wouldn't. I am merely telling you what this young man told me.'

'And now the reverend is engaged to a woman from New York, apparently. So even if he did have some kind of — of friendship with Mary, he would never admit to anything more than that.'

'No. He would not. Therefore, if it was more than that, somehow I must persuade him to confess it. If I can.'

Now, as he took his leave, she watched him with anxious eyes. After a moment, she heard him gathering his cloak and hat; then the front door slammed and he was gone.

She turned to MacKenzie and, for his sake, put on a smile. 'Well, Doctor, it seems we are on our own for a bit.'

★ ★ ★

Ames went along the square toward Mt. Vernon Street, his long legs striding fast over the uneven brick sidewalk. It had stopped raining, but the night air was raw and misting, a night to be at home beside one's own fire. Through partially opened shutters he could see lighted parlors, families gathered around. The sight held no charm for him. Tonight he wanted cold air in his lungs, he wanted to stretch his legs and pump up his blood for the confrontation — surely it would be that — with the Reverend Montgomery.

Serena Vincent's face rose up in his mind. He remembered how her eyes had met his, how her voice had enchanted him as it must enchant her audience every night, how he'd felt at her touch.

And how he'd sickened as she told him of her unwanted encounter with the reverend.

So it was not for Caroline, not for Agatha Montgomery that he ventured out this night, but for Serena Vincent. The reverend had accosted her — would probably have raped her if she'd not been a woman of his own class. If she'd been a poor, frightened girl off the streets, unable to resist a man of authority, a man who held power over her, who could deny her shelter at the Bower — oh, yes, Ames thought bitterly. Then the reverend could have had his way with her and none the wiser. Had he done that, many times, with the Bower's girls? Had he done it with Mary — had his way with her, and then, panicked at her condition, had he killed her?

He turned down Charles, crossed Beacon

— traffic, for once, was light — and plunged into the Public Garden. The misted haloes around the lamps, widely spaced apart on their tall posts along the winding paths, gave little light; the lagoon, its ice partly melted in the thaw, glimmered fitfully. Between the lamps were stretches of darkness where an unwary pedestrian, on a night like this, might be set upon by footpads. But he had spent years at Crabbe's Boxing and Fencing Club. He would give any man who accosted him a fight for his life, and the fellow would go away the worse for the encounter.

He emerged from the Garden across from the Arlington Street Church, whose tall brownstone spire was lost in the darkness and mist. He crossed and went on down Boylston Street. There were not many people about, and of those, few were women. Now, loping along, he overtook a lone female; as she realized that a man approached her from behind, she threw him a terrified glance over her shoulder and tried to walk faster. But she was encumbered by twenty pounds of clothing over a tightly laced corset, and she made no headway.

'I beg your pardon, madam,' Ames said, hurrying past and doffing his hat. She stopped short, staring after him, her face a pale blur.

He strode on, over the railroad tracks to the South End. There were even fewer pedestrians here, but at the corners, and in doorways, he could see the dark shapes of men. Menacing, threatening shapes, and might one of them be the man he sought?

No. He swerved to avoid a creature slithering across his path — a cat? a large rat? — and went on. None of these tramps and drifters was his man. He was sure of it — more sure with every passing hour.

At Columbus Avenue, he turned toward Bertram's Bower. His footsteps echoed as he went, giving him an unaccustomed sense of vulnerability. And if he felt vulnerable, what must a lone young woman feel? Anyone could step out from one of those sheltering doorways and set upon her, and she would have no defense.

He was not far, now, from the Reverend Montgomery's place. With luck the man would be at home. He was stepping off the curb to cross, when out of the night a figure appeared and seized his arm.

'What the — '

'Police, mister,' said a voice. 'Hold on now, or we'll have you in for a look-see.' An Irish voice.

Ames drew himself up. They were standing under a street-lamp. In its feeble glow, he could see that the man who had accosted him wore a policeman's uniform, but he could not make out his face.

'Have me in, by all means,' he said. 'My friend Inspector Crippen will vouch for me.'

The hand on his elbow relaxed a bit. 'Himself, is it? Well, he's hereabouts. Let's see if we can find him.'

With his free hand the policeman took out his wooden clacker and whirled it furiously. In the quiet night, the rat-tat-tat seemed very loud.

'You might let go of me,' Ames said. 'I won't run.'

'Yes, well, we'll see about that,' the policeman replied gruffly. He did not take away his hand. Ames made a mental note to speak to Cousin Wainwright about teaching a few rules of common courtesy to the police force, but then he reminded himself that this was the night watch he and Crippen had spoken of, and the man was only doing his job.

A herdic clattered by, and then another, followed by a four-wheeler. Inspector Crippen, it seemed, was elsewhere.

'Look here, Officer,' Ames said, 'I can assure you that Inspector Crippen knows me well. I am late for an appointment as it is, and I see no reason why I should be detained unless you intend to arrest me.'

'Not yet, I don't.' Ames noted that the man had not yet called him 'sir.' 'But we have to ask you your business hereabouts,' the policeman went on. 'We're questioning every man abroad in the district, and — '

He broke off at the sight of a trio of men hurrying toward them. Two were tall, and one was short, rotund. Crippen. The little inspector was panting as he came up, but when he recognized Ames, his ugly face broke into a grin.

'Well, well, well, if it isn't Mr. Ames! Getting a breath of air, are you? It's all right, Devlin, I know him.'

Ames felt the pressure on his arm fall away, and he shook his cape into place.

'Your night watch is most thorough, Inspector,' he remarked dryly. 'I consider myself fortunate not to be loaded into the paddy wagon and taken downtown for a night as a guest of the city.'

Crippen was not in the least disconcerted. 'We have to be thorough, Mr. Ames. We have our work cut out for us, and I don't mind telling you, we need to do it quickly.'

'I thought you were on the verge of making an arrest, Inspector. Or has the situation changed?'

'No.' Crippen tipped back his bowler and

rocked back on his heels as he peered up at Ames. 'No, it hasn't changed at all. I still know what I know. This little exercise here tonight won't change that. But as long as we're undertaking it, we have to make it look good, don't we?'

'You mean, this is like the line-up — strictly for appearance's sake?'

'Well, now, I wouldn't say that exactly. But what with my superiors breathing down my neck, so to speak, I want to give 'em their money's worth. I have my men on every block in this district, and I'll be surprised if we don't have a fine good haul down at the Tombs come morning.'

'But nowhere in that haul will be the man you seek?'

'Probably not, no.'

Ames thought of the drain on the city's treasury from the overtime paid this night, but he said nothing. The drain on the city's treasury was not his concern.

'May I take it that I am free to go?' Ames said, his sarcasm lost on Crippen.

'Of course you are, Mr. Ames! And you can tell your cousin who sits on the board of commissioners that we are doing our job right and proper.'

'Good hunting, Inspector.' Ames nodded to him and set off once again, aware that they still watched him. Well, that was their job, and he couldn't fault them for performing it.

His lips twitched as he thought of Caroline coming down to the Tombs to vouch for him in the morning. What with her eagerness for him to involve himself in this case, there were aspects to the business that she probably hadn't anticipated. She'd not let him into the house, he thought, if he'd spent a night in the city jail.

He rounded a corner and saw, across the street, the grim stone building that was the Reverend Montgomery's rectory. A single light shone from a downstairs window.

He crossed, opened the wrought-iron gate, and went up the path to the door. As he lifted his hand to grasp the knocker, he paused. His repugnance for this man was so great that he wondered if he could speak to him and remain civil.

But then he reminded himself that it was imperative to speak to him; this was no time to allow his feelings, no matter how strong, to keep him from doing what he must.

He lifted the knocker and brought it down sharply, twice.

No sound came from within. Perhaps the light was a ruse to ward off burglars.

He tried again, three raps this time.

Suddenly the door opened, startling him;

he'd heard no footsteps approaching.

The Reverend Randolph Montgomery stood before him.

'Yes?'

'Good evening, Reverend.'

'Who — ?' Montgomery peered out at him.

'Addington Ames.'

'Ah! Mr. Ames! I could not make out who you were. What brings you to our humble neighborhood on such a night?'

'I wanted a word with you.'

'I see. Well, I — Yes, all right. Come in.' He stepped back to allow Ames to cross over the threshold; then he led the way into the parlor, which, as before, was drab and dingy, messy, none too clean. Whatever else the reverend did with all the money he collected, Ames thought, it was not used on this house. He put his hat and gloves on a chair by the parlor door, removed his cloak, and hung it over the back.

'Now,' said the reverend, rubbing his hands as if to warm them. There was a tiny fire in the grate, not nearly enough to make the room comfortable. 'What can I give you? Brandy?'

'Nothing, thanks.'

Ames would in fact have liked a drink, but he did not want to accept Montgomery's hospitality.

'You don't mind if I do?' the reverend asked, moving toward a monumental Jacobean sideboard that took up much of one wall.

'Not at all.'

'Take a chair, then, and I'll be with you in a moment.'

On the large round table in the center of the room lay sheets of writing, illuminated by the dim light of a gas chandelier overhead. As Ames pulled out a chair, he glanced at the scattered pages.

'Sorry about these,' the reverend said, returning. He put down his brandy glass and scooped them up, putting them in a pile upside down at the far edge of the table. 'Hard to sort out my thoughts sometimes, you know. But people come to services expecting a good, rousing talk, and I have to give it to them.'

Ames nodded. 'I imagine you find a way.'

'Oh, yes. I do. And they are so appreciative, don't you know.'

The reverend took his seat and sipped his brandy. In the gaslight, his face looked smooth and bland, and his well-manicured hands — large, strong-looking hands — were steady as he held his glass.

'And what will your text be this Sunday?' Ames asked.

'This Sunday? Oh, I won't preach this Sunday. I have a substitute coming in. That sermon' — he nodded toward the pile of manuscript — 'is for the week after.'

'You will be out of the city?'

'Over in Cambridge, yes. For the annual meeting of the Congregational ministry. Members come from all over the Northeast, and we get together and say a prayer and have a good confab.'

'All day Sunday?'

'Tomorrow and Sunday, actually. We used to begin on Fridays, but some members found the lodging charge too expensive, so we've cut it to just the two days.'

'I see.'

The reverend took another sip of his brandy, and now in his pale eyes Ames could see the question: Why have you come here?

'That was a fascinating time, the other night at your place,' the reverend said. 'Please tell your sister again for me how much I enjoyed myself.'

Ames inclined his head. 'It was good of you — and Miss Montgomery — to come on such short notice.'

The reverend smiled unctuously. 'We are not proud, Mr. Ames. And for Agatha, particularly, I felt that the change of atmosphere, even just for an evening, would do her good.'

'Yes.'

An easy introduction of the subject of Bertram's Bower, then, without any awkwardness.

'How does she do, your sister?' Ames asked.

The reverend looked grave. 'Well enough, I suppose. No — that is not true. I do not suppose that. I suppose — I *know* — that she is very nearly overcome with grief, with guilt, call it what you will. She feels very strongly that she has somehow betrayed those two poor, unfortunate girls — that she has betrayed her own mission by not keeping them safe. She has always been her own harshest critic, and in this instance it is no different.'

Ames nodded. 'It is a most distressing case. I must say, the police are doing heroic duty. Coming over here just now, I was stopped and very nearly arrested.'

'You? Arrested?' The reverend appeared sincerely shocked. 'For what?'

'For being abroad in the nighttime, I imagine. They have put out a watch in the district tonight, in response to the public's panic.'

'Well! Good for them. I only hope they

have some success. Have they spoken to that typewriter salesman?'

'I don't know. But I did myself this afternoon.'

'Did you indeed? And?'

'He left for Worcester on Saturday, just after he'd had the argument with Mary. He returned this morning.'

'I see. Well, then, that would seem to eliminate him, would it not?'

'It would, yes.'

'Which leaves — who? The Irish boy, I'd say.'

'Or one of the neighborhood riffraff.'

'Yes. Well. Not likely that one of them would kill both girls, is it? One, perhaps, but not two.'

'Even less likely that one of them would have put Mary into the family way.'

'Yes. There is that to consider.' The reverend frowned, seemingly considering it.

You fraud, thought Ames. You knew Mary's condition; probably you caused it. His revulsion toward this man was so great that he found it difficult to keep his anger in check. You may fool the world, Reverend, he thought, but you no longer fool me.

'But if we are dealing with something more than riffraff,' Montgomery went on, 'if, as your guest proposed the other night, we are dealing with Jack the Ripper, either the man himself or some demented creature who seeks to imitate him — '

'It was most unfortunate that Mr. Chadwick chose to unburden himself of his theories, Reverend. And even more unfortunate that he chose to publish them. I do not believe for a moment that we have Jack the Ripper in our midst.'

Instead of replying, Montgomery rose to refill his glass. 'You're sure about that drink?' he said.

'Quite sure.'

Ames waited until he had returned. Then: 'I wonder if you could tell me, Reverend — '

'Yes?' Suddenly Montgomery was wary, sensing danger.

'Where you were last Sunday evening.' Even as Ames spoke the words, he understood how they would sound to Montgomery. They would sound impertinent — unforgivably intrusive, ill bred, rude, and altogether intolerable.

The reverend could not quite hide his shock — his anger at Ames's blunt question. He swallowed a large gulp of brandy and with great care and precision set his glass on the table.

'You told me that you were — ah — assisting the police in their investigations,

325

Mr. Ames.' The reverend's eyes were cold now, and his voice, ordinarily so rich and mellifluous, had gone very soft.

'Yes.'

'So must I assume that your question has some kind of — ah — official sanction? Did the police tell you to come here to interrogate me — '

'I would hardly call it an interrogation,' Ames broke in.

'I repeat, to interrogate me. Or did you take it upon yourself to do so?'

'I am merely doing what I can.'

'I understand that your sister, too, is poking her nose into this regrettable affair. I was told that she spent some time, yesterday, questioning people at the Bower.'

'Yes.'

Montgomery lifted his chin and stared down his fleshy nose at Ames. 'I will tell you quite frankly, Mr. Ames, I think you are seriously out of line. This is a matter for the police. Leave them to deal with it. I cannot imagine why you have concerned yourself about it in the first place. Surely a man who lives on Louisburg Square does not need to come slumming over here in the South End to keep himself amused?'

Ames smarted under this calculated insult, but he clenched his teeth and forbore to respond in kind. Of course Montgomery resented him. Probably he resented everyone who had not suffered, as the reverend's family had suffered, the humiliations of bankruptcy and consequent loss of standing in the small, circumscribed world of Boston Society into which they, like the Ameses, had been born.

'No,' he replied quietly.

'Then why do you trouble yourself, man? Two girls you never knew, never would have known, girls who came from the lowest, the humblest rung of society, who could have had no importance to you? Their deaths were admittedly horrendous crimes, but still, why do you care about them?'

Montgomery leaned forward, his eyes searching Ames's face as if he truly wanted to know the answer to his question. And perhaps, Ames thought, he did.

But I cannot tell you, Reverend. I can tell you part of the truth but not the whole of it, not the most important part of it, which is that a woman who has begun to haunt my thoughts — my dreams — asked me to involve myself in this case, and the reason she did so has partly to do with you.

And with this reflection, all his anger and disgust with the man sitting before him returned to sicken him once more, and he was forced to look away lest he betray himself.

'My sister pleaded with me — ' he began.

'Ah, but *my* sister did not, did she? I cannot imagine that Agatha has welcomed your — I must say it — your meddling in this affair.'

'No,' Ames admitted. 'She has not.'

'Well, then. Why persist, when the one person who has been most affected by these deaths gives you to understand that she does not wish you to do so? Great heaven, man, leave it to the police, and go and find something else to occupy your time!'

With that, he shoved back his chair and stood up. He was a tall man, nearly as tall as Ames, and much heavier. But I could best you in a fight, Ames thought as he stood also. You may be strong enough to overpower some poor frail girl, Reverend, but you are not in condition. You could not, if it came to that, overpower me.

'You will not tell me?' he said quietly, referring to the question that had so aroused the reverend's ire.

'Tell you what? That I can account for my time when poor Mary was being set upon and killed in the most horrible way?' The reverend's mouth was set in a hard line, and his budding jowls quivered ever so slightly.

'Very well, Mr. Ames. If you insist — yes, I can account for it.'

Ames waited.

The reverend sniffed. 'I was at the home of Mr. and Mrs. Lawrence Norton. Three-something Beacon Street, I forget the exact address. They were kind enough to hold a reception for me, with the understanding that the guests who came would be people happy to contribute to the Bower.'

'And you arrived at the Nortons' when?'

'About four o'clock.'

'And you spent the rest of the afternoon there?'

'Yes, and part of the evening as well.'

'Until?'

The reverend's nostrils flared slightly, and he sniffed again. 'Until nearly ten.'

'I see.'

'You had better see. How on earth, man — how can you come here, into my own home, and insult me by demanding that I account for my time? Which, mind you, I have already done for the police. I am under no obligation whatsoever to answer to you — none!'

The voice — that rolling, basso-profundo preacher's voice — was in full flower again as Montgomery excoriated him.

'No,' Ames replied quietly. 'You are not. But — '

'And now I suppose you will want to know where I was on the following night, when the second girl was killed.'

Ames waited.

'I was here, Mr. Ames. It is none of your business, but — Yes. I was right here in this room.'

'Alone?'

'Of course alone! I live very simply, and I never entertain.'

Wrong, thought Ames. You entertained Mary Flaherty on more than one occasion.

The Reverend Montgomery stared at him belligerently, as if he could read his thoughts. 'Now, you listen to me, Ames. You come here unannounced, you make the most monstrous accusations — '

'I have accused you of nothing, Reverend.'

'Not directly, no. But it is obvious that you believe me to be implicated in this dreadful affair. And I warn you, I will — '

'You knew Mary Flaherty fairly well, did you not?'

'How do you mean?'

'I mean, from what I have heard, she seemed to look upon you as a special friend.'

The reverend frowned, drew down his mouth. 'I am not sure I understand you.'

'It is simple enough. Were you particularly friendly with Mary Flaherty?'

'No.'

'She seemed to think otherwise.'

The reverend shrugged. 'I can hardly be held accountable for what she thought.'

'Ah, but it was more than what she thought. She told Fred Brice, for one, that she hoped to marry you.'

Montgomery started back as if he'd been slapped. 'Marry me? But that is preposterous.'

'That is what Mr. Brice thought. But Mary, apparently, had some reason to believe it. I would remind you that she was three months gone with child.'

'Now, wait a moment.' Montgomery stood and put his hands flat on the table as he leaned toward Ames in a menacing way. 'Are you trying to implicate me in that as well?' His face, which had been pale, had turned pink, and his eyes, which had been cold, suddenly blazed with anger.

'I am not — '

'Get out!' Montgomery roared. Straightening, he advanced a step, and quickly Ames stood and stepped back.

'Reverend, if you will just — '

'*Out!*' As Montgomery suddenly raised his fist, Ames put up his own to defend himself.

'And stay out!' Montgomery came at him and struck a blow that Ames easily deflected. Montgomery stopped. He was breathing heavily, and a little trickle of saliva showed at the corner of his mouth.

There seemed nothing more to be said, and so, in the next moment, with a curt farewell, Ames took his leave. He had done himself no good, he thought, and probably a great deal of harm. The reverend was on guard now — more than he had been before — and would not only refuse to help him, but would also do what he could to impede him.

So be it, Ames thought grimly as he strode down the walk and let himself out at the gate. The night was colder than before, the freezing mist turning to ice underfoot. The street was quiet, not even a passing cab to break the silence. Next to the rectory, the reverend's church stood massive and dark.

Ames crossed the street and stopped at the first doorway. From here he could see the rectory clearly, the single light still showing from the front room where he had had his unpleasant interview with the Reverend Montgomery.

It was a sizable house, built no doubt for a minister who had a large family. Double windows on either side of the front door with its small porch; a row of smaller windows on the second floor.

And above those, a third story with three gables protruding.

Ames took a few steps and then turned to look at the rectory again.

Martin Sweeney of the Green Harp Saloon would know of a man who could do the job — a sharp-witted cracksman who was not only skilled with locks, but tight-mouthed as well.

I will have you yet, Reverend, he thought as he strode rapidly away into the night.

★ ★ ★

At No. 16½, the fire burned low in the grate and the grandmother clock in the hall struck the hour: ten o'clock.

Locked into fierce combat with her opponent, Caroline lifted her eyes to his and smiled. She was winning, but only just, and not, she thought, because he was allowing her to do so.

'You have put yourself into a difficult position, Doctor,' she said. But still, she was smiling; he heard no censure in her words.

He cleared his throat. She was right: He was going to lose. Somehow, he didn't mind.

'I seem to have done, yes,' he replied,

staring at the pieces on the board.

While he considered his situation, she listened for the sound of Addington's return. What had he learned, if anything, from the Reverend Montgomery? And if a homicidal lunatic stalked the streets of the South End, looking for another victim, had Addington encountered him? What if that same lunatic decided to use his knife on a man instead of a woman? Addington was strong, and well trained in the martial arts from his years at Crabbe's, but still. An encounter with an assailant who had a weapon was hardly a fair fight. Dr. MacKenzie owned a gun. She should have insisted that he accompany Addington. Perhaps — and it was a weapon of her own that she had employed only a few times in her adult life — she should have begun to cry. Addington would have had to listen to her then.

Dr. MacKenzie was staring at her. He seemed to have forgotten about their game.

She felt a little quiver in the region of her well-protected heart. Once, long ago, she'd felt something of the kind for a young man who, in the end, had gone away. Her heart had been broken, and she'd promised herself she would not allow that to happen to her ever again. But now, in the company of this quiet, kindly man who had come so unexpectedly into their lives, Addington's and hers, she felt her heart tremble once more as she met his eyes, and she did not want to subdue it.

She held his gaze, and when she spoke, her voice was soft and (it seemed to him) resonant with meaning.

'Your move, Doctor.'

18

Beacon Street, the next morning, was busy with commercial traffic, but it was still too early for the day's parade of landaus and four-wheelers, delivering the Back Bay's fashionable ladies to make their calls.

Ames and MacKenzie, having taken the Green Trolley to Gloucester Street, mounted the tall flight of brownstone steps at the home of the Lawrence Nortons.

'Not a propitious hour,' Ames murmured as he grasped the bellpull. 'But I know Norton. He'll not be put off.'

Admitted by a surprised-looking butler still adjusting his jacket, they waited in a small room off the spacious foyer. In a moment they were shown up to the library at the front of the second floor. Norton, a lanky, loose-limbed man with gingery sideburns, greeted them cordially enough, but without troubling to hide his curiosity about their visit at such an hour.

'What's the trouble, Ames?' he said, motioning them to comfortable leather chairs before the fire. 'Since I assume this is not a social call. How do you do, Doctor?'

In a few words, Ames stated his question: Had the Reverend Montgomery attended a gathering here last Sunday?

'Why, yes,' Norton said. 'My wife, you understand, is a staunch supporter of the Bower. We hold a fund-raising social for the reverend two or three times a year.'

'And this one lasted into the evening?'

'Not very late. Until about seven.'

Ames leaned forward, his keen gaze fixed on his host. 'Can you say for certain what time the reverend left?'

Norton thought about it. 'I think I can, yes. I remember because my son broke his curfew that evening. He'd gone out in the afternoon but promised to be back by six to do his lessons. He's at the Latin School, and they work the boys pretty hard there. Just when the reverend was leaving, my son came in and I looked at the clock. It was quarter past. I was thoroughly put out with him, I don't mind telling you.'

MacKenzie had a fleeting moment of sympathy for Norton Junior, facing his father's wrath.

Norton cleared his throat. 'If you don't mind my asking, Mr. Ames, why it is that you want to know?'

'I am trying to account for his time,' Ames said simply.

'For the entire evening?'

'Yes.'

'Because?'

'Because on that night, one of the Bower's girls was murdered.'

Norton nodded vigorously. 'Yes. Terrible business. And then a second girl — '

'Was killed the next night. But for the moment, I am interested in Sunday, when the first girl was killed. I spoke to the reverend last evening, and he told me that he left here about ten on Sunday night. Now you tell me that it was quarter past.'

Norton pursed his lips. 'I believe your sister, like my wife, is active in helping Miss Montgomery in her work.'

'She is, yes.'

'Mrs. Norton is of the opinion that this scandal will hurt the Bower.'

'That is what my sister thinks also.'

'But — ' Norton's face was a study in puzzlement. 'You cannot possibly believe that the Reverend Montgomery had anything to do with these murders?'

'I do not believe anything. I am merely trying — at my cousin Wainwright's request — to assist the police in their inquiries.'

'Wainwright sits on the board of commissioners.'

'Yes. And the longer it takes for the culprit

to be apprehended, the more the police suffer in the public's trust. Naturally he wants the case brought to a conclusion as soon as possible.'

'Of course.' Norton pondered for a moment. 'And all this business about Jack the Ripper does not help matters.'

'It certainly doesn't.'

'Mr. Ames, I will be frank with you.' Norton tapped a nervous little tattoo on the arm of his chair. 'I hold these fundraisers for the Bower because my wife asks me to. And of course I cannot deny that Miss Montgomery performs a worthy service. Worthy — and, unfortunately, necessary. Do you know Miss Montgomery? Of course you do. She is a most worthy female herself, if a trifle offputting. These people who have a mission in the world are very often offputting; they cannot help it. Still, I admire her.'

He was obviously building up to something, MacKenzie thought. Get on with it, man.

'But I will tell you this as well, Mr. Ames. Even though her brother is widely admired for his own part in keeping the Bower afloat, I personally have a mental reservation about him.'

Ames cocked his head. 'And what would that be?'

'He is . . . duplicitous.'

'How?'

'He . . . does not always behave well. In fact, he sometimes behaves very badly.'

'Do you believe him capable of murder?'

Norton blinked. 'Murder? Well, now, I don't know about that. I suppose anyone is capable of murder if he's sufficiently threatened.' He leaned forward as if to impart a confidence. 'But the man is not what he seems.'

No, thought Ames, he is not. 'How do you mean?'

'I mean, my brother-in-law is active in the Watch and Ward. You know of their work?'

'Yes.'

The New England Society for the Suppression of Vice, popularly known as the Watch & Ward, was a group of men who had taken it upon themselves to guard the public morals of the city. In pursuit of their goal of absolute moral purity, they visited bookstores to demand that objectionable titles be removed from the shelves, they shut down — mostly in Scollay Square — risqué theatrical presentations, they raided houses of ill repute, they monitored the sale of indecent postcards and other pornographic material, and generally made themselves busy about minding other people's business. Privately, although Ames deplored the general coarsening of the culture, he thought the Watch & Ward was the Puritan impulse run amok, a subject perhaps for William James's studies of psychological aberrations, but he forbore to say so now.

'And what I have to tell you must be kept in absolute confidence,' Norton went on, glancing at MacKenzie.

'Of course. You may rest assured of Dr. MacKenzie's complete discretion.'

'I am sure I can. Well, my brother-in-law went with a few other men last month on a surprise visit to the Black Sea, down in South Cove. You know of it?'

'I do.'

'A district of the foulest vice if ever there was one. Disorderly houses, gambling parlors, fancy bordellos, what have you. The police make regular raids, of course, but as I don't have to tell you, a little baksheesh goes a long way with some of those officers, particularly the ones who walk a beat.'

'I imagine it does, yes.'

'In the course of this particular visit, a few so-called respectable men were discovered at one or two of the houses.'

'And among them was the Reverend Montgomery?'

'Yes.'

Ames was silent, and after a moment,

Norton said, 'You do not seem surprised, Mr. Ames.'

'I am not. To be frank, I have the same impression of him that you do — that he is not what he pretends to be. But if you knew about this — ah — discovery, may I ask why you entertained him here? Surely a man who frequents the Black Sea should not be welcomed into any decent household.'

Norton's gaze wavered, then came back. 'You are right, of course, Mr. Ames. But I had already given my wife permission to hold the event, and in all honesty, if I had demanded she cancel it, I did not feel I could tell her why. One cannot speak of such things to a lady, after all.'

'No. I suppose not. And she knows you well enough to detect it if you made up some falsehood as an excuse?'

Norton rolled his eyes. 'Yes.'

MacKenzie smothered a smile.

'So if you are looking to discover where the reverend was on Sunday evening after he left here — earlier than he said he did — I am sorry to say, Mr. Ames, that you may have to pay a visit to the Black Sea yourself.'

★ ★ ★

342

The Black Sea was a dreary area of tenements and small commercial establishments, saloons, dingy cafés, and, on the narrow side streets, three- and four-story row houses. Here and there could be seen the three gold balls of pawnbrokers' shops, and small hand-lettered signs announcing the premises of crystal-ball readers and dubious healers. Some places, lacking any advertisement, looked more prosperous than their neighbors; these, presumably, housed the area's active flesh trade.

To MacKenzie's astonishment, Ames seemed familiar with the neighborhood. Since he was sure his landlord was far too fastidious a man to frequent such a district, he had to assume that Ames was operating on hearsay and clever guesses.

The first three places they visited, while assuredly disorderly houses, had no knowledge of the Reverend Montgomery. Ames did not use the reverend's name; instead, sure that Montgomery would have come here under an alias, he described him.

At the fourth house, he found what he was looking for: a woman who said — after Ames intimated that the police might wish to pay her a visit — that yes, such a man was a regular customer.

'But who are you?' she asked. She was

middle-aged, hardlooking, with dyed black hair and pouchy eyes. 'Not the police, I know that for sure.'

'No,' Ames replied. 'Not the police. Now, tell me, my good woman, did this man visit you last Sunday night?'

She squinted, as if the daylight hurt her eyes. 'Last Sunday? I couldn't say for sure.'

'Try.'

She sniffed. 'I can't.'

'I believe you can,' Ames said. 'And my friend, Inspector Crippen, will — '

'All right!' she said quickly.

'He was here?'

'Yes.'

'What time?'

'I couldn't say.'

'No? Of course you could.'

She thought about it. 'Around nine, nine-thirty.'

'And he stayed until?'

'He's always quick about it, that one,' she said with a sour smile. 'Not after ten.'

As they turned to go, she cried, 'No trouble from the police, now, mister!'

When they were on the sidewalk once more, Ames gave himself a shake as if to slough off a film of dirt.

'I don't hold with the Watch and Ward, Doctor, but I must say, sometimes I don't object to their activities if they can rid the city of places like this.'

But they can't, MacKenzie thought, and they never will.

Ames hailed a cab on Washington Street and gave the driver the Bower's address. Despite the admission he had wrung from the brothel's owner just now, he felt oddly deflated. He'd hoped to find that the reverend had no way to account for his time on the night that Mary was killed, and now, perhaps, he had done so. That is, if Crippen would take the word of a whore. If Norton had been correct in his estimation of the hour when Montgomery had left his house. If, if, if —

The medical examiner had put the time of Mary's death at between seven and midnight — a span that easily could have allowed the reverend to leave the Nortons', make his way back to the South End to deal with Mary, and then visit the Black Sea.

But why, if indeed he had killed Mary, had he killed Bridget also?

*　*　*

'She can't see you,' snapped Matron Pratt. She stood in the hall, hands on her hips, eyes slitted nearly shut with animosity. 'She can't

345

see anyone. Why don't you leave her alone? She's near out of her mind with worry, and you come here to pester her — '

Ames inclined his head. 'I understand, Matron. I will not take up one moment of her time more than I need, I assure you.'

The Bower was quiet. From the dining hall at the rear of the building, where the girls were presumably at their noon meal, came the odor of boiled cabbage.

'She's resting,' Matron Pratt replied through clenched teeth. 'She hasn't slept a wink since — since it happened, and now for once she is, and I won't — '

She broke off as they heard voices rising, high and piercing, from the dining hall. In the next moment, they heard curses, and then the sound of what might have been someone's head hitting, very hard, a bare floor.

At once, Mrs. Pratt whirled and went at a half-run toward the back of the house.

'Stand guard,' Ames muttered to MacKenzie. In the next instant, he was inside the office. Lifting the glass door of one of the bookshelves, he took down the account book for the previous year, 1891. Quickly he scanned the pages that held the record of income and outgo for the last three months.

In a moment more, he was out in the hall once again, just in time to greet Agatha

Montgomery coming from the dining room, giving the lie to the matron's excuses.

'Mr. Ames.'

'Miss Montgomery.'

'How can I — what do you want?'

She looked worse than ever, MacKenzie thought: pale and tense, and her voice strained and thin.

'We want a few words with you, no more,' Ames said.

'You are not fit — ' Mrs. Pratt growled at her, coming up behind.

'It's all right, Matron.'

Miss Montgomery opened the door to the office and went in, Ames and MacKenzie following. She sat in the chair behind the desk — Mary Flaherty's chair — and the men seated themselves opposite. They caught sight of Matron Pratt's angry visage at the door before she slammed it shut.

For a moment, Miss Montgomery seemed to be trying to summon up the strength to speak. She sat rigid, her hands clenched on the desk before her, her long, equine face tight with strain. Her hair was straggling out of its knot, and the collar of her dark dress was crooked.

Then at last she said, 'Now, Mr. Ames. What do you want?'

He reminded himself that women were the

weaker sex. He reminded himself that Agatha Montgomery, although hardly weak in the way that most women were, was nevertheless a female herself — and, more, that during the past few days, she had been through a great deal of emotional turmoil and devastating loss. She must, he thought, be particularly vulnerable just now.

So. This was his chance, and he must take it.

'Miss Montgomery, were you aware that Mary Flaherty was expecting a child?'

Her mouth dropped open, and her pale eyes widened with shock — at what Ames had told her? MacKenzie wondered. Or at the fact that he would mention such an unmentionable thing?

Ames waited for a moment. Then he pressed on. 'Did you know that, Miss Montgomery?'

'No.' She spoke so softly that they barely heard her.

'I believe you did. Or you suspected it at least. And since your brother was friendly with Mary — '

'He — I don't know what you mean by friendly.'

'He knew her rather better than he knew most of the girls here, didn't he?'

Her eyes shifted away, to the file cabinets

and bookcases lining the walls, to her clenched hands, to the ceiling, back to her hands.

'Didn't he, Miss Montgomery?' Ames persisted. 'He had to see to the account books, after all, which Mary kept here in the office. He was in and out at all hours, and he would have met her here as she worked.'

'Yes. I suppose so.'

'And so, being friendly with her, he would have listened to her troubles.'

'What troubles?' She looked up sharply.

'I think you know.'

No answer.

'Didn't you know about Mary, Miss Montgomery? That she was expecting a child?'

'No.'

'But you must have suspected it?'

'Never. She was — No. I don't believe it.'

You are lying, MacKenzie thought.

'The medical examiner is quite sure,' Ames said.

She blazed up at him. 'Then the medical examiner is mistaken! She couldn't have been — she wouldn't — '

'No, Miss Montgomery. The medical examiner is not mistaken,' Ames said softly. 'And I believe you know he is not.'

She made no reply. She sat immobile; after

a moment, they saw tears begin to slide down her thin, sallow cheeks. She made no move to stop them or to wipe them away. She simply sat, without speaking, without making a sound, letting her tears fall — and what bitter tears they must be, Ames thought. It was almost as if she were mourning, not Mary's death, or Bridget's, but the whole wreckage of her life, all her years of effort and toil to establish this place, this 'bower' of refuge for girls who might, in the end, throw that effort back in her face. Other girls had left the Bower because they'd been pregnant, but those other girls had not been Mary Flaherty: her pet, her prize girl.

Gently, Ames said, 'Did you ever talk to Mary about her condition, Miss Montgomery?'

She shook her head. Then she fumbled in her cuff for a handkerchief, withdrew it, and wiped her eyes. She looked old — older than she did ordinarily, and somehow beaten.

'But you knew,' he said.

'I did not!' Suddenly she was infused with a dreadful energizing anger. She sat up straight and glared at Ames as if he and he alone were the source of all her woe.

'But if I had known, I can assure you I would have expelled her at once! At once! To have allowed her to stay — and with a bastard child — never! To see her, like *that* — ! No,

Mr. Ames. If what you say is true, she would have gone at once.'

'It is true,' he said. 'Believe me. And what I am trying to discover is if you have any idea who the man might have been.'

She stared at him as if he had taken leave of his senses. 'How can you ask such a thing, Mr. Ames? How would I know that? The girls are strictly monitored — '

'Ah, but Mary was not, was she?'

They watched, fascinated, as a series of emotions passed over her face: anger, bewilderment, a kind of cunning. And finally, once more, that look of defeat.

'No,' she said. 'She was not. Let it be a lesson to me, never again to allow a girl to be so free. I thought I could trust her.'

'But she betrayed you.'

'If what you say is true — yes, she did.'

'With whom, Miss Montgomery? That is what I need to know. Who was the man?'

She shook her head. 'It seems impossible. For her to — ' She caught herself. 'What about that typewriter salesman? He was hanging around, making a nuisance of himself. If anyone got Mary into trouble, I would wager on him.'

'I agree with you that at first glance he would seem a likely candidate, but I have spoken to him, I have asked him that very question, and he denies it. For the moment, at least, I am inclined to believe him.'

'Well, then, who?' She thought about it. 'There is a boy who works here — '

'Garrett O'Reilly? I don't believe it was he.'

'Why not?'

'I have character references for him which lead me to believe that he would not be so rash as to — ah — become intimate with one of the girls here.'

Miss Montgomery's mouth twisted in a bitter smile. 'Because they are not good enough for him? An Irish boy?'

'For the moment, at least, let us eliminate him. Can you think of anyone else?'

'No.'

'And your brother — ?'

She sucked in her breath with a loud hiss. 'My brother! My *brother*? Are you suggesting that my brother, who is the very heart and soul of this establishment, had anything to do with Mary's condition? You come here to insult me, to insult him — '

A sedative, thought MacKenzie; she needs a strong dose of chloral hydrate and twenty-four hours in her bed.

'I am not trying to insult anyone,' Ames retorted. 'I beg you to believe that. I am merely trying to help the police — '

'Where you are not wanted! I told you

before, I do not want you interfering — '

'Miss Montgomery, do you realize the seriousness of this situation? The Bower is in danger of losing its support if Mary's killer — and Bridget's as well — is not swiftly apprehended.'

'Then go and apprehend him, and leave my brother out of it! It is outrageous that he must be dragged into this affair when he is the best man in the world, devoted to us, to our work! He has been my strong right hand from the beginning, and to have you insinuate such things about him is more than I can bear!'

She turned her head away from them. When, after a moment, she had quieted a little, Ames said, 'He might, in fact, know something that can help us.'

'If he does, he would have told it to you — or to the police — already.'

Although she had calmed, still she twisted her hands, hard, until MacKenzie thought they must hurt her.

'My brother, Mr. Ames, is a very different person from me. Yes — I know it. I accept it. He was always, from the time he was born, a charming, personable boy. Everyone always liked him. They didn't like me particularly — charm is not one of my virtues — but they liked him. He has always made his way in the world on the strength of that charm — his ability to bring people over to his side. That is why he is so successful at raising funds. People naturally want to help him, and, by extension, the Bower.'

She paused, distracted by her thoughts. For a moment, the ghost of a smile flitted across her face.

'It is not Randolph's fault that people find him attractive,' she went on. 'Women in particular seem to throw themselves at him. Oh, yes. More than one woman has tried to befriend me in the hope that I will connect her to him. I never do, of course. Why should I?'

'And yet, one woman has — ah — connected herself to him on her own, has she not?' Ames asked. 'Just the other evening, at Caroline's dinner party, we learned that he is engaged to be married.'

Miss Montgomery's face darkened, her mouth tightened — with anger, MacKenzie thought — but she made no reply.

'Did we not?' Ames persisted. He felt, just then, like a bully — something he never wanted to be — but he was coming close to something, he didn't know what, and he needed to keep on until he found it.

'We did — yes,' Miss Montgomery replied reluctantly.

'You were not aware of it before Wednesday evening?'

'No.'

Why not? Ames wondered. Why did your precious brother keep it secret? To avoid your wrath?

'You do not know the lady?'

'No.'

'Nor anything about her?'

'No. Except that she is a widow. Randolph told me that later. And quite wealthy.'

'I see.' Ames's pulse quickened at the thought of the Reverend Montgomery, a wealthy widow within his grasp. And if a girl from the Bower — a girl who was inconveniently in the family way, and perhaps by him — threatened to be an impediment to that match, what would the reverend have done to get rid of her?

'It will be a splendid marriage for him.' Miss Montgomery seemed to have forgotten her anger, her distress. She spoke now in a singsong voice, her eyes gazing into the middle distance, seeing, perhaps, the advantageous match that her brother had achieved. 'And when they marry, they will live here in Boston, they will not go to New York. Randolph would never leave me here alone. He always promised me — '

'He promised you what?'

They had not heard him open the door. Now he came in, closing it behind him.

Miss Montgomery started. 'Randolph!'

'Good morning, sister.' His eyes raked Ames and MacKenzie, but he did not greet them.

'We were just — Mr. Ames came to — ' Suddenly, she was afraid. Of the reverend? Ames wondered. And if so, why?

'Mr. Ames came to — what?' Montgomery's voice was soft, but they heard the threat in it.

'To ask Miss Montgomery — ' Ames began.

'To harass her, you mean.' Montgomery was breathing hard, as if he were trying to contain anger he did not want to reveal. 'To hound her — to pester her once more, when in fact you have done enough pestering already, sir.'

He glanced at his sister, who sat immobile. Only the rapid blinking of her eyes showed that she, too, labored under some considerable stress.

'And so, Mr. Ames — Doctor — I ask you to leave. At once.'

Ames rose, and MacKenzie did likewise. 'Of course,' Ames said. 'Since you request it. But as long as you are here, Reverend, I wonder if I might prevail a trifle more upon your patience — '

'My patience is at an end, sir! I told you that last night! I order you to leave. Now!'

They were moving toward the door, and the reverend stepped aside to allow them to go out. But as Ames passed by, he murmured, 'Only a moment, Reverend.'

In the hall, Ames and the doctor continued on to the front door, opened it, and went out. Montgomery stood by the office door, glaring at them. At last, as if he had come to some difficult decision, he joined them.

The three men went down the tall flight of brownstone steps to the sidewalk. At first glance, the square was deserted, only a lone grocer's wagon trundling down the opposite side. Then MacKenzie saw a rather slovenly looking man leaning against a tree, facing the Bower. A neighborhood tramp? Doubtful, he thought. The fellow seemed to be waiting for something — or someone.

'Well?' Montgomery demanded.

Ames walked a few doors down, MacKenzie and the reverend behind. Then Ames stopped and turned to face Montgomery.

'I have spoken to Lawrence Norton,' he said.

Montgomery's eyes, meeting his own, did not waver. 'And?' he said.

'And he told me that last Sunday evening you left his house shortly after seven.'

'Perhaps he is mistaken.'

'I do not believe so.'

A dull red had begun to spread over the reverend's fleshy face, and his eyes, so pale, so cold, seemed no more than two chips of flinty stone.

'What business of yours — I ask you, Ames — what earthly business of yours is it at what hour I left the Nortons'? You barge into my home, you come here, you harass my sister, you poke and pry — '

He raised his clenched, gloved fist and shook it under Ames's nose. 'Get out!' he said, his voice choked with fury.

'This is a public walkway, Reverend.'

The man leaning against the tree straightened.

'I do not care what it is! Get out! Or by God I will have you arrested for trespassing at the Bower!'

'The Black Sea, Reverend.'

This threw Montgomery off guard. 'What?'

'The Black Sea. I believe you know it. They certainly know you.'

Montgomery's face was bright red now. 'Get out!' he shouted. A woman just emerging from an areaway across the square stopped in astonishment as she heard him.

'I warn you, Ames!' Montgomery advanced, fist raised. 'Once and for all!'

Ames held up his hands, palms out. 'We are going, Reverend. Do not excite yourself further. Good morning to you.'

He turned and walked swiftly toward the end of the square. MacKenzie, hurrying to keep up, saw out of the corner of his eye the man who had been leaning against the tree begin to head in their direction. And now he thought he recognized him.

'Excuse me — '

Ames looked around, but he did not pause. He knew this man: Babcock, from the *Globe*.

'Mr. Ames, is it? I wonder if I could have a word — '

'No.'

'But I'll pay — '

'No.'

'Make it worth your while, sir, if you'd just give me — '

With a snarl, Ames dismissed him. The journalist stood in the middle of the sidewalk, staring after them, shaking his head.

It was not until they had turned into Columbus Avenue that Ames spoke. His face was taut, his eyes flashing with anger.

'A — what would you call him, Doctor? A mountebank? I don't mean that damned scribbler back there. I mean the reverend. Yes. That is what he is. A perfect charlatan. I smell fraud about his person — stinking fraud, and worse besides.'

'Nevertheless, he has his prospects,' MacKenzie replied.

'Indeed he does. And, having them — her, rather, that wealthy widow — he would not want his plans spoiled by the inconvenience of a poor girl at the Bower who presented herself to him in a scandalous condition.'

'You mean a condition for which he was responsible?'

'Exactly, Doctor. A condition into which, if I am not mistaken, the good reverend put her.'

'His sister will never believe it.'

'No, she will not. Her faith in him is absolute.'

'To the point that if that faith were destroyed, her world would come crashing down around her.'

'Yes. Precisely.' Ames lifted his arm, and a herdic-phaeton veered toward them. 'I have another errand, but you, I imagine, will be glad to go home. Tell Caro that I will be back at some point, I do not know when. She is not to worry.'

The last MacKenzie saw of him was his tall, dark-clad figure loping at a rapid clip down the avenue in the rain.

19

MacKenzie gazed through the lavender glass at the purplish winter-dead greenery behind the black iron fence of the oval. The rain continued unabated, the gray skies emptying sheets of water onto the square. Already now, at two o'clock, the afternoon was growing dark. Soon the streetlamps would glow, casting their pale illumination through the downpour. Lights would go on in the windows of the houses ringing the square; people would hurry home to the peace and comfort of their firesides.

But not here. Here was tension and worry, no hope of peace. As he turned back to the room, he saw that Caroline had picked up her knitting. After completing a row or two, she put it down, took up one of her beloved Diana Strangeways novels, and tried to read. He did the same, seating himself in his Morris rocker and opening the pages of the life of Lincoln that he seemed unable to finish. The words danced before his eyes in a senseless jumble, and he kept going over the same sentence, the same paragraph, without understanding what he read. A half hour passed; three-quarters. At last he put the volume aside and looked up to find her watching him.

'Where is Addington?' she said.

He saw the worry in her eyes, he heard the tension in her voice, and he longed to find the words to reassure her that her brother was safe.

'I don't know.'

'But surely he should be back by now? I wish he'd told you where he was going. It isn't prudent to go who-knows-where, and possibly — '

A knock at the front door interrupted her. She broke off, her hand flown to her bosom, listening — hoping — for a friendly voice instead of word of some disaster. They heard Margaret hurrying to answer. When, after a moment, she did not announce the caller, Caroline stood up.

'Who do you suppose — ' she began, but just then the pocket doors slid open to reveal Margaret, her face unwontedly grim.

'Yes, Margaret? Who is it?'

'It's an Irish, miss,' the maid said disapprovingly.

'Well, who, Margaret? Does he want to see Mr. Ames?'

'Him — or you, miss.'

Caroline pushed past her. The vestibule

was empty, the front door closed. She opened it.

On the front step, shivering, hatless, wearing only a thin jacket and soaked to the skin, stood Garrett O'Reilly.

'Garrett! What on earth — come in, you'll catch your death!'

He dripped puddles onto the tiled vestibule floor, and his teeth were chattering so badly, he could hardly speak. When Caroline turned to lead him into the hall, she confronted Margaret's scowl.

'It's all right, Margaret. Would you bring tea, please?' But tea hardly seemed adequate to Garrett's condition, and so she added, 'And would you go up to the fourth floor, to the box room, and see if you can find any of Mr. Ames's old clothing?'

Not that there would be much to choose from, she thought; Addington, like so many men of his class, wore his things year in and year out. He didn't have many castoffs.

'Yes, miss. But you remember — '

'What, Margaret?'

'I'm catching the train, miss. To my sister's.'

'Oh, yes. I'd forgotten. But the train doesn't leave until nine o'clock, does it?' Even in the present emergency, Caroline hadn't the heart to forbid Margaret's long-anticipated visit.

Margaret disappeared, and Caroline led the shivering young man into the parlor, where MacKenzie was pulling up a side chair to the fire. He shoveled more coal onto the low flames, stirred them up, and said, 'Well, my lad, you're a candidate for pneumonia. Come here and warm yourself.'

'Yes, sir.'

Caroline introduced them, and Garrett limped across the rug, shedding water as he went, to take MacKenzie's outstretched hand — with no hesitation, the doctor noted. Once seated, Garrett held out his thin, chapped hands to the flames. He couldn't seem to stop shivering.

Caroline gave him a moment, and then, unable to contain her curiosity, she said, 'What is it, Garrett? Why have you come?'

He looked up at her. He was trembling, MacKenzie thought, from more than cold.

'It's the police, miss.'

'What happened?' Caroline asked. 'Did they question you?'

'Yes, miss.'

'Just now?'

'Yes. It was that inspector — Crippen, is it? He thinks — ' His voice broke, and he swallowed hard. 'He thinks I did it. He was that nasty, miss.'

'I'm sure he was.'

'He wanted to know — like, did I know the girls. Did I talk to them. Where was I on Sunday night.'

'Well?' said MacKenzie. 'And where were you?'

Garrett shot him an inscrutable look. 'At home, sir. Where else would I be?'

'Any number of places, I imagine. Did Crippen believe you?'

'No, sir. He said family alibi isn't good enough. Any mother would lie to save her son, he said.'

'Hmmm. True enough, I suppose. What else did he want to know?'

'Just — things,' Garrett muttered, shaking his head.

Like whether you had intimate relations with Mary Flaherty, MacKenzie thought. Hardly a topic to discuss in front of Caroline Ames.

Margaret came in, then, with the tea tray. She was still scowling with disapproval, and she put it down with an unnecessarily loud thud and left the room without her usual curtsy.

Scalding hot as it was, Garrett greedily drank the full cup that Caroline gave to him and accepted another. She waited until he had stopped shivering somewhat, and then she said, 'Garrett, what did you tell Inspector Crippen?'

'I told him the truth, miss. That I didn't do it — didn't have anything to do with either of 'em.'

'But you did,' she said.

He looked away.

'You sometimes spoke to Bridget, didn't you? I have been told that you sometimes asked her questions. Is that so?'

And now they saw the first hint of truculence in him. He stared at them as if he were trying to judge the degree of danger they posed to him, instead of being the source of help he'd sought.

'What if I did?' he said at last. 'What difference does that make?'

'None,' she replied, 'except that it gives the lie to your statement that you had nothing to do with her. And that makes people suspicious. Surely you can understand that.'

That, and a good deal more, MacKenzie thought. He could almost see the rapid workings of Garrett's mind as the lad considered what to say next.

After a long moment, Garrett said, 'I had my reasons to speak to her. It doesn't mean that I — that I did her in.'

'Of course it doesn't,' said Caroline warmly. MacKenzie could see that she was genuinely troubled about this boy, and he was touched by her compassion.

'Why did you?' he asked Garrett. 'Speak to her, I mean.'

Garrett hesitated. Then: 'Because I was asking her about the new girl.'

'New girl? Who was that?'

'Peg Corcoran.'

'And why were you asking about her?' Caroline said.

'I wanted to see if she was getting along.' It seemed a tremendous effort for him to get out the words. 'She's my cousin,' he added, obviously with great reluctance.

'Your — oh, dear. I am sorry.'

'It was — you understand — a disgrace to us. To our family. My ma didn't know, y'see. Peg is her niece — her brother's child. They live in South Boston. My uncle Frank near died when he found out about Peg. Last year, it was. She'd gone into service with a family over in Cambridge. But then something happened, I don't know what, and they put her out. She couldn't bear to go home like that — a failure. So she took to the streets. Lived with three other girls in a room. She was arrested once or twice, and one time she was sent up for thirty days. Then she got sick. She went to Uncle Frank for help, but he turned her out. Said she was no daughter of his no more. He told me about it, made me promise not to tell my ma. That must'v' frightened her more than anything, I think — that she was so far gone, her own family didn't want her. She must'v' seen she was headed straight for Potter's Field if she didn't straighten herself out. That's when she came to the Bower.'

'Did she know you worked there?' MacKenzie asked.

'No, sir, she didn't. I saw her in the dining room one day when I was washin' windows. I almost fell off my ladder, I can tell you. But I never spoke to her, not once. I wouldn't want her to think I'd let on to the family she was there. Though it mightn't have made any difference, seein' as how they considered her dead. An' anyways, the Bower's better than the streets, isn't it?'

'So it was simply out of concern for her that you asked Bridget about her,' MacKenzie said.

'Yes, sir. I just wanted to make sure she was all right.'

It seemed an innocent enough explanation, and yet MacKenzie doubted Inspector Crippen would accept it if he had already made up his mind, as he seemed to have done, that the lad was the Bower killer.

'And now with all this goin' on,' Garrett

added, 'how do I know she's safe at all? Any of the Bower's girls might be the next.'

'If there is to be another, yes,' Caroline replied, suppressing a shudder. Another — but there couldn't be. There mustn't be.

'Inspector Crippen let you go in the end,' MacKenzie said.

'Yes, sir.' Garrett nodded at him. 'But he said I must stay in Boston. I shouldn't think of tryin' to run away, he said, because he could find me anywhere. But where would I go anyways?'

Caroline went to the bellpull by the fireplace and pulled it twice sharply. Then she said to Garrett, 'You must stay here.'

'Do you not think — ' MacKenzie began, but he broke off as she gave him a look. It was not, after all, his affair if she chose to offer shelter to this lad.

'Yes, I do think, Doctor,' she said, and that, he understood, was the end of it.

When Margaret came, she still had that stubborn, mutinous look. 'Yes, miss?'

'Have you found any dry clothing, Margaret?' The way to deal with the maid's attitude, Caroline believed, was to ignore it.

'Not yet, miss.'

'Please do so immediately. And then make up the bed in Henry's old room' — this was the chamber, next to the kitchen, that had once housed the family's butler — 'and tell Cook to find something for this young man to eat. He will be staying with us for a day or two.'

If not longer, she thought, and she momentarily quailed at the thought of her brother's reaction when he learned of Garrett's presence in the household.

'Cook is gettin' dinner, miss, an' then she'll be on her way home.'

Caroline stared at her. 'Then tell her to put something out before she goes! Really, Margaret!'

'Yes, miss.' Margaret shot a hostile glance toward Garrett as she left the room.

In all Margaret's years with the family, Caroline had never had trouble with her. Well, she'd deal with her when she came back from her sister's; she hadn't time to soothe the maid's obviously ruffled feathers now. 'Do you understand, Garrett?' she said. 'If you are here with us, we can vouch for you in the event of another — '

'I can't stay, miss.'

'But why not?'

'My ma'll be worried crazy if I don't come home.'

'We could send her a note,' MacKenzie offered.

'She can't read.'

'Send it anyway. Where do you live?'

'Salem Street.'

A street of tenements in the North End. 'Well, then, surely someone in her building can read. Or she could take it to one of the neighborhood shopkeepers, perhaps, to read to her.'

Caroline went to the little desk in the corner and took out a sheet of paper. 'If you go down to Charles Street, Doctor,' she said, 'you will find a runner at Bright's Apothecary. Tell them you know me. They always have a supply of boys to run messages, and they won't charge you more than a nickel.'

She wrote a few lines, folded the paper, and sealed it into an envelope. 'What is the address, Garrett?'

He told her and she printed it large and clear. 'There, Doctor,' she said, handing the envelope to him. For once, she didn't smile at him, and for once, he didn't mind.

Out-of-doors, he pulled his muffler more tightly around his neck as he made his way down the hill. The rain had stopped, but the air was raw, filled with a tangy, salt-smelling mist that overlay the odor of horse dung.

Charles Street was thronged with Saturday afternoon shoppers and pedestrians; a seller of roasted chestnuts was doing a brisk business. At Bright's Apothecary, the clerk acknowledged knowing the Ameses, but this was a particularly busy day, he said, and he didn't have a lad handy. Could the gentleman wait for a moment while he finished up with this customer?

Impatiently, MacKenzie tapped his fingers on the polished wooden counter. He hadn't thought to be delayed; he needed to get back to No. 16½. He didn't like leaving Caroline Ames alone with that Irish lad, no matter how innocent he seemed to be. Margaret was there, of course, and Cook, but still. Not a good arrangement. And he was certain that Ames would be unhappy when he learned that Caroline had asked Garrett to stay, no matter that he himself had offered to help the lad.

Five minutes passed; ten. MacKenzie stared at the shelves of tall glass apothecary jars containing various colored liquids and powders and bits of vegetation — roots, stems, ugly-looking dried things. The place had a musty, medicinal smell. MacKenzie wanted to be outdoors; he felt confined in here, too nerved up to wait patiently. He spoke to the clerk again: Could a lad be found to take this note?

At last the door burst open and a whey-faced little boy came trotting in. This, it seemed, was the runner for whom MacKenzie waited. He handed over the note and a nickel, and at last the message to Garrett's mother was on its way to the North End. He stepped outside to watch the child set off at a rapid clip, and then he rounded the corner to climb Mt. Vernon Street. He'd been gone almost half an hour, he estimated. Too long.

He was slightly out of breath when he reached Louisburg Square. He lumbered along the uneven brick sidewalk toward No. 16½, peering eagerly at the welcoming light shining through the lavender windowpanes. She'd be worried, he thought, wondering what had become of him.

But when he greeted her at last, he saw that she wasn't worried after all — or not about him at any rate. She was alone, Garrett presumably having gone down to the kitchen to be fed, and she was standing by the fire, holding a flimsy scrap of yellow paper: a telegram.

'What is it?' he said, still puffing a little.

'The Ladies' Committee at the church.'

Not some further crisis at the Bower, then. He was relieved to hear it, but in the next moment his anxiety returned when she added, 'They want me to make a visit.'

'A visit? To whom?'

'To the family I saw on Monday. Oh, I hope he hasn't come back!'

'Who?'

'The husband.' Her sweet, pretty face was suddenly grim. 'He has been warned repeatedly to stay away from them, but when he is inebriated, he comes back and beats her. The eldest son is fifteen now, so he can defend her — his mother — fairly well, but still, I must go.'

'When? Now?'

'Yes.'

'But — late on a Saturday afternoon? Can it not wait until tomorrow?'

'I am afraid not. People generally don't call on us unless it is an emergency. They have no place else to turn, you see.'

He was not convinced. 'Surely you can ask someone else to go. You should not be burdened with such a request at a time like this.' He was pulling at one end of his mustache, a sure sign of his distress.

'Oh, I couldn't do that,' she said hastily, looking slightly shocked, as if he had suggested some truly outrageous thing. 'This family is mine — assigned to me, my responsibility. I must go.'

'Then I will come with you.'

'Oh, no, Doctor. Thank you, but no. I won't be long. I know these people fairly well. The woman is very self-reliant, she wouldn't call on us — on me — if it weren't absolutely necessary.'

She tucked the telegram into the pocket of her skirt and started for the door. MacKenzie, seized with a sudden dread, threw propriety to the winds and put his hand on her arm. 'Where do they live?'

'On West Newton Street.'

He was familiar enough with the city, by now, to know where that was. 'In the South End.'

'Yes.'

Where, in the past week, two women had been brutally murdered. What would her brother do? he wondered. Forbid her to go? Could he act in Ames's place and do the same?

Before he'd decided how to proceed, she had gently removed his hand and was going out into the vestibule to collect her things from the hall tree. Struggling with his rising sense of helpless panic, he followed her.

'Miss Ames, I am sure — I am absolutely positive — that your brother would not want you to go on this — this errand of mercy.'

She had been pulling on her overshoes. Now she straightened, one on, one off, and said with no little dignity, 'My brother does not need to know about it.'

'Yes, but if he should return and find you gone — or if, God forbid, you should come to some harm — '

'I will not come to harm.'

'How can you say that?' He was aware that he was shouting. He couldn't help it. 'You know as well as I do that a homicidal lunatic is at large in that district! He has killed two women in the most brutal fashion. Undoubtedly, if the police do not apprehend him, he will kill a third. I cannot — I will not — allow you to put yourself in danger like this.'

He had maneuvered himself past her as he spoke, and now he stood before the front door. If she insisted upon going out, she would have to push him aside.

Or —

'Very well, Doctor,' she said after a moment. She stared at him, outraged. Her voice was cold and hard. Furious, he thought. She is furious with me. In that moment he realized, too late, that in opposing her he had pitted himself against a woman who embodied generations — centuries — of stern New England resolve. Briefly his courage failed him as he saw the wreckage of all his dreams. He would lose her either way, he thought: If she went out, she'd come to harm sure enough, and if — at his insistence — she stayed, she would never forgive him for meddling in her affairs.

'Please, Miss Ames,' he begged, his voice little more than a hoarse croak. 'Please do not go on this errand, no matter how much an errand of mercy you believe it to be. Are this family's troubles worth your life? At least let me come with you.'

'It is far more important, Doctor, that you stay here with Garrett. I will be quite all right on my own. I understand your concern, but this is a summons I must obey. It is my Christian duty to go, can you not understand that? We — the ladies on the committee — are responsible for these families. I have no idea what this summons is about. Perhaps it is simply a problem with one of the children that can be solved quickly. Or perhaps the husband has returned, after all. But whatever it is, I must tend to it. If you insist on barring my way, I will go down to the kitchen and leave from the areaway.'

She turned her back to him, pulled on the other overshoe, and lifted down her waterproof and bonnet.

Utterly defeated, and still struggling with himself — should he risk her further wrath by forcibly restraining her? — MacKenzie watched her. She was the only woman who had ever captured his heart, and now — he was sure — he was going to lose her. Probably he had lost her already.

'Good-bye, Doctor,' she said. She lifted her chin as she met his eyes. Her voice was quiet

— deadly quiet — but still very cold, and her eyes were filled with contempt.

Contempt for him, he thought miserably as the door closed behind her. He was certain he'd ruined himself in her opinion. She'd never think of him now as anything but a coward.

Raw with self-reproach, his conscience wracked with guilt, he lingered by the lavender-glass bow window until she disappeared around the corner of Mt. Vernon Street. Then he turned back to the empty room. Where was Ames? he thought as he began to pace. Up to something, undoubtedly. Why wasn't he here, where he should be, to protect his sister? Ames had the authority to dictate to her which he, John MacKenzie, did not. Fat lot of good it did, that authority, when Ames wasn't here to exercise it.

His knee was aching. He came to a stop by his chair and, with an audible sigh, settled into it. He wondered if he should go down to the kitchen to see how the Irish lad did. Perhaps, after a while, he would.

He rested his head on the antimacassar. Exhausted by the emotional turmoil of the past half hour, he let the warmth of the simmering sea-coal fire envelop him.

He closed his eyes and slept.

He was startled into wakefulness by the

sound of the front door slamming. At once he felt a wave of relief: She'd come back, then, safe and sound. He heaved himself up, preparing to greet her, but his welcoming words died on his lips as Addington Ames walked into the room.

'What is it, Doctor?' Ames asked.

'Nothing,' MacKenzie stammered. 'I thought it was Miss Ames, returning.'

'Returning! Where did she go?'

Ames frowned as MacKenzie told him of the summons from the Ladies' Committee. 'Confound it! And to the South End — you couldn't prevent her going?' Instantly he corrected himself. 'No — no, of course you couldn't. When Caroline sets her mind on something — you don't know the name of the family?'

MacKenzie was embarrassed to admit that he hadn't thought of asking for it.

'Never mind. Even if we went after her we'd probably cross paths and miss her anyway. Well! Shall we have tea?' He stood before the fire, rubbing warmth back into his frozen hands.

And where have you been, MacKenzie thought, and doing what? But he didn't ask, because tea made him think of the kitchen, and the kitchen made him remember Garrett O'Reilly.

'There is something else you should know,' he said.

Ames turned a wary eye to him. 'What?'

'The Irish boy came, in a fright because he'd been roughly questioned by Crippen. Your sister told him to stay here. He is downstairs.'

Ames had taken hold of the bellpull to summon Margaret, but now he let it go.

'What? Garrett is here?'

'Yes.'

Without a reply, Ames turned and swiftly left the room. MacKenzie could hear him clattering down the back stairs; in what seemed too short a time, he had returned.

'Gone!' he exclaimed.

'What? I didn't hear him go out.' But you were asleep, his conscience told him.

'He ducked out at the front areaway, no doubt,' Ames said. 'Damned young fool! I don't like the thought of sheltering him, but even less do I like the thought of him abroad in the city. He will put himself into Crippen's hands by his own foolhardiness if he doesn't watch out.'

Margaret appeared, then, bearing their tea. Her face wore an expression that MacKenzie, in his present state of unease, read as 'This is what comes of trying to help someone from the lower orders.'

'No point in trying to go after him either,' Ames commented gloomily as he surveyed the plate of lace cookies and sliced fruit cake. 'Tea, Doctor? Help yourself. We are captive here, I am afraid, until either Caroline or that young Irish scamp sees fit to rejoin us. We can do nothing but wait.'

20

It was dark on Warren Avenue, darker than usual because along this stretch, a whole row of streetlamps had gone out. As Caroline hurried along, she had only the pale illumination from an unshuttered window, here and there, to see by. Not so fast, she told herself; the last thing you need is to trip and fall. At the corner, up ahead, she saw the welcome glow of a lamp on every side, and she kept her eyes fixed there, a beacon in this dark night.

Dr. MacKenzie had been right: She shouldn't have come. The emergency had turned out to be not so very urgent after all; it could easily have been tended to the following day or even the day after. Christian charity was one thing; waste of it was another.

She heard the sound of a carriage behind her, and she turned to look. It was a four-wheeler — a private carriage, not a cab. She'd taken a herdic earlier because she'd wanted to save time, but when she'd left the cold, cheerless room where the objects of her charity lived, she'd been so annoyed — with herself, with them, with the Ladies' Committee — that she'd thought to punish herself by denying herself a cab to get home.

But now, on this dark, deserted street, she thought better of it. If a herdic came by, she'd hail it, never mind the expense.

She started to walk once more. In the silence, her footsteps sounded very loud. Then, from a nearby church, she heard the bell begin to toll the hour: six o'clock. For a moment, a scene from home flashed across her mind's eye: the warm, bright parlor, Dr. MacKenzie — and perhaps, by this time, Addington too — sitting by the fire, awaiting her. Oh, how she longed to be there with them! Why had she come out — and for nothing after all?

A heretical thought came to her: She would quit the Ladies' Committee. She'd served on it for years; surely she'd done her share. Someone new could take her place.

She reached the lighted corner, crossed, and went on. Darkness again. The bell had stopped, but now suddenly, out of the silent night, came the angry screech of a yowling cat. Dear heaven, what a noise! It was an unnerving sound at any time, but particularly now, when she was a solitary female abroad in the nighttime, a foolish female to have come here alone. What had she been thinking of? She should have allowed Dr. MacKenzie to come with her. Better yet, she should have listened to him and not come at all.

The yowling reached a high pitch and then suddenly stopped. *Clomp-clomp-clomp* went her galoshes on the brick sidewalk. *Thud-thud-thud* went her heart, as if in answer. Only a little way now until she came to Dartmouth Street, where she could cross over into Copley Square. It would be safer there, more people, brightly lighted, and well away from this district where those two girls, those poor, unfortunate girls, had been so atrociously murdered.

Someone was following her. Over the sound of her pounding heart, over the sound of her clomping galoshes, she heard footsteps. A man's footsteps, much too heavy to be a woman's. They were gaining on her.

Her heart jumped into her throat, and for a moment, she thought she would choke.

Stop and turn to look? Or ignore him and keep going fast, faster, as if she hadn't heard? If he sees that you are frightened, she told herself, that in itself may spur him to some reckless — some unthinkable — act.

The footsteps ceased. He must have turned a corner or gone into one of the tall, poorly lighted row houses that lined the street. Glancing back, she saw the sidewalk stretching empty behind her. The lights from the streetlamps — those that worked — glimmered on the deserted cobblestones of the street.

Despite the cold, the raw night air, she was perspiring. Sweat trickled uncomfortably down her face and neck. She wiped at her upper lip, but her fingers, encased in her kid glove, did no good. Perhaps she could find her handkerchief in her carpetbag.

She fumbled at it, scrabbled for the scrap of cloth. But she couldn't find it, and now, to her horror, she heard footsteps again — a man's again, but with a different rhythm to them.

Fearful, terrified of what she would see, she glanced over her shoulder. Coming at her, very fast, was a tall, solid figure. He was no tramp, no riffraff from the rails, but a confident, long-striding male dressed in a tall hat and well-fitting overcoat. He was perhaps half a block away, and gaining rapidly.

Hurriedly she closed her bag and started to walk again, faster than before. But still she heard his footsteps; he was gaining on her. Suddenly seized by panic, she started to run. No, she thought. It isn't possible. Please let him not be —

She thought she heard him call to her, but she ignored him. She was running hard now, pain stabbing at her side, her lungs throbbing, her corset cruelly cutting her. She must draw a full breath or she would faint. But she mustn't faint, she must run — run for her life, because she was being chased by this man who was running, now, himself, and in a moment he was going to catch her.

Her overshoe caught on a protruding brick, and she went down. Her shoulder hit the ground with a heavy thud; then her head hit, but the rim of her bonnet kept her from serious injury.

But she was stunned, what little breath she'd had knocked out of her, and for a long, terrible moment she lay prostrate. Her heart hammered, ready to burst, and her mouth went dry as she heard the footsteps coming closer and closer . . .

She looked up. Just before she fainted she saw, looming over her, the faceless figure of the man who had pursued her.

21

She might have been young, but her face was frozen into a grotesque mask of terror so that it was impossible at first to tell her age. Her throat was slashed, her abdomen ripped open.

At first, when he'd spotted the crumpled heap halfway down the alley, he'd paused in his search, afraid of what he would see. But then, drawn by his need to know, slowly, cautiously, near paralyzed with dread, he crept down the narrow way until he reached the thing lying on the ground. His knees were so weak that he almost collapsed, and for a moment he leaned against the wall to steady himself. With trembling hands he fished a box of matches from his pocket, but it was nearly a minute before he managed to get one lit.

He heard a low, keening sound — a despairing wail of grief and loss — and he knew that it came from him. He sank onto his knees beside her, heedless of the muck and filth of the alley, heedless of her blood, and struck match after match. In the damp, misty night they went out quickly, and so he needed to keep striking them. With a shaking hand he held them close to her face. He still could not believe it. He kept thinking he had wandered into some nightmare, and any moment now he would awake and find himself safe in the Ameses' kitchen.

'No,' he crooned, 'no, no, no . . . ' He rocked back and forth on his knees, overcome with grief. 'No, no, no . . . '

He never heard the commotion at the end of the alley, never heard the approach of the men's heavy steps. He was startled when they seized him by the arms and hauled him up. He looked wildly around at their stern, accusing faces; in the flickering light of their lanterns, they looked like a trio of executioners.

He started to protest, but they ignored him. As they dragged him away, his shouts echoing off the walls of the alley, they were sure they had found the Bower killer at last.

22

Caroline groaned, and then bit her lip to keep from groaning again. In the parlor of No. 16½, she sat in MacKenzie's chair while he knelt at her feet, gently exploring with his fingertips her swollen — and quite naked — right ankle.

'No breakage,' he said, smiling up at her. 'But you've had a nasty sprain. You should soak this for a while, and then I will bind it.'

From his place by the fire, Ames clucked in disapproval. 'I cannot emphasize enough, Caroline, how fortunate you were.'

To have been pursued by the man he believed responsible for the Bower murders? How did that make her fortunate?

But she'd been frightened enough, he thought as he saw her disconsolate face. Even as disapproving as he was of her recklessness, he wouldn't chastise her further.

She'd arrived half an hour ago in a herdic. The driver had come to the door to ask assistance because she'd been unable to walk across the sidewalk. When at last she was safe inside, and had gasped out the details of her misadventure, Ames and MacKenzie had been appalled — horrified at her narrow escape.

'The Reverend Montgomery?' Ames had said.

'Yes, Addington. He — I thought he was pursuing me. That's why I ran. And then I fell, and he caught up with me. He was almost as upset as you are now to find me there. He was very kind. He helped me up, and he stayed with me until a herdic came by. He was going to accompany me here — he insisted upon doing so — but I would not allow it. He told me he was overdue at some conference, and he'd been kind enough already. I didn't want to delay him any longer.'

The reverend had said he was to spend this day and the next at a conference in Cambridge. Some urgent reason must have detained him in Boston. And so, stalking the streets of the South End, he had come upon Caroline, alone and defenseless . . .

Suddenly Ames's throat constricted, and he swallowed painfully.

MacKenzie stood up. They should ring for Margaret to bring a basin of warm water, he said, and meanwhile he would fetch a wrapping from his bag of medical supplies.

A short while later, the soaking completed, Caroline allowed him to bind her ankle. The

390

intimacy of this act had at first given her pause; for a man to see her bare leg and foot protruding from her petticoats would have been, in ordinary circumstances, indescribably embarrassing. But MacKenzie was a doctor, after all, and so kind, so gentle, so thoroughly professional, she hardly minded at all. She reminded herself that he'd seen more of her than her ankle when, two months before, he'd tended to the bullet wound in her shoulder.

'There.' He fastened the wrap with a metal clip and gently placed her foot on a low stool. 'You'll need to stay off it for a day or two, or possibly longer. But there has been no permanent damage.'

'You were fortunate, Caroline,' Ames said grimly.

'I know that,' she said, and her voice was not sharp, as it might have been, but low, subdued. 'You were right, Doctor, to say that I should not have gone. The errand was not truly necessary. I shall speak to the committee, to ask them to clarify the rules whereby we may be called upon. And I am sorry that I — spoke harshly to you.'

'Am I forgiven, then?' MacKenzie wanted to clasp her hand, but he did not quite dare.

'Yes. Completely.'

He felt an enormous sense of relief, as if a

heavy weight had been lifted from his heart. He was not to be banished from her good graces after all. And perhaps, someday . . .

She sat back, suddenly exhausted, accepting the cup of tea that Ames put into her hands. It was hot, reviving; she sipped it gratefully as she glanced around the familiar, welcoming room. How inexpressibly glad she was to be here, with these two men who cared for her — she took Ames's caring for granted; she'd come to appreciate MacKenzie's — safe from the terrors of the night, the dark, rain-swept streets.

Suddenly, although she was not cold, she shuddered.

'What is it?' said Ames.

'I was thinking of Agatha. And the girls at the Bower. Even if the police catch this man — '

'When,' he interjected. 'When they catch him.'

'Yes. When. But forever afterward, for a long time, the girls at the Bower will not be able to go out without the memory of — of Mary and Bridget.'

'But in time — ' MacKenzie began, looking for some way to banish her dark thoughts. But just then they heard the door knocker — loud, peremptory — and he broke off.

They heard Margaret going along the hall

to answer. They heard her startled exclamation, and then a man's voice, stern, demanding. Without waiting for Margaret to announce the caller, Ames strode to the closed pocket doors and slid them open.

'Desmond! What is it?'

Delahanty stared at each of them in turn, as if he were looking for someone. He'd been running; he was breathing hard, and his hair was disheveled and damp, long, straggling red locks falling over his high forehead.

'Is Garrett here?' he demanded.

And when they did not answer at once: 'For God's sake, Ames! Is he here or not?'

'He was,' Ames replied. 'But not now.'

'What do you mean, not now? Where is he?'

'We don't know,' Caroline said. 'He came — at your direction, he told me — but then he went away again.'

'Why?' barked Delahanty.

'We don't know that, either.'

Delahanty's thin shoulders slumped, and suddenly he looked defeated. He shook his head.

'What is it, Desmond?' Ames asked. He'd never seen his friend so distraught, and he was sincerely alarmed.

Delahanty took a deep breath. 'There has been another murder,' he said quietly.

There was a moment's shocked silence. Then: 'Oh, *no*,' breathed Caroline. For a moment, she was back in the dark streets of the South End, fleeing a faceless pursuer.

'The same?' Ames asked. But of course it was the same; Delahanty would not have come here to announce, say, the death of some roisterer down in Roxbury.

'Yes. I had word just now, down in Washington Street. The *Globe* has a line to the police. As I was leaving my office, their men were running out. When I asked them where they were going — it was almost as if I knew before they spoke — they told me that another girl has been killed over in the South End.'

Caroline tried to speak, but her throat was dry and she could not get out the words. At last: 'You mean, another of Agatha Montgomery's?'

'Yes. Another girl from Bertram's Bower.'

23

Two police wagons stood at the curb, the horses' breath rising in small columns in the raw night air. Several uniformed men stood guard along the sidewalk. For what? thought Ames as he stepped from the herdic-phaeton. The damage, once again, had been done, and once again the police were too late to prevent it.

Beyond the police line stood a crowd of restless men: journalists. Damnation! Some of them shouted at him, but he ignored them.

'There's Babcock, from the *Globe*,' muttered Delahanty at his elbow. 'And Hibbens, from the *Post* — watch out for him, he'll misquote you every time.'

'Comment, gentlemen?' shouted a journalist.

'Connected to the case?' shouted another.

'Related to the girl?'

'Give us a statement!'

A brief scuffle erupted as two of them tried — and failed — to break through the police barrier.

'Carrion crow,' muttered MacKenzie. He saw Crippen hurrying down the Bower's steps, followed by two plain-clothes-men.

Behind them, at the open door at the top, stood the forbidding figure of Matron Pratt.

' 'Evening, Inspector.'

'Ah! Mr. Ames.' Crippen came to an abrupt halt.

'There has been another murder,' Ames said.

Crippen allowed himself half a grin. 'That's right. But this time, we've got him dead to rights. He's down at headquarters now, being booked. We caught him red-handed.'

'Who?' Ames asked, dreading to hear the answer.

Crippen nodded in a self-satisfied way. 'Why, the fellow I've had in my sights all along, that's who. That Irish lad. Who else?'

'Impossible!' Delahanty blurted, pushing forward past MacKenzie. 'You cannot mean — ' He stopped as Ames put a warning hand on his arm.

Crippen turned his gaze to Delahanty, and now his face was grim. 'I cannot mean what, sir?'

'He is not your man,' Delahanty said.

'Oh? Is he not, indeed? I think otherwise, Mr. — ah — '

Hastily Ames introduced them, but Crippen had no time for social niceties. He had started to move toward his carriage, when Ames said, 'Who was the girl, Inspector? Do you know?'

'Oh, yes.' Crippen turned back, and again they saw that unsettling half-grin. 'We know. Her name was Peg Corcoran.'

Peg Corcoran. Who, MacKenzie had said, was Garrett O'Reilly's cousin.

Ames was glad of the dark, glad that Crippen could not see his face clearly. With a word to his companions, he stepped toward the little police inspector and walked with him to his waiting carriage.

'Inspector, I would ask you — my cousin Wainwright, as you know, does not want this case to blow up in our faces.'

'Blow up in our faces, Mr. Ames? How do you mean?'

'I mean, the Irish population of Boston is restless enough. The three girls who were murdered were Irish, and now you have arrested an Irish lad in their deaths. If it should happen that he is not in fact guilty — '

Crippen had been walking with his head slightly tilted toward Ames, as if he were listening carefully, but now he came to an abrupt halt and thrust out his chin in an antagonistic way.

'Mr. Ames, you surprise me.'

'How is that, Inspector?'

'Because you are an intelligent man. Even, if I may say so, a very clever man, which is something else entirely. Do you think I don't know what you're telling me? I need to be sure when I make an arrest in a case like this, and I can tell you right now I am very sure indeed.' He thrust his hand into his inside jacket pocket and took out something small that glittered in the dim light from the streetlamp.

'Have a look at this.' He gave it to Ames, adding, 'It's some kind of religious medal apparently — and you know how religious the Irish are. The girl had it clutched in her hand, like she grabbed it off him. It's almost like she was trying to identify him.'

Ames stopped under the light to look at it, and as he did so, something tugged at the edges of his memory. A small, glittering disc — where had he seen it?

'It is not a religious medal, Inspector.'

Crippen's face sagged with disappointment. 'It's not? What is it, then?'

'It is a coin — a very ancient one. If I am not mistaken, it is third or fourth century B.C. — the head of Medusa, an idealized version of the dread monster, Gorgo. The later Greeks rendered her as a beautiful young woman facing death, as she is here. Rather appropriate, wouldn't you say?'

He handed it back, and Crippen took it and slipped it back into his inside jacket pocket. 'Whatever you say, Mr. Ames. We'll get it all sorted out later.' It was obvious that he did not believe what Ames had told him.

Crippen's uniformed driver clucked to the horses to bring the carriage near. On the door, Ames could see the words BOSTON POLICE. With a curt 'good-night,' Crippen clambered up, and the driver ordered the horses to walk on. Ames stood at the curb, watching the vehicle move away until it disappeared into the darkness. The other police vans followed, and then the square was left with only a lone uniform patrolling. Already the journalists had begun to drift away.

'We must do something about that boy, Ames,' said Delahanty.

'Indeed we must,' Ames replied. 'And quickly. Once Crippen learns that the murdered girl, this time, was Garrett's cousin — '

'What!' exclaimed Delahanty. 'His cousin? Are you sure?'

'Fairly. He told Caroline that, at any rate.' Ames thought for a moment. 'I am going to speak briefly to Miss Montgomery, if she will see me. And I will ask you, Desmond, to run an errand for me, if you will.'

In a moment more, he had given Delahanty his instructions, and the Irishman set off at a fast clip.

Then Ames turned to glance up at Bertram's Bower. The place was brightly illuminated, every window ablaze behind drawn shades.

'They must be terrified, poor things,' said MacKenzie as he saw the shadow of a female form.

'Undoubtedly,' Ames replied. 'And Miss Montgomery may be indisposed — I would not be surprised if she were — but let us just see for ourselves.'

As they ascended the steps, he thought of Caroline. She was alone at Louisburg Square. He had warned her to admit no one, and he assumed that she had the good sense for once to obey him. And if the house was locked and secure, with the faithful Margaret there, then Caroline would be safe until he returned.

'Yes?'

It was Matron Pratt herself, thinking, no doubt, that the police had returned.

'Good evening, Matron. I wonder if we could impose briefly upon Miss Montgomery.'

She started to snap a refusal, but then, to their surprise, she thought better of it and stepped back to admit them. Inside, in the dim light of the hall gas jets, they saw that her face, ordinarily so hostile and belligerent, was sunk into what looked like despair.

'In her room at the back,' she said dully, not meeting their eyes. Before they could say anything more, she had disappeared into the office.

Agatha Montgomery sat with two of the Bower's girls. Side by side on the sofa, they were crying — loudly sobbing, their faces red and wet with tears. Across from them, Miss Montgomery sat with her hands folded in her lap. She was leaning toward them as if she had been speaking to them, but as Ames and MacKenzie knocked and entered, she looked up. Her expression was calm, her eyes clear.

'Miss Montgomery,' Ames began, 'we do not mean to trouble you — '

'It is no trouble, Mr. Ames.' She inclined her head toward the two girls. 'They were just leaving.' And when they did not move, she said in a sharper tone, 'All right, girls. Go on, now.'

After they had gone, she sat back in her chair and closed her eyes. She was pale but composed. She looked like a woman of a certain age who had had a tiring day, but nothing more than that.

Ames cleared his throat. She opened her eyes and looked up at him. 'Mr. Ames,' she said flatly.

'I wanted first to extend my sympathy — '

She stopped him with a wave of her hand.

401

'Do you know where I went this afternoon? I went to the Women's Industrial Union. They have invited us to join their sewing cooperative. We will be able to make some money, they tell me, and so we will not need to depend so heavily on charity. That should improve our fortunes, do you not think?' She smiled a small, bitter smile.

It seemed odd, thought MacKenzie, for her to be speaking of sewing cooperatives and charity, when the Bower had just suffered another hideous crime against one of its own. Perhaps she was still in such shock that she could not face the truth of what had happened.

Ames glanced at the doctor, quirked an eyebrow, and tried again.

'I am very sorry to trouble you at this time, but — ' He seated himself on the sofa opposite her. MacKenzie cautiously took a chair nearer the door.

'But I understand the police have spoken to you just now,' Ames went on.

She came back from someplace far away. 'Yes?'

He saw that she had not grasped what he'd said, and so he repeated it.

'Oh — the police,' she said. 'Yes, I have seen them. Such a tiresome little man, isn't he? That inspector, whatever his name is.'

'Crippen.'

She nodded vaguely.

Ames gritted his teeth. He desperately needed this woman's help, but she seemed in no condition to give it.

'They have made an arrest, but I believe they have the wrong man. Or boy, rather.'

She frowned at him, puzzled, but she did not reply.

'Miss Montgomery, they have arrested Garrett O'Reilly for that girl's death tonight. And I have no doubt that Crippen will find a way to charge him with the murders of Mary Flaherty and Bridget Brown as well.'

She shook her head, but she did not reply.

'Miss Montgomery? Are you listening?' Ames hunched forward on the sofa, fixing her in his dark gaze. For a moment, she struggled to come to grips with what he was saying; then, as her eyes met his, some spark of his own energy, his own determination, seemed to leap from him to her, and she snapped to.

'Yes, Mr. Ames. I am listening.' She folded her hands in her lap like a dutiful pupil.

'They have arrested the wrong person.'

'Yes, I believe they have,' she replied.

'You believe Garrett is innocent?' he asked sharply.

'Yes, I do.'

'Did you tell Inspector Crippen so?'

She faded again; she shook her head and began to twist her hands in her lap — that restless, obsessive habit of hers, profoundly unsettling to see.

'Did you?' Ames persisted.

'No.'

'But why not? It is very important that you, his employer, vouch for him to the police. They intend to convict him — and he is innocent, I am sure of it.'

She came back a little. 'Yes,' she said, nodding. 'I believe that too.'

'Well, then. You must say so — and as forcefully as you can. May I send word to Inspector Crippen that you will go down to police headquarters?'

'Oh, I couldn't do that!'

He leaned toward her and seized her hands. She started and tried to pull away, but she could not.

'Miss Montgomery, listen to me. Yes — listen! A young man who is probably innocent has been arrested for the murder of three of the Bower's girls. He is poor, illiterate, the sole support of his family. He will be put on trial for his life, and public sentiment being what it is, he will very likely be convicted. If he is convicted, he will very likely be hanged. You said just now that you

404

do not believe he is guilty. Why? Why did you say that, Miss Montgomery? Do you have some suspicion about who is?'

She stared at him. Her mouth worked, but no words came. She blinked several times, as if she were trying to order her thoughts.

Then she began to laugh. It was a horrible sound, harsh and cackling, that made the hair rise on the back of Ames's neck.

He had let go of her hands, and now he rose and stood over her. He glanced at MacKenzie, hoping perhaps for some helpful word. 'Doctor — ?' he began, but before he could say more, the door flew open and Matron Pratt rushed in.

'There!' she snapped at Ames with some of her former vituperousness. 'You see what you've done!'

She bent over Miss Montgomery, put her arms around her, and tenderly embraced her. 'There,' she said again, but softly now, almost singing, in the tone used to soothe a troubled child.

Miss Montgomery went on laughing for a moment, but then her laughter changed to deep, wrenching sobs that from someone else would have been heartbreaking. From this woman, MacKenzie thought, they were faintly revolting.

But he was amazed at Matron Pratt, who

apparently had some human feeling after all. He found that notion oddly reassuring.

Suddenly Matron Pratt reverted to form. Still shielding Miss Montgomery with one arm, she straightened and half turned to the two men. 'Go away!' she snapped. 'She's in no condition to speak to you!'

Since this was so obviously true, they left. As MacKenzie glanced back, he saw that Matron Pratt had both arms around Miss Montgomery and was bending over her, embracing her, crooning softly to her. He shook his head. Amazing, to see such tenderness from that dragon.

It had begun to rain again. As they went down the steps, the uniformed patrolman was just passing; he nodded to them and touched the brim of his helmet.

'All quiet, Officer?' Ames asked.

'Yes, sir.'

They watched him as he walked on. The square was dark, deserted.

'Come along, Doctor,' Ames said. 'We've work to do.'

24

'There he is,' muttered Ames. 'On Martin Sweeney's personal assurance, he's the best cracksman in the business.'

They had come to a corner a few blocks from the Bower. Briefly, MacKenzie had been disoriented, but now, as he peered through the darkness and rain, across the stretch of wet, glistening cobblestones, he saw that they stood across the street from the Reverend Montgomery's rectory.

'He' was a short, stubby man in a tweed cap and shapeless jacket. He stood a little away from the streetlamp, so that they could not see his face clearly, but obviously he recognized Ames, for he approached them now as they crossed. MacKenzie noted that he carried a dark lantern, unlit. Without a word of greeting he put out his hand, and Ames shook it briefly.

Then Ames led the way to an alley halfway down the block, and they went along the high wooden fence until they came to the gate behind the church property. Ames pushed it open. They were in a small garden whose stone benches and lone marble statue were evidence that someone — the Reverend Montgomery? some of his female parishioners? — cared for it more than for the bleak, inhospitable rectory itself.

In a moment more they were at the rectory's basement door. MacKenzie waited, holding the dark lantern, while Ames went down the small flight of stone steps with their companion. After a moment, there was the sound of metal scraping on metal. To MacKenzie's ears, acutely attuned to the danger of their situation, it sounded very loud. Hurry, he thought, or Garrett O'Reilly will not be the only one arrested this night.

After what seemed an endless time but was probably no more than thirty seconds or so, Sweeney's cracksman gave a small grunt of satisfaction, and MacKenzie heard the door creak open.

There was a moment's pause during which Ames, after a muttered word or two, slipped a folded banknote to their silent companion. Then the cracksman, without a word, came up the steps, slipped past MacKenzie, and disappeared through the gate, carefully and silently closing it behind him.

'Well, Doctor,' said Ames quietly, 'shall we proceed?'

As well be hung for a sheep as a lamb,

MacKenzie thought as he slipped into the darkened rectory.

'Here,' muttered Ames. 'Hold the lantern.' He struck a match, and the lantern's dim light blossomed in the gloom.

They were in a back passageway. Doors led off it, all closed. Ames tried one and then another until he found the way to the rectory's kitchen. 'Come,' he said softly — although why he troubled to lower his voice, MacKenzie did not know. Either they were alone in the house, in which case Ames could speak in a normal tone, or they were not, in which case they would inevitably be discovered.

MacKenzie held the lantern high while Ames prowled the room. He stopped by a large butcher's block, above which hung a rack of knives. He pulled them out one by one, examined them closely, and then, shrugging, moved on. He opened a cabinet door and peered at its contents: bottles and jars of various sizes, some labeled — SODA, CINNAMON, SALT — some not.

'The reverend suffers from toothache apparently,' Ames murmured, turning away. Glancing in, MacKenzie saw a bottle labeled CHLOROFORM. It was not significant; half the households in America had chloroform on hand.

With a final glance around the shadowy room, Ames motioned for MacKenzie to follow him out into the passageway once more and up a flight of stairs that led to the first-floor hall.

'Now,' said Ames. 'Just bring the lantern over here, Doctor, if you will.' He stepped to a place by the wall, toward the front door, and, crouching, struck a match. Holding it close to the wall, he peered intently at the heavy, dark, leathery paper. When the match had burned down to his fingers, he dropped it into his pocket and lit another, and then another.

'What is it?' asked MacKenzie. His knee was hurting, and although the rectory was nearly as cold as the streets, sweat trickled uncomfortably down his face and neck.

'Or what is it not?' Ames replied. 'Set the lantern down, Doctor, and — here — light matches for me.'

Ames was on his hands and knees now, his face only a few inches from the red-and-black tile floor where it met the wall.

After MacKenzie had lighted four matches, Ames got to his feet.

'Enough,' he said. Taking back the matchbox and picking up the lantern, he led the way upstairs. As MacKenzie followed, his feeling of unease grew with every step, until by the time they had reached the second-floor hall, he was as nervous as a cat in a dog pound. Ames must have believed that they had enough time to make their break-and-entry exploration, or he would not have attempted it; nevertheless, MacKenzie liked to think of himself as a law-abiding man, and this exercise unnerved him. Well-connected though Ames might be to the police and the other power centers of the city, MacKenzie knew that their presence here, if it were discovered, would not be looked upon as anything but criminal.

Ames opened the door to the front bedroom. Like every other room they'd seen in the rectory, this was a bare, dreary chamber with little attempt at adornment or decoration. A sagging bed in an iron bed-frame stood against one wall, a tall chiffonier against another. The blinds and curtains at the front windows were drawn shut, but a dim light from the streetlamp outside shone around the edges.

Handing the lantern to the doctor, Ames went to a door and opened it: the reverend's clothes closet. Rapidly he rummaged among the frock coats and trousers hanging there; after a moment, he turned away. He opened the drawers of the chiffonier, riffled through the contents, and shut them. Nothing.

In the hall once more, Ames turned toward the rear, where, opening a door, he saw not a closet but a flight of stairs leading up.

'Now we may find something of interest,' he said, starting up ahead of MacKenzie. The steps were narrow and high-risered; once, MacKenzie stumbled and nearly dropped the lantern.

At the top was a door — locked. There was no landing, so MacKenzie waited behind on the stairs while Ames took from his trouser pocket a small ring of skeleton keys.

'Fortunately I persuaded Sweeney's man to lend these to me for the night,' he said. 'Now the question is, can I get one of them to work?'

Carefully he inserted one key into the lock, fiddled with it with no success, took it out and tried another, and another. At last, with a small exclamation of triumph, he turned the lock, turned the knob, and pushed open the door.

They were in a large room, richly furnished — how richly they could not at first discern in the dim light of the dark lantern. After making sure that no light would show from the heavily curtained windows, Ames turned the gas jets on the wall sconces by the fireplace, and with the turning rod illuminated the large chandelier in the center of the room.

MacKenzie caught his breath. Richly furnished indeed — an exquisite Turkish carpet woven in shades of red and topaz and indigo; velvet and brocade furniture in the latest, most ornate styles, including a fringed ottoman and a sofa with a high, carved rosewood back; marble-topped ebony tables; lamps with multicolored glass shades in the fashionable Tiffany style.

A tiled fireplace took up much of the wall opposite the windows, while on the other two hung a number of paintings framed in heavy carved and gilded wood. A large table in the center of the room held several books bound in fine tooled leather.

Ames, muttering under his breath, had been prowling the room, but now he stopped before a table on which was propped a small painting.

'Look at this!' he exclaimed.

MacKenzie looked. It was an antique-looking scene of dainty, half-clad maidens cavorting in a misty wood.

'What is it?' he said.

'The Watteau,' Ames replied. 'Do you remember, just — what was it? — three nights ago, when Caroline had her dinner party for that rapscallion Englishman? He spoke of an art auction in New York. He was beat out by a Boston man, he said, whose name he never learned. I could give it to him now, sure enough. There hasn't been time to find a place to hang it, I assume.'

Ames moved to a bookshelf beside the fireplace. 'Doctor, look here.' He pulled out a large volume and carried it to the center table. 'This is the Bower's account book for the last year. I have seen its twin at the Bower's office.'

He opened it and began rapidly to scan its closely written pages. 'Yes — here — and, yes — why, the man has no shame. None at all.'

MacKenzie stepped to his side. He saw columns of names with sums of money entered next to them. Quite large sums of money, and many names.

'Look at the last month of the year,' Ames said. 'For December — the total receipts are listed as — ah — one thousand four hundred and seventy-five dollars. But I distinctly remember that in the account book at the Bower, the receipts for December were only three hundred and something. And the expenditure column in that book matched the receipts exactly, whereas here, there are no expenditures listed at all. Only the intake.'

'One wonders why the man bothered to record it,' MacKenzie said.

'This,' said Ames, stabbing at the page with his forefinger, 'this is the real amount that the reverend has brought in for the Bower. The one at the office is false. And it is from these sums — these moneys given by the good people of Boston — that the reverend affords all this.' His angry gaze swept around the room. 'The man is a thief for certain. And far worse than that, if I am not mistaken,' he added grimly.

He returned the account book to its place and moved to a small rolltop desk. Pushing up the slatted lid, he plucked from among the littered papers there a small manual.

'If I am not mistaken, the reverend used this to compose his coded notes to Mary Flaherty. I wonder if he might have a sample.'

He rummaged among the papers — bills from Brooks Brothers, from Locke-Ober's restaurant, from a wine merchant in Brookline — without success. No matter. The manual was evidence enough.

'I wonder — ' he began, but MacKenzie never learned what Ames planned to say next, for at that moment they heard, from below, the sound of the front door slamming. The reverberation carried up through the house.

For a fraction of a second their eyes met. Then Ames darted to the gas jets, turned down the lights by the mantel, and reached with the rod to extinguish the chandelier.

In the near darkness, illuminated only by

the dark lantern, they listened. They heard a heavy footfall — surely the reverend's — upon the stairs leading to the second floor.

MacKenzie's heart hammered painfully in his chest, and his mouth was dry. They were caught in a trap of their own making, and if Ames could not bluff their way out — but what possible excuse could he give for their being here, having broken into the place, in stealth, by night, if not to burgle then at the very least to pry?

The reverend's footsteps had not stopped at the second floor. Now they were on the stairs leading to this room, and now MacKenzie could hear the reverend's voice, and the soft sound of laughter — female laughter — in reply.

Ames had closed the door when they came in. They heard the reverend insert a key into the lock, turn it, and turn the doorknob to push open the door. But the reverend had not unlocked but locked the door, and he cursed softly now, with a querulous tone to his voice.

The key turned in the lock again, and with a horrid fascination, MacKenzie watched as the door opened.

★　★　★

416

'Thank you, Margaret,' Caroline said as the maid came in to fetch her supper tray. She leaned back in her chair, comfortably nourished on beef tea and scrambled eggs, ready to pick up a Diana Strangeways until her menfolk returned.

'I'll be leaving soon, miss,' Margaret said.

'Yes, of course. Go ahead.'

As the maid went out, Caroline heard the grandmother clock in the hall strike the hour: eight o'clock. Surely, Addington and Dr. MacKenzie would be home soon.

Rain spattered on the lavender-glass windows, shuttered now against the dark, and the sea-coal fire murmured soothingly in the grate. Her ankle hurt a bit, but not as much as before. She wouldn't try to walk down the hill to church tomorrow, however; she'd rest at home. She was safe here, she knew that, and yet —

She thought of them now, with Mr. Delahanty, returning to the South End, those dark, dangerous streets where another girl had been caught and killed. Oh, poor Agatha! However would she recover from this dreadful time?

Poor you, she corrected herself. If it had not been the Reverend Montgomery who came upon you . . . if it had been that homicidal lunatic —

Stop it. Addington would deal with it; she could do nothing more. Resolutely forcing her thoughts away from the scene at the Bower, she opened her book.

A short while later, she heard the front door knocker, and she looked up in alarm. Who had come? Not Addington and the doctor, safely home at last, for they had a key. Someone else, then, who might bring bad news, fresh news of disaster —

She heard Margaret going to answer. She strained to hear the caller's voice, but the pocket doors were closed and she could hear nothing.

The doors slid open, but instead of Margaret, it was someone else who came into the room. She was breathing hard, and her eyes were wide — with fear? What had happened? Her cloak and bonnet, wet from the rain, dripped onto the carpet.

Caroline spoke first. 'I can't get up, Agatha. I twisted my ankle, and I — '

'There has been another death,' Miss Montgomery said abruptly.

Caroline saw Margaret hovering behind. Their eyes met, and Margaret was nodding even before Caroline could ask her to bring the universal prescription for all crises — which this obviously was — a tray of tea and cakes. Somehow, Margaret would manage to produce it before she left. She took a step back into the hall and pulled shut the doors, leaving Caroline and her friend alone.

'Yes. I know,' Caroline said to Miss Montgomery.

'You do?' For a moment, Miss Montgomery looked puzzled, but then she went on. 'It was another one of our girls.'

'I know that too. Agatha, do come and sit down. Take off your things — why, you are soaked! Just put them on that chair.'

Caroline thought of the damage her friend's dripping cloak would do to the already well-worn brocade — the dye would run, she just knew it — but this was no time, she chided herself, to be house-proud. Agatha was clearly in a state, and the important thing was to help her through it.

Miss Montgomery did not move at first. Then, as if at last she understood what Caroline had said, she unfastened her cape and let it fall to the floor. Slowly, as if she moved in a dream, she untied the strings of her bonnet, took it off, and dropped it onto the cloak.

'That's right,' Caroline said soothingly. 'Now come and sit down.'

Still moving slowly, one cautious step at a time, Miss Montgomery approached. With

419

great care, as if every bone in her bony frame hurt her, she lowered herself onto the sofa opposite Caroline.

'How did you know?' she asked dully.

'Mr. Delahanty came to tell us. He has his office down in Newspaper Row, and he had word when the reporters were alerted. Agatha, I really do think — '

'Her name was Peg Corcoran,' Miss Montgomery said, still in that flat, deadened voice that Caroline found quite alarming.

'Peg — Oh, no!'

This seemed to jolt Miss Montgomery. 'You knew her?'

'She was — yes, she was in my embroidery class, but worse than that — Agatha, I don't imagine you knew it, but she was Garrett O'Reilly's cousin.'

Miss Montgomery absorbed this in silence, her eyes darting back and forth as if she were trying to adjust her obviously erratic thoughts.

'His cousin?' she said slowly.

'Yes. He didn't want it known, but — '

'They have arrested him.'

'Arrested him? Garrett? But that is wrong!'

'They said they caught him red-handed.'

'But that is monstrous!' In her agitation, Caroline had shifted slightly in her chair, and she winced at the pain in her ankle. Then she rushed on. 'Agatha, I must tell you, Garrett was here earlier. Inspector Crippen interrogated him. He — Garrett — was badly frightened. Mr. Delahanty had told him to come to Addington if he needed help.'

'Is he here?' Miss Montgomery demanded.

'Who? Addington? No. Did you want to speak with him? I'm sure he'll be back soon.'

They heard a soft rapping at the pocket doors, and in the next moment Margaret came in bearing the tea tray, which she set on the low table beside Caroline's chair.

'I'll be off now, miss,' she said. 'Cook's on her way too. She says the gentlemen's dinner is in the warming oven.'

'Yes, yes, go on, Margaret. And remember me to your sister.'

Miss Montgomery did not appear to notice the interruption. She stared at Caroline, blinking, her mouth working, her uncorseted body under her drab black dress as rigid as if she suffered rigor mortis.

Caroline glanced at the tea tray. Margaret had had the sense to supply a plate of sandwiches, thick and meaty. Agatha probably hadn't eaten any dinner. A nourishing cold roast sandwich would do her good, and several cups of steaming Darjeeling, and a piece of lemon pound cake.

'Agatha, you must eat something. And then

when Addington gets back, we'll sort this out. I simply don't believe that Garrett is capable — '

She had lifted the plate of sandwiches, and now she held it out to her friend. Miss Montgomery ignored it.

'Agatha, please. You must keep your strength up.'

'You are right, Caroline.' Agatha wasn't talking about the food, Caroline realized. 'Garrett didn't kill that girl tonight — or the others.'

'No, of course he didn't,' Caroline replied. The plate seemed very heavy, and so after a moment, she put it back on the tray. 'So in that case — ' She didn't know how to continue. In that case, what? Or, more to the point, who?

'Do you know what that policeman told me?' Miss Montgomery asked.

'No.' Caroline cringed a little as Miss Montgomery's pale, intense eyes fixed on her own. Of course, Agatha was always very intense, very driven, but just now she looked —

'He told me they found something clutched in Peg's hand. He said it was a religious medal of some kind, but it wasn't that.'

Not a religious medal. Caroline's thoughts

raced. She saw something small and round, glittering on her dining room carpet. She saw Agatha, bending down to pick it up.

Suddenly she felt ill, and the feeling had nothing to do with her injured ankle.

'Agatha — '

'Yes.' Miss Montgomery nodded, as if satisfied that Caroline had understood. 'It was Randolph's watch fob. If you remember, I told you I would return it to him, after he dropped it' — she looked around with a vaguely baffled expression, as if she had only just realized where she was — 'at your dinner.'

Caroline swallowed hard, but the lump in her throat did not go away. Earlier that night, she had thought she was being pursued by the Bower killer. *Had she been?*

'When the police realize what it is,' Miss Montgomery went on, 'they will trace it to him. He will say he lost it, of course. As he did.'

'Agatha — '

Suddenly Miss Montgomery's face convulsed into a rictus of hate. 'I didn't know,' she gasped.

'Know what, Agatha?' Caroline's voice sounded odd in her ears, tinny and faint.

'That he planned to marry that woman in New York. He never told me. If it hadn't been mentioned the other night, I might not know about it even now.'

'Agatha, about his watch fob — did you give it back to him?'

'That is what I will tell the police.' Miss Montgomery nodded again, as if she had settled something in her mind. 'Not that I had it, but that he told me he'd lost it and then that he found it again.'

'But — '

'The only person who knows I had it is you, Caroline.'

Caroline tried to speak, but for a moment her voice wouldn't come. She tried again. 'You did return it to him?'

'No.'

The word hung in the air between them, echoing over and over again: Nonono.

25

At the rectory, the tall, bulky form of the Reverend Randolph Montgomery came into the third floor room, followed by a female.

'What the — ' Montgomery's hand went to his coat pocket as if he reached for a weapon, but no weapon was forthcoming. Instead, he called: 'Who's there? Who is it?'

'Good evening, Reverend,' Ames replied with what MacKenzie thought was admirable calm. He reached up and turned on the gas in the lamps over the mantel. In the sudden, harsh illumination, MacKenzie saw that the female who had accompanied the reverend was young, tastelessly overdressed, and certainly no lady.

For a moment Montgomery did not reply; he stared, open-mouthed, as if Ames were an apparition.

Then: 'What the devil — Ames?'

'I am afraid so, Reverend.'

'But — what are you doing here? How did you get in?'

'I hired a cracksman.'

The reverend had gone pale, but now a flush mounted to his cheeks, and his

425

hands clenched and unclenched at his sides. MacKenzie remembered his previous burst of temper — his sudden, alarming loss of control.

Montgomery took the female by the arm and shoved her toward the door. 'Get downstairs,' he said brusquely.

With a frightened whimper, she obeyed. He shut the door behind her.

'Now,' he said heavily, turning back to Ames. 'Explain yourself, if you can.'

Ames waited for a moment, as if he were trying to gauge the extent of the reverend's anger.

'Another girl from the Bower has been murdered,' he began.

The reverend started at that; he blinked several times and ran his tongue over his lips.

'You didn't know?' Ames asked.

'No.'

'I don't believe you.'

'What do you mean, you don't believe me? Why should I know that?'

'Because I believe you killed her.'

Montgomery did not reply at once. His mouth opened and shut, his eyes darted back and forth as if he sought escape — and yet he stood still, rooted to the spot. As if, MacKenzie thought, all his strength had been suddenly drained away, rendering him immobile.

Then at last he said, 'You have taken leave of your senses, Ames.'

'I think not. I am merely trying to prevent a miscarriage of justice. The police have arrested one of your candidates in the case — '

'My candidate?'

'Yes. The Irish lad, Garrett O'Reilly.'

'Well, then, the case is settled, is it not?'

'Hardly.' Ames put out a warning hand. 'Before you say anything more, Reverend, I should tell you that the police found an incriminating piece of evidence on the girl who died tonight. They believe that it was a religious medal of some kind, but I told them they were wrong. It was a gold coin of the Hellenistic period, a very fine Medusa head.'

Montgomery seemed to crumple. He remained standing, but he visibly withered, as if he had had some devastating emotional blow.

'That was your coin, Reverend, was it not?' Ames said quietly.

Montgomery put out his hand, still in its glove, and like a blind man feeling his way, moved into the room until he came to a tall-backed, brocade Queen Anne chair. For a moment, he gripped its back; then he came around and, with a groan, lowered himself onto the seat. He sat slumped, one hand covering his eyes. Ames shot a glance at MacKenzie as if to say, Be ready in case he begins to rage again.

But the reverend did not rage. He sat for a moment more, the picture of miserable dejection; then slowly, deliberately, he began to remove his gloves. They were very fine gloves, MacKenzie noted: soft black kid, looking brand new. He thought of the account book with its record of generous donations, and his mouth twisted in revulsion. Did Agatha Montgomery know of her brother's thievery? Did she know and yet allow him to cheat her so that on the meager funds that remained after he'd taken his lion's share, she could continue to pursue her life's work?

'Brandy,' said the reverend hoarsely. 'In the cupboard.'

Ames nodded to MacKenzie, who went to the sideboard, where he found a half-full bottle of Courvoisier. Pour for one or for all of us? he wondered. All of us, definitely. This night is only just beginning, and we all have a long way to go.

He gave snifters to Ames and the reverend and took his own. His knee was acting up very badly, and he wondered if Ames would mind if he sat. Easing himself onto a chair across from the reverend, he glanced at Ames, but Ames paid him no mind. All his attention was on Montgomery, who, now that he had taken a few restorative sips, seemed more like himself.

'A Medusa head,' he said to Ames.

'Yes.'

The reverend fiddled at his coat buttons and drew back the garment's edges to reveal his watch chain stretched across his middle. 'I had such a coin on this chain,' he said slowly.

'I know you did. I saw it.'

'But at some point in the last few days, I lost it.'

Ames regarded him, disbelief plain on his face.

'Damn you!' The reverend had regained his strength, and now he set down his glass and leaned forward in his chair, glaring at Ames. 'Yes — I lost it. It dropped off, I don't know where. I looked all over this place, I looked in the church, and at Agatha's. Finally, I decided it must have fallen off in the street, and I gave up trying to find it.'

'Or possibly you lost it when Peg Corcoran was trying to fend you off,' Ames said.

'No!' thundered the reverend, in full-throated voice once more. 'God damn you for the meddling, interfering bounder that you are, Ames!'

Meddling and interfering, possibly, thought MacKenzie, but bounder? No.

'What are you trying to do, man?' the reverend demanded. 'Destroy me? Why?'

Ames glanced toward the bookcase. 'Not that, Reverend, but I am trying to save an innocent lad from the gallows. I came here tonight — yes, we broke in, I admit it, and you are free to report me to the authorities — to look for evidence against you in the death of the Bower's girls. As I was examining this room, I came upon a set of account books that record the sums you have collected for the Bower. More, I might add, than is shown in the book for the same year in the Bower's office.'

The reverend gave a short laugh. 'The books here will be destroyed this night, Ames, and where will you find your proof then?'

'By interrogating every person in the city who has ever given a penny to you,' Ames said. 'And I promise you, Reverend, I will do that if I must.'

'A lengthy task,' the reverend replied. 'You will be lucky to finish — '

'Before you hang,' Ames said flatly.

Only a faint tremor around Montgomery's eyes betrayed any reaction to this. 'Before I hang?' he replied. 'Before *I* hang? Ye gods, man, you most certainly have taken leave of

430

your senses! You come here and accuse me — '

'There is blood on the wallpaper downstairs,' Ames said. 'And the floor tiles have been freshly scrubbed — but not enough. You missed a place next to the wainscoting.'

A sound like a low growl came from the reverend. MacKenzie set down his glass and prepared to rise, ready to spring to Ames's aid when Montgomery exploded.

But Montgomery did not explode. He sat tensed in his chair, that eerie, inhuman sound issuing from his throat, staring at Ames as if by his mere look, he could cause Ames to disappear.

'You seduced Mary,' Ames said.

The growling grew louder.

'And, having come upon a rich widow willing to marry you, you could not afford to have Mary inconveniently in the way,' Ames went on.

'No!' And now the reverend did explode. He sprang to his feet and faced Ames for a moment, glaring at him. Then with an oath he whirled, as if he were about to run down the stairs. But they could not lead him to safety, not while Ames lived.

He began to pace. Like an animal, MacKenzie thought: growling, every nerve alive with tension, ready to spring, ready to attack . . .

At last he came to a stop in front of the fireplace and put his hand on the mantel as if to steady himself.

'This is the hardest thing I have ever done,' he said. His tone had changed once more, as if, now, he were speaking to himself.

He paused, shaking his head as he peered at Ames. 'She betrayed me,' he said.

'Who did? Mary? Under the circumstances — '

'No, no. Not Mary. Agatha.'

Through the heavy draperies they heard the bell in the church next door begin to toll the hour: eight o'clock.

Ames waited until the tolling stopped. Then: 'How did she do that, Reverend?'

'She knew Mary was pregnant. She was unable to deal with that fact. Apparently, Mary not only told Agatha about her condition, she named me as the man responsible.'

'And were you?'

The reverend's hand tightened on the mantel as if he were afraid he would collapse, but his gaze did not falter.

'Yes.'

'I see.'

'No. You cannot possibly see.' Montgomery

shook his head violently, as if he would shake all his bad memories away. 'Agatha is so very . . . involved with the Bower. It is all she has — all she needs. She is not afflicted, as I am, with a taste for — ' His eyes swept the room. 'For all this. I cannot help it, Mr. Ames. I cannot live, as she does, a life deprived of beauty. Of beauty in all its forms — fine paintings, objets d'art, elegant clothes. Agatha can wear the same dress day in, day out, and never notice. She can live in one bare room at the Bower and never really see it, much less hate it. But I — I am different, you see.'

Let us get to the point, MacKenzie thought; we are not your congregation, to be swayed by your eloquence.

'And Mary was a very pretty girl,' Montgomery went on. 'Very pretty indeed. When she came to us, she was quite ill. We — Agatha, I mean — brought her back to health. And then one day, in the late summer, I went to the Bower on some business or other, and it was as if I were seeing her for the first time. She put herself in my way, of course. She wanted me to notice her, and I did. I did . . . '

He trailed off.

Ames glanced at MacKenzie, and a wordless message passed between them: Say nothing, no matter how long he rambles on, say nothing to distract him from what he will tell us in the end.

'She was not an innocent,' Montgomery said. 'Oh, no. Far from it. But you know what they are, those girls at the Bower. Their innocence has been destroyed long before Agatha takes them in. It can never be restored, never repaired. But the odd thing is — Mary *looked* innocent. She had that fresh-faced, girlish appearance, as if she'd never known a man in her life. And when she — when she put herself in my way, I thought, why not? It was not as if I were deflowering her, after all. She'd made her living on the streets before she came to Agatha's, and she knew a few tricks too, I don't mind telling you.'

Suddenly, horribly, he leered at them.

'So I took her,' he said. 'Why not? She was a . . . reward, of a kind, for all my years of devotion to the Bower.'

Ames thought of what Serena Vincent had told him, he thought of what Dr. Hannah had told Caroline, but he gritted his teeth and stayed silent.

'Yes,' Montgomery said. 'A reward. It never occurred to me that she would let herself become pregnant. They have ways, don't they, those girls on the streets, of preventing it? Sinful as they are, what is one more little sin like that — interfering with Nature? I thought Mary would do the same. It never occurred to me that she had another agenda entirely.'

'Which was marriage,' Ames said.

Montgomery grimaced. 'Yes,' he said. 'The slut wanted to marry me. Can you imagine? I would as soon marry that old battle-ax Carry Nation.'

'And Miss Montgomery knew all this?'

'Eventually — I suppose inevitably — yes.'

'Even the coded notes?'

'Mary must have told her about those. Certainly I never did.'

'Why do you say that your sister betrayed you, Reverend?'

'Because — ' Montgomery paused, wiped his hand down over his face, and took a deep breath. 'The Medusa head,' he said simply.

'I don't follow.'

'Damn it, man! Don't you see? I didn't kill that girl tonight! And when it becomes necessary, as it undoubtedly will, for me to account for my time, I will do so, no matter the embarrassment. Yes — I was at the Black Sea just now. I admit it. I often take dinner there. Then I find a girl and bring her back here for the evening. The atmosphere is somewhat better here than there.' He thought for a moment. 'I was on my way there tonight, when I came upon your sister. It was most foolhardy of her to be out alone after dark, particularly in this district. She began to run away from me. She must have feared that I was about to attack her. She tripped and fell. Fortunately for her I am not the Bower killer, or I would have had an easy victim. She refused to allow me to accompany her home, but at least I was able to help her into a herdic. She has told you about it? Yes. After that, I went to the Black Sea.'

'And the conference in Cambridge?' Ames asked.

'I planned to join them tomorrow. To be frank, two days in the company of my fellow ministers is more than I can endure.'

He peered at Ames, squinting a little, as if his vision had suddenly clouded.

'So you see, Mr. Ames, I did not kill that girl tonight. I lost the coin a few days ago. Someone found it and planted it on the girl's body — someone who knew it was mine, someone who wanted to implicate me in her death.'

Ames waited. Then, when Montgomery did not continue, he said, 'Your sister?'

'Yes.' The reverend's eyes were blank, his voice — his fine preacher's voice — hollow.

'It was my impression that Miss Montgomery is devoted to you. Why would she try to implicate you in a murder?'

Montgomery gave a short, harsh laugh. 'You do not know Agatha very well, Mr. Ames. She is — was, I should say — exceptionally devoted to me, yes. Or she always has been, until — what was it? Three days ago? When one of your guests spoke out of turn, and tactlessly brought up the subject of my impending marriage to Mrs. Wilson.'

'The wealthy widow in New York.'

'Yes.'

'Miss Montgomery had not known of your plans?'

'No. I had intended to tell her, of course, but not so soon. I suppose she felt . . . betrayed, in some sense. Abandoned, perhaps.'

'It hardly seems sufficient reason — '

'As I said, Mr. Ames, you do not know Agatha. I suppose she saw the collapse of all her life's work if I should cease my efforts in her behalf. My so very successful' — he swept his hand to encompass the room — 'financial efforts.'

She saw something more even than that, MacKenzie thought. She loved you for more than your fund-raising, Reverend. Did you know that? Do you know it now?

'And so she took her revenge by making it

look as if you killed Peg Corcoran tonight,'
Ames said.

'Was that her name? I can't place her. But,
yes, it was Agatha — it must have been
— taking her revenge on me. For my sins,' he
added sarcastically.

'And the other girls?' Ames said quietly.
'Mary? Bridget?'

Montgomery took a deep breath. 'I knew
nothing of how Mary met her death until the
next evening, when the girl who roomed with
her — Bridget Brown — came hammering at
my door. She had known, apparently, of
Mary's condition — and of my part in it. She
was overcome with grief, with anger. She
came to accuse me, to threaten to expose me
to the authorities. But she hardly had time to
say more than a few words, when Agatha
came.' He paused, remembering. 'We were
standing in the front hall. Agatha came
rushing in. Before I realized what she meant
to do, she had attacked the girl.' He spoke as
if he were reciting a dream, thought
MacKenzie. A nightmare.

'I must have worked half the night to wash
the floor,' Montgomery went on. 'Fortunately, I do not keep servants, so there was no
one to see . . . what I did.'

'And the body?' said Ames.

'The body. Yes. Dear God, the body.' He

438

drew a deep, harsh breath. 'I waited until — until much later that night. Then I took it to — I don't remember. An alley.'

'Miss Montgomery?'

'Returned to the Bower. They had seen her run out after Bridget. She told them she'd searched for her without success. They accepted it.'

'Her skirts must have been soaked with blood.'

'Yes. She washed them in the kitchen sink here. I imagine that at the Bower, they thought her dress had gotten wet — very wet — in the rain.'

'Was it then she told you about Mary?'

'You mean that she'd killed her? Yes. I could not believe it at first, but after seeing how she'd attacked Bridget — in a frenzy, a madness — I did.'

'But her murder of Mary was not a sudden frenzy. It was planned. She lured her out of the Bower with a coded note — '

'Yes. She feared that Mary would disgrace me — and the Bower as well. As she might have done in the end, of course. So Agatha was angry with Mary, but even more, she feared her.'

'And when she discovered your plans to marry, she felt betrayed by you as well, and turned on you? You believe that she killed a third girl for no reason but to throw suspicion on you?'

'It seems so, yes.' The reverend's face was bleak, his voice flat with exhaustion.

'Crippen has arrested the Irish boy,' Ames said. 'But when I spoke to Miss Montgomery this evening, she said she did not believe Garrett was guilty.'

'Did she say whom she suspected?'

'No.'

'She means to implicate me. That is obvious.' Montgomery looked suddenly afraid. 'When the police realize that the coin is mine — '

'We must go to her — we must confront her, insist that she confess — take her to Crippen!'

'But — '

'What, man? Come on, we must go at once!'

'Then I will be — what do they call it? An accessory.'

'Yes, undoubtedly you will.' Ames threw him a scornful glance. 'But the authorities have ways of dealing with accessories. As I understand it, they will treat you gently if you provide them with evidence against her.'

Both Ames and MacKenzie were appalled to see the look of relief that passed over the reverend's face.

'All right,' Montgomery muttered. 'Let us go to her and get done with this miserable business once and for all.'

★ ★ ★

At Bertram's Bower, the windows were still brightly illuminated behind the drawn shades. As the three men approached, the uniformed patrolman intercepted them and ordered them to halt. He was appeased when Ames stepped forward to identify himself.

'Beg your pardon, sir,' he said. 'I'm ordered to question everyone, you understand.'

They hurried up the steps, and Ames sharply brought down the brass knocker. He had no idea what to expect from Agatha Montgomery: hysterics, denial, an attempt to implicate someone — anyone — else?

The door flew open.

'You've come back — ' It was Matron Pratt. When she saw who they were, she collected herself and assumed her normal hostile demeanor. 'Mr. Ames,' she said curtly. 'And Reverend — '

'Whom were you expecting, Matron?' Ames asked, but already he knew, and his heart sank.

'She went out,' Mrs. Pratt said, not moving aside to allow them to enter.

441

'When?'

'I don't know. A while ago.'

'Why?'

'I don't know that either. She said she had an errand to do.'

'At this hour of a Saturday night?' said Ames. 'And after — ' He turned to the reverend, who stood on the step below him. 'Where could she have gone? Have you any idea?'

'None. I cannot imagine — '

But Ames, suddenly, could. Into his mind's eye had come a vision of the company at Caroline's dinner party three nights before. He saw the ladies in their finery, the men in their more subdued attire. And very distinctly, he saw the Reverend Randolph Montgomery, standing with the others in the parlor before they went in to dinner. He was certain — yes, absolutely — that Montgomery had had a gold disc dangling from his watch chain.

'Reverend, when did you say you first missed the Medusa head?'

He heard the Bower's door slam shut behind them as they descended to the sidewalk.

'I'm not sure,' Montgomery replied. 'Thursday, I think.'

'So you probably had it on Wednesday.'

442

'Yes. In fact, I am sure I did, because someone admired it on Wednesday afternoon.'

'So. Between then and Thursday — '

'What are you getting at, Mr. Ames?'

'I am getting at — ' Suddenly it came to him in a rush, and he nearly choked on it.

'Doctor — you have your weapon at home?'

'Yes.'

'I pray you won't need it, but — you must go there at once. Only hope you arrive in time, before she — '

'Who, Ames?' said the reverend. Already MacKenzie, disregarding the pain in his knee, was hurrying down the square in search of a herdic.

'Why — your sister, man!' Ames was nearly shouting now. 'If I am not mistaken, she has gone to Caroline to make sure — Go on! Go with MacKenzie! You may need to deal with her! She is your sister after all. She may listen to you. Go on!'

Finally Montgomery seemed to understand. With an exclamation of alarm, he hurried after the doctor, down to the avenue where a herdic, on this foul night, might be found.

Ames bounded back up the Bower's steps and, ignoring the door knocker, pounded on the wooden panel.

'Matron!' he called. 'Open — at once!'

The door swung back.

'What?' Mrs. Pratt began, but Ames pushed past her, into the hall where the Bower's telephone was. He'd never used a telephone, and so now he hesitated, but only for a moment, as he stared at the wooden box and its appendages.

'How does this thing work?' he demanded. Matron Pratt had followed him and stood now at his side, breathing heavily.

'Why?'

'Damnation, woman! Never mind why! This is an emergency, and if you do not tell me how to operate this confounded contraption, I will have you charged with interfering with a police investigation!'

Seeming unintimidated by his threat, still she stepped forward, seized the handle attached to one side of the box, and cranked it hard, four times. Then she lifted a black earpiece attached to a tube and held it out to him. 'Hold this to your ear. Speak here, into this. Tell the operator who you want.'

In an amazingly short time, Ames was connected, but the connection was so poor he could hardly understand what the person on the other end of the line was saying, and it was obvious that person could not understand him either, even when he shouted. Which he felt he needed to do, else how could someone a mile and more distant — two miles — ever hear him? After a moment more of frustration, he slammed down the earpiece and without a further word to Mrs. Pratt, hurried out.

At the other end of the square, the patrolman was just finishing a circuit. When Ames insisted that he needed to get to Inspector Crippen at once, the man produced his clacker and whirled it rapidly, making a tremendous noise in the quiet night. In no more than a few seconds, a police wagon appeared and Ames clambered in.

'Whip up the horses, man! There is no time to lose!'

26

In the parlor at No. 16½, Agatha Montgomery leaned forward and rested her elbows on her knees, which poked up sharply through the thin stuff of her skirt, not properly swaddled in layers of petticoats as they should have been. But she has no money for petticoats, Caroline thought; she has no money for anything except the Bower. And what money she has, she gets from the reverend.

'Caroline, can you imagine how I felt when I learned of Mary's condition?'

'Her condition?' Caroline repeated faintly. Had Agatha known it all the time?

'No. Of course you cannot. No one can. That girl whom I had rescued from the streets — as I rescue all of them, but — she was different. She was — ' Miss Montgomery broke off as if she were remembering what Mary had been. 'Do you know, I actually thought that someday, Mary might take my place as directress of the Bower? Can you imagine such foolishness?'

She paused. She was breathing heavily.

Tea, Caroline thought. If only I could get

her to drink a cup of tea, and eat something —

'She was a slut!' snarled Miss Montgomery, her pale eyes blazing. 'A vicious little trollop who tried to blackmail him into marriage!'

Her voice broke, and for a moment, she clapped her hand over her mouth as if she were ashamed of her weakness.

A cup of hot tea, Caroline thought. And then Dr. MacKenzie, when he comes back, can tend to her professionally, give her a few drops of chloral hydrate to sedate her.

'As if my brother — *my brother* — would ever allow himself to be trapped like that! You have taken leave of your senses, Mary my girl, I told her. She defied me. She threw it up to me — that she carried his child. Can you imagine? She thought she would get him in the end, but she was wrong. I could never have allowed her to do that, could I?'

Miss Montgomery wiped away a tear. 'Don't you understand, Caroline? I could never have allowed her to marry my Randolph. It would have been his ruin — and ours. Not that I had any sympathy for him, mind you. No, indeed. Men are so weak, aren't they? So weak, so easily taken in by a scheming female.'

The bellpull, Caroline thought. It was only a few steps away, hanging by the mantel. If she could stand up, surely she could bear to put her weight on her foot for just a step or two, and then Margaret would come —

But then she remembered that surely, by now, Margaret had gone, and Cook along with her.

'Bridget knew,' Miss Montgomery said. 'She confronted me the day after Mary's death. She knew of Randolph's involvement with Mary, and she knew of Mary's condition. She said she intended to go to Randolph and make him confess. Confess! Can you picture it?'

She paused, as if she were reordering her thoughts. A sudden burst of rain spattered against the windows, sounding very loud in the silent room.

Caroline realized that she had been clenching her hands. She looked down and saw the small, bright red half-moon cuts where her nails had dug into her palms.

'Randolph had to work half the night to clean up her blood,' Miss Montgomery went on. 'We were indoors — in his front hall — and so there was no rain to wash it away. He was very good about it. He never complained. He said it would be our secret, his and mine. No one would ever know, he said. But all the time he had another secret of his own that he never told me.'

She had begun to cry. She made small, wheezing, whistling sounds — horrid sounds — while her mouth quivered and tears ran down her long, pale cheeks.

Caroline fumbled in her sleeve for a handkerchief. For once in her life, she didn't have one. A napkin, then, from the tea tray —

'Don't you understand, Caroline?' Miss Montgomery sobbed. 'He was going to leave me — to marry that woman in New York and move away! He said he would stay here, but I didn't believe him. I knew he would go in the end. But he won't be able to do that now, will he? Not now. Not after — They will think he killed her, this girl tonight. And they will think that if he killed her, he must have killed the other two as well. It didn't matter who it was, I had to provide a third girl, and I had to make sure that something would connect her to Randolph.'

'Agatha, what are you saying? If you did not return that coin to him, then — '

Caroline saw the gleaming metal blade in her friend's hand, and for a moment, before her brain registered it, she did not know what it was. She stared at it, fascinated; then she jumped as the grandmother clock in the hall struck the half hour.

'Agatha . . .'

'You and your meddling brother,' said Miss

Montgomery. 'If only you had stayed out of it, Caroline. Why couldn't you do that? But no. You had to intrude yourselves, you had to poke and pry — '

She raised the knife and lunged.

In the same instant, Caroline seized the hot-water pot and threw its contents into Miss Montgomery's face.

She heard a scream, saw the blade come at her.

'Miss Ames!'

Dr. MacKenzie stood at the open pocket doors, another man behind him. Not Addington. In one bound the Reverend Montgomery pushed MacKenzie aside, crossed the room, and seized his sister's wrist to wrench the knife from her grasp.

But she was as strong as he — stronger, perhaps, in her madness. Blinded by the boiling water, her face scalded, still she clutched her weapon, and as she wrestled with him, she cried, 'Randolph, how could you?'

They fell in a death struggle to the floor.

'Miss Ames!' MacKenzie exclaimed again.

He was at her side, helping her up. She managed to stand, and in the next instant she and MacKenzie were across the room and out into the hall. She felt a sharp stab of pain in her ankle, but she ignored it.

'Hurry!' he said. His knee was on fire, and he didn't know how much longer he could bear her weight leaning on his arm. Pray the elevator was on this floor and not stopped somewhere above. He couldn't remember when he'd used it last, but — Yes. Here it was.

As he pulled open the door, they heard a cry from the parlor — the reverend, he thought — but they had no time to stop, they must get into the elevator cab.

'Can you stand?' he asked.

'Yes.'

Her face was as pale as Death, but her voice was steady. He pulled the door shut and grasped the lever. Slowly they began to go up.

'What will we do, Doctor?' Caroline asked. It had all happened so quickly that her mind was a blur.

'We are safe here,' he said. Safe — but in this very small space. Already he was beginning to feel trapped — uncomfortably confined. 'Your brother will come directly. He asked me to get my weapon. It is in my room. I will — '

His voice died in his throat. Something was on the stairs that curved around the elevator shaft. He could dimly see its dark form, and he heard its harsh and painful breathing. Then he saw the gleam of a knife blade.

Agatha Montgomery.

451

The knife flashed through the grille, narrowly missing his midriff. With alacrity he stepped back, but he could not step far enough for safety because he needed to keep his hand on the lever.

The elevator kept on rising, but too slowly. Sweat trickled down his neck, down his back. I will not panic, he thought.

What had happened to the reverend? Had she killed him?

The blade flashed again, and this time it nicked his hand just above the thumb. In the dim light he saw the dark spurt of blood, and he fumbled with his free hand for his handkerchief to stanch it.

'Doctor — your hand!' Caroline exclaimed behind him.

He half turned to her. 'It is nothing. You must keep quiet.'

As they kept on going up, he caught a glimpse of the creature on the stairs. He saw the dark, shapeless mass of her clothing, and for an instant he saw her face, which bore the blistering red wounds from the scalding water. She was muttering, but so low they could not make out her words. Every few seconds she emitted a low moan, as if she were in great pain.

As she is, thought Caroline. She is in agony, and not just from her burns. But her natural feelings of compassion for her friend — for the woman who had been her friend, she corrected herself — were overcome by her terror, for this thing crouching on the stairs was not the Agatha Montgomery she had known. This was an alien creature, all her obsessions — with her life's work, with the reverend — transformed into a murderous madness.

Like the flickering tongue of a deadly serpent, the knife blade flashed through the grille again, this time at their feet. Keep going, MacKenzie told himself. But what would they do when they reached the top? With his game knee, he would never be able to reach his room in time to fetch his pistol, not with Agatha Montgomery hot on his heels, intent on stabbing him to death.

The elevator whined and moaned. Miss Montgomery panted up the stairs alongside them. The blade flashed again through the grille, and then again. Then her dark shape passed them, heading on up.

'She will wait for us above,' MacKenzie said in a low voice.

'Then do not go all the way up!' Caroline whispered. 'Stop — stop now.'

With a little jolt, he did. They were just short of the third story, with the hall floor at eye level. They could see Miss Montgomery's worn boots, the sodden hem of her skirts.

'Go down,' Caroline whispered. 'We cannot get out while she is there. We must just keep going up and down until Addington comes.'

If he does, MacKenzie thought.

He reversed the lever, and with agonizing slowness they descended toward the second floor. As they did so, they saw a movement — a shadow — on the stairs: Miss Montgomery, following them down. She stood a little below the cab, awaiting them.

He stopped. In the sudden silence they could hear Miss Montgomery's breath come heavy and hard. It was her madness that sustained her, thought MacKenzie — that gave her the strength to fight her exhaustion, her pain.

Suddenly she came back and thrust at them again. The blood-tipped blade slipped into the elevator at their feet.

With his good leg, he stepped on it — put his booted foot down hard. He heard Miss Montgomery grunt as she tried to pull the knife free. He started up the elevator again. Miss Montgomery held on to the knife with a death grip. He bore down on the blade with all his weight. Suddenly they heard a sharp snap! as the blade broke, and with a cry of anger Miss Montgomery fell back onto the stairs, still clutching the handle. A small portion of the blade was attached to it; the rest lay under MacKenzie's heel.

'We must — ' Caroline began, but then she heard a sound on the stairs below. She peered out.

It was the reverend.

He was on his hands and knees, crawling up, trying to reach his sister. They heard his gasping, agonized breath, and when he managed to utter a few words, his voice was weak.

'Agatha . . . stop . . . you must stop . . . '

She made no reply — not in words — but they heard a snarl like the snarl of a devil hound, and then a strange, high sobbing as if she felt not remorse but some faint memory of remorse.

'Agatha . . . '

Somehow the reverend had managed to get to his feet. He staggered up a step or two, bracing himself against the banister. His sister waited for him. He put out a hand and seized the hem of her skirts, but he had no strength to pull her down. Caroline, craning her neck, saw dark red stains on the stair carpet. Agatha must have wounded him very badly, she thought. He must be attended to, or he will bleed to death.

With a sudden movement, Miss Montgomery pulled away from his grasp and he fell facedown onto the stairs, his arms thrust up in front of him.

And now — most horrible of all, to Caroline — Miss Montgomery began to curse him.

'Damn you, Randolph! Damn you to eternal hell! Why? *Why?*'

He lifted his head. His eyes, caught in the light of the hall gas jets, seemed to blaze with an anger equal to her own.

'It would have been — ' he began, but then he broke off, as if he were saving what little strength he had left for his last effort.

Groaning, he braced himself and slowly got to his feet. He took one step up, and then another.

Miss Montgomery backed away.

He went after her.

She turned and scrambled to the second-floor hall. To Caroline's amazement, the reverend kept on.

'Doctor,' she whispered, 'do you think — '

'Yes,' he said. He shifted the lever and they began to rise again. Above them now, they heard Agatha Montgomery and her brother stumbling up the stairs. The sound of their footsteps had an erratic rhythm: She ran up a few steps, then waited for him nearly to catch her; when he had staggered up and was almost upon her, she ran up a little farther.

Caroline heard them even as she heard her heart pounding, pounding, the sound of it mingling in an eerie way with the footsteps, and with the whine and moan of the elevator, until it was all one sound in her ears.

Then she heard something new. 'Listen!' she said.

A key in the front door lock, the door bursting open —

'Addington — at last!' she cried, no longer caring if Miss Montgomery heard her. Relief flooded over her, making her suddenly weak, and she clung to MacKenzie's arm.

And pray he is not too late, MacKenzie thought. He was exquisitely conscious of her presence, her touch, but this was not the moment to respond to it. They were nearly at the third floor now; he heard Miss Montgomery in the hall there, the dragging steps of the reverend in pursuit.

'Addington!' Caroline called. 'We are here — in the elevator! And the reverend is on the stairs, and he is wounded! Be careful — Agatha has a knife!'

Broken the knife might be, it was still a weapon that could inflict a serious wound.

In no more than an instant, Ames was bounding up, calling to her. 'Are you safe?' he cried. 'Stay there! Crippen is with me!'

And now she heard someone else, and she caught a glimpse of the little inspector, close on Ames's heels as they raced up the stairs past the elevator.

Footsteps thudded along the third-floor hall. The elevator shuddered to a stop. MacKenzie pulled open the door and stepped out, wincing at the pain in his knee but unutterably relieved to be free of that small, panic-making space. Above, on the stairs to the fourth floor, he heard Crippen's voice: 'Halt! Halt, I say!'

Intending to get his weapon, MacKenzie limped to the door of his room. Before he could utter a word of warning, Caroline had slipped past him and was heading up to the fourth floor behind the others.

Please, she thought, gritting her teeth against the pain in her ankle. Please let them stop. Let Agatha not harm anyone — not anyone else.

When she was halfway up the stairs, she felt a sudden draft of cold air. She came into the fourth-floor hall just in time to see Addington and Crippen disappear up the last little half-flight of stairs to the roof.

As fast as she could, she hobbled up behind them. She heard Agatha's voice — 'Randolph!' — and his reply — 'You fool!

See what you have done!'

She heard a warning shout from Addington, a single explosive oath from Crippen.

She came out onto the roof.

She felt the cold night wind on her face, and a spattering of rain. She saw two dark forms grappling near the edge. They might have been lovers entwined in a deadly embrace. They swayed back and forth — they staggered and teetered — they fell, still clutching each other — rolled over — and then —

Agatha went over the edge.

But she did not fall far, because she held on to the reverend, truly in a death grip now, both hands grasping his above the wrists while he sprawled flat on his stomach. She had dropped her broken knife; it lay, gleaming dully, halfway across the rooftop.

In two steps, Ames reached them. With a warning cry, he seized the reverend's legs. Caroline started to shout — 'No, Addington!' — but then, afraid of startling him, she bit back her words.

They will all three fall to their death, she thought. Please, Addington, let him go, let Agatha go —

Ames hauled back on the reverend, and for

a moment it seemed that Agatha could be saved as well.

But she could hold on no longer. They heard her scream — a sound that would haunt Caroline to her grave — and then she was gone.

27

Early the next afternoon, a cold, cloudy day with the wind strong from the north, Ames strode purposefully across the Public Garden and exited through the tall iron gates at the Commonwealth Avenue Mall. The city was Sunday-quiet, which suited his pensive mood.

How could he tell her what had happened? She was convinced of Agatha Montgomery's near sainthood. How could he find the words to say that far from being some kind of saint, the proprietress of Bertram's Bower had been a woman who, tormented by her demons, had committed murder three times over and possibly four?

He paused to allow a brougham to pass at Arlington Street, and then, buffeted by the wind, crossed and strode on down the avenue. Snow by nightfall, he thought. Well, he didn't mind snow. Winter in New England wouldn't be right without it. Some of his friends had taken to wintering in the South. He'd had jolly notes postmarked from Charleston and Savannah. Unnatural, he thought: a winter of sunshine and mild breezes, weather warm enough to sit out-doors.

He rounded the corner and crossed in the middle of the block to the Berkeley Arms. He hadn't thought to send a telegram warning her of his arrival, but surely she'd be at home.

The concierge announced him and he went up. She'd opened the door before he reached it, and she welcomed him with a heart-quivering smile.

'Mr. Ames,' she said softly, giving him her hand. She wore a dark green velvet tea gown and a necklace of baroque pearls. Her eyes were shadowed with sorrow, and her lush, beautiful mouth trembled a bit. 'What has happened?'

'I cannot stay long. But I wanted to — I did not want you to — '

Already he was bungling it; he should not have spoken so abruptly. He deposited his cloak and hat and gloves with the maid and followed Mrs. Vincent into her warm, expensively elegant parlor. Her little dog, who was apparently becoming used to him, lifted its head and yawned.

'Can I give you lunch, Mr. Ames?'

'No, thank you.' He looked around. He saw a stack of Sunday newspapers on a low table. 'You have seen the news?'

'Yes. But the news is not the whole story, I imagine.'

'No. The whole story — Perhaps you had better sit down.'

Her eyes widened in surprise, but she did as he suggested, and with a graceful gesture waved him to a seat opposite.

He hesitated, wanting to get it right, conscious that he had her fixed attention. Many men, he knew, would have given much for that. As he always did in her presence, he felt awkward, like a gawking schoolboy.

'Well, Mr. Ames? What is it? I cannot believe that Agatha Montgomery is dead, and yet the Sunday *Herald* prints it, so it must be so.'

'Yes. She is dead.'

'Did she really fall from your roof? Or . . . '

She held his gaze, wanting him not only to finish her question but to answer it. But when he kept quiet, she said, 'Or was she pushed?' Her voice — her splendid actress's voice — was low and throbbing and filled with emotion. As it always did, it set his pulses racing even as he reminded himself that this was a woman beyond the bounds of polite society. Polite society be damned, he thought. If he was going to cause her pain — and he was — he wanted that pain to be as brief as possible.

'She was not pushed,' he said curtly.

'Then — how did she fall?'

'She was struggling with her brother — trying to kill him.'

Mrs. Vincent was obviously shocked at that, but quickly she collected herself and said, 'So she found out about him at last?'

'You mean about his — ah — tendency to take liberties?'

'Yes.'

'At least one person — Dr. Hannah Bigelow, a friend of my sister's — tried to warn Miss Montgomery about that, but Miss Montgomery would not listen. This episode last night occurred not because of his liberties, however, but because he planned to marry a woman from New York. And perhaps — so Miss Montgomery feared — to move there. Thus, in her view, deserting her.'

'But surely — ' She broke off, trying to make sense of it.

Ames leaned forward, his elbows on his knees. He wanted very much to take her hand, but he did not quite dare. He hated to distress her with what more he had to tell her, and yet he must do it; he couldn't let her learn it from the newspapers.

'Mrs. Vincent, I came here today to tell you what all the city will know soon enough. I didn't want you to see it first in the public prints, because I know how much you admired Miss Montgomery, and I know it will hurt you to learn that she ... was capable of ... what she did.'

'What she did?' she repeated.

Make it quick and clean, he thought. 'She was the Bower killer.'

She went quite pale, and her face — her beautiful face, beauty beyond men's dreams, beauty a man could die for, and had — froze as she absorbed what he'd said.

Quick and clean, and tell it all. 'She killed all three of those girls, and she may have killed her brother. He is at Mass General now, near death.'

'But — why?'

'I don't know. I don't really know, I mean. The facts of the case — ' He spread his hands in a gesture of futility. He saw the rapid rise and fall of her bosom, and he wished he could comfort her somehow, make it up to her for shattering her faith in the woman she'd called a saint.

Failing that, he tried to explain it to her: Mary's pregnancy, Bridget's threats, Peg Corcoran's bad luck to be at hand when Miss Montgomery needed a third victim to avenge herself on her brother.

She heard him out in silence, her hands folded in her lap, her eyes never wavering from his — very strong, she seemed, and yet he could not help thinking that even as he spoke, he was watching some part of her wither and die: the part that had believed in Agatha Montgomery.

At last he came to the end of it, and he fell silent. I have failed her, he thought. She asked my assistance, and instead —

'I owe you a debt of thanks,' she said softly.

'Not at all. I merely tried to help.'

'And you did. It is not your fault that things turned out rather differently than either of us expected.'

Abruptly she rose and went to the hearth, where a sea-coal fire simmered with a steady warmth. After a moment he realized, with a stab of dismay, that she was weeping. At once he was on his feet and at her side, and then, without knowing how it happened, she was in his arms and sobbing against his shoulder. He felt her shuddering, trembling body all down the length of his own, and he realized with another sharp little stab that she was uncorseted.

Holding her was unlike anything he'd ever experienced. For a long moment, as he rested his cheek against her glorious hair, he breathed in her scent — some heavy, sensuous scent that no proper Boston lady would wear — and he murmured to her he didn't know what, anything to ease her grief, her very real heartbreak.

Gradually her sobs quieted, and after a moment more she pulled away from him a little, but without leaving his embrace entirely. With no embarrassment she gave him a small, tremulous smile. He reminded himself that she was accustomed to displaying all kinds of emotion to perfect strangers, all the time. He reminded himself that she had a string of lovers, a supply of men eager to be where he was now, with her in his arms.

None of that mattered. What mattered at this moment was that he must leave her, and he had no idea when he might see her again.

Could he ask her to call at Louisburg Square? No. Impossible. Caroline would never —

'I must go,' he said.

'Yes,' she said.

'I am sorry if I — '

She shook her head, dismissing any apology he might have made. She stepped back, free of his embrace, and his empty arms dropped to his sides. 'You were kind to come, Mr. Ames.'

Kind. Was that what he wanted to be to her?

'It was — I felt that I — ' He cleared his throat, trying to recover his equilibrium.

Having her stand so near, with the memory of her in his arms, was an assault on his senses that made it difficult to think.

'Will you stay in touch with me?' she said.

In touch. What did that mean? 'Yes, of course.'

'Thank you.' She held out her hand, sending him on his way. In her eyes he thought he saw not sorrow, not pain at what he'd had to tell her, but a curious kind of understanding. Beyond understanding. Sympathy, he thought as he went out into the cold once more, heading home. Not for Agatha Montgomery, but for him.

Yes. Sympathy — and something even more than that. Why? Because she knew how he felt about her? He didn't know that himself. Because she knew he was in danger of falling in love with her?

She was right. He was in danger of that. And now at last he realized what he'd seen as she'd said good-bye to him: not understanding, not sympathy. What he'd seen in her beautiful eyes — and how the realization galled him! — had been pity.

★   ★   ★

Wincing at the pain in his knee, MacKenzie heaved himself up from his chair, seized the poker, and stirred up the coals in the hearth. He heard the grandmother clock in the hall strike the half hour: three-thirty, nearly dusk. When he turned to speak to his companion, he saw that she was gazing up at him, and because of what they'd recently endured together, because of the fate they'd narrowly escaped, it seemed to him that in her face he saw some feeling for him that had not been there, or at least not so strongly, before their harrowing adventure last night. Affection? Perhaps. Or, at the very least, a comforting kind of trust.

She is still afraid, he thought. But surely they were done with it now; she need fear nothing more.

Until early that morning, and all the long night before, they had had chaos: curious neighbors, swarming police, medical teams, ambulances, hordes of reporters tipped off to a sensational story.

But now at last they were at peace. Ames had gone out and had not yet returned. He was all right, he'd said; he merely wanted an hour or so of quiet. Caroline agreed: quiet was what she wanted, too, more than anything.

'Would you like tea, Doctor?' she asked.

'If you would,' he replied. 'Shall I ring?'

'Please.'

The household might have been severely discommoded because of Margaret's absence, but their neighbor across the square, Dr. Warren, had kindly sent one of his servants to assist.

After they were alone once more, MacKenzie carefully lowered himself into his chair. His knee was throbbing; he could only imagine what Dr. Warren would say to him about it.

Although it was growing dark, he had not wanted to turn up the gas. He liked sitting in this shadowy room with Caroline Ames. He liked knowing that when he spoke, she was there to answer him. That in the normal routine of their lives, when he went out, she would be there to greet him on his return.

Suddenly he shuddered, thinking of what had happened in this room last night: Agatha Montgomery in a murderous fury, wielding her knife.

'Are you cold, Doctor?' Caroline asked.

'No. Not — not cold.' He searched for the words to tell her what he felt, but they eluded him.

The pocket doors slid open, and Ames stood there, surveying the quiet domestic scene. MacKenzie, just at that moment, would not have dreamed of asking where he'd been, but he could guess. She will cause you

470

to suffer, my friend, he thought but did not say, and then, for fear his thoughts showed on his face, he looked away.

Ames turned up the gas a little and took his accustomed place by the hearth, one slim, booted foot resting on the brass fender. 'I must send to the hospital to see how the reverend does,' he said.

'And if he lives — ?' asked MacKenzie.

'If he lives, I suppose he will tell his story to Crippen. Whether he will be believed is another matter.'

'I wonder what he will say about the account books,' MacKenzie ventured.

'What can he say? At the very least, the man is a thief — and a blackguard.' Ames's long, lean face drew down into lines of disgust. He felt dirty even thinking about the reverend, never mind talking about him.

'Poor Agatha,' Caroline murmured. She caught MacKenzie's eye and added, 'I know, Doctor. I know what she did. But she was driven to it.'

'She lived in a fantasy world,' Ames said sharply. 'She believed in something that bore no relation to reality.'

'She loved him,' Caroline said. And when both men looked at her sharply, she raised her chin and added, 'Well, she *did*.'

'Unwisely — and far too well,' Ames said.

'And until she turned against him, she would have been willing to allow an innocent lad to be hanged for murders he did not commit.'

'Yes,' she replied softly. 'I know.'

So much for Miss Montgomery's putative sainthood, thought Ames. Serena Vincent's face rose in his mind, and with an almost physical effort, he banished it.

They heard the front door knocker, and when the borrowed servant did not answer, Ames went himself. They heard him in the vestibule welcoming the caller, and Caroline could tell from the sound of his genuine pleasure that it was not Inspector Crippen. Thank goodness, she thought. She did not feel strong enough, just yet, to deal with him.

In another moment, Ames ushered in Desmond Delahanty.

'Miss Ames — Doctor — what a time of it, yes?'

As usual, he was hatless, his hair windblown, his long blue muffler wrapped around his neck.

'Mr. Delahanty, how good to see you,' Caroline said, giving him her hand. 'What news?'

'Well, the lad's free, and that's something.'

Delahanty shook hands and then went to the fire to warm himself. 'And it took them a good long time to do it, mind you. I went down to the Tombs myself to speak for him. You wouldn't believe the paperwork they had to go through just to release an innocent boy.'

Their tea came then, and the men helped themselves to Sally Lunn and lace cookies while Caroline poured. Then Delahanty, perched on the edge of the sofa, looked around at them and they knew that not all his news was good.

'What else, Desmond?' asked Ames.

'The Reverend Montgomery died just after noon.'

'Ah.' Ames realized he was disappointed that the reverend had so easily escaped the law. 'Hardly surprising, considering his wounds.'

Good riddance, thought MacKenzie, and yet he found Delahanty's news somewhat disturbing. Despite his aching knee, he heaved himself up once more and went to stand at the lavender-glass bow window. It was dusk; the streetlamps had just come on. In the oval behind the high iron fence, the purplish trees thrashed in the wind, and a few snowflakes whirled in the lamplight. Across the square, he could see lights in the houses opposite — a comforting sight, the blessed tranquillity of ordinary lives.

And yet —

'Will the Bower continue, do you think?' Delahanty asked.

'I don't know,' Caroline replied. They heard the sadness in her voice. 'Agatha was its heart and soul.'

'It is a very worthy cause. Surely some other dedicated female might be found to keep it going.'

'Yes.' Caroline thought of the Bower's girls, of Liza and Katy. She would talk to Edward and Imogen Boylston, she thought, and perhaps — 'Perhaps,' she said.

MacKenzie looked back at the little group in the parlor. The firelight illuminated the men in their dark clothing, edging them with light; it gilded Caroline's hair and played over her face, her dress. It was like a painting, he thought: The Angel of the Hearth.

His Angel?

Perhaps. With luck — and time.

He left the window and went back to her, back to the warmth and the light, and she turned up her face to smile at him. And then, gladdening his heart, she gave him her hand, and eagerly he grasped it.

A gust of wind blew down the chimney, causing a shower of sparks. The thaw was past; winter had come again.

Author's Note

'Boston,' wrote an anonymous commentator in 1879, 'in spite of the organized efforts of thoughtful and good people, and the annual expenditure of large sums of money, has its full share of unrelieved suffering and want.'

In an age without modern-day 'safety nets,' the Victorian impulse for doing good, in Boston as elsewhere, found many outlets. Most of them were bluntly, even crudely named: orphanages, workhouses and almshouses, lunatic asylums, homes for 'aged females' and 'children of the destitute,' and, as in *Murder at Bertram's Bower*, refuges for 'fallen women.'

There really was such a place in Boston in the late nineteenth century, a 'bower' in the South End.

Today we might ask, 'Fallen? From what? Into what?'

From virtue into sin, the Victorians would have replied. And for them, sin, particularly women's sin, was almost always sexual. In that age, so similar to and yet so different from our own, women were ruled by a social code far more constricting than the corsets that crushed their bodies into unnatural shapes to please the eyes of men. High on the pedestals where men put them and tried to keep them, women perched so precariously that one slip could cause them to fall into a chasm of ostracism and shame.

To our somewhat jaded modern sensibilities, the Victorian code of conduct for women, both written and unwritten, seems faintly ridiculous, not to say inhumane. But it ruled the lives of women then, as well they knew, and they violated it at their peril.

As for Jack the Ripper, the most famous criminal of all time: He haunts us still. The faceless, nameless killer stalking his female victims in London's nighttime streets is the very image of terror. Despite more than a century of sleuthing both amateur and professional, he is still a mystery. Who was he? Why did he kill in such a dreadful, bloody way? Why did he stop? What happened to him? Probably, now, we will never know.

One thing we do know, however, is that Scotland Yard believed he might have escaped to America; they even sent a man here to search for him. And so I took that intriguing possibility, together with the fact of a home for 'fallen women' in Boston's

South End, and combined them to make
this tale.

What if . . . ? I thought.

What if, indeed?

— Cynthia Peale

We do hope that you have enjoyed reading this large print book.

Did you know that all of our titles are available for purchase?

We publish a wide range of high quality large print books including:
Romances, Mysteries, Classics
General Fiction
Non Fiction and Westerns

Special interest titles available in large print are:
The Little Oxford Dictionary
Music Book
Song Book
Hymn Book
Service Book

Also available from us courtesy of Oxford University Press:
Young Readers' Dictionary
(large print edition)
Young Readers' Thesaurus
(large print edition)

For further information or a free brochure, please contact us at:
Ulverscroft Large Print Books Ltd.,
The Green, Bradgate Road, Anstey,
Leicester, LE7 7FU, England.
Tel: (00 44) 0116 236 4325
Fax: (00 44) 0116 234 0205